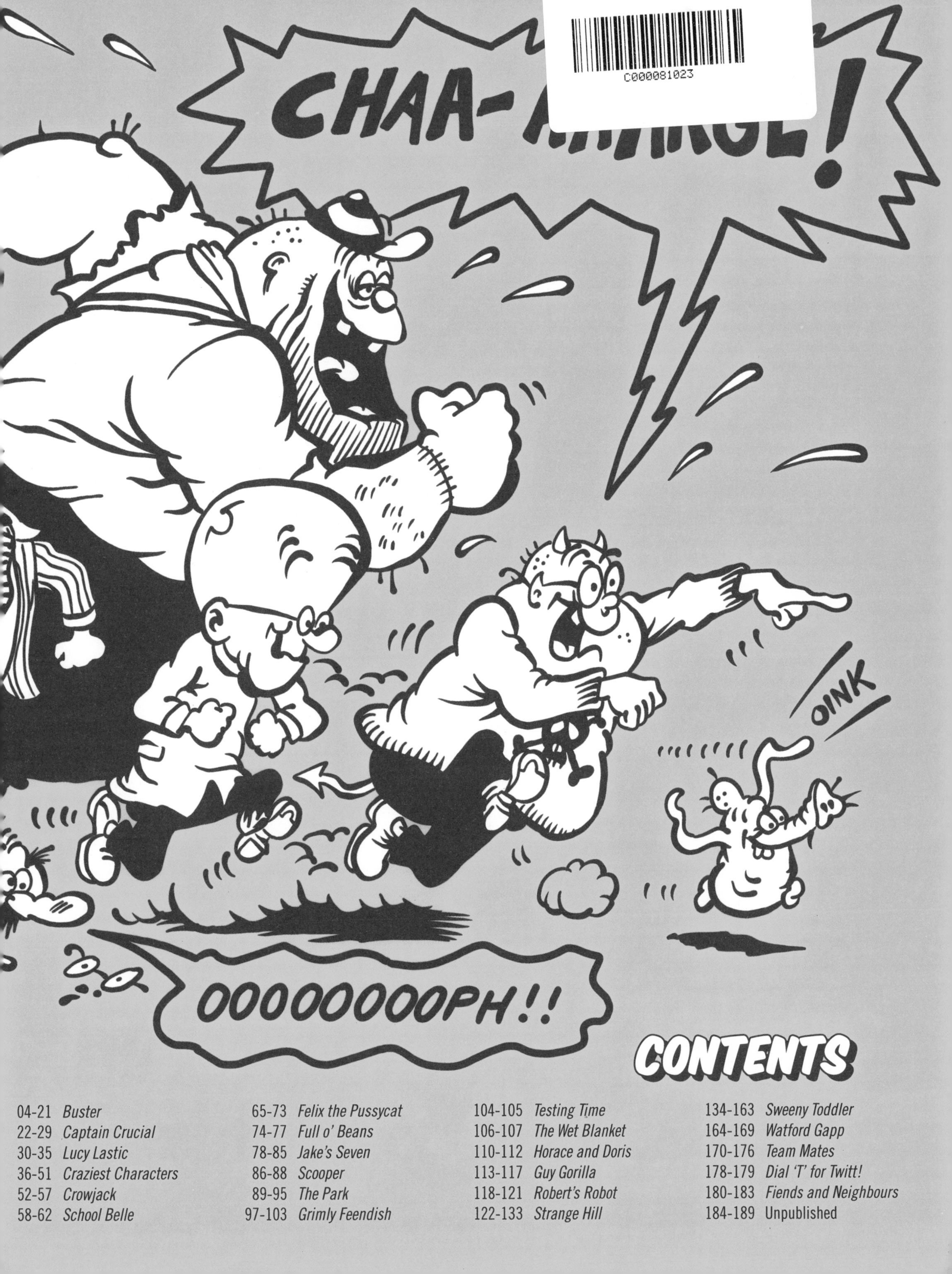
CHAA-
OINK
OOOOOOOOPH!!



# CONTENTS

**TOM PATERSON • MARK BENNINGTON • ROGER FITTON • GRAHAM EXTON • MARK RODGERS**
Writers

**TOM PATERSON**
Artist

**REBELLiON®**

Creative Director and CEO: Jason Kingsley
Chief Technical Officer: Chris Kingsley
Head of Publishing: Ben Smith
Publishing Manager: Beth Lewis
Senior Graphic Novels Editor: Keith Richardson
Graphic Novels Editors: Oliver Pickles & Olivia Hicks
Graphic Design: Oz Osborne, Sam Gretton & Gemma Sheldrake
Reprographics: Joseph Morgan, Emma Denton & Richard Tustian
Production Manager: Dagna Dlubak
PR: Michael Molcher
PR Assistant: Rosie Peat
Publishing Coordinator: Owen Johnson
Archivist: Charlene Taylor

The Treasury of British Comics Presents: The Tom Paterson Collection is ™ Rebellion Publishing Ltd, copyright © Rebellion Publishing Ltd, all rights reserved.
Published by Rebellion, Riverside House, Osney Mead, Oxford, UK. OX2 0ES
**www.rebellion.co.uk**

ISBN: 978-1-78108-940-8

Printed in Malta by Gutenberg Press
Manufactured in the EU by LPPS Ltd., Wellingborough, NN8 3PJ, UK.

Special thanks to: Lew Stringer, Allen Cummings and Tom Paterson

First published: November 2021
10 9 8 7 6 5 4 3 2 1
Printed on FSC Accredited Paper
A CIP catalogue record for this book is available from the British Library.
For information on other Rebellion graphic novels visit **2000adonline.com**, or if you have any comments on this book, please email **books@2000ADonline.com**

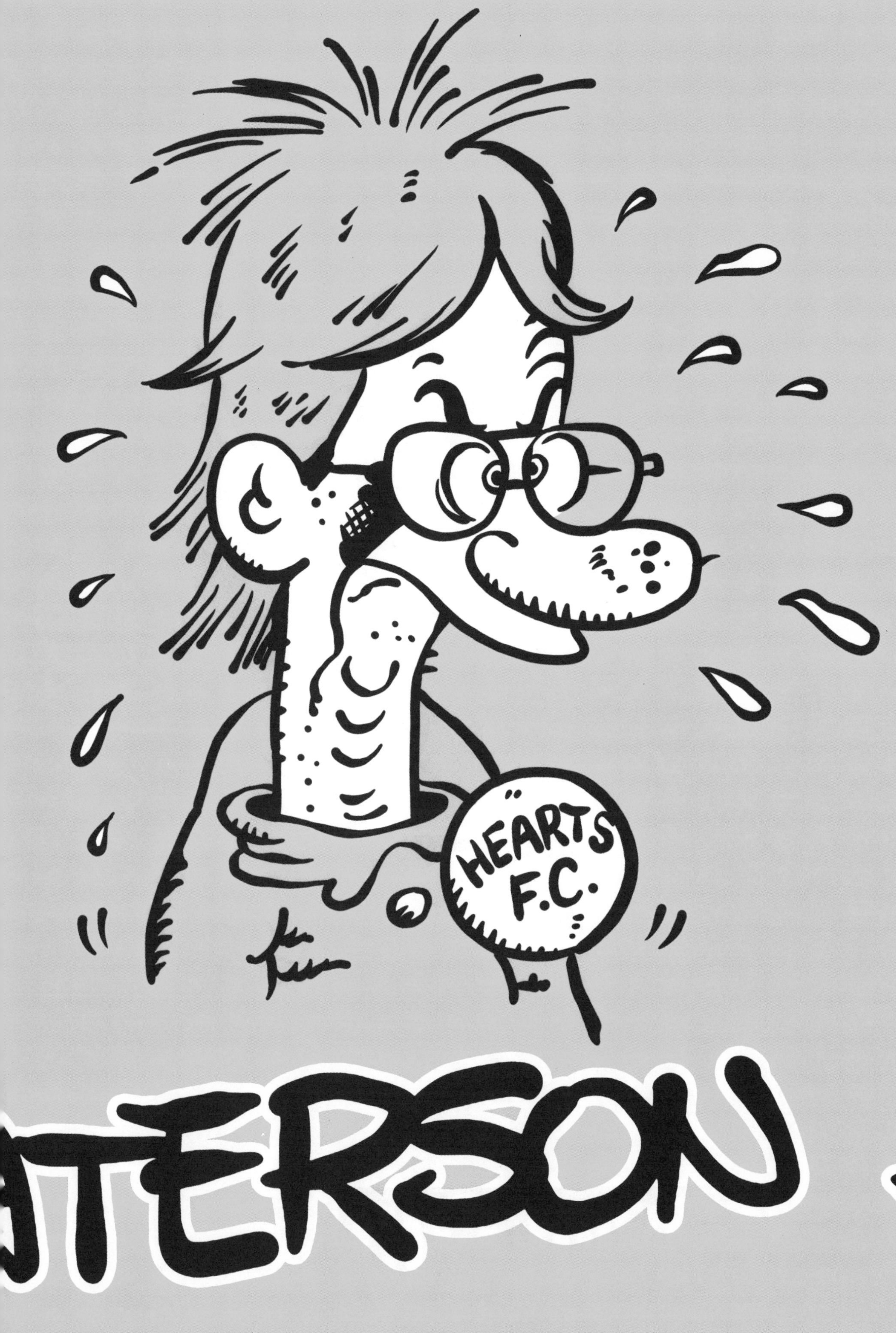
HEARTS F.C.

# TERSON –

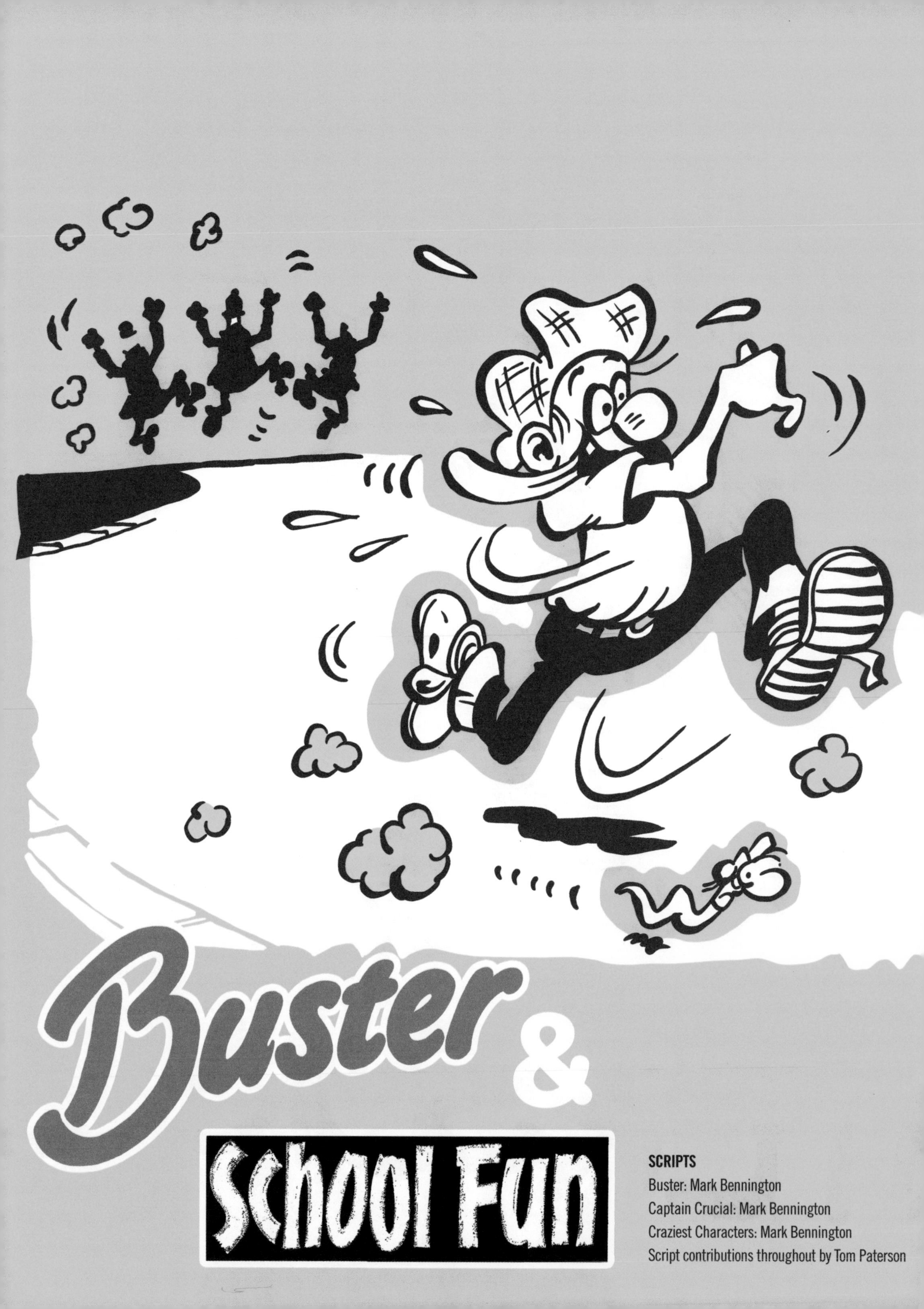

# Buster & School Fun

**SCRIPTS**

Buster: Mark Bennington

Captain Crucial: Mark Bennington

Craziest Characters: Mark Bennington

Script contributions throughout by Tom Paterson

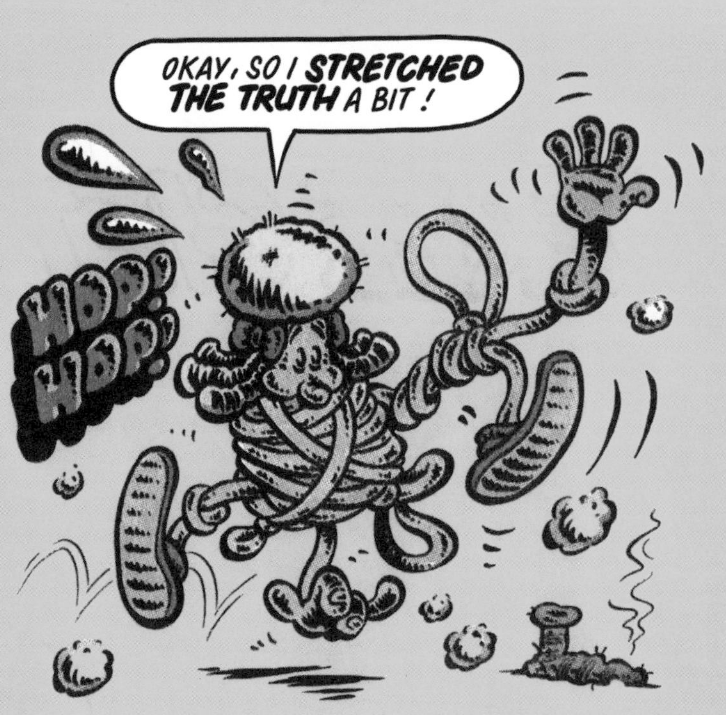
OKAY, SO I STRETCHED THE TRUTH A BIT!
HOP! HOP!

# MARK BENNINGTON

## ARTIST/WRITER – BUSTER, CAPTAIN CRUCIAL, X-RAY SPECS

**OM PATERSON…ABSOLUTE** master of British cartooning...I was artist and criptwriter on the **Buster** comic and Fleetway titles in the mid-80s onwards nd was teamed up with Tom for **Buster**'s title strip. Tom had the uncanny kill of making static characters appear animated on the page with his antastic facial expressions and anatomical drawings. I was the new guy and earnt a great deal from Tom's work in mastering the art of cartoons.

He also drew my crazy centre spread characters…and he brought my reatest creation, *Lucy Lastic* to life. *Captain Crucial* was another of ur creations...at the time an innovative, contemporary and a ground-reaking character of colour...anyone wanting to become a cartoonist hould study Tom's work.

# JAMIE SMART

## WRITER/ARTIST – DESPERATE DAN, BEAR, LOOSHKIN, BUNNY VS. MONKEY

**I CAN'T THINK** of any cartoonist who has affected me more deeply than Tom Paterson. His work reaches right into your very soul and wibbles it. Every panel he draws is so crammed with energy, all the grotesque hooting, the squelching rasps and the honking shrieks, the characters squashed and contorted, their faces joyously pummelled from one emotion to the next. It's breathless to read. It's intense. It's utterly, utterly thrilling. And when you're a young, impressionable comic reader it blasts your brain right out of its skull.

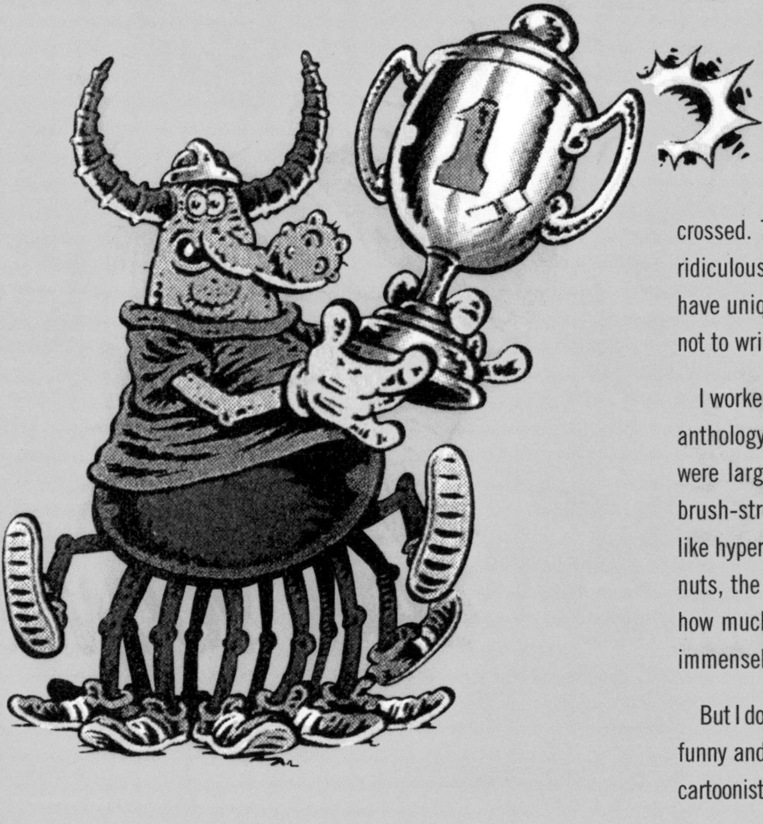

When I first discovered Tom's work I was equal parts baffled, excited and awe-struck, laughing too much to take a breath between pages. Tom showed me all that comics could do, how boundless they could be, how relentlessly bonkers. He taught me that the panel of a comic wasn't a constraint, it was a line to be crossed. That there's always room to hammer in one more gag, one more ridiculous, raspberry-blowing sentient dollop. Tom understood that comics have unique access to an almost cosmic anarchy, and it would be a tragedy not to wring it dry.

I worked, very briefly, with Tom, when he contributed to my children's comic anthology **Moose Kid Comics**. When the original artwork arrived the pages were large, hand-painted, and magnificent. I could see every detail, every brush-stroke, I could follow the colour bleeding into each gag. It may sound like hyperbole, but I felt like I was privy to the inner workings of a comic. The nuts, the bolts, the secret mechanisms which pinpoint the jokes. And given how much I'd admired Tom's work for most of my life, there was something immensely moving about being this close to it.

But I doubt Tom would want me to fawn this much. He's been creating brilliantly funny and anarchic comics for years, he's influenced a whole swathe of British cartoonists, and maybe all that needs saying is thank you, Tom.

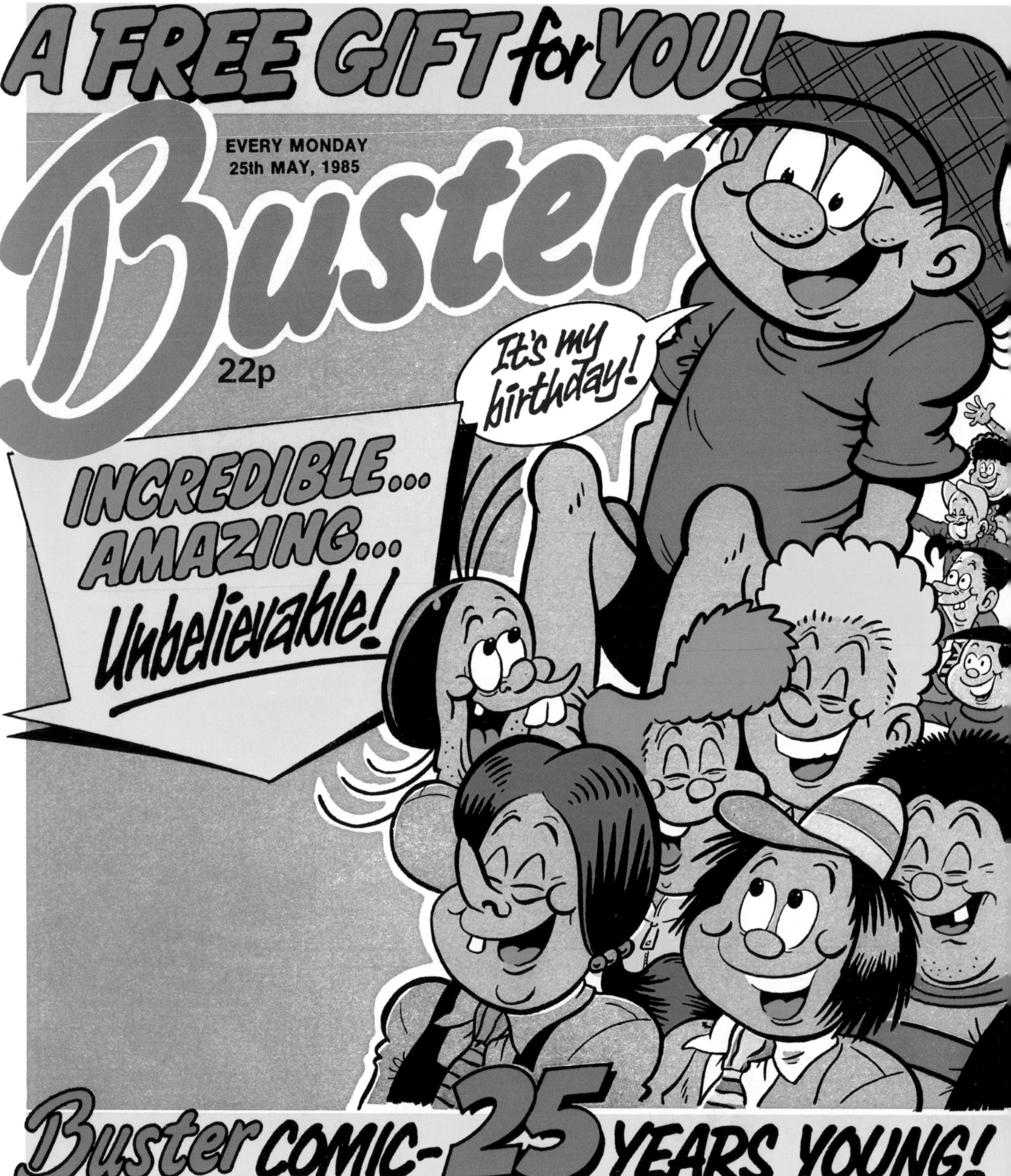
A FREE GIFT for YOU!
Buster
EVERY MONDAY
25th MAY, 1985
22p
It's my birthday!
INCREDIBLE...
AMAZING...
Unbelievable!
Buster COMIC-25 YEARS YOUNG!

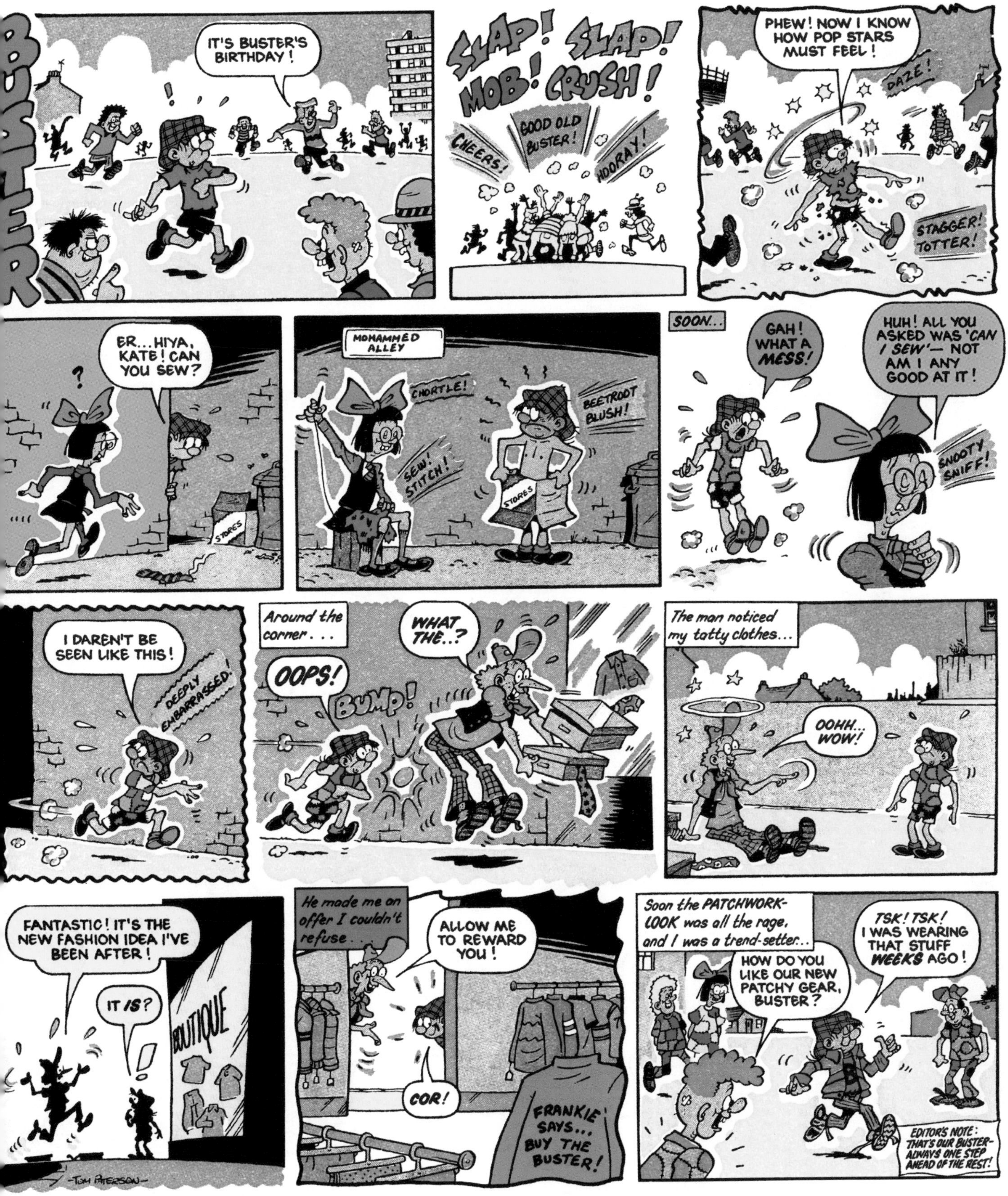
BUSTER
IT'S BUSTER'S BIRTHDAY!
SLAP! SLAP!
MOB! CRUSH!
GOOD OLD BUSTER!
CHEERS!
HOORAY!
PHEW! NOW I KNOW HOW POP STARS MUST FEEL!
DAZE!
STAGGER! TOTTER!
ER... HIYA, KATE! CAN YOU SEW?
STORES
MOHAMMED ALLEY
CHORTLE!
SEW! STITCH!
BEETROOT BLUSH!
STORES
SOON...
GAH! WHAT A MESS!
HUH! ALL YOU ASKED WAS 'CAN I SEW'— NOT AM I ANY GOOD AT IT!
SNOOTY SNIFF!
I DAREN'T BE SEEN LIKE THIS!
DEEPLY EMBARRASSED!
Around the corner...
WHAT THE..?
OOPS!
BUMP!
The man noticed my tatty clothes...
OOHH... WOW!
FANTASTIC! IT'S THE NEW FASHION IDEA I'VE BEEN AFTER!
IT IS?
BOUTIQUE
-TOM PATERSON-
He made me an offer I couldn't refuse...
ALLOW ME TO REWARD YOU!
COR!
FRANKIE SAYS... BUY THE BUSTER!
Soon the PATCHWORK-LOOK was all the rage, and I was a trend-setter...
HOW DO YOU LIKE OUR NEW PATCHY GEAR, BUSTER?
TSK! TSK! I WAS WEARING THAT STUFF WEEKS AGO!
EDITOR'S NOTE: THAT'S OUR BUSTER- ALWAYS ONE STEP AHEAD OF THE REST!

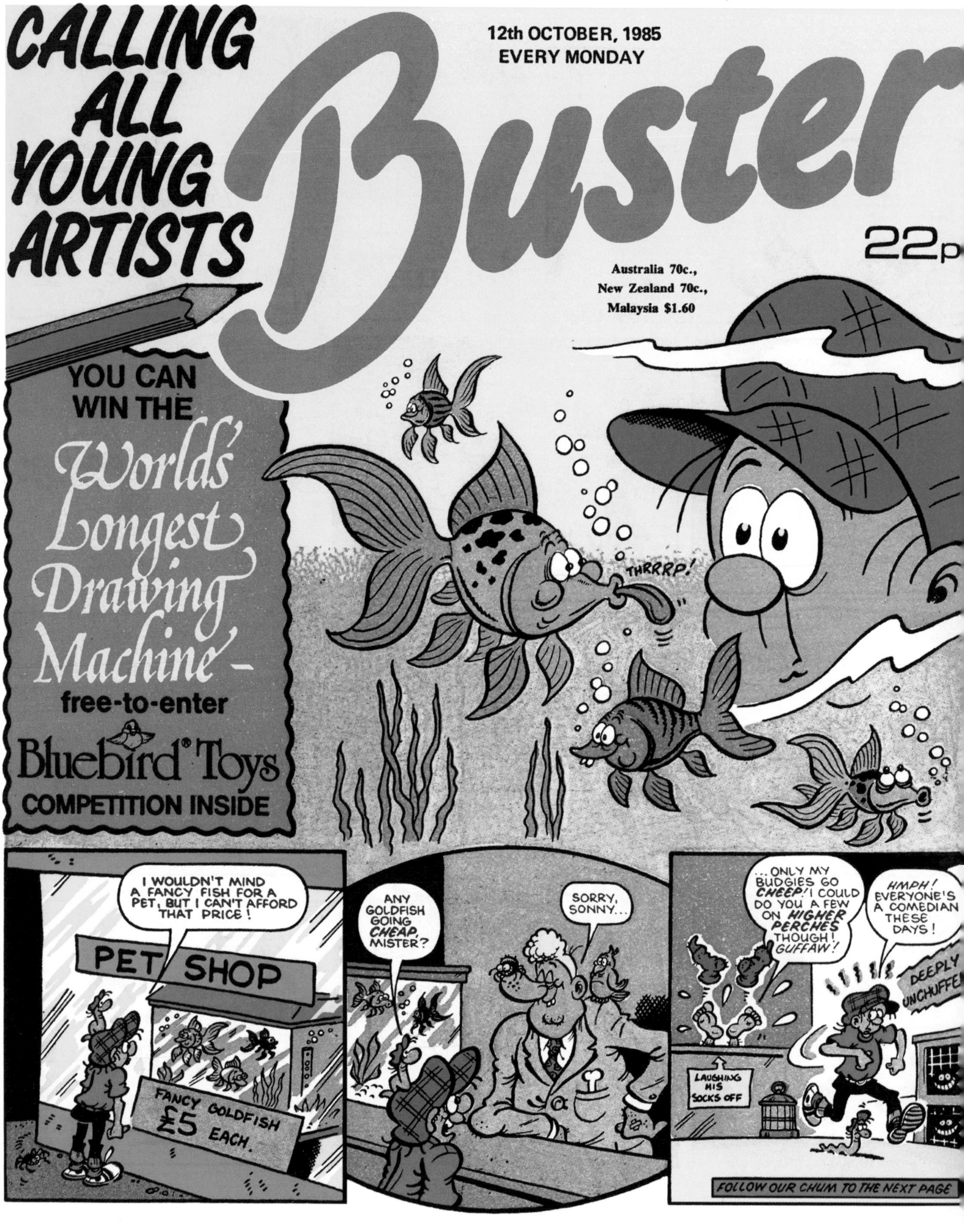
CALLING ALL YOUNG ARTISTS
12th OCTOBER, 1985
EVERY MONDAY
Buster
22p
Australia 70c.,
New Zealand 70c.,
Malaysia $1.60
YOU CAN WIN THE
World's Longest Drawing Machine -
free-to-enter
Bluebird® Toys
COMPETITION INSIDE
THRRRP!
I WOULDN'T MIND A FANCY FISH FOR A PET, BUT I CAN'T AFFORD THAT PRICE!
PET SHOP
FANCY GOLDFISH £5 EACH.
ANY GOLDFISH GOING CHEAP, MISTER?
SORRY, SONNY...
...ONLY MY BUDGIES GO CHEEP! I COULD DO YOU A FEW ON HIGHER PERCHES THOUGH! GUFFAW!
HMPH! EVERYONE'S A COMEDIAN THESE DAYS!
DEEPLY UNCHUFFED
LAUGHING HIS SOCKS OFF
FOLLOW OUR CHUM TO THE NEXT PAGE

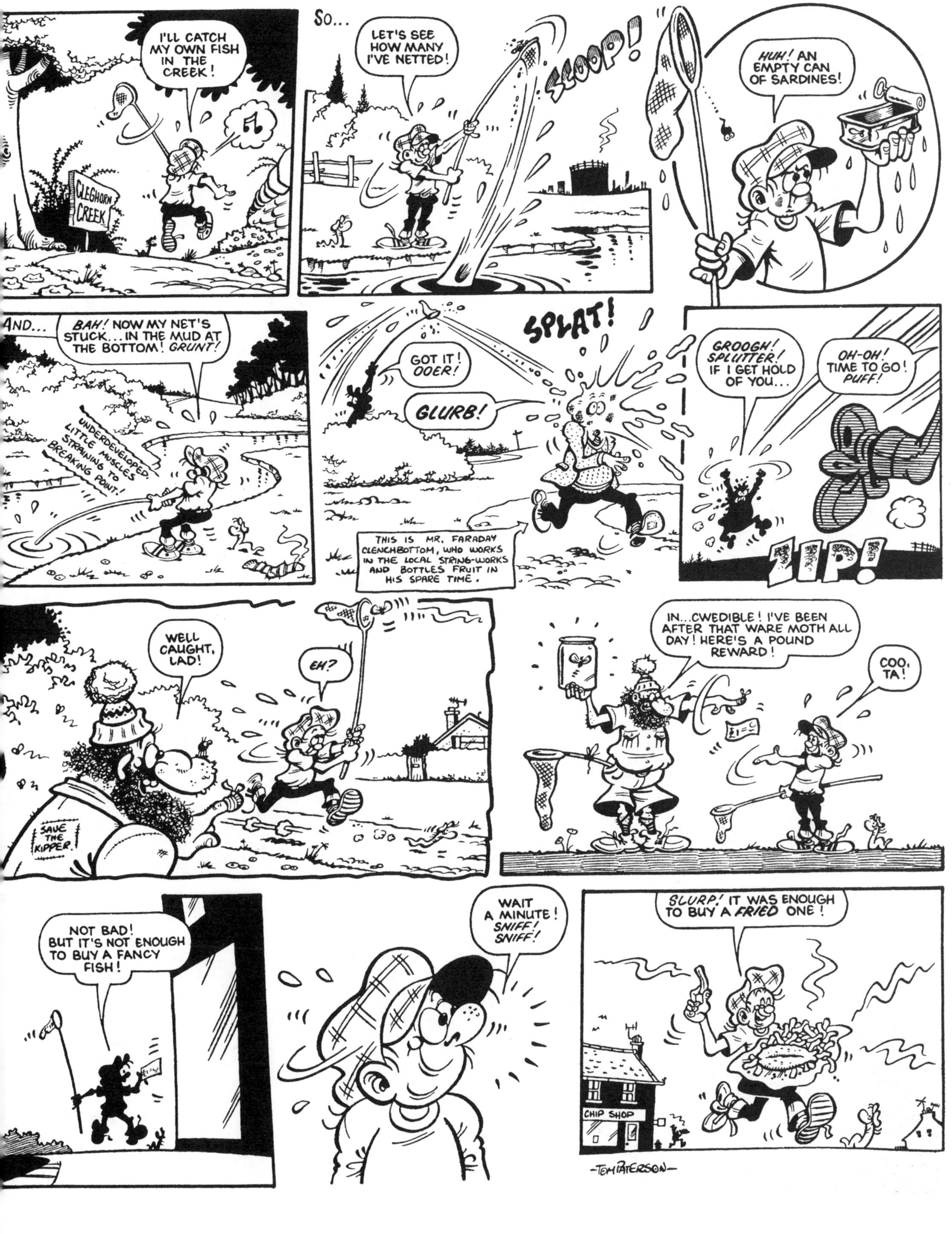
I'LL CATCH MY OWN FISH IN THE CREEK!
CLEGHORN CREEK
SO...
LET'S SEE HOW MANY I'VE NETTED!
SCOOP!
HUH! AN EMPTY CAN OF SARDINES!
AND...
BAH! NOW MY NET'S STUCK... IN THE MUD AT THE BOTTOM! GRUNT!
UNDERDEVELOPED LITTLE MUSCLES STRAINING TO BREAKING POINT!
GOT IT! OOER!
GLURB!
SPLAT!
THIS IS MR. FARADAY CLENCHBOTTOM, WHO WORKS IN THE LOCAL STRING-WORKS AND BOTTLES FRUIT IN HIS SPARE TIME.
GROOGH! SPLUTTER! IF I GET HOLD OF YOU...
OH-OH! TIME TO GO! PUFF!
ZIP!
WELL CAUGHT, LAD!
EH?
SAVE THE KIPPER
IN...CWEDIBLE! I'VE BEEN AFTER THAT WARE MOTH ALL DAY! HERE'S A POUND REWARD!
COO, TA!
NOT BAD! BUT IT'S NOT ENOUGH TO BUY A FANCY FISH!
WAIT A MINUTE! SNIFF! SNIFF!
SLURP! IT WAS ENOUGH TO BUY A FRIED ONE!
CHIP SHOP
-TOM PATERSON-

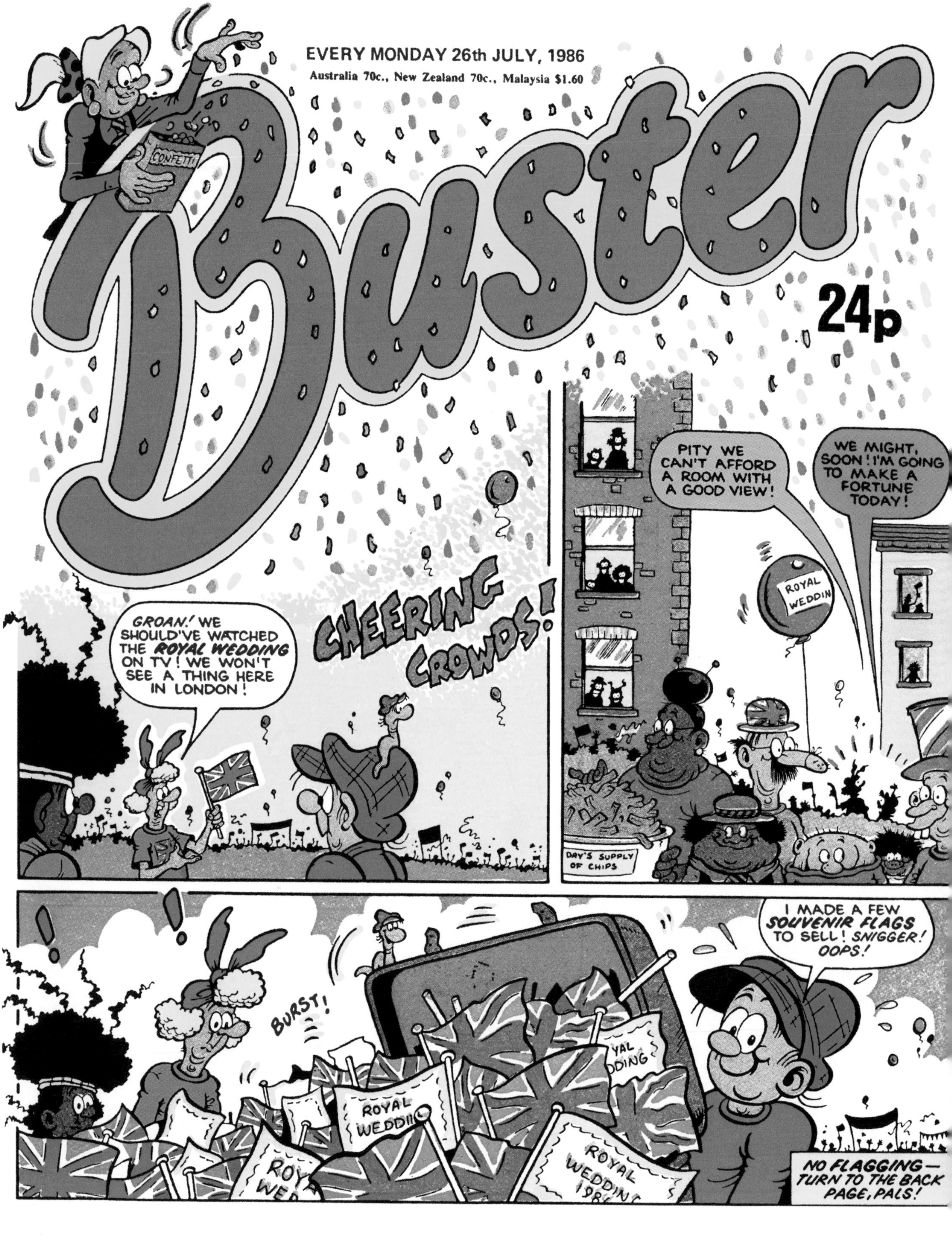
EVERY MONDAY 26th JULY, 1986
Australia 70c., New Zealand 70c., Malaysia $1.60
Buster
24p
CONFETTI
GROAN! WE SHOULD'VE WATCHED THE ROYAL WEDDING ON TV! WE WON'T SEE A THING HERE IN LONDON!
CHEERING CROWDS!
PITY WE CAN'T AFFORD A ROOM WITH A GOOD VIEW!
WE MIGHT, SOON! I'M GOING TO MAKE A FORTUNE TODAY!
ROYAL WEDDIN
DAY'S SUPPLY OF CHIPS
BURST!
I MADE A FEW SOUVENIR FLAGS TO SELL! SNIGGER! OOPS!
ROYAL WEDDII
ROYAL WEDDIN 198
NO FLAGGING— TURN TO THE BACK PAGE, PALS!

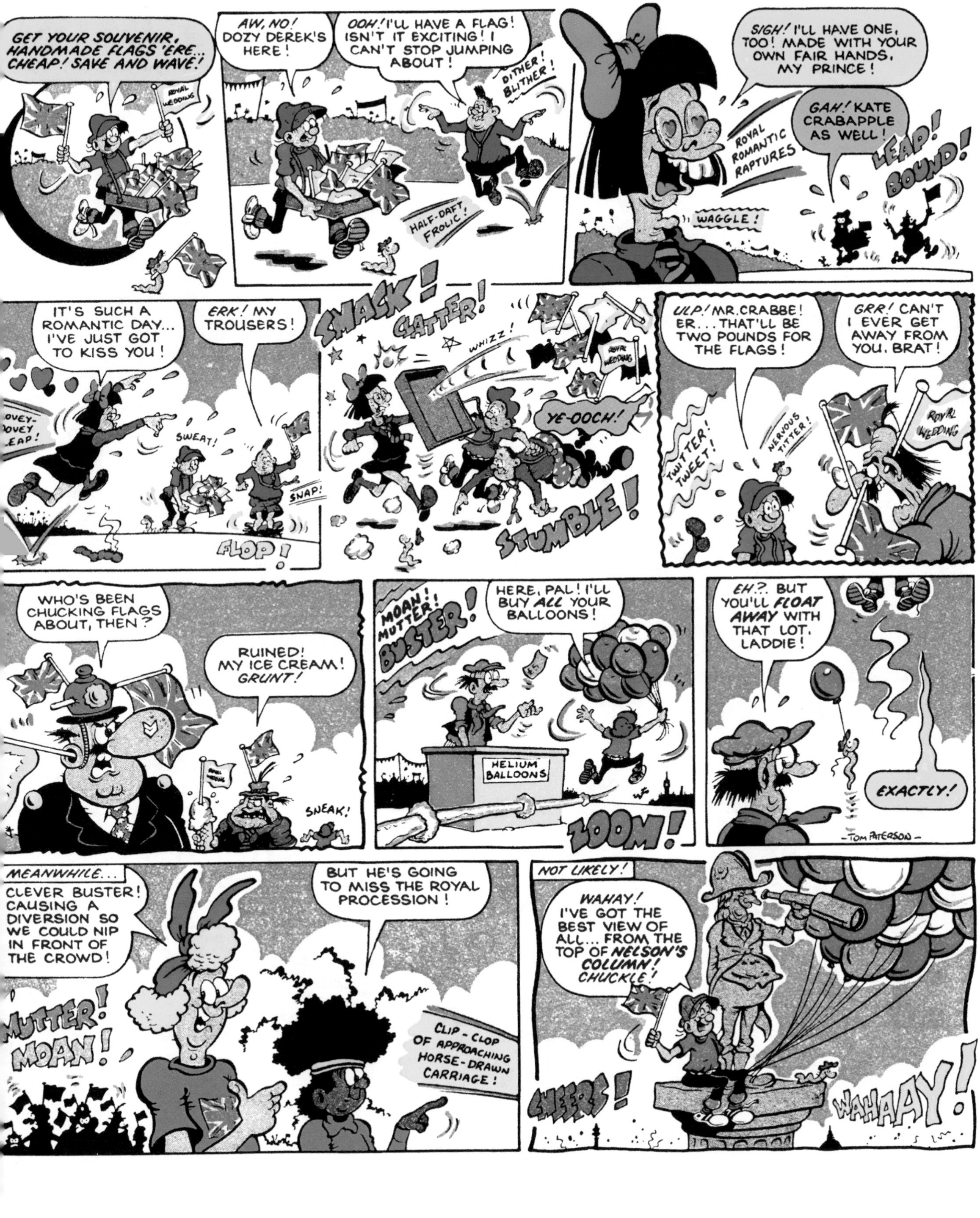
GET YOUR SOUVENIR, HANDMADE FLAGS 'ERE... CHEAP! SAVE AND WAVE!
ROYAL WEDDING
AW, NO! DOZY DEREK'S HERE!
OOH! I'LL HAVE A FLAG! ISN'T IT EXCITING! I CAN'T STOP JUMPING ABOUT!
DITHER! BLITHER!
HALF-DAFT FROLIC!
SIGH! I'LL HAVE ONE, TOO! MADE WITH YOUR OWN FAIR HANDS, MY PRINCE!
ROYAL ROMANTIC RAPTURES
GAH! KATE CRABAPPLE AS WELL!
WAGGLE!
LEAP! BOUND!
IT'S SUCH A ROMANTIC DAY... I'VE JUST GOT TO KISS YOU!
ERK! MY TROUSERS!
SWEAT!
SNAP!
FLOP!
SMACK! CLATTER!
WHIZZ!
ROYAL WEDDING
YE-OOCH!
STUMBLE!
ULP! MR.CRABBE! ER... THAT'LL BE TWO POUNDS FOR THE FLAGS!
GRR! CAN'T I EVER GET AWAY FROM YOU, BRAT!
TWITTER! TWEET!
NERVOUS TITTER!
ROYAL WEDDING
WHO'S BEEN CHUCKING FLAGS ABOUT, THEN?
RUINED! MY ICE CREAM! GRUNT!
SNEAK!
MOAN! MUTTER! BUSTER!
HERE, PAL! I'LL BUY ALL YOUR BALLOONS!
HELIUM BALLOONS
ZOOM!
EH?.. BUT YOU'LL FLOAT AWAY WITH THAT LOT, LADDIE!
EXACTLY!
—TOM PATERSON—
MEANWHILE...
CLEVER BUSTER! CAUSING A DIVERSION SO WE COULD NIP IN FRONT OF THE CROWD!
BUT HE'S GOING TO MISS THE ROYAL PROCESSION!
MUTTER! MOAN!
CLIP-CLOP OF APPROACHING HORSE-DRAWN CARRIAGE!
NOT LIKELY!
WAHAY! I'VE GOT THE BEST VIEW OF ALL... FROM THE TOP OF NELSON'S COLUMN! CHUCKLE!
CHEERS!
WAHAAY!

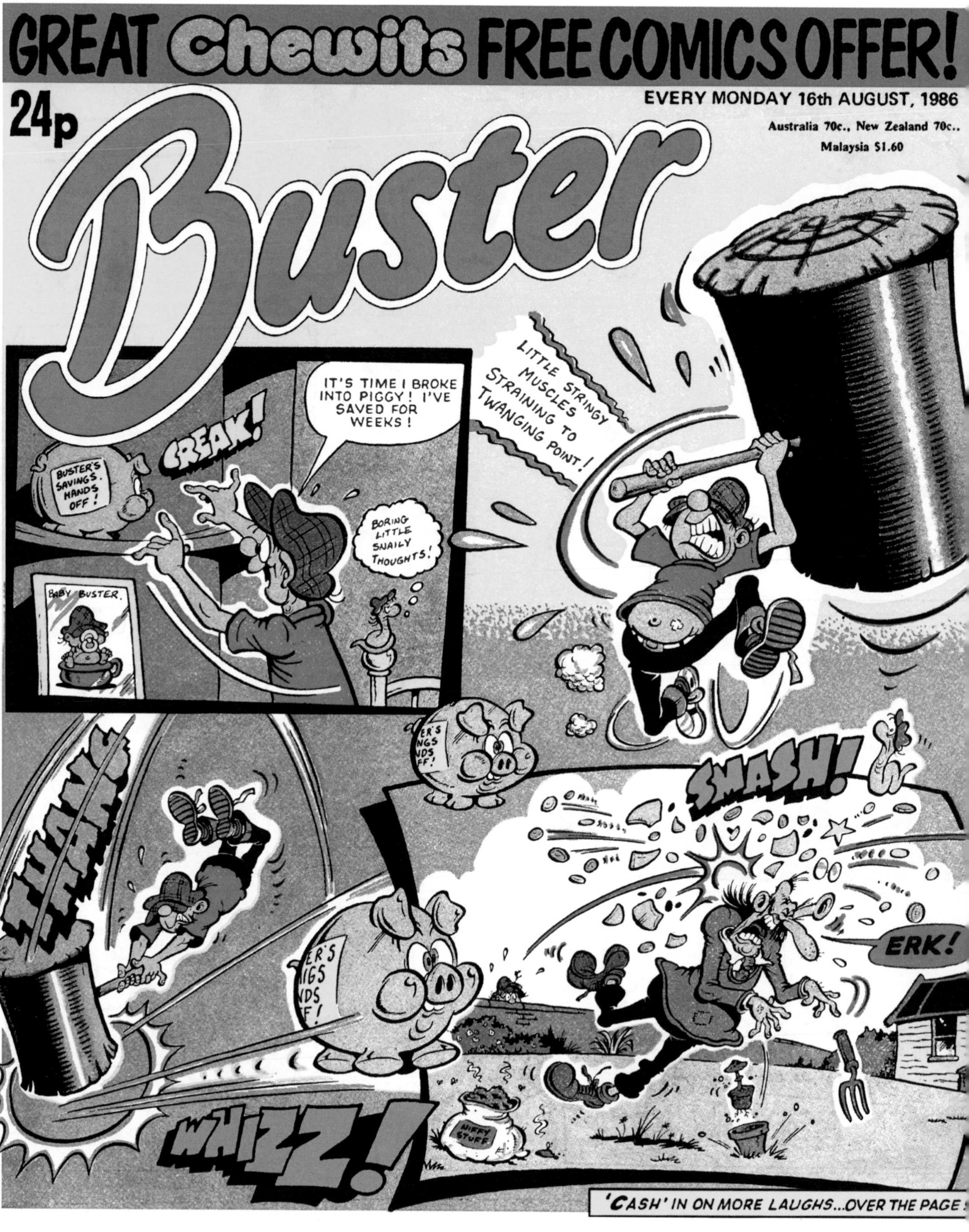

GREAT Chewits FREE COMICS OFFER!
24p
EVERY MONDAY 16th AUGUST, 1986
Australia 70c., New Zealand 70c.,
Malaysia $1.60
Buster
IT'S TIME I BROKE INTO PIGGY! I'VE SAVED FOR WEEKS!
BUSTER'S SAVINGS. HANDS OFF!
CREAK!
BORING LITTLE SNAILY THOUGHTS!
BABY BUSTER.
LITTLE STRINGY MUSCLES STRAINING TO TWANGING POINT!
SMASH!
ERK!
WHIZZ!
NIFFY STUFF
'CASH' IN ON MORE LAUGHS...OVER THE PAGE

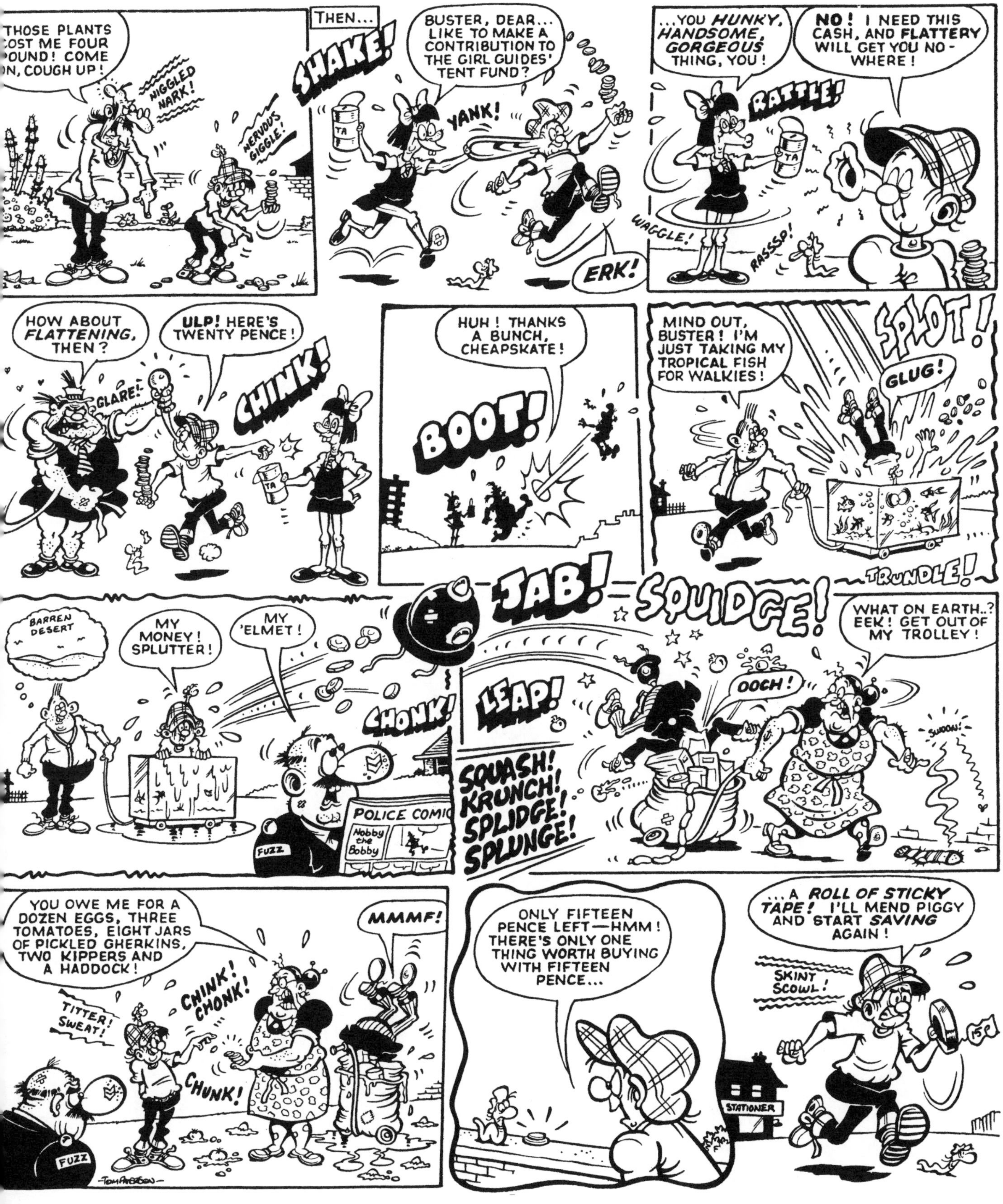
THOSE PLANTS COST ME FOUR POUND! COME ON, COUGH UP!
NIGGLED NARK!
NERVOUS GIGGLE!
THEN...
SHAKE!
BUSTER, DEAR... LIKE TO MAKE A CONTRIBUTION TO THE GIRL GUIDES' TENT FUND?
YANK!
ERK!
...YOU HUNKY, HANDSOME, GORGEOUS THING, YOU!
NO! I NEED THIS CASH, AND FLATTERY WILL GET YOU NOWHERE!
RATTLE!
WAGGLE!
RASSSP!
HOW ABOUT FLATTENING, THEN?
GLARE!
ULP! HERE'S TWENTY PENCE!
CHINK!
HUH! THANKS A BUNCH, CHEAPSKATE!
BOOT!
MIND OUT, BUSTER! I'M JUST TAKING MY TROPICAL FISH FOR WALKIES!
SPLOT!
GLUG!
TRUNDLE!
BARREN DESERT
MY MONEY! SPLUTTER!
MY 'ELMET!
JAB!
CHONK!
POLICE COMIC
Nobby the Bobby
FUZZ
SQUIDGE!
LEAP!
SQUASH! KRUNCH! SPLIDGE! SPLUNGE!
OOCH!
WHAT ON EARTH..? EEK! GET OUT OF MY TROLLEY!
YOU OWE ME FOR A DOZEN EGGS, THREE TOMATOES, EIGHT JARS OF PICKLED GHERKINS, TWO KIPPERS AND A HADDOCK!
MMMF!
TITTER! SWEAT!
CHINK! CHONK!
CHUNK!
FUZZ
ONLY FIFTEEN PENCE LEFT—HMM! THERE'S ONLY ONE THING WORTH BUYING WITH FIFTEEN PENCE...
STATIONER
...A ROLL OF STICKY TAPE! I'LL MEND PIGGY AND START SAVING AGAIN!
SKINT SCOWL!
15p

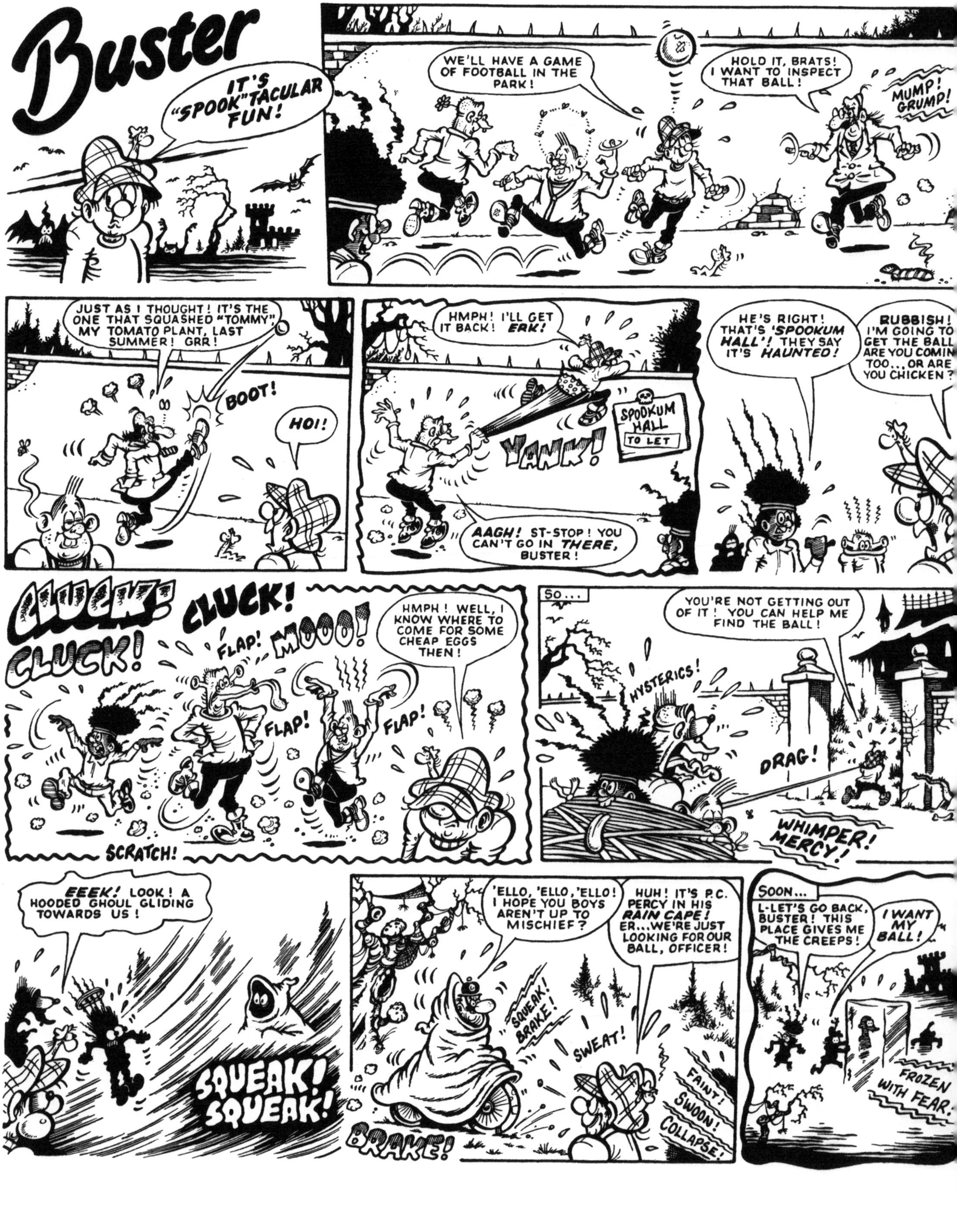
Buster
IT'S "SPOOK"TACULAR FUN!
WE'LL HAVE A GAME OF FOOTBALL IN THE PARK!
HOLD IT, BRATS! I WANT TO INSPECT THAT BALL!
MUMP! GRUMP!
JUST AS I THOUGHT! IT'S THE ONE THAT SQUASHED "TOMMY" MY TOMATO PLANT, LAST SUMMER! GRR!
BOOT!
HOI!
HMPH! I'LL GET IT BACK! ERK!
SPOOKUM HALL
TO LET
YANK!
AAGH! ST-STOP! YOU CAN'T GO IN THERE, BUSTER!
HE'S RIGHT! THAT'S 'SPOOKUM HALL'! THEY SAY IT'S HAUNTED!
RUBBISH! I'M GOING TO GET THE BALL ARE YOU COMIN TOO... OR ARE YOU CHICKEN?
CLUCK! CLUCK! CLUCK!
FLAP! MOOO!
FLAP!
FLAP!
HMPH! WELL, I KNOW WHERE TO COME FOR SOME CHEAP EGGS THEN!
SCRATCH!
SO...
YOU'RE NOT GETTING OUT OF IT! YOU CAN HELP ME FIND THE BALL!
HYSTERICS!
DRAG!
WHIMPER! MERCY!
EEEK! LOOK! A HOODED GHOUL GLIDING TOWARDS US!
SQUEAK! SQUEAK!
'ELLO, 'ELLO, 'ELLO! I HOPE YOU BOYS AREN'T UP TO MISCHIEF?
HUH! IT'S P.C. PERCY IN HIS RAIN CAPE! ER...WE'RE JUST LOOKING FOR OUR BALL, OFFICER!
SQUEAK! BRAKE!
SWEAT!
FAINT! SWOON! COLLAPSE!
BRAKE!
SOON...
L-LET'S GO BACK, BUSTER! THIS PLACE GIVES ME THE CREEPS!
I WANT MY BALL!
FROZEN WITH FEAR.

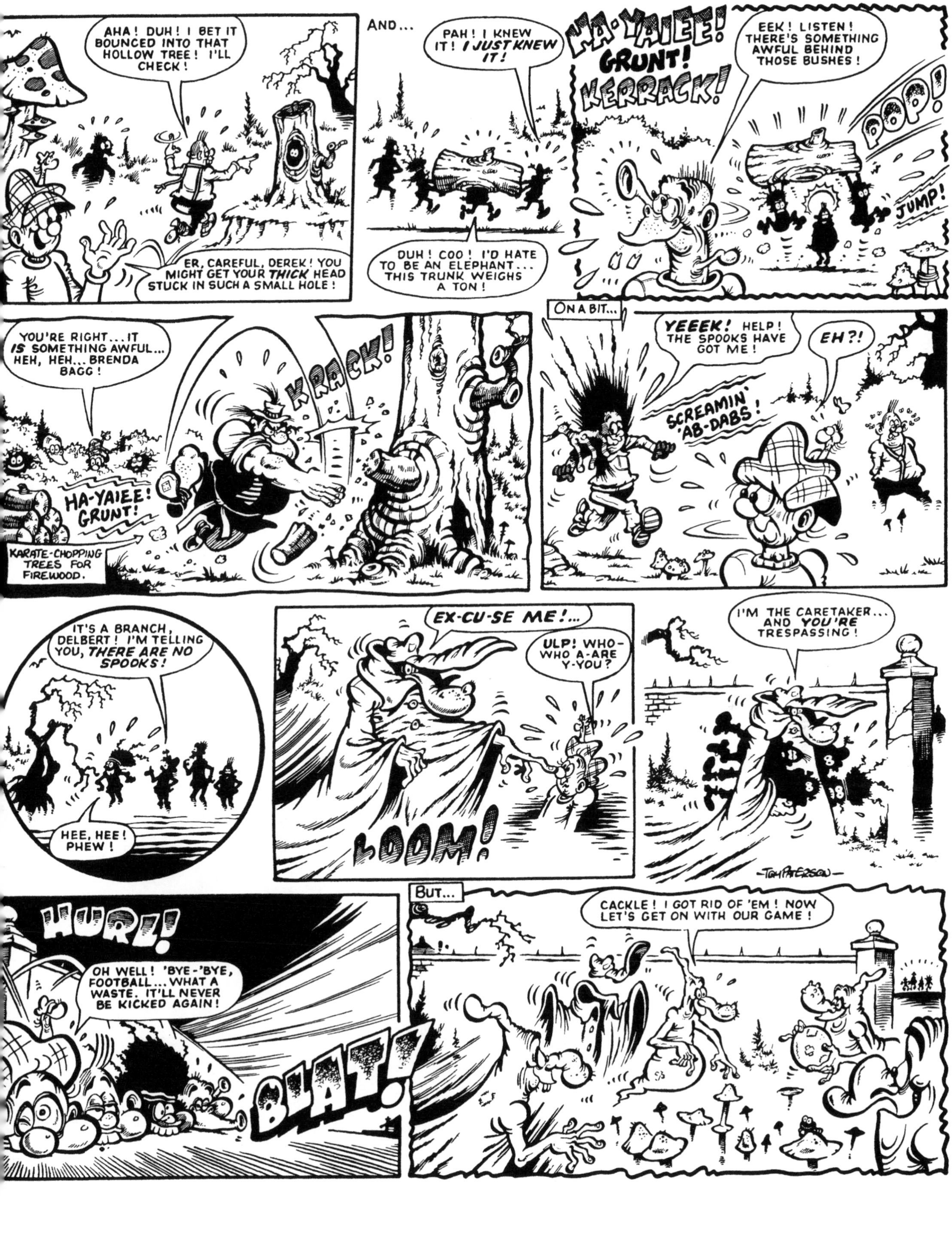

AHA! DUH! I BET IT BOUNCED INTO THAT HOLLOW TREE! I'LL CHECK!
ER, CAREFUL, DEREK! YOU MIGHT GET YOUR THICK HEAD STUCK IN SUCH A SMALL HOLE!
AND...
PAH! I KNEW IT! I JUST KNEW IT!
DUH! COO! I'D HATE TO BE AN ELEPHANT... THIS TRUNK WEIGHS A TON!
HA-YAIEE! GRUNT! KERRACK!
EEK! LISTEN! THERE'S SOMETHING AWFUL BEHIND THOSE BUSHES!
POP!
JUMP!
YOU'RE RIGHT... IT IS SOMETHING AWFUL... HEH, HEH... BRENDA BAGG!
KRACK!
HA-YAIEE! GRUNT!
KARATE-CHOPPING TREES FOR FIREWOOD.
ON A BIT...
YEEEK! HELP! THE SPOOKS HAVE GOT ME!
EH?!
SCREAMIN' 'AB-DABS!
IT'S A BRANCH, DELBERT! I'M TELLING YOU, THERE ARE NO SPOOKS!
HEE, HEE! PHEW!
EX-CU-SE ME!...
ULP! WHO-WHO A-ARE Y-YOU?
LOOM!
I'M THE CARETAKER... AND YOU'RE TRESPASSING!
TOM PATERSON
HURL!
OH WELL! 'BYE-'BYE, FOOTBALL... WHAT A WASTE. IT'LL NEVER BE KICKED AGAIN!
BLAT!
BUT...
CACKLE! I GOT RID OF 'EM! NOW LET'S GET ON WITH OUR GAME!

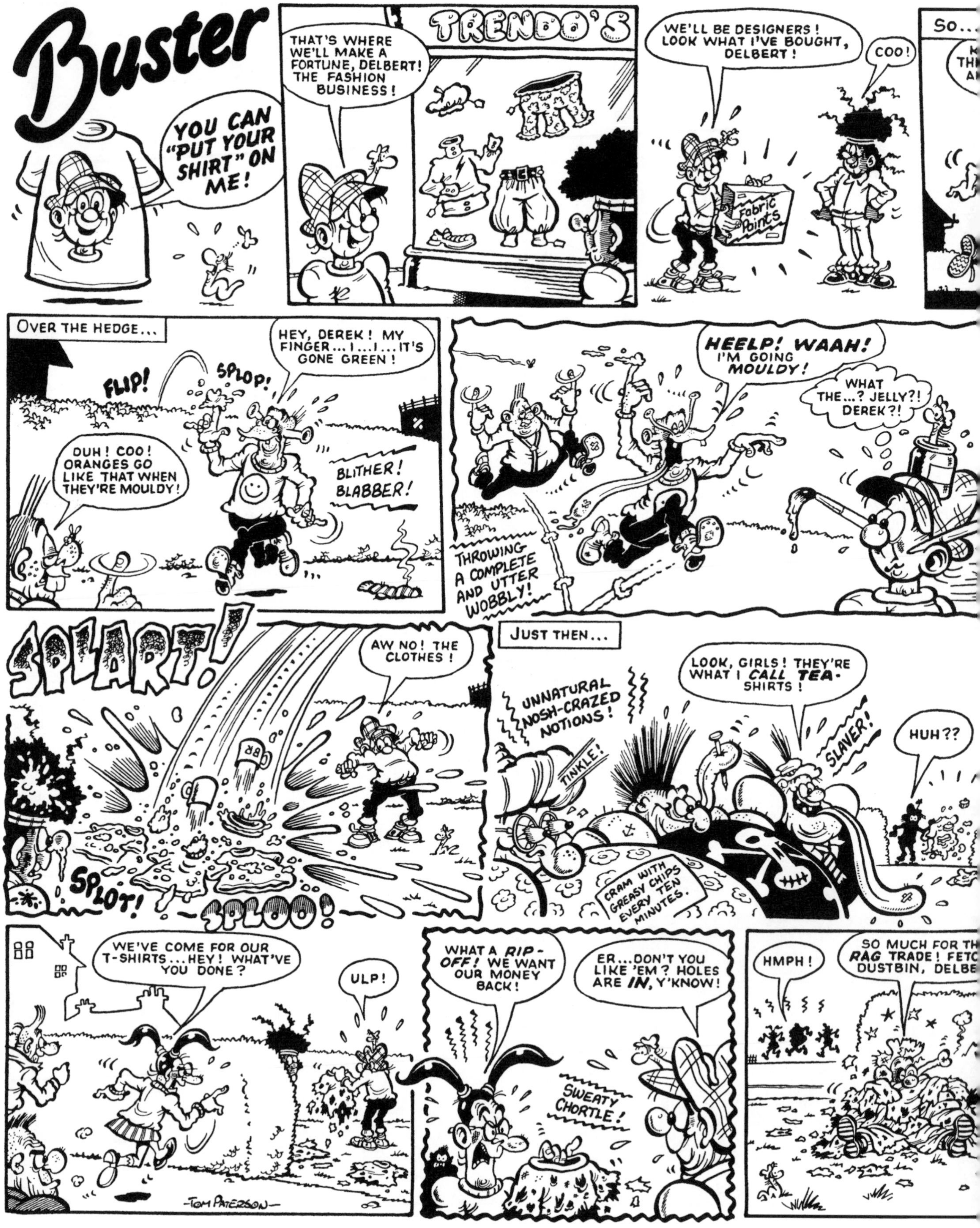

Buster
YOU CAN "PUT YOUR SHIRT" ON ME!
THAT'S WHERE WE'LL MAKE A FORTUNE, DELBERT! THE FASHION BUSINESS!
TRENDO'S
WE'LL BE DESIGNERS! LOOK WHAT I'VE BOUGHT, DELBERT!
COO!
Fabric Paints
SO...
OVER THE HEDGE...
FLIP!
SPLOP!
HEY, DEREK! MY FINGER...I...I...IT'S GONE GREEN!
DUH! COO! ORANGES GO LIKE THAT WHEN THEY'RE MOULDY!
BLITHER! BLABBER!
HEELP! WAAH! I'M GOING MOULDY!
WHAT THE...? JELLY?! DEREK?!
THROWING A COMPLETE AND UTTER WOBBLY!
SPLART!
AW NO! THE CLOTHES!
SPLOT!
SPLOO!
JUST THEN...
UNNATURAL NOSH-CRAZED NOTIONS!
TINKLE!
LOOK, GIRLS! THEY'RE WHAT I CALL TEA-SHIRTS!
SLAVER!
HUH??
CRAM WITH GREASY CHIPS EVERY TEN MINUTES.
WE'VE COME FOR OUR T-SHIRTS...HEY! WHAT'VE YOU DONE?
ULP!
-TOM PATERSON-
WHAT A RIP-OFF! WE WANT OUR MONEY BACK!
ER...DON'T YOU LIKE 'EM? HOLES ARE IN, Y'KNOW!
SWEATY CHORTLE!
HMPH!
SO MUCH FOR TH
RAG TRADE! FETC
DUSTBIN, DELBE

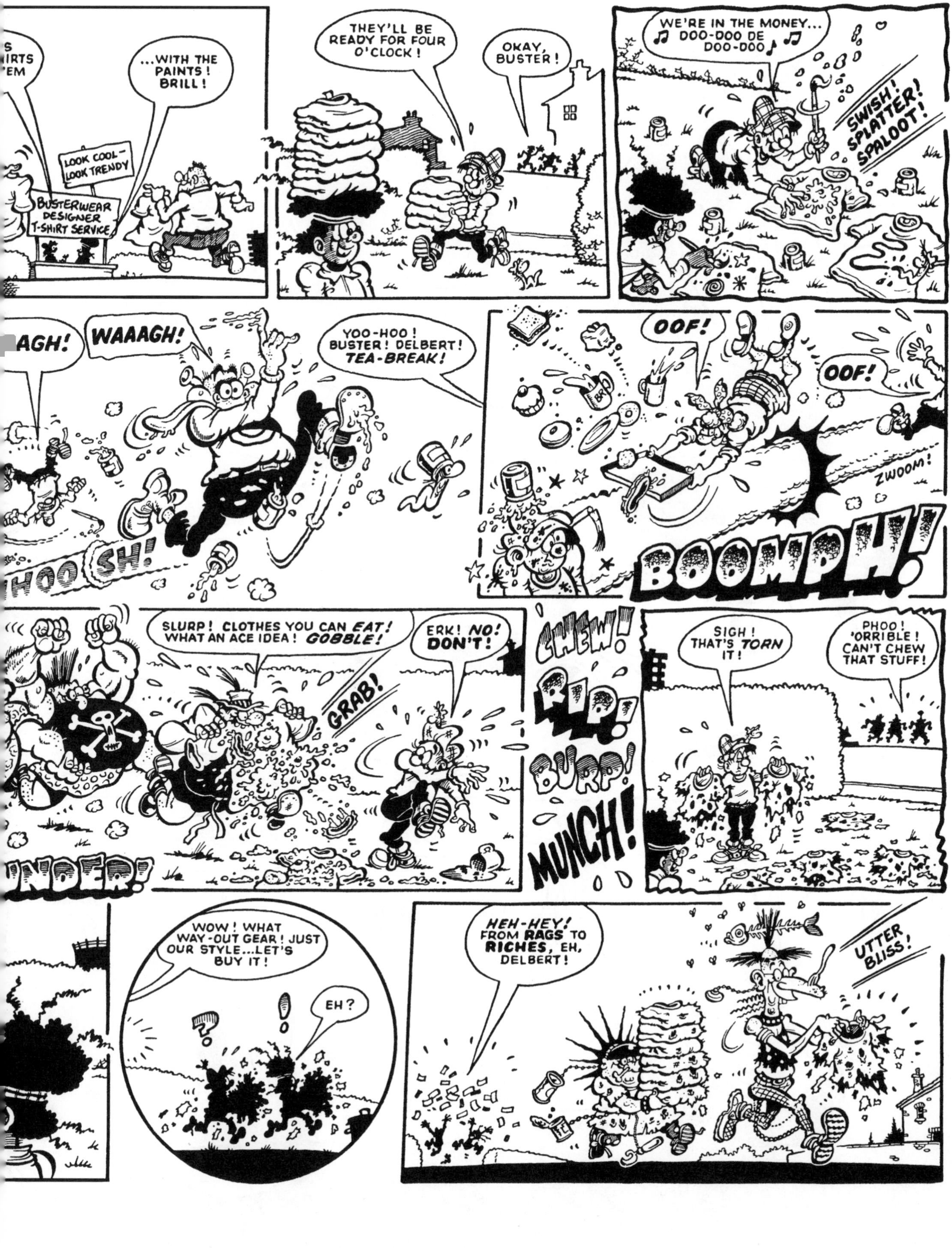

LOOK COOL - LOOK TRENDY
BUSTERWEAR DESIGNER T-SHIRT SERVICE
...WITH THE PAINTS! BRILL!
THEY'LL BE READY FOR FOUR O'CLOCK!
OKAY, BUSTER!
WE'RE IN THE MONEY... DOO-DOO DE DOO-DOO
SWISH! SPLATTER! SPALOOT!
AGH!
WAAAGH!
YOO-HOO! BUSTER! DELBERT! TEA-BREAK!
SH!
OOF!
OOF!
ZWOOM!
BOOMPH!
SLURP! CLOTHES YOU CAN EAT! WHAT AN ACE IDEA! GOBBLE!
ERK! NO! DON'T!
GRAB!
CHEW! RIP! BURP! MUNCH!
SIGH! THAT'S TORN IT!
PHOO! 'ORRIBLE! CAN'T CHEW THAT STUFF!
WOW! WHAT WAY-OUT GEAR! JUST OUR STYLE...LET'S BUY IT!
EH?
HEH-HEY! FROM RAGS TO RICHES, EH, DELBERT!
UTTER BLISS!

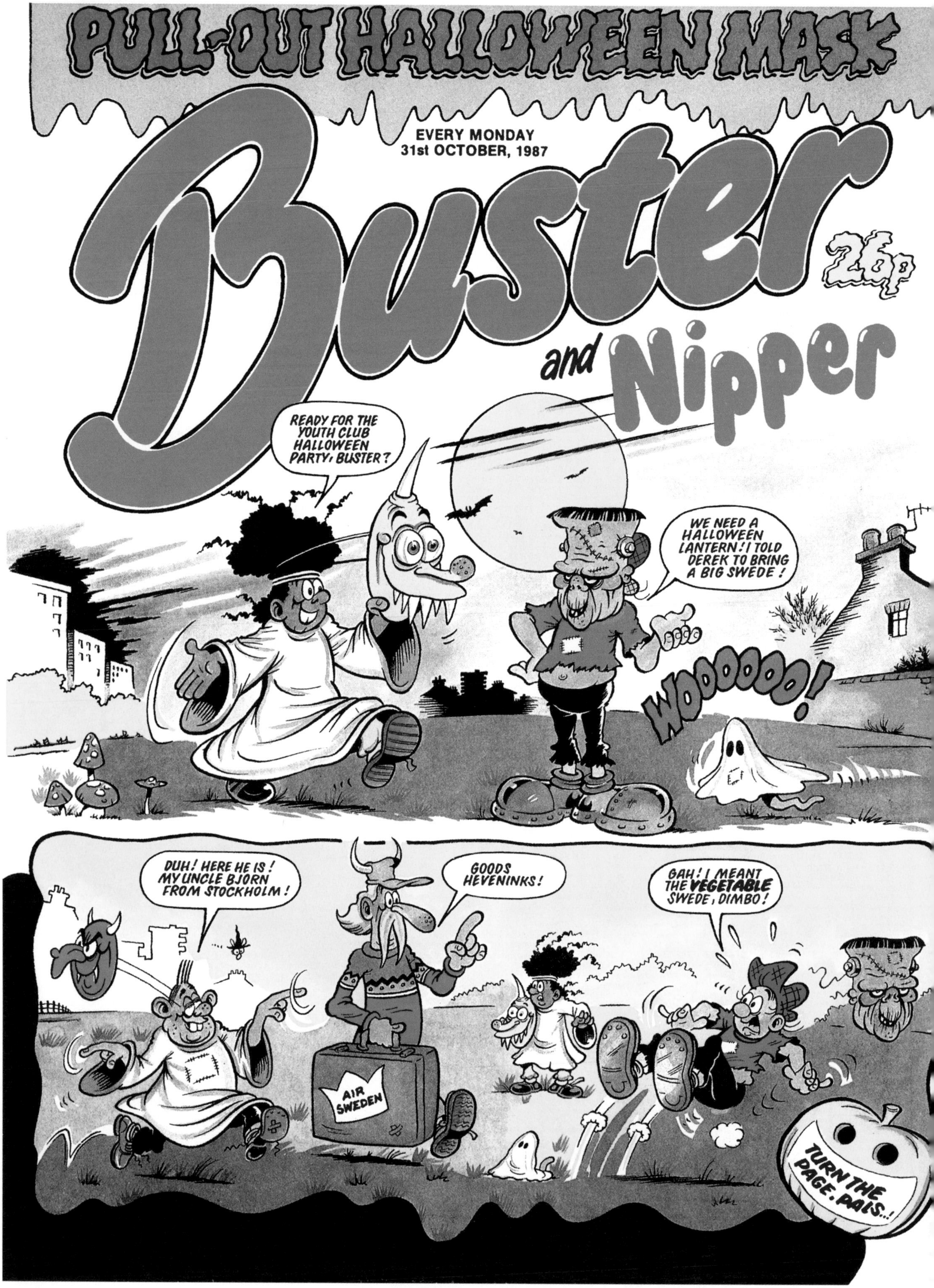
PULL-OUT HALLOWEEN MASK
EVERY MONDAY
31st OCTOBER, 1987
Buster
26p
and Nipper
READY FOR THE YOUTH CLUB HALLOWEEN PARTY, BUSTER?
WE NEED A HALLOWEEN LANTERN! I TOLD DEREK TO BRING A BIG SWEDE!
WOOOOOO!
DUH! HERE HE IS! MY UNCLE BJORN FROM STOCKHOLM!
GOODS HEVENINKS!
GAH! I MEANT THE VEGETABLE SWEDE, DIMBO!
AIR SWEDEN
TURN THE PAGE, PALS...!

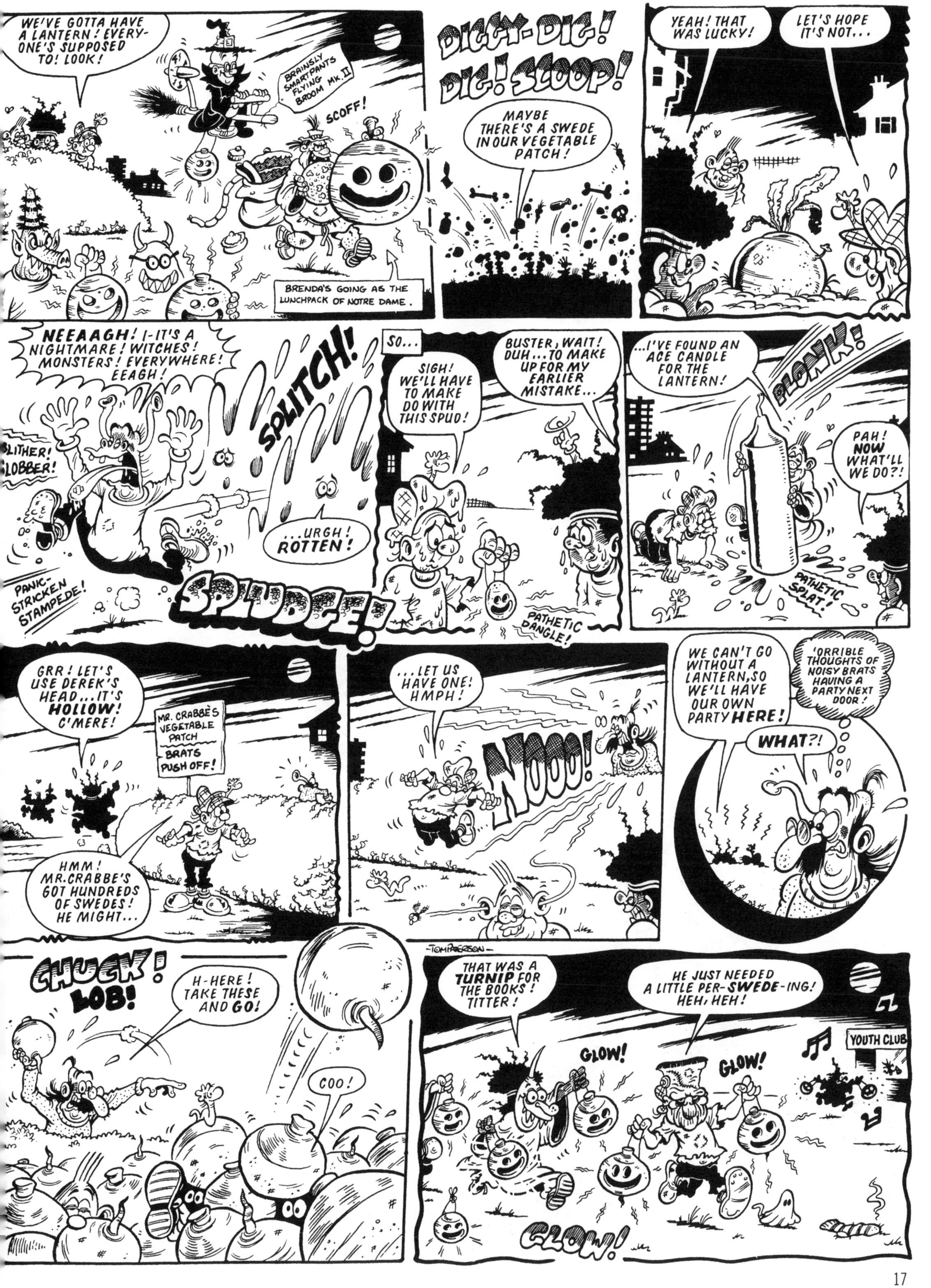

WE'VE GOTTA HAVE A LANTERN! EVERYONE'S SUPPOSED TO! LOOK!
BRAINSLY SMARTPANTS FLYING BROOM MK. II
SCOFF!
BRENDA'S GOING AS THE LUNCHPACK OF NOTRE DAME.
DIGGY-DIG! DIG! SLOOP!
MAYBE THERE'S A SWEDE IN OUR VEGETABLE PATCH!
YEAH! THAT WAS LUCKY!
LET'S HOPE IT'S NOT...
NEEAAGH! I-IT'S A NIGHTMARE! WITCHES! MONSTERS! EVERYWHERE! EEAGH!
SPLITCH!
SLITHER! SLOBBER!
...URGH! ROTTEN!
PANIC-STRICKEN STAMPEDE!
SPLUDGE!
SO...
SIGH! WE'LL HAVE TO MAKE DO WITH THIS SPUD!
BUSTER, WAIT! DUH... TO MAKE UP FOR MY EARLIER MISTAKE...
PATHETIC DANGLE!
...I'VE FOUND AN ACE CANDLE FOR THE LANTERN!
BLONK!
PAH! NOW WHAT'LL WE DO?!
PATHETIC SPLAT!
GRR! LET'S USE DEREK'S HEAD... IT'S HOLLOW! C'MERE!
MR. CRABBE'S VEGETABLE PATCH
BRATS PUSH OFF!
HMM! MR. CRABBE'S GOT HUNDREDS OF SWEDES! HE MIGHT...
...LET US HAVE ONE! HMPH!
NOOO!
WE CAN'T GO WITHOUT A LANTERN, SO WE'LL HAVE OUR OWN PARTY HERE!
'ORRIBLE THOUGHTS OF NOISY BRATS HAVING A PARTY NEXT DOOR!
WHAT?!
-TOM PATERSON-
CHUCK! LOB!
H-HERE! TAKE THESE AND GO!
COO!
THAT WAS A TURNIP FOR THE BOOKS! TITTER!
HE JUST NEEDED A LITTLE PER-SWEDE-ING! HEH, HEH!
GLOW!
GLOW!
YOUTH CLUB
GLOW!

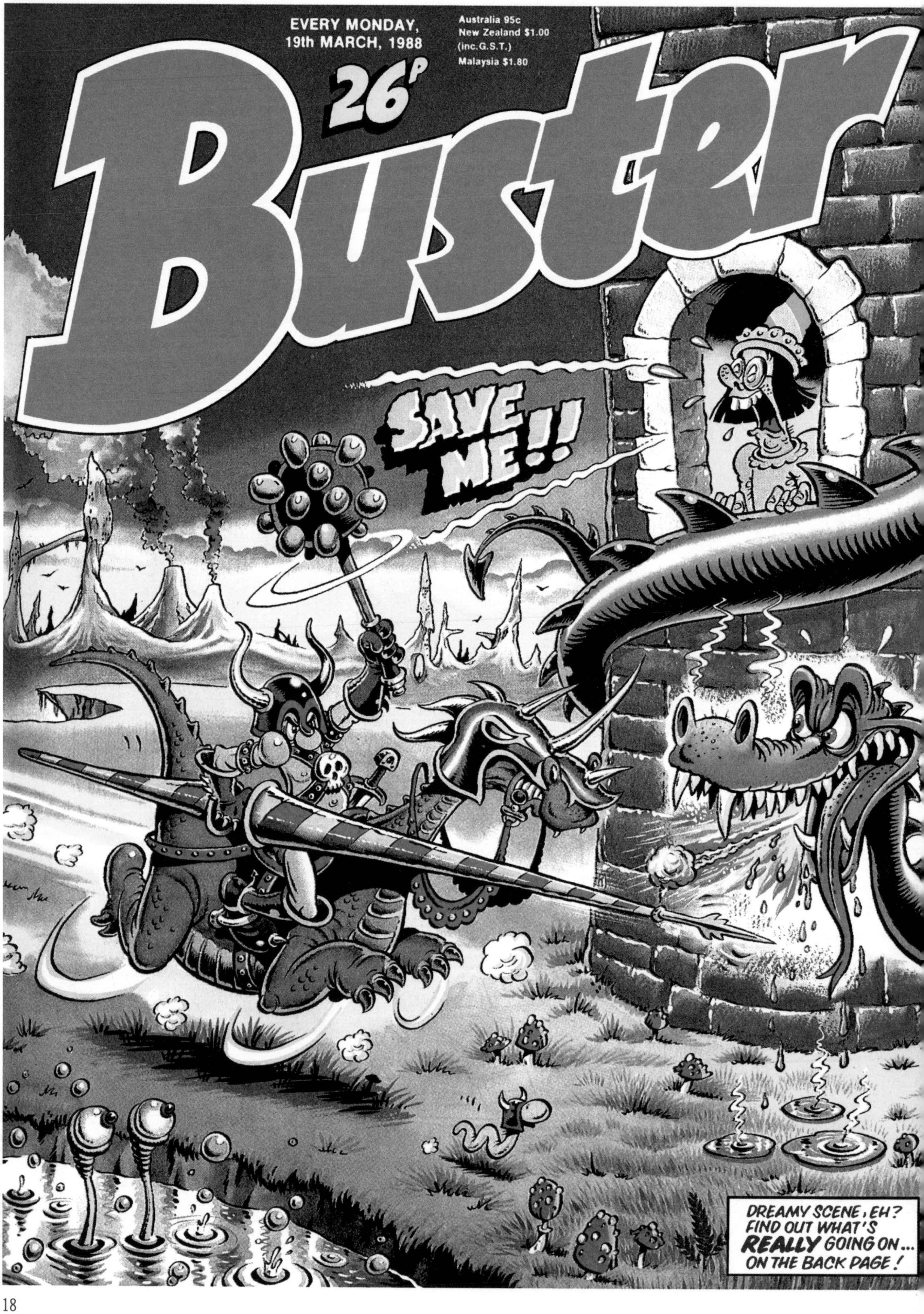
EVERY MONDAY,
19th MARCH, 1988
Australia 95c
New Zealand $1.00
(inc.G.S.T.)
Malaysia $1.80
26p
Buster
SAVE ME!!
DREAMY SCENE, EH? FIND OUT WHAT'S REALLY GOING ON... ON THE BACK PAGE!

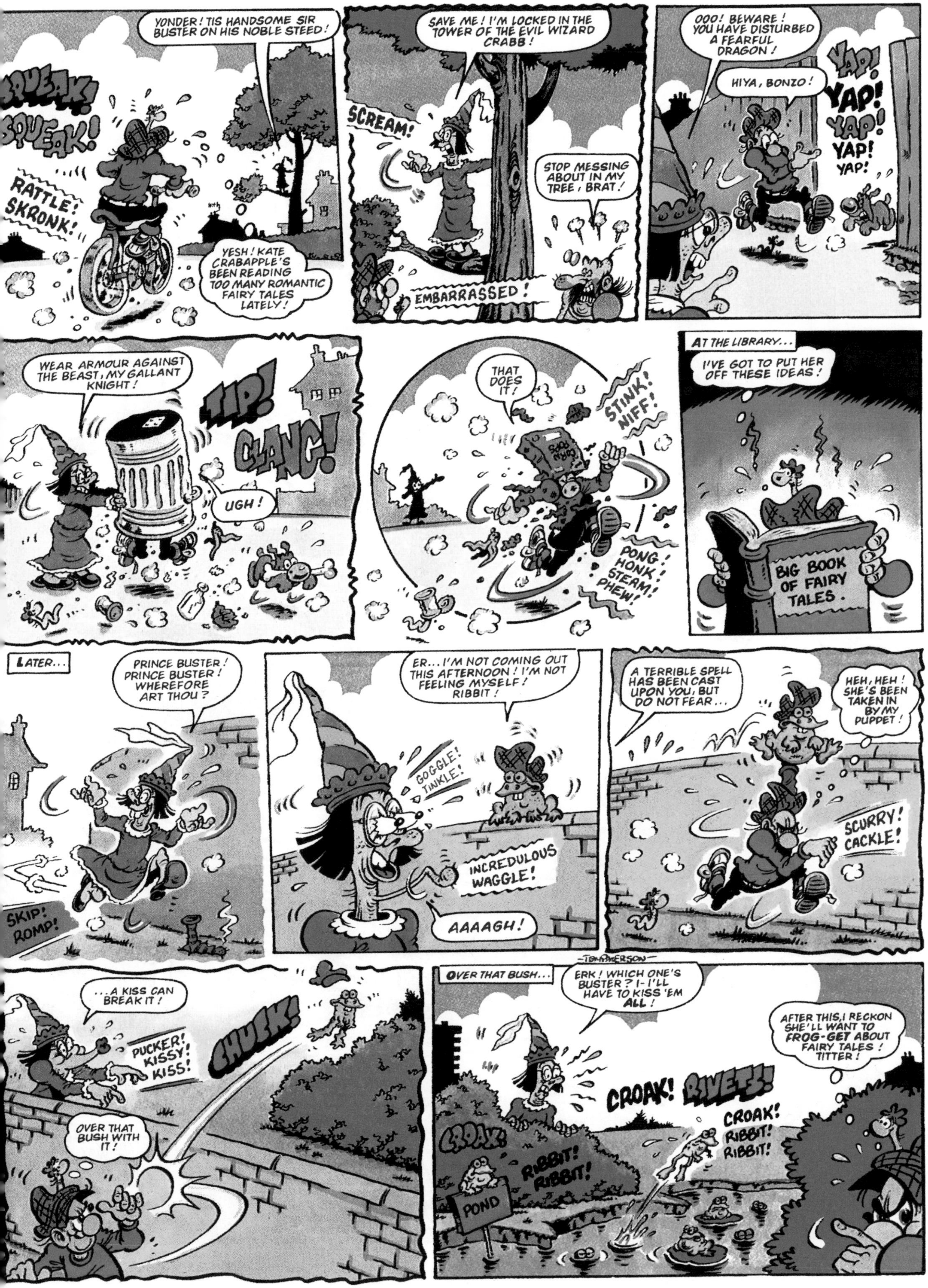
YONDER! TIS HANDSOME SIR BUSTER ON HIS NOBLE STEED!
SQUEAK! SQUEAK!
RATTLE! SKRONK!
YESH! KATE CRABAPPLE'S BEEN READING TOO MANY ROMANTIC FAIRY TALES LATELY!
SAVE ME! I'M LOCKED IN THE TOWER OF THE EVIL WIZARD CRABB!
SCREAM!
STOP MESSING ABOUT IN MY TREE, BRAT!
EMBARRASSED!
OOO! BEWARE! YOU HAVE DISTURBED A FEARFUL DRAGON!
HIYA, BONZO!
YAP! YAP! YAP! YAP! YAP!
WEAR ARMOUR AGAINST THE BEAST, MY GALLANT KNIGHT!
TIP! CLANG!
UGH!
THAT DOES IT!
STINK! NIFF!
CORN POPS
PONG! HONK! STEAM! PHEW!
AT THE LIBRARY...
I'VE GOT TO PUT HER OFF THESE IDEAS!
BIG BOOK OF FAIRY TALES.
LATER...
PRINCE BUSTER! PRINCE BUSTER! WHEREFORE ART THOU?
SKIP! ROMP!
ER... I'M NOT COMING OUT THIS AFTERNOON! I'M NOT FEELING MYSELF! RIBBIT!
GOGGLE! TINKLE!
INCREDULOUS WAGGLE!
AAAAGH!
A TERRIBLE SPELL HAS BEEN CAST UPON YOU, BUT DO NOT FEAR...
HEH, HEH! SHE'S BEEN TAKEN IN BY MY PUPPET!
SCURRY! CACKLE!
...A KISS CAN BREAK IT!
PUCKER! KISSY! KISS!
CHUCK!
OVER THAT BUSH WITH IT!
OVER THAT BUSH...
ERK! WHICH ONE'S BUSTER? I-I'LL HAVE TO KISS 'EM ALL!
AFTER THIS, I RECKON SHE'LL WANT TO FROG-GET ABOUT FAIRY TALES! TITTER!
CROAK! RIVETS!
CROAK!
CROAK! RIBBIT! RIBBIT!
RIBBIT! RIBBIT!
POND

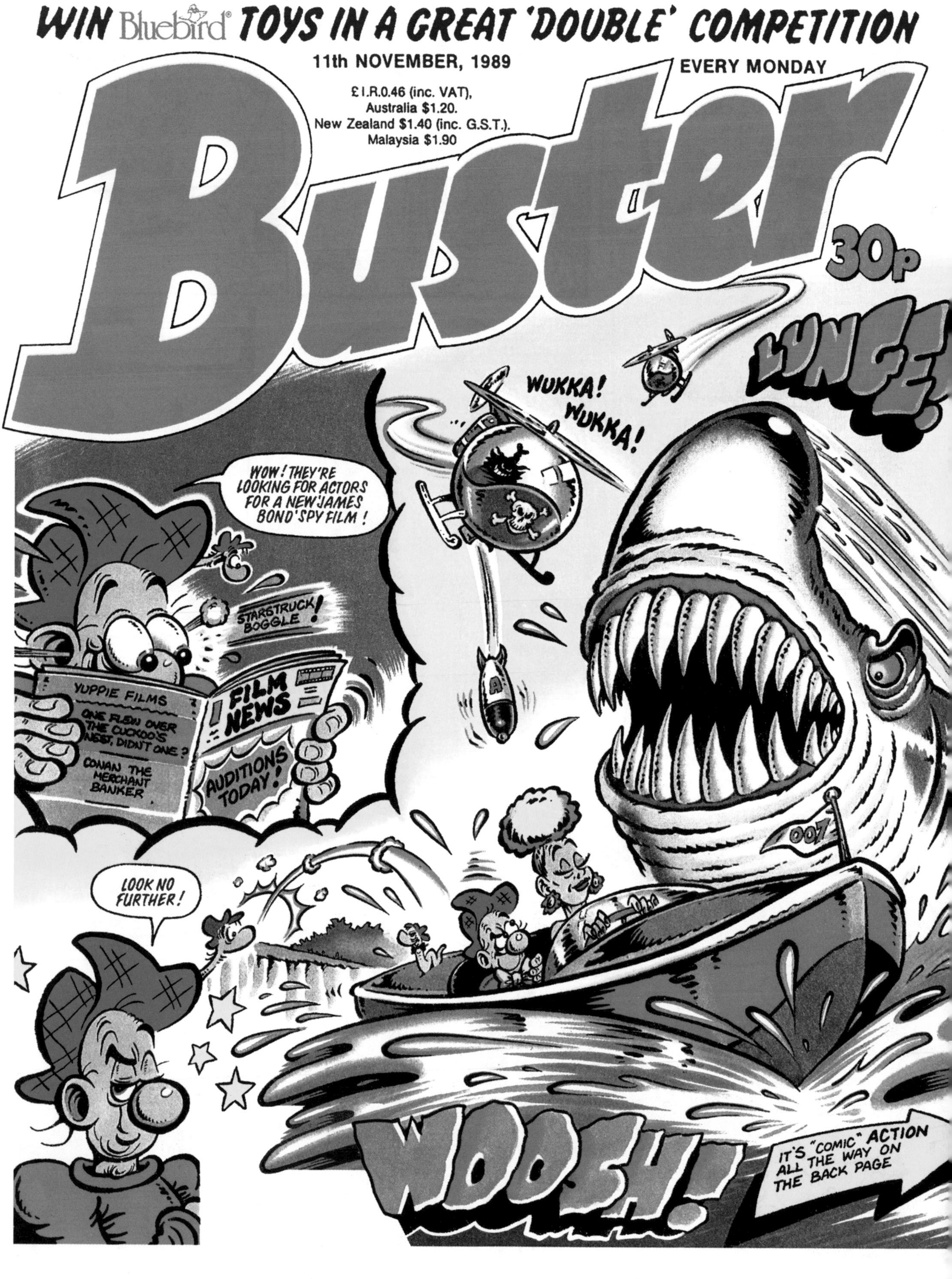
WIN Bluebird TOYS IN A GREAT 'DOUBLE' COMPETITION
11th NOVEMBER, 1989
EVERY MONDAY
£I.R.0.46 (inc. VAT), Australia $1.20. New Zealand $1.40 (inc. G.S.T.). Malaysia $1.90
Buster
30p
LUNGE!
WUKKA! WUKKA!
WOW! THEY'RE LOOKING FOR ACTORS FOR A NEW 'JAMES BOND' SPY FILM!
STARSTRUCK! BOGGLE!
YUPPIE FILMS
ONE FLEW OVER THE CUCKOO'S NEST, DIDN'T ONE?
CONAN THE MERCHANT BANKER
FILM NEWS
AUDITIONS TODAY!
007
LOOK NO FURTHER!
WOOSH!
IT'S "COMIC" ACTION ALL THE WAY ON THE BACK PAGE

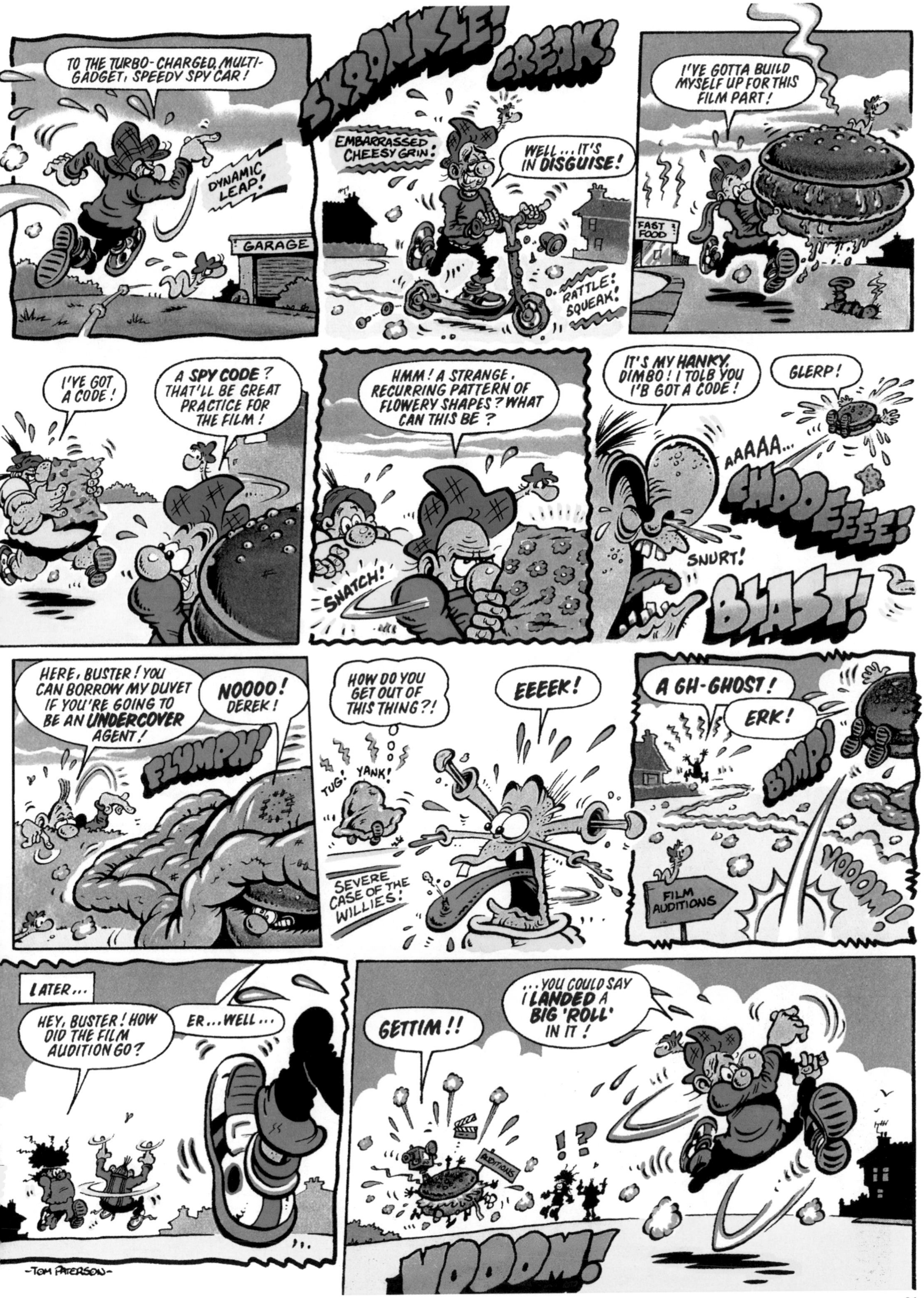

TO THE TURBO-CHARGED, MULTI-GADGET, SPEEDY SPY CAR!
DYNAMIC LEAP!
GARAGE
SKRONKLE!
CREAK!
EMBARRASSED CHEESY GRIN!
WELL... IT'S IN DISGUISE!
RATTLE! SQUEAK!
I'VE GOTTA BUILD MYSELF UP FOR THIS FILM PART!
FAST FOOD
I'VE GOT A CODE!
A SPY CODE? THAT'LL BE GREAT PRACTICE FOR THE FILM!
HMM! A STRANGE, RECURRING PATTERN OF FLOWERY SHAPES? WHAT CAN THIS BE?
SNATCH!
IT'S MY HANKY, DIMBO! I TOLB YOU I'B GOT A CODE!
GLERP!
AAAAA... CHOOEEEE!
SNURT!
BLAST!
HERE, BUSTER! YOU CAN BORROW MY DUVET IF YOU'RE GOING TO BE AN UNDERCOVER AGENT!
NOOOO! DEREK!
FLUMPH!
HOW DO YOU GET OUT OF THIS THING?!
TUG! YANK!
EEEEK!
SEVERE CASE OF THE WILLIES!
A GH-GHOST!
ERK!
BUMP!
FILM AUDITIONS
VOOOM!
LATER...
HEY, BUSTER! HOW DID THE FILM AUDITION GO?
ER... WELL...
...YOU COULD SAY I LANDED A BIG 'ROLL' IN IT!
GETTIM!!
AUDITIONS
!?
VOOOM!
-TOM PATERSON-

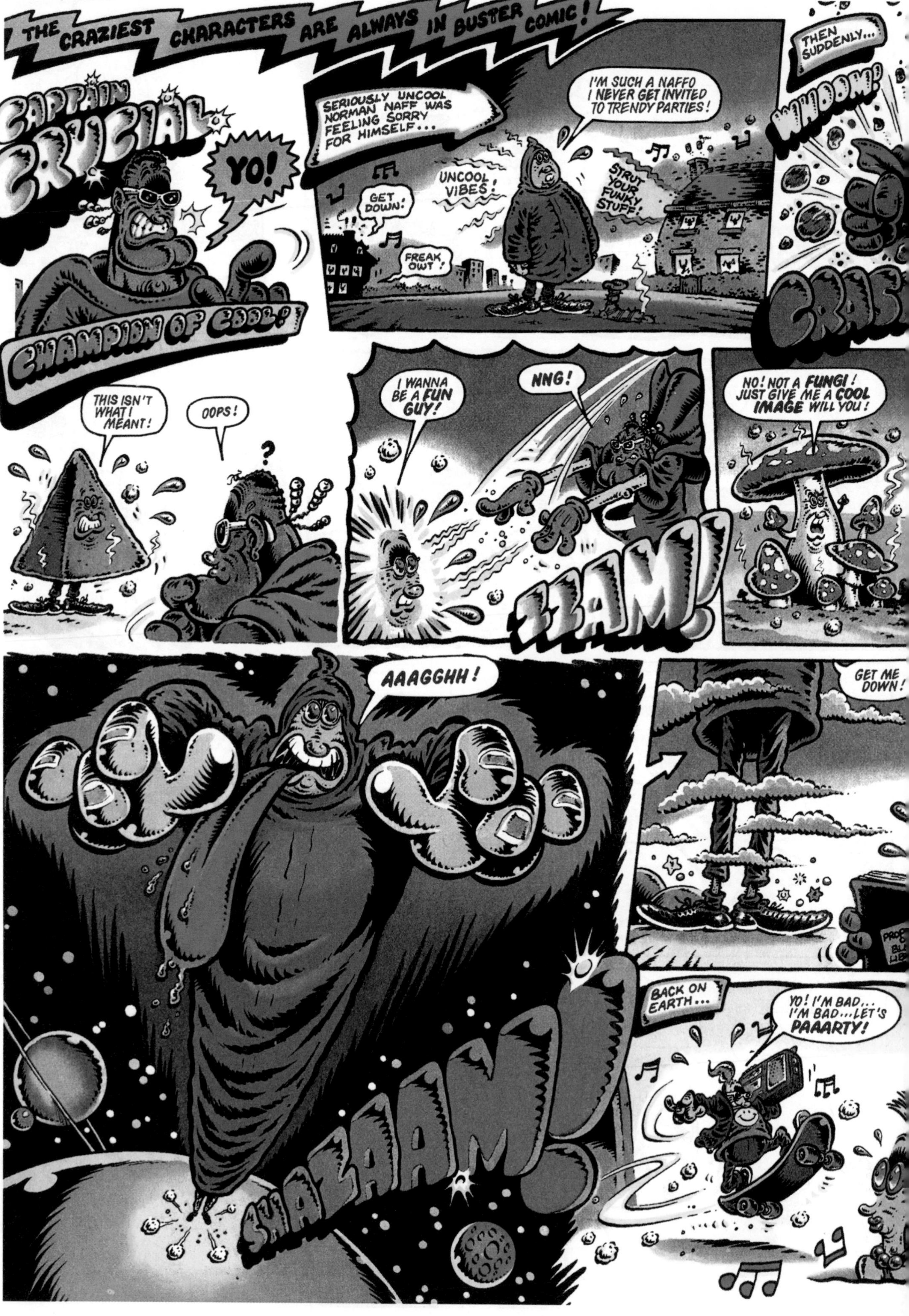
THE CRAZIEST CHARACTERS ARE ALWAYS IN BUSTER COMIC!
CAPTAIN CRUCIAL
YO!
CHAMPION OF COOL!
SERIOUSLY UNCOOL NORMAN NAFF WAS FEELING SORRY FOR HIMSELF...
I'M SUCH A NAFFO I NEVER GET INVITED TO TRENDY PARTIES!
GET DOWN!
UNCOOL VIBES!
FREAK OWT!
STRUT YOUR FUNKY STUFF!
THEN SUDDENLY...
WHOOM!
THIS ISN'T WHAT I MEANT!
OOPS!
I WANNA BE A FUN GUY!
NNG!
ZZAM!
NO! NOT A FUNGI! JUST GIVE ME A COOL IMAGE WILL YOU!
AAAGGHH!
SHAZAAAM!
GET ME DOWN!
BACK ON EARTH...
YO! I'M BAD... I'M BAD... LET'S PAAARTY!

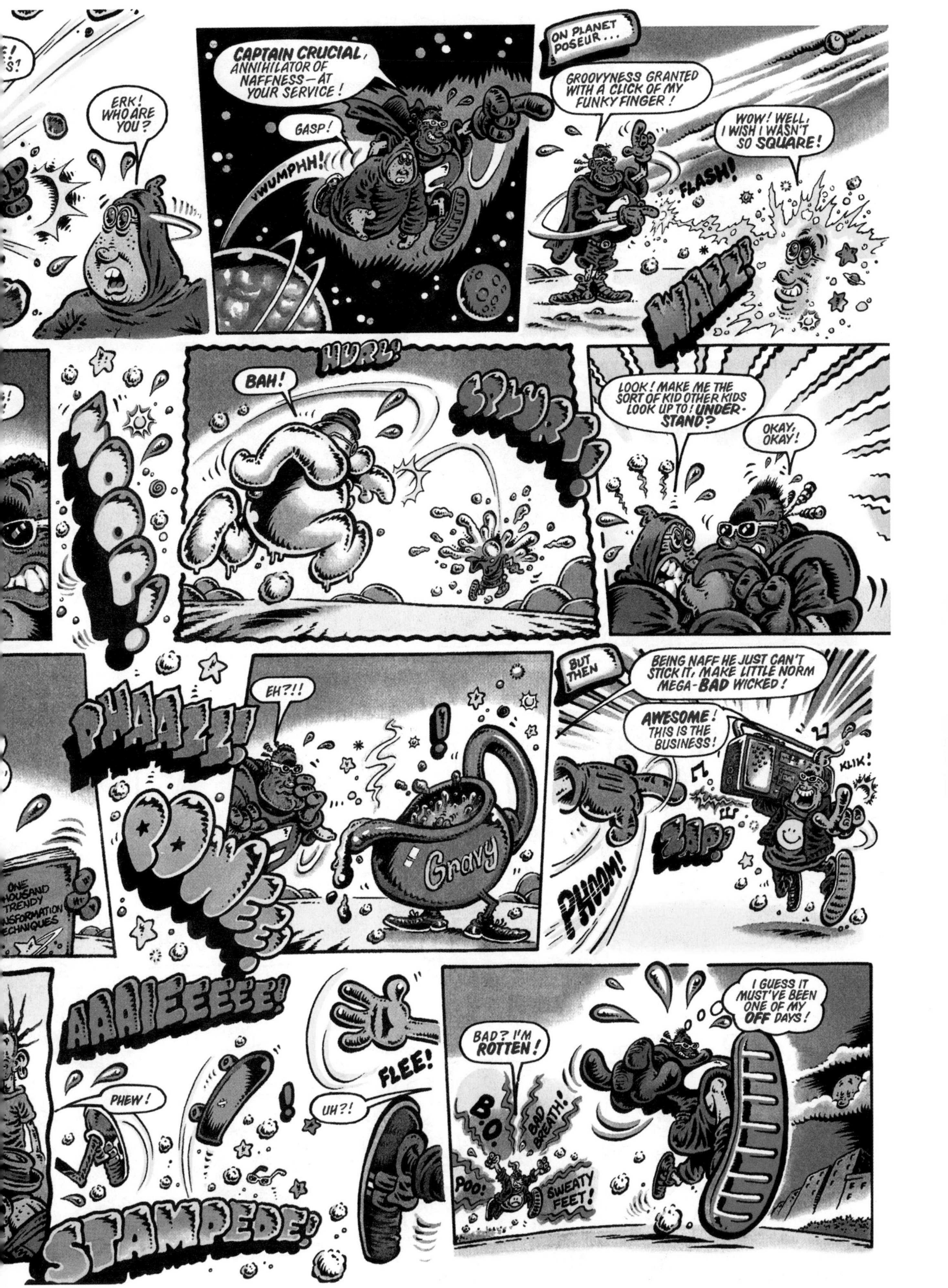
ERK! WHO ARE YOU?
CAPTAIN CRUCIAL, ANNIHILATOR OF NAFFNESS—AT YOUR SERVICE!
GASP!
WUMPHH!
ON PLANET POSEUR...
GROOVYNESS GRANTED WITH A CLICK OF MY FUNKY FINGER!
WOW! WELL, I WISH I WASN'T SO SQUARE!
FLASH!
ZOOP!
HURL!
BAH!
SPLURT!
LOOK! MAKE ME THE SORT OF KID OTHER KIDS LOOK UP TO! UNDERSTAND?
OKAY, OKAY!
PHAAZZ!
EH?!!
POWEEE
ONE THOUSAND TRENDY TRANSFORMATION TECHNIQUES
Gravy
BUT THEN
BEING NAFF HE JUST CAN'T STICK IT, MAKE LITTLE NORM MEGA-BAD WICKED!
AWESOME! THIS IS THE BUSINESS!
KLIK!
ZAP!
PHOOM!
AAAIEEEEE!
PHEW!
FLEE!
UH?!
STAMPEDE!
BAD? I'M ROTTEN!
B.O.
BAD BREATH!
POO!
SWEATY FEET!
I GUESS IT MUST'VE BEEN ONE OF MY OFF DAYS!

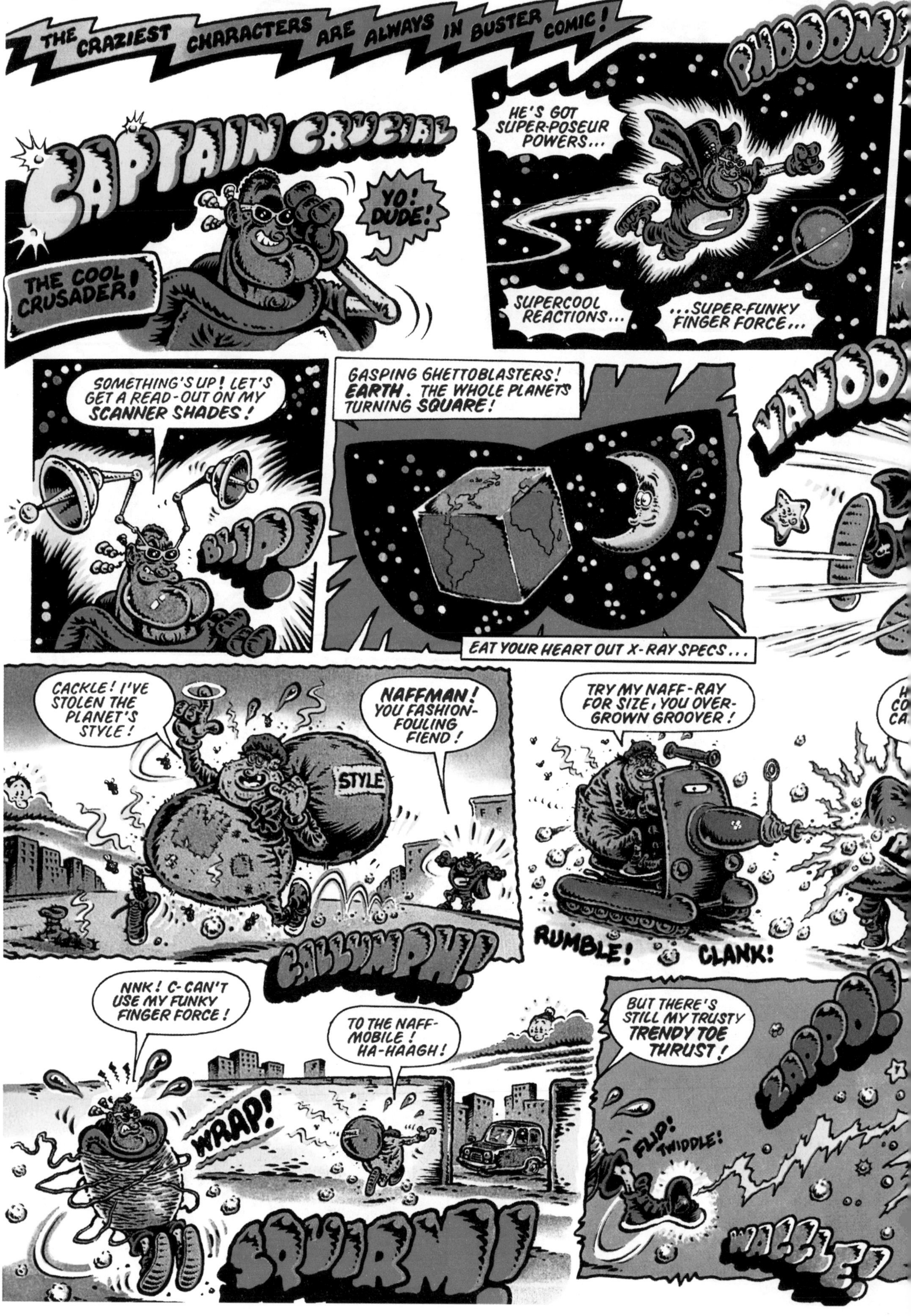
THE CRAZIEST CHARACTERS ARE ALWAYS IN BUSTER COMIC!
CAPTAIN CRUCIAL
YO! DUDE!
THE COOL CRUSADER!
HE'S GOT SUPER-POSEUR POWERS...
SUPERCOOL REACTIONS...
...SUPER-FUNKY FINGER FORCE...
SOMETHING'S UP! LET'S GET A READ-OUT ON MY SCANNER SHADES!
BLIP!
GASPING GHETTOBLASTERS! EARTH. THE WHOLE PLANET'S TURNING SQUARE!
EAT YOUR HEART OUT X-RAY SPECS...
CACKLE! I'VE STOLEN THE PLANET'S STYLE!
STYLE
NAFFMAN! YOU FASHION-FOULING FIEND!
CALLUMPH!
TRY MY NAFF-RAY FOR SIZE, YOU OVER-GROWN GROOVER!
RUMBLE!
CLANK!
NNK! C-CAN'T USE MY FUNKY FINGER FORCE!
TO THE NAFF-MOBILE! HA-HAAGH!
WRAP!
SQUIRM!
BUT THERE'S STILL MY TRUSTY TRENDY TOE THRUST!
ZAPPO!
FLIP! TWIDDLE!

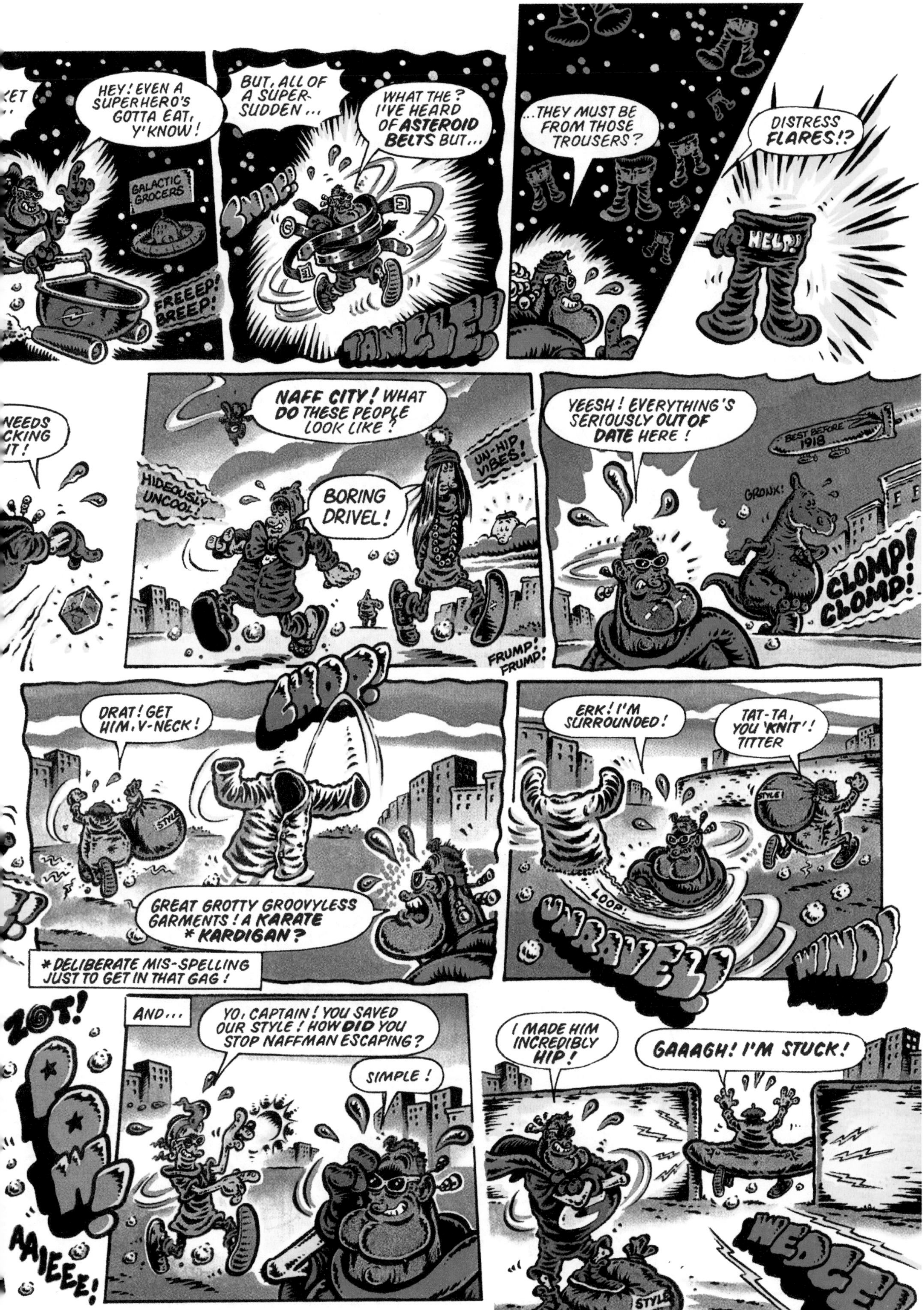
HEY! EVEN A SUPERHERO'S GOTTA EAT, Y'KNOW!
GALACTIC GROCERS
FREEEP! BREEP!
BUT, ALL OF A SUPER-SUDDEN...
WHAT THE? I'VE HEARD OF ASTEROID BELTS BUT...
TANGLE!
...THEY MUST BE FROM THOSE TROUSERS?
DISTRESS FLARES!?
HELP!
NEEDS
NAFF CITY! WHAT DO THESE PEOPLE LOOK LIKE?
HIDEOUSLY UNCOOL!
BORING DRIVEL!
UN-HIP VIBES!
FRUMP! FRUMP!
YEESH! EVERYTHING'S SERIOUSLY OUT OF DATE HERE!
BEST BEFORE 1918
GRONK!
CLOMP! CLOMP!
DRAT! GET HIM, V-NECK!
STYLE
GREAT GROTTY GROOVYLESS GARMENTS! A KARATE *KARDIGAN?
*DELIBERATE MIS-SPELLING JUST TO GET IN THAT GAG!
ERK! I'M SURROUNDED!
TAT-TA, YOU 'KNIT'! TITTER
STYLE
LOOP!
UNRAVEL!
WIND!
ZOT!
POW!
AAIEEEE!
AND...
YO, CAPTAIN! YOU SAVED OUR STYLE! HOW DID YOU STOP NAFFMAN ESCAPING?
SIMPLE!
I MADE HIM INCREDIBLY HIP!
GAAAGH! I'M STUCK!
WEDGE!
STYLE

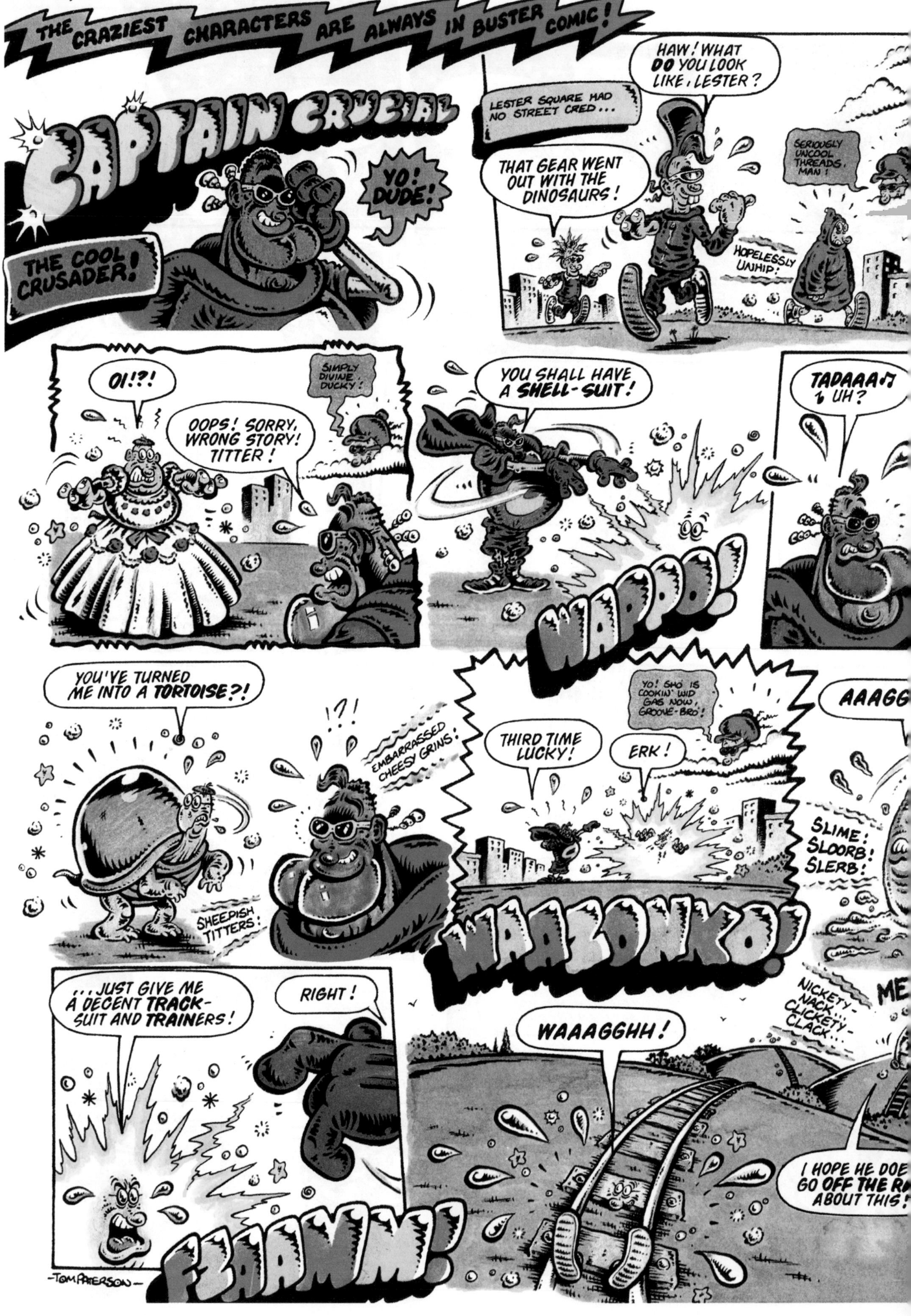

THE CRAZIEST CHARACTERS ARE ALWAYS IN BUSTER COMIC!
CAPTAIN CRUCIAL
THE COOL CRUSADER!
YO! DUDE!
LESTER SQUARE HAD NO STREET CRED...
HAW! WHAT DO YOU LOOK LIKE, LESTER?
THAT GEAR WENT OUT WITH THE DINOSAURS!
SERIOUSLY UNCOOL THREADS, MAN!
HOPELESSLY UNHIP!
OI!?!
SIMPLY DIVINE, DUCKY!
OOPS! SORRY, WRONG STORY! TITTER!
YOU SHALL HAVE A SHELL-SUIT!
WAPOO!
TADAAA ♪ UH?
YOU'VE TURNED ME INTO A TORTOISE?!
!?!
EMBARRASSED CHEESY GRINS!
SHEEPISH TITTERS!
YO! SHO' IS COOKIN' WID GAS NOW, GROOVE-BRO!
THIRD TIME LUCKY!
ERK!
WAAZONKO!
AAAGG
SLIME! SLOORB! SLERB!
...JUST GIVE ME A DECENT TRACK-SUIT AND TRAINERS!
RIGHT!
FZZAMM!
WAAAGGHH!
NICKETY-NACK, CLICKETY-CLACK...
ME
I HOPE HE DOE GO OFF THE RA ABOUT THIS!
-TOM PATERSON-

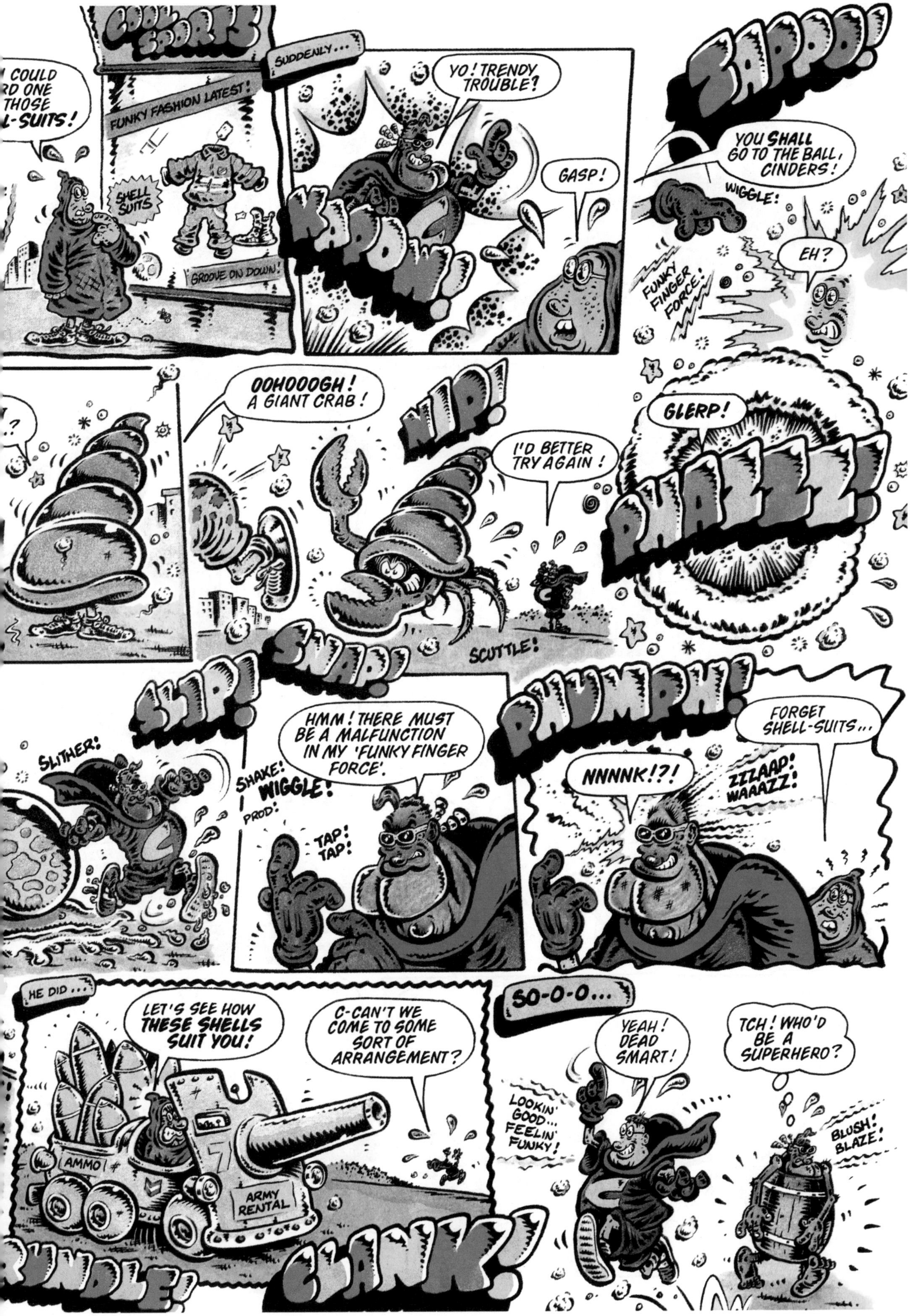
COOL SPORTS
FUNKY FASHION LATEST!
SHELL SUITS
GROOVE ON DOWN!
COULD
RD ONE
THOSE
L-SUITS!
SUDDENLY...
YO! TRENDY TROUBLE?
KAPOW!
GASP!
ZAPPO!
YOU SHALL GO TO THE BALL, CINDERS!
WIGGLE!
FUNKY FINGER FORCE!
EH?
OOHOOOGH! A GIANT CRAB!
NIP!
SNAP!
SCUTTLE!
I'D BETTER TRY AGAIN!
GLERP!
PHAZZZ!
SLIP!
SLITHER!
HMM! THERE MUST BE A MALFUNCTION IN MY 'FUNKY FINGER FORCE'.
SHAKE! WIGGLE!
PROD!
TAP! TAP!
PHUMPH!
NNNNK!?!
ZZZAAP! WAAAZZ!
FORGET SHELL-SUITS...
HE DID...
LET'S SEE HOW THESE SHELLS SUIT YOU!
C-CAN'T WE COME TO SOME SORT OF ARRANGEMENT?
AMMO
ARMY RENTAL
CLANK!
SO-O-O...
YEAH! DEAD SMART!
LOOKIN' GOOD... FEELIN' FUNKY!
TCH! WHO'D BE A SUPERHERO?
BLUSH! BLAZE!

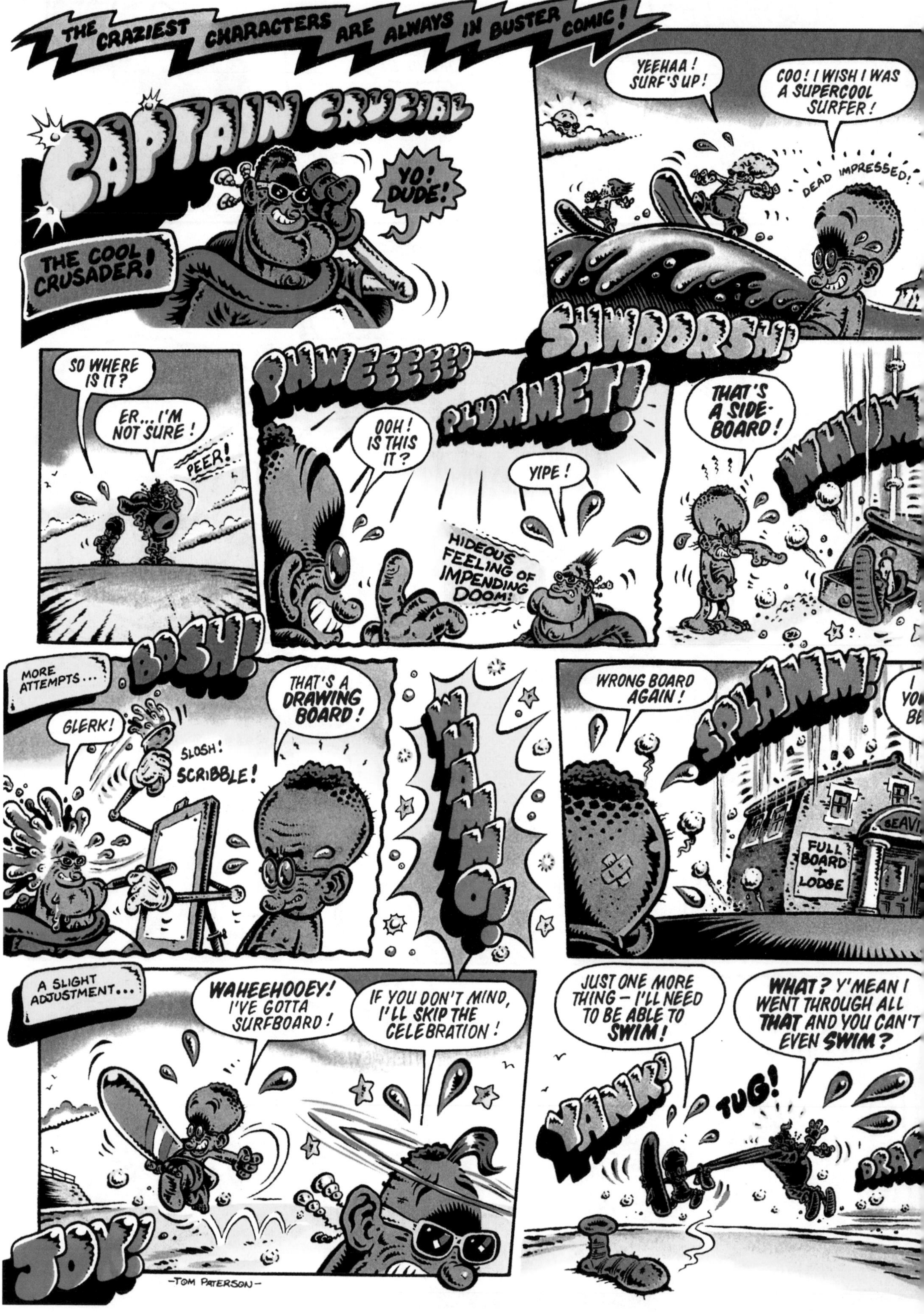
THE CRAZIEST CHARACTERS ARE ALWAYS IN BUSTER COMIC!
CAPTAIN CRUCIAL
THE COOL CRUSADER!
YO! DUDE!
YEEHAA! SURF'S UP!
COO! I WISH I WAS A SUPERCOOL SURFER!
DEAD IMPRESSED!
SHNOORSH!
SO WHERE IS IT?
ER... I'M NOT SURE!
PEER!
PHWEEEEE!
PLUMMET!
OOH! IS THIS IT?
YIPE!
HIDEOUS FEELING OF IMPENDING DOOM!
THAT'S A SIDE-BOARD!
MORE ATTEMPTS...
BOSH!
GLERK!
SLOSH!
SCRIBBLE!
THAT'S A DRAWING BOARD!
WHAMMO!
WRONG BOARD AGAIN!
SPLAMM!
FULL BOARD + LODGE
A SLIGHT ADJUSTMENT...
WAHEEHOOEY! I'VE GOTTA SURFBOARD!
IF YOU DON'T MIND, I'LL SKIP THE CELEBRATION!
JOY!
-TOM PATERSON-
JUST ONE MORE THING – I'LL NEED TO BE ABLE TO SWIM!
WHAT? Y'MEAN I WENT THROUGH ALL THAT AND YOU CAN'T EVEN SWIM?
YANK!
TUG!

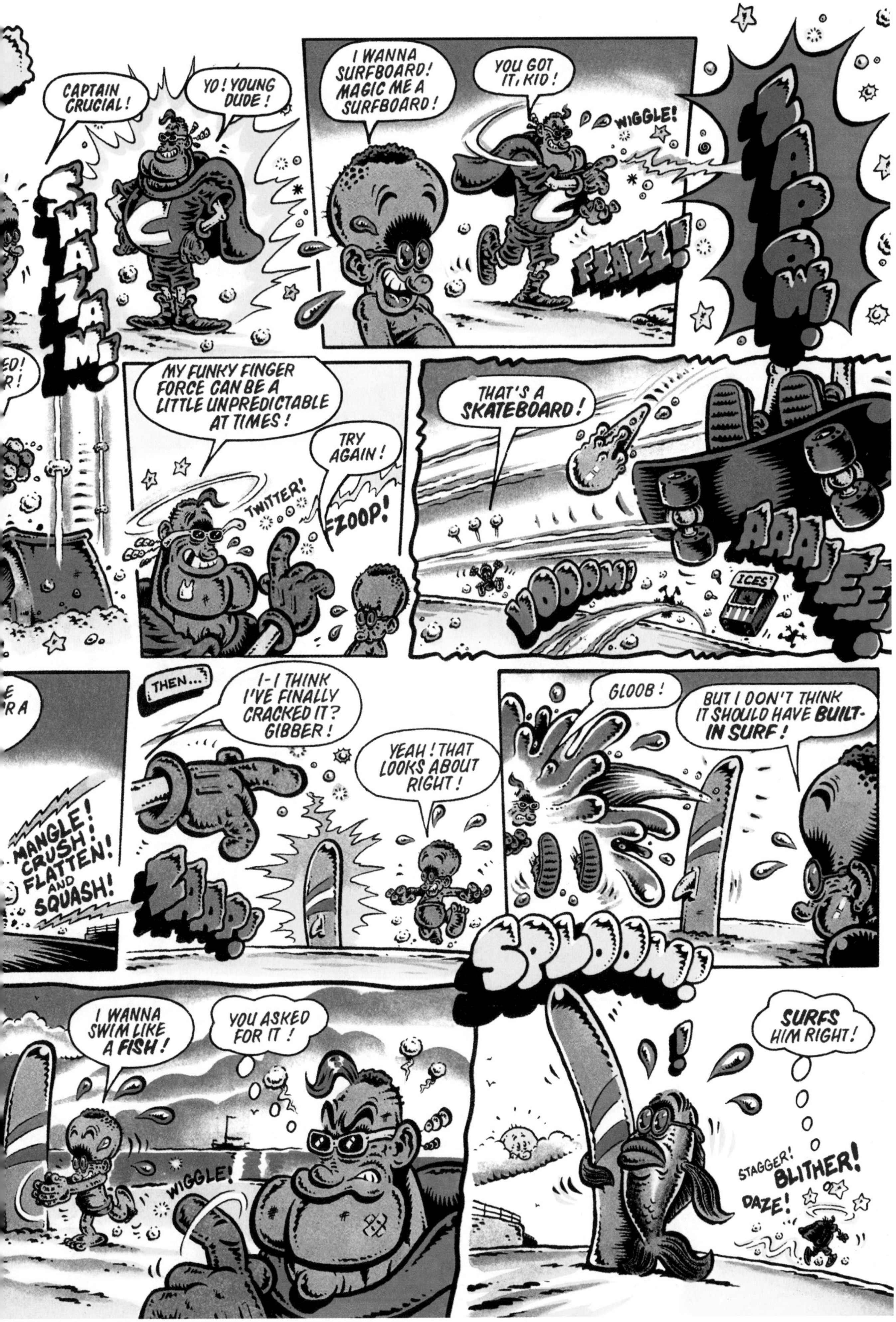
CAPTAIN CRUCIAL!
YO! YOUNG DUDE!
SHAZAAM!
I WANNA SURFBOARD! MAGIC ME A SURFBOARD!
YOU GOT IT, KID!
WIGGLE!
FZAZZ!
ZAPOW!
MY FUNKY FINGER FORCE CAN BE A LITTLE UNPREDICTABLE AT TIMES!
TRY AGAIN!
TWITTER!
FZOOP!
THAT'S A SKATEBOARD!
WOOOOM!
AAAIEEE!
ICES
THEN...
I-I THINK I'VE FINALLY CRACKED IT? GIBBER!
MANGLE! CRUSH! FLATTEN! AND SQUASH!
ZAP
YEAH! THAT LOOKS ABOUT RIGHT!
GLOOB!
BUT I DON'T THINK IT SHOULD HAVE BUILT-IN SURF!
SPLOOOM!
I WANNA SWIM LIKE A FISH!
YOU ASKED FOR IT!
WIGGLE!
SURFS HIM RIGHT!
STAGGER! BLITHER! DAZE!

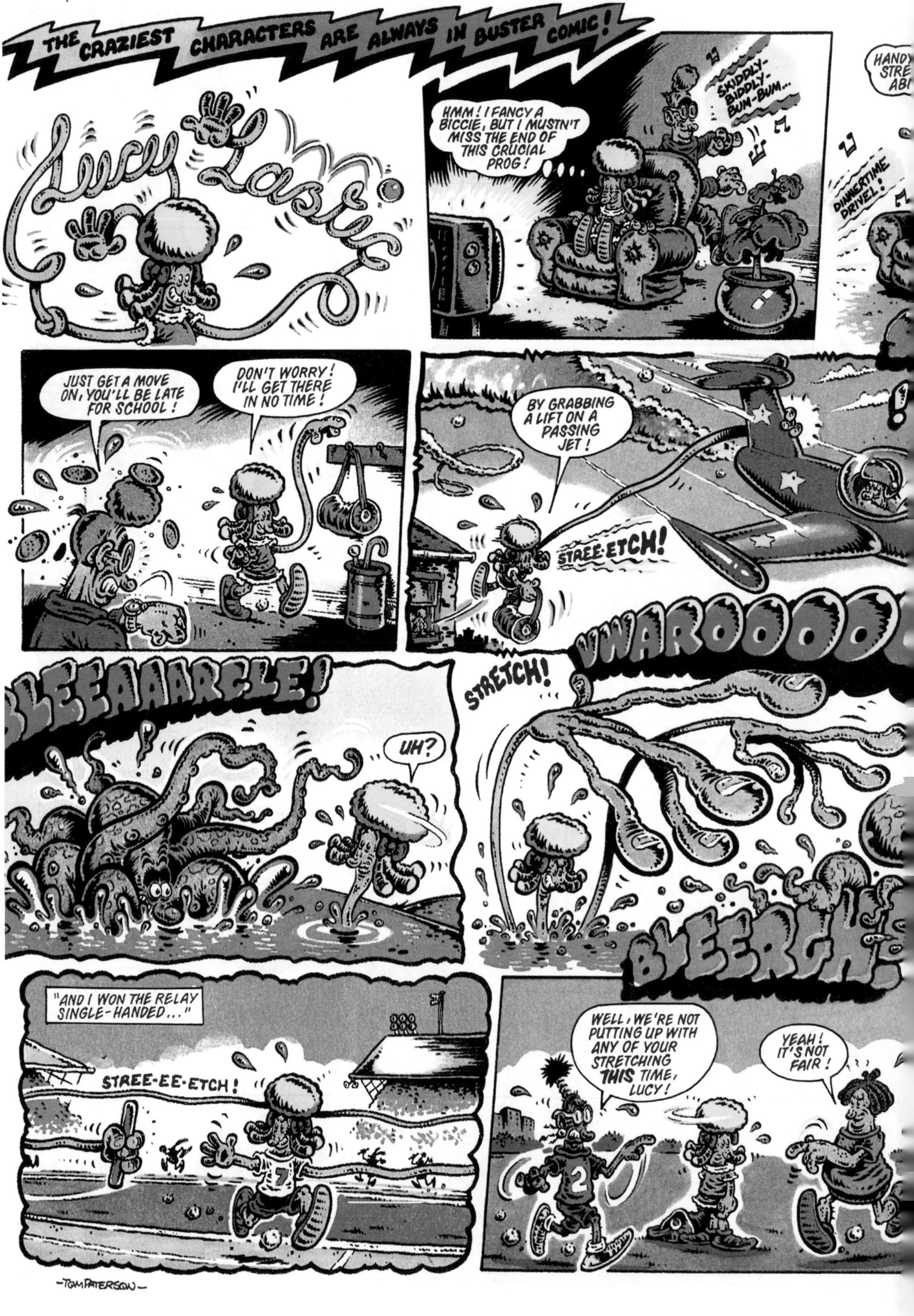
THE CRAZIEST CHARACTERS ARE ALWAYS IN BUSTER COMIC!
Lucy Lastic
HMM! I FANCY A BICCIE, BUT I MUSTN'T MISS THE END OF THIS CRUCIAL PROG!
SKIDDLY-BIDDLY-BUM-BUM...
DINNERTIME DRIVEL!
JUST GET A MOVE ON, YOU'LL BE LATE FOR SCHOOL!
DON'T WORRY! I'LL GET THERE IN NO TIME!
BY GRABBING A LIFT ON A PASSING JET!
STREE-ETCH!
BLEEAAARGLE!
UH?
STRETCH!
BLEERCH!
"AND I WON THE RELAY SINGLE-HANDED..."
STREE-EE-ETCH!
WELL, WE'RE NOT PUTTING UP WITH ANY OF YOUR STRETCHING THIS TIME, LUCY!
YEAH! IT'S NOT FAIR!
-TOM PATERSON-

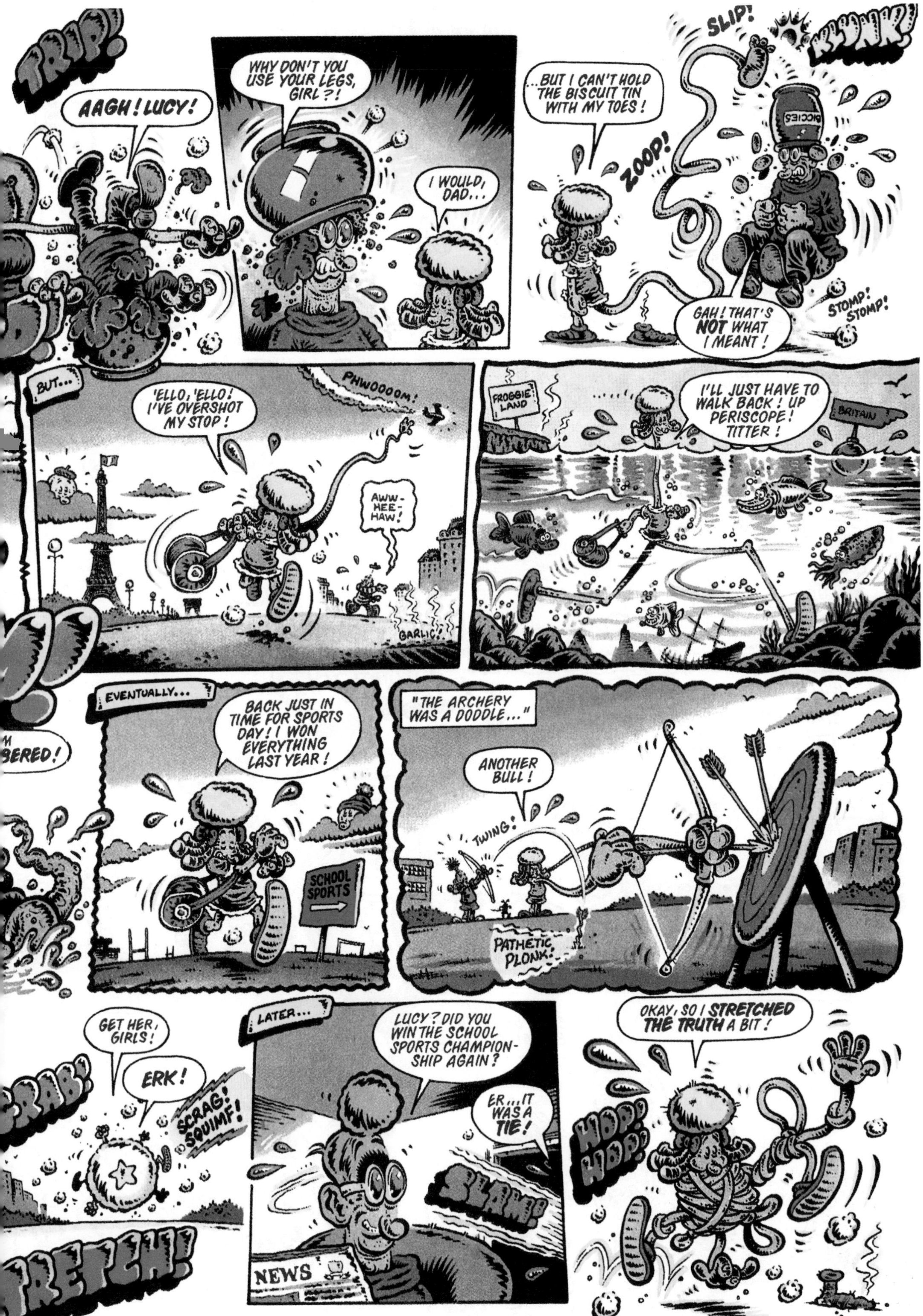

TRIP!
AAGH! LUCY!
WHY DON'T YOU USE YOUR LEGS, GIRL?!
I WOULD, DAD...
...BUT I CAN'T HOLD THE BISCUIT TIN WITH MY TOES!
ZOOP!
SLIP!
KLONK!
BICCIES
GAH! THAT'S NOT WHAT I MEANT!
STOMP! STOMP!
BUT...
PHWOOOOM!
'ELLO, 'ELLO! I'VE OVERSHOT MY STOP!
AWW-HEE-HAW!
GARLIC!
FROGGIE LAND
I'LL JUST HAVE TO WALK BACK! UP PERISCOPE! TITTER!
BRITAIN
EVENTUALLY...
BACK JUST IN TIME FOR SPORTS DAY! I WON EVERYTHING LAST YEAR!
SCHOOL SPORTS
"THE ARCHERY WAS A DODDLE..."
ANOTHER BULL!
TWING!
PATHETIC PLONK!
GET HER, GIRLS!
ERK!
SCRAG! SQUIMF!
LATER...
LUCY? DID YOU WIN THE SCHOOL SPORTS CHAMPIONSHIP AGAIN?
ER...IT WAS A TIE!
SLAM!
NEWS
OKAY, SO I STRETCHED THE TRUTH A BIT!
HOP! HOP!

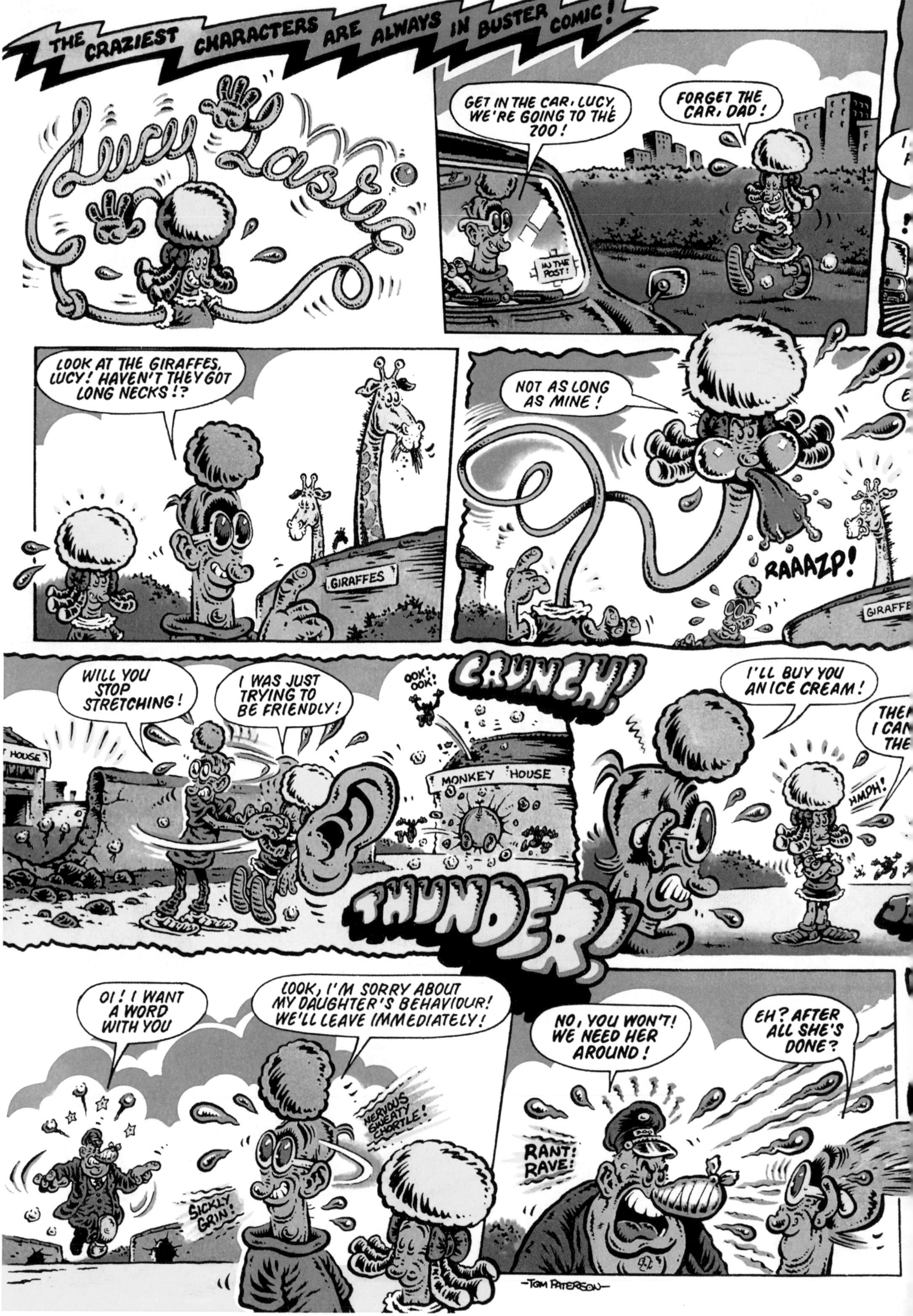
THE CRAZIEST CHARACTERS ARE ALWAYS IN BUSTER COMIC!
Lucy Lastic
GET IN THE CAR, LUCY, WE'RE GOING TO THE ZOO!
FORGET THE CAR, DAD!
IN THE POST!
LOOK AT THE GIRAFFES, LUCY! HAVEN'T THEY GOT LONG NECKS!?
GIRAFFES
NOT AS LONG AS MINE!
RAAAZP!
WILL YOU STOP STRETCHING!
I WAS JUST TRYING TO BE FRIENDLY!
OOK! OOK!
CRUNCH!
MONKEY HOUSE
THUNDER!
I'LL BUY YOU AN ICE CREAM!
HMPH!
OI! I WANT A WORD WITH YOU
LOOK, I'M SORRY ABOUT MY DAUGHTER'S BEHAVIOUR! WE'LL LEAVE IMMEDIATELY!
NERVOUS SWEATY CHORTLE!
SICKLY GRIN!
NO, YOU WON'T! WE NEED HER AROUND!
RANT! RAVE!
EH? AFTER ALL SHE'S DONE?
TOM PATERSON

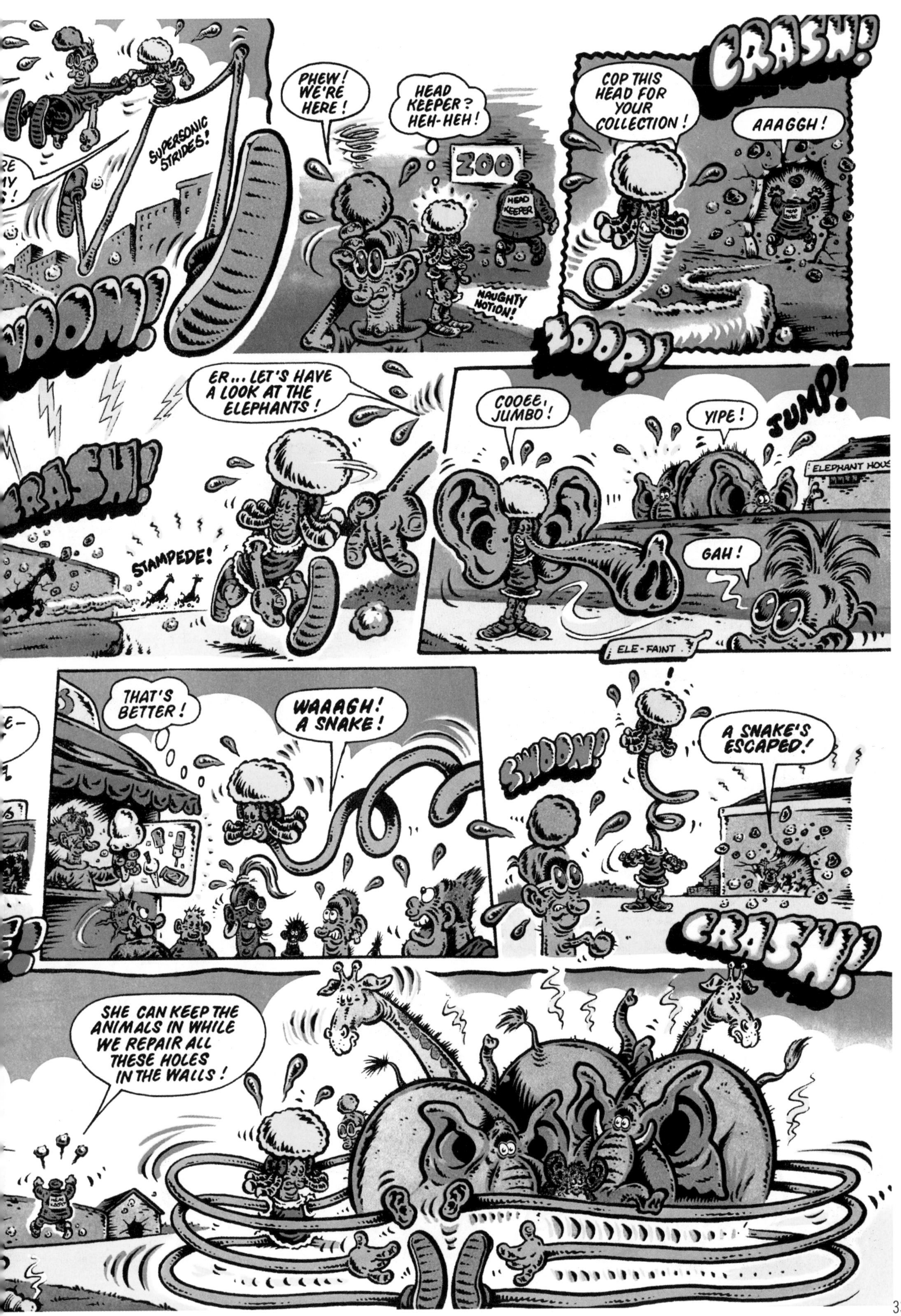
SUPERSONIC STRIDES!
PHEW! WE'RE HERE!
HEAD KEEPER? HEH-HEH!
ZOO
HEAD KEEPER
NAUGHTY NOTION!
CRASH!
COP THIS HEAD FOR YOUR COLLECTION!
AAAGGH!
ZOOP!
ER... LET'S HAVE A LOOK AT THE ELEPHANTS!
STAMPEDE!
COOEE, JUMBO!
YIPE!
JUMP!
GAH!
ELE-FAINT
THAT'S BETTER!
WAAAGH! A SNAKE!
SWOON!
A SNAKE'S ESCAPED!
CRASH!
SHE CAN KEEP THE ANIMALS IN WHILE WE REPAIR ALL THESE HOLES IN THE WALLS!

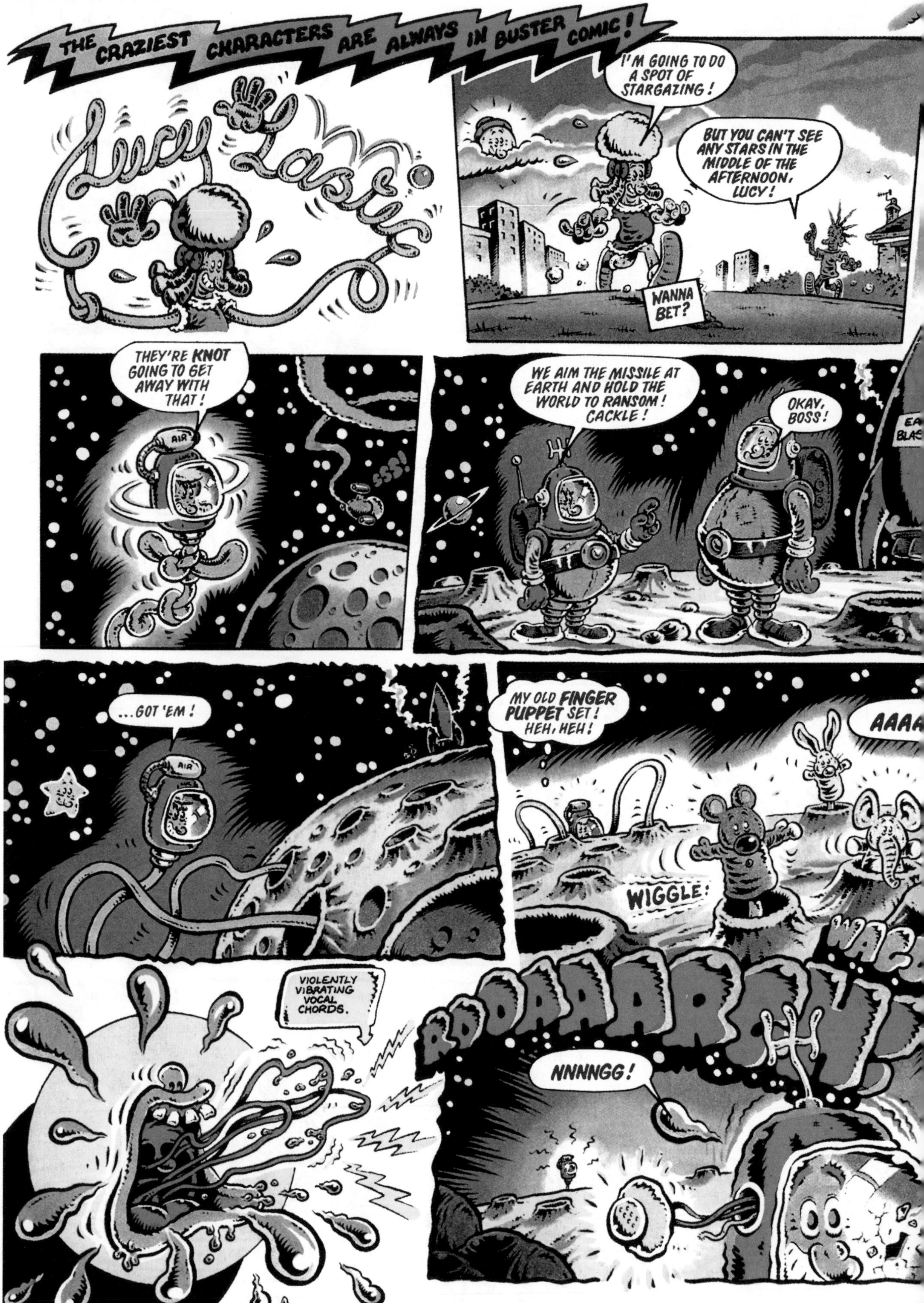
THE CRAZIEST CHARACTERS ARE ALWAYS IN BUSTER COMIC!
Lucy Lastic
I'M GOING TO DO A SPOT OF STARGAZING!
BUT YOU CAN'T SEE ANY STARS IN THE MIDDLE OF THE AFTERNOON, LUCY!
WANNA BET?
THEY'RE KNOT GOING TO GET AWAY WITH THAT!
SSS!
WE AIM THE MISSILE AT EARTH AND HOLD THE WORLD TO RANSOM! CACKLE!
OKAY, BOSS!
...GOT 'EM!
MY OLD FINGER PUPPET SET! HEH, HEH!
WIGGLE!
VIOLENTLY VIBRATING VOCAL CHORDS.
NNNNGG!

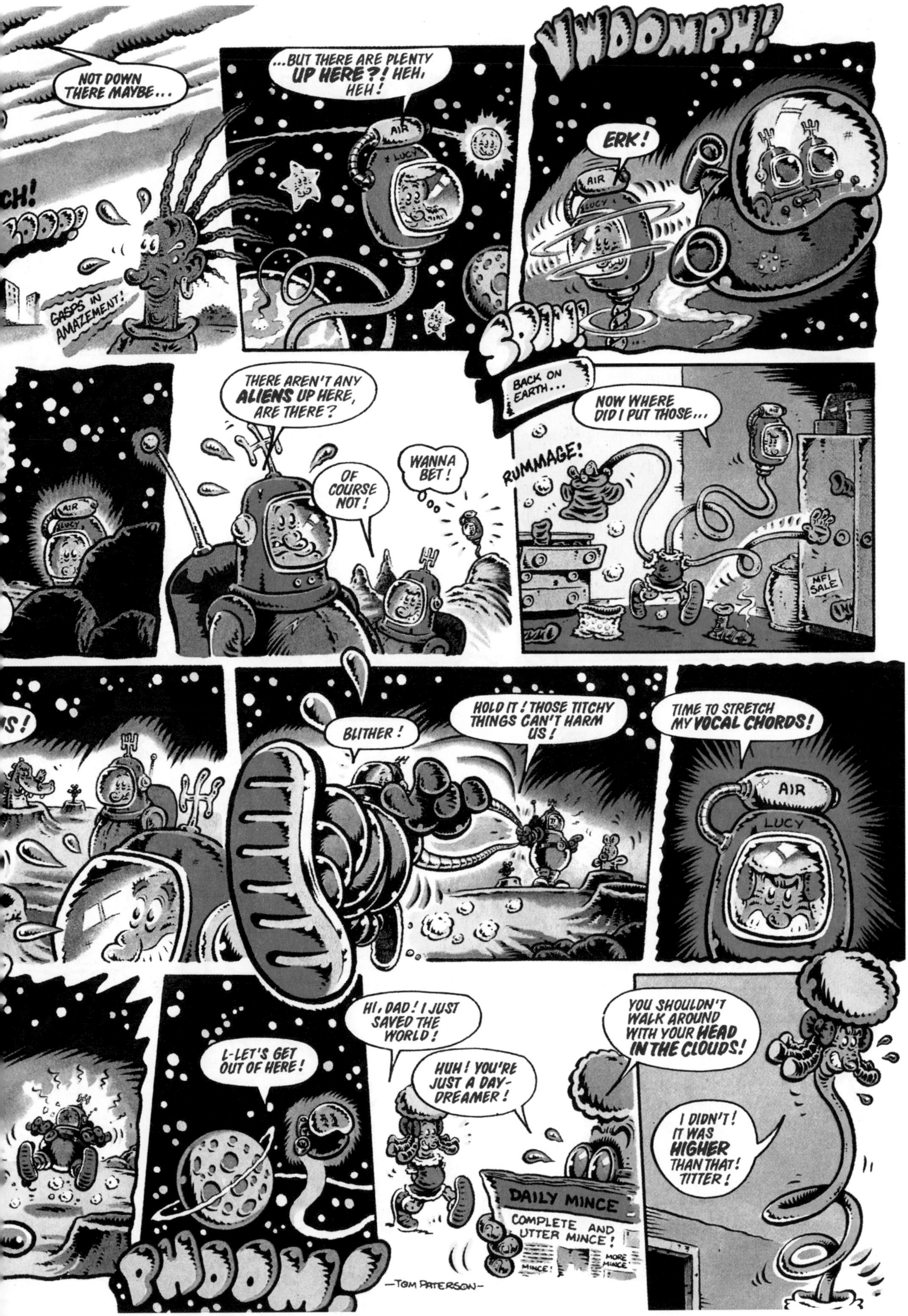
NOT DOWN THERE MAYBE...
GASPS IN AMAZEMENT!
...BUT THERE ARE PLENTY UP HERE?! HEH, HEH!
AIR
LUCY
VWOOMPH!
ERK!
AIR
LUCY
SPIN!
THERE AREN'T ANY ALIENS UP HERE, ARE THERE?
AIR
LUCY
OF COURSE NOT!
WANNA BET!
BACK ON EARTH...
NOW WHERE DID I PUT THOSE...
RUMMAGE!
MFI SALE
BLITHER!
HOLD IT! THOSE TITCHY THINGS CAN'T HARM US!
TIME TO STRETCH MY VOCAL CHORDS!
AIR
LUCY
L-LET'S GET OUT OF HERE!
PHOOM!
HI, DAD! I JUST SAVED THE WORLD!
HUH! YOU'RE JUST A DAY-DREAMER!
DAILY MINCE
COMPLETE AND UTTER MINCE!
MINCE!
MORE MINCE
YOU SHOULDN'T WALK AROUND WITH YOUR HEAD IN THE CLOUDS!
I DIDN'T! IT WAS HIGHER THAN THAT! TITTER!
—TOM PATERSON—

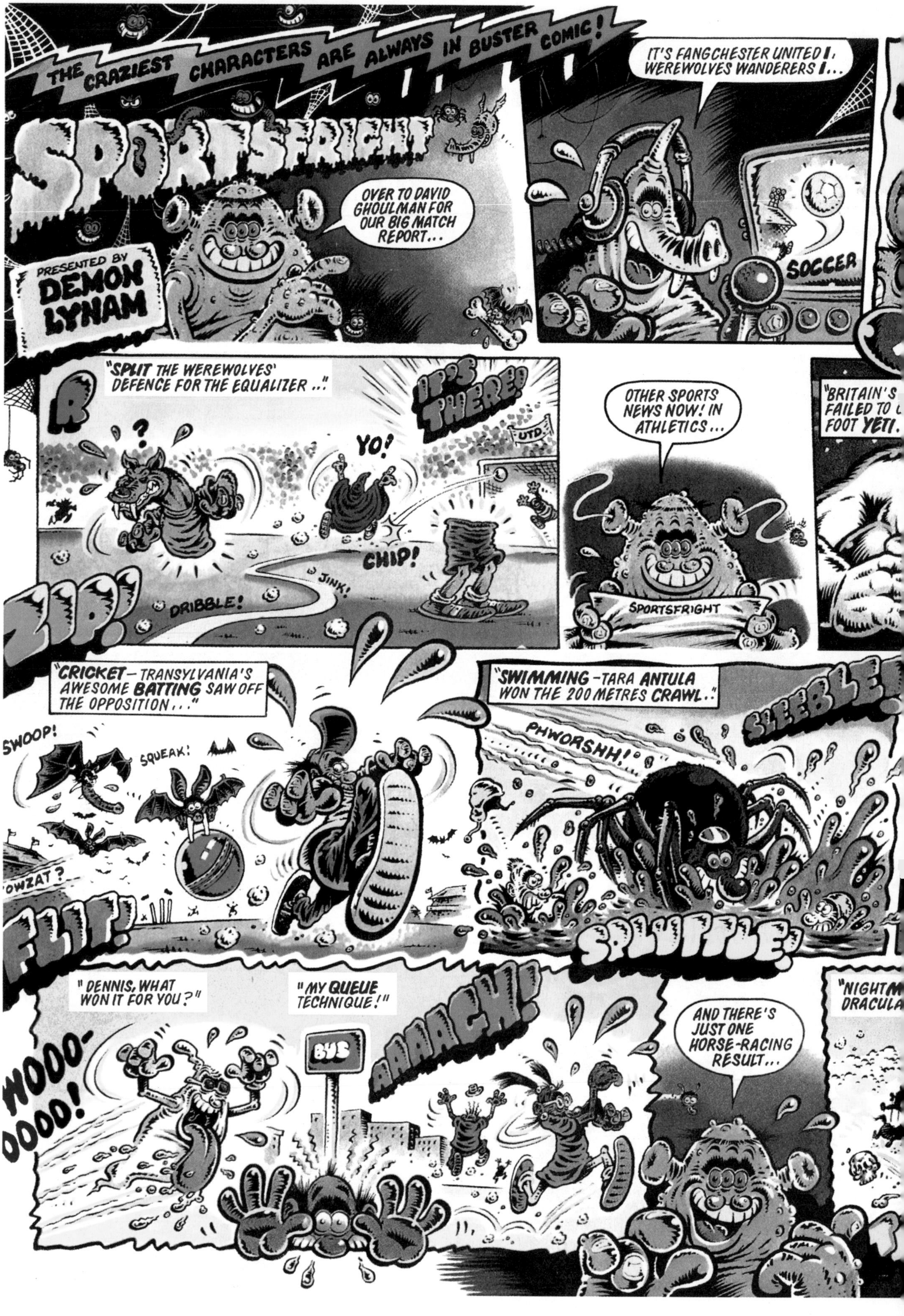
THE CRAZIEST CHARACTERS ARE ALWAYS IN BUSTER COMIC!
SPORTSFRIGHT
PRESENTED BY DEMON LYNAM
OVER TO DAVID GHOULMAN FOR OUR BIG MATCH REPORT...
IT'S FANGCHESTER UNITED 1, WEREWOLVES WANDERERS 1...
SOCCER
"SPLIT THE WEREWOLVES' DEFENCE FOR THE EQUALIZER ..."
IT'S THERE!
UTD
YO!
CHIP!
JINK!
DRIBBLE!
ZIP!
OTHER SPORTS NEWS NOW! IN ATHLETICS...
SPORTSFRIGHT
"BRITAIN'S
FAILED TO
FOOT YETI.
"CRICKET — TRANSYLVANIA'S AWESOME BATTING SAW OFF THE OPPOSITION..."
SWOOP!
SQUEAK!
OWZAT?
FLIT!
"SWIMMING — TARA ANTULA WON THE 200 METRES CRAWL."
PHWORSHH!
SPLUTTLE!
"DENNIS, WHAT WON IT FOR YOU?"
"MY QUEUE TECHNIQUE!"
HOOO-OOOD!
BUS
AAAAACH!
AND THERE'S JUST ONE HORSE-RACING RESULT...
"NIGHT
DRACULA

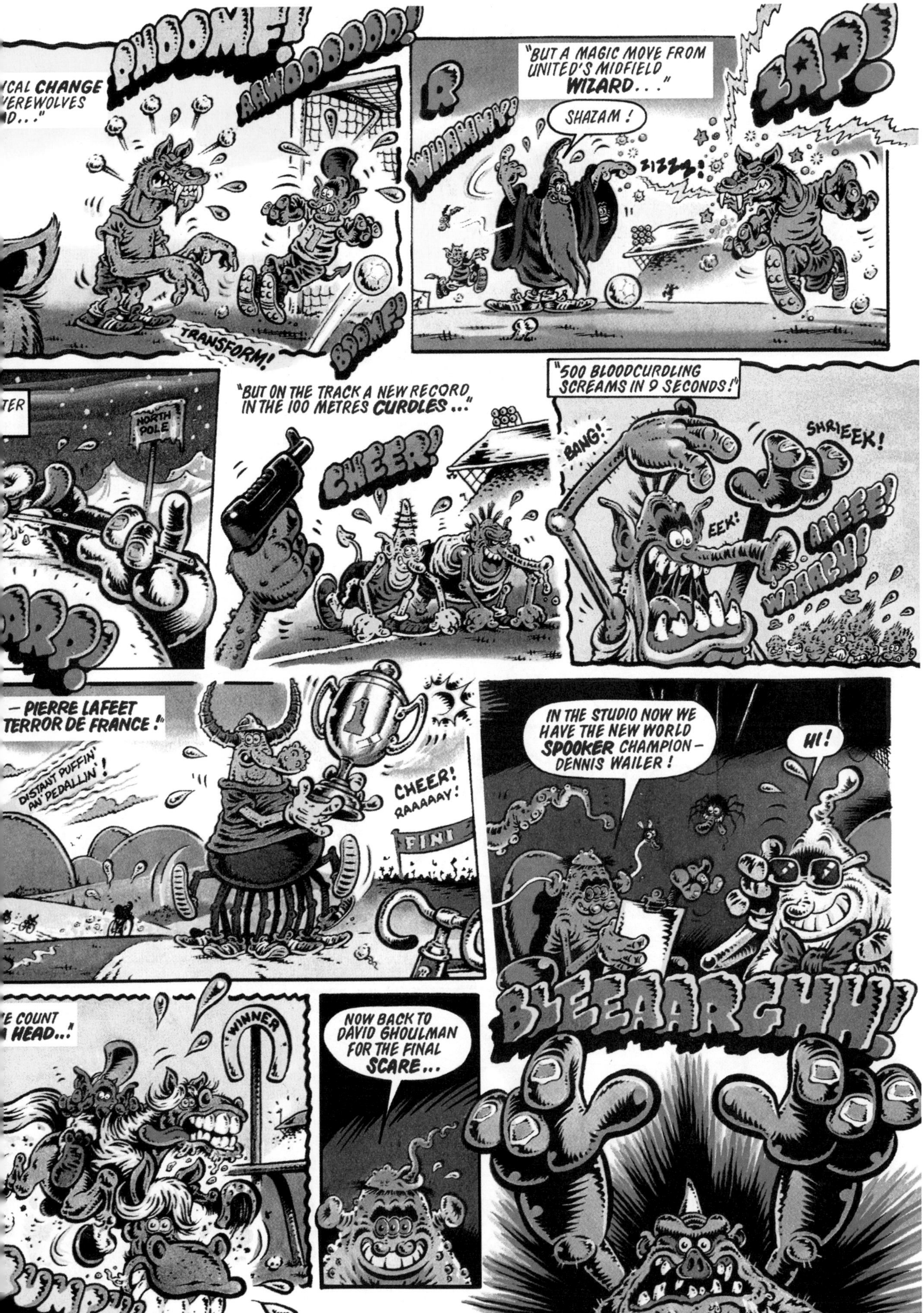

ICAL CHANGE
VEREWOLVES
D..."
PHOOMF!
AAWOOOOOOO!
TRANSFORM!
BOOMF!
"BUT A MAGIC MOVE FROM UNITED'S MIDFIELD WIZARD..."
WHAMMY!
SHAZAM!
ZIZZZ!
ZAP!
TER
NORTH POLE
"BUT ON THE TRACK A NEW RECORD IN THE 100 METRES CURDLES..."
CHEER!
"500 BLOODCURDLING SCREAMS IN 9 SECONDS!"
BANG!
SHRIEEK!
EEK!
AAIEEE!
WAAAGH!
– PIERRE LAFEET TERROR DE FRANCE!"
DISTANT PUFFIN' AN' PEDALLIN'!
CHEER! RAAAAAY!
FINI
IN THE STUDIO NOW WE HAVE THE NEW WORLD SPOOKER CHAMPION – DENNIS WAILER!
HI!
BLEEAARGHH!
E COUNT
HEAD..."
WINNER
NOW BACK TO DAVID GHOULMAN FOR THE FINAL SCARE...

THE CRAZIEST CHARACTERS ARE ALWAYS IN BUSTER COMIC!

THINGUMMY-BLOB

THE WHO-KNOWS-WHAT FROM WHO-KNOWS-WHERE.

WHERE DID I COME FROM? WHAT AM I MEANT TO BE?

SHPLECHHH!

ROOM!

LIKE THIS, YOU MEAN?

ROOAAAR!

THAT'S FLYING! YOU MUST BE A BIRD!

YOU NEED TO IMPROVE YOUR LANDING, THOUGH!

SHPLURP!

PXWAART!

OOPS! SORRY, I GOT CARRIED AWAY!

GAH!

SQUAARK!

GO AND GET THE DINNER IN, WE'RE SHORT OF WORMS!

I'M ON MY WAY!

SALUTE!

STILL, IT'LL MAKE A NICE CHANGE FROM WORM, WON'T IT?

...THAT'S AN ELEPHANT!

IS IT? I WONDERED WHY IT HAD A BIG LUMP ON THE END!

OINKLE!

FEED THIS END

SPLUMP!

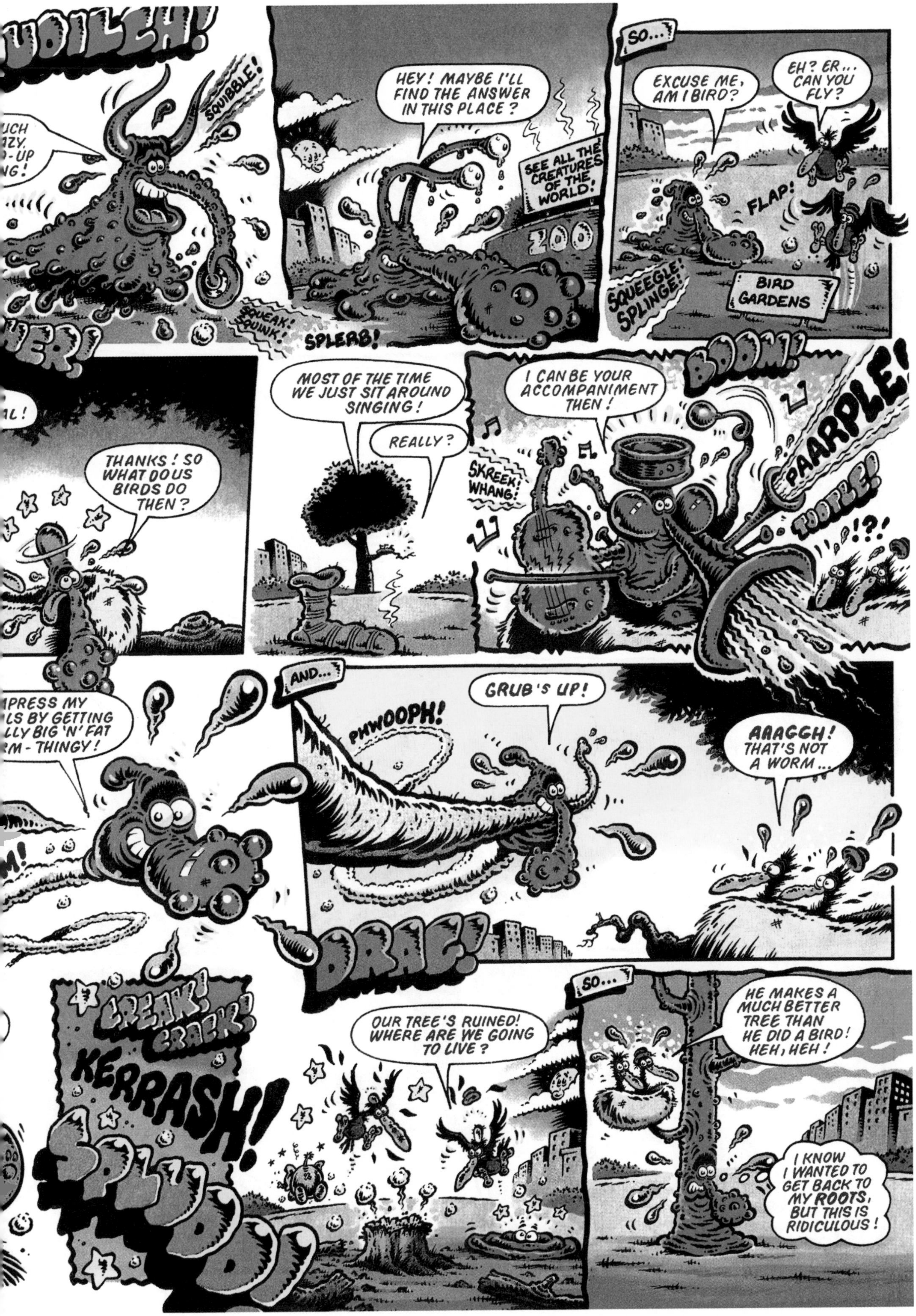
SQUIBBLE!
SQUEAK! SQUINK!
HEY! MAYBE I'LL FIND THE ANSWER IN THIS PLACE?
SEE ALL THE CREATURES OF THE WORLD!
ZOO
SPLERB!
SO...
EXCUSE ME, AM I BIRD?
EH? ER... CAN YOU FLY?
FLAP!
SQUEEGLE SPLINGE!
BIRD GARDENS
THANKS! SO WHAT DO US BIRDS DO THEN?
MOST OF THE TIME WE JUST SIT AROUND SINGING!
REALLY?
I CAN BE YOUR ACCOMPANIMENT THEN!
BOOM!
SKREEK! WHANG!
PAARPLE!
TOOTLE!
AND...
GRUB'S UP!
PHWOOPH!
AAAGGH! THAT'S NOT A WORM...
DRAG!
CREAK! CRACK!
KERRASH!
OUR TREE'S RUINED! WHERE ARE WE GOING TO LIVE?
SO...
HE MAKES A MUCH BETTER TREE THAN HE DID A BIRD! HEH, HEH!
I KNOW I WANTED TO GET BACK TO MY ROOTS, BUT THIS IS RIDICULOUS!

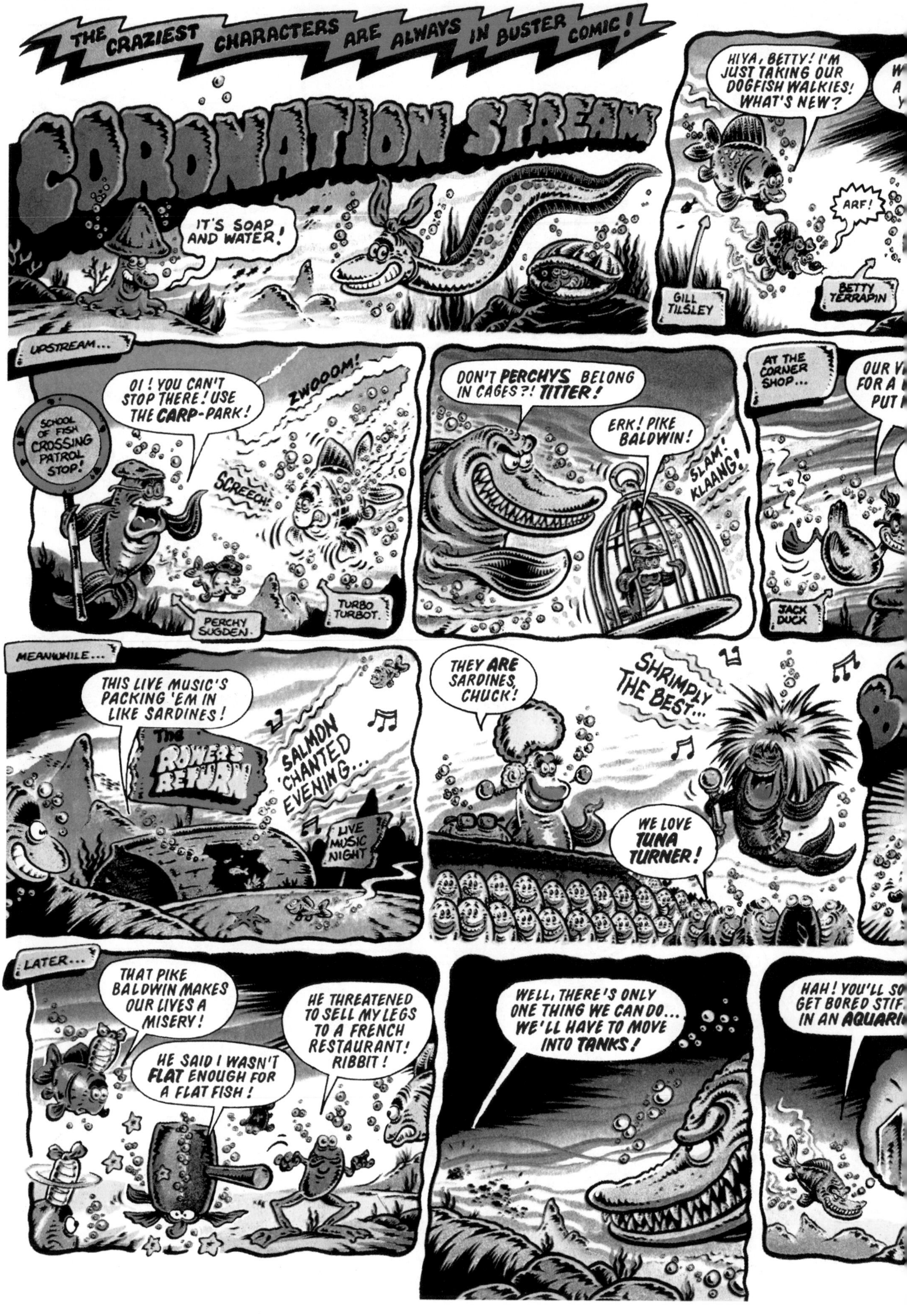
THE CRAZIEST CHARACTERS ARE ALWAYS IN BUSTER COMIC!
CORONATION STREAM
IT'S SOAP AND WATER!
HIYA, BETTY! I'M JUST TAKING OUR DOGFISH WALKIES! WHAT'S NEW?
ARF!
GILL TILSLEY
BETTY TERRAPIN
UPSTREAM...
SCHOOL OF FISH CROSSING PATROL STOP!
OI! YOU CAN'T STOP THERE! USE THE CARP-PARK!
ZWOOOM!
SCREECH!
PERCHY SUGDEN
TURBO TURBOT
DON'T PERCHYS BELONG IN CAGES?! TITTER!
ERK! PIKE BALDWIN!
SLAM! KLAANG!
AT THE CORNER SHOP...
JACK DUCK
MEANWHILE...
THIS LIVE MUSIC'S PACKING 'EM IN LIKE SARDINES!
THE ROVER'S RETURN
SALMON CHANTED EVENING...
LIVE MUSIC NIGHT
THEY ARE SARDINES, CHUCK!
SHRIMPLY THE BEST...
WE LOVE TUNA TURNER!
LATER...
THAT PIKE BALDWIN MAKES OUR LIVES A MISERY!
HE SAID I WASN'T FLAT ENOUGH FOR A FLAT FISH!
HE THREATENED TO SELL MY LEGS TO A FRENCH RESTAURANT! RIBBIT!
WELL, THERE'S ONLY ONE THING WE CAN DO... WE'LL HAVE TO MOVE INTO TANKS!

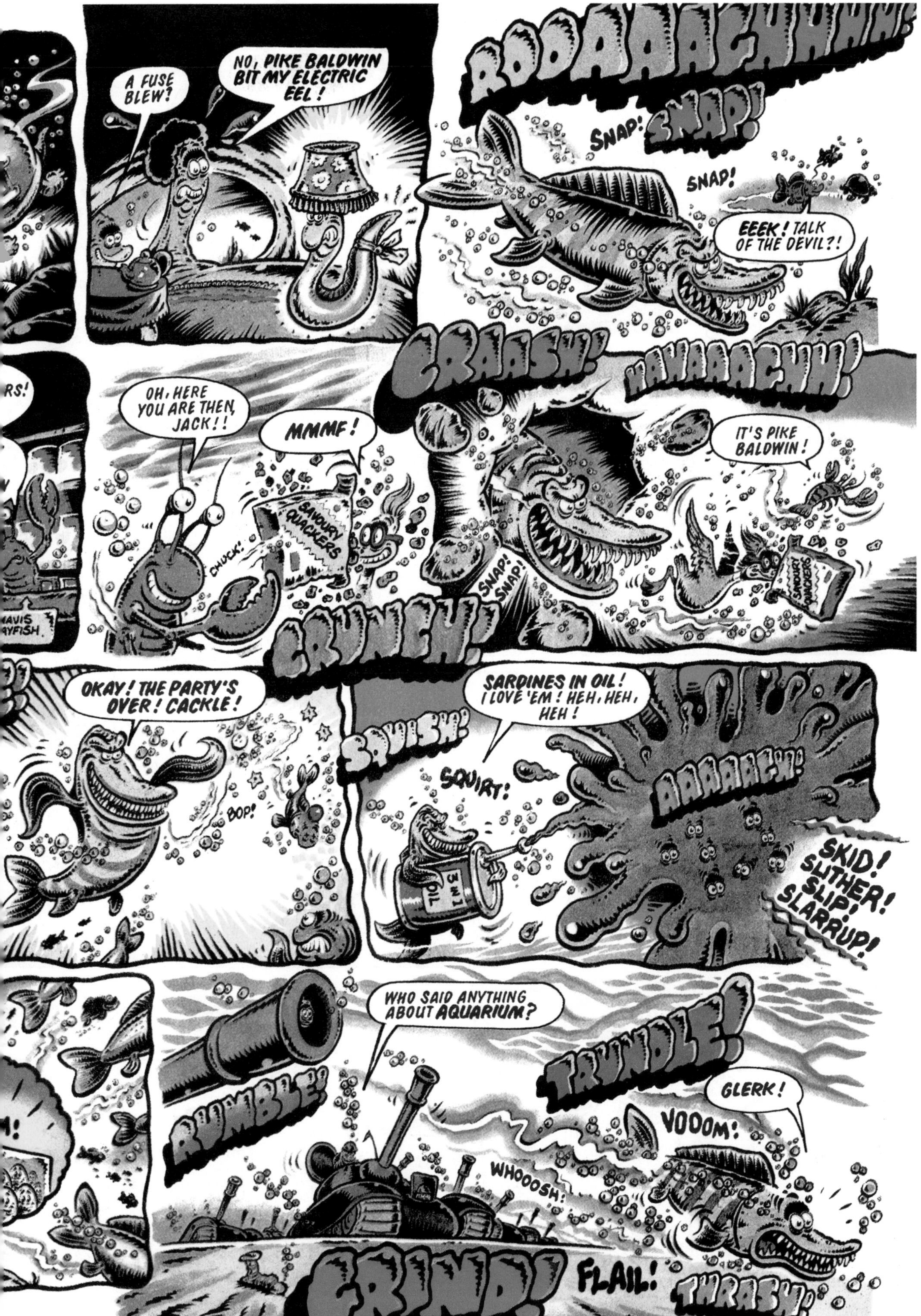
A FUSE BLEW?
NO, PIKE BALDWIN BIT MY ELECTRIC EEL!
SNAP! SNAP!
SNAP!
EEEK! TALK OF THE DEVIL?!
OH, HERE YOU ARE THEN, JACK!!
MMMF!
CHUCK!
SAVOURY QUACKERS
CRAASH!
IT'S PIKE BALDWIN!
SNAP! SNAP!
CRUNCH!
SAVOURY QUACKERS
OKAY! THE PARTY'S OVER! CACKLE!
BOP!
SQUISH!
SARDINES IN OIL! I LOVE 'EM! HEH, HEH, HEH!
SQUIRT!
3 IN 1 OIL
SKID! SLITHER! SLIP! SLARRUP!
WHO SAID ANYTHING ABOUT AQUARIUM?
RUMBLE!
TRUNDLE!
GLERK!
VOOOM!
WHOOOSH!
GRIND!
FLAIL!
THRASH!

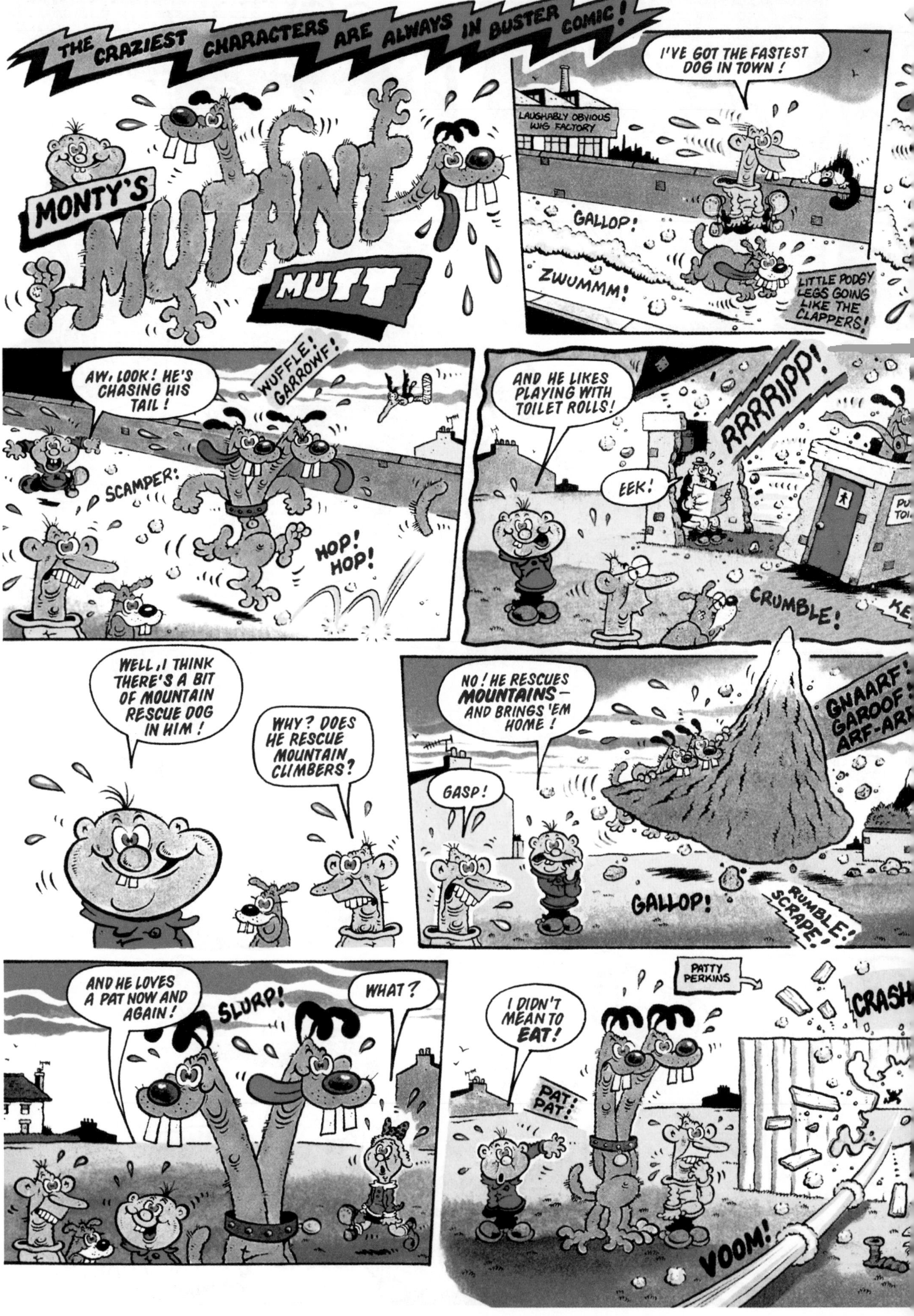
THE CRAZIEST CHARACTERS ARE ALWAYS IN BUSTER COMIC!
MONTY'S
MUTANT
MUTT
I'VE GOT THE FASTEST DOG IN TOWN!
LAUGHABLY OBVIOUS WIG FACTORY
GALLOP!
ZWUMMM!
LITTLE PODGY LEGS GOING LIKE THE CLAPPERS!
AW, LOOK! HE'S CHASING HIS TAIL!
WUFFLE! GARROWF!
SCAMPER!
HOP! HOP!
AND HE LIKES PLAYING WITH TOILET ROLLS!
RRRRIPP!
EEK!
CRUMBLE!
WELL, I THINK THERE'S A BIT OF MOUNTAIN RESCUE DOG IN HIM!
WHY? DOES HE RESCUE MOUNTAIN CLIMBERS?
NO! HE RESCUES MOUNTAINS — AND BRINGS 'EM HOME!
GNAARF! GAROOF!
GASP!
GALLOP!
RUMBLE! SCRAPE!
AND HE LOVES A PAT NOW AND AGAIN!
SLURP!
WHAT?
PATTY PERKINS
I DIDN'T MEAN TO EAT!
PAT! PAT!
VOOM!

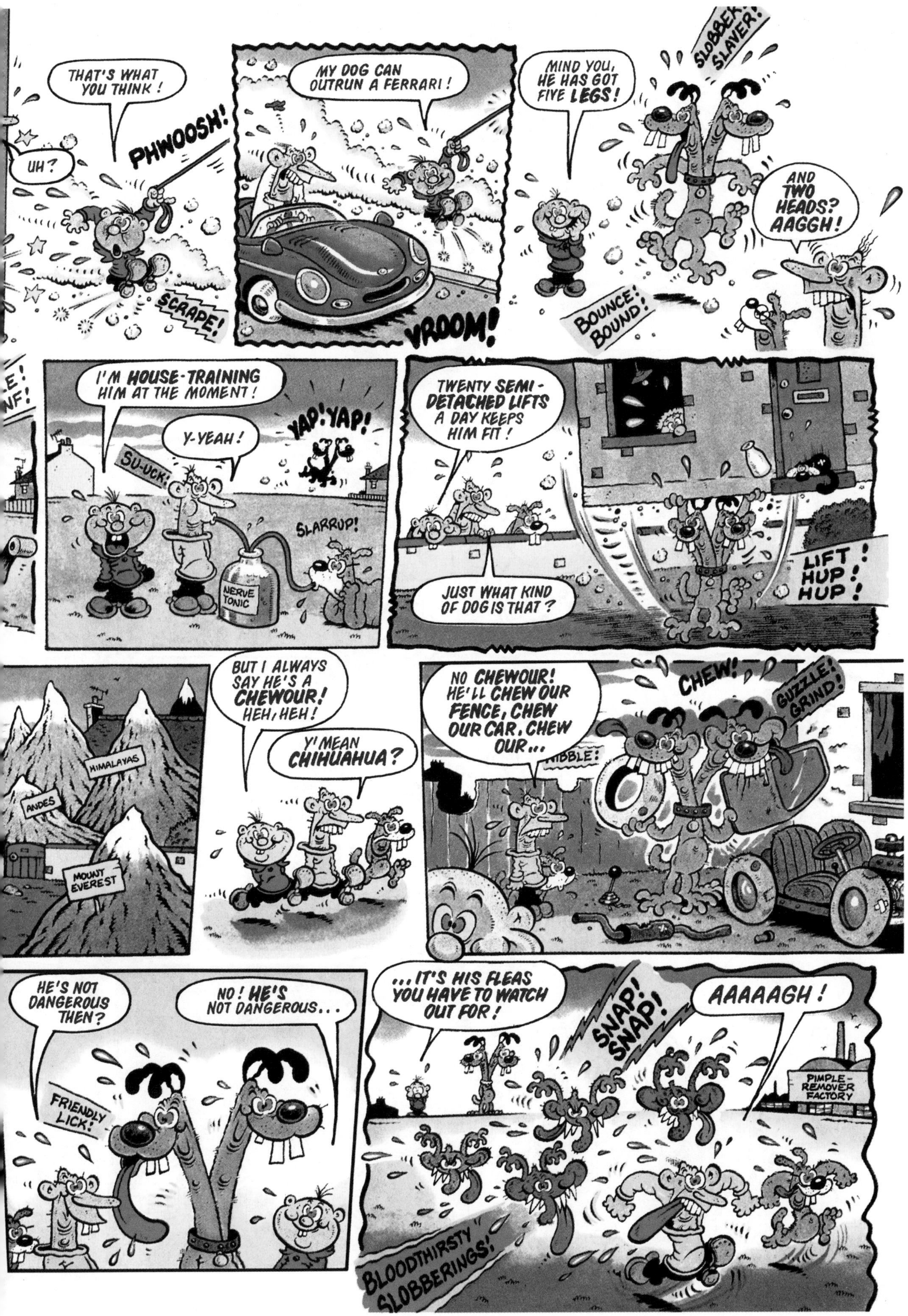

THAT'S WHAT YOU THINK!
UH?
PHWOOSH!
SCRAPE!
MY DOG CAN OUTRUN A FERRARI!
VROOM!
MIND YOU, HE HAS GOT FIVE LEGS!
SLOBBER! SLAVER!
AND TWO HEADS? AAGGH!
BOUNCE! BOUND!
I'M HOUSE-TRAINING HIM AT THE MOMENT!
Y-YEAH!
YAP! YAP!
SU-UCK!
SLARRUP!
NERVE TONIC
TWENTY SEMI-DETACHED LIFTS A DAY KEEPS HIM FIT!
JUST WHAT KIND OF DOG IS THAT?
LIFT! HUP! HUP!
HIMALAYAS
ANDES
MOUNT EVEREST
BUT I ALWAYS SAY HE'S A CHEWOUR! HEH, HEH!
Y'MEAN CHIHUAHUA?
NO CHEWOUR! HE'LL CHEW OUR FENCE, CHEW OUR CAR, CHEW OUR...
CHEW!
GUZZLE! GRIND!
HE'S NOT DANGEROUS THEN?
NO! HE'S NOT DANGEROUS...
FRIENDLY LICK!
...IT'S HIS FLEAS YOU HAVE TO WATCH OUT FOR!
SNAP! SNAP!
AAAAAGH!
PIMPLE-REMOVER FACTORY
BLOODTHIRSTY SLOBBERINGS!

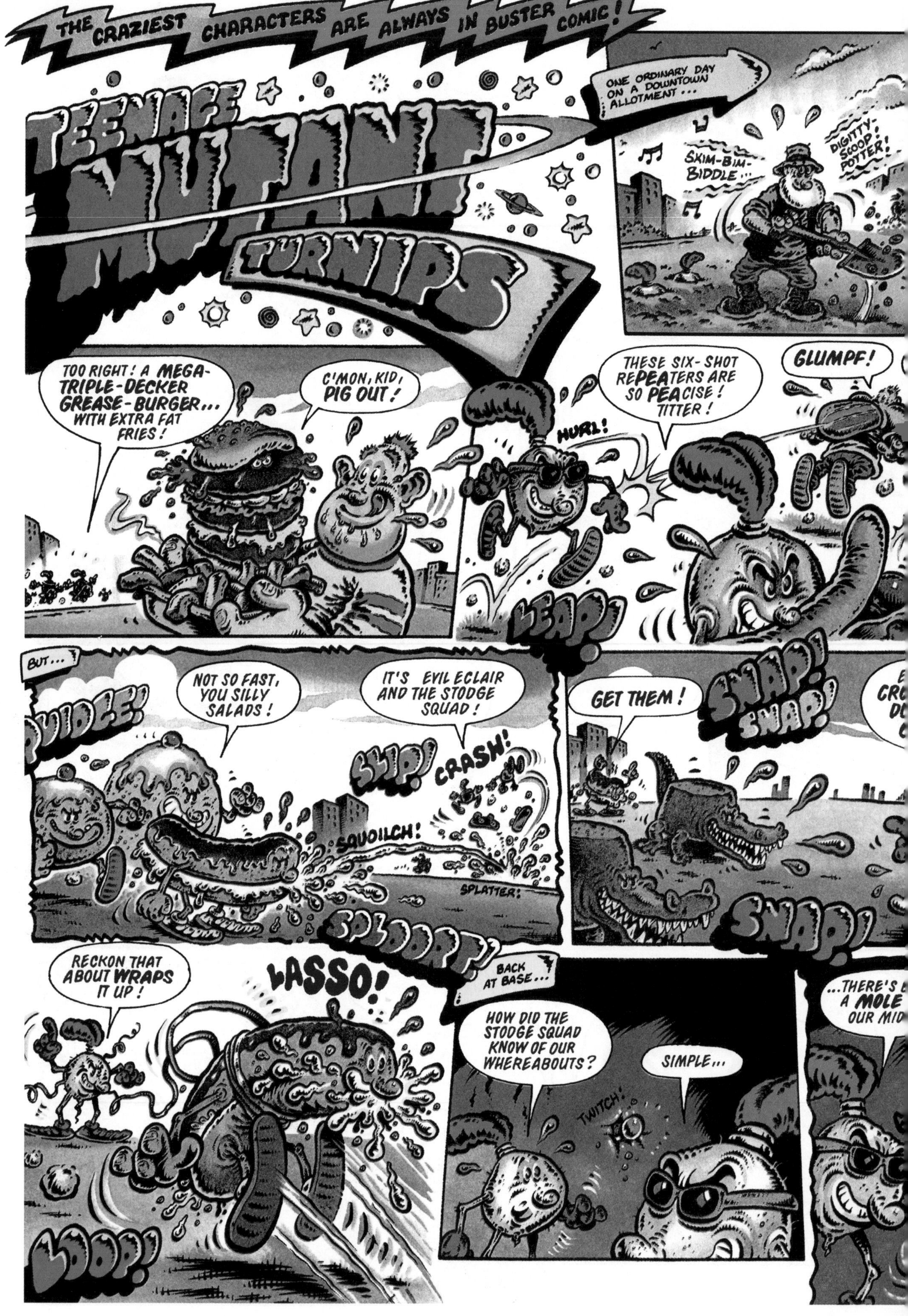

THE CRAZIEST CHARACTERS ARE ALWAYS IN BUSTER COMIC!
TEENAGE MUTANT TURNIPS
ONE ORDINARY DAY ON A DOWNTOWN ALLOTMENT...
SKIM-BIM-BIDDLE...
DIGITTY-SCOOP-POTTER!
TOO RIGHT! A MEGA-TRIPLE-DECKER GREASE-BURGER... WITH EXTRA FAT FRIES!
C'MON, KID, PIG OUT!
HURL!
THESE SIX-SHOT REPEATERS ARE SO PEACISE! TITTER!
GLUMPF!
LEAP!
BUT...
NOT SO FAST, YOU SILLY SALADS!
IT'S EVIL ECLAIR AND THE STODGE SQUAD!
SLIP!
CRASH!
SQUOILCH!
SPLATTER!
SPLOOORT!
GET THEM!
SNAP! SNAP!
SNAP!
RECKON THAT ABOUT WRAPS IT UP!
LASSO!
LOOP!
BACK AT BASE...
HOW DID THE STODGE SQUAD KNOW OF OUR WHEREABOUTS?
SIMPLE...
TWITCH!
...THERE'S
A MOLE

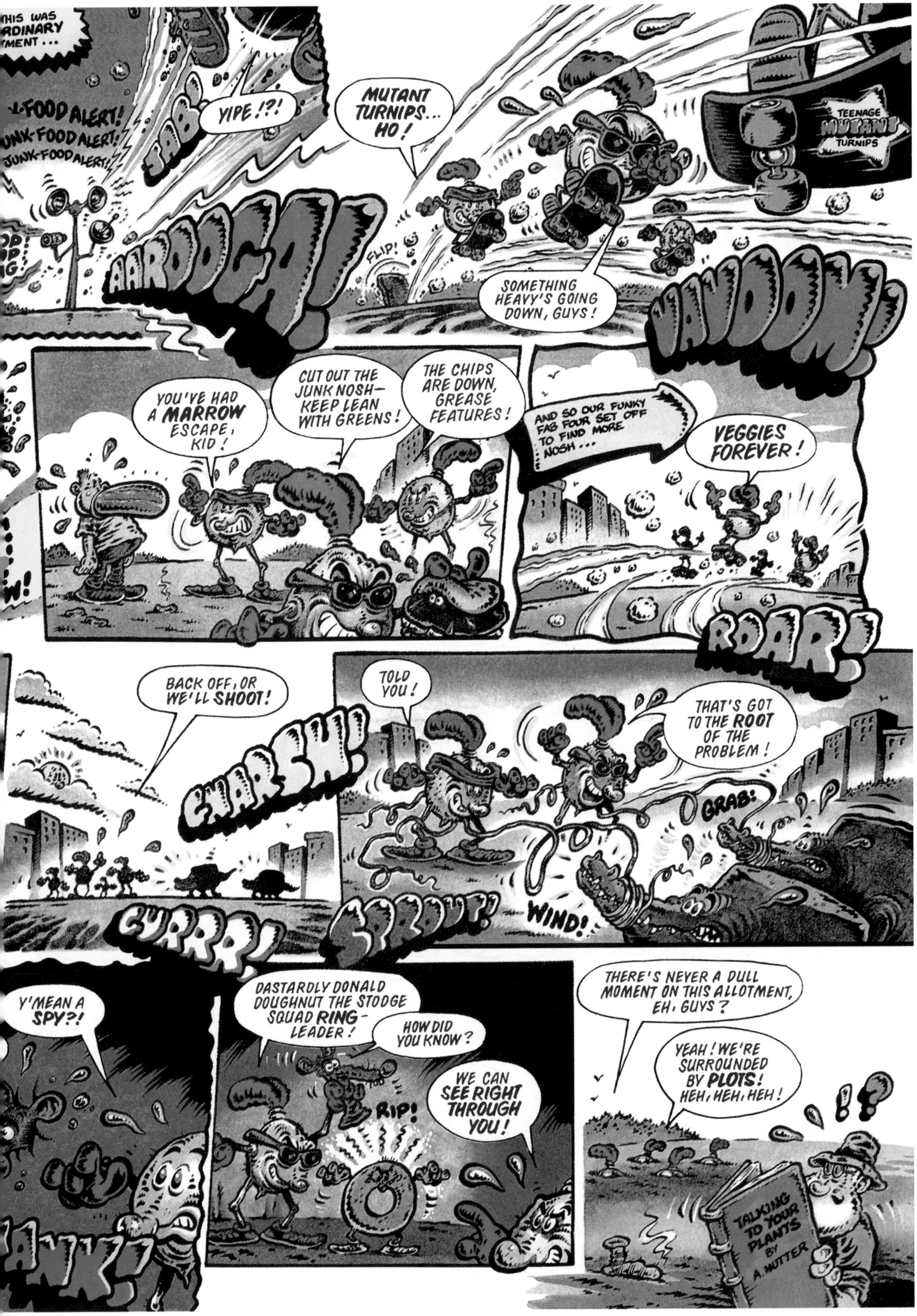
THIS WAS
RDINARY
TMENT...
-FOOD ALERT!
UNK-FOOD ALERT!
JUNK-FOOD ALERT!
JAB!
YIPE!?!
MUTANT TURNIPS... HO!
TEENAGE MUTANT TURNIPS
AAROOGA!
FLIP!
SOMETHING HEAVY'S GOING DOWN, GUYS!
VAVOOM!
YOU'VE HAD A MARROW ESCAPE, KID!
CUT OUT THE JUNK NOSH— KEEP LEAN WITH GREENS!
THE CHIPS ARE DOWN, GREASE FEATURES!
AND SO OUR FUNKY FAB FOUR SET OFF TO FIND MORE NOSH...
VEGGIES FOREVER!
ROAR!
BACK OFF, OR WE'LL SHOOT!
CHARSH!
TOLD YOU!
THAT'S GOT TO THE ROOT OF THE PROBLEM!
GRAB!
CURRR!
SPLOUT!
WIND!
Y'MEAN A SPY?!
DASTARDLY DONALD DOUGHNUT THE STODGE SQUAD RING-LEADER!
HOW DID YOU KNOW?
WE CAN SEE RIGHT THROUGH YOU!
RIP!
THERE'S NEVER A DULL MOMENT ON THIS ALLOTMENT, EH, GUYS?
YEAH! WE'RE SURROUNDED BY PLOTS! HEH, HEH, HEH!
TALKING TO YOUR PLANTS BY A. NUTTER

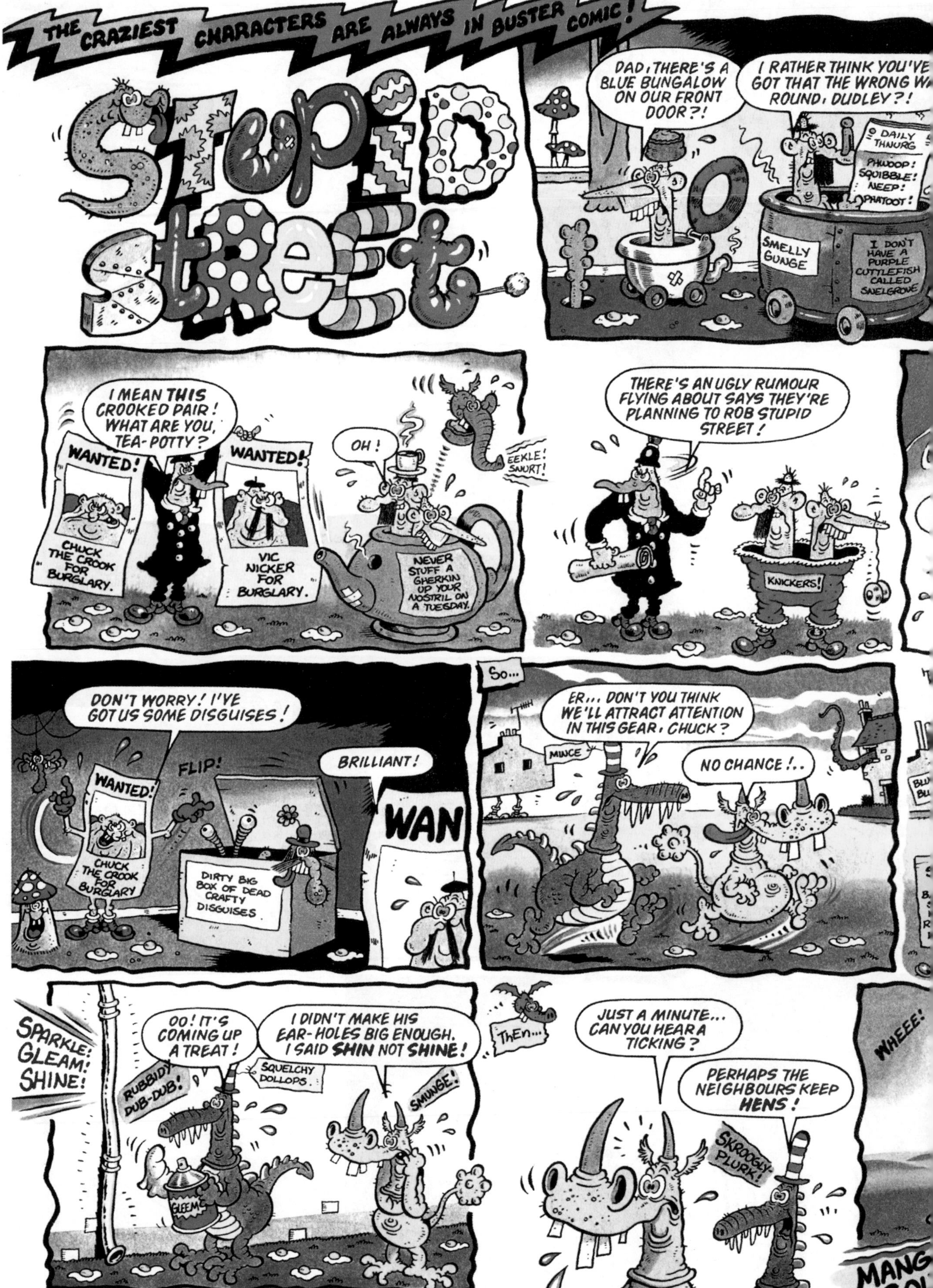
THE CRAZIEST CHARACTERS ARE ALWAYS IN BUSTER COMIC!
STUPID STREET
DAD, THERE'S A BLUE BUNGALOW ON OUR FRONT DOOR?!
I RATHER THINK YOU'VE GOT THAT THE WRONG WA ROUND, DUDLEY?!
DAILY THNURG
PHWOOP! SQUIBBLE! NEEP! PHATOOT!
SMELLY GUNGE
I DON'T HAVE A PURPLE CUTTLEFISH CALLED SNELGROVE
I MEAN THIS CROOKED PAIR! WHAT ARE YOU, TEA-POTTY?
WANTED! CHUCK THE CROOK FOR BURGLARY.
WANTED! VIC NICKER FOR BURGLARY.
OH!
EEKLE! SNURT!
NEVER STUFF A GHERKIN UP YOUR NOSTRIL ON A TUESDAY.
THERE'S AN UGLY RUMOUR FLYING ABOUT SAYS THEY'RE PLANNING TO ROB STUPID STREET!
KNICKERS!
DON'T WORRY! I'VE GOT US SOME DISGUISES!
FLIP!
BRILLIANT!
WANTED! CHUCK THE CROOK FOR BURGLARY
DIRTY BIG BOX OF DEAD CRAFTY DISGUISES
WAN
So...
ER... DON'T YOU THINK WE'LL ATTRACT ATTENTION IN THIS GEAR, CHUCK?
MINCE
NO CHANCE!..
SPARKLE! GLEAM! SHINE!
OO! IT'S COMING UP A TREAT!
I DIDN'T MAKE HIS EAR-HOLES BIG ENOUGH. I SAID SHIN NOT SHINE!
RUBBIDY DUB-DUB!
SQUELCHY DOLLOPS.
SMUNGE!
GLEEM
Then...
JUST A MINUTE... CAN YOU HEAR A TICKING?
PERHAPS THE NEIGHBOURS KEEP HENS!
SKROOGLY-PLURK!
WHEEE!
MANG SQU F

— ARTWORK BY FESTUS, THE TRAMPOLINING LIMPET —

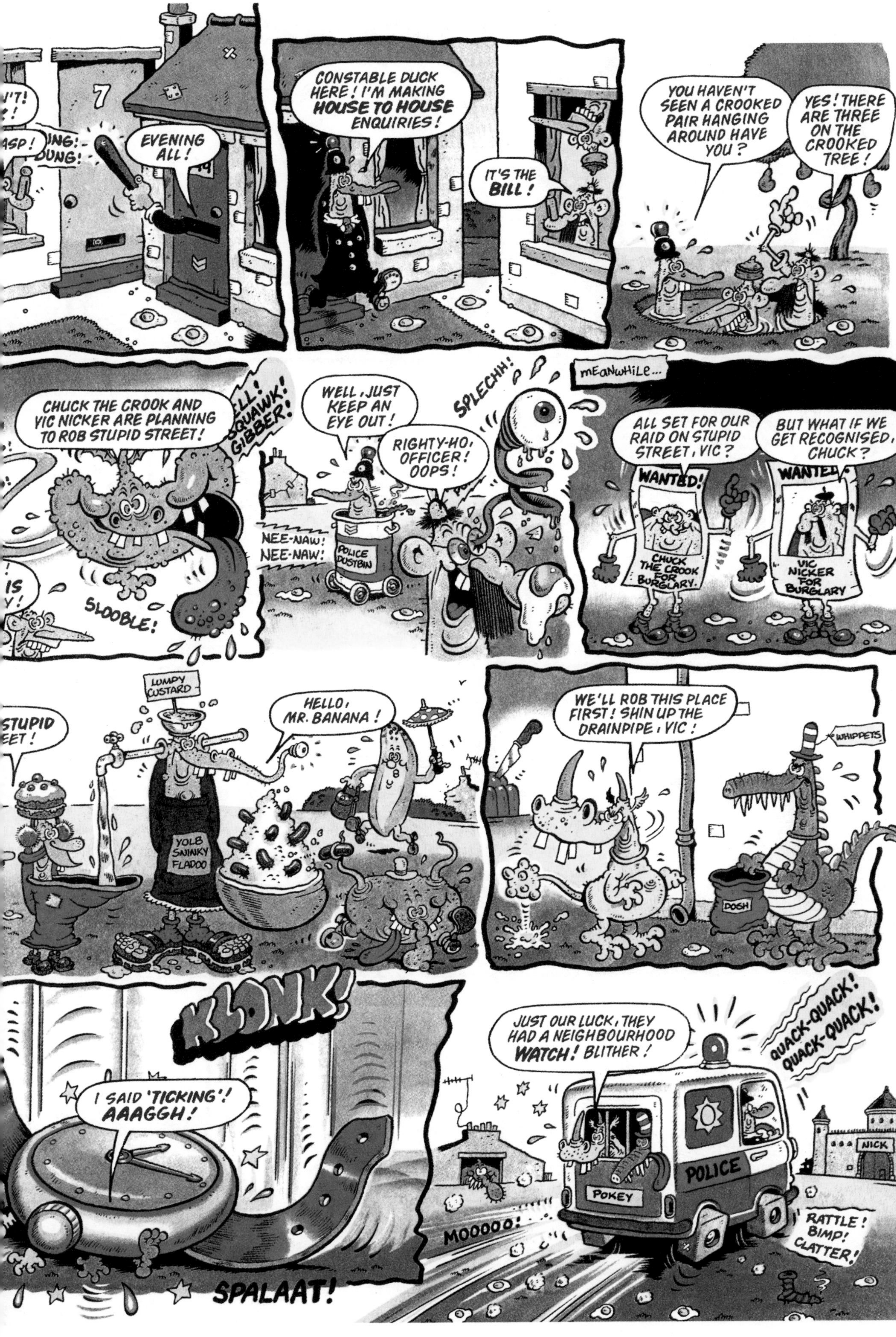
7
EVENING ALL!
14
CONSTABLE DUCK HERE! I'M MAKING HOUSE TO HOUSE ENQUIRIES!
IT'S THE BILL!
YOU HAVEN'T SEEN A CROOKED PAIR HANGING AROUND HAVE YOU?
YES! THERE ARE THREE ON THE CROOKED TREE!
CHUCK THE CROOK AND VIC NICKER ARE PLANNING TO ROB STUPID STREET!
SQUAWK! GIBBER!
SLOOBLE!
WELL, JUST KEEP AN EYE OUT!
RIGHTY-HO, OFFICER! OOPS!
NEE-NAW! NEE-NAW!
POLICE DUSTBIN
SPLECHH!
MEANWHILE...
ALL SET FOR OUR RAID ON STUPID STREET, VIC?
BUT WHAT IF WE GET RECOGNISED, CHUCK?
WANTED! CHUCK THE CROOK FOR BURGLARY.
WANTED VIC NICKER FOR BURGLARY
LUMPY CUSTARD
HELLO, MR. BANANA!
YOLB SNINKY FLADOO
WE'LL ROB THIS PLACE FIRST! SHIN UP THE DRAINPIPE, VIC!
WHIPPETS
DOSH
KLONK!
I SAID 'TICKING'! AAAGGH!
SPALAAT!
JUST OUR LUCK, THEY HAD A NEIGHBOURHOOD WATCH! BLITHER!
QUACK-QUACK! QUACK-QUACK!
POLICE
POKEY
NICK
MOOOOO!
RATTLE! BIMP! CLATTER!

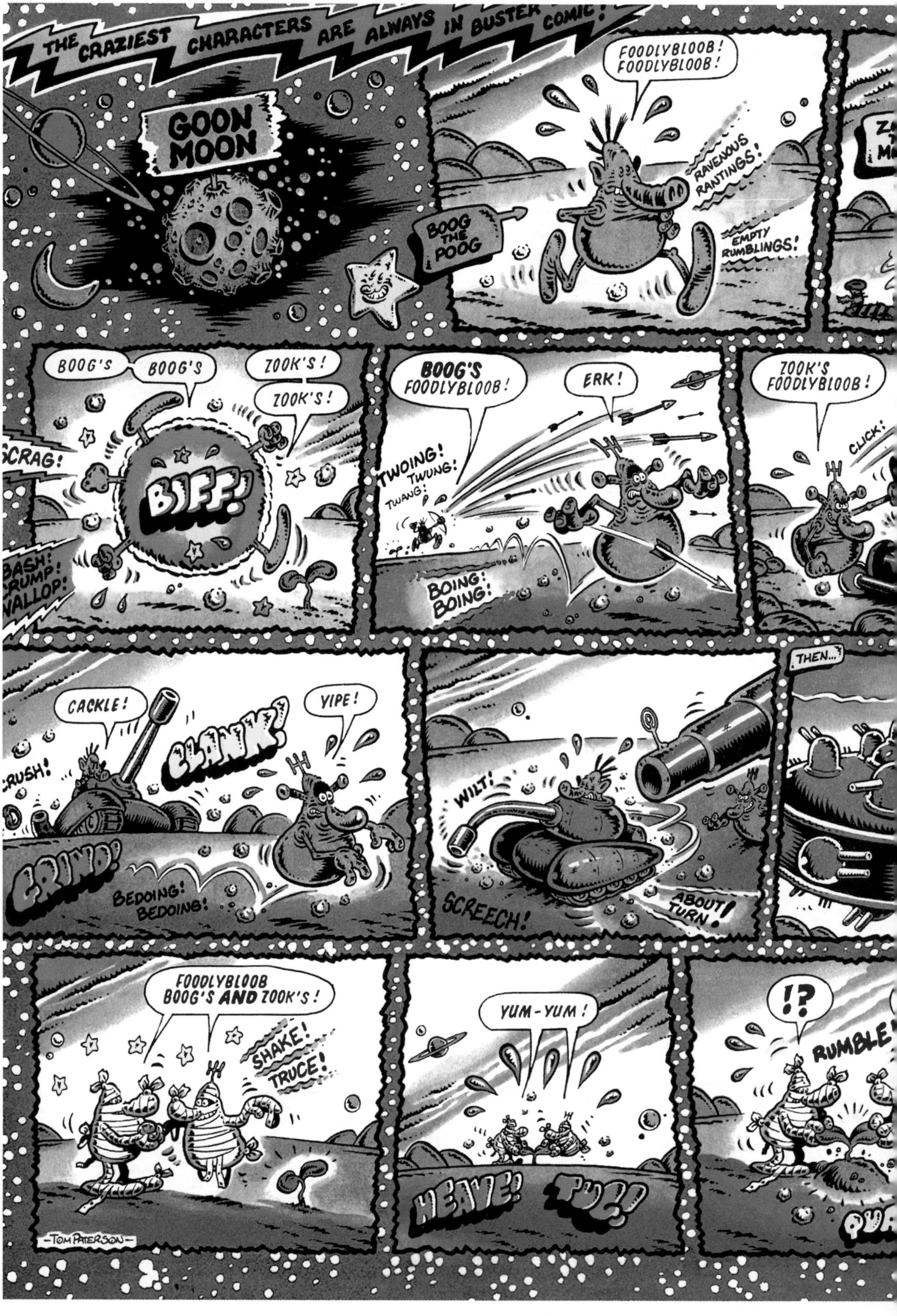
THE CRAZIEST CHARACTERS ARE ALWAYS IN BUSTER COMIC!
GOON MOON
BOOG THE POOG
FOODLYBLOOB! FOODLYBLOOB!
RAVENOUS RANTINGS!
EMPTY RUMBLINGS!
BOOG'S
BOOG'S
ZOOK'S!
ZOOK'S!
SCRAG!
BIFF!
BASH! CRUMP! WALLOP!
BOOG'S FOODLYBLOOB!
ERK!
TWOING! TWUNG! TWANG!
BOING! BOING!
ZOOK'S FOODLYBLOOB!
CLICK!
CACKLE!
CLANK!
YIPE!
CRUSH!
GRIND!
BEDOING! BEDOING!
WILT!
SCREECH!
ABOUT TURN!
THEN...
FOODLYBLOOB BOOG'S **AND** ZOOK'S!
SHAKE! TRUCE!
-TOM PATERSON-
YUM-YUM!
HEAVE! TUG!
!?
RUMBLE

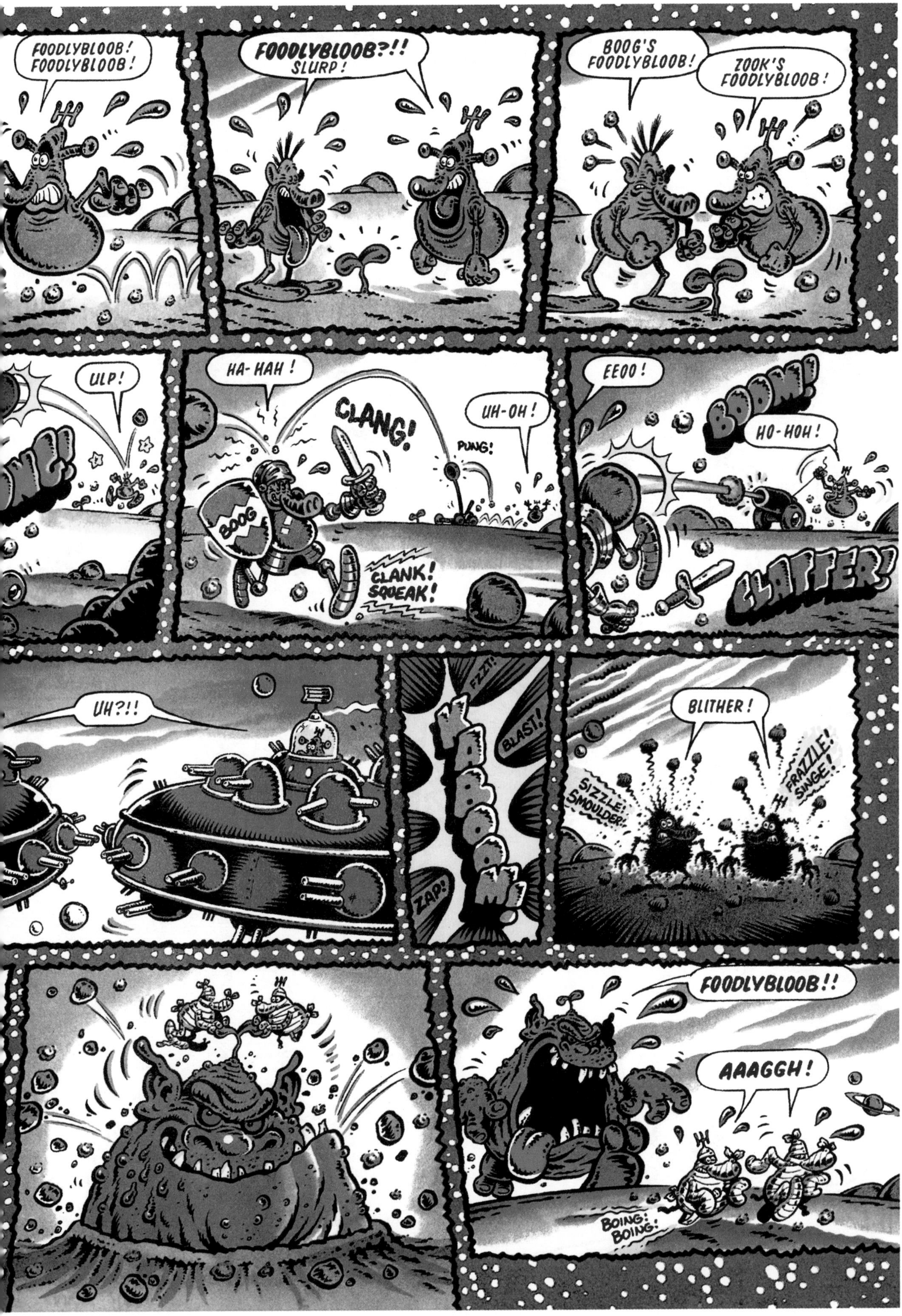
FOODLYBLOOB! FOODLYBLOOB!
FOODLYBLOOB?!! SLURP!
BOOG'S FOODLYBLOOB!
ZOOK'S FOODLYBLOOB!
ULP!
HA-HAH!
CLANG!
BOOG
PUNG!
UH-OH!
CLANK! SQUEAK!
EEOO!
BOOM!
HO-HOH!
CLATTER!
UH?!!
FZZT!
BLAST!
ZAP!
BLITHER!
SIZZLE! SMOULDER!
FRAZZLE! SINGE!
FOODLYBLOOB!!
AAAGGH!
BOING! BOING!

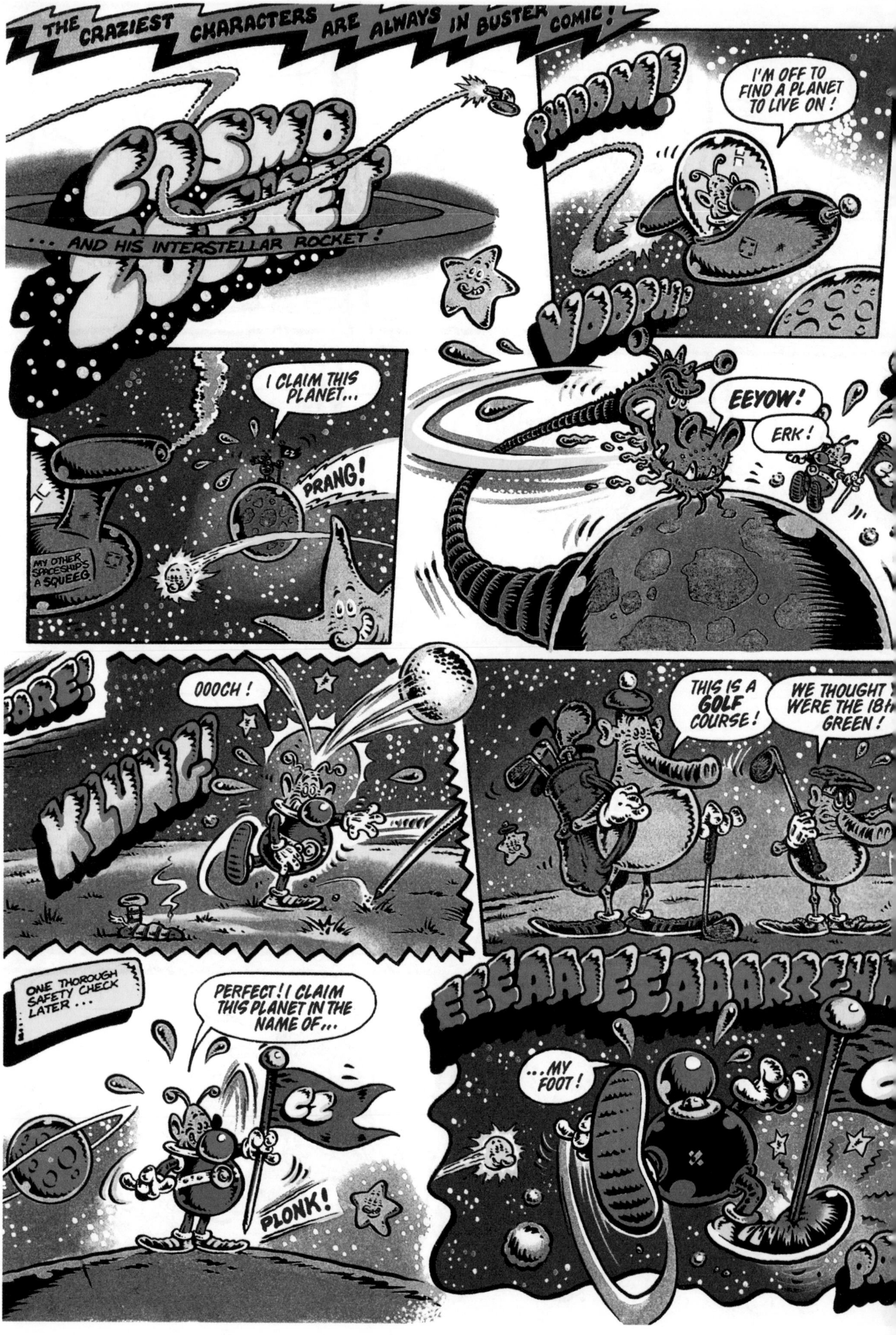
THE CRAZIEST CHARACTERS ARE ALWAYS IN BUSTER COMIC!
COSMO ZOCKET
... AND HIS INTERSTELLAR ROCKET!
PHOOM!
I'M OFF TO FIND A PLANET TO LIVE ON!
VOOPH!
I CLAIM THIS PLANET...
PRANG!
MY OTHER SPACESHIP'S A SQUEEG
EEYOW!
ERK!
OOOCH!
KLUNG!
THIS IS A GOLF COURSE!
ONE THOROUGH SAFETY CHECK LATER...
PERFECT! I CLAIM THIS PLANET IN THE NAME OF...
PLONK!
...MY FOOT!

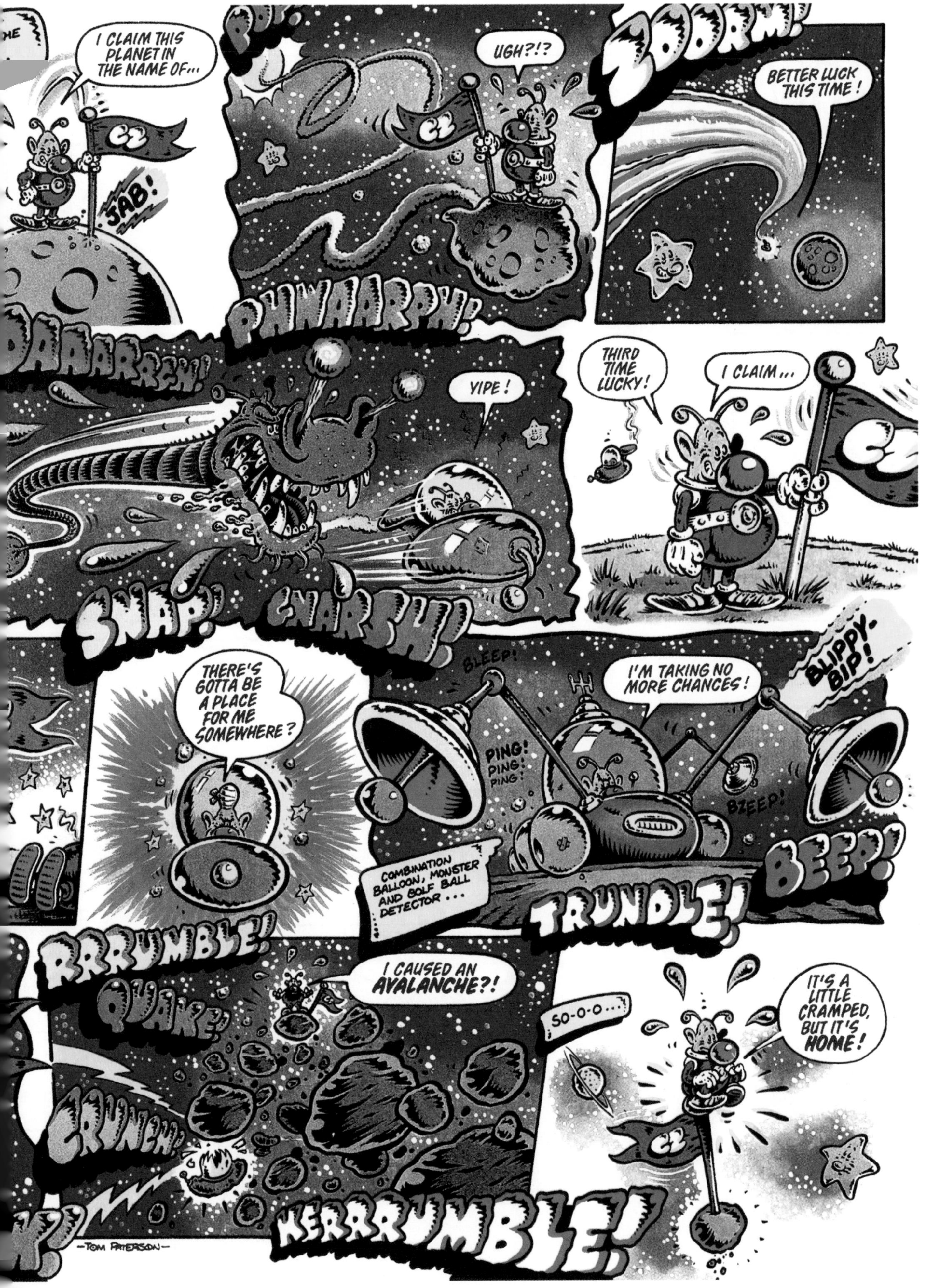
I CLAIM THIS PLANET IN THE NAME OF...
JAB!
UGH?!?
BETTER LUCK THIS TIME!
ZOOOM!
PHWAARPH!
DAAARRGH!
YIPE!
SNAP!
GNARSH!
THIRD TIME LUCKY!
I CLAIM...
THERE'S GOTTA BE A PLACE FOR ME SOMEWHERE?
BLEEP!
I'M TAKING NO MORE CHANCES!
BLIPPY-BIP!
PING! PING! PING!
BZEEP!
COMBINATION BALLOON, MONSTER AND GOLF BALL DETECTOR...
TRUNDLE!
BEEP!
RRRUMBLE!
QUAKE!
I CAUSED AN AVALANCHE?!
SO-O-O...
IT'S A LITTLE CRAMPED, BUT IT'S HOME!
CRUNCH!
KERRRUMBLE!
-TOM PATERSON-

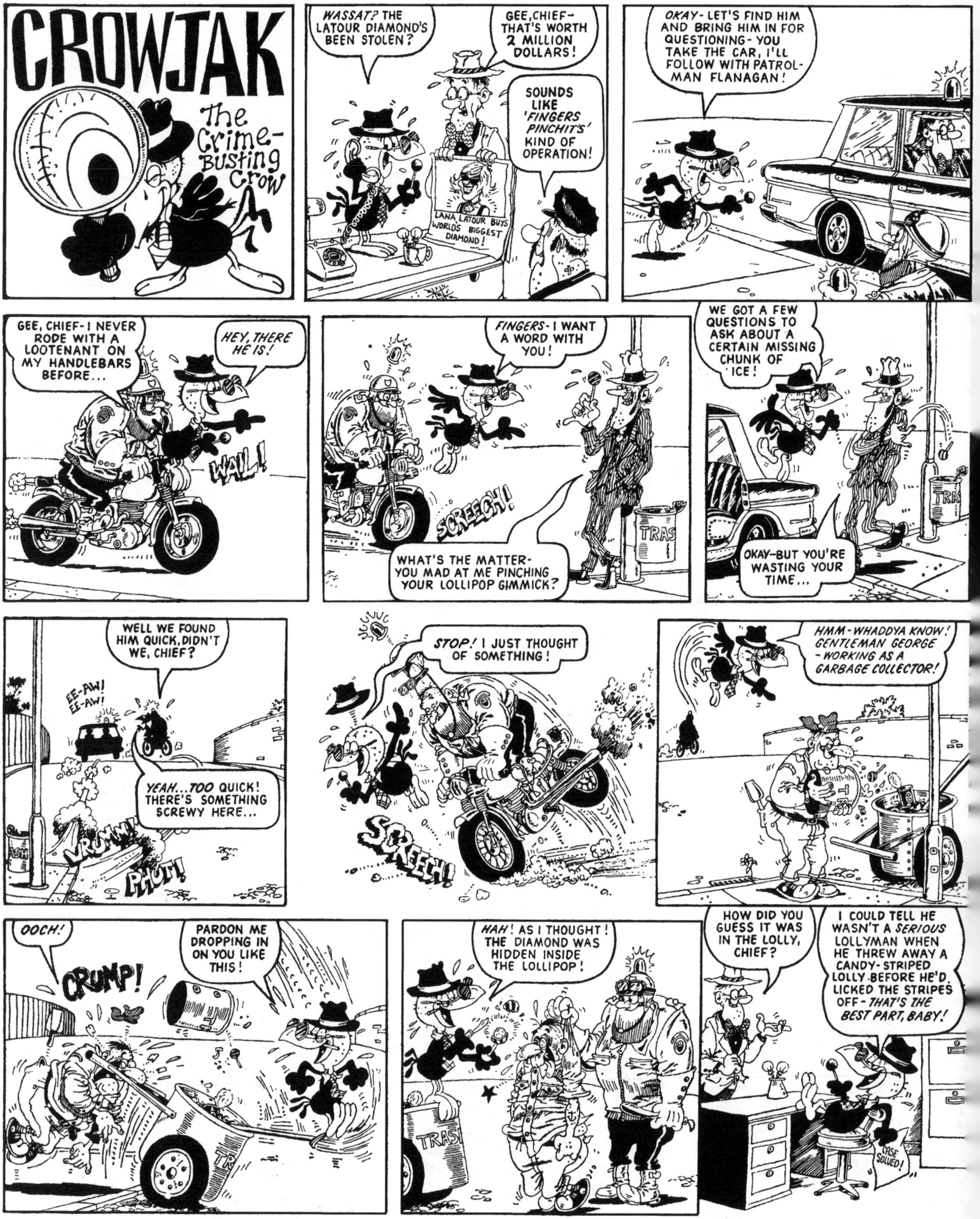
CROWJAK
The Crime-Busting Crow
WASSAT? THE LATOUR DIAMOND'S BEEN STOLEN?
GEE, CHIEF- THAT'S WORTH 2 MILLION DOLLARS!
LANA LATOUR BUYS WORLD'S BIGGEST DIAMOND!
SOUNDS LIKE 'FINGERS PINCHITS' KIND OF OPERATION!
OKAY- LET'S FIND HIM AND BRING HIM IN FOR QUESTIONING- YOU TAKE THE CAR, I'LL FOLLOW WITH PATROLMAN FLANAGAN!
GEE, CHIEF- I NEVER RODE WITH A LOOTENANT ON MY HANDLEBARS BEFORE...
HEY, THERE HE IS!
WAIL!
FINGERS- I WANT A WORD WITH YOU!
SCREECH!
WHAT'S THE MATTER- YOU MAD AT ME PINCHING YOUR LOLLIPOP GIMMICK?
WE GOT A FEW QUESTIONS TO ASK ABOUT A CERTAIN MISSING CHUNK OF ICE!
OKAY-BUT YOU'RE WASTING YOUR TIME...
WELL WE FOUND HIM QUICK, DIDN'T WE, CHIEF?
EE-AW! EE-AW!
YEAH...TOO QUICK! THERE'S SOMETHING SCREWY HERE...
VRUMM!
PHUT!
STOP! I JUST THOUGHT OF SOMETHING!
SCREECH!
HMM-WHADDYA KNOW! GENTLEMAN GEORGE - WORKING AS A GARBAGE COLLECTOR!
OOCH!
CRUMP!
PARDON ME DROPPING IN ON YOU LIKE THIS!
HAH! AS I THOUGHT! THE DIAMOND WAS HIDDEN INSIDE THE LOLLIPOP!
HOW DID YOU GUESS IT WAS IN THE LOLLY, CHIEF?
I COULD TELL HE WASN'T A SERIOUS LOLLYMAN WHEN HE THREW AWAY A CANDY-STRIPED LOLLY BEFORE HE'D LICKED THE STRIPES OFF - THAT'S THE BEST PART, BABY!
CASE SOLVED!

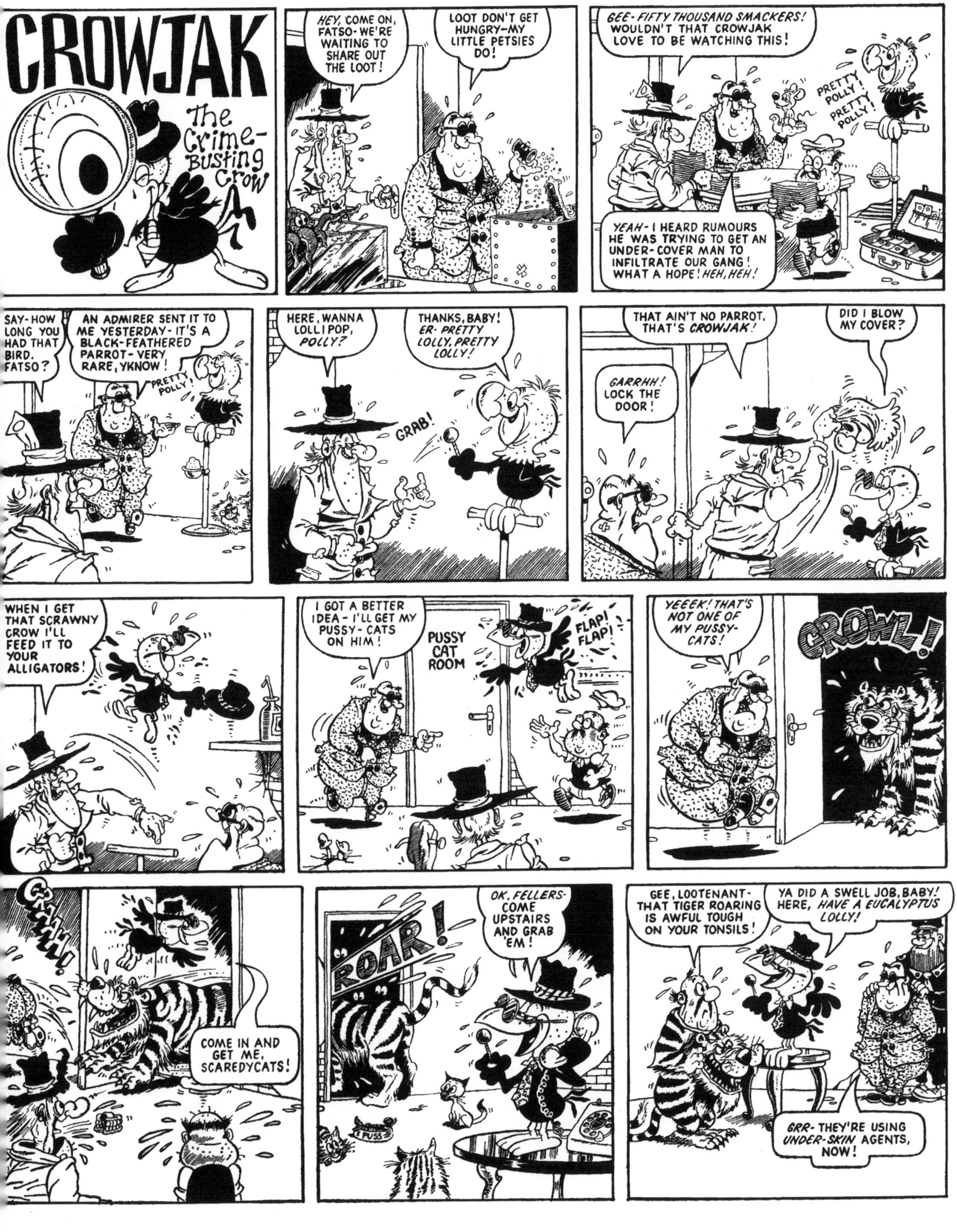
CROWJAK
The Crime-Busting Crow
HEY, COME ON, FATSO- WE'RE WAITING TO SHARE OUT THE LOOT!
LOOT DON'T GET HUNGRY-MY LITTLE PETSIES DO!
GEE- FIFTY THOUSAND SMACKERS! WOULDN'T THAT CROWJAK LOVE TO BE WATCHING THIS!
PRETTY POLLY! PRETTY POLLY!
YEAH- I HEARD RUMOURS HE WAS TRYING TO GET AN UNDER-COVER MAN TO INFILTRATE OUR GANG! WHAT A HOPE! HEH, HEH!
SAY- HOW LONG YOU HAD THAT BIRD, FATSO?
AN ADMIRER SENT IT TO ME YESTERDAY- IT'S A BLACK-FEATHERED PARROT- VERY RARE, YKNOW!
PRETTY POLLY!
HERE, WANNA LOLLIPOP, POLLY?
THANKS, BABY! ER- PRETTY LOLLY, PRETTY LOLLY!
GRAB!
THAT AIN'T NO PARROT, THAT'S CROWJAK!
DID I BLOW MY COVER?
GARRHH! LOCK THE DOOR!
WHEN I GET THAT SCRAWNY CROW I'LL FEED IT TO YOUR ALLIGATORS!
I GOT A BETTER IDEA - I'LL GET MY PUSSY- CATS ON HIM!
PUSSY CAT ROOM
FLAP! FLAP!
YEEEK! THAT'S NOT ONE OF MY PUSSY-CATS!
GROWL!
COME IN AND GET ME, SCAREDYCATS!
ROAR!
OK, FELLERS- COME UPSTAIRS AND GRAB 'EM!
PUSS
GEE, LOOTENANT- THAT TIGER ROARING IS AWFUL TOUGH ON YOUR TONSILS!
YA DID A SWELL JOB, BABY! HERE, HAVE A EUCALYPTUS LOLLY!
GRR- THEY'RE USING UNDER-SKIN AGENTS, NOW!

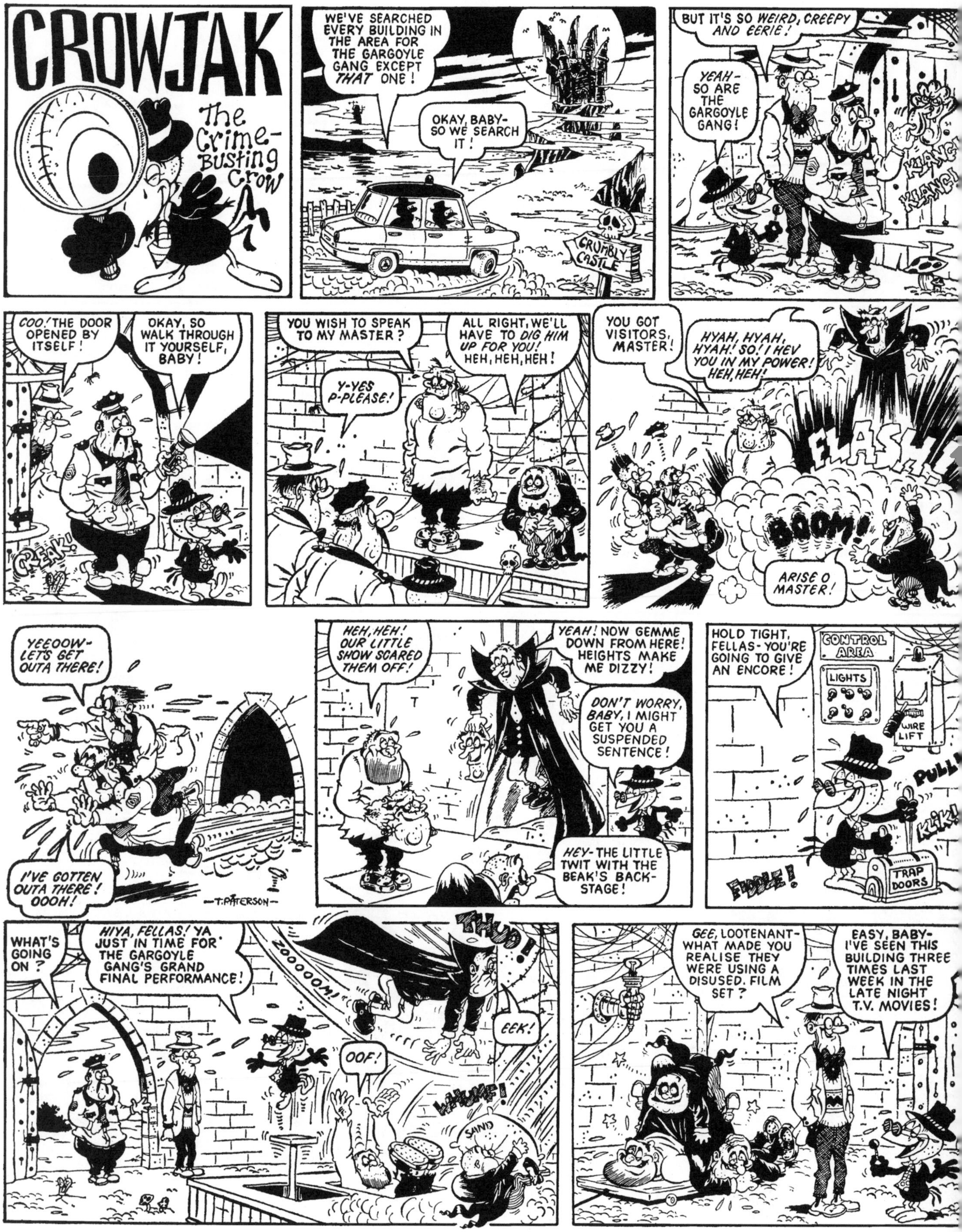
CROWJAK
The Crime-Busting Crow
WE'VE SEARCHED EVERY BUILDING IN THE AREA FOR THE GARGOYLE GANG EXCEPT THAT ONE!
OKAY, BABY- SO WE SEARCH IT!
CRUMBLY CASTLE
BUT IT'S SO WEIRD, CREEPY AND EERIE!
YEAH- SO ARE THE GARGOYLE GANG!
KLANG!
KLANG!
COO! THE DOOR OPENED BY ITSELF!
OKAY, SO WALK THROUGH IT YOURSELF, BABY!
CREAK!
YOU WISH TO SPEAK TO MY MASTER?
ALL RIGHT, WE'LL HAVE TO DIG HIM UP FOR YOU! HEH, HEH, HEH!
Y-YES P-PLEASE!
YOU GOT VISITORS, MASTER!
HYAH, HYAH, HYAH! SO! I HEV YOU IN MY POWER! HEH, HEH!
FLASH!
BOOM!
ARISE O MASTER!
YEEOOW- LET'S GET OUTA THERE!
I'VE GOTTEN OUTA THERE! OOOH!
T. PATERSON
HEH, HEH! OUR LITTLE SHOW SCARED THEM OFF!
YEAH! NOW GEMME DOWN FROM HERE! HEIGHTS MAKE ME DIZZY!
DON'T WORRY, BABY, I MIGHT GET YOU A SUSPENDED SENTENCE!
HEY- THE LITTLE TWIT WITH THE BEAK'S BACKSTAGE!
HOLD TIGHT, FELLAS- YOU'RE GOING TO GIVE AN ENCORE!
CONTROL AREA
LIGHTS
WIRE LIFT
PULL!
KLIK!
FIDDLE!
TRAP DOORS
WHAT'S GOING ON?
HIYA, FELLAS! YA JUST IN TIME FOR THE GARGOYLE GANG'S GRAND FINAL PERFORMANCE!
THUD!
ZOOOOOOM!
EEK!
OOF!
WHUMF!
SAND
GEE, LOOTENANT- WHAT MADE YOU REALISE THEY WERE USING A DISUSED FILM SET?
EASY, BABY- I'VE SEEN THIS BUILDING THREE TIMES LAST WEEK IN THE LATE NIGHT T.V. MOVIES!

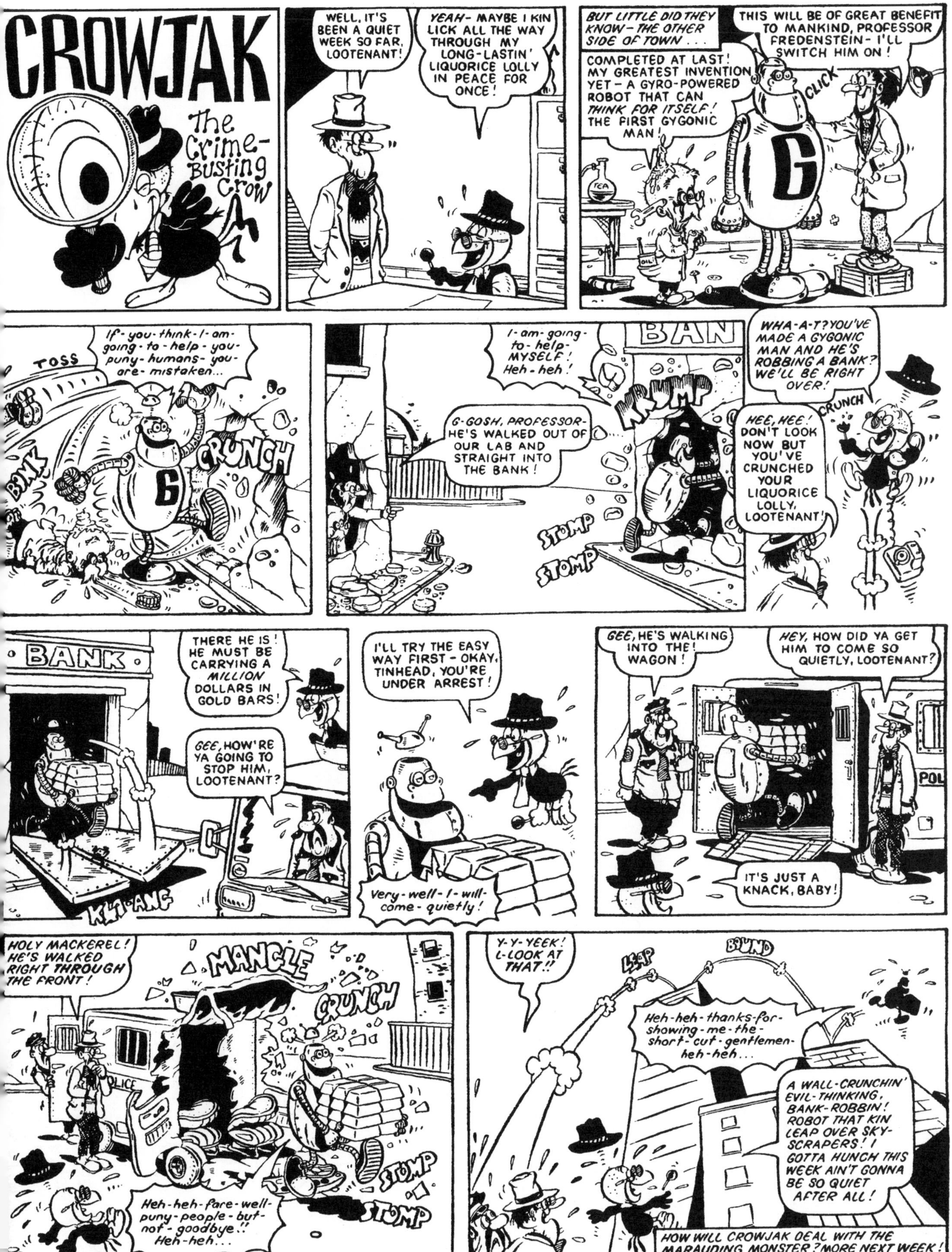
CROWJAK
The Crime-Busting Crow
WELL, IT'S BEEN A QUIET WEEK SO FAR, LOOTENANT!
YEAH- MAYBE I KIN LICK ALL THE WAY THROUGH MY LONG-LASTIN' LIQUORICE LOLLY IN PEACE FOR ONCE!
BUT LITTLE DID THEY KNOW – THE OTHER SIDE OF TOWN . . .
COMPLETED AT LAST! MY GREATEST INVENTION YET – A GYRO-POWERED ROBOT THAT CAN THINK FOR ITSELF! THE FIRST GYGONIC MAN!
THIS WILL BE OF GREAT BENEFIT TO MANKIND, PROFESSOR FREDENSTEIN- I'LL SWITCH HIM ON!
CLICK
G
TEA
OIL
TOSS
If-you-think-I-am-going-to-help-you-puny-humans-you-are-mistaken...
BONK
CRUNCH
G
I-am-going-to-help-MYSELF! Heh-heh!
G-GOSH, PROFESSOR- HE'S WALKED OUT OF OUR LAB AND STRAIGHT INTO THE BANK!
BAN
KRUMP
STOMP
STOMP
WHA-A-T? YOU'VE MADE A GYGONIC MAN AND HE'S ROBBING A BANK? WE'LL BE RIGHT OVER!
CRUNCH
HEE, HEE! DON'T LOOK NOW BUT YOU'VE CRUNCHED YOUR LIQUORICE LOLLY, LOOTENANT!
BANK
THERE HE IS! HE MUST BE CARRYING A MILLION DOLLARS IN GOLD BARS!
GEE, HOW'RE YA GOING TO STOP HIM, LOOTENANT?
KLANG
I'LL TRY THE EASY WAY FIRST – OKAY, TINHEAD, YOU'RE UNDER ARREST!
Very-well-I-will-come-quietly!
GEE, HE'S WALKING INTO THE! WAGON!
HEY, HOW DID YA GET HIM TO COME SO QUIETLY, LOOTENANT?
POL
IT'S JUST A KNACK, BABY!
HOLY MACKEREL! HE'S WALKED RIGHT THROUGH THE FRONT!
MANGLE
CRUNCH
OLICE
STOMP
STOMP
Heh-heh-fare-well-puny-people-but-not-goodbye!! Heh-heh...
Y-Y-YEEK! L-LOOK AT THAT!!
LEAP
BOUND
Heh-heh-thanks-for-showing-me-the-short-cut-gentlemen-heh-heh...
A WALL-CRUNCHIN' EVIL-THINKING, BANK-ROBBIN' ROBOT THAT KIN LEAP OVER SKY-SCRAPERS! I GOTTA HUNCH THIS WEEK AIN'T GONNA BE SO QUIET AFTER ALL!
HOW WILL CROWJAK DEAL WITH THE MARAUDING MONSTER? MORE NEXT WEEK!

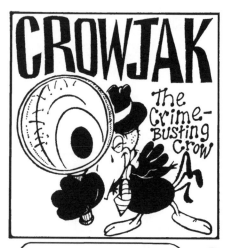

CROWJAK
The Crime-Busting Crow
STORY SO FAR... PROFESSOR FREDENSTEIN'S LATEST INVENTION IS THE GYGON-POWERED ROBOT THAT CAN THINK FOR ITSELF. UNFORTUNATLY IT SEEMS TO HAVE TAKEN TO A LIFE OF CRIME AND CROWJAK CAN'T STOP HIM!
NOW LISTEN, CROWJAK - YOU GOTTA STOP THIS NUTTY ROBOT GOIN' AROUND ROBBING PLACES! I WANNA SEE SOME ACTION, D'YA HEAR?
DAILY TRASH
RUNAWAY ROBOT ROBS ANOTHER WAREHOUSE!
THUMP
I HEAR YA LOUD AN' CLEAR, MAYOR, BABY!
MAYOR
NAH! GOT YOU AT LAST!
BONK
BONK
AWK! I THINK I FOUND SOME ACTION!
HOW DARE YOU WASTE THE TAXPAYERS' MONEY, BUILDING NEW BRIDGES IN THE MIDDLE OF NOWHERE! WHAT'S THE USE OF A BRIDGE IN MUDPACK SWAMP, EH, MR. MAYOR?
WHACK
THWOP
BONK
OO! OWCH!
KNOCK IT OFF, LADY! THAT AIN'T THE MAYOR- THAT'S LOOTENANT CROWJAK!
I CAN'T FIGURE OUT WHY THAT GYGONIC ROBOT IS PULLING SUCH PECULIAR ROBBERIES, LOOTENANT! TRUCK-LOADS OF NUTS AND BOLTS - A WAREHOUSE FULL OF ELECTRONIC GEAR - A TRAINLOAD OF ALUMINIUM...
REPORT
SCREWY ROBOTS AND NUTTY OLD LADIES - THIS AIN'T MY DAY!
-T. PATERSON-
HEY! MAYBE THAT OLD LADY PUT US ON TA SOMETHING! WE'RE GOIN' OVER TO MUDPACK SWAMP, BABY!
YOU SURE THAT OLD LADY DIDN'T HIT YOU TOO HARD, LOOTENANT?
WELL, SHE WAS RIGHT! THERE IS A NEW BRIDGE IN THE MIDDLE OF NOWHERE - BUT WHERE DOES THAT LEAD US, LOOTENANT?
OVER TA THE OTHER SIDE OF COURSE - C'MON LET'S GO VISIT MUDPACK ISLAND!
STOMP STOMP STOMP STOMP
GEE, LOOTENANT! WHAT'S THAT STRANGE THUMPING NOISE COMIN' FROM THE ISLAND?
IF IT'S WHAT I THINK IT IS - WE GOT TROUBLE!
YEAH! MY HUNCH WUZ RIGHT! THAT GYGONIC ROBOT'S BEEN BUILDING A WHOLE ARMY OF ROBOTS ON THAT DESERTED ISLAND - JUST LIKE HIMSELF! ONLY BIGGER!
TROMP
TROMP
STOMP
STOMP
POLICE
GEE, SO THAT'S WHY HE STOLE ALL THAT EQUIPMENT AND STUFF!
CLANG
AND THAT'S WHY HE BUILT THE BRIDGE - TO TAKE THE WEIGHT OF THESE GIANT TINNIES!
QUIT STRAININ' YA BRAINS WITH ALL THAT THINKIN' AND JUMP OUTA THE WAY - FAST!
KRUNCH
STOMP
CLANG
MANGLE
TROMP
CRUNCH
GEE, LOOTENANT! THEY'RE HEADIN' STRAIGHT FOR NEW YORK!
I TELL YA ONE THING - I AIN'T GONNA RUSH TA TELL THE MAYOR ABOUT THIS...
THEY'LL TEAR THE PLACE APART! WHAT CAN WE DO?
STOMP
CRUNCH
IS THIS THING TOO BIG FOR OUR LOLLY-LICKIN' TEC TO HANDLE? SEE NEXT WEEK...

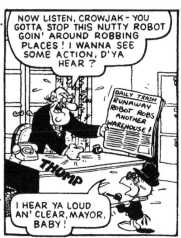

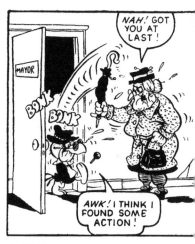

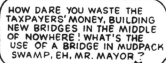

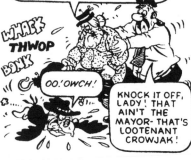

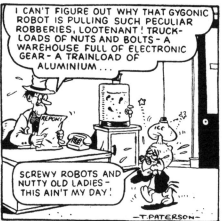

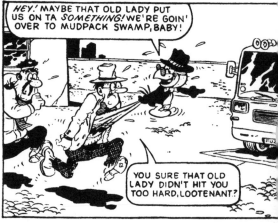

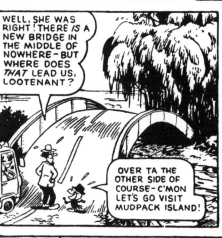

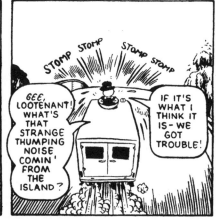

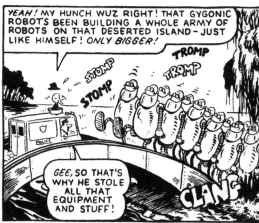

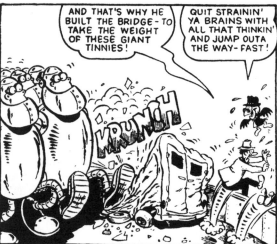

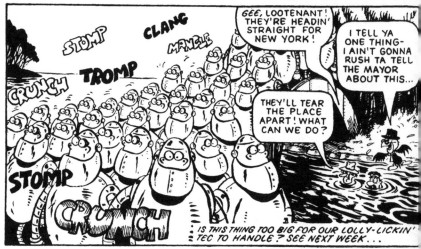

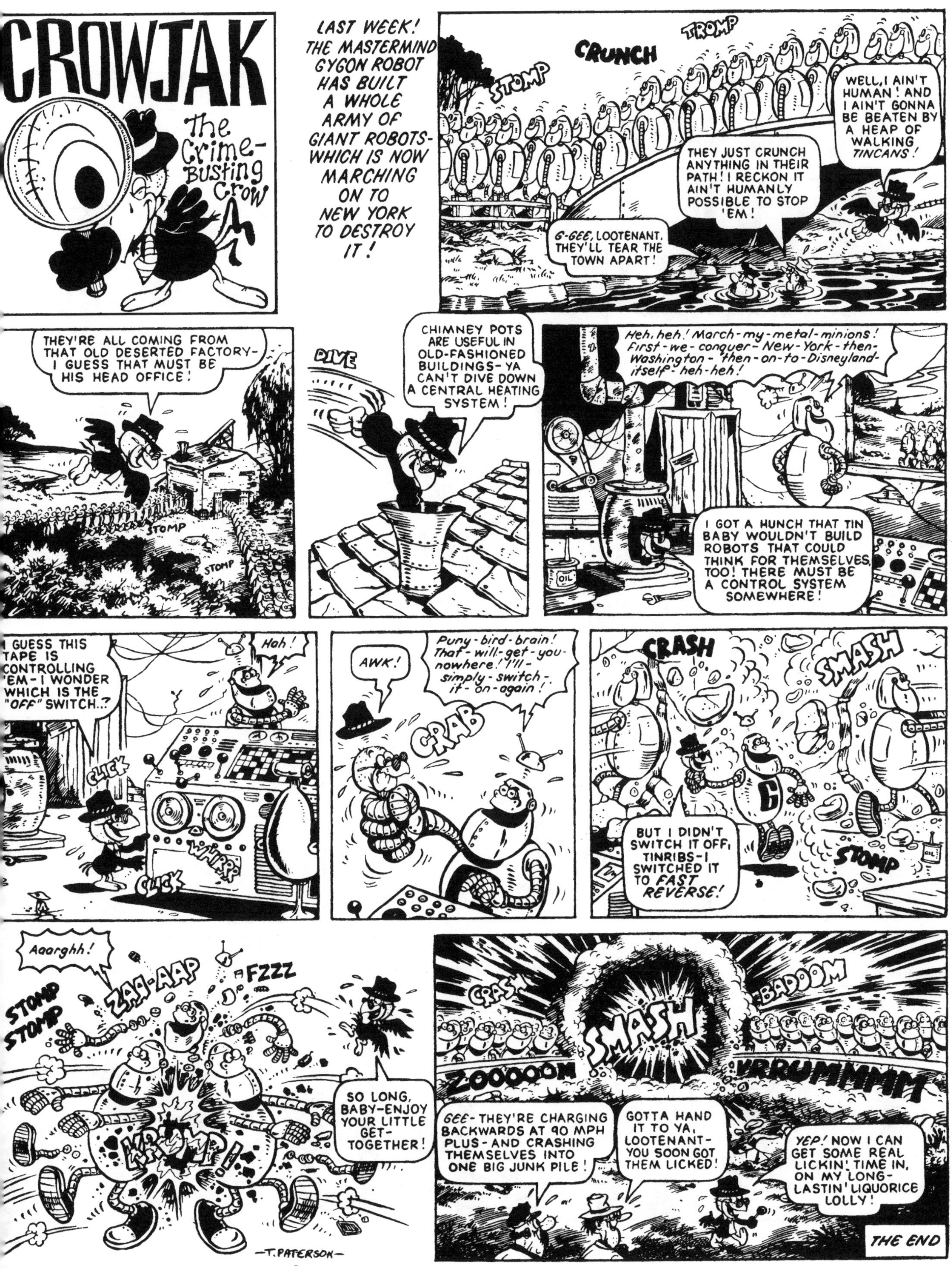
CROWJAK
The Crime-Busting Crow
LAST WEEK! THE MASTERMIND GYGON ROBOT HAS BUILT A WHOLE ARMY OF GIANT ROBOTS-WHICH IS NOW MARCHING ON TO NEW YORK TO DESTROY IT!
STOMP
CRUNCH
TROMP
G-GEE, LOOTENANT, THEY'LL TEAR THE TOWN APART!
THEY JUST CRUNCH ANYTHING IN THEIR PATH! I RECKON IT AIN'T HUMANLY POSSIBLE TO STOP 'EM!
WELL, I AIN'T HUMAN! AND I AIN'T GONNA BE BEATEN BY A HEAP OF WALKING TINCANS!
THEY'RE ALL COMING FROM THAT OLD DESERTED FACTORY-I GUESS THAT MUST BE HIS HEAD OFFICE!
STOMP
STOMP
DIVE
CHIMNEY POTS ARE USEFUL IN OLD-FASHIONED BUILDINGS-YA CAN'T DIVE DOWN A CENTRAL HEATING SYSTEM!
Heh, heh! March-my-metal-minions! First-we-conquer-New-York-then-Washington-then-on-to-Disneyland-itself-heh-heh!
I GOT A HUNCH THAT TIN BABY WOULDN'T BUILD ROBOTS THAT COULD THINK FOR THEMSELVES, TOO! THERE MUST BE A CONTROL SYSTEM SOMEWHERE!
OIL
I GUESS THIS TAPE IS CONTROLLING 'EM-I WONDER WHICH IS THE "OFF" SWITCH..?
Hah!
CLICK
WHIRR
CLICK
AWK!
Puny-bird-brain! That-will-get-you-nowhere! I'll-simply-switch-it-on-again!
GRAB
CRASH
SMASH
BUT I DIDN'T SWITCH IT OFF, TINRIBS-I SWITCHED IT TO FAST REVERSE!
STOMP
OIL
Aaarghh!
ZAA-AAP
FZZZ
STOMP
STOMP
KER-UMP!
SO LONG, BABY-ENJOY YOUR LITTLE GET-TOGETHER!
-T. PATERSON-
CRASH
SMASH
BADOOM
ZOOOOOM
VRRUMMMM
GEE-THEY'RE CHARGING BACKWARDS AT 90 MPH PLUS-AND CRASHING THEMSELVES INTO ONE BIG JUNK PILE!
GOTTA HAND IT TO YA, LOOTENANT-YOU SOON GOT THEM LICKED!
YEP! NOW I CAN GET SOME REAL LICKIN' TIME IN, ON MY LONG-LASTIN' LIQUORICE LOLLY!
THE END

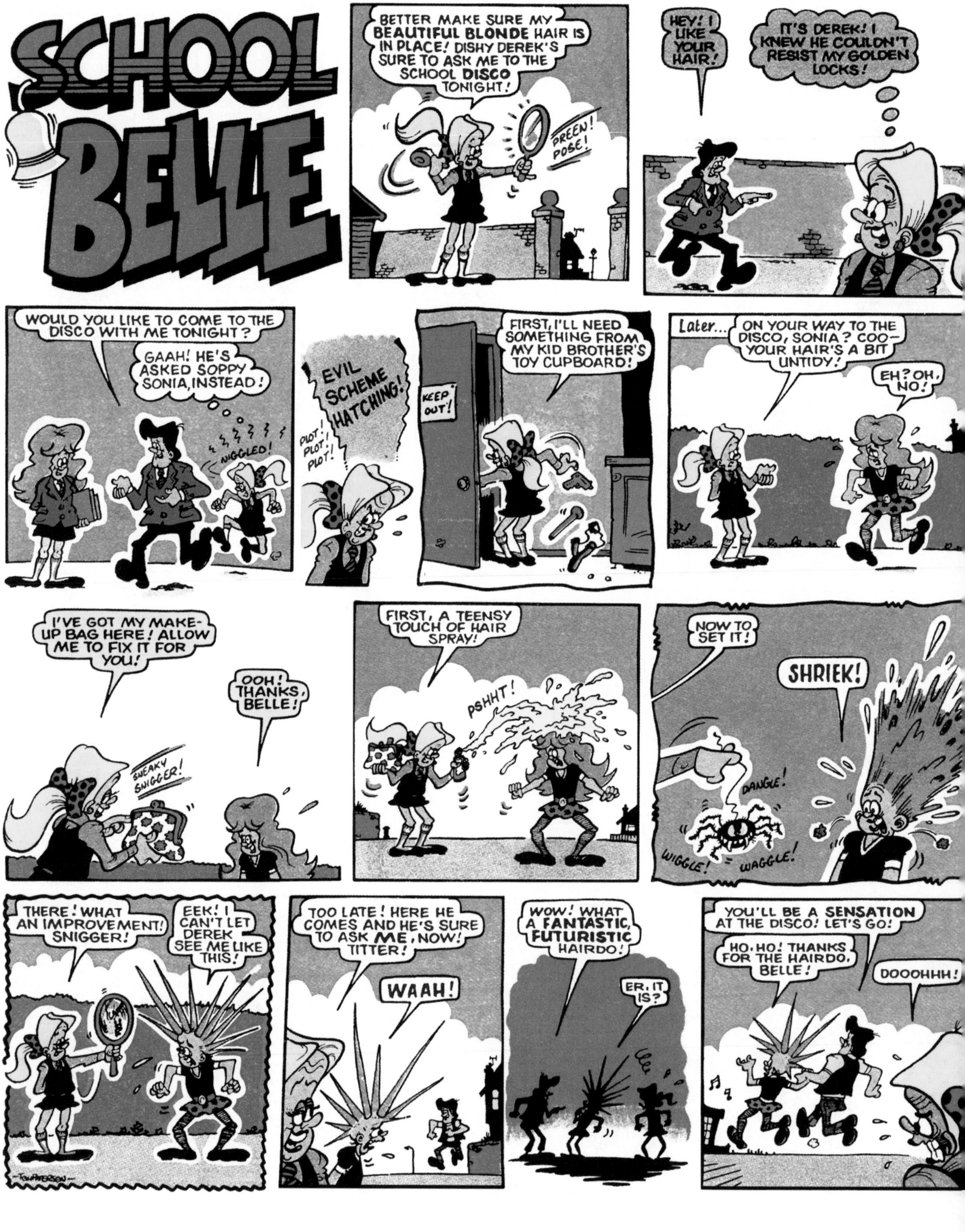
SCHOOL BELLE
BETTER MAKE SURE MY BEAUTIFUL BLONDE HAIR IS IN PLACE! DISHY DEREK'S SURE TO ASK ME TO THE SCHOOL DISCO TONIGHT!
PREEN! POSE!
HEY! I LIKE YOUR HAIR!
IT'S DEREK! I KNEW HE COULDN'T RESIST MY GOLDEN LOCKS!
WOULD YOU LIKE TO COME TO THE DISCO WITH ME TONIGHT?
GAAH! HE'S ASKED SOPPY SONIA, INSTEAD!
NIGGLED!
EVIL SCHEME HATCHING!
PLOT! PLOT! PLOT!
FIRST, I'LL NEED SOMETHING FROM MY KID BROTHER'S TOY CUPBOARD!
KEEP OUT!
Later...
ON YOUR WAY TO THE DISCO, SONIA? COO— YOUR HAIR'S A BIT UNTIDY!
EH? OH, NO!
I'VE GOT MY MAKE-UP BAG HERE! ALLOW ME TO FIX IT FOR YOU!
SNEAKY SNIGGER!
OOH! THANKS, BELLE!
FIRST, A TEENSY TOUCH OF HAIR SPRAY!
PSHHT!
NOW TO SET IT!
SHRIEK!
DANGLE!
WIGGLE! WAGGLE!
THERE! WHAT AN IMPROVEMENT! SNIGGER!
EEK! I CAN'T LET DEREK SEE ME LIKE THIS!
TOO LATE! HERE HE COMES AND HE'S SURE TO ASK ME, NOW! TITTER!
WAAH!
WOW! WHAT A FANTASTIC, FUTURISTIC HAIRDO!
ER, IT IS?
YOU'LL BE A SENSATION AT THE DISCO! LET'S GO!
HO, HO! THANKS FOR THE HAIRDO, BELLE!
DOOOHHH!

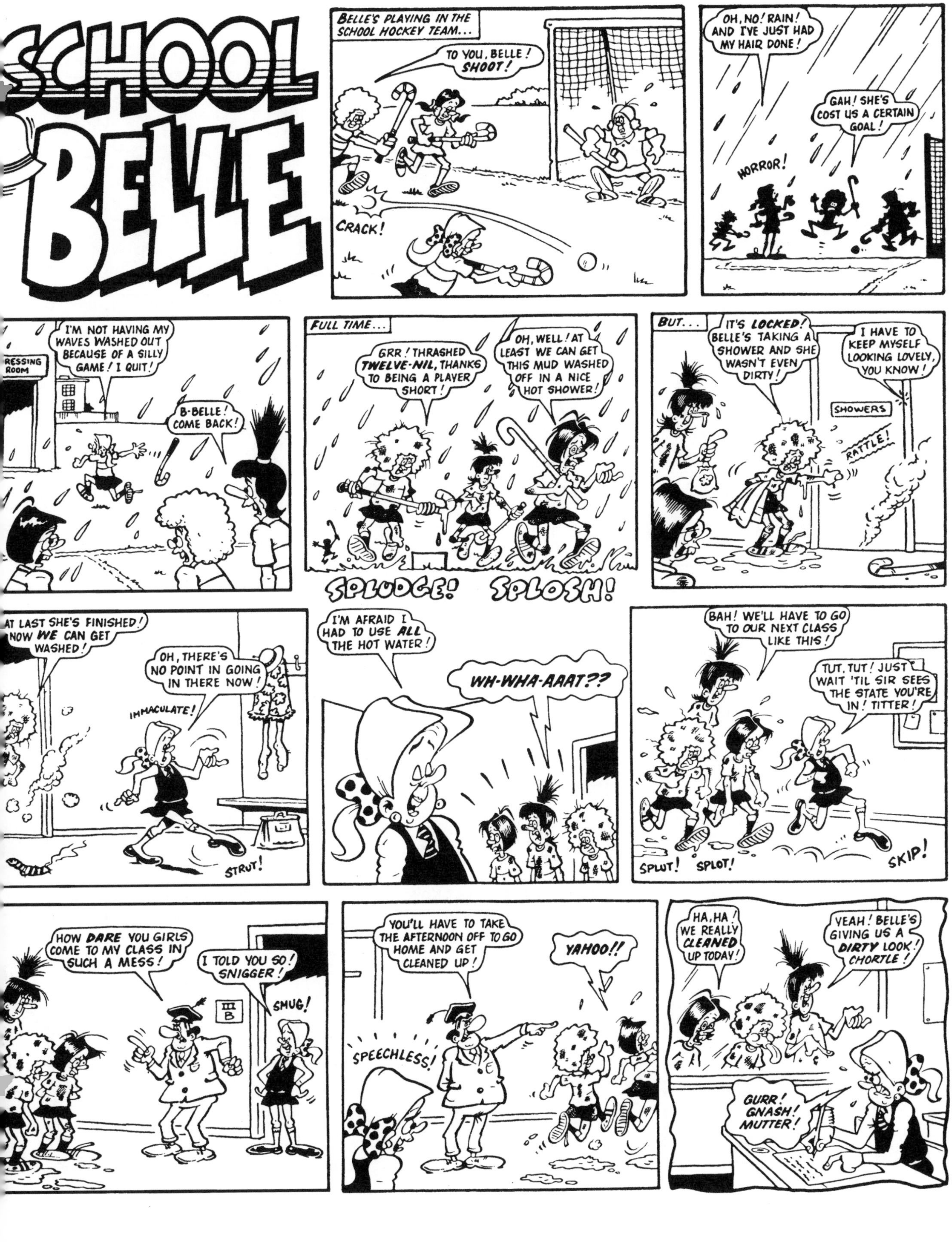
SCHOOL BELLE
BELLE'S PLAYING IN THE SCHOOL HOCKEY TEAM...
TO YOU, BELLE! SHOOT!
CRACK!
OH, NO! RAIN! AND I'VE JUST HAD MY HAIR DONE!
GAH! SHE'S COST US A CERTAIN GOAL!
HORROR!
I'M NOT HAVING MY WAVES WASHED OUT BECAUSE OF A SILLY GAME! I QUIT!
RESSING ROOM
B-BELLE! COME BACK!
FULL TIME...
GRR! THRASHED TWELVE-NIL, THANKS TO BEING A PLAYER SHORT!
OH, WELL! AT LEAST WE CAN GET THIS MUD WASHED OFF IN A NICE HOT SHOWER!
SPLUDGE! SPLOSH!
BUT...
IT'S LOCKED! BELLE'S TAKING A SHOWER AND SHE WASN'T EVEN DIRTY!
I HAVE TO KEEP MYSELF LOOKING LOVELY, YOU KNOW!
SHOWERS
RATTLE!
AT LAST SHE'S FINISHED! NOW WE CAN GET WASHED!
OH, THERE'S NO POINT IN GOING IN THERE NOW!
IMMACULATE!
STRUT!
I'M AFRAID I HAD TO USE ALL THE HOT WATER!
WH-WHA-AAAT??
BAH! WE'LL HAVE TO GO TO OUR NEXT CLASS LIKE THIS!
TUT, TUT! JUST WAIT 'TIL SIR SEES THE STATE YOU'RE IN! TITTER!
SPLUT! SPLOT!
SKIP!
HOW DARE YOU GIRLS COME TO MY CLASS IN SUCH A MESS!
I TOLD YOU SO! SNIGGER!
III B
SMUG!
YOU'LL HAVE TO TAKE THE AFTERNOON OFF TO GO HOME AND GET CLEANED UP!
YAHOO!!
SPEECHLESS!
HA, HA! WE REALLY CLEANED UP TODAY!
YEAH! BELLE'S GIVING US A DIRTY LOOK! CHORTLE!
GURR! GNASH! MUTTER!

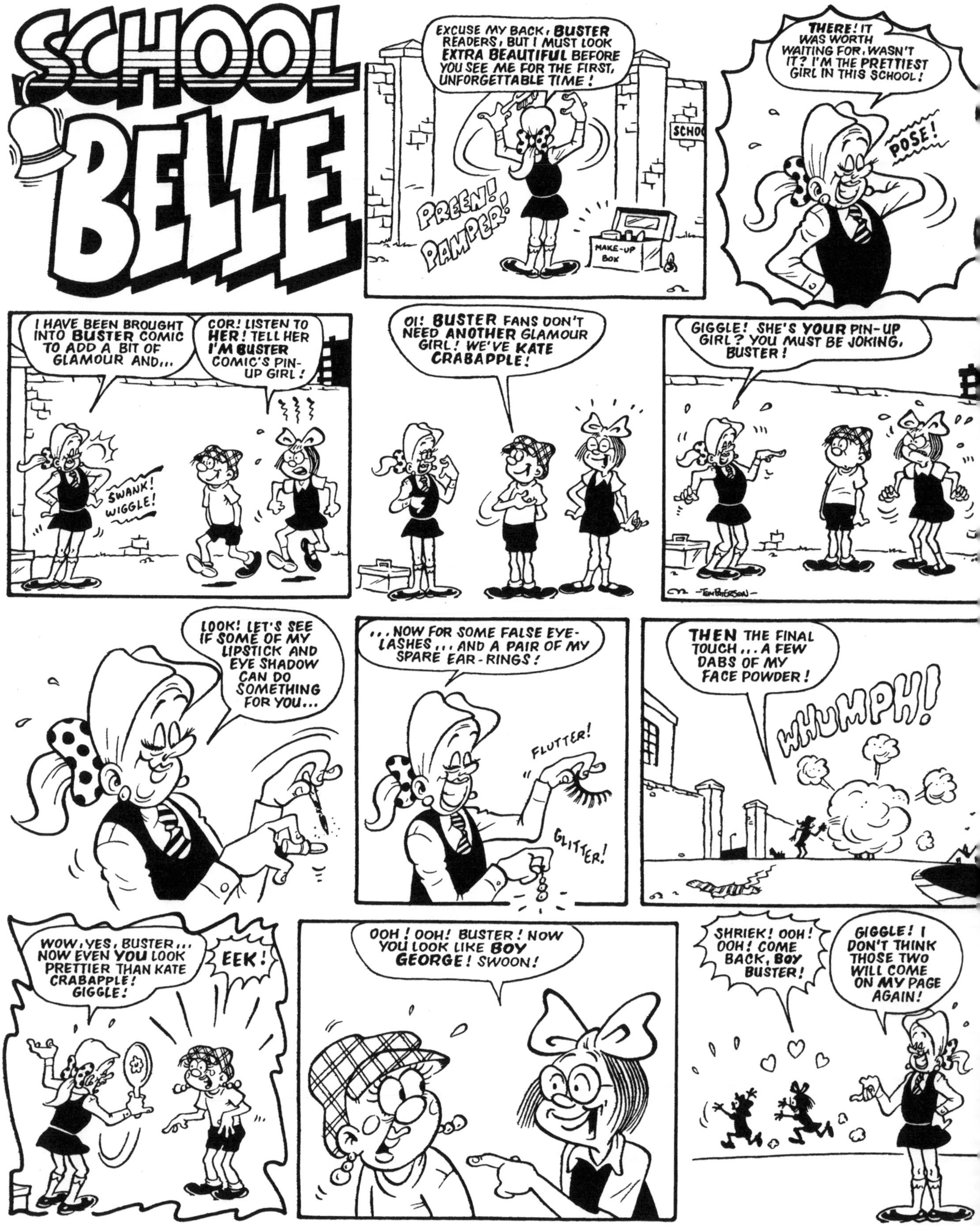
SCHOOL BELLE
EXCUSE MY BACK, BUSTER READERS, BUT I MUST LOOK EXTRA BEAUTIFUL BEFORE YOU SEE ME FOR THE FIRST, UNFORGETTABLE TIME!
SCHOO
PREEN! PAMPER!
MAKE-UP BOX
THERE! IT WAS WORTH WAITING FOR, WASN'T IT? I'M THE PRETTIEST GIRL IN THIS SCHOOL!
POSE!
I HAVE BEEN BROUGHT INTO BUSTER COMIC TO ADD A BIT OF GLAMOUR AND...
COR! LISTEN TO HER! TELL HER I'M BUSTER COMIC'S PIN-UP GIRL!
SWANK! WIGGLE!
OI! BUSTER FANS DON'T NEED ANOTHER GLAMOUR GIRL! WE'VE KATE CRABAPPLE!
GIGGLE! SHE'S YOUR PIN-UP GIRL? YOU MUST BE JOKING, BUSTER!
LOOK! LET'S SEE IF SOME OF MY LIPSTICK AND EYE SHADOW CAN DO SOMETHING FOR YOU...
...NOW FOR SOME FALSE EYE-LASHES... AND A PAIR OF MY SPARE EAR-RINGS!
FLUTTER!
GLITTER!
THEN THE FINAL TOUCH... A FEW DABS OF MY FACE POWDER!
WHUMPH!
WOW, YES, BUSTER... NOW EVEN YOU LOOK PRETTIER THAN KATE CRABAPPLE! GIGGLE!
EEK!
OOH! OOH! BUSTER! NOW YOU LOOK LIKE BOY GEORGE! SWOON!
SHRIEK! OOH! OOH! COME BACK, BOY BUSTER!
GIGGLE! I DON'T THINK THOSE TWO WILL COME ON MY PAGE AGAIN!

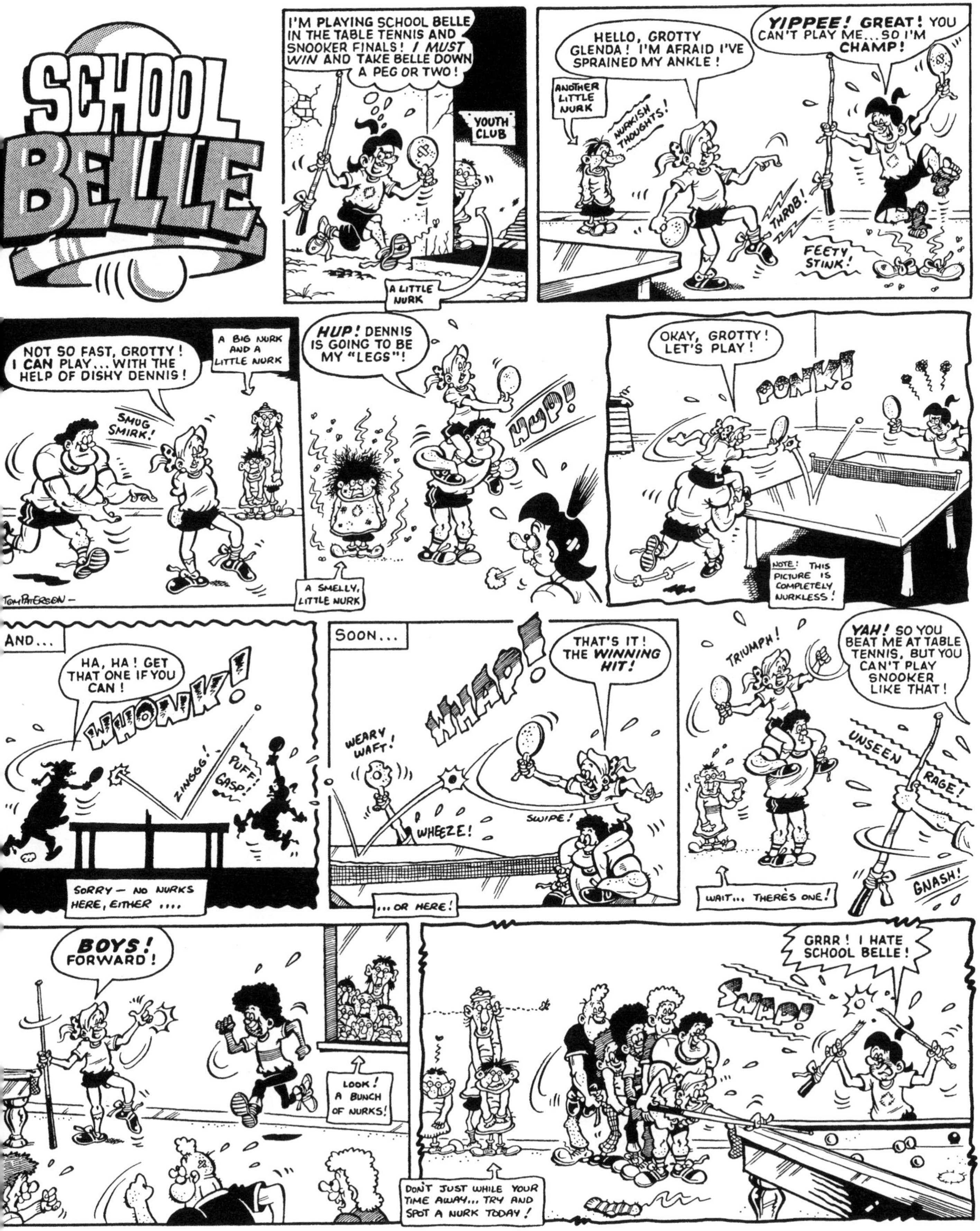
SCHOOL BELLE
I'M PLAYING SCHOOL BELLE IN THE TABLE TENNIS AND SNOOKER FINALS! I MUST WIN AND TAKE BELLE DOWN A PEG OR TWO!
YOUTH CLUB
A LITTLE NURK
HELLO, GROTTY GLENDA! I'M AFRAID I'VE SPRAINED MY ANKLE!
ANOTHER LITTLE NURK
NURKISH THOUGHTS!
THROB!
YIPPEE! GREAT! YOU CAN'T PLAY ME... SO I'M CHAMP!
FEETY STINK!
NOT SO FAST, GROTTY! I CAN PLAY... WITH THE HELP OF DISHY DENNIS!
A BIG NURK AND A LITTLE NURK
SMUG SMIRK!
TOM PATERSON
HUP! DENNIS IS GOING TO BE MY "LEGS"!
HUP!
A SMELLY, LITTLE NURK
OKAY, GROTTY! LET'S PLAY!
PONK!
NOTE: THIS PICTURE IS COMPLETELY NURKLESS!
AND...
HA, HA! GET THAT ONE IF YOU CAN!
WHONK!
ZINGGG!
PUFF! GASP!
SORRY — NO NURKS HERE, EITHER ....
SOON...
WEARY WAFT!
WHAP!
THAT'S IT! THE WINNING HIT!
WHEEZE!
SWIPE!
...OR HERE!
TRIUMPH!
YAH! SO YOU BEAT ME AT TABLE TENNIS, BUT YOU CAN'T PLAY SNOOKER LIKE THAT!
UNSEEN RAGE!
GNASH!
WAIT... THERE'S ONE!
BOYS! FORWARD!
LOOK! A BUNCH OF NURKS!
GRRR! I HATE SCHOOL BELLE!
SMAP!
DON'T JUST WHILE YOUR TIME AWAY... TRY AND SPOT A NURK TODAY!

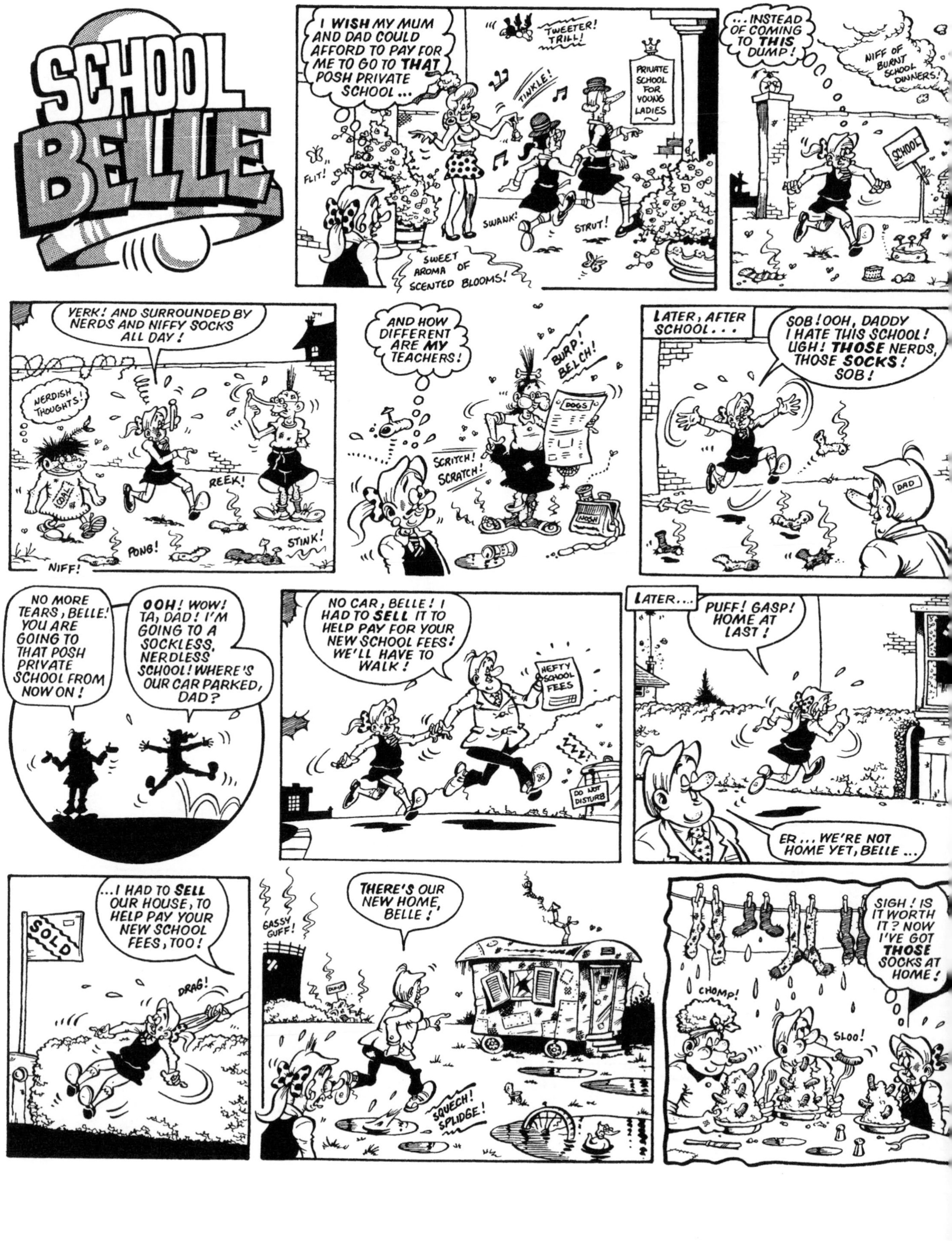
SCHOOL BELLE
I WISH MY MUM AND DAD COULD AFFORD TO PAY FOR ME TO GO TO THAT POSH PRIVATE SCHOOL ...
TWEETER! TRILL!
PRIVATE SCHOOL FOR YOUNG LADIES
TINKLE!
FLIT!
SWANK!
STRUT!
SWEET AROMA OF SCENTED BLOOMS!
... INSTEAD OF COMING TO THIS DUMP!
NIFF OF BURNT SCHOOL DINNERS!
SCHOOL
YERK! AND SURROUNDED BY NERDS AND NIFFY SOCKS ALL DAY!
NERDISH THOUGHTS!
REEK!
PONG!
STINK!
NIFF!
AND HOW DIFFERENT ARE MY TEACHERS!
BURP! BELCH!
DOGS
SCRITCH! SCRATCH!
NOSH
LATER, AFTER SCHOOL...
SOB! OOH, DADDY I HATE THIS SCHOOL! UGH! THOSE NERDS, THOSE SOCKS! SOB!
DAD
NO MORE TEARS, BELLE! YOU ARE GOING TO THAT POSH PRIVATE SCHOOL FROM NOW ON!
OOH! WOW! TA, DAD! I'M GOING TO A SOCKLESS, NERDLESS SCHOOL! WHERE'S OUR CAR PARKED, DAD?
NO CAR, BELLE! I HAD TO SELL IT TO HELP PAY FOR YOUR NEW SCHOOL FEES! WE'LL HAVE TO WALK!
HEFTY SCHOOL FEES
DO NOT DISTURB
LATER...
PUFF! GASP! HOME AT LAST!
ER... WE'RE NOT HOME YET, BELLE...
...I HAD TO SELL OUR HOUSE, TO HELP PAY YOUR NEW SCHOOL FEES, TOO!
SOLD
DRAG!
GASSY GUFF!
THERE'S OUR NEW HOME, BELLE!
DUMP
SQUELCH! SPLIDGE!
SIGH! IS IT WORTH IT? NOW I'VE GOT THOSE SOCKS AT HOME!
CHOMP!
SLOO!

DOGSBODY!! WHERE ARE YOU, YOU LAZY SO-AND-SO?
CLUMP CLUMP

# Nipper & JACKPOT

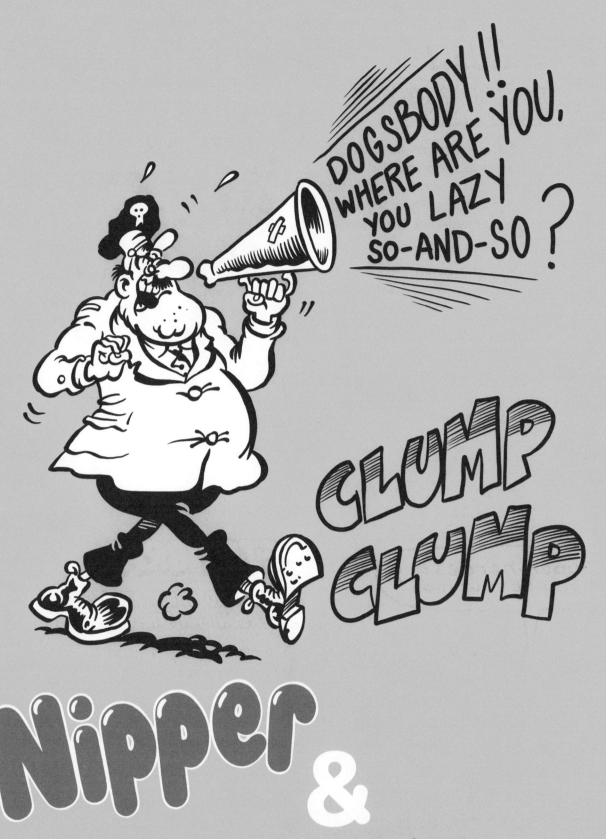

**SCRIPTS**

Script contributions throughout by Tom Paterson.

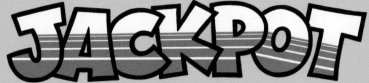

# LEW STRINGER

## WRITER/ARTIST – COMBAT COLIN, DEREK THE TROLL, BRICKMAN

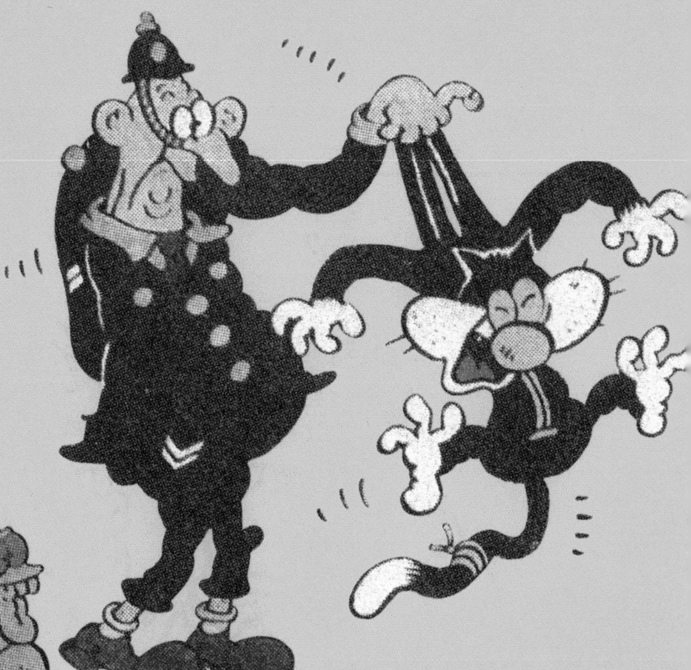

**IT WASN'T IMMEDIATELY** evident when Tom Paterson started his career ghosting strips such as *Grimly Feendish* and *Sweeny Toddler* that he'd soon develop into one of the best humour artists in comics but his own distinct touches soon came to the fore. I'd go as far to say that his *Sweeny Toddler* strips are easily on a par with any of Baxendale's work. Devilish humour is there in every panel.

The amazing thing about Tom's work is not only that it's genuinely funny, but how he's re-invented his style several times to suit the tone of whatever series he's drawing. His revamp of the *Buster* character had a completely different style to his *Sweeny Toddler* strips, but maintained the same hilarious energy. Then he evolved his style further, bringing in touches of a Robert Crumb influence, but establishing his own approach with *Captain Crucial* and *Watford Gapp*. The brilliant thing is Tom can switch between styles, as is evident from his recent *Grimly Feendish* strips for the **Cor!! Buster** Specials. A true comics great!

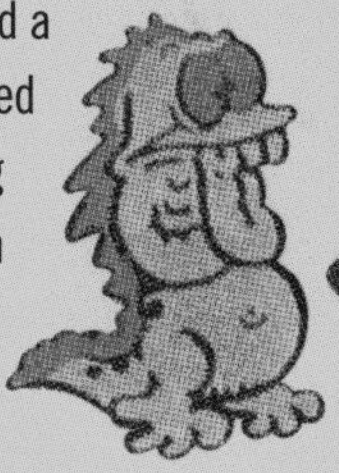

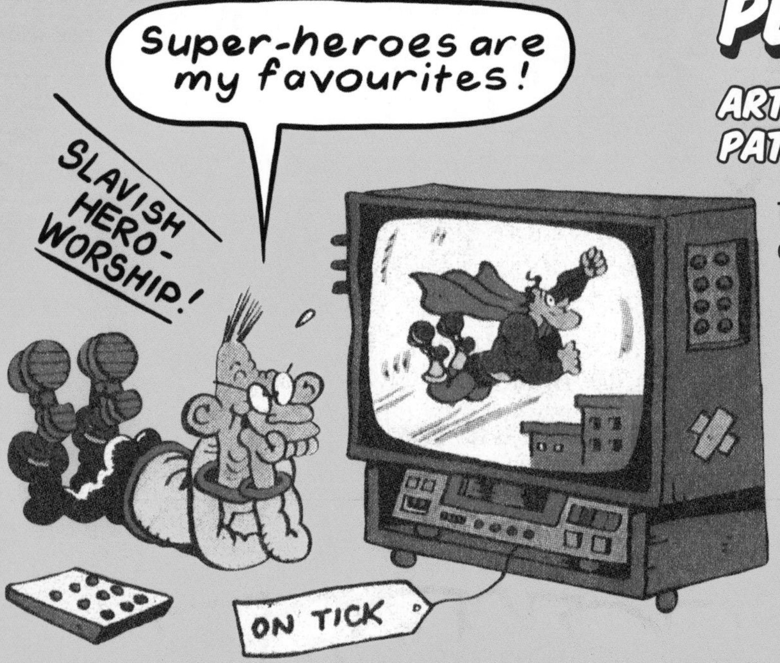
Super-heroes are my favourites!
SLAVISH HERO-WORSHIP!
ON TICK

# PETER GRAY

## ARTIST AND ORIGINATOR OF THE TOM PATERSON FAN SITE ON FACEBOOK

**TOM PATERSON DESERVES** this book, his cartoony art stood out in comic and no wonder he got the covers and centre pages.

Every panel is filled to the brim with humorous silly fun and cra descriptive words. His work surprises you and makes you laugh out lou Seeing new things each time you read it… a brilliant body of work.

Tom Paterson is a close second to Leo Baxendale and you can't g any higher praise than that.

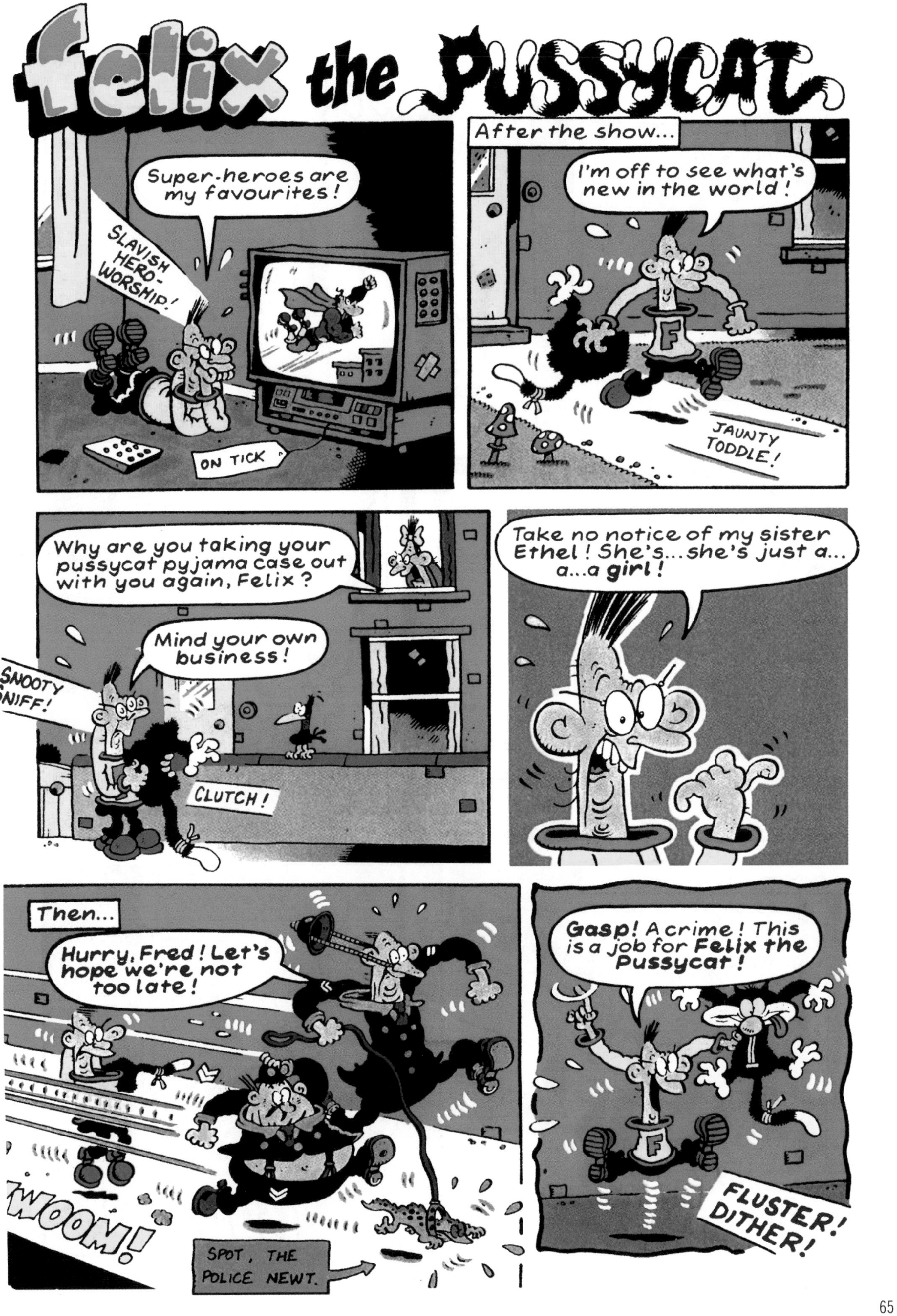
felix the PUSSYCAT
Super-heroes are my favourites!
SLAVISH HERO-WORSHIP!
ON TICK
After the show...
I'm off to see what's new in the world!
JAUNTY TODDLE!
Why are you taking your pussycat pyjama case out with you again, Felix?
Mind your own business!
SNOOTY SNIFF!
CLUTCH!
Take no notice of my sister Ethel! She's... she's just a... a...a **girl**!
Then...
Hurry, Fred! Let's hope we're not too late!
WOOM!
SPOT, THE POLICE NEWT.
**Gasp!** A crime! This is a job for **Felix the Pussycat**!
FLUSTER! DITHER!

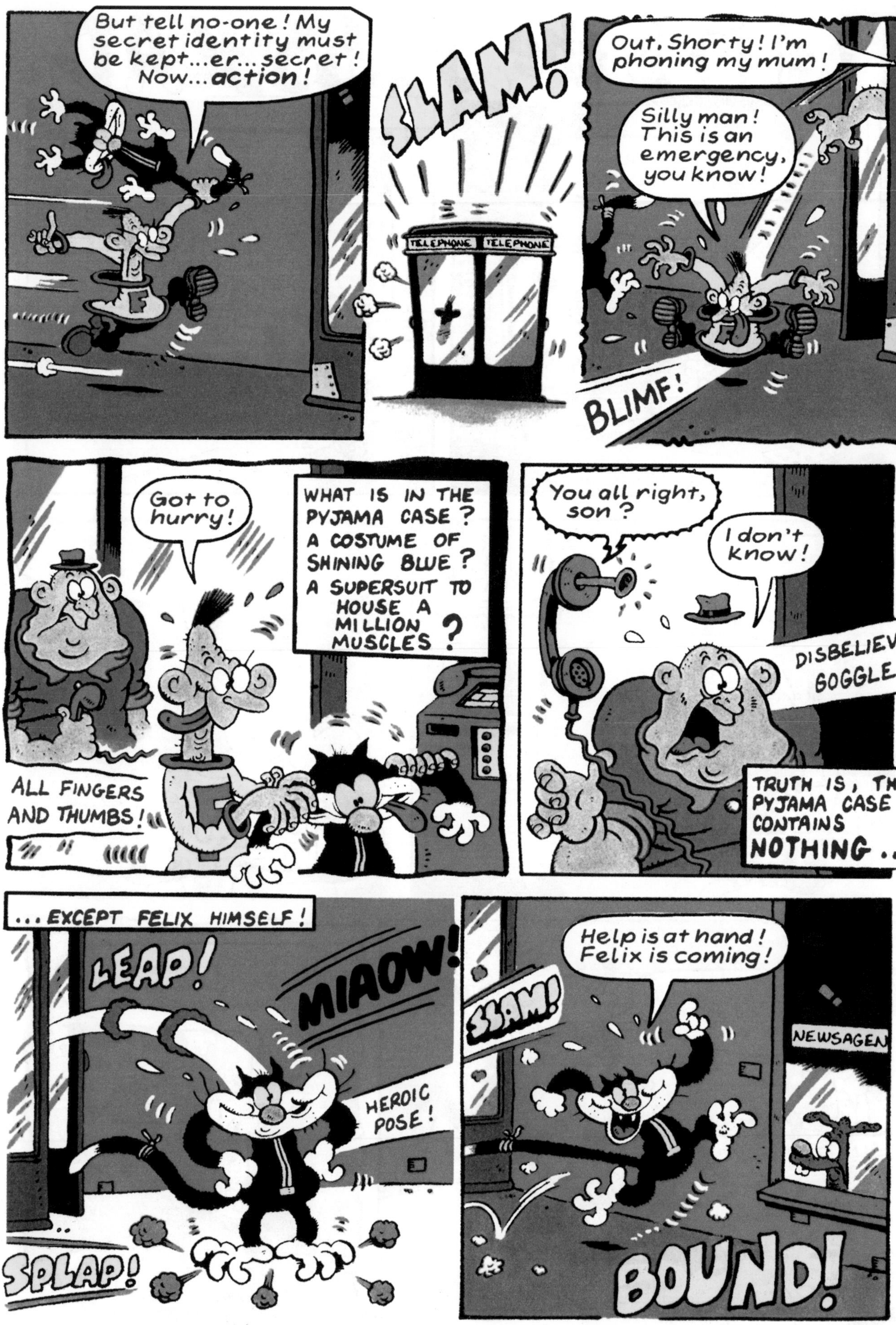
But tell no-one! My secret identity must be kept...er...secret! Now...action!
SLAM!
TELEPHONE TELEPHONE
Out, Shorty! I'm phoning my mum!
Silly man! This is an emergency, you know!
BLIMF!
Got to hurry!
WHAT IS IN THE PYJAMA CASE? A COSTUME OF SHINING BLUE? A SUPERSUIT TO HOUSE A MILLION MUSCLES?
ALL FINGERS AND THUMBS!
You all right, son?
I don't know!
DISBELIEVING GOGGLE!
TRUTH IS, THE PYJAMA CASE CONTAINS NOTHING...
...EXCEPT FELIX HIMSELF!
LEAP!
MIAOW!
HEROIC POSE!
SPLAP!
Help is at hand! Felix is coming!
SLAM!
NEWSAGEN
BOUND!

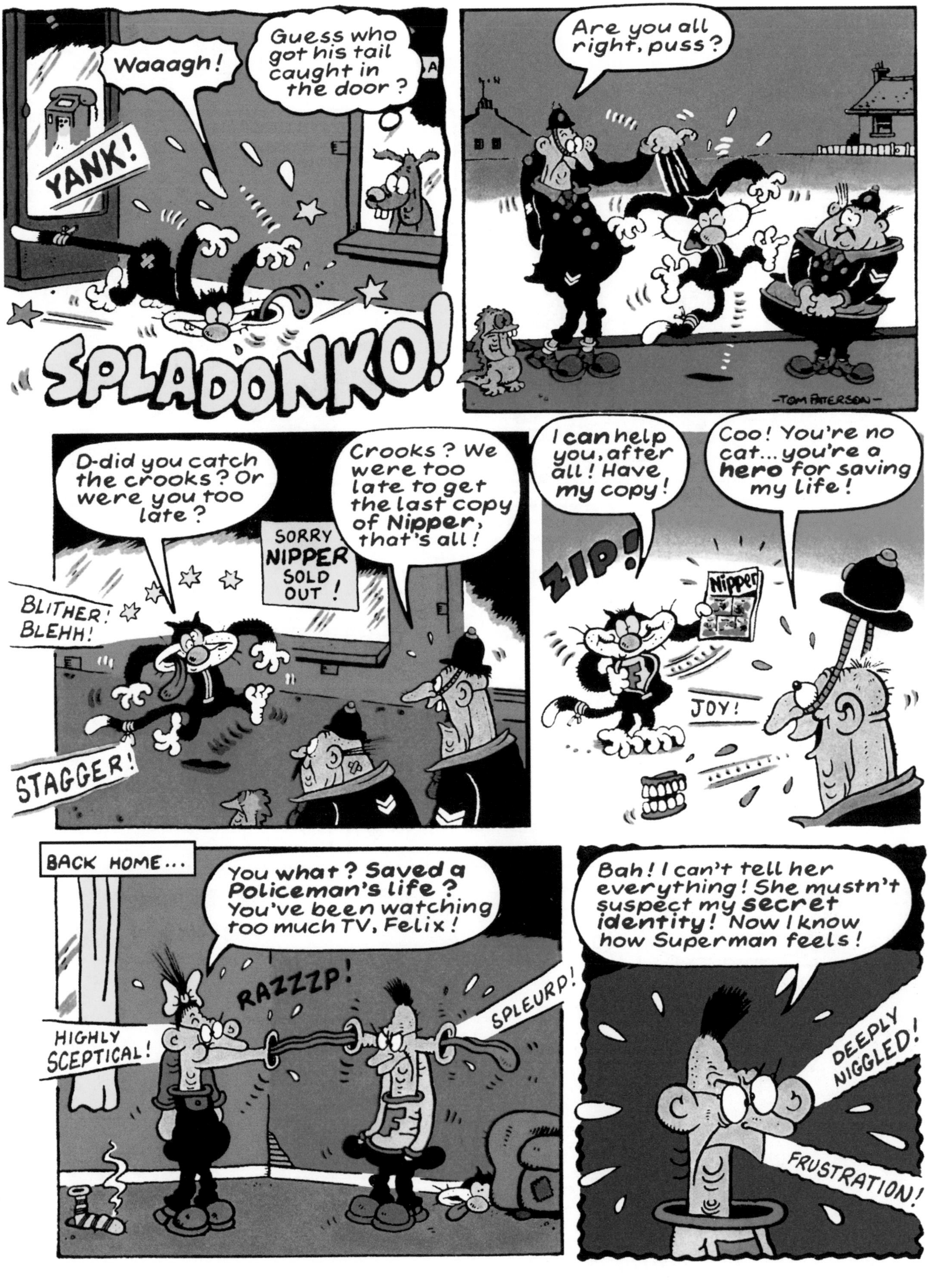

Waaagh!
Guess who got his tail caught in the door?
YANK!
SPLADONKO!
Are you all right, puss?
-TOM PATERSON-
D-did you catch the crooks? Or were you too late?
Crooks? We were too late to get the last copy of Nipper, that's all!
SORRY NIPPER SOLD OUT!
BLITHER! BLEHH!
STAGGER!
I can help you, after all! Have my copy!
Coo! You're no cat... you're a hero for saving my life!
ZIP!
Nipper
JOY!
BACK HOME...
You what? Saved a Policeman's life? You've been watching too much TV, Felix!
RAZZZP!
SPLEURP!
HIGHLY SCEPTICAL!
Bah! I can't tell her everything! She mustn't suspect my secret identity! Now I know how Superman feels!
DEEPLY NIGGLED!
FRUSTRATION!

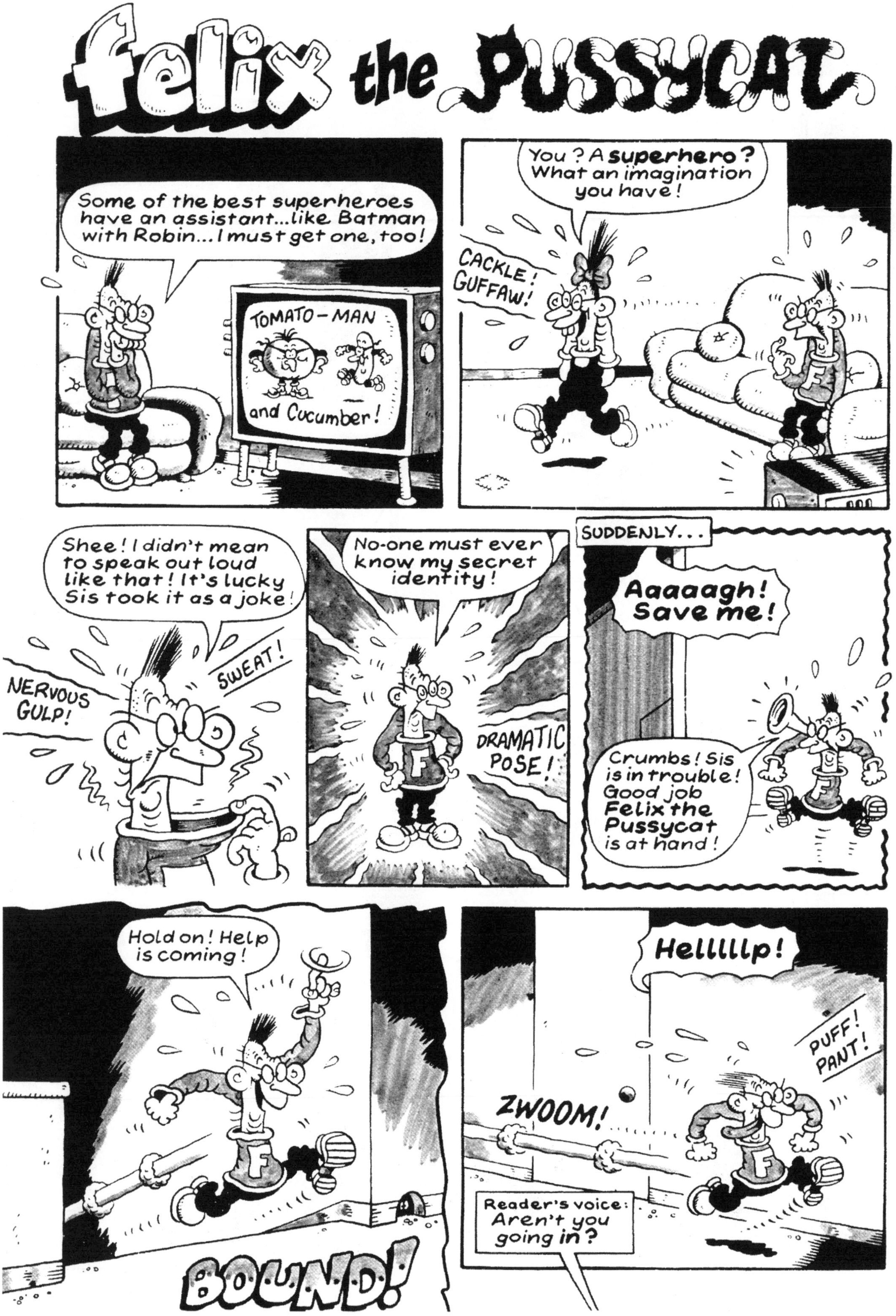
felix the PUSSYCAT
Some of the best superheroes have an assistant...like Batman with Robin...I must get one, too!
TOMATO-MAN
and Cucumber!
You? A superhero? What an imagination you have!
CACKLE! GUFFAW!
Shee! I didn't mean to speak out loud like that! It's lucky Sis took it as a joke!
NERVOUS GULP!
SWEAT!
No-one must ever know my secret identity!
DRAMATIC POSE!
SUDDENLY...
Aaaaagh! Save me!
Crumbs! Sis is in trouble! Good job Felix the Pussycat is at hand!
Hold on! Help is coming!
BOUND!
Hellllllp!
PUFF! PANT!
ZWOOM!
Reader's voice: Aren't you going in?

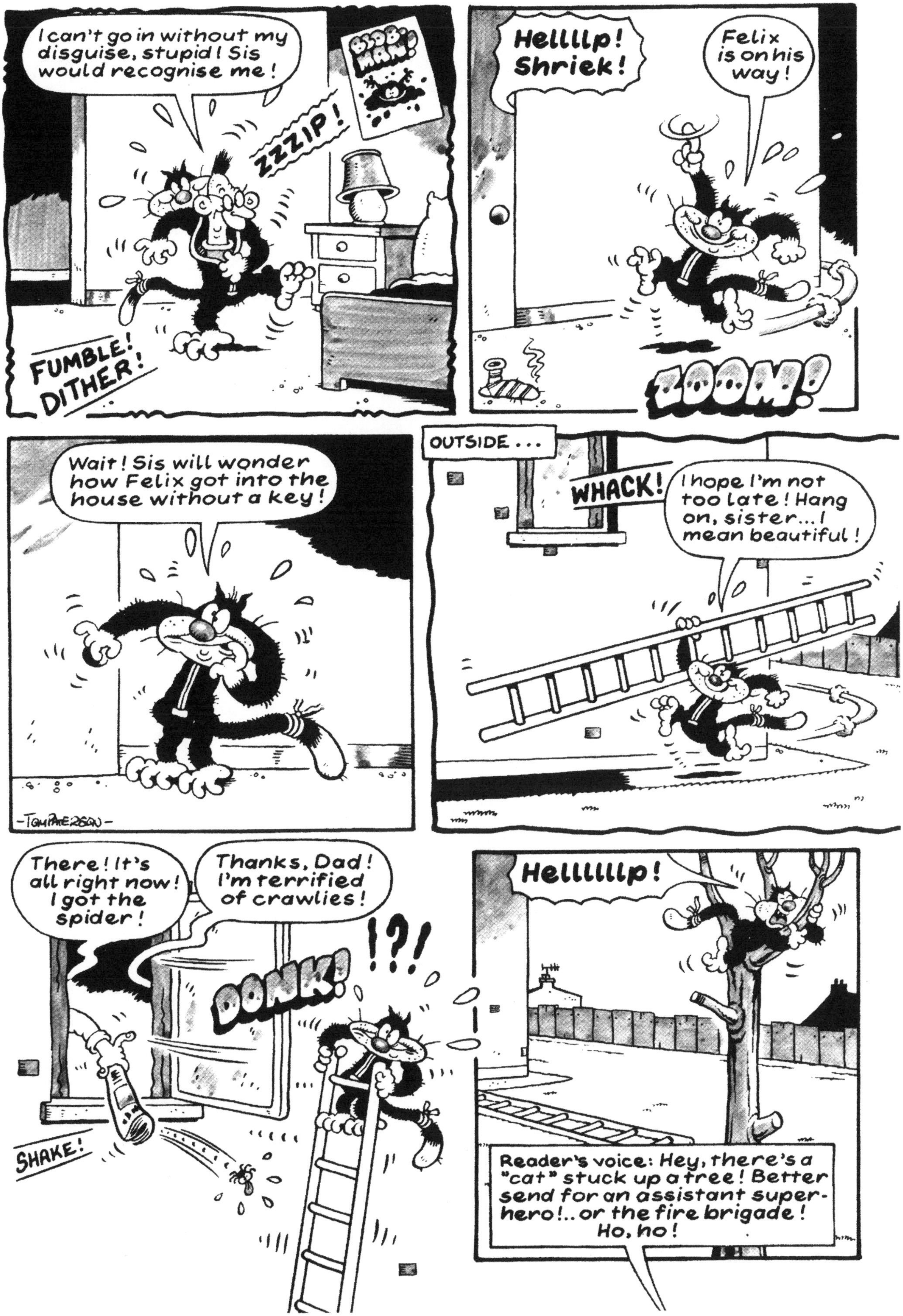

I can't go in without my disguise, stupid! Sis would recognise me!
BLOB-MAN!
ZZZIP!
FUMBLE! DITHER!
Hellllp! Shriek!
Felix is on his way!
ZOOM!
Wait! Sis will wonder how Felix got into the house without a key!
-TOM PATERSON-
OUTSIDE...
WHACK!
I hope I'm not too late! Hang on, sister... I mean beautiful!
There! It's all right now! I got the spider!
Thanks, Dad! I'm terrified of crawlies!
DONK!
!?!
SHAKE!
Hellllllp!
Reader's voice: Hey, there's a "cat" stuck up a tree! Better send for an assistant super-hero!.. or the fire brigade! Ho, ho!

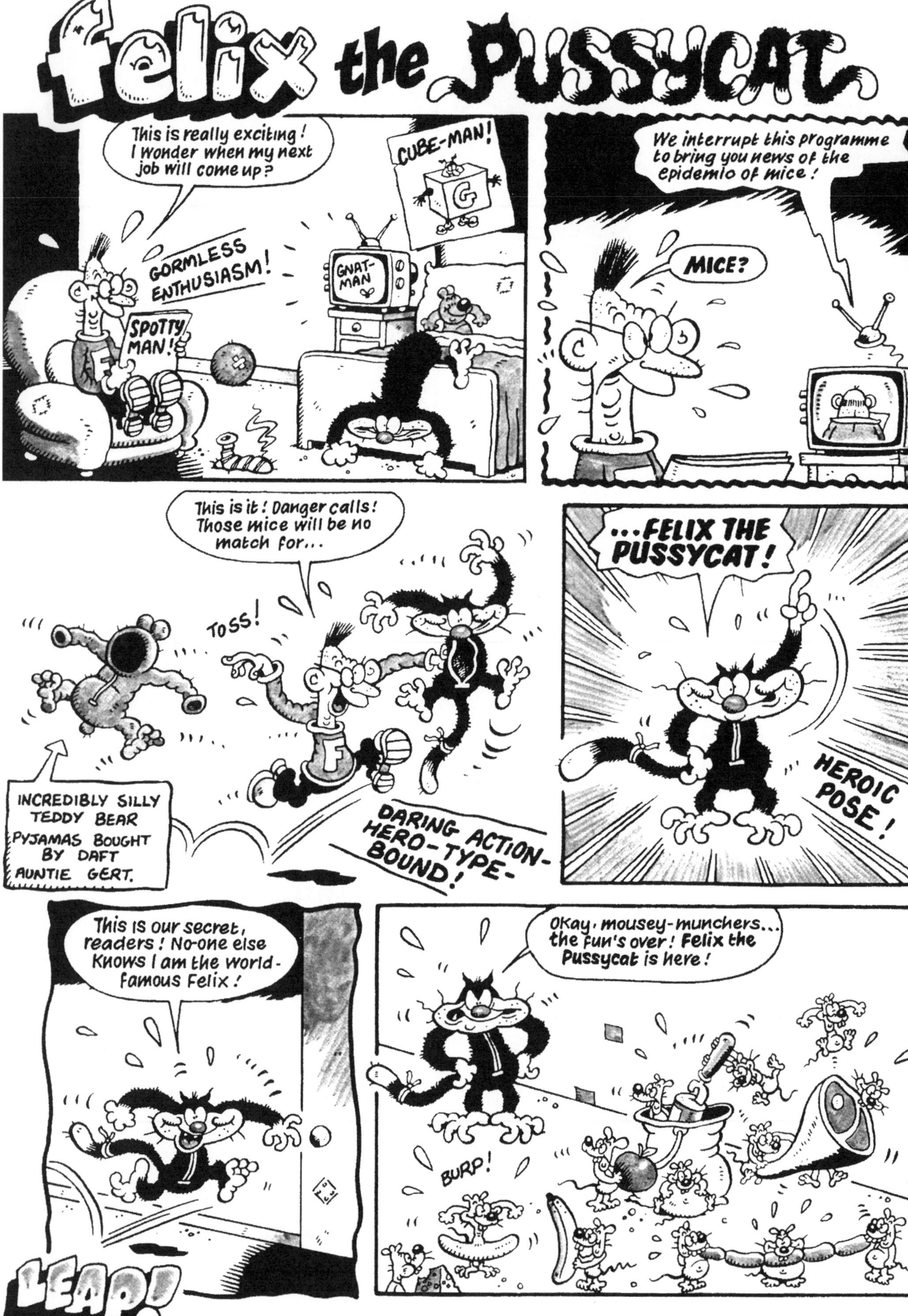

felix the PUSSYCAT
This is really exciting! I wonder when my next job will come up?
CUBE-MAN!
G
GORMLESS ENTHUSIASM!
GNAT-MAN
SPOTTY MAN!
F
We interrupt this programme to bring you news of the epidemic of mice!
MICE?
This is it! Danger calls! Those mice will be no match for...
TOSS!
F
INCREDIBLY SILLY TEDDY BEAR PYJAMAS BOUGHT BY DAFT AUNTIE GERT.
DARING ACTION-HERO-TYPE-BOUND!
...FELIX THE PUSSYCAT!
HEROIC POSE!
This is our secret, readers! No-one else knows I am the world-famous Felix!
LEAP!
Okay, mousey-munchers... the fun's over! Felix the Pussycat is here!
BURP!

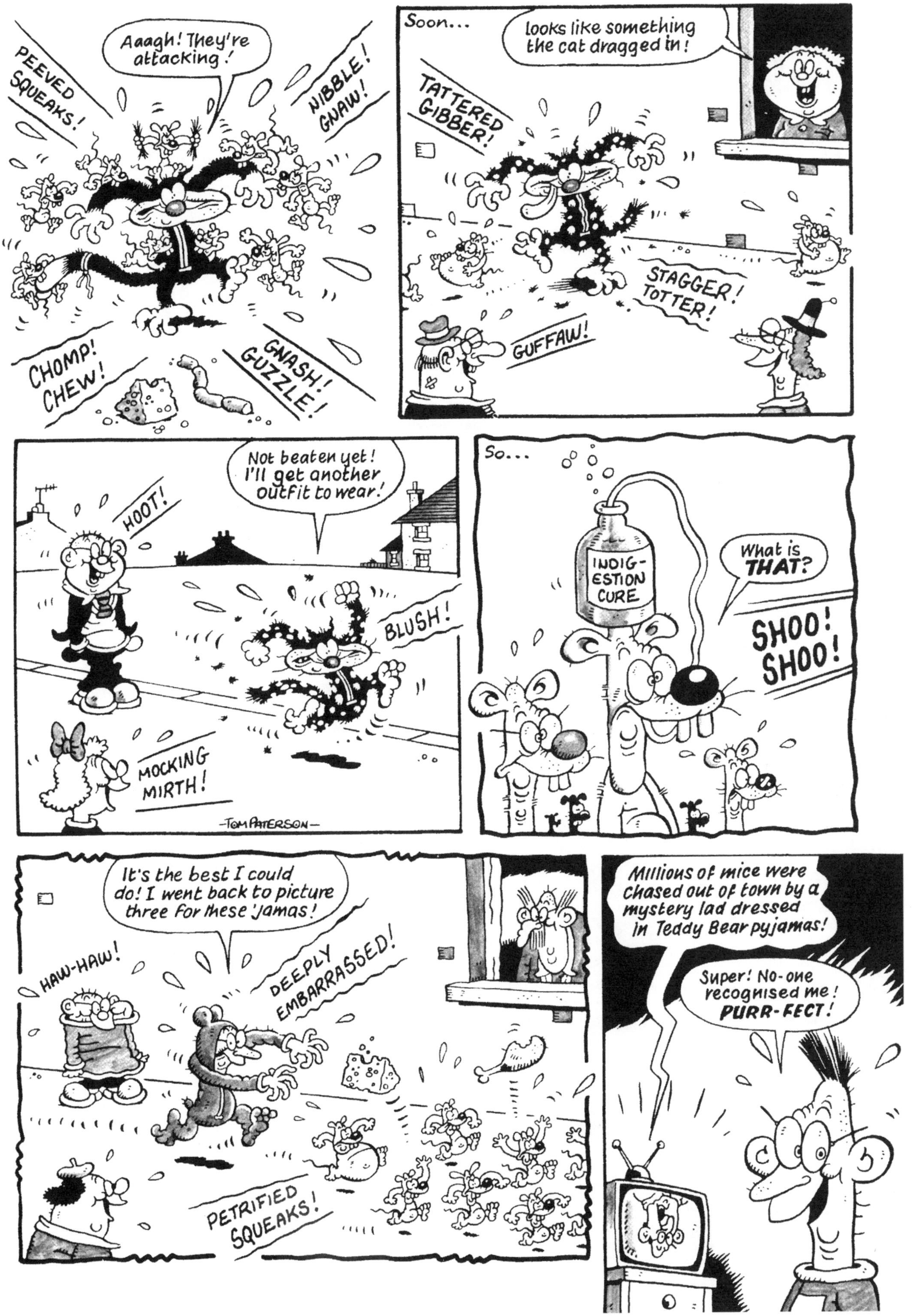

PEEVED SQUEAKS!
Aaagh! They're attacking!
NIBBLE! GNAW!
CHOMP! CHEW!
GNASH! GUZZLE!
Soon...
looks like something the cat dragged in!
TATTERED GIBBER!
STAGGER! TOTTER!
GUFFAW!
HOOT!
Not beaten yet! I'll get another outfit to wear!
BLUSH!
MOCKING MIRTH!
-TOM PATERSON-
So...
INDIG-ESTION CURE
What is THAT?
SHOO! SHOO!
It's the best I could do! I went back to picture three for these 'jamas!
HAW-HAW!
DEEPLY EMBARRASSED!
PETRIFIED SQUEAKS!
Millions of mice were chased out of town by a mystery lad dressed in Teddy Bear pyjamas!
Super! No-one recognised me! PURR-FECT!

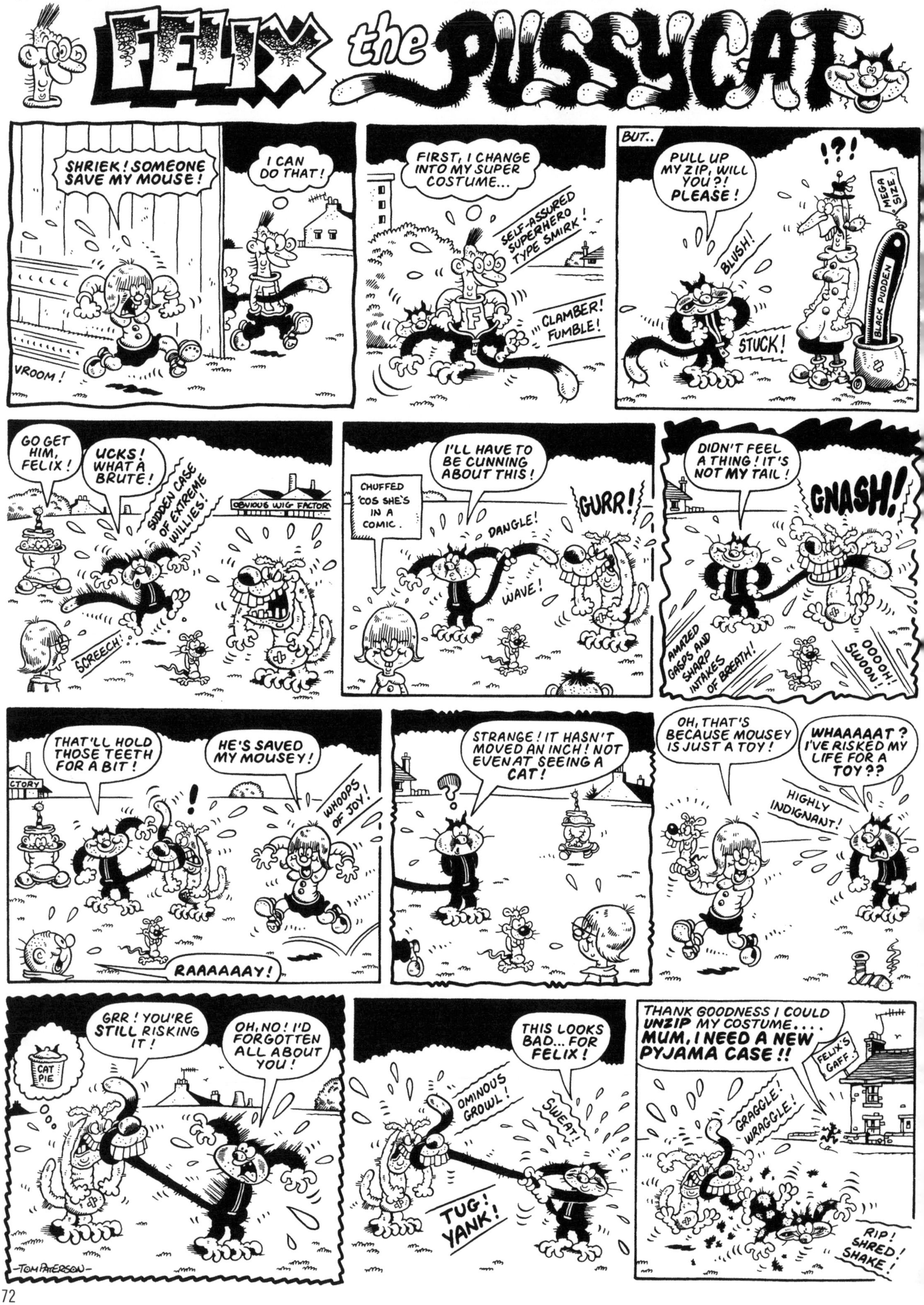
FELIX the PUSSYCAT
SHRIEK! SOMEONE SAVE MY MOUSE!
VROOM!
I CAN DO THAT!
FIRST, I CHANGE INTO MY SUPER COSTUME...
SELF-ASSURED SUPERHERO TYPE SMIRK!
CLAMBER! FUMBLE!
BUT..
PULL UP MY ZIP, WILL YOU?! PLEASE!
!?!
BLUSH!
STUCK!
MEGA SIZE
BLACK PUDDEN
GO GET HIM, FELIX!
UCKS! WHAT A BRUTE!
SUDDEN CASE OF EXTREME WILLIES!
OBVIOUS WIG FACTOR
SCREECH!
CHUFFED 'COS SHE'S IN A COMIC.
I'LL HAVE TO BE CUNNING ABOUT THIS!
DANGLE!
GURR!
WAVE!
DIDN'T FEEL A THING! IT'S NOT MY TAIL!
GNASH!
AMAZED GASPS AND SHARP INTAKES OF BREATH!
OOOOH! SWOON!
THAT'LL HOLD THOSE TEETH FOR A BIT!
CTORY
HE'S SAVED MY MOUSEY!
WHOOPS OF JOY!
RAAAAAAY!
STRANGE! IT HASN'T MOVED AN INCH! NOT EVEN AT SEEING A CAT!
OH, THAT'S BECAUSE MOUSEY IS JUST A TOY!
WHAAAAAT? I'VE RISKED MY LIFE FOR A TOY??
HIGHLY INDIGNANT!
CAT PIE
GRR! YOU'RE STILL RISKING IT!
OH, NO! I'D FORGOTTEN ALL ABOUT YOU!
-TOM PATERSON-
THIS LOOKS BAD... FOR FELIX!
OMINOUS GROWL!
SWEAT!
TUG! YANK!
THANK GOODNESS I COULD UNZIP MY COSTUME.... MUM, I NEED A NEW PYJAMA CASE!!
FELIX'S GAFF.
GRAGGLE! WRAGGLE!
RIP! SHRED! SHAKE!

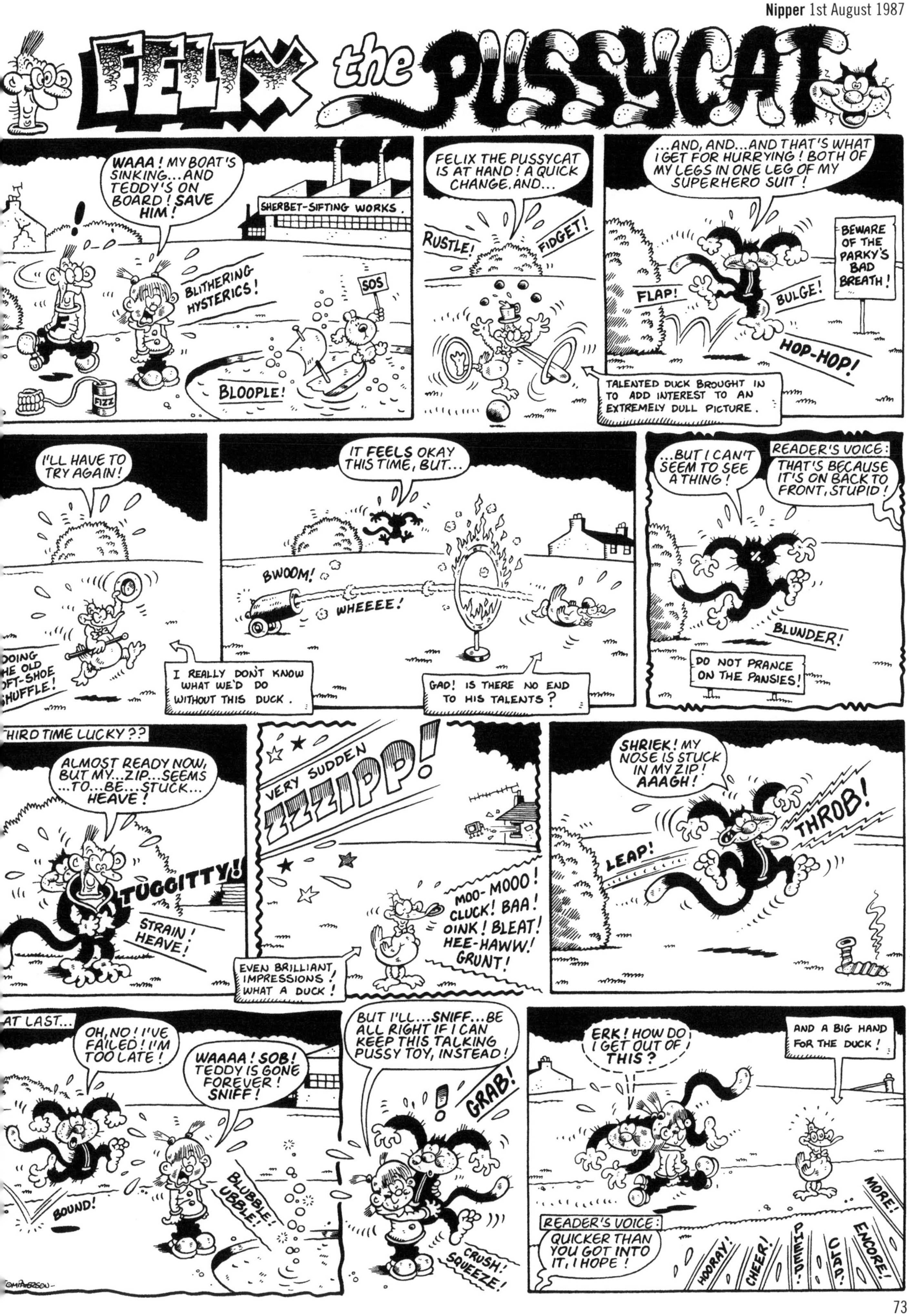
FELIX the PUSSYCAT
WAAA! MY BOAT'S SINKING... AND TEDDY'S ON BOARD! SAVE HIM!
SHERBET-SIFTING WORKS
BLITHERING HYSTERICS!
SOS
FIZZ
BLOOPLE!
FELIX THE PUSSYCAT IS AT HAND! A QUICK CHANGE, AND...
RUSTLE!
FIDGET!
TALENTED DUCK BROUGHT IN TO ADD INTEREST TO AN EXTREMELY DULL PICTURE.
...AND, AND... AND THAT'S WHAT I GET FOR HURRYING! BOTH OF MY LEGS IN ONE LEG OF MY SUPERHERO SUIT!
BEWARE OF THE PARKY'S BAD BREATH!
FLAP!
BULGE!
HOP-HOP!
I'LL HAVE TO TRY AGAIN!
DOING HE OLD OFT-SHOE SHUFFLE!
I REALLY DON'T KNOW WHAT WE'D DO WITHOUT THIS DUCK.
IT FEELS OKAY THIS TIME, BUT...
BWOOM!
WHEEEE!
GAD! IS THERE NO END TO HIS TALENTS?
...BUT I CAN'T SEEM TO SEE A THING!
READER'S VOICE: THAT'S BECAUSE IT'S ON BACK TO FRONT, STUPID!
BLUNDER!
DO NOT PRANCE ON THE PANSIES!
THIRD TIME LUCKY??
ALMOST READY NOW, BUT MY... ZIP... SEEMS ...TO... BE... STUCK... HEAVE!
TUGGITTY!
STRAIN! HEAVE!
VERY SUDDEN ZZZIPP!
MOO-MOOO! CLUCK! BAA! OINK! BLEAT! HEE-HAWW! GRUNT!
EVEN BRILLIANT IMPRESSIONS! WHAT A DUCK!
SHRIEK! MY NOSE IS STUCK IN MY ZIP! AAAGH!
THROB!
LEAP!
AT LAST...
OH, NO! I'VE FAILED! I'M TOO LATE!
WAAAA! SOB! TEDDY IS GONE FOREVER! SNIFF!
BOUND!
BLUBBLE! UBBLE!
BUT I'LL... SNIFF... BE ALL RIGHT IF I CAN KEEP THIS TALKING PUSSY TOY, INSTEAD!
GRAB!
CRUSH! SQUEEZE!
ERK! HOW DO I GET OUT OF THIS?
AND A BIG HAND FOR THE DUCK!
READER'S VOICE: QUICKER THAN YOU GOT INTO IT, I HOPE!
HOORAY! CHEER! PHEEP! CLAP! ENCORE! MORE!

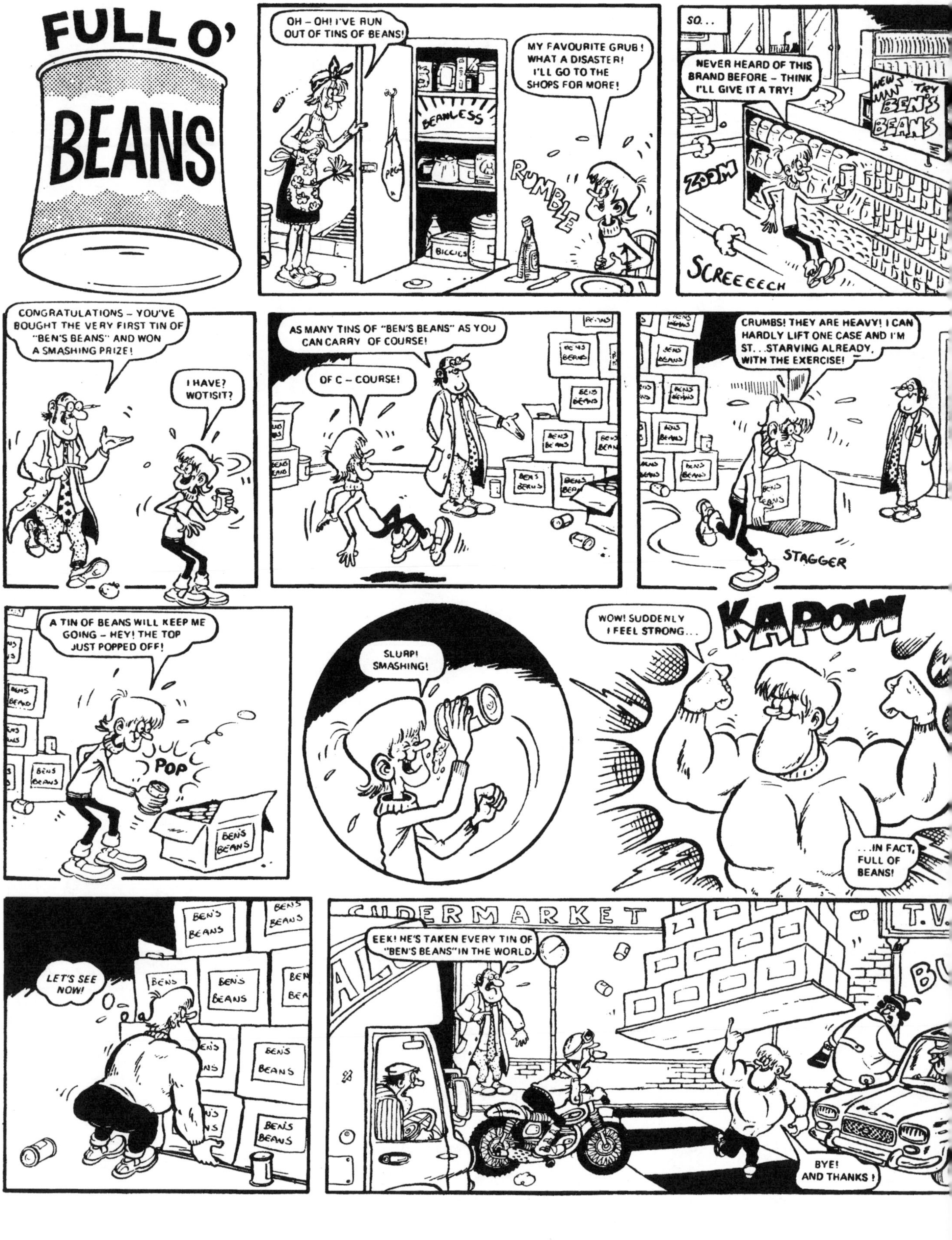
FULL O'
BEANS
OH – OH! I'VE RUN OUT OF TINS OF BEANS!
BEANLESS
PEGS
BICCIES
MY FAVOURITE GRUB! WHAT A DISASTER! I'LL GO TO THE SHOPS FOR MORE!
RUMBLE
SO...
NEVER HEARD OF THIS BRAND BEFORE – THINK I'LL GIVE IT A TRY!
NEW TRY BEN'S BEANS
ZOOM
SCREEEEECH
CONGRATULATIONS – YOU'VE BOUGHT THE VERY FIRST TIN OF "BEN'S BEANS" AND WON A SMASHING PRIZE!
I HAVE? WOTISIT?
AS MANY TINS OF "BEN'S BEANS" AS YOU CAN CARRY OF COURSE!
OF C – COURSE!
CRUMBS! THEY ARE HEAVY! I CAN HARDLY LIFT ONE CASE AND I'M ST...STARVING ALREADY, WITH THE EXERCISE!
STAGGER
A TIN OF BEANS WILL KEEP ME GOING – HEY! THE TOP JUST POPPED OFF!
POP
SLURP! SMASHING!
WOW! SUDDENLY I FEEL STRONG...
KAPOW
...IN FACT, FULL OF BEANS!
LET'S SEE NOW!
BEN'S BEANS
EEK! HE'S TAKEN EVERY TIN OF "BEN'S BEANS" IN THE WORLD.
T.V.
BYE! AND THANKS!

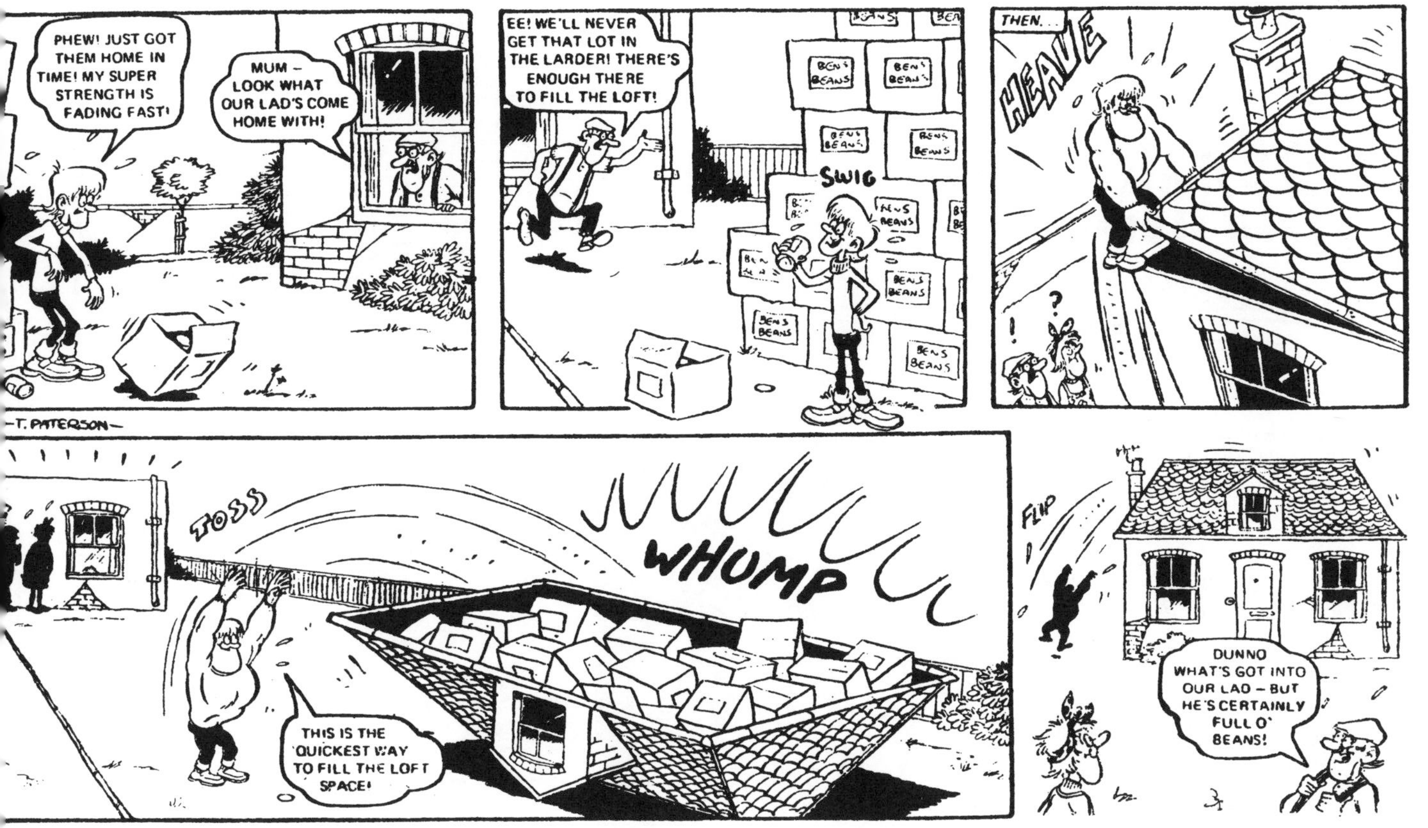
PHEW! JUST GOT THEM HOME IN TIME! MY SUPER STRENGTH IS FADING FAST!
MUM – LOOK WHAT OUR LAD'S COME HOME WITH!
EE! WE'LL NEVER GET THAT LOT IN THE LARDER! THERE'S ENOUGH THERE TO FILL THE LOFT!
SWIG
THEN. . .
HEAVE
T. PATERSON
TOSS
WHUMP
THIS IS THE QUICKEST WAY TO FILL THE LOFT SPACE!
FLIP
DUNNO WHAT'S GOT INTO OUR LAD – BUT HE'S CERTAINLY FULL O' BEANS!

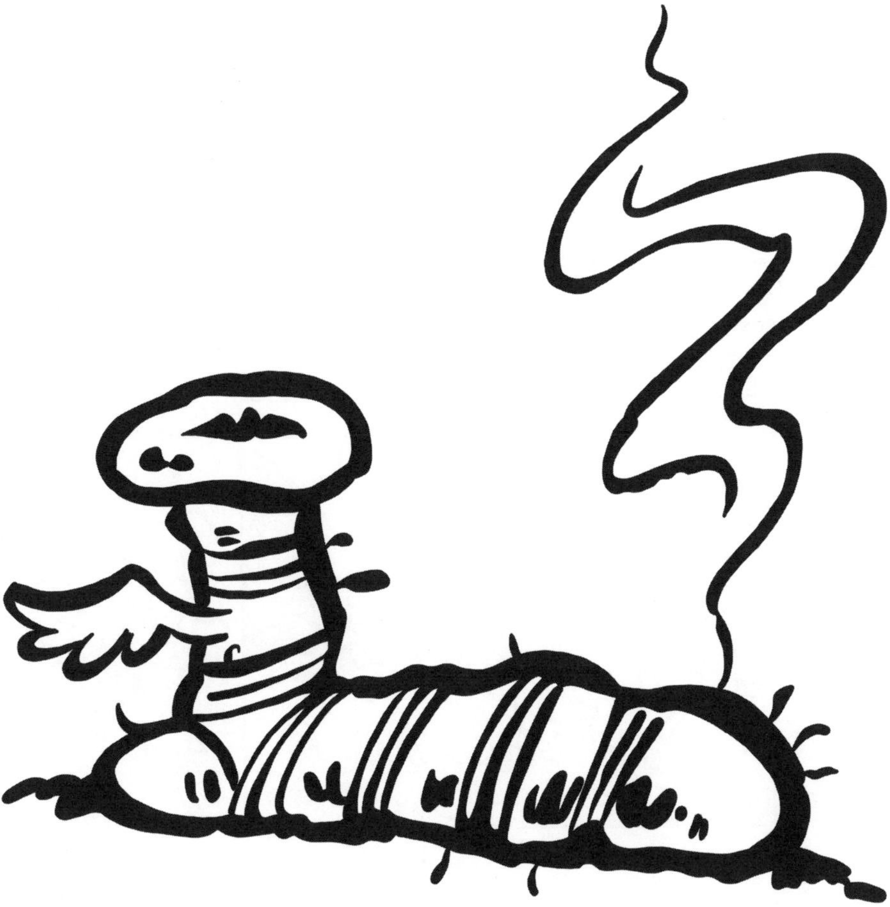

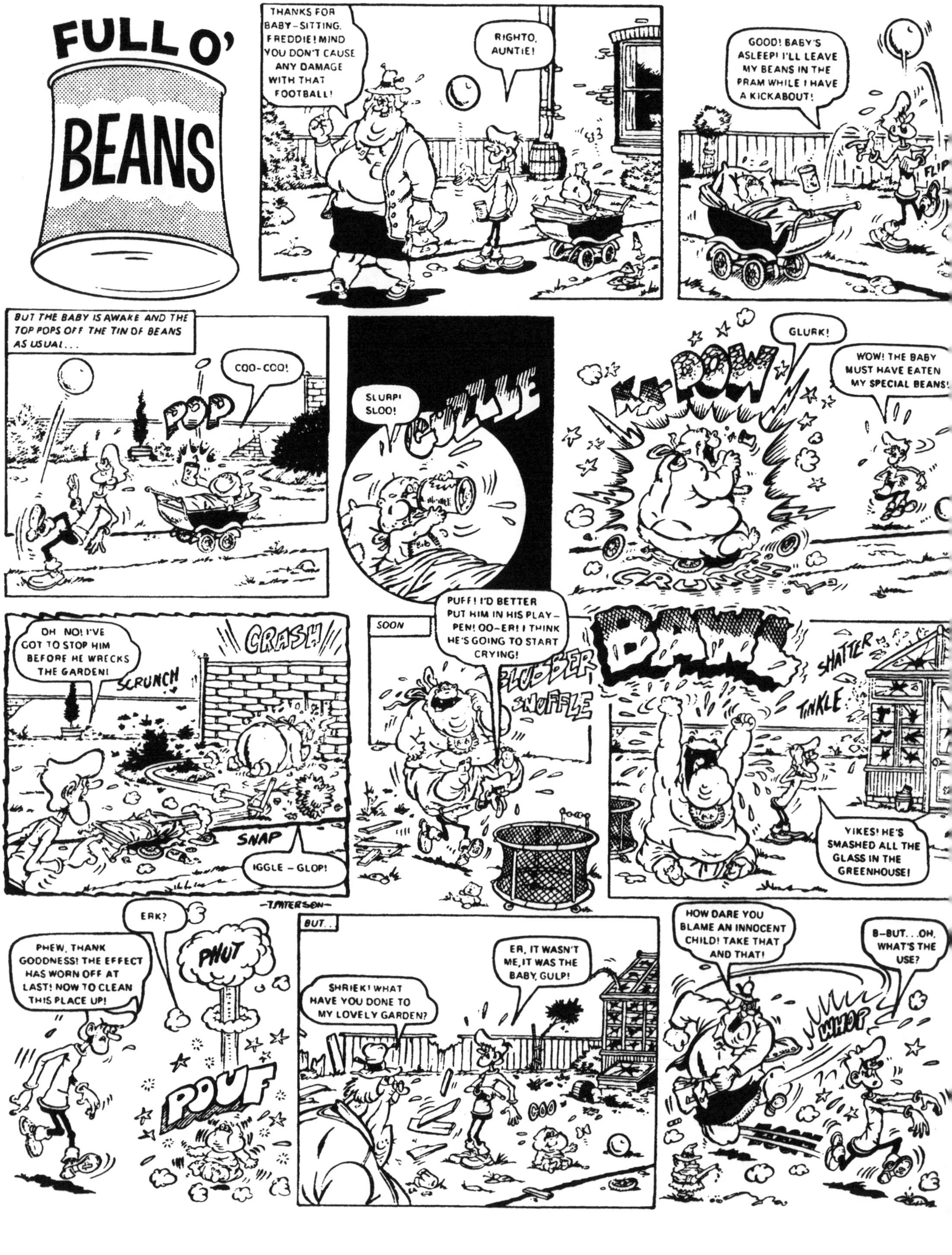
FULL O' BEANS
THANKS FOR BABY-SITTING, FREDDIE! MIND YOU DON'T CAUSE ANY DAMAGE WITH THAT FOOTBALL!
RIGHTO, AUNTIE!
GOOD! BABY'S ASLEEP! I'LL LEAVE MY BEANS IN THE PRAM WHILE I HAVE A KICKABOUT!
FLIP
BUT THE BABY IS AWAKE AND THE TOP POPS OFF THE TIN OF BEANS AS USUAL...
COO-COO!
POP
SLURP! SLOO!
GULP
GLURK!
KA-BOOM
WOW! THE BABY MUST HAVE EATEN MY SPECIAL BEANS!
CRUNCH
OH NO! I'VE GOT TO STOP HIM BEFORE HE WRECKS THE GARDEN!
CRASH
SCRUNCH
SNAP
IGGLE-GLOP!
SOON
PUFF! I'D BETTER PUT HIM IN HIS PLAY-PEN! OO-ER! I THINK HE'S GOING TO START CRYING!
BLUBBER
SNUFFLE
BAWL
SHATTER
TINKLE
YIKES! HE'S SMASHED ALL THE GLASS IN THE GREENHOUSE!
-T.PATERSON-
PHEW, THANK GOODNESS! THE EFFECT HAS WORN OFF AT LAST! NOW TO CLEAN THIS PLACE UP!
ERK?
PHUT
POUF
BUT...
SHRIEK! WHAT HAVE YOU DONE TO MY LOVELY GARDEN?
ER, IT WASN'T ME, IT WAS THE BABY, GULP!
GOO
HOW DARE YOU BLAME AN INNOCENT CHILD! TAKE THAT AND THAT!
B-BUT...OH, WHAT'S THE USE?
WHOP

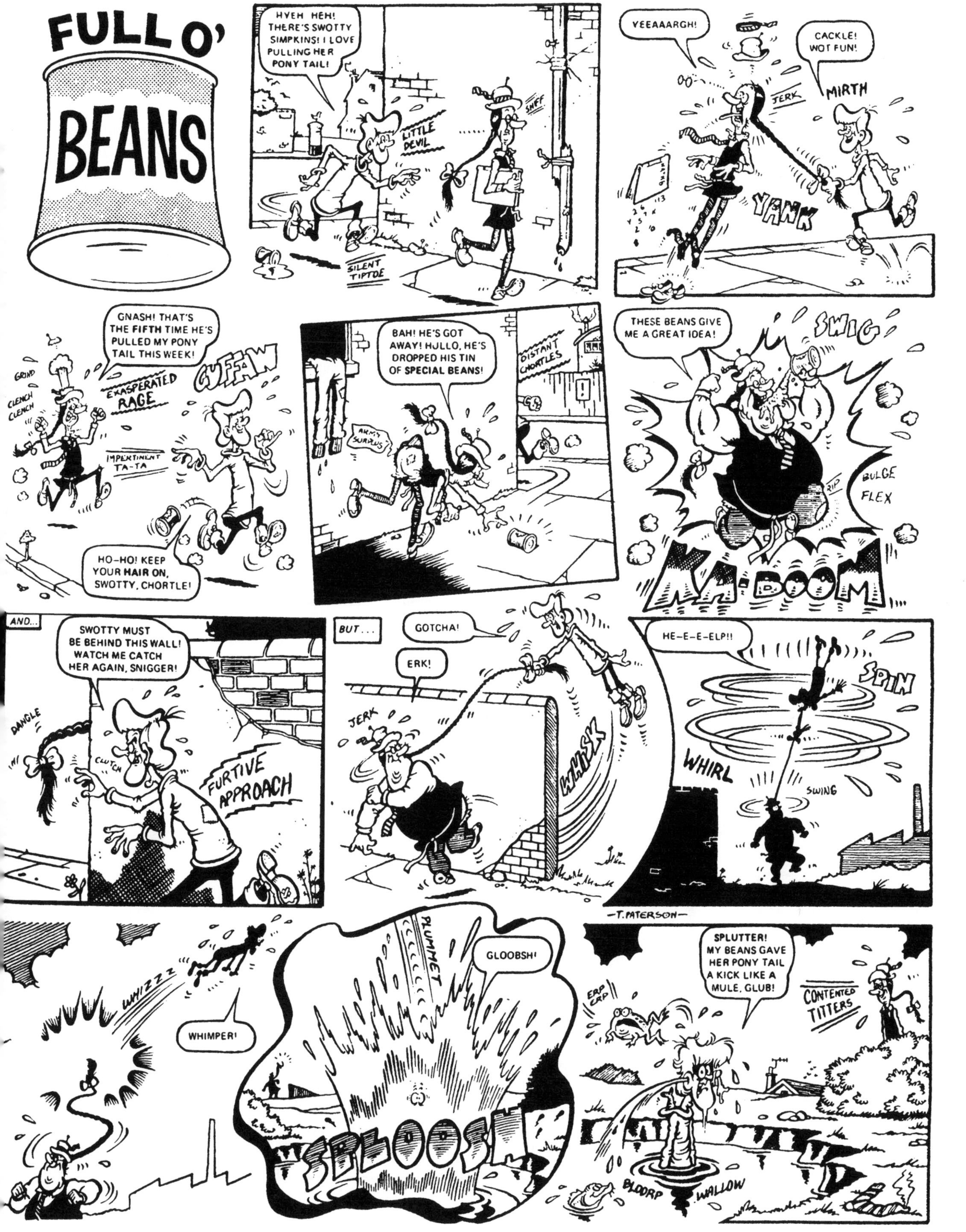

FULL O' BEANS
HYEH HEH! THERE'S SWOTTY SIMPKINS! I LOVE PULLING HER PONY TAIL!
LITTLE DEVIL
SNIFF
SILENT TIPTOE
YEEAAARGH!
CACKLE! WOT FUN!
JERK
MIRTH
YANK
GNASH! THAT'S THE FIFTH TIME HE'S PULLED MY PONY TAIL THIS WEEK!
GRIND
CLENCH CLENCH
EXASPERATED RAGE
GUFFAW
IMPERTINENT TA-TA
HO-HO! KEEP YOUR HAIR ON, SWOTTY, CHORTLE!
BAH! HE'S GOT AWAY! HULLO, HE'S DROPPED HIS TIN OF SPECIAL BEANS!
DISTANT CHORTLES
ARMY SURPLUS
THESE BEANS GIVE ME A GREAT IDEA!
SWIG
RIP
BULGE
FLEX
KA-BOOM
AND...
SWOTTY MUST BE BEHIND THIS WALL! WATCH ME CATCH HER AGAIN, SNIGGER!
DANGLE
CLUTCH
FURTIVE APPROACH
BUT...
GOTCHA!
ERK!
JERK
WHISK
HE-E-E-ELP!!
SPIN
WHIRL
SWING
—T. PATERSON—
WHIZZZ
WHIMPER!
PLUMMET
GLOOBSH!
SPLOOSH
SPLUTTER! MY BEANS GAVE HER PONY TAIL A KICK LIKE A MULE, GLUB!
ERP ERP
CONTENTED TITTERS
BLOORP
WALLOW

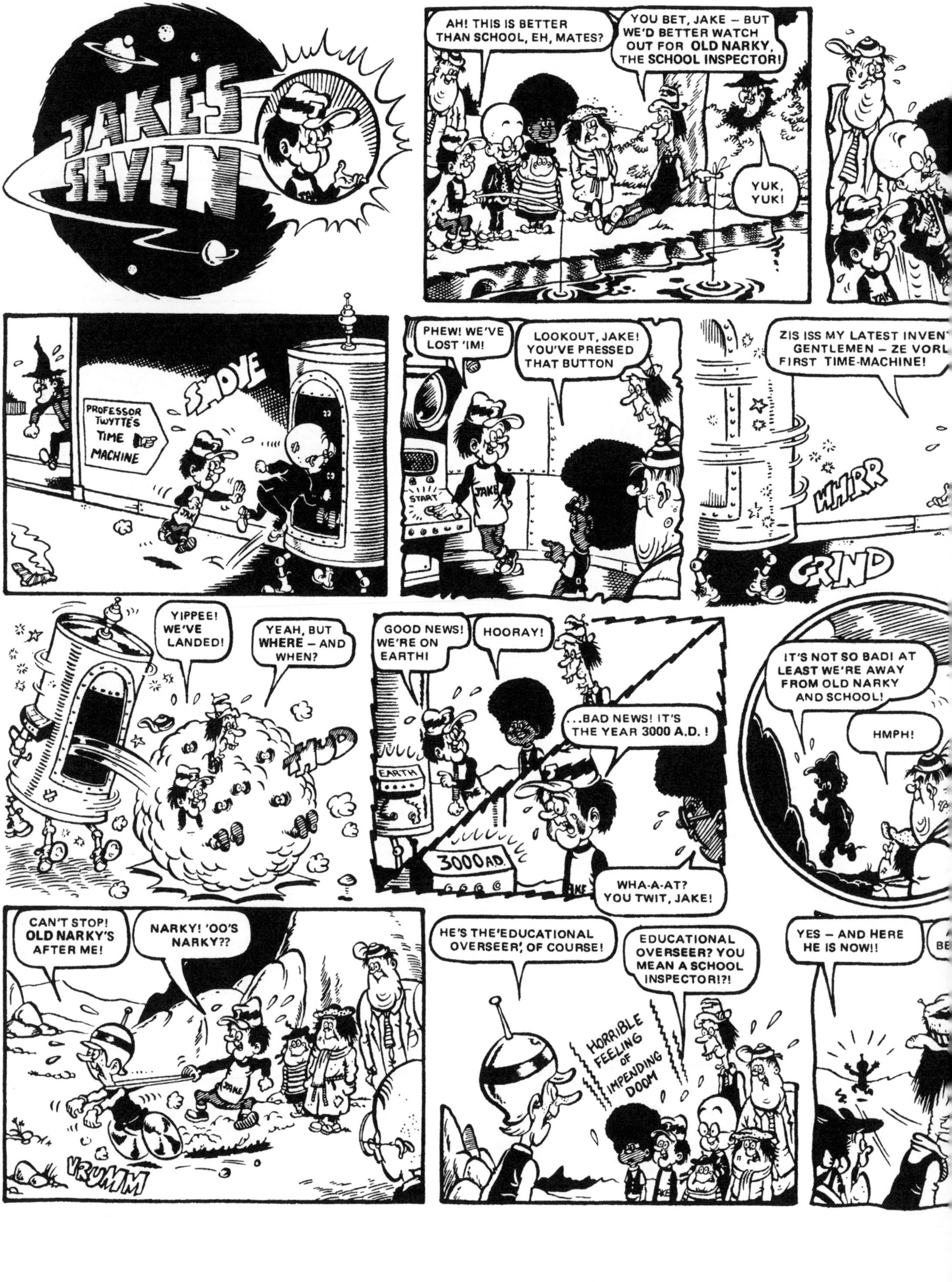
JAKE'S SEVEN
AH! THIS IS BETTER THAN SCHOOL, EH, MATES?
YOU BET, JAKE – BUT WE'D BETTER WATCH OUT FOR OLD NARKY, THE SCHOOL INSPECTOR!
SHOVE
YUK, YUK!
PROFESSOR TWYTTE'S TIME MACHINE
SHOVE
PHEW! WE'VE LOST 'IM!
LOOKOUT, JAKE! YOU'VE PRESSED THAT BUTTON
START
JAKE
ZIS ISS MY LATEST INVENT
GENTLEMEN – ZE VORL
FIRST TIME-MACHINE!
WHIRR
GRIND
YIPPEE! WE'VE LANDED!
YEAH, BUT WHERE – AND WHEN?
GOOD NEWS! WE'RE ON EARTH!
HOORAY!
...BAD NEWS! IT'S THE YEAR 3000 A.D. !
EARTH
3000 AD
WHA-A-AT? YOU TWIT, JAKE!
IT'S NOT SO BAD! AT LEAST WE'RE AWAY FROM OLD NARKY AND SCHOOL!
HMPH!
CAN'T STOP! OLD NARKY'S AFTER ME!
NARKY! 'OO'S NARKY??
JAKE
VRUMM
HE'S THE 'EDUCATIONAL OVERSEER', OF COURSE!
EDUCATIONAL OVERSEER? YOU MEAN A SCHOOL INSPECTOR!?!
HORRIBLE FEELING OF IMPENDING DOOM
YES – AND HERE HE IS NOW!!

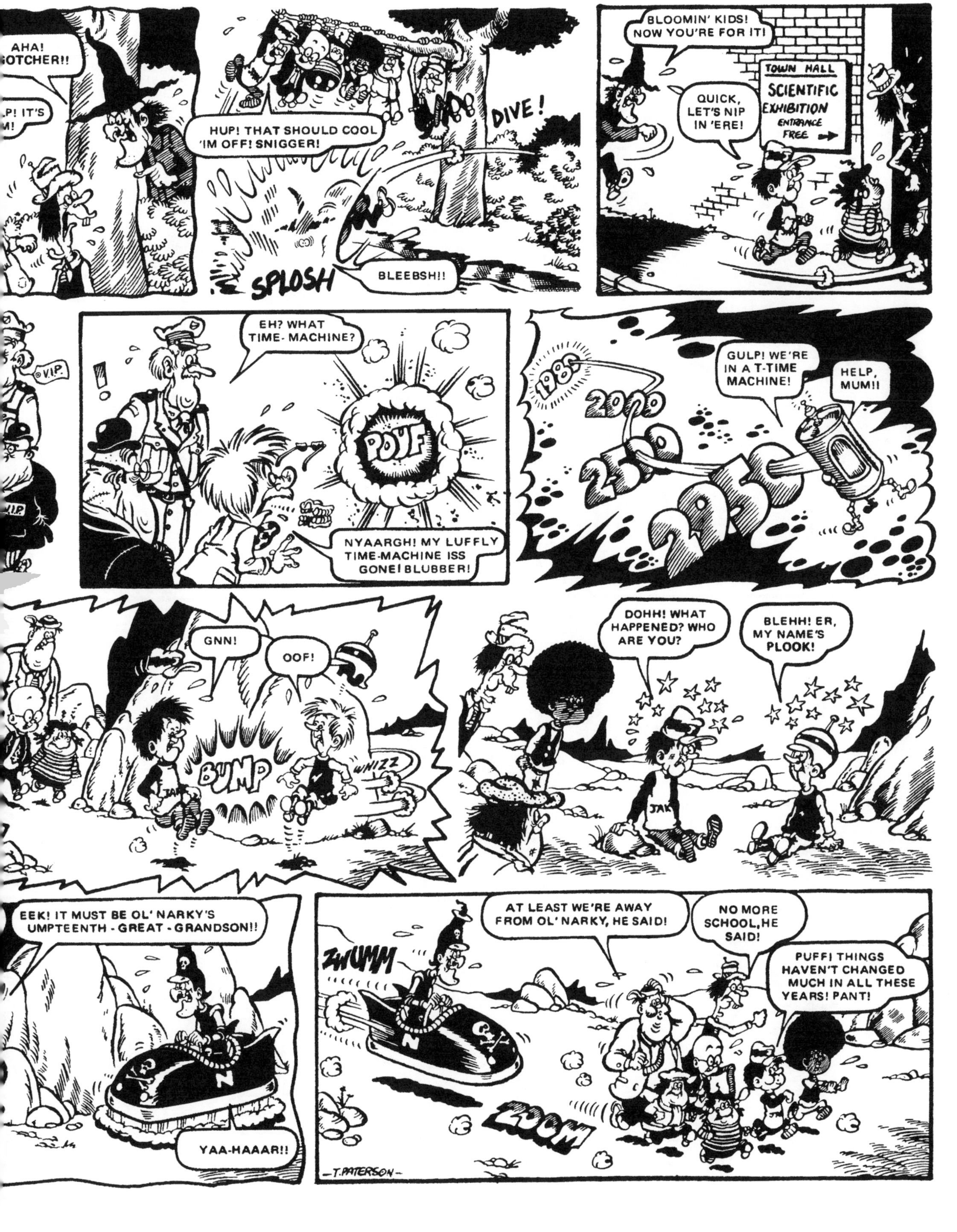

AHA! GOTCHER!!
..P! IT'S ..M!
HUP! THAT SHOULD COOL 'IM OFF! SNIGGER!
DIVE!
SPLOSH
BLEEBSH!!
BLOOMIN' KIDS! NOW YOU'RE FOR IT!
TOWN HALL
SCIENTIFIC EXHIBITION ENTRANCE FREE
QUICK, LET'S NIP IN 'ERE!
V.I.P.
EH? WHAT TIME-MACHINE?
POUF
NYAARGH! MY LUFFLY TIME-MACHINE ISS GONE! BLUBBER!
1980
2000
2500
2950
GULP! WE'RE IN A T-TIME MACHINE!
HELP, MUM!!
GNN!
OOF!
BUMP
WHIZZ
DOHH! WHAT HAPPENED? WHO ARE YOU?
BLEHH! ER, MY NAME'S PLOOK!
EEK! IT MUST BE OL' NARKY'S UMPTEENTH-GREAT-GRANDSON!!
YAA-HAAAR!!
ZWUMM
AT LEAST WE'RE AWAY FROM OL' NARKY, HE SAID!
NO MORE SCHOOL, HE SAID!
PUFF! THINGS HAVEN'T CHANGED MUCH IN ALL THESE YEARS! PANT!
ZOOM
T. PATERSON

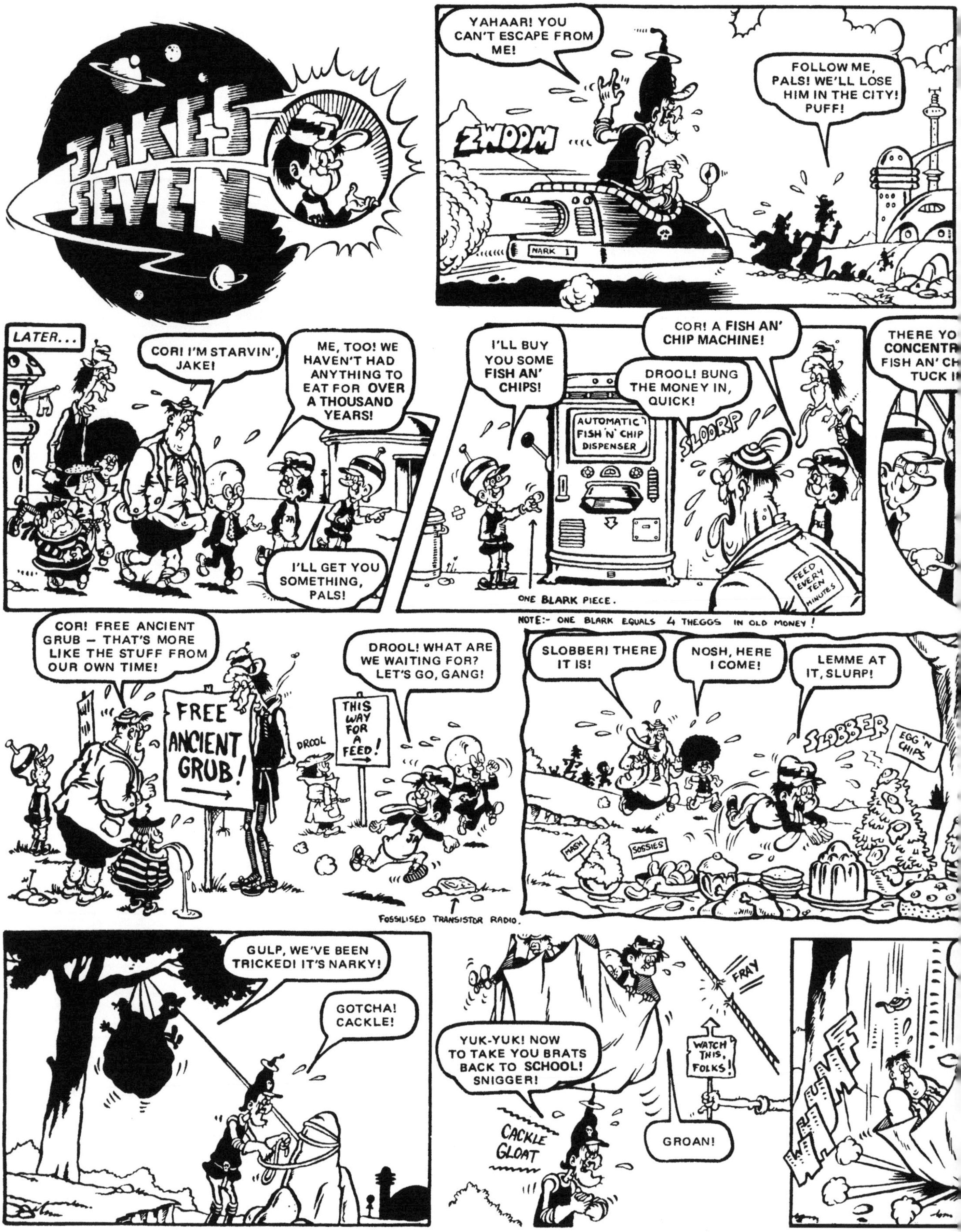
JAKE'S SEVEN
YAHAAR! YOU CAN'T ESCAPE FROM ME!
ZWOOM
MARK 1
FOLLOW ME, PALS! WE'LL LOSE HIM IN THE CITY! PUFF!
LATER...
COR! I'M STARVIN', JAKE!
ME, TOO! WE HAVEN'T HAD ANYTHING TO EAT FOR OVER A THOUSAND YEARS!
I'LL GET YOU SOMETHING, PALS!
I'LL BUY YOU SOME FISH AN' CHIPS!
AUTOMATIC FISH 'N' CHIP DISPENSER
ONE BLARK PIECE.
COR! A FISH AN' CHIP MACHINE!
DROOL! BUNG THE MONEY IN, QUICK!
SLOORP
FEED EVERY TEN MINUTES
NOTE:- ONE BLARK EQUALS 4 THEGGS IN OLD MONEY!
COR! FREE ANCIENT GRUB – THAT'S MORE LIKE THE STUFF FROM OUR OWN TIME!
FREE ANCIENT GRUB!
DROOL
DROOL! WHAT ARE WE WAITING FOR? LET'S GO, GANG!
THIS WAY FOR A FEED!
FOSSILISED TRANSISTOR RADIO.
SLOBBER! THERE IT IS!
NOSH, HERE I COME!
LEMME AT IT, SLURP!
SLOBBER
EGG 'N CHIPS
MASH
SOSSIES
GULP, WE'VE BEEN TRICKED! IT'S NARKY!
GOTCHA! CACKLE!
YUK-YUK! NOW TO TAKE YOU BRATS BACK TO SCHOOL! SNIGGER!
CACKLE GLOAT
FRAY
WATCH THIS, FOLKS!
GROAN!

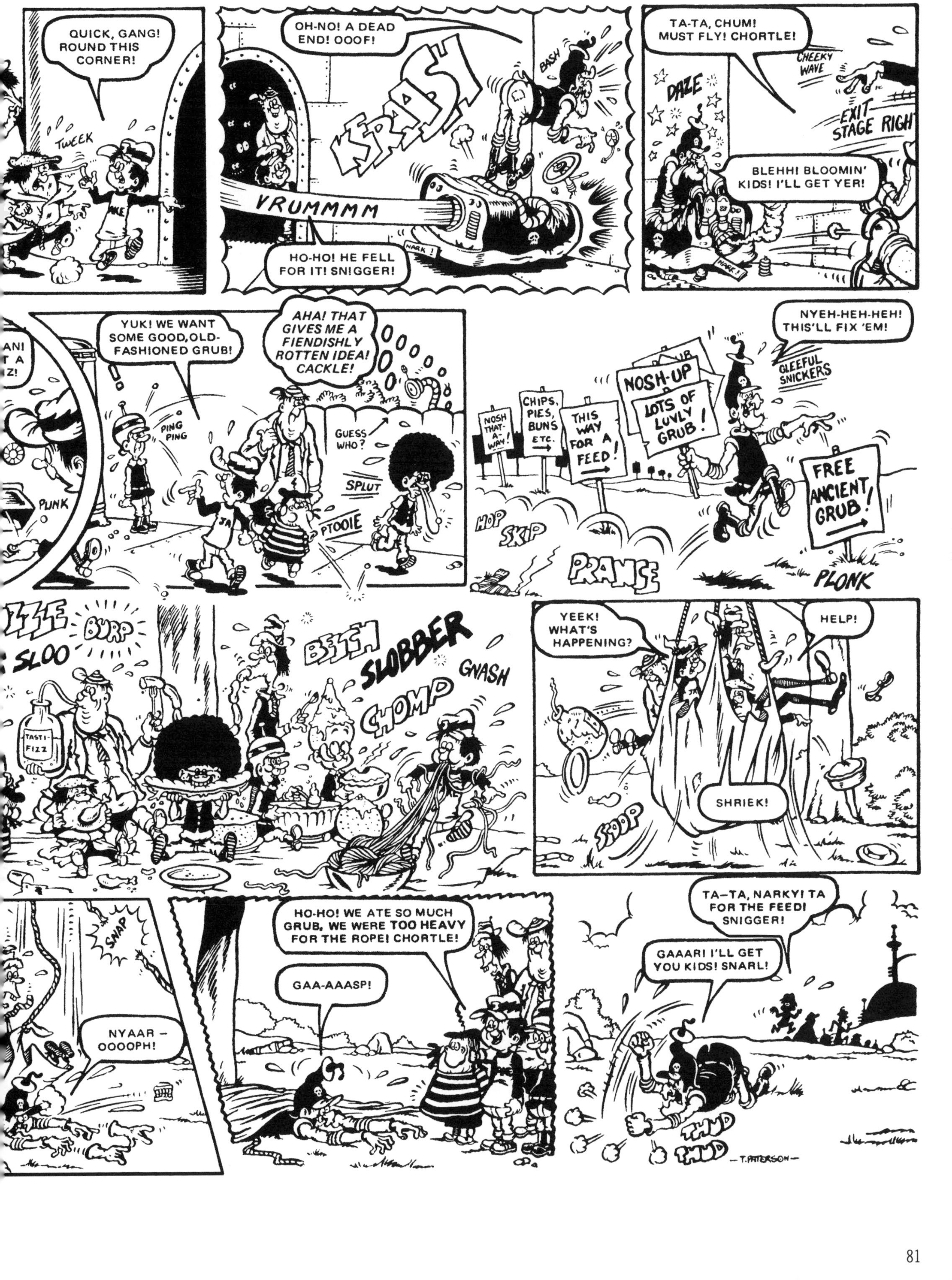

QUICK, GANG! ROUND THIS CORNER!
TWEEK
OH-NO! A DEAD END! OOOF!
KRASH
BASH
VRUMMMM
HO-HO! HE FELL FOR IT! SNIGGER!
NARK!
TA-TA, CHUM! MUST FLY! CHORTLE!
CHEEKY WAVE
DAZE
EXIT STAGE RIGHT
BLEHH! BLOOMIN' KIDS! I'LL GET YER!
NARK!
PUNK
YUK! WE WANT SOME GOOD, OLD-FASHIONED GRUB!
PING PING
AHA! THAT GIVES ME A FIENDISHLY ROTTEN IDEA! CACKLE!
GUESS WHO?
SPLUT
PTOOIE
NYEH-HEH-HEH! THIS'LL FIX 'EM!
GLEEFUL SNICKERS
NOSH THAT-A-WAY!
CHIPS, PIES, BUNS ETC.
THIS WAY FOR A FEED!
NOSH-UP
LOTS OF LUVLY GRUB!
FREE ANCIENT GRUB!
HOP
SKIP
PRANCE
PLONK
BURP
SLOO
BELCH
SLOBBER
GNASH
CHOMP
TASTI-FIZZ
YEEK! WHAT'S HAPPENING?
HELP!
SHRIEK!
SWOOP
SNAP
NYAAR — OOOOPH!
HO-HO! WE ATE SO MUCH GRUB, WE WERE TOO HEAVY FOR THE ROPE! CHORTLE!
GAA-AAASP!
TA—TA, NARKY! TA FOR THE FEED! SNIGGER!
GAAAR! I'LL GET YOU KIDS! SNARL!
THUD
THUD
T. PATERSON

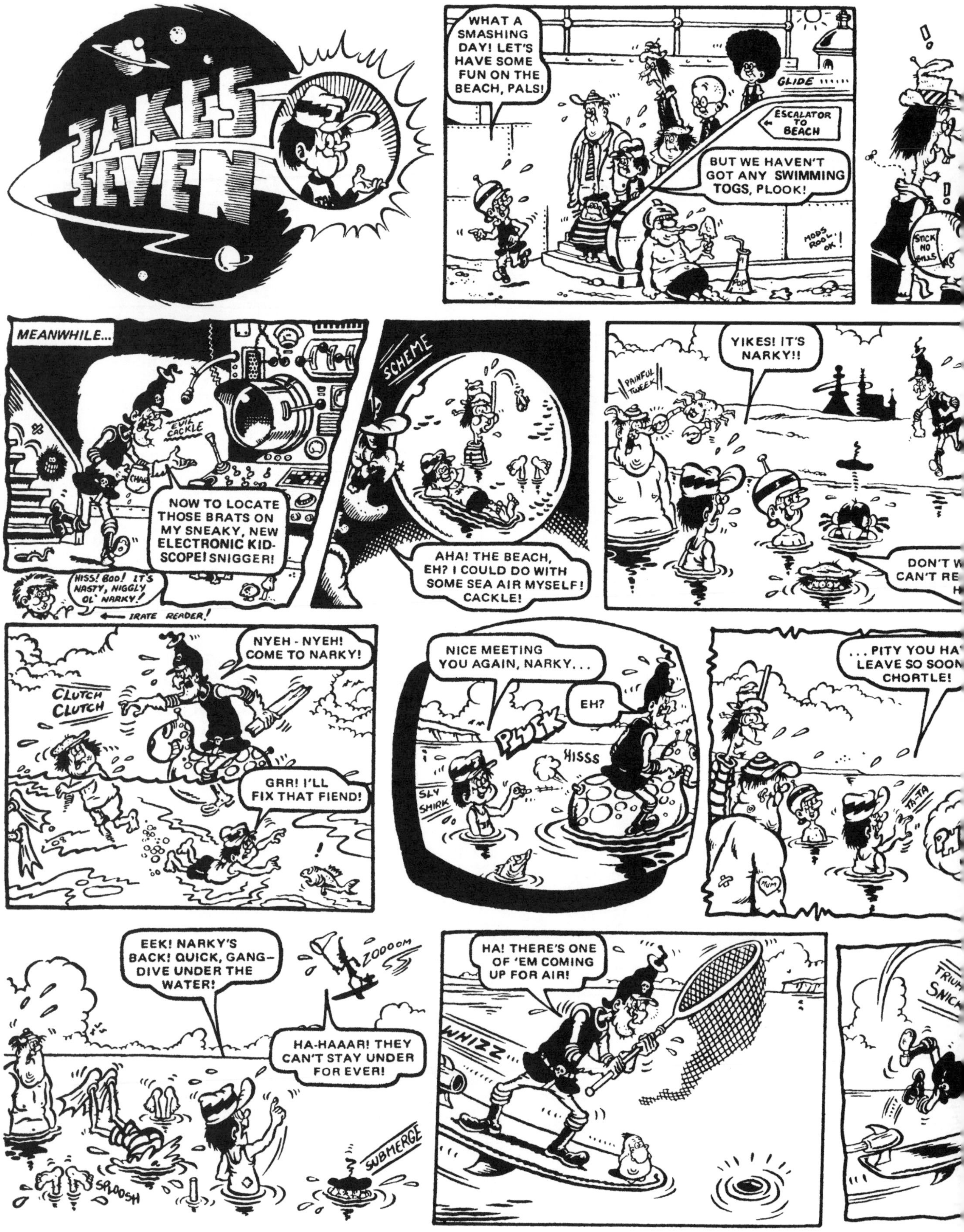
JAKE'S SEVEN
WHAT A SMASHING DAY! LET'S HAVE SOME FUN ON THE BEACH, PALS!
GLIDE
ESCALATOR TO BEACH
BUT WE HAVEN'T GOT ANY SWIMMING TOGS, PLOOK!
MODS ROOL OK!
POP
STICK NO BILLS
MEANWHILE...
EVIL CACKLE
NOW TO LOCATE THOSE BRATS ON MY SNEAKY, NEW ELECTRONIC KID-SCOPE! SNIGGER!
HISS! BOO! IT'S NASTY, NIGGLY OL' NARKY!
IRATE READER!
SCHEME
AHA! THE BEACH, EH? I COULD DO WITH SOME SEA AIR MYSELF! CACKLE!
YIKES! IT'S NARKY!!
PAINFUL TWEEK
DON'T W
CAN'T RE
NYEH - NYEH! COME TO NARKY!
CLUTCH CLUTCH
GRR! I'LL FIX THAT FIEND!
NICE MEETING YOU AGAIN, NARKY...
EH?
PLUCK
HISSS
SLY SMIRK
... PITY YOU HA
LEAVE SO SOON
CHORTLE!
TA-TA
MUM
EEK! NARKY'S BACK! QUICK, GANG-DIVE UNDER THE WATER!
ZOOOOM
HA-HAAAR! THEY CAN'T STAY UNDER FOR EVER!
SPLOOSH
SUBMERGE
HA! THERE'S ONE OF 'EM COMING UP FOR AIR!
WHIZZ

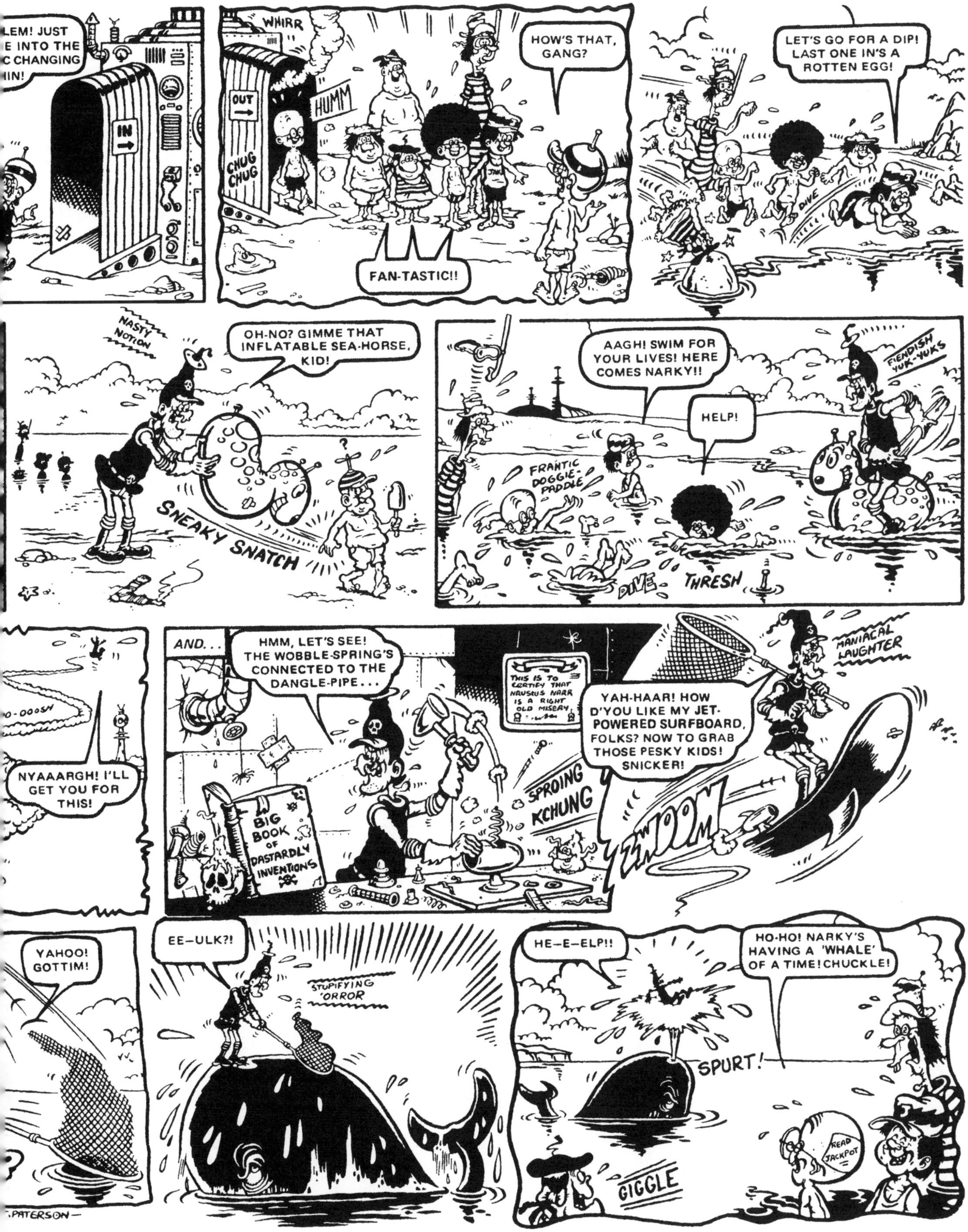

LEM! JUST
E INTO THE
C CHANGING
HIN!
IN
WHIRR
OUT
HUMM
CHUG CHUG
HOW'S THAT, GANG?
FAN-TASTIC!!
LET'S GO FOR A DIP! LAST ONE IN'S A ROTTEN EGG!
DIVE
NASTY NOTION
OH-NO? GIMME THAT INFLATABLE SEA-HORSE, KID!
SNEAKY SNATCH
AAGH! SWIM FOR YOUR LIVES! HERE COMES NARKY!!
FIENDISH YUK-YUKS
HELP!
FRANTIC DOGGIE-PADDLE
DIVE
THRESH
NYAAARGH! I'LL GET YOU FOR THIS!
AND...
HMM, LET'S SEE! THE WOBBLE-SPRING'S CONNECTED TO THE DANGLE-PIPE...
THIS IS TO CERTIFY THAT NAUSEUS NARR IS A RIGHT OLD MISERY
BIG BOOK OF DASTARDLY INVENTIONS
SPROING
KCHUNG
MANIACAL LAUGHTER
YAH-HAAR! HOW D'YOU LIKE MY JET-POWERED SURFBOARD, FOLKS? NOW TO GRAB THOSE PESKY KIDS! SNICKER!
ZWOOM
YAHOO! GOTTIM!
EE-ULK?!
STUPIFYING 'ORROR
HE-E-ELP!!
HO-HO! NARKY'S HAVING A 'WHALE' OF A TIME! CHUCKLE!
SPURT!
READ JACKPOT
GIGGLE
PATERSON

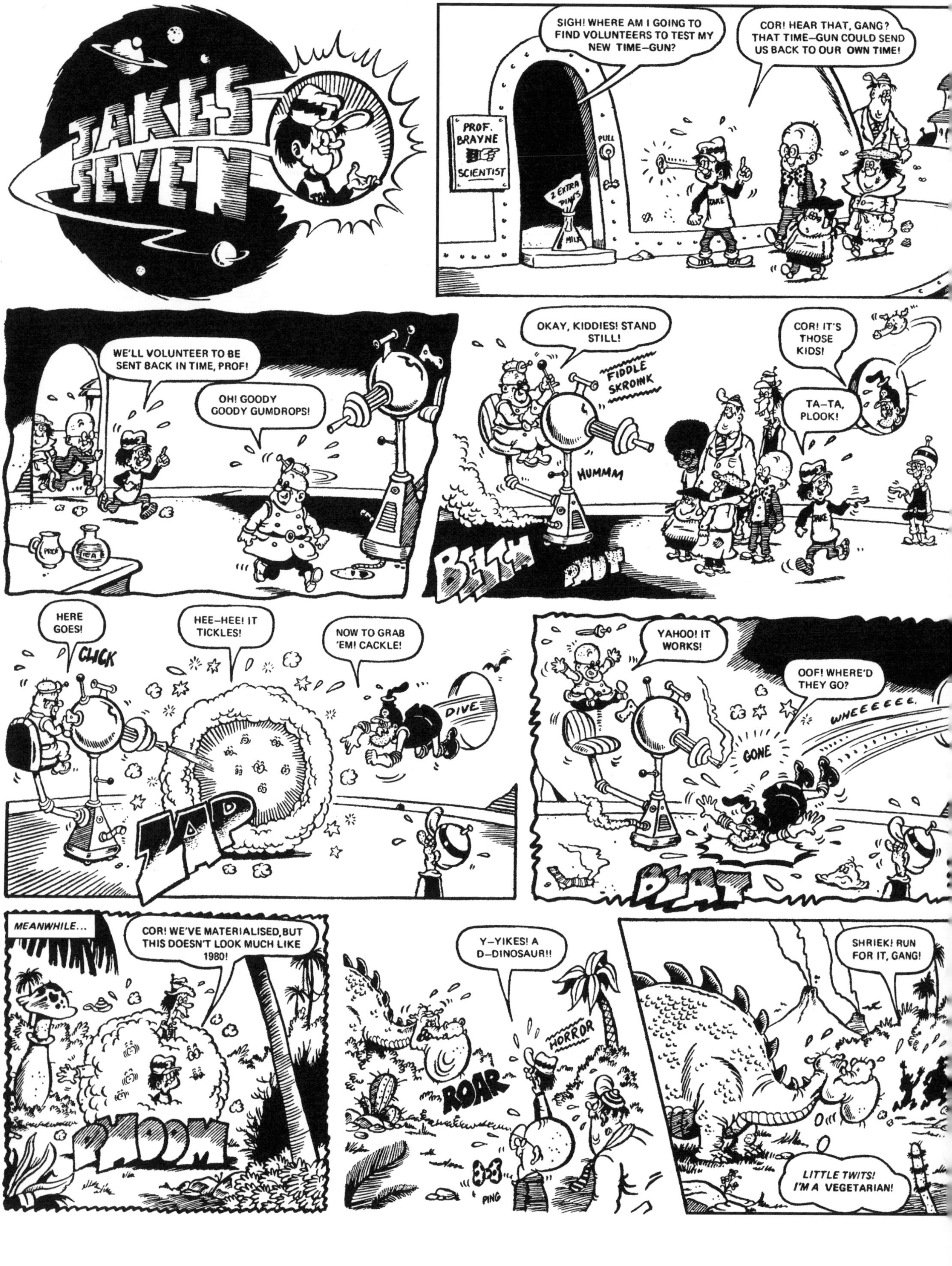
JAKE'S SEVEN
SIGH! WHERE AM I GOING TO FIND VOLUNTEERS TO TEST MY NEW TIME-GUN?
PROF. BRAYNE SCIENTIST
PULL
2 EXTRA PINTS
MILK
COR! HEAR THAT, GANG? THAT TIME-GUN COULD SEND US BACK TO OUR OWN TIME!
JAKE
WE'LL VOLUNTEER TO BE SENT BACK IN TIME, PROF!
OH! GOODY GOODY GUMDROPS!
PROF
TEA
OKAY, KIDDIES! STAND STILL!
FIDDLE SKROINK
HUMMM
COR! IT'S THOSE KIDS!
TA-TA, PLOOK!
HERE GOES!
CLICK
HEE-HEE! IT TICKLES!
NOW TO GRAB 'EM! CACKLE!
DIVE
ZAP
YAHOO! IT WORKS!
OOF! WHERE'D THEY GO?
WHEEEEEE
GONE
MEANWHILE...
COR! WE'VE MATERIALISED, BUT THIS DOESN'T LOOK MUCH LIKE 1980!
Y-YIKES! A D-DINOSAUR!!
HORROR
ROAR
PING
SHRIEK! RUN FOR IT, GANG!
LITTLE TWITS! I'M A VEGETARIAN!

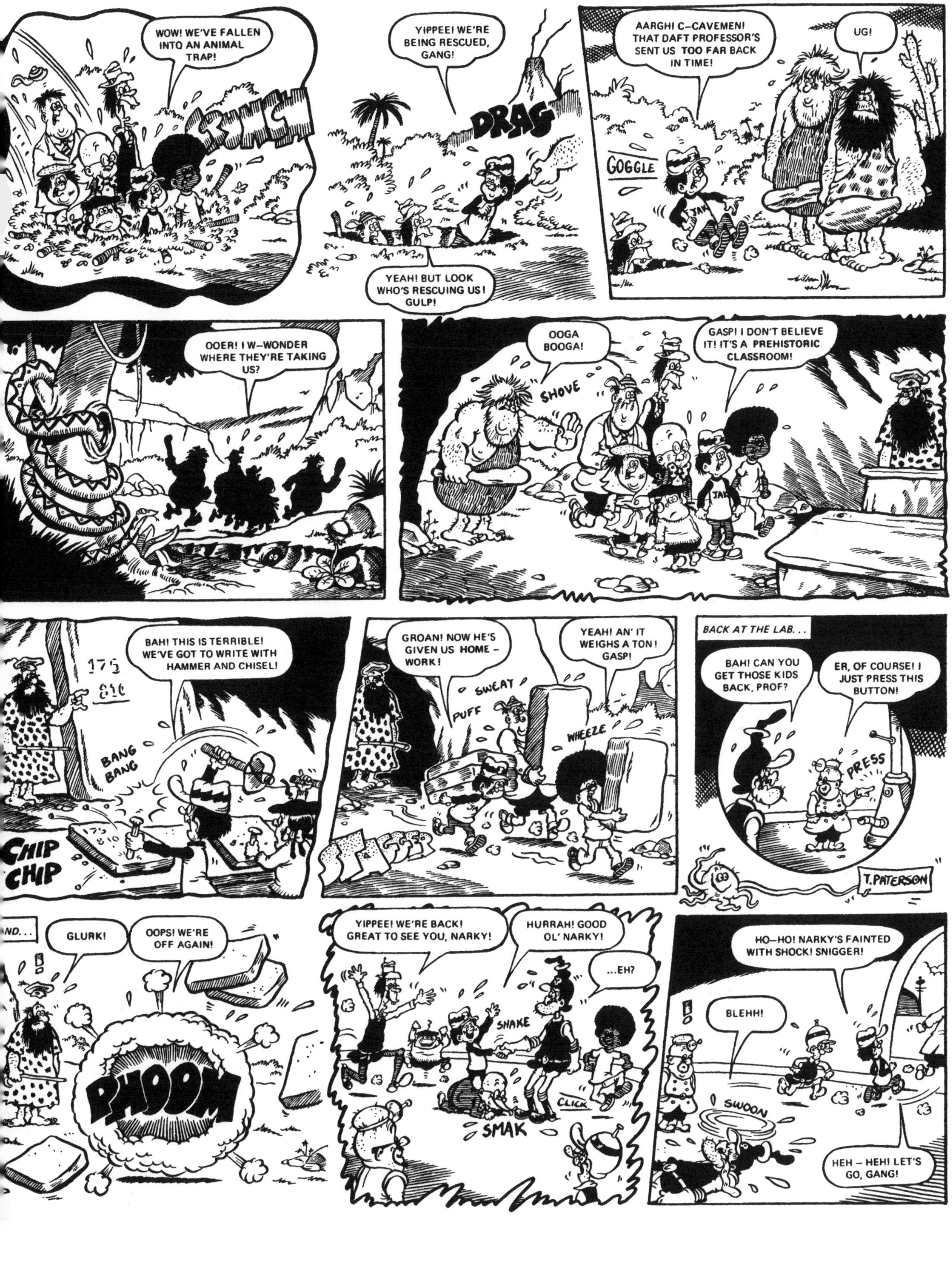

WOW! WE'VE FALLEN INTO AN ANIMAL TRAP!
YIPPEE! WE'RE BEING RESCUED, GANG!
DRAG
YEAH! BUT LOOK WHO'S RESCUING US! GULP!
AARGH! C-CAVEMEN! THAT DAFT PROFESSOR'S SENT US TOO FAR BACK IN TIME!
UG!
GOGGLE
OOER! I W-WONDER WHERE THEY'RE TAKING US?
OOGA BOOGA!
SHOVE
GASP! I DON'T BELIEVE IT! IT'S A PREHISTORIC CLASSROOM!
BAH! THIS IS TERRIBLE! WE'VE GOT TO WRITE WITH HAMMER AND CHISEL!
BANG BANG
CHIP CHIP
GROAN! NOW HE'S GIVEN US HOME-WORK!
YEAH! AN' IT WEIGHS A TON! GASP!
SWEAT
PUFF
WHEEZE
BACK AT THE LAB...
BAH! CAN YOU GET THOSE KIDS BACK, PROF?
ER, OF COURSE! I JUST PRESS THIS BUTTON!
PRESS
T. PATERSON
ND...
GLURK!
OOPS! WE'RE OFF AGAIN!
PHOOM
YIPPEE! WE'RE BACK! GREAT TO SEE YOU, NARKY!
HURRAH! GOOD OL' NARKY!
...EH?
SHAKE
CLICK
SMAK
HO-HO! NARKY'S FAINTED WITH SHOCK! SNIGGER!
BLEHH!
SWOON
HEH-HEH! LET'S GO, GANG!

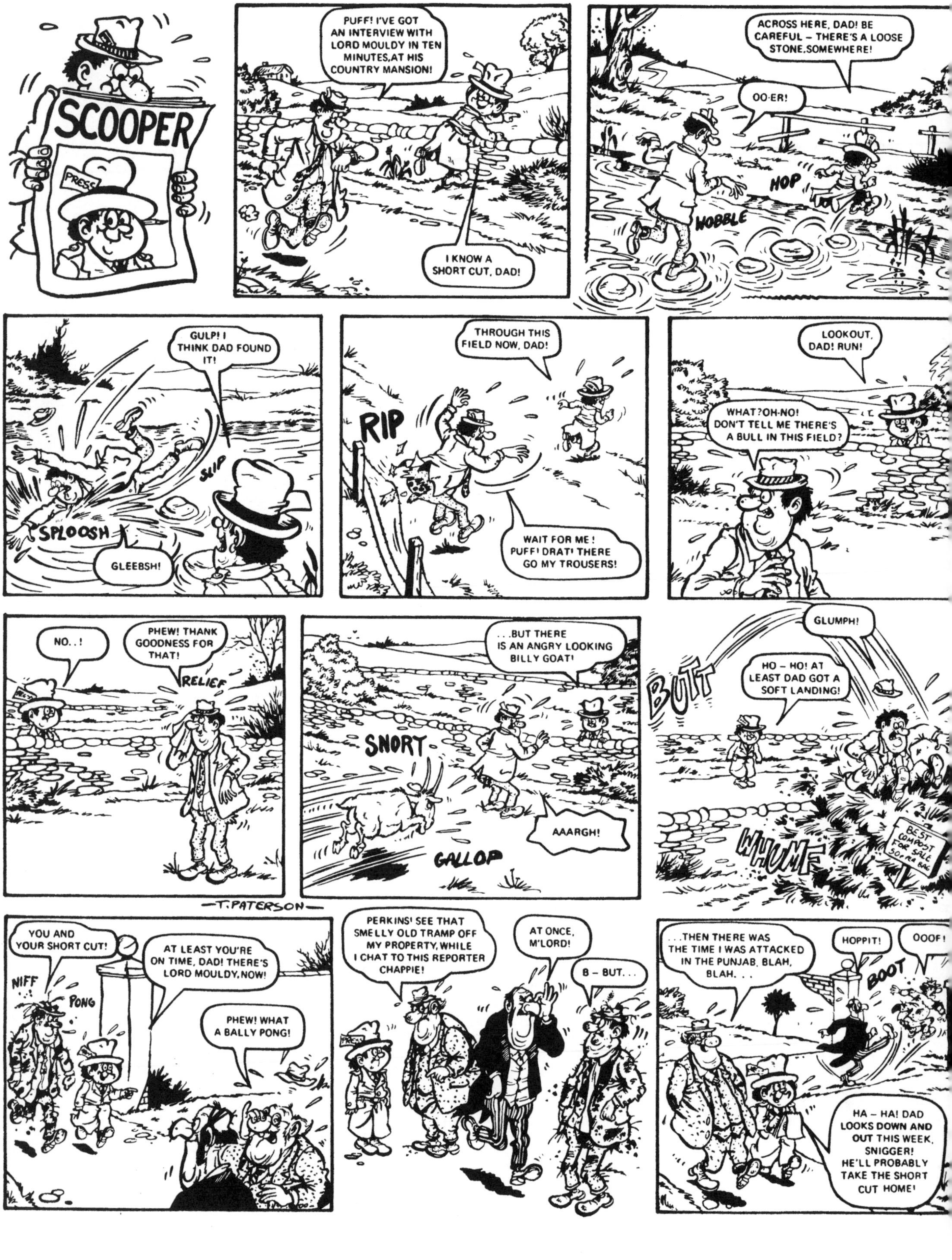
SCOOPER
PRESS
PUFF! I'VE GOT AN INTERVIEW WITH LORD MOULDY IN TEN MINUTES, AT HIS COUNTRY MANSION!
I KNOW A SHORT CUT, DAD!
ACROSS HERE, DAD! BE CAREFUL – THERE'S A LOOSE STONE, SOMEWHERE!
OO-ER!
HOP
WOBBLE
GULP! I THINK DAD FOUND IT!
SLIP
SPLOOSH
GLEEBSH!
THROUGH THIS FIELD NOW, DAD!
RIP
WAIT FOR ME! PUFF! DRAT! THERE GO MY TROUSERS!
LOOKOUT, DAD! RUN!
WHAT? OH-NO! DON'T TELL ME THERE'S A BULL IN THIS FIELD?
NO..!
PHEW! THANK GOODNESS FOR THAT!
RELIEF
...BUT THERE IS AN ANGRY LOOKING BILLY GOAT!
SNORT
AAARGH!
GALLOP
GLUMPH!
BUTT
HO – HO! AT LEAST DAD GOT A SOFT LANDING!
WHUMF
BEST COMPOST FOR SALE 50p A BAG
T. PATERSON
YOU AND YOUR SHORT CUT!
NIFF
PONG
AT LEAST YOU'RE ON TIME, DAD! THERE'S LORD MOULDY, NOW!
PHEW! WHAT A BALLY PONG!
PERKINS! SEE THAT SMELLY OLD TRAMP OFF MY PROPERTY, WHILE I CHAT TO THIS REPORTER CHAPPIE!
AT ONCE, M'LORD!
B – BUT...
...THEN THERE WAS THE TIME I WAS ATTACKED IN THE PUNJAB, BLAH, BLAH...
HOPPIT!
OOOF!
BOOT
HA – HA! DAD LOOKS DOWN AND OUT THIS WEEK, SNIGGER! HE'LL PROBABLY TAKE THE SHORT CUT HOME!

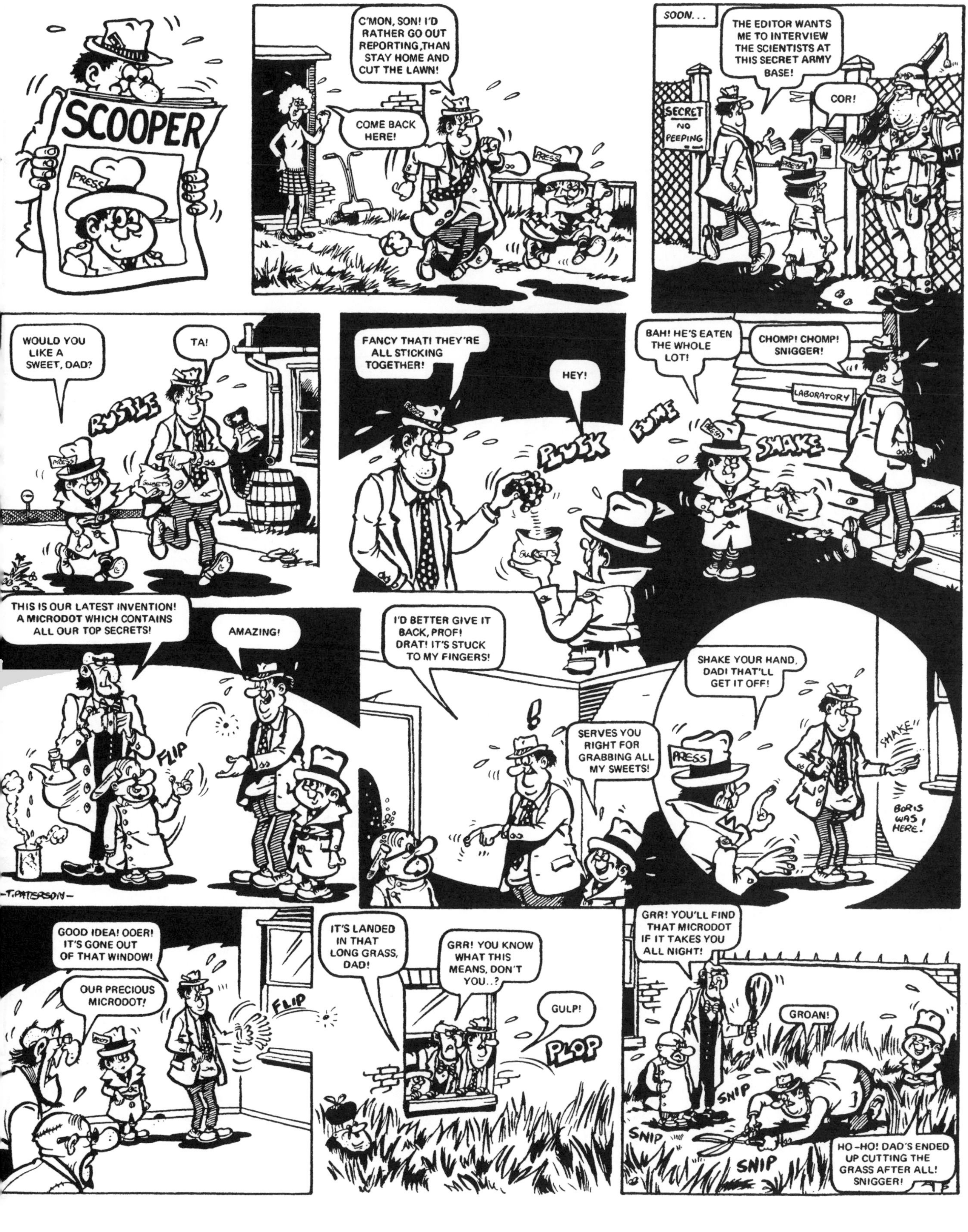
SCOOPER
PRESS
C'MON, SON! I'D RATHER GO OUT REPORTING, THAN STAY HOME AND CUT THE LAWN!
COME BACK HERE!
PRESS
SOON...
THE EDITOR WANTS ME TO INTERVIEW THE SCIENTISTS AT THIS SECRET ARMY BASE!
COR!
SECRET NO PEEPING
MP
WOULD YOU LIKE A SWEET, DAD?
TA!
RUSTLE
PRESS
SWEETS
FANCY THAT! THEY'RE ALL STICKING TOGETHER!
HEY!
PLUCK
SWEETS
BAH! HE'S EATEN THE WHOLE LOT!
CHOMP! CHOMP! SNIGGER!
LABORATORY
FUME
SHAKE
THIS IS OUR LATEST INVENTION! A MICRODOT WHICH CONTAINS ALL OUR TOP SECRETS!
AMAZING!
FLIP
-T.PATERSON-
I'D BETTER GIVE IT BACK, PROF! DRAT! IT'S STUCK TO MY FINGERS!
!
SERVES YOU RIGHT FOR GRABBING ALL MY SWEETS!
SHAKE YOUR HAND, DAD! THAT'LL GET IT OFF!
PRESS
SHAKE
BORIS WAS HERE!
GOOD IDEA! OOER! IT'S GONE OUT OF THAT WINDOW!
OUR PRECIOUS MICRODOT!
FLIP
IT'S LANDED IN THAT LONG GRASS, DAD!
GRR! YOU KNOW WHAT THIS MEANS, DON'T YOU..?
GULP!
PLOP
GRR! YOU'LL FIND THAT MICRODOT IF IT TAKES YOU ALL NIGHT!
GROAN!
SNIP
SNIP
SNIP
HO-HO! DAD'S ENDED UP CUTTING THE GRASS AFTER ALL! SNIGGER!

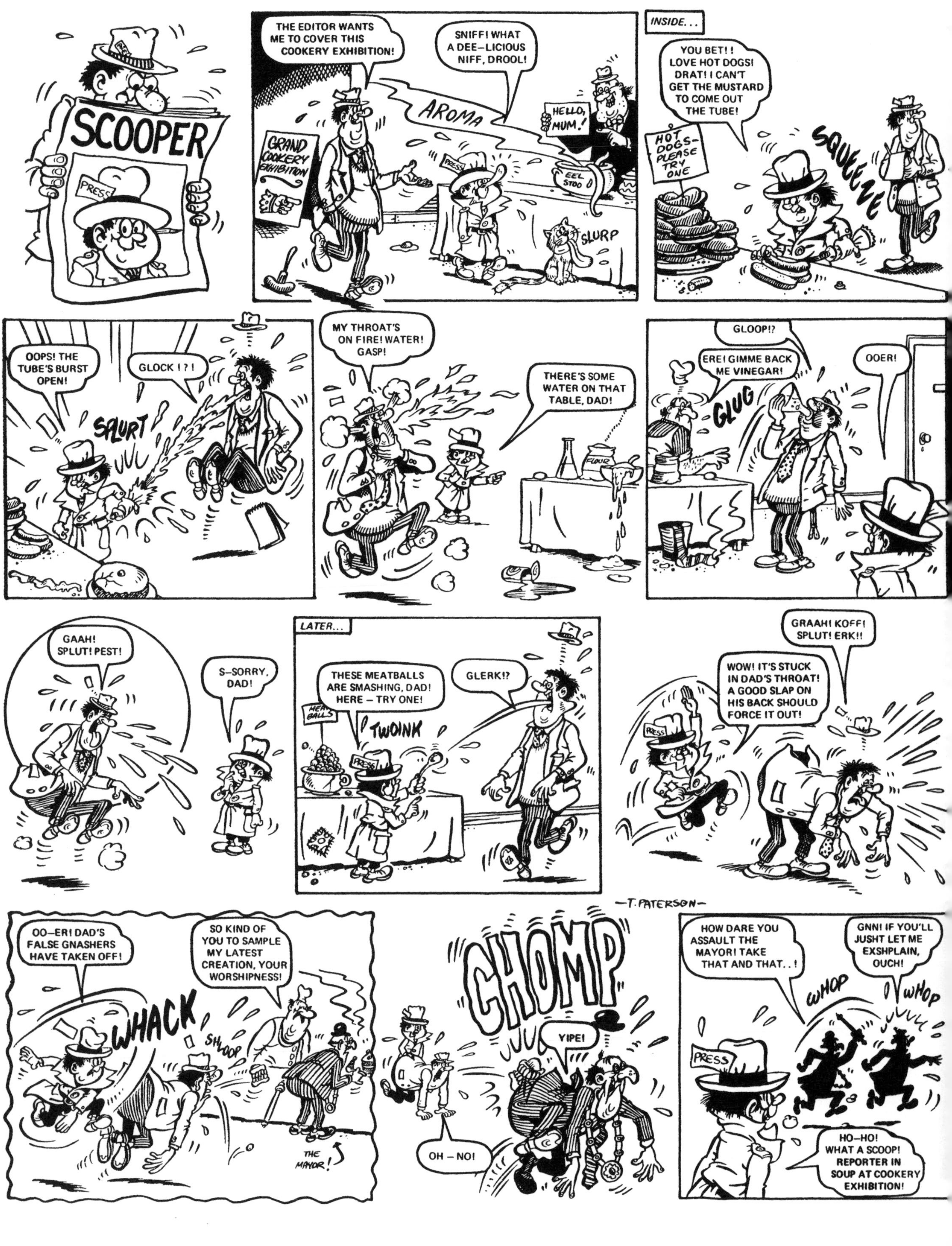
SCOOPER
PRESS
THE EDITOR WANTS ME TO COVER THIS COOKERY EXHIBITION!
SNIFF! WHAT A DEE-LICIOUS NIFF, DROOL!
AROMA
GRAND COOKERY EXHIBITION
HELLO, MUM!
EEL STOO
SLURP
INSIDE...
YOU BET!! LOVE HOT DOGS! DRAT! I CAN'T GET THE MUSTARD TO COME OUT THE TUBE!
HOT DOGS-PLEASE TRY ONE
SQUEEZE
OOPS! THE TUBE'S BURST OPEN!
GLOCK!?!
SPLURT
MY THROAT'S ON FIRE! WATER! GASP!
THERE'S SOME WATER ON THAT TABLE, DAD!
FLOUR
GLOOP!?
ERE! GIMME BACK ME VINEGAR!
OOER!
GLUG
GAAH! SPLUT! PEST!
S-SORRY, DAD!
LATER...
THESE MEATBALLS ARE SMASHING, DAD! HERE – TRY ONE!
GLERK!?
TWOINK
GRAAH! KOFF! SPLUT! ERK!!
WOW! IT'S STUCK IN DAD'S THROAT! A GOOD SLAP ON HIS BACK SHOULD FORCE IT OUT!
-T. PATERSON-
OO-ER! DAD'S FALSE GNASHERS HAVE TAKEN OFF!
SO KIND OF YOU TO SAMPLE MY LATEST CREATION, YOUR WORSHIPNESS!
WHACK
SHLOOP
THE MAYOR!
CHOMP
YIPE!
OH – NO!
HOW DARE YOU ASSAULT THE MAYOR! TAKE THAT AND THAT..!
GNN! IF YOU'LL JUSHT LET ME EXSHPLAIN, OUCH!
WHOP
WHOP
HO-HO! WHAT A SCOOP! REPORTER IN SOUP AT COOKERY EXHIBITION!

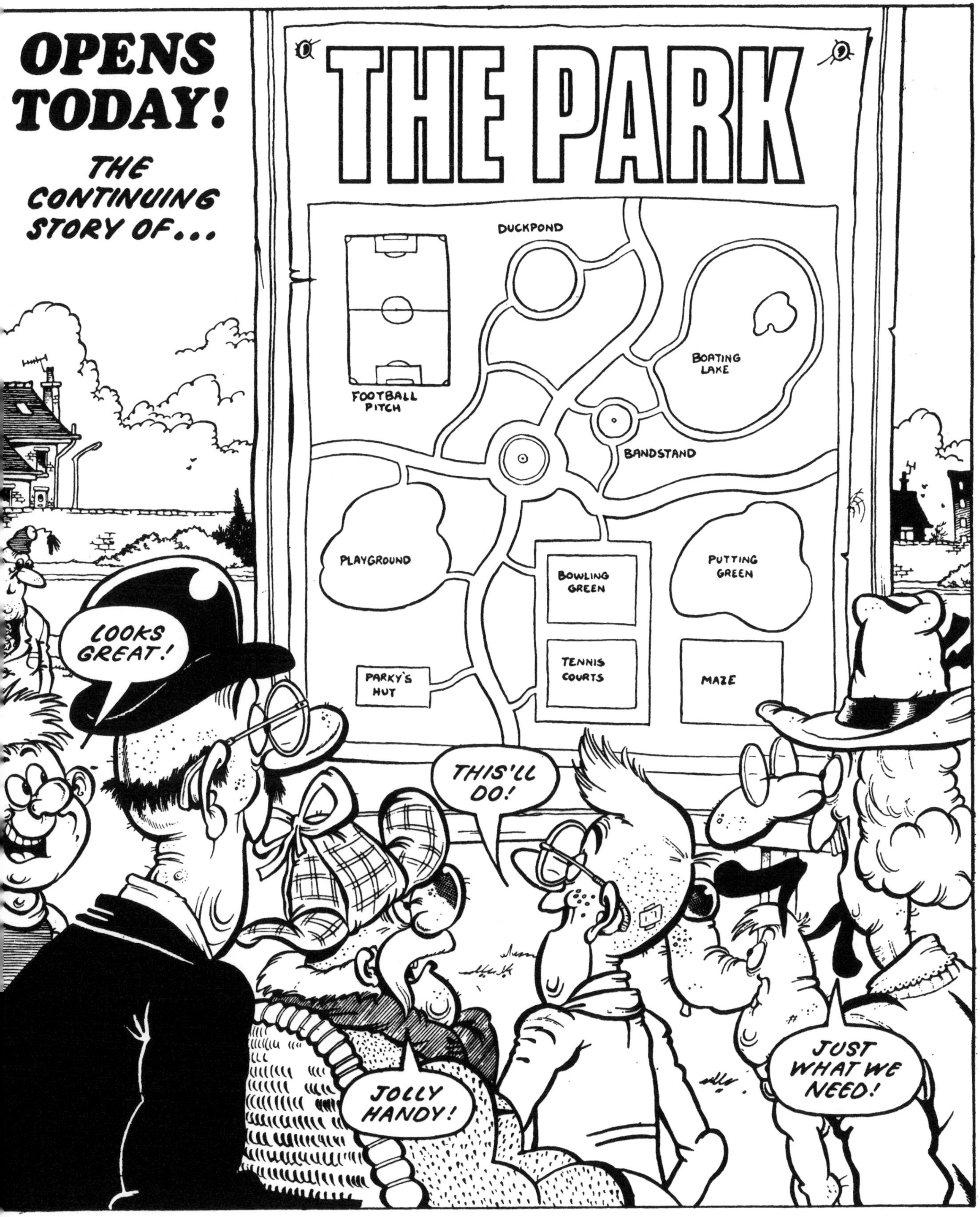
OPENS TODAY!
THE CONTINUING STORY OF...
THE PARK
DUCKPOND
FOOTBALL PITCH
BOATING LAKE
BANDSTAND
PLAYGROUND
PUTTING GREEN
BOWLING GREEN
TENNIS COURTS
PARKY'S HUT
MAZE
LOOKS GREAT!
THIS'LL DO!
JOLLY HANDY!
JUST WHAT WE NEED!

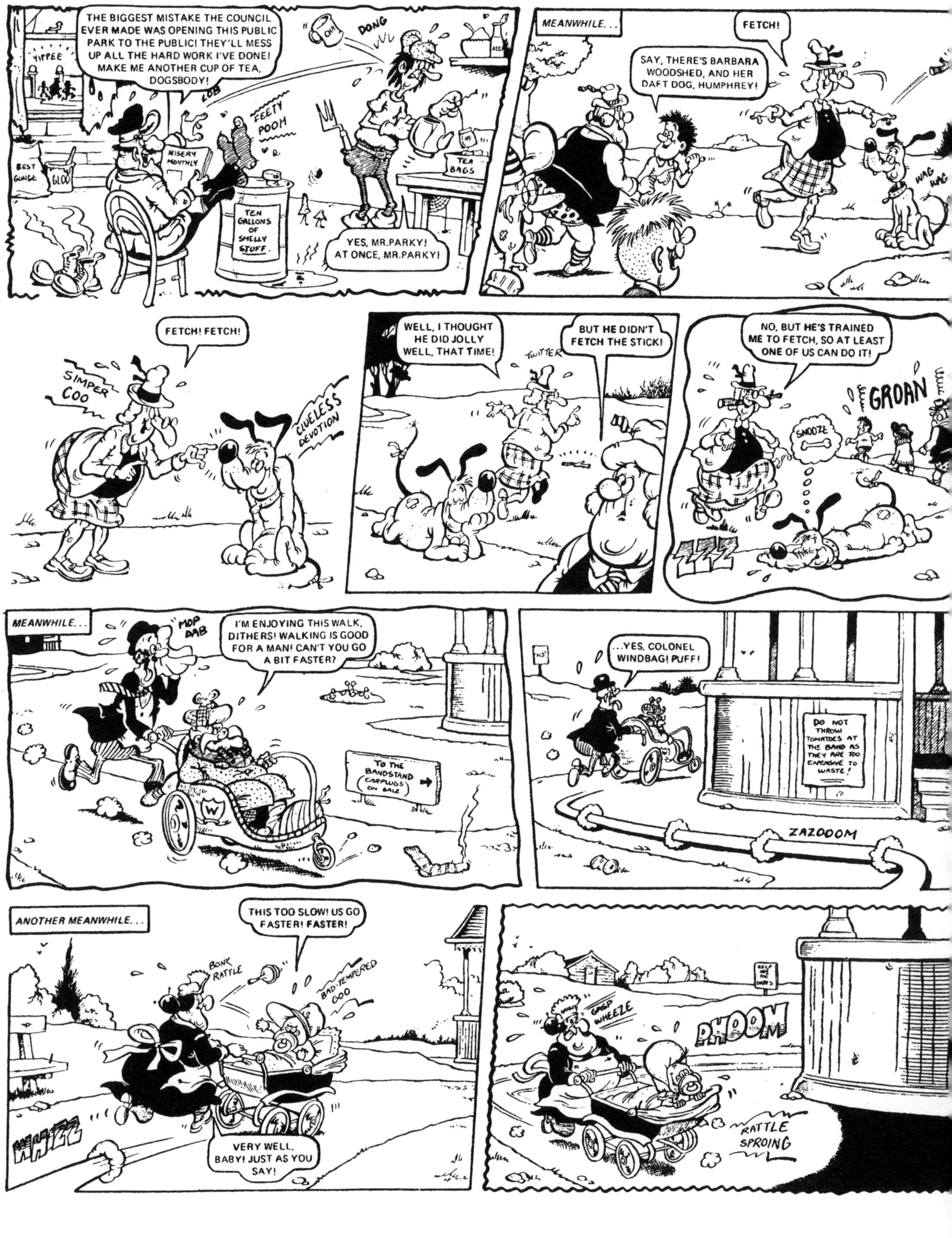

THE BIGGEST MISTAKE THE COUNCIL EVER MADE WAS OPENING THIS PUBLIC PARK TO THE PUBLIC! THEY'LL MESS UP ALL THE HARD WORK I'VE DONE! MAKE ME ANOTHER CUP OF TEA, DOGSBODY!
YIPPEE
BEST GUNGE
GLOO
MISERY MONTHLY
FEETY POOH
DONG
TEN GALLONS OF SMELLY STUFF.
TEA BAGS
YES, MR.PARKY! AT ONCE, MR.PARKY!
MEANWHILE...
SAY, THERE'S BARBARA WOODSHED, AND HER DAFT DOG, HUMPHREY!
FETCH!
WAG WAG
FETCH! FETCH!
SIMPER COO
CLUELESS DEVOTION
WELL, I THOUGHT HE DID JOLLY WELL, THAT TIME!
TWITTER
BUT HE DIDN'T FETCH THE STICK!
NO, BUT HE'S TRAINED ME TO FETCH, SO AT LEAST ONE OF US CAN DO IT!
GROAN
SNOOZE
ZZZ
MEANWHILE...
MOP DAB
I'M ENJOYING THIS WALK, DITHERS! WALKING IS GOOD FOR A MAN! CAN'T YOU GO A BIT FASTER?
TO THE BANDSTAND (EARPLUGS ON SALE)
...YES, COLONEL WINDBAG! PUFF!
DO NOT THROW TOMATOES AT THE BAND AS THEY ARE TOO EXPENSIVE TO WASTE!
ZAZOOOM
ANOTHER MEANWHILE...
THIS TOO SLOW! US GO FASTER! FASTER!
BONK RATTLE
BAD-TEMPERED GOO
VERY WELL, BABY! JUST AS YOU SAY!
GASP WHEEZE
PHOOM
RATTLE SPROING

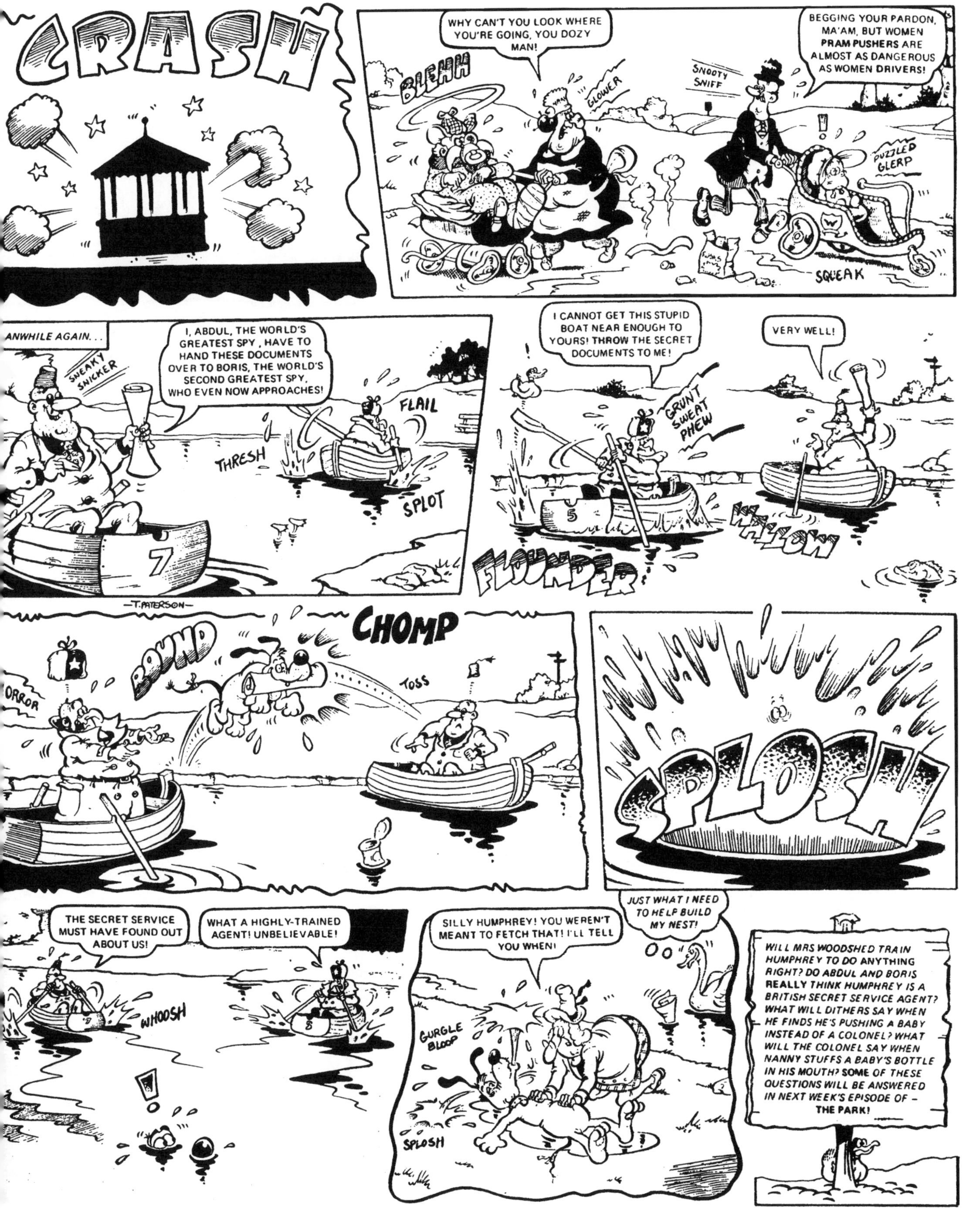

CRASH
WHY CAN'T YOU LOOK WHERE YOU'RE GOING, YOU DOZY MAN!
BLEHH
GLOWER
SNOOTY SNIFF
BEGGING YOUR PARDON, MA'AM, BUT WOMEN PRAM PUSHERS ARE ALMOST AS DANGEROUS AS WOMEN DRIVERS!
!
PUZZLED GLERP
SQUEAK
ANWHILE AGAIN. . .
SNEAKY SNICKER
I, ABDUL, THE WORLD'S GREATEST SPY, HAVE TO HAND THESE DOCUMENTS OVER TO BORIS, THE WORLD'S SECOND GREATEST SPY, WHO EVEN NOW APPROACHES!
FLAIL
THRESH
SPLOT
7
I CANNOT GET THIS STUPID BOAT NEAR ENOUGH TO YOURS! THROW THE SECRET DOCUMENTS TO ME!
VERY WELL!
GRUNT SWEAT PHEW
5
WALLOW
FLOUNDER
-T. PATERSON-
CHOMP
BOUND
ORROR
TOSS
SPLOSH
THE SECRET SERVICE MUST HAVE FOUND OUT ABOUT US!
WHAT A HIGHLY-TRAINED AGENT! UNBELIEVABLE!
WHOOSH
!
SILLY HUMPHREY! YOU WEREN'T MEANT TO FETCH THAT! I'LL TELL YOU WHEN!
JUST WHAT I NEED TO HELP BUILD MY NEST!
GURGLE BLOOP
SPLOSH
WILL MRS WOODSHED TRAIN HUMPHREY TO DO ANYTHING RIGHT? DO ABDUL AND BORIS REALLY THINK HUMPHREY IS A BRITISH SECRET SERVICE AGENT? WHAT WILL DITHERS SAY WHEN HE FINDS HE'S PUSHING A BABY INSTEAD OF A COLONEL? WHAT WILL THE COLONEL SAY WHEN NANNY STUFFS A BABY'S BOTTLE IN HIS MOUTH? SOME OF THESE QUESTIONS WILL BE ANSWERED IN NEXT WEEK'S EPISODE OF - THE PARK!

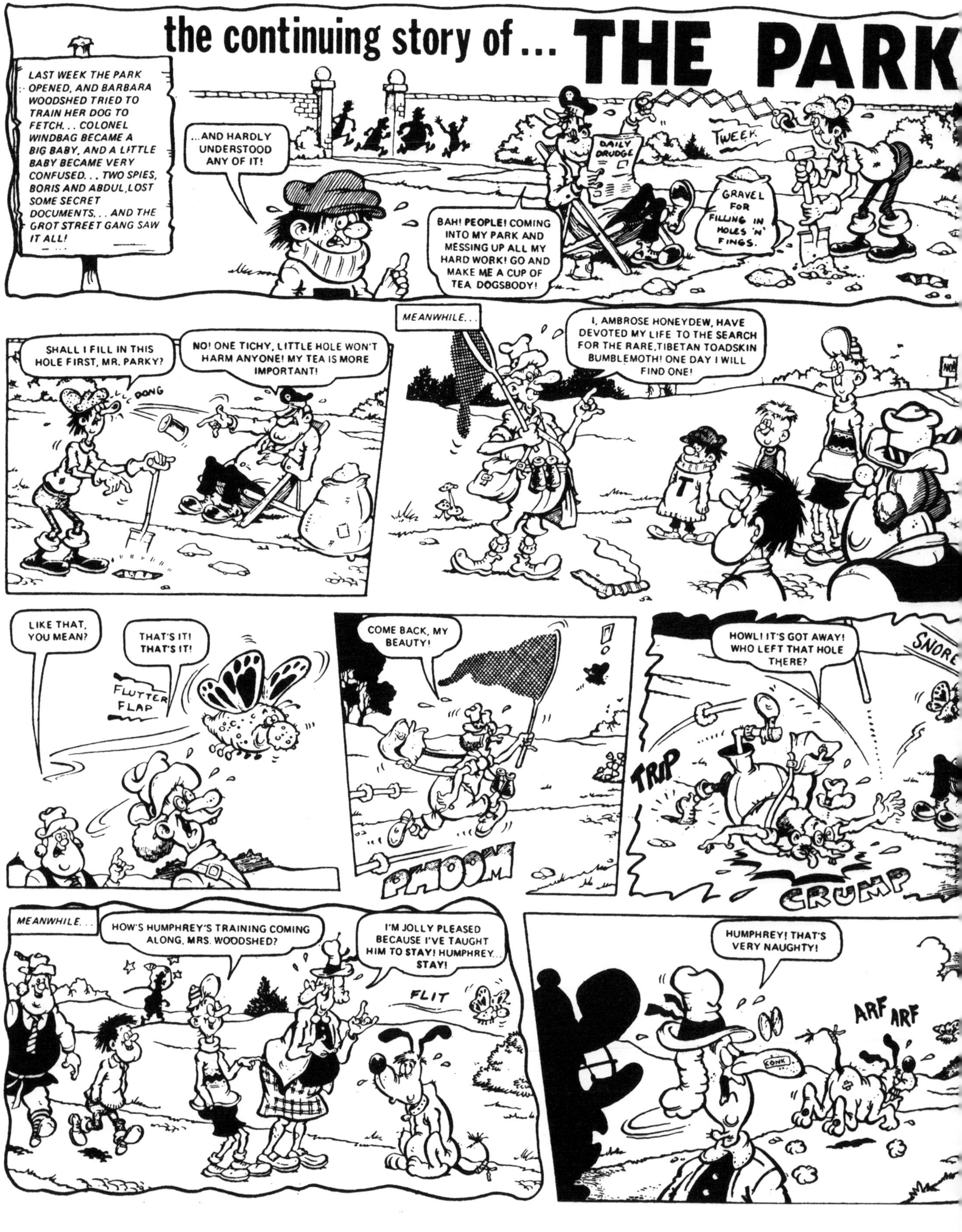
the continuing story of... THE PARK
LAST WEEK THE PARK OPENED, AND BARBARA WOODSHED TRIED TO TRAIN HER DOG TO FETCH... COLONEL WINDBAG BECAME A BIG BABY, AND A LITTLE BABY BECAME VERY CONFUSED... TWO SPIES, BORIS AND ABDUL, LOST SOME SECRET DOCUMENTS... AND THE GROT STREET GANG SAW IT ALL!
...AND HARDLY UNDERSTOOD ANY OF IT!
DAILY DRUDGE
TWEEK
GRAVEL FOR FILLING IN HOLES 'N' FINGS.
BAH! PEOPLE! COMING INTO MY PARK AND MESSING UP ALL MY HARD WORK! GO AND MAKE ME A CUP OF TEA DOGSBODY!
SHALL I FILL IN THIS HOLE FIRST, MR. PARKY?
DONG
NO! ONE TICHY, LITTLE HOLE WON'T HARM ANYONE! MY TEA IS MORE IMPORTANT!
MEANWHILE...
I, AMBROSE HONEYDEW, HAVE DEVOTED MY LIFE TO THE SEARCH FOR THE RARE, TIBETAN TOADSKIN BUMBLEMOTH! ONE DAY I WILL FIND ONE!
LIKE THAT, YOU MEAN?
THAT'S IT! THAT'S IT!
FLUTTER FLAP
COME BACK, MY BEAUTY!
PHOOM
HOWL! IT'S GOT AWAY! WHO LEFT THAT HOLE THERE?
SNORE
TRIP
CRUMP
MEANWHILE...
HOW'S HUMPHREY'S TRAINING COMING ALONG, MRS. WOODSHED?
I'M JOLLY PLEASED BECAUSE I'VE TAUGHT HIM TO STAY! HUMPHREY... STAY!
FLIT
HUMPHREY! THAT'S VERY NAUGHTY!
KONK
ARF ARF

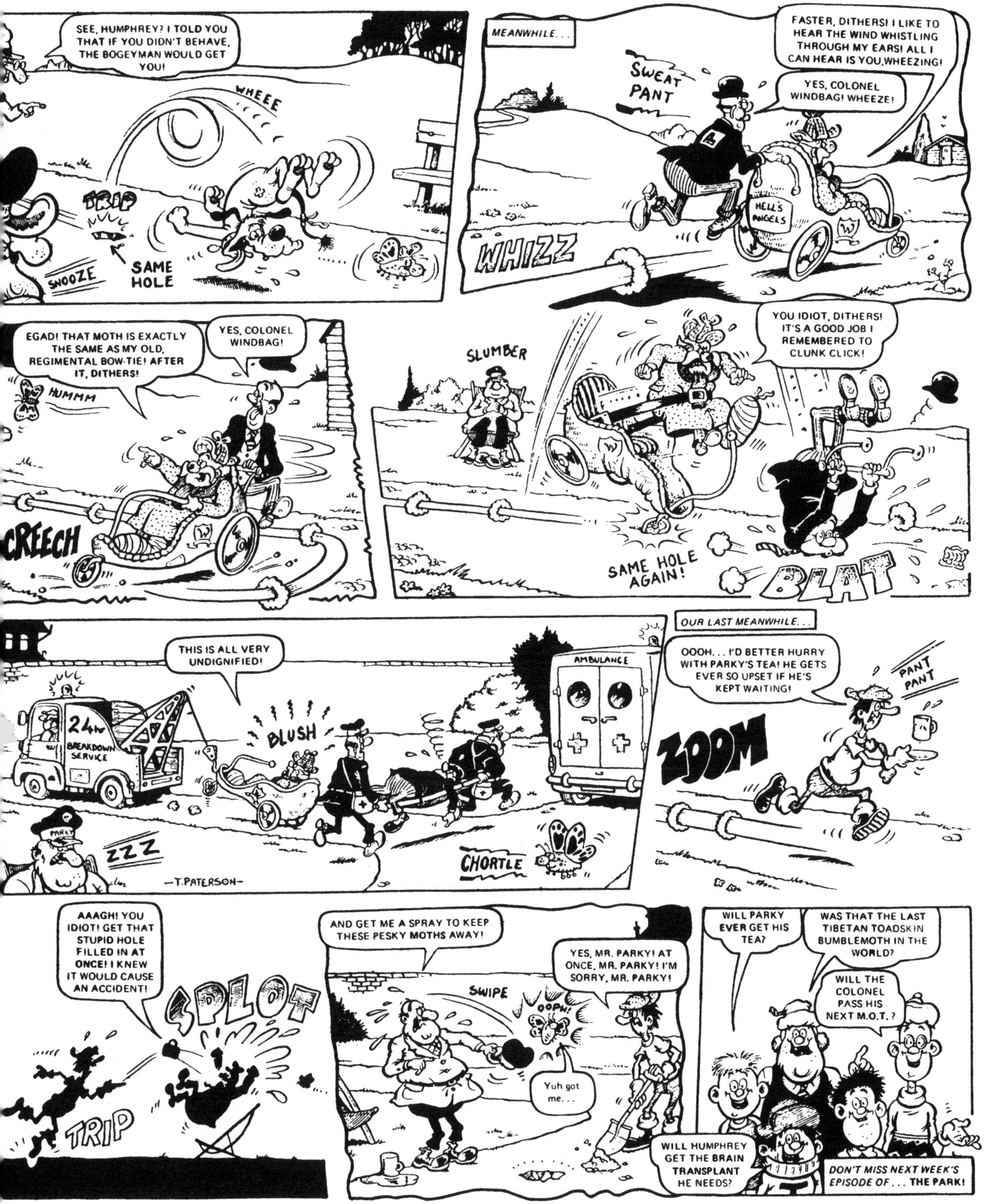

SEE, HUMPHREY? I TOLD YOU THAT IF YOU DIDN'T BEHAVE, THE BOGEYMAN WOULD GET YOU!
WHEEE
TRIP
SAME HOLE
SNOOZE
MEANWHILE...
FASTER, DITHERS! I LIKE TO HEAR THE WIND WHISTLING THROUGH MY EARS! ALL I CAN HEAR IS YOU, WHEEZING!
YES, COLONEL WINDBAG! WHEEZE!
SWEAT PANT
HELL'S ANGELS
WHIZZ
EGAD! THAT MOTH IS EXACTLY THE SAME AS MY OLD, REGIMENTAL BOW-TIE! AFTER IT, DITHERS!
YES, COLONEL WINDBAG!
HUMMM
CREECH
SLUMBER
YOU IDIOT, DITHERS! IT'S A GOOD JOB I REMEMBERED TO CLUNK CLICK!
SAME HOLE AGAIN!
BLAT
THIS IS ALL VERY UNDIGNIFIED!
24hr BREAKDOWN SERVICE
BLUSH
AMBULANCE
PARKY
ZZZ
CHORTLE
—T.PATERSON—
OUR LAST MEANWHILE...
OOOH... I'D BETTER HURRY WITH PARKY'S TEA! HE GETS EVER SO UPSET IF HE'S KEPT WAITING!
PANT PANT
ZOOM
AAAGH! YOU IDIOT! GET THAT STUPID HOLE FILLED IN AT ONCE! I KNEW IT WOULD CAUSE AN ACCIDENT!
SPLOT
TRIP
AND GET ME A SPRAY TO KEEP THESE PESKY MOTHS AWAY!
YES, MR. PARKY! AT ONCE, MR. PARKY! I'M SORRY, MR. PARKY!
SWIPE
OOPH!
Yuh got me...
WILL PARKY EVER GET HIS TEA?
WAS THAT THE LAST TIBETAN TOADSKIN BUMBLEMOTH IN THE WORLD?
WILL THE COLONEL PASS HIS NEXT M.O.T.?
WILL HUMPHREY GET THE BRAIN TRANSPLANT HE NEEDS?
DON'T MISS NEXT WEEK'S EPISODE OF... THE PARK!

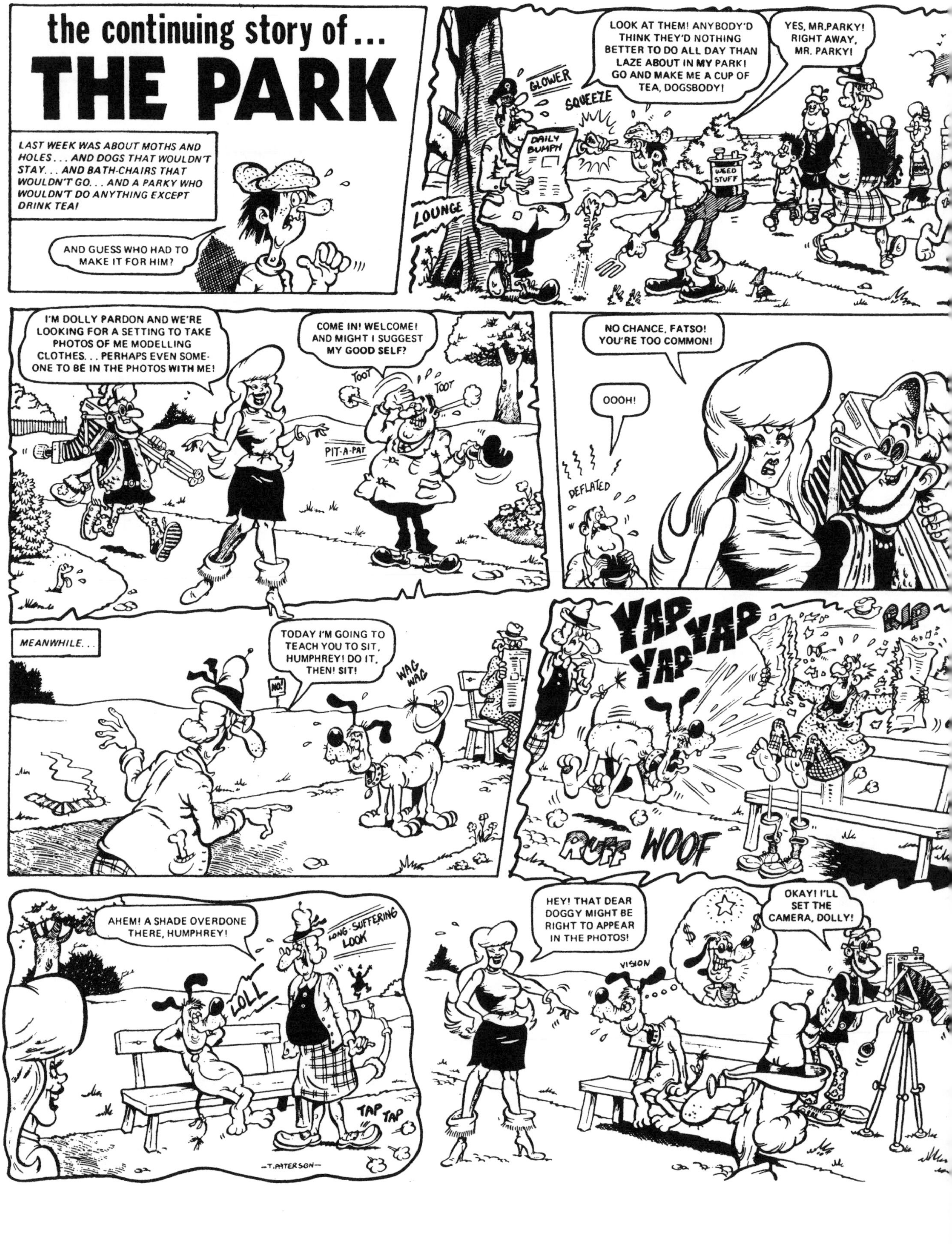
the continuing story of...
THE PARK
LAST WEEK WAS ABOUT MOTHS AND HOLES... AND DOGS THAT WOULDN'T STAY... AND BATH-CHAIRS THAT WOULDN'T GO... AND A PARKY WHO WOULDN'T DO ANYTHING EXCEPT DRINK TEA!
AND GUESS WHO HAD TO MAKE IT FOR HIM?
LOOK AT THEM! ANYBODY'D THINK THEY'D NOTHING BETTER TO DO ALL DAY THAN LAZE ABOUT IN MY PARK! GO AND MAKE ME A CUP OF TEA, DOGSBODY!
YES, MR.PARKY! RIGHT AWAY, MR. PARKY!
GLOWER
SQUEEZE
DAILY BUMPH
WEED STUFF
LOUNGE
I'M DOLLY PARDON AND WE'RE LOOKING FOR A SETTING TO TAKE PHOTOS OF ME MODELLING CLOTHES... PERHAPS EVEN SOME-ONE TO BE IN THE PHOTOS WITH ME!
COME IN! WELCOME! AND MIGHT I SUGGEST MY GOOD SELF?
TOOT
TOOT
PIT-A-PAT
NO CHANCE, FATSO! YOU'RE TOO COMMON!
OOOH!
DEFLATED
MEANWHILE...
TODAY I'M GOING TO TEACH YOU TO SIT, HUMPHREY! DO IT, THEN! SIT!
NO!
WAG WAG
YAP YAP YAP
RIP
RUFF WOOF
AHEM! A SHADE OVERDONE THERE, HUMPHREY!
LONG-SUFFERING LOOK
LOLL
TAP TAP
-T. PATERSON-
HEY! THAT DEAR DOGGY MIGHT BE RIGHT TO APPEAR IN THE PHOTOS!
OKAY! I'LL SET THE CAMERA, DOLLY!
VISION

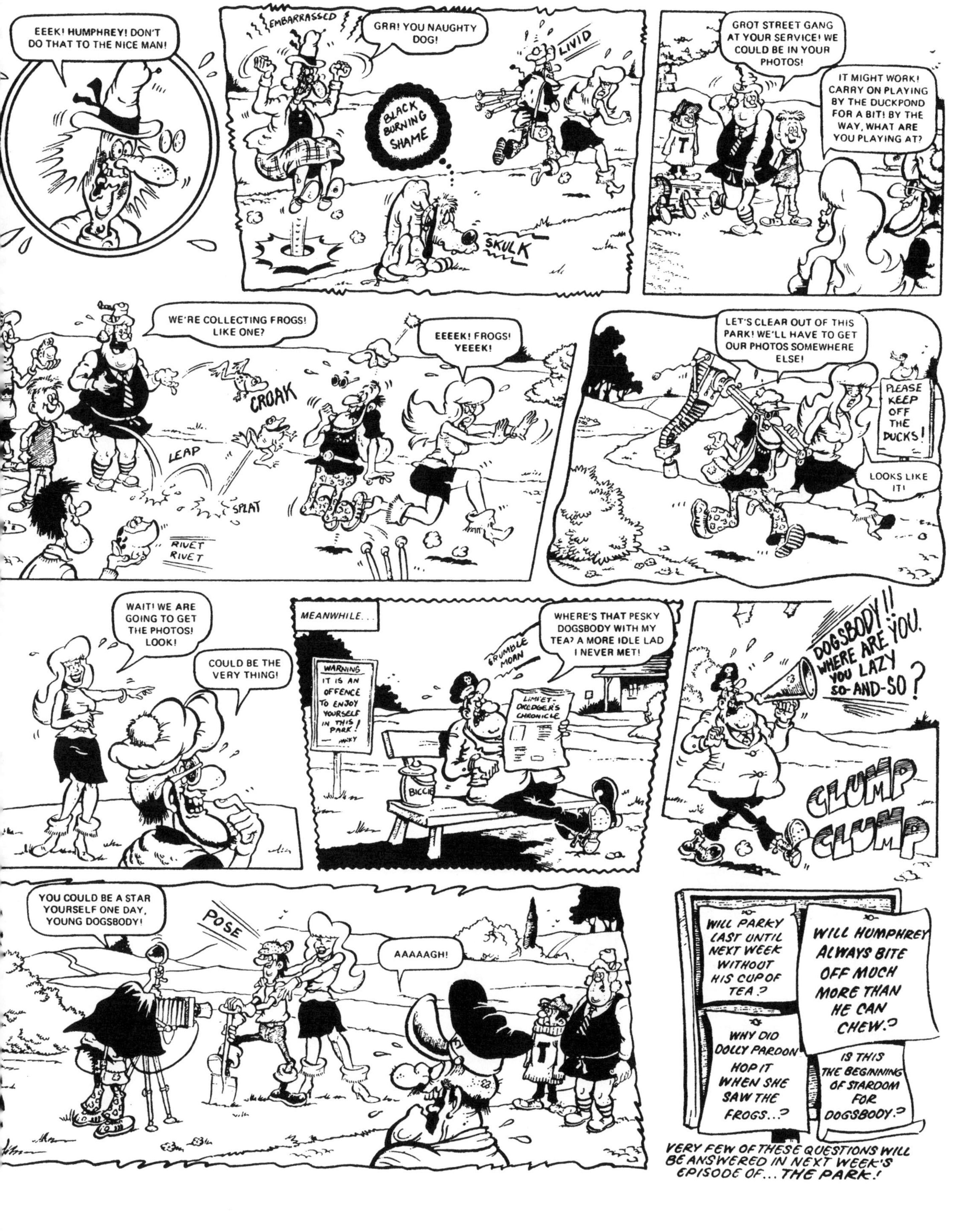
EEEK! HUMPHREY! DON'T DO THAT TO THE NICE MAN!
EMBARRASSED
GRR! YOU NAUGHTY DOG!
LIVID
BLACK BURNING SHAME
SKULK
GROT STREET GANG AT YOUR SERVICE! WE COULD BE IN YOUR PHOTOS!
IT MIGHT WORK! CARRY ON PLAYING BY THE DUCKPOND FOR A BIT! BY THE WAY, WHAT ARE YOU PLAYING AT?
WE'RE COLLECTING FROGS! LIKE ONE?
EEEEK! FROGS! YEEEK!
CROAK
LEAP
SPLAT
RIVET RIVET
LET'S CLEAR OUT OF THIS PARK! WE'LL HAVE TO GET OUR PHOTOS SOMEWHERE ELSE!
PLEASE KEEP OFF THE DUCKS!
LOOKS LIKE IT!
WAIT! WE ARE GOING TO GET THE PHOTOS! LOOK!
COULD BE THE VERY THING!
MEANWHILE...
WARNING IT IS AN OFFENCE TO ENJOY YOURSELF IN THIS PARK!
GRUMBLE MOAN
WHERE'S THAT PESKY DOGSBODY WITH MY TEA? A MORE IDLE LAD I NEVER MET!
LIMEY-DREDGER'S CHRONICLE
BICCIE
DOGSBODY!! WHERE ARE YOU, YOU LAZY SO-AND-SO?
CLUMP CLUMP
YOU COULD BE A STAR YOURSELF ONE DAY, YOUNG DOGSBODY!
POSE
AAAAAGH!
WILL PARKY LAST UNTIL NEXT WEEK WITHOUT HIS CUP OF TEA?
WILL HUMPHREY ALWAYS BITE OFF MUCH MORE THAN HE CAN CHEW?
WHY DID DOLLY PARDON HOP IT WHEN SHE SAW THE FROGS...?
IS THIS THE BEGINNING OF STARDOM FOR DOGSBODY?
VERY FEW OF THESE QUESTIONS WILL BE ANSWERED IN NEXT WEEK'S EPISODE OF... THE PARK!

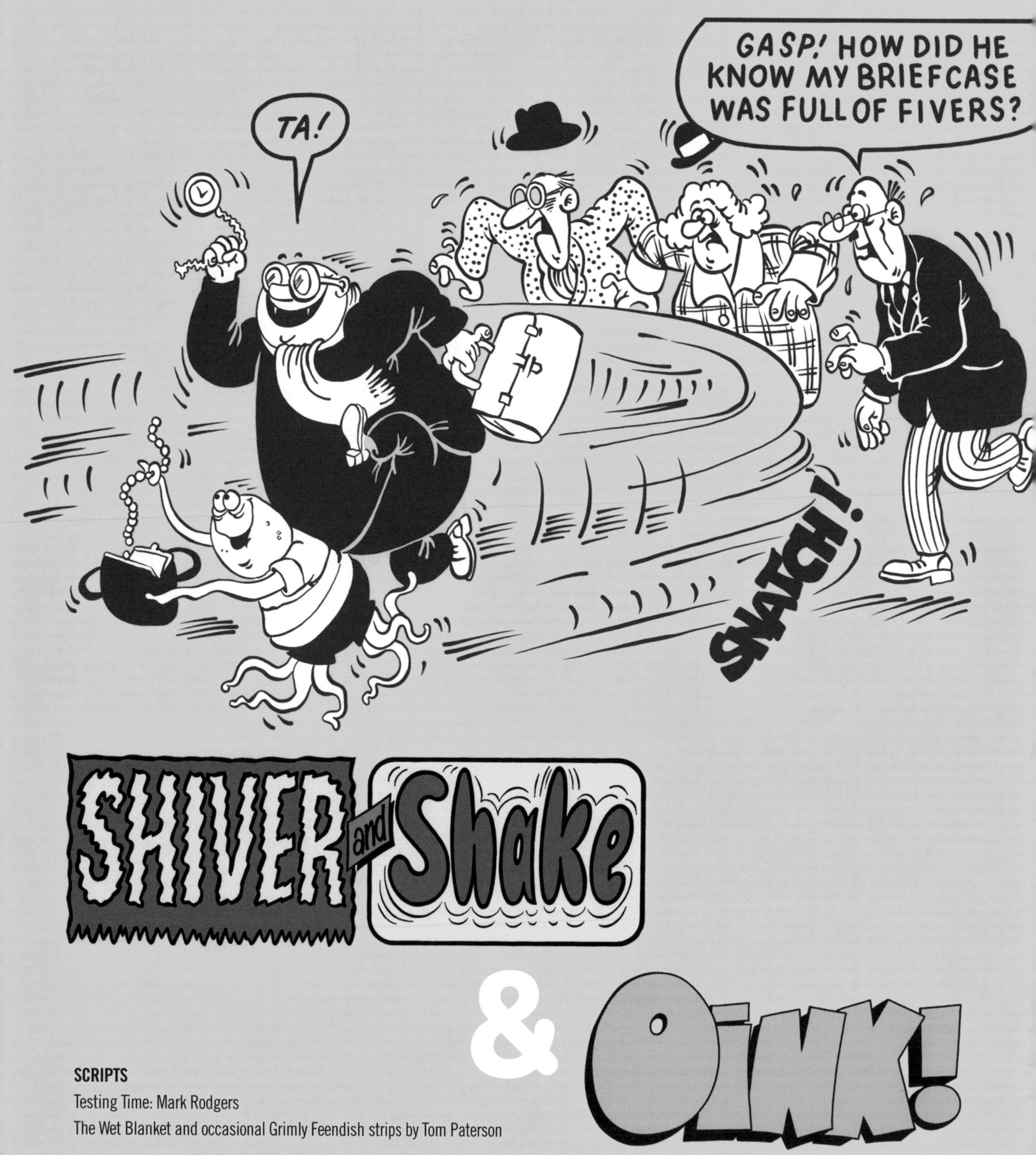
TA!
GASP! HOW DID HE KNOW MY BRIEFCASE WAS FULL OF FIVERS?
SNATCH!

# SHIVER and Shake & OINK!

**SCRIPTS**

Testing Time: Mark Rodgers

The Wet Blanket and occasional Grimly Feendish strips by Tom Paterson

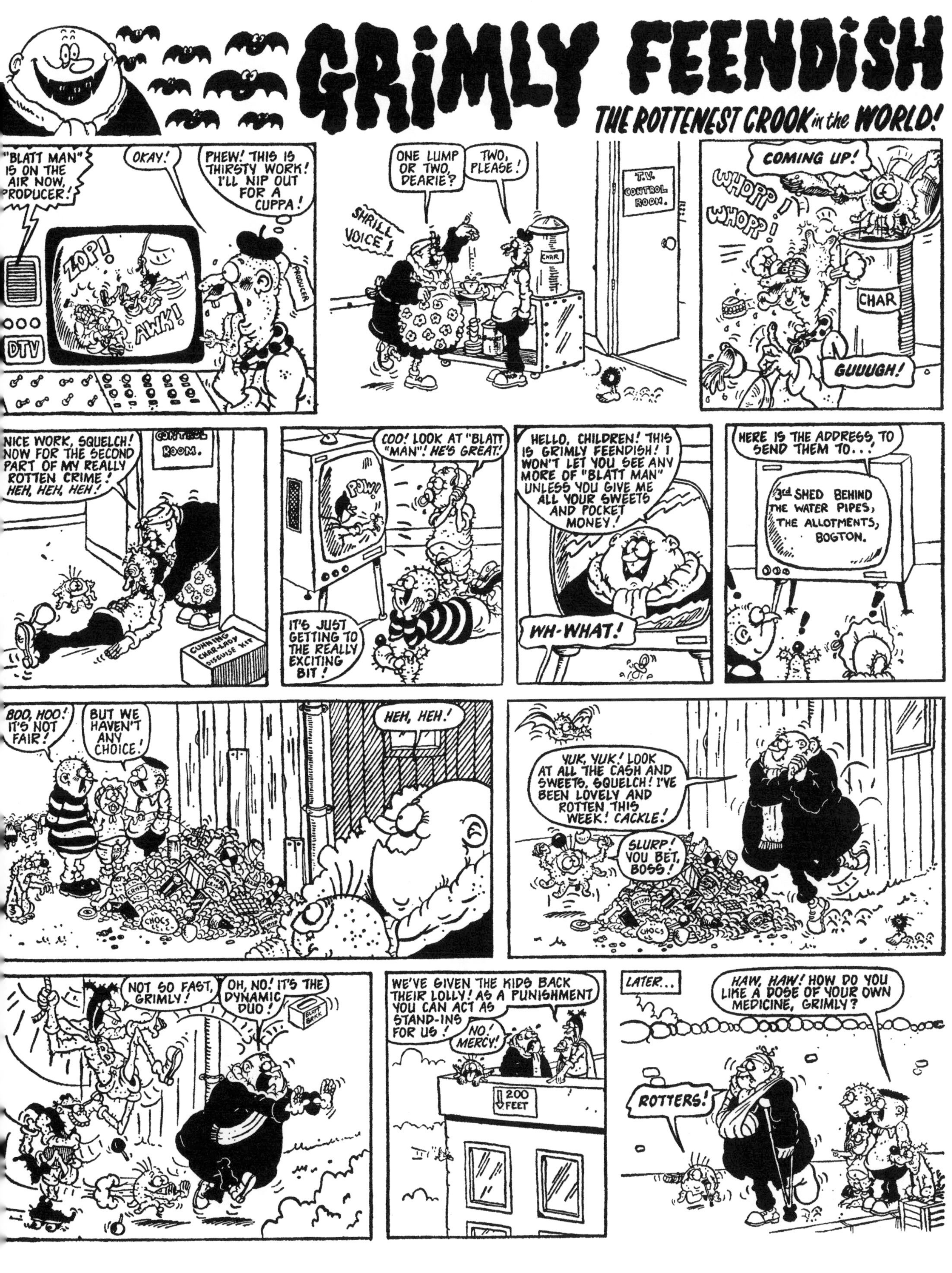
GRIMLY FEENDISH
THE ROTTENEST CROOK in the WORLD!
"BLATT MAN" IS ON THE AIR NOW, PRODUCER!
OKAY!
PHEW! THIS IS THIRSTY WORK! I'LL NIP OUT FOR A CUPPA!
ZOP!
AWK!
DTV
PRODUCER
ONE LUMP OR TWO, DEARIE?
TWO, PLEASE!
SHRILL VOICE!
CHAR
T.V. CONTROL ROOM.
COMING UP!
WHOPP! WHOPP!
CHAR
GUUUGH!
NICE WORK, SQUELCH! NOW FOR THE SECOND PART OF MY REALLY ROTTEN CRIME! HEH, HEH, HEH!
CONTROL ROOM.
CUNNING CHAR-LADY DISGUISE KIT
COO! LOOK AT "BLATT MAN"! HE'S GREAT!
POW!
IT'S JUST GETTING TO THE REALLY EXCITING BIT!
HELLO, CHILDREN! THIS IS GRIMLY FEENDISH! I WON'T LET YOU SEE ANY MORE OF "BLATT MAN" UNLESS YOU GIVE ME ALL YOUR SWEETS AND POCKET MONEY!
WH-WHAT!
HERE IS THE ADDRESS, TO SEND THEM TO...
3rd SHED BEHIND THE WATER PIPES, THE ALLOTMENTS, BOGTON.
BOO, HOO! IT'S NOT FAIR!
BUT WE HAVEN'T ANY CHOICE!
HEH, HEH!
CRISPS
CHOCS
YUK, YUK! LOOK AT ALL THE CASH AND SWEETS, SQUELCH! I'VE BEEN LOVELY AND ROTTEN THIS WEEK! CACKLE!
SLURP! YOU BET, BOSS!
CRISPS
CHOCS
NOT SO FAST, GRIMLY!
OH, NO! IT'S THE DYNAMIC DUO!
WE'VE GIVEN THE KIDS BACK THEIR LOLLY! AS A PUNISHMENT YOU CAN ACT AS STAND-INS FOR US!
NO! MERCY!
200 FEET
LATER...
HAW, HAW! HOW DO YOU LIKE A DOSE OF YOUR OWN MEDICINE, GRIMLY?
ROTTERS!

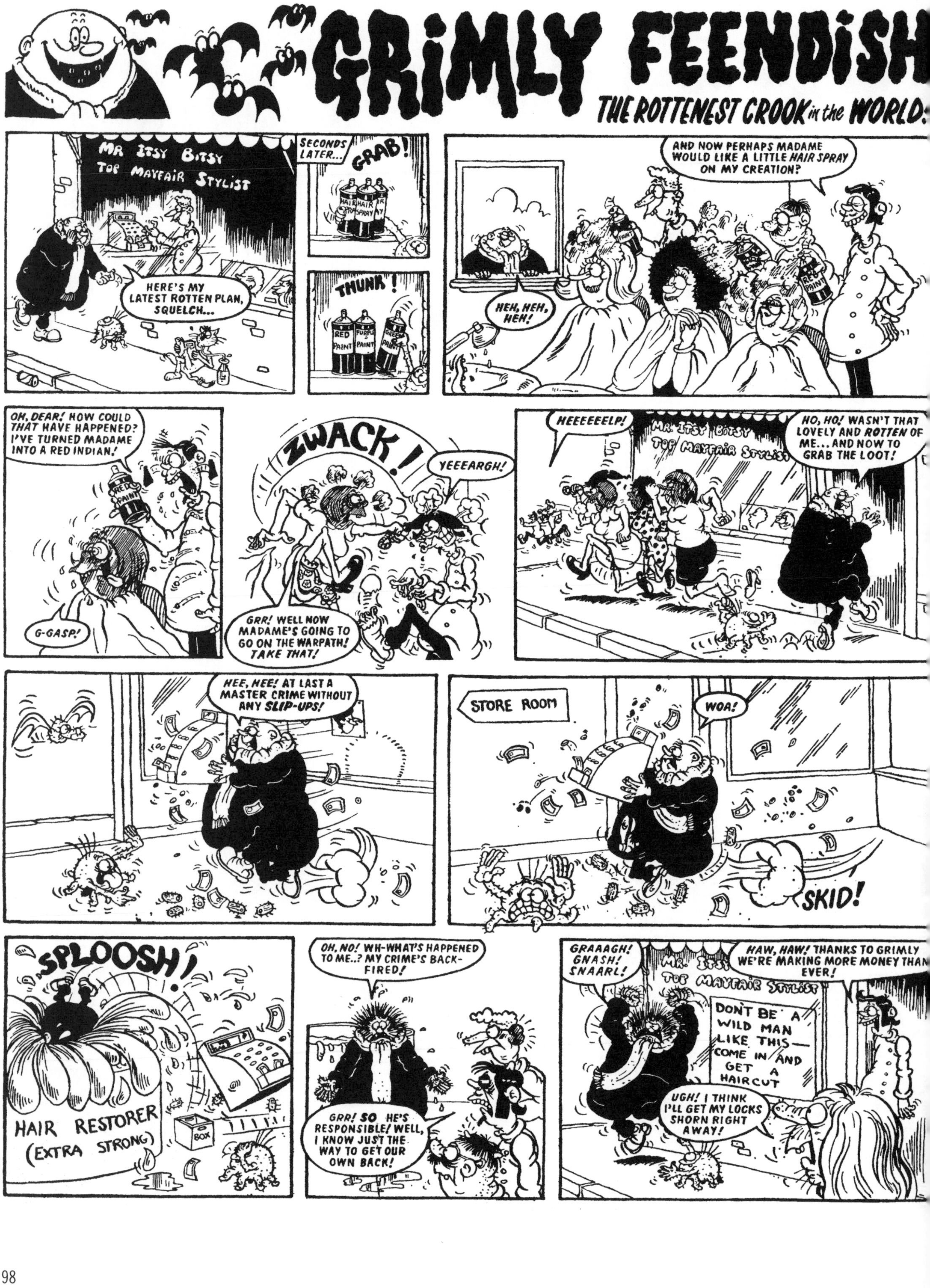
GRIMLY FEENDISH
THE ROTTENEST CROOK in the WORLD!
MR ITSY BITSY
TOP MAYFAIR STYLIST
HERE'S MY LATEST ROTTEN PLAN, SQUELCH...
SECONDS LATER...
GRAB!
HAIR SPRAY
THUNK!
RED PAINT
PURPLE PAINT
GREEN PAINT
AND NOW PERHAPS MADAME WOULD LIKE A LITTLE HAIR SPRAY ON MY CREATION?
HEH, HEH, HEH!
RED PAINT
OH, DEAR! HOW COULD THAT HAVE HAPPENED? I'VE TURNED MADAME INTO A RED INDIAN!
G-GASP!
ZWACK!
YEEEARGH!
GRR! WELL NOW MADAME'S GOING TO GO ON THE WARPATH! TAKE THAT!
HEEEEEELP!
MR. ITSY BITSY
TOP MAYFAIR STYLIST
HO, HO! WASN'T THAT LOVELY AND ROTTEN OF ME... AND NOW TO GRAB THE LOOT!
HEE, HEE! AT LAST A MASTER CRIME WITHOUT ANY SLIP-UPS!
STORE ROOM
WOA!
SKID!
SPLOOSH!
HAIR RESTORER (EXTRA STRONG)
BOX
OH, NO! WH-WHAT'S HAPPENED TO ME..? MY CRIME'S BACK-FIRED!
GRR! SO HE'S RESPONSIBLE! WELL, I KNOW JUST THE WAY TO GET OUR OWN BACK!
GRAAAGH! GNASH! SNAARL!
TOP MAYFAIR STYLIST
HAW, HAW! THANKS TO GRIMLY WE'RE MAKING MORE MONEY THAN EVER!
DON'T BE A WILD MAN LIKE THIS— COME IN AND GET A HAIRCUT
UGH! I THINK I'LL GET MY LOCKS SHORN RIGHT AWAY!

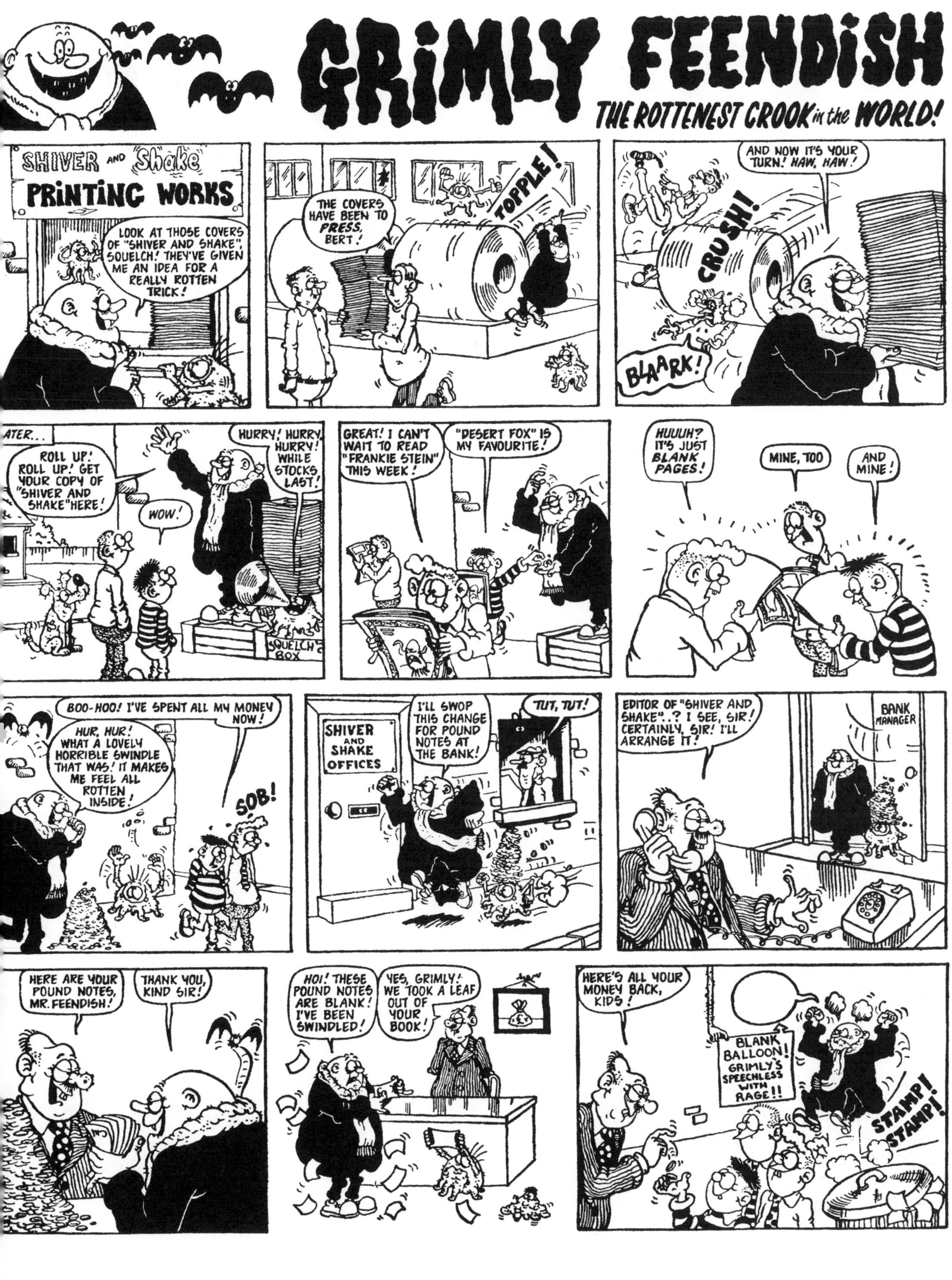
GRIMLY FEENDISH
THE ROTTENEST CROOK in the WORLD!
SHIVER AND Shake PRINTING WORKS
LOOK AT THOSE COVERS OF "SHIVER AND SHAKE", SQUELCH! THEY'VE GIVEN ME AN IDEA FOR A REALLY ROTTEN TRICK!
THE COVERS HAVE BEEN TO PRESS, BERT!
TOPPLE!
AND NOW IT'S YOUR TURN! HAW, HAW!
CRUSH!
BLAARK!
LATER...
ROLL UP! ROLL UP! GET YOUR COPY OF "SHIVER AND SHAKE" HERE!
HURRY! HURRY! HURRY! WHILE STOCKS LAST!
WOW!
SQUELCH'S BOX
GREAT! I CAN'T WAIT TO READ "FRANKIE STEIN" THIS WEEK!
"DESERT FOX" IS MY FAVOURITE!
HUUUH? IT'S JUST BLANK PAGES!
MINE, TOO
AND MINE!
BOO-HOO! I'VE SPENT ALL MY MONEY NOW!
HUR, HUR! WHAT A LOVELY HORRIBLE SWINDLE THAT WAS! IT MAKES ME FEEL ALL ROTTEN INSIDE!
SOB!
SHIVER AND SHAKE OFFICES
I'LL SWOP THIS CHANGE FOR POUND NOTES AT THE BANK!
TUT, TUT!
EDITOR OF "SHIVER AND SHAKE"..? I SEE, SIR! CERTAINLY, SIR! I'LL ARRANGE IT!
BANK MANAGER
HERE ARE YOUR POUND NOTES, MR. FEENDISH!
THANK YOU, KIND SIR!
HOI! THESE POUND NOTES ARE BLANK! I'VE BEEN SWINDLED!
YES, GRIMLY! WE TOOK A LEAF OUT OF YOUR BOOK!
HERE'S ALL YOUR MONEY BACK, KIDS!
BLANK BALLOON! GRIMLY'S SPEECHLESS WITH RAGE!!
STAMP! STAMP!

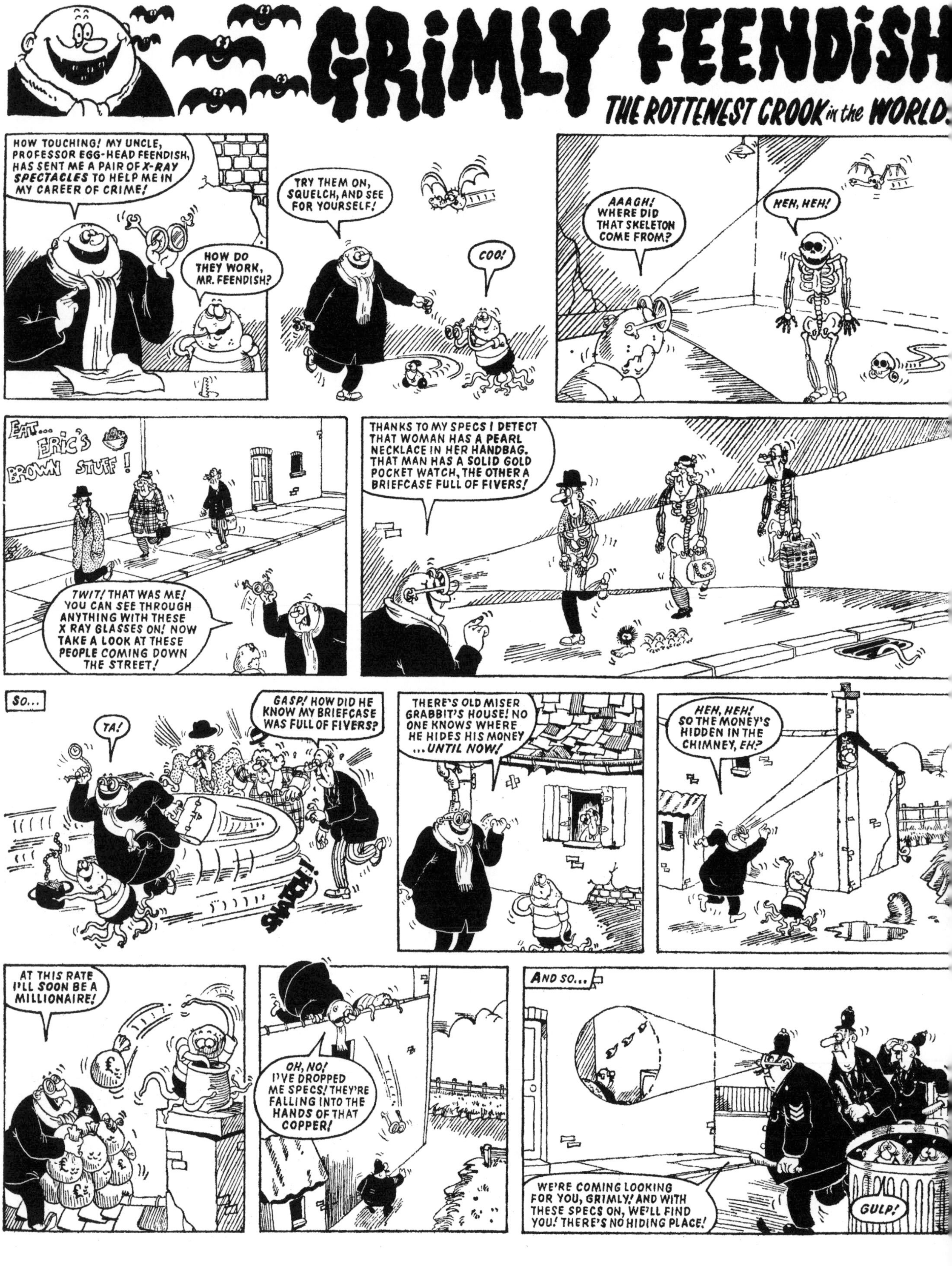
GRIMLY FEENDISH
THE ROTTENEST CROOK in the WORLD.
HOW TOUCHING! MY UNCLE, PROFESSOR EGG-HEAD FEENDISH, HAS SENT ME A PAIR OF X-RAY SPECTACLES TO HELP ME IN MY CAREER OF CRIME!
HOW DO THEY WORK, MR. FEENDISH?
TRY THEM ON, SQUELCH, AND SEE FOR YOURSELF!
COO!
AAAGH! WHERE DID THAT SKELETON COME FROM?
HEH, HEH!
EAT... ERIC'S BROWN STUFF!
TWIT! THAT WAS ME! YOU CAN SEE THROUGH ANYTHING WITH THESE X RAY GLASSES ON! NOW TAKE A LOOK AT THESE PEOPLE COMING DOWN THE STREET!
THANKS TO MY SPECS I DETECT THAT WOMAN HAS A PEARL NECKLACE IN HER HANDBAG. THAT MAN HAS A SOLID GOLD POCKET WATCH, THE OTHER A BRIEFCASE FULL OF FIVERS!
SO...
TA!
GASP! HOW DID HE KNOW MY BRIEFCASE WAS FULL OF FIVERS?
SNATCH!
THERE'S OLD MISER GRABBIT'S HOUSE! NO ONE KNOWS WHERE HE HIDES HIS MONEY ...UNTIL NOW!
HEH, HEH! SO THE MONEY'S HIDDEN IN THE CHIMNEY, EH?
AT THIS RATE I'LL SOON BE A MILLIONAIRE!
OH, NO! I'VE DROPPED ME SPECS! THEY'RE FALLING INTO THE HANDS OF THAT COPPER!
AND SO...
WE'RE COMING LOOKING FOR YOU, GRIMLY! AND WITH THESE SPECS ON, WE'LL FIND YOU! THERE'S NO HIDING PLACE!
GULP!

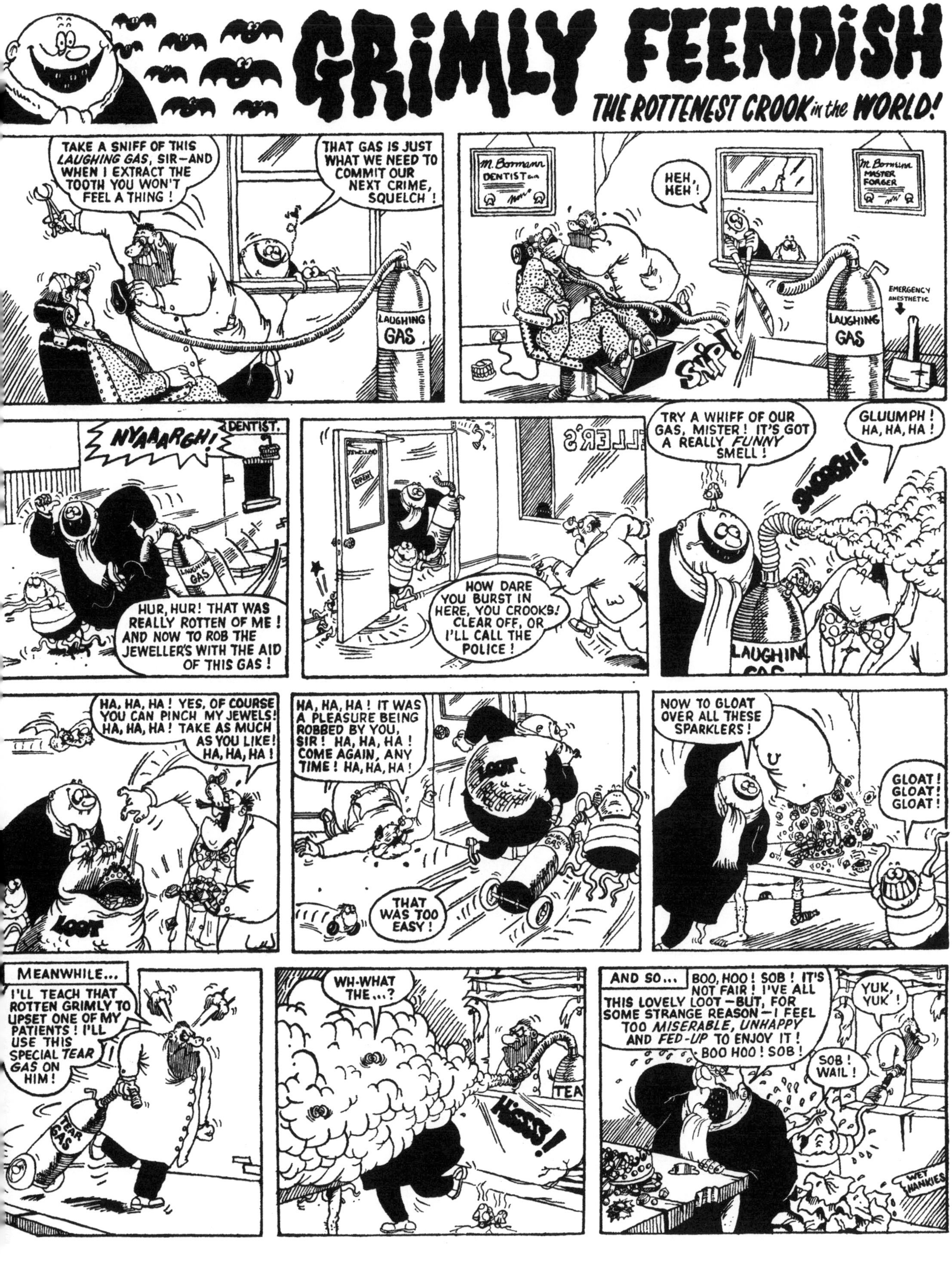
GRIMLY FEENDISH
THE ROTTENEST CROOK in the WORLD!
TAKE A SNIFF OF THIS *LAUGHING GAS*, SIR—AND WHEN I EXTRACT THE TOOTH YOU WON'T FEEL A THING!
THAT GAS IS JUST WHAT WE NEED TO COMMIT OUR NEXT CRIME, SQUELCH!
LAUGHING GAS
M. Bormann DENTIST
HEH, HEH!
M. Bormann MASTER FORGER
EMERGENCY ANESTHETIC
SNIP!
LAUGHING GAS
NYAAARGH!
DENTIST.
HUR, HUR! THAT WAS REALLY ROTTEN OF ME! AND NOW TO ROB THE JEWELLER'S WITH THE AID OF THIS GAS!
HOW DARE YOU BURST IN HERE, YOU CROOKS! CLEAR OFF, OR I'LL CALL THE POLICE!
TRY A WHIFF OF OUR GAS, MISTER! IT'S GOT A REALLY *FUNNY* SMELL!
GLUUMPH! HA, HA, HA!
SWOOSH!
LAUGHING GAS
HA, HA, HA! YES, OF COURSE YOU CAN PINCH MY JEWELS! HA, HA, HA! TAKE AS MUCH AS YOU LIKE! HA, HA, HA!
LOOT
HA, HA, HA! IT WAS A PLEASURE BEING ROBBED BY YOU, SIR! HA, HA, HA! COME AGAIN, ANY TIME! HA, HA, HA!
LOOT
THAT WAS TOO EASY!
NOW TO GLOAT OVER ALL THESE SPARKLERS!
GLOAT! GLOAT! GLOAT!
MEANWHILE...
I'LL TEACH THAT ROTTEN GRIMLY TO UPSET ONE OF MY PATIENTS! I'LL USE THIS SPECIAL *TEAR GAS* ON HIM!
TEAR GAS
WH-WHAT THE...?
TEAR
HISSS!
AND SO...
BOO, HOO! SOB! IT'S NOT FAIR! I'VE ALL THIS LOVELY LOOT—BUT, FOR SOME STRANGE REASON—I FEEL TOO *MISERABLE*, *UNHAPPY* AND *FED-UP* TO ENJOY IT! BOO HOO! SOB!
YUK, YUK!
SOB! WAIL!
WET HANKIES

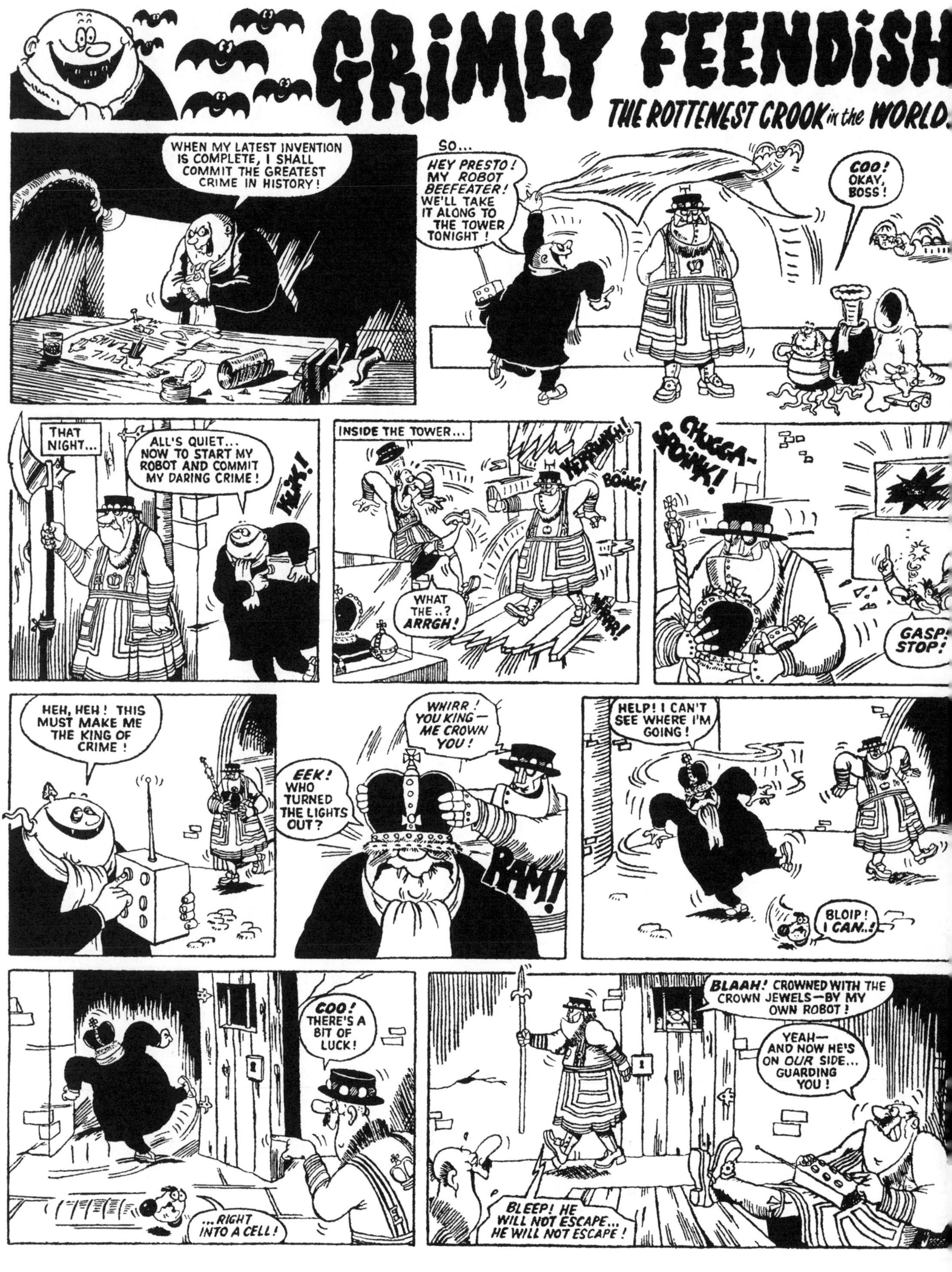
GRIMLY FEENDISH
THE ROTTENEST CROOK in the WORLD
WHEN MY LATEST INVENTION IS COMPLETE, I SHALL COMMIT THE GREATEST CRIME IN HISTORY!
EVIL PLANS
SO...
HEY PRESTO! MY ROBOT BEEFEATER! WE'LL TAKE IT ALONG TO THE TOWER TONIGHT!
COO! OKAY, BOSS!
THAT NIGHT...
ALL'S QUIET... NOW TO START MY ROBOT AND COMMIT MY DARING CRIME!
INSIDE THE TOWER...
BOING!
WHAT THE..? ARRGH!
WHIRR!
CHUGGA-SPOINK!
GASP! STOP!
HEH, HEH! THIS MUST MAKE ME THE KING OF CRIME!
WHIRR! YOU KING— ME CROWN YOU!
EEK! WHO TURNED THE LIGHTS OUT?
RAM!
HELP! I CAN'T SEE WHERE I'M GOING!
BLOIP! I CAN..!
COO! THERE'S A BIT OF LUCK!
...RIGHT INTO A CELL!
BLAAH! CROWNED WITH THE CROWN JEWELS—BY MY OWN ROBOT!
YEAH— AND NOW HE'S ON OUR SIDE... GUARDING YOU!
BLEEP! HE WILL NOT ESCAPE... HE WILL NOT ESCAPE!

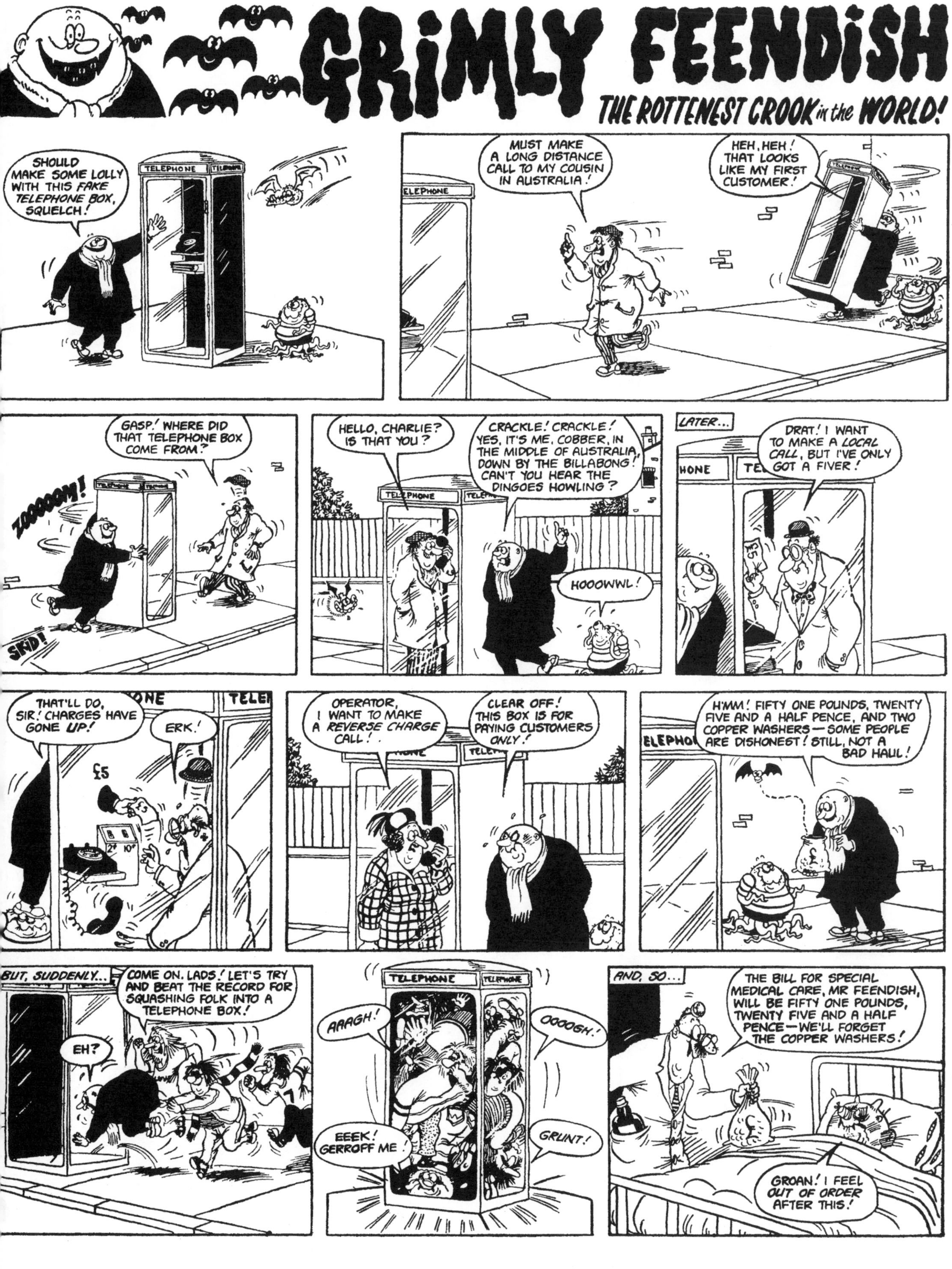
GRIMLY FEENDISH
THE ROTTENEST CROOK in the WORLD!
SHOULD MAKE SOME LOLLY WITH THIS FAKE TELEPHONE BOX, SQUELCH!
TELEPHONE
MUST MAKE A LONG DISTANCE CALL TO MY COUSIN IN AUSTRALIA!
HEH, HEH! THAT LOOKS LIKE MY FIRST CUSTOMER!
GASP! WHERE DID THAT TELEPHONE BOX COME FROM?
ZOOOOOM!
SKID!
HELLO, CHARLIE? IS THAT YOU?
CRACKLE! CRACKLE! YES, IT'S ME, COBBER, IN THE MIDDLE OF AUSTRALIA DOWN BY THE BILLABONG! CAN'T YOU HEAR THE DINGOES HOWLING?
HOOOWWL!
LATER...
DRAT! I WANT TO MAKE A LOCAL CALL, BUT I'VE ONLY GOT A FIVER!
THAT'LL DO, SIR! CHARGES HAVE GONE UP!
ERK!
OPERATOR, I WANT TO MAKE A REVERSE CHARGE CALL!
CLEAR OFF! THIS BOX IS FOR PAYING CUSTOMERS ONLY!
H'MM! FIFTY ONE POUNDS, TWENTY FIVE AND A HALF PENCE, AND TWO COPPER WASHERS—SOME PEOPLE ARE DISHONEST! STILL, NOT A BAD HAUL!
BUT, SUDDENLY...
COME ON, LADS! LET'S TRY AND BEAT THE RECORD FOR SQUASHING FOLK INTO A TELEPHONE BOX!
EH?
AAAGH!
OOOOGH!
EEEK! GERROFF ME!
GRUNT!
AND, SO...
THE BILL FOR SPECIAL MEDICAL CARE, MR FEENDISH, WILL BE FIFTY ONE POUNDS, TWENTY FIVE AND A HALF PENCE—WE'LL FORGET THE COPPER WASHERS!
GROAN! I FEEL OUT OF ORDER AFTER THIS!

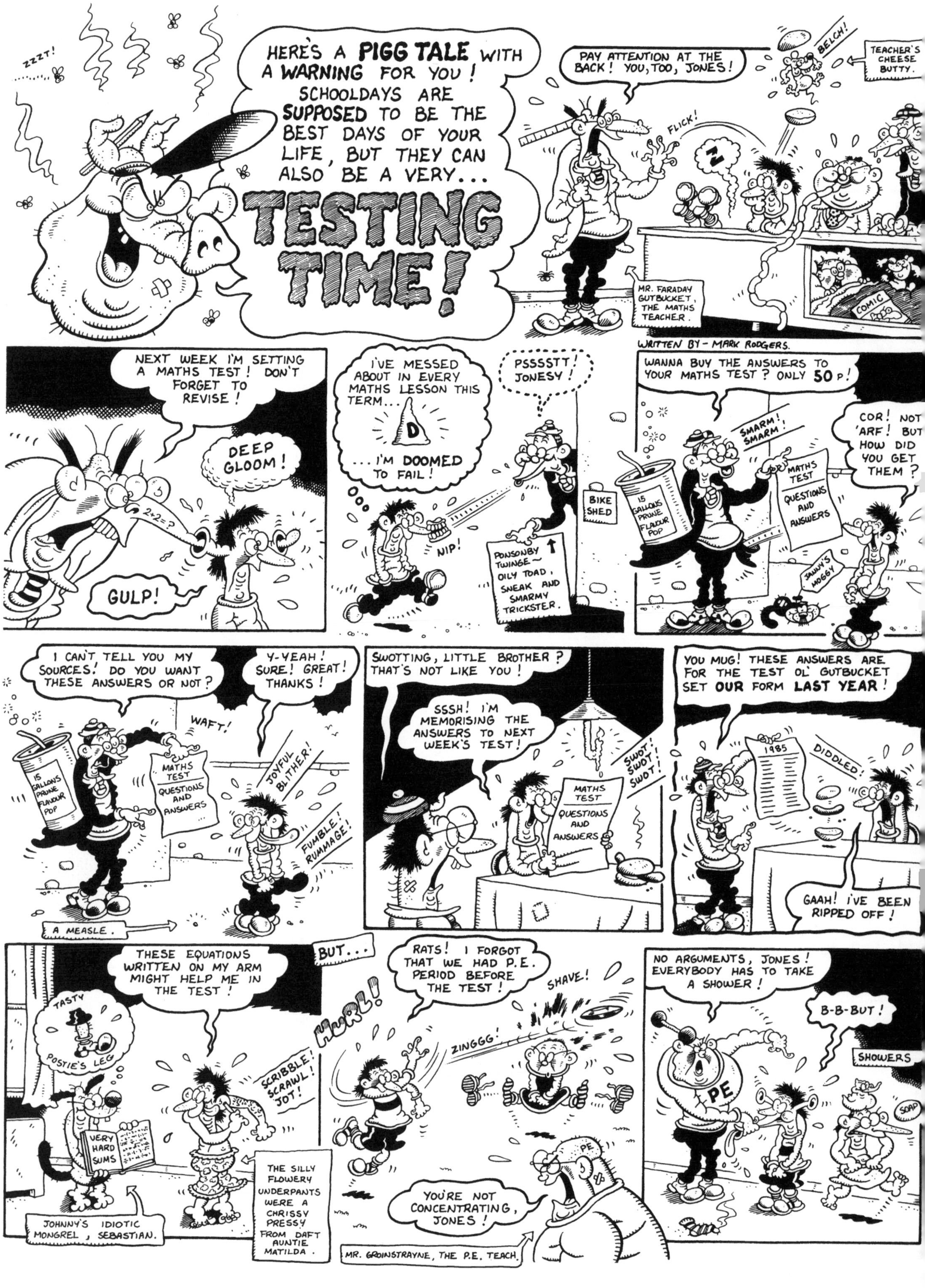
ZZZT!
HERE'S A PIGG TALE WITH A WARNING FOR YOU! SCHOOLDAYS ARE SUPPOSED TO BE THE BEST DAYS OF YOUR LIFE, BUT THEY CAN ALSO BE A VERY...
TESTING TIME!
PAY ATTENTION AT THE BACK! YOU, TOO, JONES!
BELCH!
TEACHER'S CHEESE BUTTY.
FLICK!
Z
MR. FARADAY GUTBUCKET, THE MATHS TEACHER.
COMIC
WRITTEN BY - MARK RODGERS.
NEXT WEEK I'M SETTING A MATHS TEST! DON'T FORGET TO REVISE!
DEEP GLOOM!
2+2=?
GULP!
I'VE MESSED ABOUT IN EVERY MATHS LESSON THIS TERM... D ...I'M DOOMED TO FAIL!
OOO
NIP!
PSSSSTT! JONESY!
BIKE SHED
PONSONBY TWINGE ~ OILY TOAD, SNEAK AND SMARMY TRICKSTER.
WANNA BUY THE ANSWERS TO YOUR MATHS TEST? ONLY 50 P!
SMARM! SMARM!
15 GALLONS PRUNE FLAVOUR POP
MATHS TEST QUESTIONS AND ANSWERS
COR! NOT 'ARF! BUT HOW DID YOU GET THEM?
JANNY'S MOGGY
I CAN'T TELL YOU MY SOURCES! DO YOU WANT THESE ANSWERS OR NOT?
Y-YEAH! SURE! GREAT! THANKS!
WAFT!
15 GALLONS PRUNE FLAVOUR POP
MATHS TEST QUESTIONS AND ANSWERS
JOYFUL BLITHER!
FUMBLE! RUMMAGE!
A MEASLE.
SWOTTING, LITTLE BROTHER? THAT'S NOT LIKE YOU!
SSSH! I'M MEMORISING THE ANSWERS TO NEXT WEEK'S TEST!
SWOT! SWOT! SWOT!
MATHS TEST QUESTIONS AND ANSWERS
YOU MUG! THESE ANSWERS ARE FOR THE TEST OL' GUTBUCKET SET OUR FORM LAST YEAR!
1985
DIDDLED!
GAAH! I'VE BEEN RIPPED OFF!
THESE EQUATIONS WRITTEN ON MY ARM MIGHT HELP ME IN THE TEST!
TASTY POSTIE'S LEG
VERY HARD SUMS
SCRIBBLE! SCRAWL! JOT!
JOHNNY'S IDIOTIC MONGREL, SEBASTIAN.
THE SILLY FLOWERY UNDERPANTS WERE A CHRISSY PRESSY FROM DAFT AUNTIE MATILDA.
BUT...
HURL!
RATS! I FORGOT THAT WE HAD P.E. PERIOD BEFORE THE TEST!
SHAVE!
ZINGGG!
PE
YOU'RE NOT CONCENTRATING, JONES!
MR. GROINSTRAYNE, THE P.E. TEACH.
NO ARGUMENTS, JONES! EVERYBODY HAS TO TAKE A SHOWER!
B-B-BUT!
SHOWERS
PE
SOAP

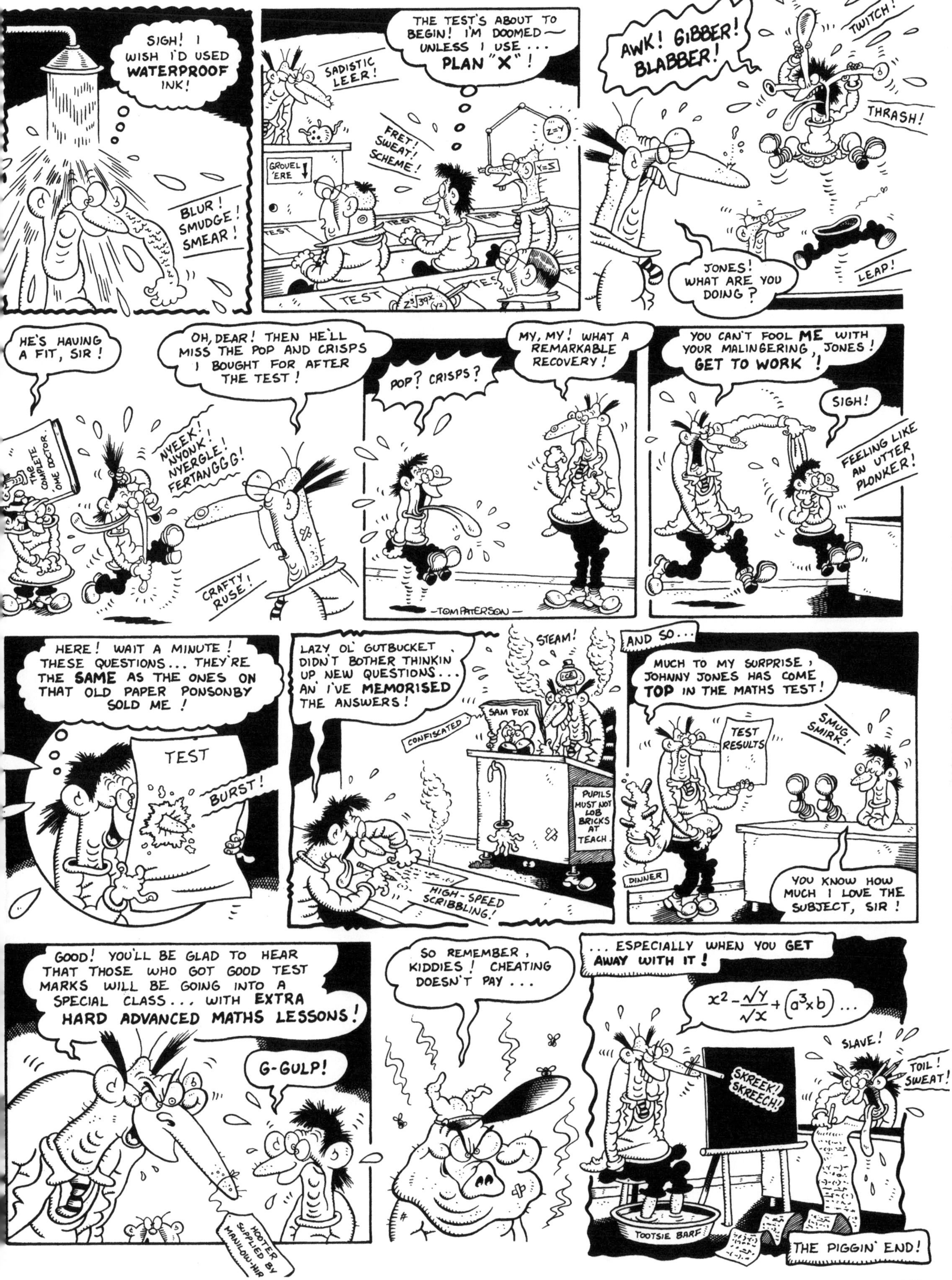

SIGH! I WISH I'D USED WATERPROOF INK!
BLUR! SMUDGE! SMEAR!
THE TEST'S ABOUT TO BEGIN! I'M DOOMED — UNLESS I USE... PLAN "X"!
SADISTIC LEER!
FRET! SWEAT! SCHEME!
GROUEL 'ERE
TEST
AWK! GIBBER! BLABBER!
TWITCH!
THRASH!
JONES! WHAT ARE YOU DOING?
LEAP!
HE'S HAVING A FIT, SIR!
THE COMPLETE 'OME DOCTOR
OH, DEAR! THEN HE'LL MISS THE POP AND CRISPS I BOUGHT FOR AFTER THE TEST!
NYEEK! NYONK! NYERGLE! FERTANGGG!
CRAFTY RUSE!
POP? CRISPS?
MY, MY! WHAT A REMARKABLE RECOVERY!
—TOM PATERSON—
YOU CAN'T FOOL ME WITH YOUR MALINGERING, JONES! GET TO WORK!
SIGH!
FEELING LIKE AN UTTER PLONKER!
HERE! WAIT A MINUTE! THESE QUESTIONS... THEY'RE THE SAME AS THE ONES ON THAT OLD PAPER PONSONBY SOLD ME!
TEST
BURST!
LAZY OL' GUTBUCKET DIDN'T BOTHER THINKIN UP NEW QUESTIONS... AN' I'VE MEMORISED THE ANSWERS!
STEAM!
SAM FOX
CONFISCATED
PUPILS MUST NOT LOB BRICKS AT TEACH.
HIGH-SPEED SCRIBBLING!
AND SO...
MUCH TO MY SURPRISE, JOHNNY JONES HAS COME TOP IN THE MATHS TEST!
TEST RESULTS
SMUG SMIRK!
DINNER
YOU KNOW HOW MUCH I LOVE THE SUBJECT, SIR!
GOOD! YOU'LL BE GLAD TO HEAR THAT THOSE WHO GOT GOOD TEST MARKS WILL BE GOING INTO A SPECIAL CLASS... WITH EXTRA HARD ADVANCED MATHS LESSONS!
G-GULP!
HOOTER SUPPLIED BY MANILOW-HIR
SO REMEMBER, KIDDIES! CHEATING DOESN'T PAY...
... ESPECIALLY WHEN YOU GET AWAY WITH IT!
SLAVE!
SKREEK! SKREECH!
TOIL! SWEAT!
TOOTSIE BARF
THE PIGGIN' END!

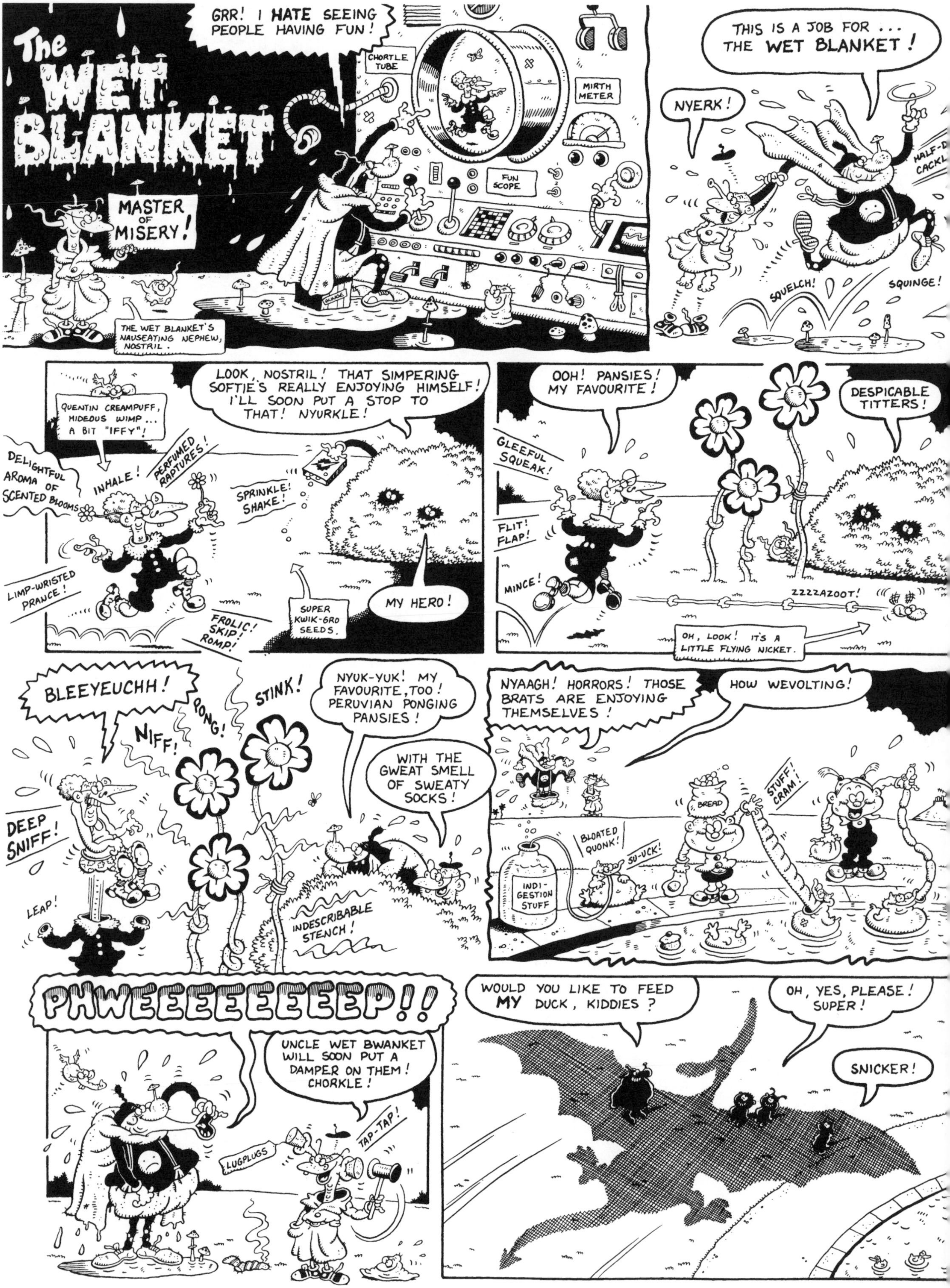
The WET BLANKET
MASTER OF MISERY!
GRR! I HATE SEEING PEOPLE HAVING FUN!
CHORTLE TUBE
MIRTH METER
FUN SCOPE
THE WET BLANKET'S NAUSEATING NEPHEW, NOSTRIL.
THIS IS A JOB FOR ... THE WET BLANKET!
NYERK!
SQUELCH!
SQUINGE!
QUENTIN CREAMPUFF, HIDEOUS WIMP ... A BIT "IFFY"!
LOOK, NOSTRIL! THAT SIMPERING SOFTIE'S REALLY ENJOYING HIMSELF! I'LL SOON PUT A STOP TO THAT! NYURKLE!
DELIGHTFUL AROMA OF SCENTED BLOOMS
INHALE!
PERFUMED RAPTURES!
SPRINKLE! SHAKE!
LIMP-WRISTED PRANCE!
FROLIC! SKIP! ROMP!
SUPER KWIK-GRO SEEDS.
MY HERO!
OOH! PANSIES! MY FAVOURITE!
DESPICABLE TITTERS!
GLEEFUL SQUEAK!
FLIT! FLAP!
MINCE!
ZZZZAZOOT!
OH, LOOK! IT'S A LITTLE FLYING NICKET.
BLEEYEUCHH!
STINK!
PONG!
NIFF!
NYUK-YUK! MY FAVOURITE, TOO! PERUVIAN PONGING PANSIES!
WITH THE GWEAT SMELL OF SWEATY SOCKS!
DEEP SNIFF!
LEAP!
INDESCRIBABLE STENCH!
NYAAGH! HORRORS! THOSE BRATS ARE ENJOYING THEMSELVES!
HOW WEVOLTING!
BREAD
STUFF! CRAM!
BLOATED QUONK!
SU-UCK!
INDI-GESTION STUFF
PHWEEEEEEEEEP!!
UNCLE WET BWANKET WILL SOON PUT A DAMPER ON THEM! CHORKLE!
LUGPLUGS
TAP-TAP!
WOULD YOU LIKE TO FEED MY DUCK, KIDDIES?
OH, YES, PLEASE! SUPER!
SNICKER!

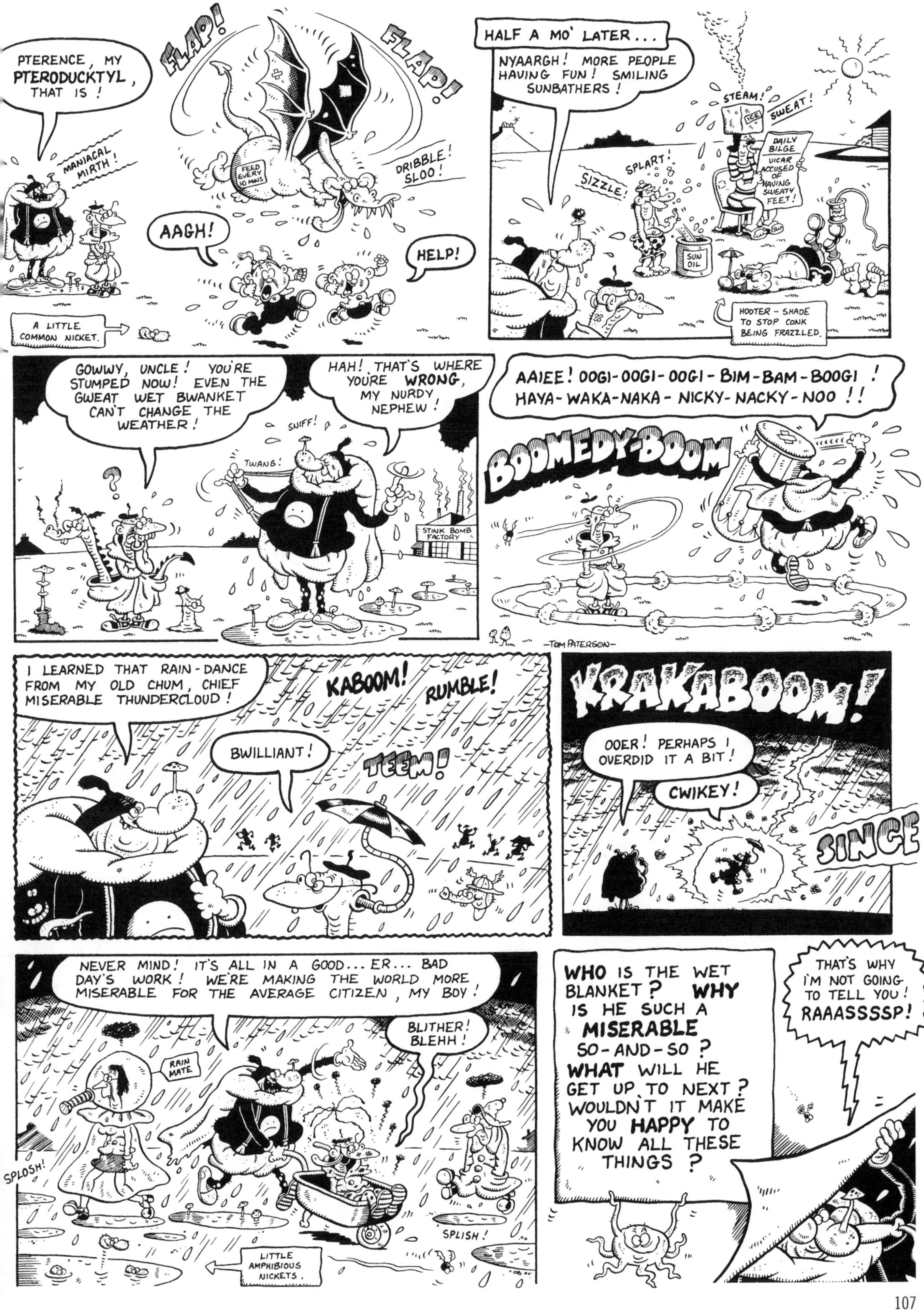

PTERENCE, MY PTERODUCKTYL, THAT IS!
FLAP! FLAP!
MANIACAL MIRTH!
FEED EVERY 10 MINS
DRIBBLE! SLOO!
AAGH!
HELP!
A LITTLE COMMON NICKET.
HALF A MO' LATER...
NYAARGH! MORE PEOPLE HAVING FUN! SMILING SUNBATHERS!
STEAM!
ICE
SWEAT!
DAILY BILGE VICAR ACCUSED OF HAVING SWEATY FEET!
SPLART!
SIZZLE!
SUN OIL
HOOTER - SHADE TO STOP CONK BEING FRAZZLED.
GOWWY, UNCLE! YOU'RE STUMPED NOW! EVEN THE GWEAT WET BWANKET CAN'T CHANGE THE WEATHER!
HAH! THAT'S WHERE YOU'RE WRONG, MY NURDY NEPHEW!
SNIFF!
TWANG!
STINK BOMB FACTORY
AAIEE! OOGI-OOGI-OOGI-BIM-BAM-BOOGI! HAYA-WAKA-NAKA-NICKY-NACKY-NOO!!
BOOMEDY-BOOM
-TOM PATERSON-
I LEARNED THAT RAIN-DANCE FROM MY OLD CHUM, CHIEF MISERABLE THUNDERCLOUD!
KABOOM!
RUMBLE!
BWILLIANT!
TEEM!
KRAKABOOM!
OOER! PERHAPS I OVERDID IT A BIT!
CWIKEY!
SINGE
NEVER MIND! IT'S ALL IN A GOOD... ER... BAD DAY'S WORK! WE'RE MAKING THE WORLD MORE MISERABLE FOR THE AVERAGE CITIZEN, MY BOY!
BLITHER! BLEHH!
RAIN MATE
SPLOSH!
SPLISH!
LITTLE AMPHIBIOUS NICKETS.
WHO IS THE WET BLANKET? WHY IS HE SUCH A MISERABLE SO-AND-SO? WHAT WILL HE GET UP TO NEXT? WOULDN'T IT MAKE YOU HAPPY TO KNOW ALL THESE THINGS?
THAT'S WHY I'M NOT GOING TO TELL YOU! RAAASSSSP!

# WHIZZER AND CHIPS

# & WHOOPEE!

# & WOW!

**SCRIPTS**

Sweeny Toddler: Graham Exton

Watford Gapp: Roger Fitton

Script contributions throughout by Tom Paterson

# ROGER FITTON
## WRITER — TARMAN, BUMPKIN BILLIONAIRES, WATFORD GAPP

**NEVER HAD** any direct contact with Tom — in the pre-internet age, it was relatively easy to stop people communicating with each other in the way that is commonplace now. All I ever heard about him was that he liked drawing scenes involving Outer Space — according to my first IPC Editor Bob Paynter and that he was `difficult' according to the second one, John Smith. I have guessed — perhaps wrongly — that John's idea of `difficult' actually meant that Tom was not prepared to accept less than the pittance he was almost certainly being paid for the brilliant stuff he produced. (I was desperate at the time and I did.) But I may be mistaken...

# GRAHAM EXTON
## WRITER — SWEENY TODDLER, GUMS, FACEACHE, SID'S SNAKE

**TOM AND I** have never communicated like normal people. It was always through the medium of *Sweeny Toddler*. As we got to know one another the strips got better and better. One example is the Judge Sweeny cover for **Whoopee** comic. I had done a few fill - in scripts for *Sweeny*, but it was the Judge Sweeny one that got me the gig full -time. I did a mock- up of the front page and Tom drew it properly (and hilariously.) *Sweeny*'s imagination got wackier and wackier, Henry Dog and Tiddles had their own subplots and Dozy Dad collected toads.

Such was my regard for Tom's work that I lost interest in *Sweeny* when he moved to Thomsons. The new artists were competent, but the sweaty socks and animal antics (sometimes scripted but often not) were missing, and it became just another strip.

LEAP!

POLICE

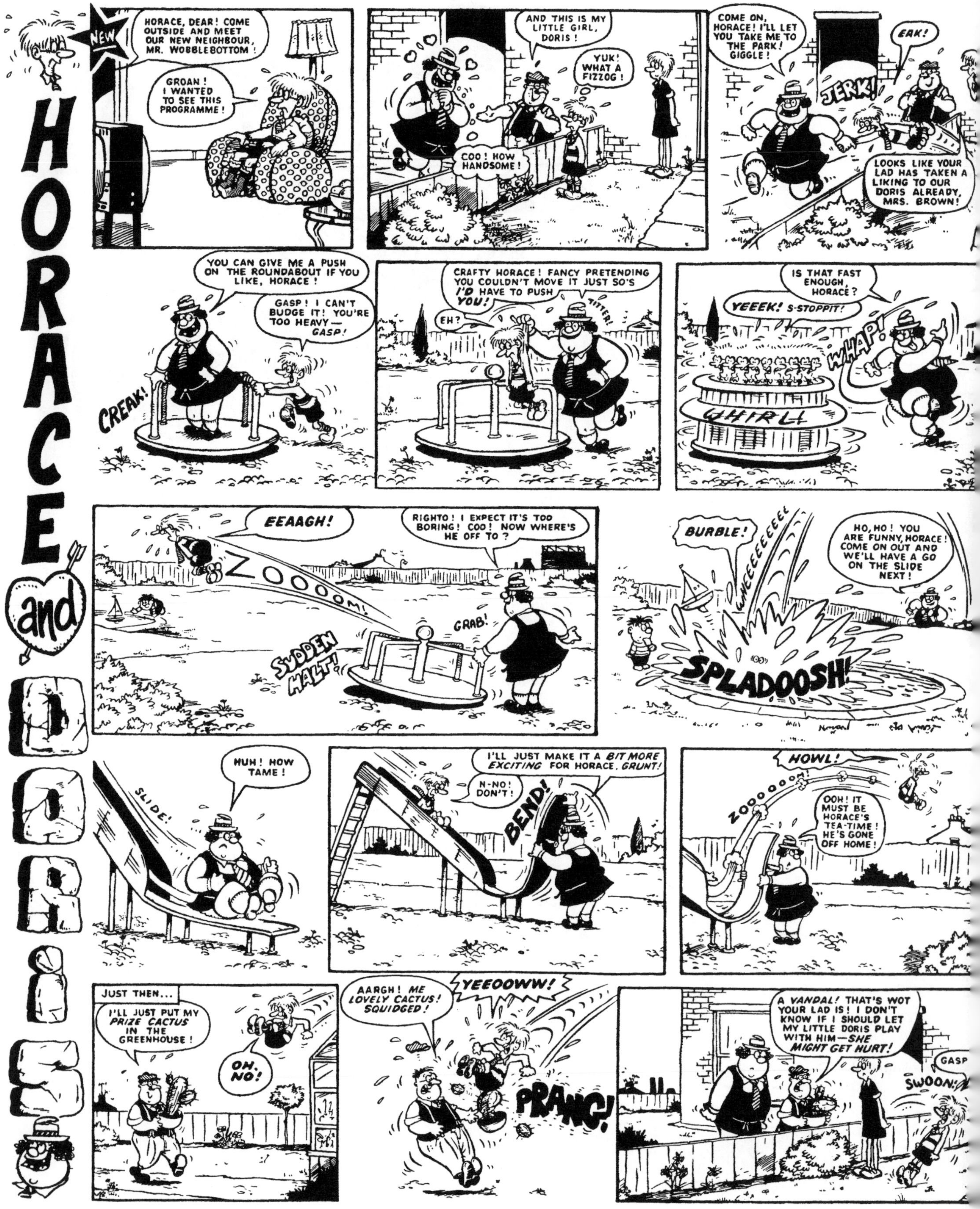
NEW
HORACE and DORIS
HORACE, DEAR! COME OUTSIDE AND MEET OUR NEW NEIGHBOUR, MR. WOBBLEBOTTOM!
GROAN! I WANTED TO SEE THIS PROGRAMME!
AND THIS IS MY LITTLE GIRL, DORIS!
YUK! WHAT A FIZZOG!
COO! HOW HANDSOME!
COME ON, HORACE! I'LL LET YOU TAKE ME TO THE PARK! GIGGLE!
EAK!
JERK!
LOOKS LIKE YOUR LAD HAS TAKEN A LIKING TO OUR DORIS ALREADY, MRS. BROWN!
YOU CAN GIVE ME A PUSH ON THE ROUNDABOUT IF YOU LIKE, HORACE!
GASP! I CAN'T BUDGE IT! YOU'RE TOO HEAVY— GASP!
CREAK!
CRAFTY HORACE! FANCY PRETENDING YOU COULDN'T MOVE IT JUST SO'S I'D HAVE TO PUSH YOU!
EH?
TITTER!
IS THAT FAST ENOUGH, HORACE?
YEEEK! S-STOPPIT!
WHAP!
WHIRL
EEAAGH!
RIGHTO! I EXPECT IT'S TOO BORING! COO! NOW WHERE'S HE OFF TO?
ZOOOOOM!
GRAB!
SUDDEN HALT!
BURBLE!
WHEEEEEEEEEE
HO, HO! YOU ARE FUNNY, HORACE! COME ON OUT AND WE'LL HAVE A GO ON THE SLIDE NEXT!
SPLADOOSH!
HUH! HOW TAME!
SLIDE!
I'LL JUST MAKE IT A BIT MORE EXCITING FOR HORACE. GRUNT!
N-NO! DON'T!
BEND!
HOWL!
ZOOOOOOM!
OOH! IT MUST BE HORACE'S TEA-TIME! HE'S GONE OFF HOME!
JUST THEN...
I'LL JUST PUT MY PRIZE CACTUS IN THE GREENHOUSE!
OH, NO!
AARGH! ME LOVELY CACTUS! SQUIDGED!
YEEOOWW!
PRANG!
A VANDAL! THAT'S WOT YOUR LAD IS! I DON'T KNOW IF I SHOULD LET MY LITTLE DORIS PLAY WITH HIM—SHE MIGHT GET HURT!
GASP
SWOON!

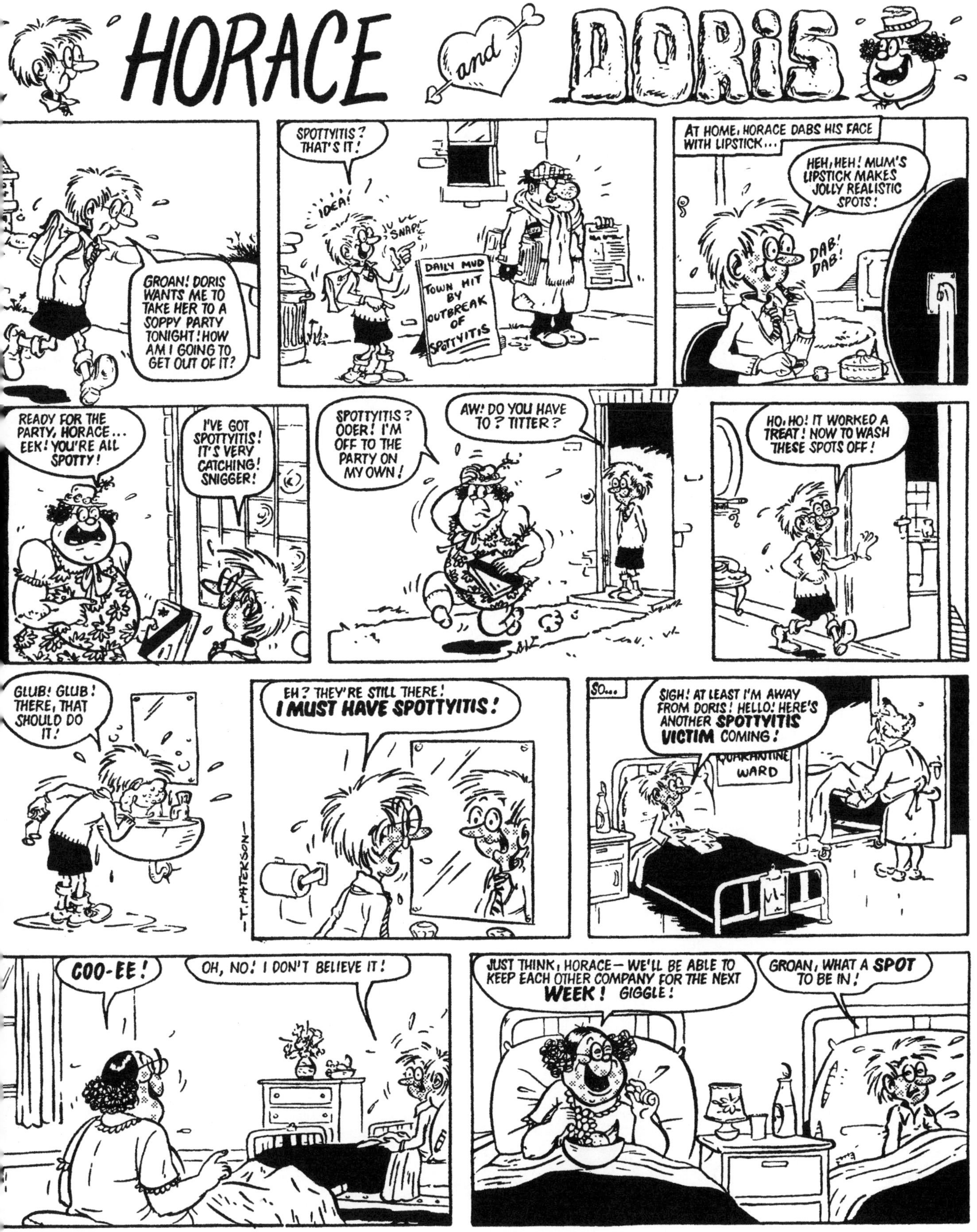
HORACE and DORIS
GROAN! DORIS WANTS ME TO TAKE HER TO A SOPPY PARTY TONIGHT! HOW AM I GOING TO GET OUT OF IT?
SPOTTYITIS? THAT'S IT!
IDEA!
SNAP!
DAILY MUD
TOWN HIT BY OUTBREAK OF SPOTTYITIS
AT HOME, HORACE DABS HIS FACE WITH LIPSTICK...
HEH, HEH! MUM'S LIPSTICK MAKES JOLLY REALISTIC SPOTS!
DAB! DAB!
READY FOR THE PARTY, HORACE... EEK! YOU'RE ALL SPOTTY!
I'VE GOT SPOTTYITIS! IT'S VERY CATCHING! SNIGGER!
SPOTTYITIS? OOER! I'M OFF TO THE PARTY ON MY OWN!
AW! DO YOU HAVE TO? TITTER?
HO, HO! IT WORKED A TREAT! NOW TO WASH THESE SPOTS OFF!
GLUB! GLUB! THERE, THAT SHOULD DO IT!
T. PATERSON
EH? THEY'RE STILL THERE! I MUST HAVE SPOTTYITIS!
SO...
SIGH! AT LEAST I'M AWAY FROM DORIS! HELLO! HERE'S ANOTHER SPOTTYITIS VICTIM COMING!
QUARANTINE WARD
COO-EE!
OH, NO! I DON'T BELIEVE IT!
JUST THINK, HORACE— WE'LL BE ABLE TO KEEP EACH OTHER COMPANY FOR THE NEXT WEEK! GIGGLE!
GROAN, WHAT A SPOT TO BE IN!

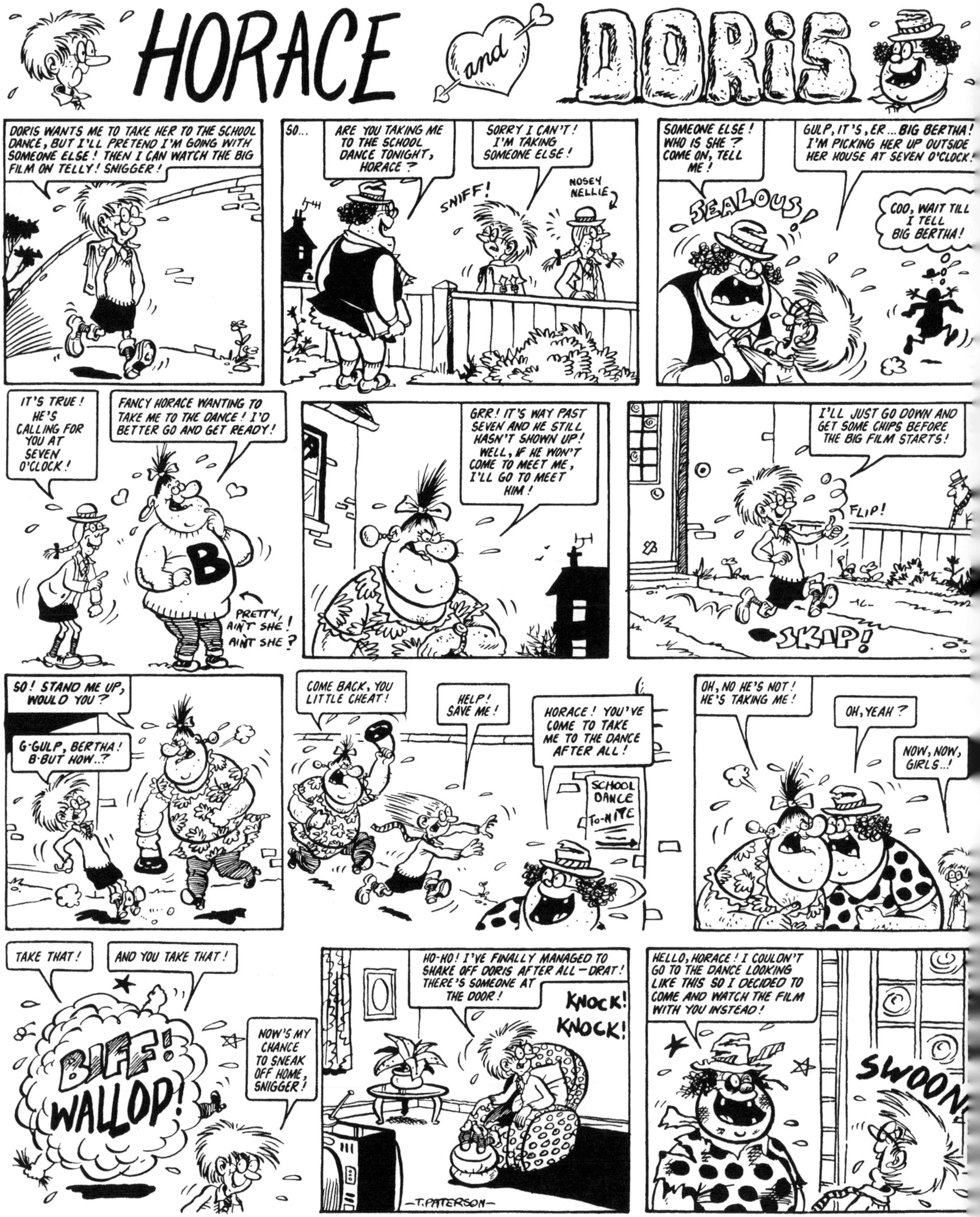
HORACE
and
DORIS
DORIS WANTS ME TO TAKE HER TO THE SCHOOL DANCE, BUT I'LL PRETEND I'M GOING WITH SOMEONE ELSE! THEN I CAN WATCH THE BIG FILM ON TELLY! SNIGGER!
SO...
ARE YOU TAKING ME TO THE SCHOOL DANCE TONIGHT, HORACE?
SORRY I CAN'T! I'M TAKING SOMEONE ELSE!
SNIFF!
NOSEY NELLIE
SOMEONE ELSE! WHO IS SHE? COME ON, TELL ME!
GULP, IT'S, ER... BIG BERTHA! I'M PICKING HER UP OUTSIDE HER HOUSE AT SEVEN O'CLOCK!
JEALOUS!
COO, WAIT TILL I TELL BIG BERTHA!
IT'S TRUE! HE'S CALLING FOR YOU AT SEVEN O'CLOCK!
FANCY HORACE WANTING TO TAKE ME TO THE DANCE! I'D BETTER GO AND GET READY!
B
PRETTY, AIN'T SHE! AIN'T SHE?
GRR! IT'S WAY PAST SEVEN AND HE STILL HASN'T SHOWN UP! WELL, IF HE WON'T COME TO MEET ME, I'LL GO TO MEET HIM!
I'LL JUST GO DOWN AND GET SOME CHIPS BEFORE THE BIG FILM STARTS!
FLIP!
SKIP!
SO! STAND ME UP, WOULD YOU?
G-GULP, BERTHA! B-BUT HOW..?
COME BACK, YOU LITTLE CHEAT!
HELP! SAVE ME!
HORACE! YOU'VE COME TO TAKE ME TO THE DANCE AFTER ALL!
SCHOOL DANCE TO-NITE
OH, NO HE'S NOT! HE'S TAKING ME!
OH, YEAH?
NOW, NOW, GIRLS..!
TAKE THAT!
AND YOU TAKE THAT!
BIFF! WALLOP!
NOW'S MY CHANCE TO SNEAK OFF HOME, SNIGGER!
HO-HO! I'VE FINALLY MANAGED TO SHAKE OFF DORIS AFTER ALL — DRAT! THERE'S SOMEONE AT THE DOOR!
KNOCK! KNOCK!
—T. PATERSON—
HELLO, HORACE! I COULDN'T GO TO THE DANCE LOOKING LIKE THIS SO I DECIDED TO COME AND WATCH THE FILM WITH YOU INSTEAD!
SWOON!

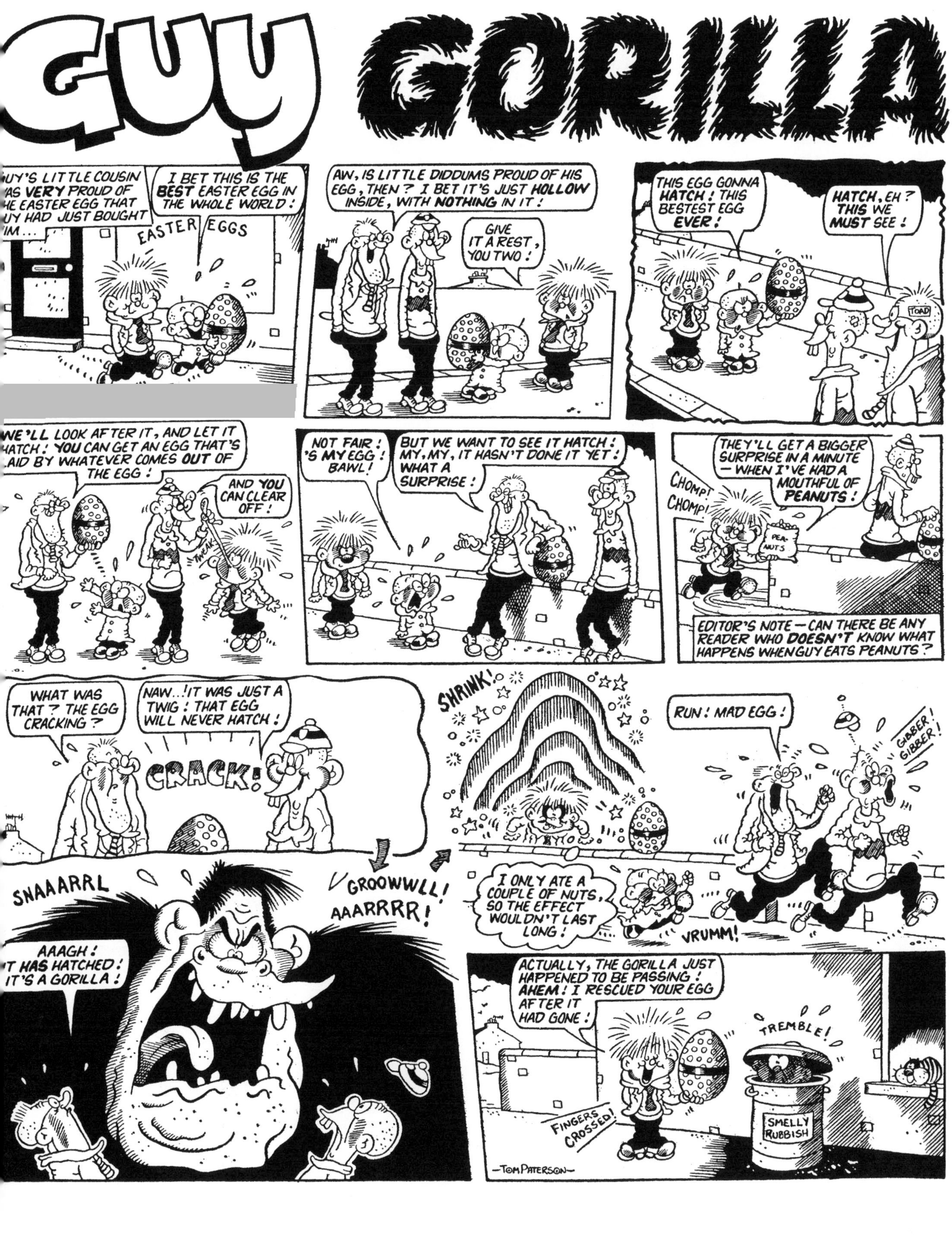
GUY GORILLA
UY'S LITTLE COUSIN AS VERY PROUD OF HE EASTER EGG THAT UY HAD JUST BOUGHT IM...
I BET THIS IS THE BEST EASTER EGG IN THE WHOLE WORLD!
EASTER EGGS
AW, IS LITTLE DIDDUMS PROUD OF HIS EGG, THEN? I BET IT'S JUST HOLLOW INSIDE, WITH NOTHING IN IT!
GIVE IT A REST, YOU TWO!
THIS EGG GONNA HATCH! THIS BESTEST EGG EVER!
HATCH, EH? THIS WE MUST SEE!
TOAD
WE'LL LOOK AFTER IT, AND LET IT HATCH! YOU CAN GET AN EGG THAT'S LAID BY WHATEVER COMES OUT OF THE EGG!
AND YOU CAN CLEAR OFF!
TWEAK
NOT FAIR! 'S MY EGG! BAWL!
BUT WE WANT TO SEE IT HATCH! MY, MY, IT HASN'T DONE IT YET! WHAT A SURPRISE!
CHOMP! CHOMP!
THEY'LL GET A BIGGER SURPRISE IN A MINUTE — WHEN I'VE HAD A MOUTHFUL OF PEANUTS!
PEA-NUTS
EDITOR'S NOTE — CAN THERE BE ANY READER WHO DOESN'T KNOW WHAT HAPPENS WHEN GUY EATS PEANUTS?
WHAT WAS THAT? THE EGG CRACKING?
NAW...!IT WAS JUST A TWIG! THAT EGG WILL NEVER HATCH!
CRACK!
SNAAARRL
GROOWWLL!
AAARRRR!
AAAGH! T HAS HATCHED! IT'S A GORILLA!
SHRINK!
RUN! MAD EGG!
GIBBER! GIBBER!
I ONLY ATE A COUPLE OF NUTS, SO THE EFFECT WOULDN'T LAST LONG!
VRUMM!
ACTUALLY, THE GORILLA JUST HAPPENED TO BE PASSING! AHEM! I RESCUED YOUR EGG AFTER IT HAD GONE!
TREMBLE!
FINGERS CROSSED!
SMELLY RUBBISH
—TOM PATERSON—

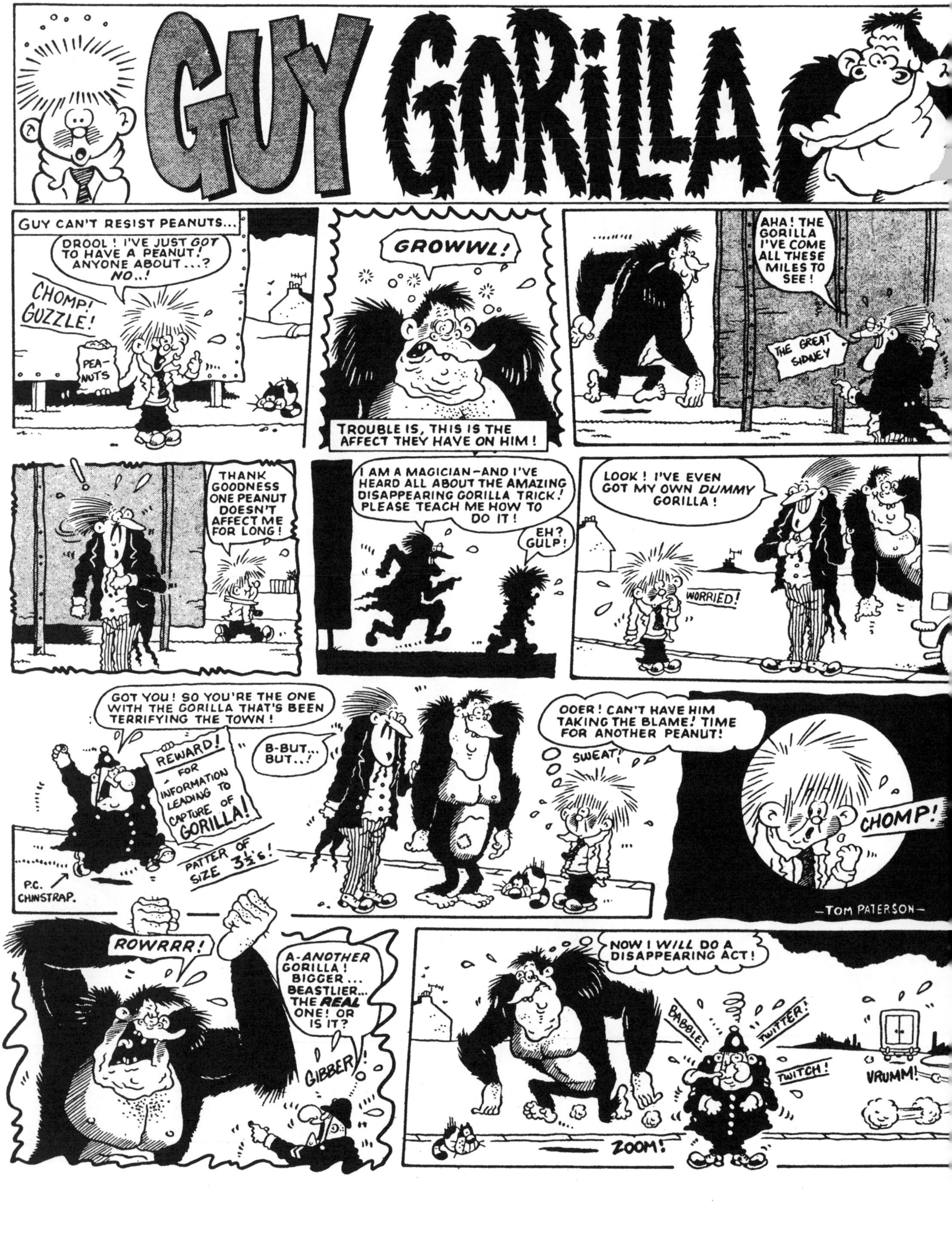
GUY GORILLA
GUY CAN'T RESIST PEANUTS...
DROOL! I'VE JUST GOT TO HAVE A PEANUT! ANYONE ABOUT...? NO..!
CHOMP! GUZZLE!
PEA-NUTS
GROWWL!
TROUBLE IS, THIS IS THE AFFECT THEY HAVE ON HIM!
AHA! THE GORILLA I'VE COME ALL THESE MILES TO SEE!
THE GREAT SIDNEY
THANK GOODNESS ONE PEANUT DOESN'T AFFECT ME FOR LONG!
I AM A MAGICIAN—AND I'VE HEARD ALL ABOUT THE AMAZING DISAPPEARING GORILLA TRICK! PLEASE TEACH ME HOW TO DO IT!
EH? GULP!
LOOK! I'VE EVEN GOT MY OWN DUMMY GORILLA!
WORRIED!
GOT YOU! SO YOU'RE THE ONE WITH THE GORILLA THAT'S BEEN TERRIFYING THE TOWN!
REWARD! FOR INFORMATION LEADING TO CAPTURE OF GORILLA!
PATTER OF SIZE 3½'6'
P.C. CHINSTRAP.
B-BUT... BUT..!
OOER! CAN'T HAVE HIM TAKING THE BLAME! TIME FOR ANOTHER PEANUT!
SWEAT!
CHOMP!
—TOM PATERSON—
ROWRRR!
A-ANOTHER GORILLA! BIGGER... BEASTLIER... THE REAL ONE! OR IS IT?
GIBBER!
NOW I WILL DO A DISAPPEARING ACT!
BABBLE!
TWITTER!
TWITCH!
VRUMM!
ZOOM!

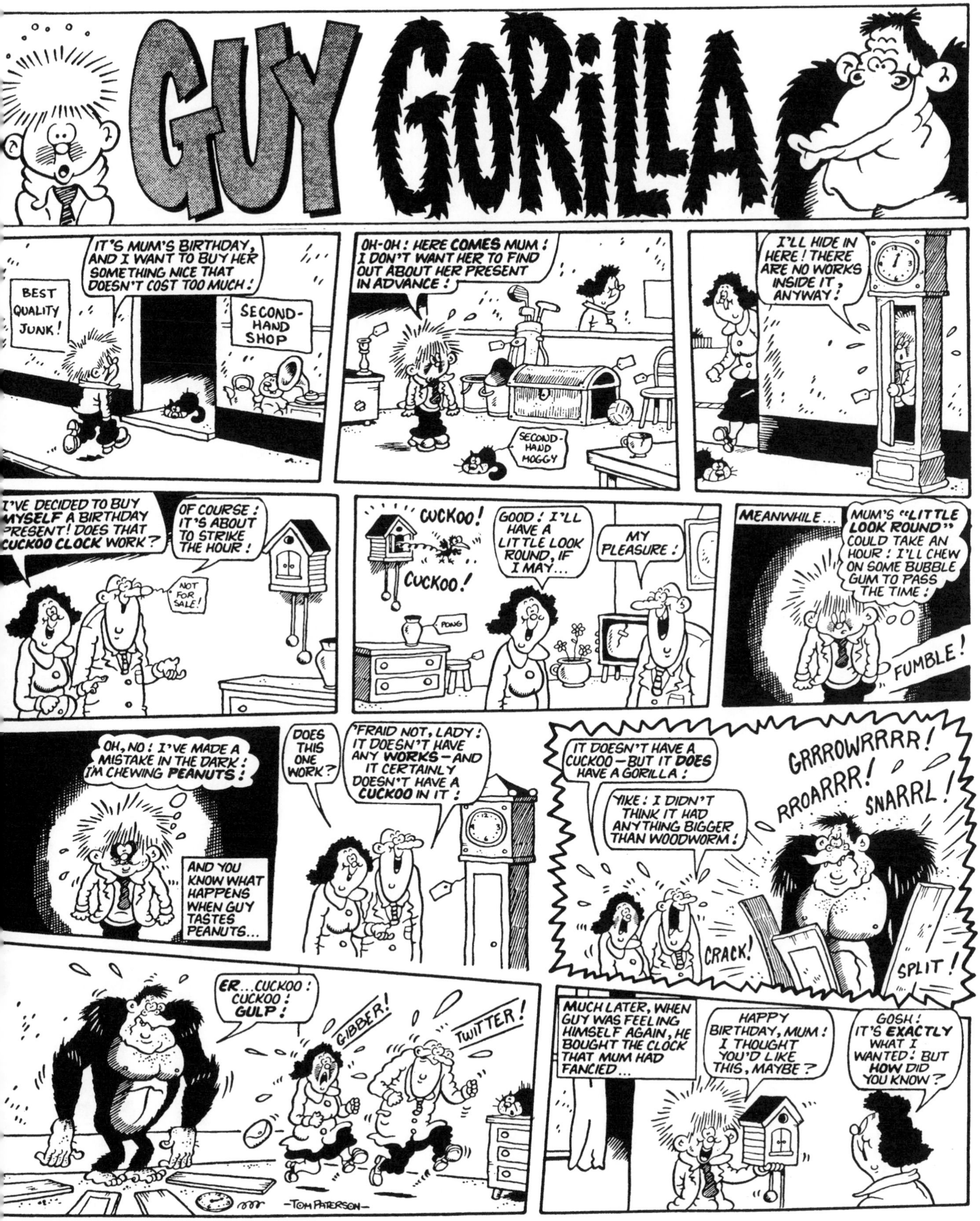
GUY GORILLA
IT'S MUM'S BIRTHDAY, AND I WANT TO BUY HER SOMETHING NICE THAT DOESN'T COST TOO MUCH!
BEST QUALITY JUNK!
SECOND-HAND SHOP
OH-OH: HERE COMES MUM! I DON'T WANT HER TO FIND OUT ABOUT HER PRESENT IN ADVANCE!
SECOND-HAND MOGGY
I'LL HIDE IN HERE! THERE ARE NO WORKS INSIDE IT, ANYWAY!
I'VE DECIDED TO BUY MYSELF A BIRTHDAY PRESENT! DOES THAT CUCKOO CLOCK WORK?
OF COURSE! IT'S ABOUT TO STRIKE THE HOUR!
NOT FOR SALE!
CUCKOO!
CUCKOO!
PONG
GOOD! I'LL HAVE A LITTLE LOOK ROUND, IF I MAY...
MY PLEASURE!
MEANWHILE...
MUM'S "LITTLE LOOK ROUND" COULD TAKE AN HOUR! I'LL CHEW ON SOME BUBBLE GUM TO PASS THE TIME!
FUMBLE!
OH, NO! I'VE MADE A MISTAKE IN THE DARK! I'M CHEWING PEANUTS!
AND YOU KNOW WHAT HAPPENS WHEN GUY TASTES PEANUTS...
DOES THIS ONE WORK?
'FRAID NOT, LADY! IT DOESN'T HAVE ANY WORKS—AND IT CERTAINLY DOESN'T HAVE A CUCKOO IN IT!
IT DOESN'T HAVE A CUCKOO—BUT IT DOES HAVE A GORILLA!
YIKE! I DIDN'T THINK IT HAD ANYTHING BIGGER THAN WOODWORM!
GRRROWRRRR!
RROARRR!
SNARRL!
CRACK!
SPLIT!
ER...CUCKOO! CUCKOO! GULP!
GIBBER!
TWITTER!
—TOM PATERSON—
MUCH LATER, WHEN GUY WAS FEELING HIMSELF AGAIN, HE BOUGHT THE CLOCK THAT MUM HAD FANCIED...
HAPPY BIRTHDAY, MUM! I THOUGHT YOU'D LIKE THIS, MAYBE?
GOSH! IT'S EXACTLY WHAT I WANTED! BUT HOW DID YOU KNOW?

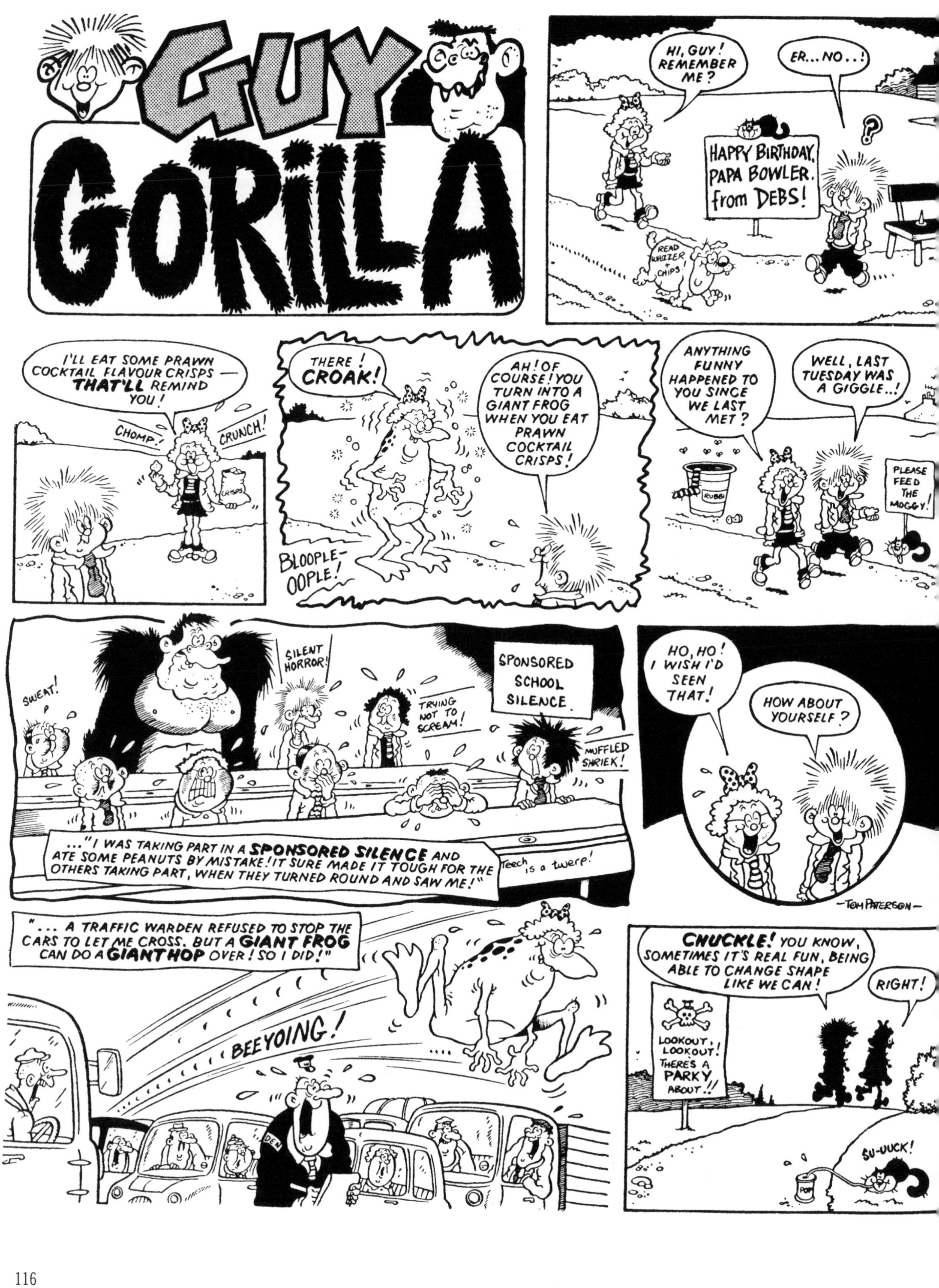
GUY GORILLA
HI, GUY! REMEMBER ME?
ER... NO..!
HAPPY BIRTHDAY, PAPA BOWLER. from DEBS!
READ WHIZZER + CHIPS!
I'LL EAT SOME PRAWN COCKTAIL FLAVOUR CRISPS — THAT'LL REMIND YOU!
CHOMP!
CRUNCH!
CRISPS
THERE! CROAK!
AH! OF COURSE! YOU TURN INTO A GIANT FROG WHEN YOU EAT PRAWN COCKTAIL CRISPS!
BLOOPLE-OOPLE!
ANYTHING FUNNY HAPPENED TO YOU SINCE WE LAST MET?
WELL, LAST TUESDAY WAS A GIGGLE..!
PLEASE FEED THE MOGGY!
SWEAT!
SILENT HORROR!
TRYING NOT TO SCREAM!
SPONSORED SCHOOL SILENCE
MUFFLED SHRIEK!
..."I WAS TAKING PART IN A SPONSORED SILENCE AND ATE SOME PEANUTS BY MISTAKE! IT SURE MADE IT TOUGH FOR THE OTHERS TAKING PART, WHEN THEY TURNED ROUND AND SAW ME!"
Teech is a twerp!
HO, HO! I WISH I'D SEEN THAT!
HOW ABOUT YOURSELF?
-TOM PATERSON-
"... A TRAFFIC WARDEN REFUSED TO STOP THE CARS TO LET ME CROSS. BUT A GIANT FROG CAN DO A GIANT HOP OVER! SO I DID!"
BEEYOING!
DEN
CHUCKLE! YOU KNOW, SOMETIMES IT'S REAL FUN, BEING ABLE TO CHANGE SHAPE LIKE WE CAN!
RIGHT!
LOOKOUT, LOOKOUT! THERE'S A PARKY ABOUT!!
SU-UUCK!
POP

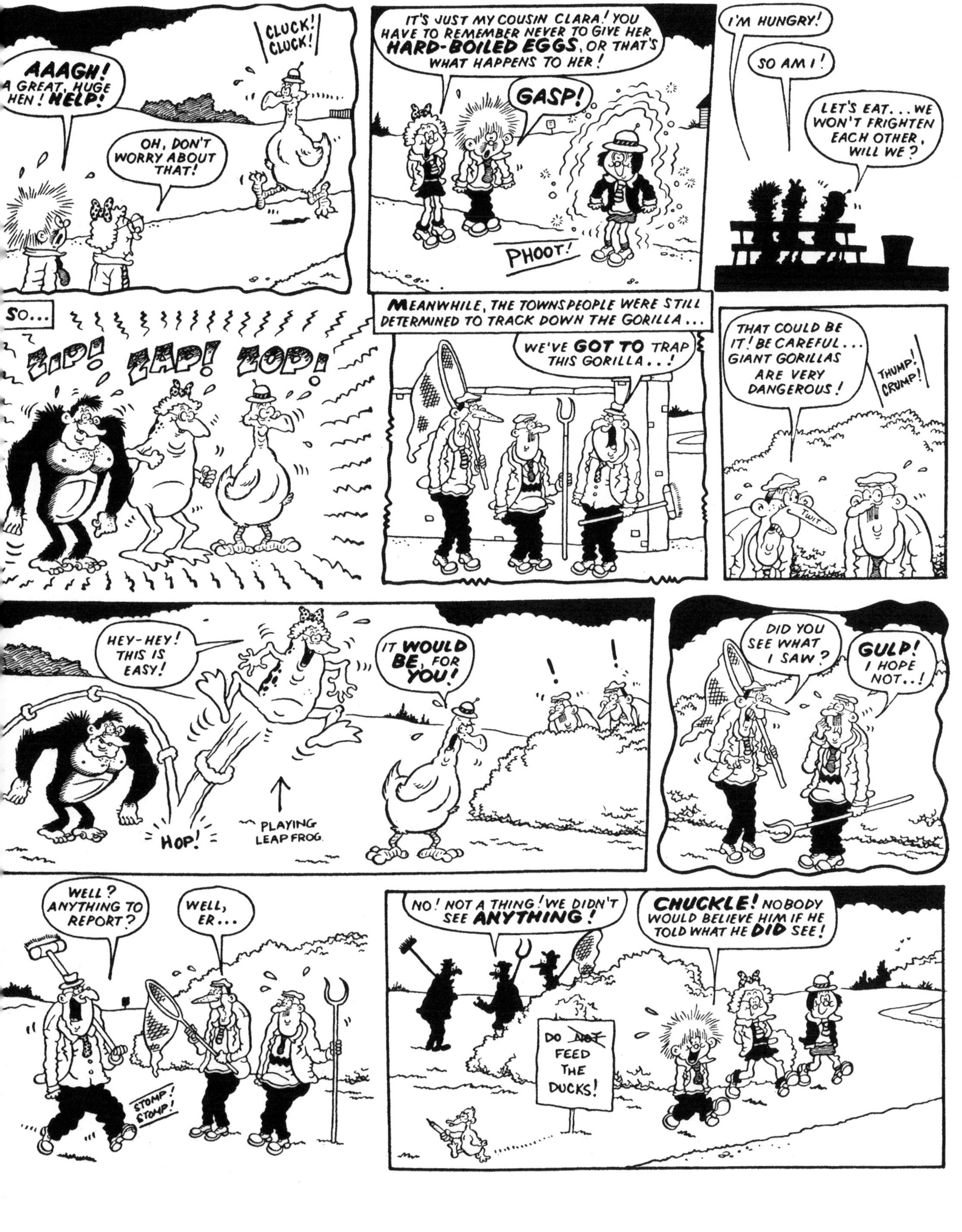
CLUCK! CLUCK!
AAAGH! A GREAT, HUGE HEN! HELP!
OH, DON'T WORRY ABOUT THAT!
IT'S JUST MY COUSIN CLARA! YOU HAVE TO REMEMBER NEVER TO GIVE HER HARD-BOILED EGGS, OR THAT'S WHAT HAPPENS TO HER!
GASP!
PHOOT!
I'M HUNGRY!
SO AM I!
LET'S EAT... WE WON'T FRIGHTEN EACH OTHER, WILL WE?
SO...
ZIP! ZAP! ZOP!
MEANWHILE, THE TOWNSPEOPLE WERE STILL DETERMINED TO TRACK DOWN THE GORILLA...
WE'VE GOT TO TRAP THIS GORILLA..!
THAT COULD BE IT! BE CAREFUL... GIANT GORILLAS ARE VERY DANGEROUS!
THUMP! CRUMP!
TWIT
HEY-HEY! THIS IS EASY!
IT WOULD BE, FOR YOU!
HOP!
PLAYING LEAP FROG
DID YOU SEE WHAT I SAW?
GULP! I HOPE NOT..!
WELL? ANYTHING TO REPORT?
WELL, ER...
STOMP! STOMP!
NO! NOT A THING! WE DIDN'T SEE ANYTHING!
CHUCKLE! NOBODY WOULD BELIEVE HIM IF HE TOLD WHAT HE DID SEE!
DO NOT FEED THE DUCKS!

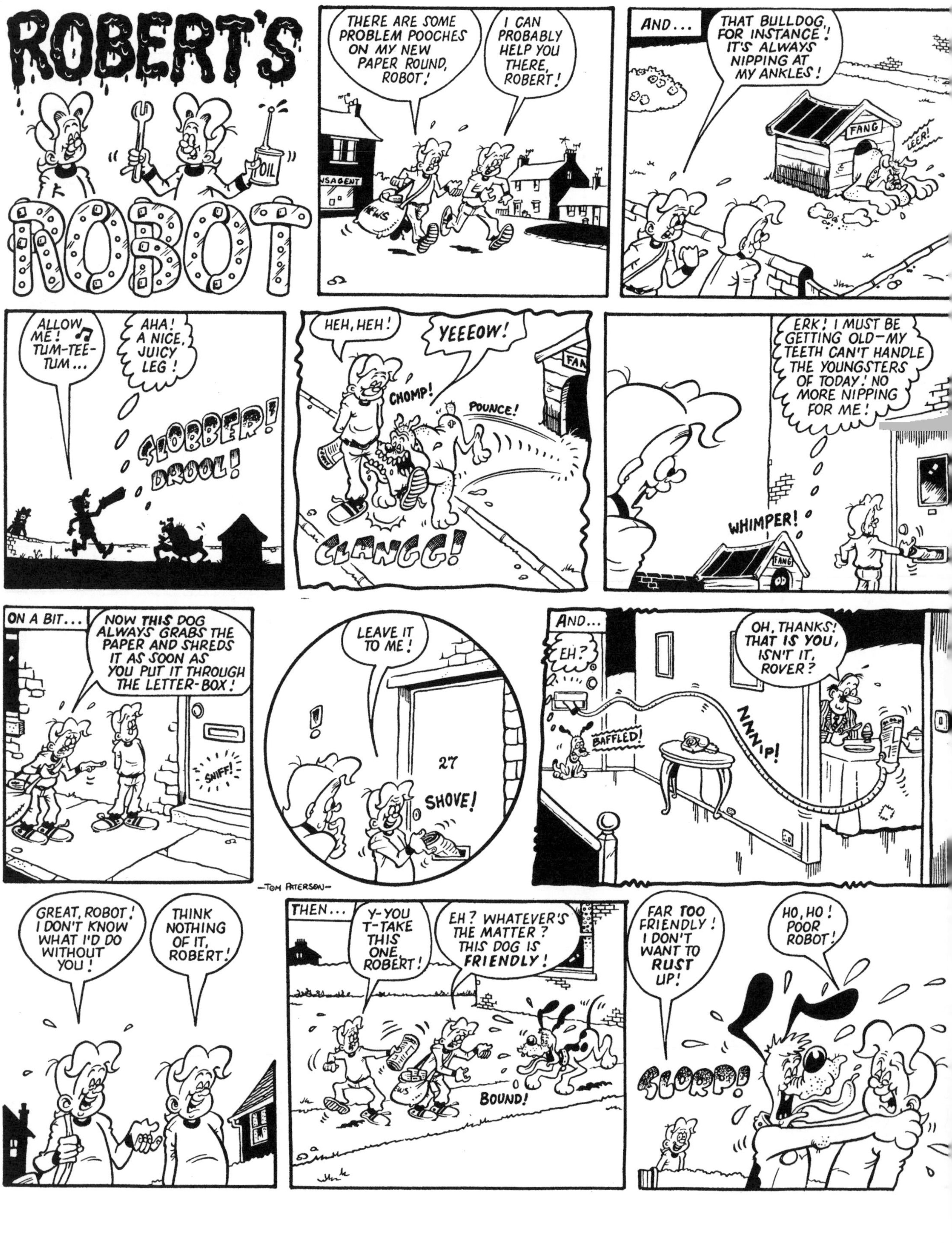
ROBERT'S ROBOT
OIL
THERE ARE SOME PROBLEM POOCHES ON MY NEW PAPER ROUND, ROBOT!
I CAN PROBABLY HELP YOU THERE, ROBERT!
NEWSAGENT
NEWS
AND...
THAT BULLDOG, FOR INSTANCE! IT'S ALWAYS NIPPING AT MY ANKLES!
FANG
LEER!
ALLOW ME! TUM-TEE-TUM...
AHA! A NICE, JUICY LEG!
SLOBBER! DROOL!
HEH, HEH!
YEEEOW!
CHOMP!
POUNCE!
CLANGG!
ERK! I MUST BE GETTING OLD—MY TEETH CAN'T HANDLE THE YOUNGSTERS OF TODAY! NO MORE NIPPING FOR ME!
WHIMPER!
FANG
ON A BIT...
NOW THIS DOG ALWAYS GRABS THE PAPER AND SHREDS IT AS SOON AS YOU PUT IT THROUGH THE LETTER-BOX!
SNIFF!
LEAVE IT TO ME!
27
SHOVE!
AND...
EH?
OH, THANKS! THAT IS YOU, ISN'T IT, ROVER?
BAFFLED!
NNNNIP!
—TOM PATERSON—
GREAT, ROBOT! I DON'T KNOW WHAT I'D DO WITHOUT YOU!
THINK NOTHING OF IT, ROBERT!
THEN...
Y-YOU T-TAKE THIS ONE, ROBERT!
EH? WHATEVER'S THE MATTER? THIS DOG IS FRIENDLY!
BOUND!
FAR TOO FRIENDLY! I DON'T WANT TO RUST UP!
HO, HO! POOR ROBOT!
SLOPP!

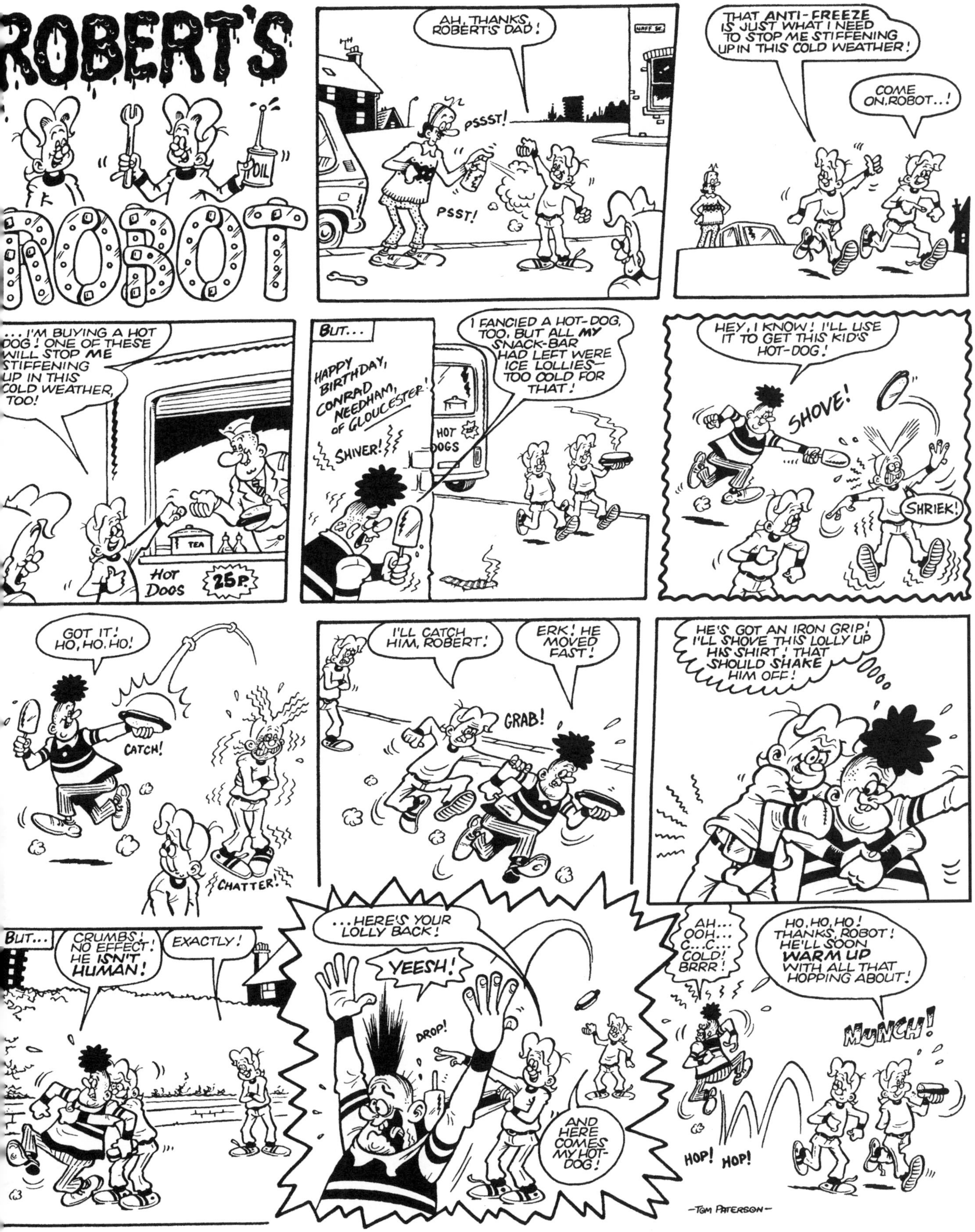
ROBERT'S ROBOT
OIL
AH, THANKS, ROBERT'S DAD!
PSSST!
PSST!
THAT ANTI-FREEZE IS JUST WHAT I NEED TO STOP ME STIFFENING UP IN THIS COLD WEATHER!
COME ON, ROBOT..!
...I'M BUYING A HOT DOG! ONE OF THESE WILL STOP ME STIFFENING UP IN THIS COLD WEATHER, TOO!
TEA
HOT DOGS 25P.
BUT...
HAPPY BIRTHDAY, CONRAD NEEDHAM, OF GLOUCESTER!
SHIVER!
I FANCIED A HOT-DOG, TOO, BUT ALL MY SNACK-BAR HAD LEFT WERE ICE LOLLIES— TOO COLD FOR THAT!
HOT DOGS
HEY, I KNOW! I'LL USE IT TO GET THIS KID'S HOT-DOG!
SHOVE!
SHRIEK!
GOT IT! HO, HO, HO!
CATCH!
CHATTER!
I'LL CATCH HIM, ROBERT!
ERK! HE MOVED FAST!
GRAB!
HE'S GOT AN IRON GRIP! I'LL SHOVE THIS LOLLY UP HIS SHIRT! THAT SHOULD SHAKE HIM OFF!
BUT...
CRUMBS! NO EFFECT! HE ISN'T HUMAN!
EXACTLY!
...HERE'S YOUR LOLLY BACK!
YEESH!
DROP!
AND HERE COMES MY HOT-DOG!
AH... OOH... C...C... COLD! BRRR!
HOP! HOP!
HO, HO, HO! THANKS, ROBOT! HE'LL SOON WARM UP WITH ALL THAT HOPPING ABOUT!
MUNCH!
—TOM PATERSON—

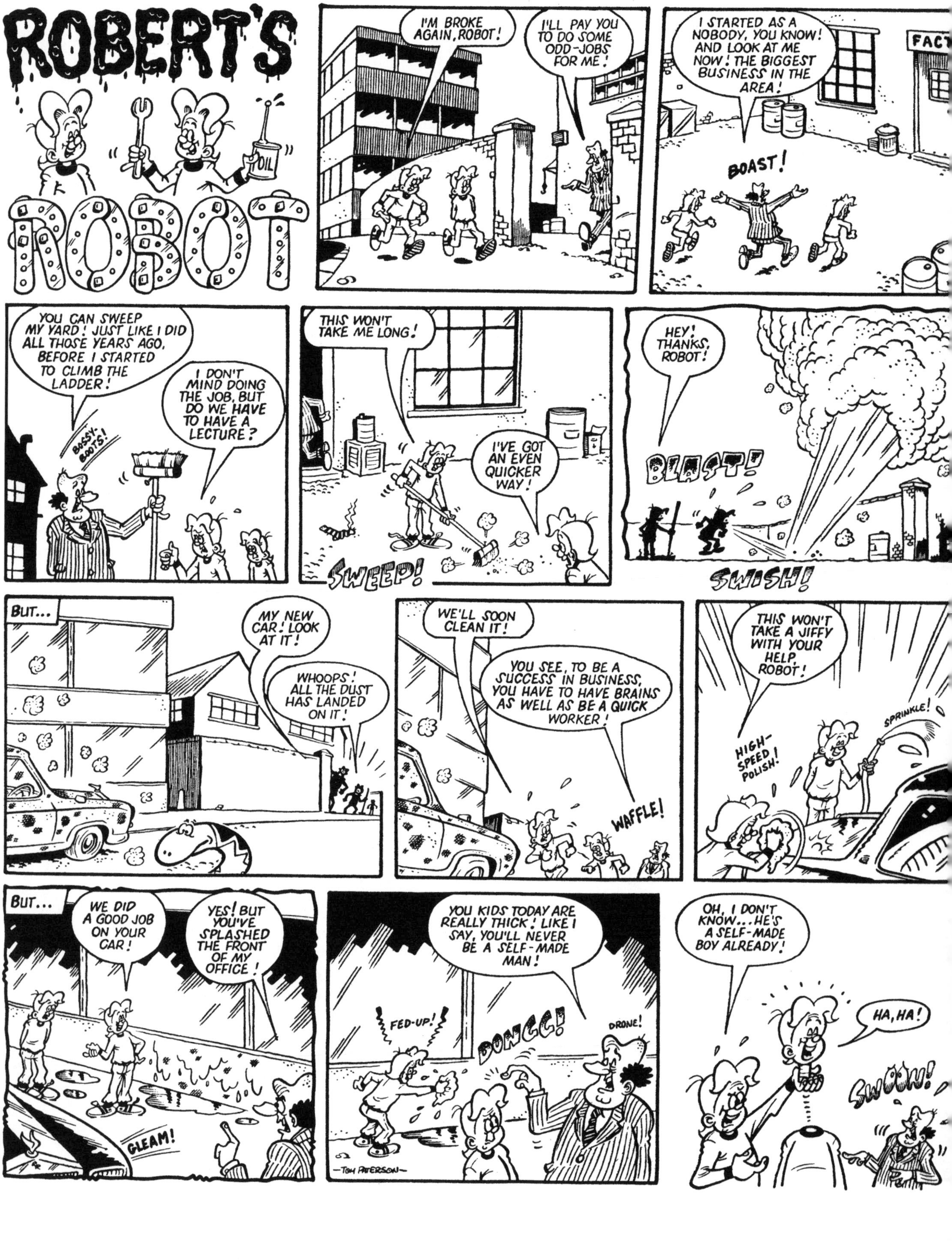
ROBERT'S ROBOT
OIL
I'M BROKE AGAIN, ROBOT!
I'LL PAY YOU TO DO SOME ODD-JOBS FOR ME!
I STARTED AS A NOBODY, YOU KNOW! AND LOOK AT ME NOW! THE BIGGEST BUSINESS IN THE AREA!
BOAST!
YOU CAN SWEEP MY YARD! JUST LIKE I DID ALL THOSE YEARS AGO, BEFORE I STARTED TO CLIMB THE LADDER!
BOSSY-BOOTS!
I DON'T MIND DOING THE JOB, BUT DO WE HAVE TO HAVE A LECTURE?
THIS WON'T TAKE ME LONG!
I'VE GOT AN EVEN QUICKER WAY!
SWEEP!
HEY! THANKS, ROBOT!
BLAST!
SWISH!
BUT...
MY NEW CAR! LOOK AT IT!
WHOOPS! ALL THE DUST HAS LANDED ON IT!
WE'LL SOON CLEAN IT!
YOU SEE, TO BE A SUCCESS IN BUSINESS, YOU HAVE TO HAVE BRAINS AS WELL AS BE A QUICK WORKER!
WAFFLE!
THIS WON'T TAKE A JIFFY WITH YOUR HELP, ROBOT!
HIGH-SPEED POLISH!
SPRINKLE!
BUT...
WE DID A GOOD JOB ON YOUR CAR!
YES! BUT YOU'VE SPLASHED THE FRONT OF MY OFFICE!
GLEAM!
YOU KIDS TODAY ARE REALLY THICK! LIKE I SAY, YOU'LL NEVER BE A SELF-MADE MAN!
FED-UP!
DONGG!
DRONE!
TOM PATERSON
OH, I DON'T KNOW... HE'S A SELF-MADE BOY ALREADY!
HA, HA!
SWOOSH!

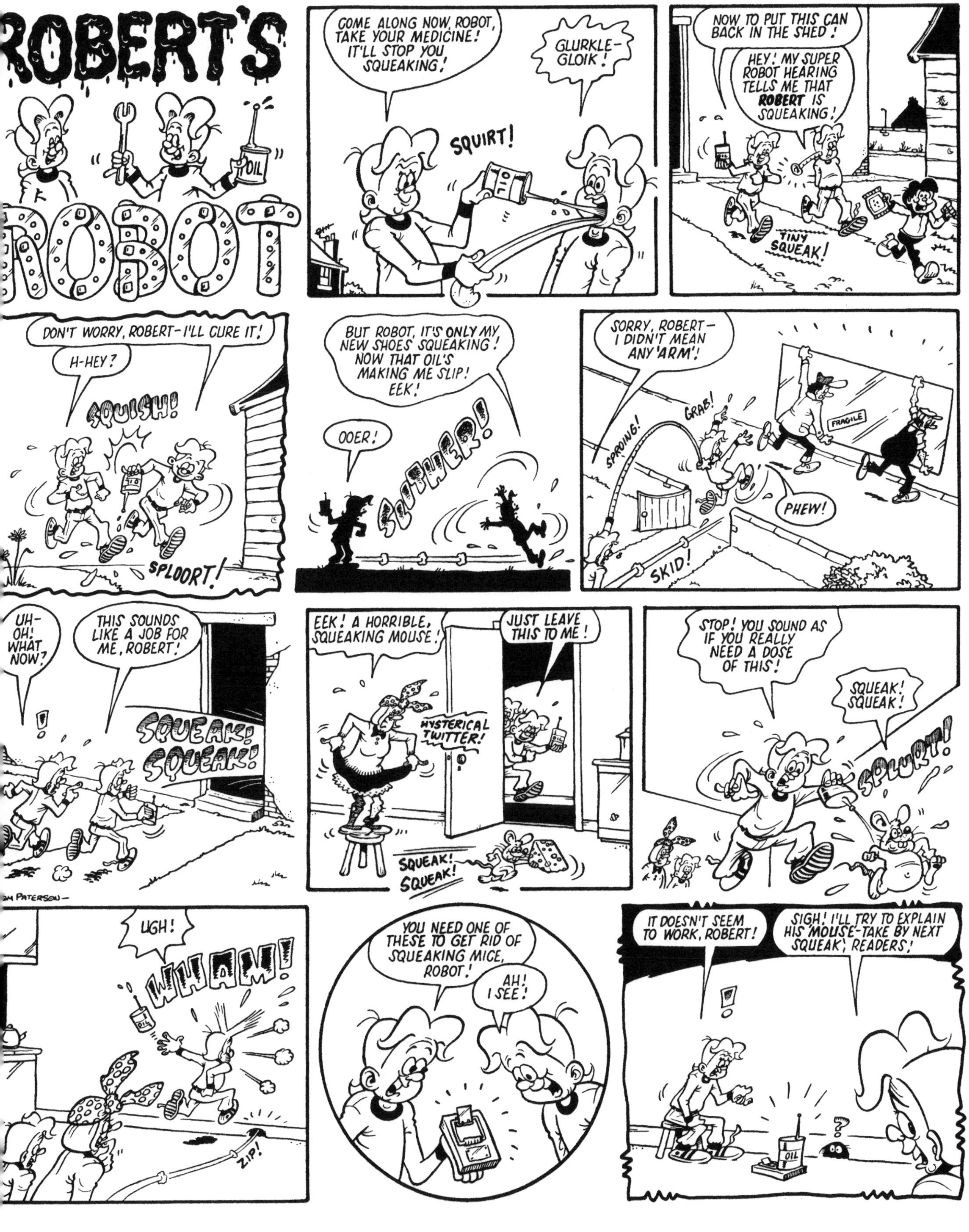
ROBERT'S ROBOT
OIL
COME ALONG NOW, ROBOT, TAKE YOUR MEDICINE! IT'LL STOP YOU SQUEAKING!
GLURKLE-GLOIK!
SQUIRT!
NOW TO PUT THIS CAN BACK IN THE SHED!
HEY! MY SUPER ROBOT HEARING TELLS ME THAT ROBERT IS SQUEAKING!
TINY SQUEAK!
DON'T WORRY, ROBERT-I'LL CURE IT!
H-HEY?
SQUISH!
SPLOORT!
BUT ROBOT, IT'S ONLY MY NEW SHOES SQUEAKING! NOW THAT OIL'S MAKING ME SLIP! EEK!
OOER!
SORRY, ROBERT-I DIDN'T MEAN ANY 'ARM'!
GRAB!
SPROING!
FRAGILE
PHEW!
SKID!
UH-OH! WHAT NOW?
THIS SOUNDS LIKE A JOB FOR ME, ROBERT!
SQUEAK! SQUEAK!
EEK! A HORRIBLE, SQUEAKING MOUSE!
JUST LEAVE THIS TO ME!
HYSTERICAL TWITTER!
SQUEAK! SQUEAK!
STOP! YOU SOUND AS IF YOU REALLY NEED A DOSE OF THIS!
SQUEAK! SQUEAK!
SPLURT!
UGH!
WHAM!
ZIP!
YOU NEED ONE OF THESE TO GET RID OF SQUEAKING MICE, ROBOT!
AH! I SEE!
IT DOESN'T SEEM TO WORK, ROBERT!
SIGH! I'LL TRY TO EXPLAIN HIS MOUSE-TAKE BY NEXT SQUEAK, READERS!
OIL

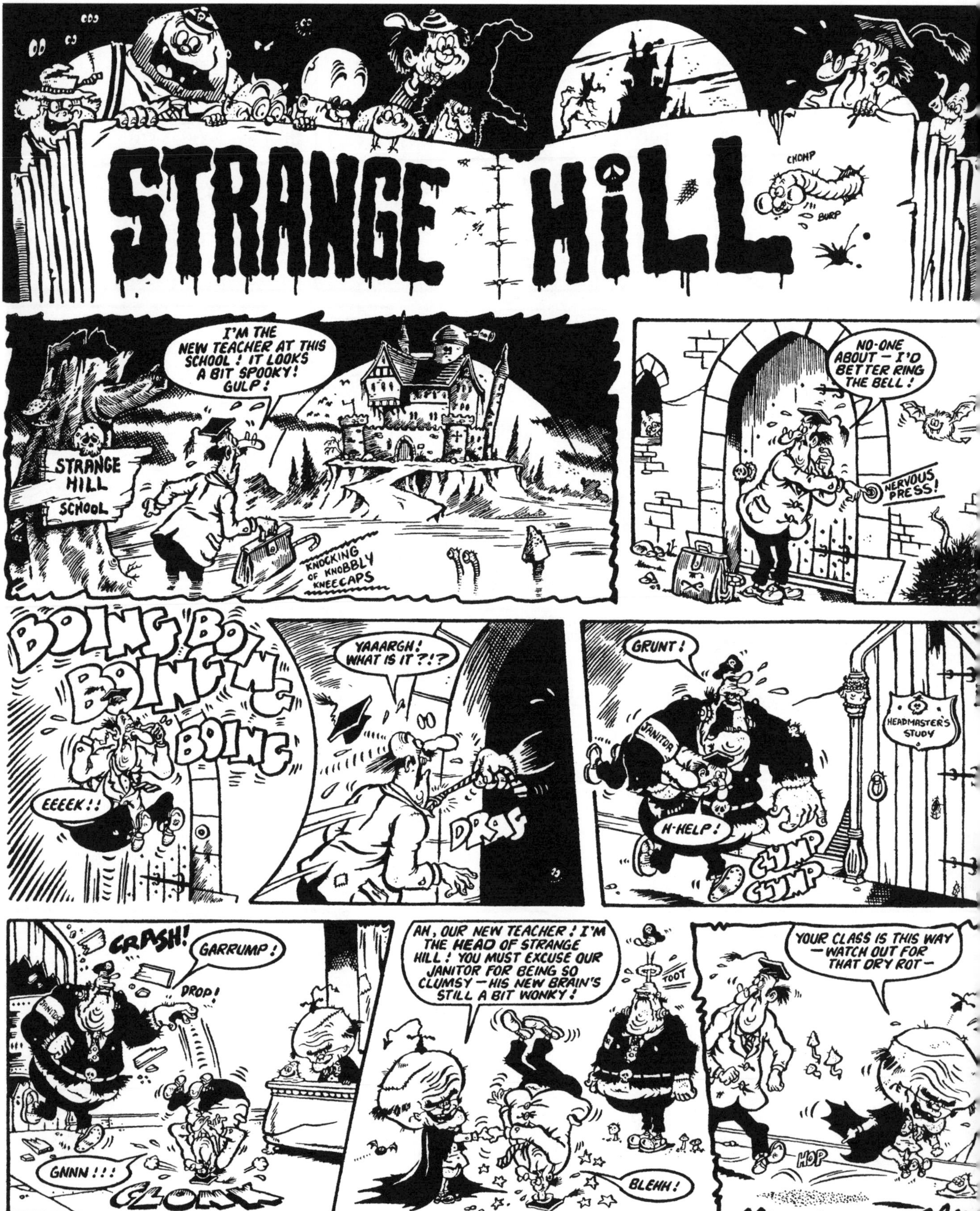
STRANGE HILL
CHOMP
BURP
I'M THE NEW TEACHER AT THIS SCHOOL ! IT LOOKS A BIT SPOOKY! GULP !
STRANGE HILL SCHOOL
KNOCKING OF KNOBBLY KNEECAPS
NO-ONE ABOUT — I'D BETTER RING THE BELL !
NERVOUS PRESS!
BOING BOING BOING BOING
BOING
EEEEK !!
YAAARGH! WHAT IS IT ?!?
DRAG
GRUNT !
JANITOR
HEADMASTER'S STUDY
H-HELP !
CLUMP CLUMP
CRASH!
GARRUMP !
DROP !
JANITOR
GNNN !!!
CLONK
AH, OUR NEW TEACHER ! I'M THE HEAD OF STRANGE HILL ! YOU MUST EXCUSE OUR JANITOR FOR BEING SO CLUMSY — HIS NEW BRAIN'S STILL A BIT WONKY !
TOOT
BLEHH !
YOUR CLASS IS THIS WAY — WATCH OUT FOR THAT DRY ROT —
HOP

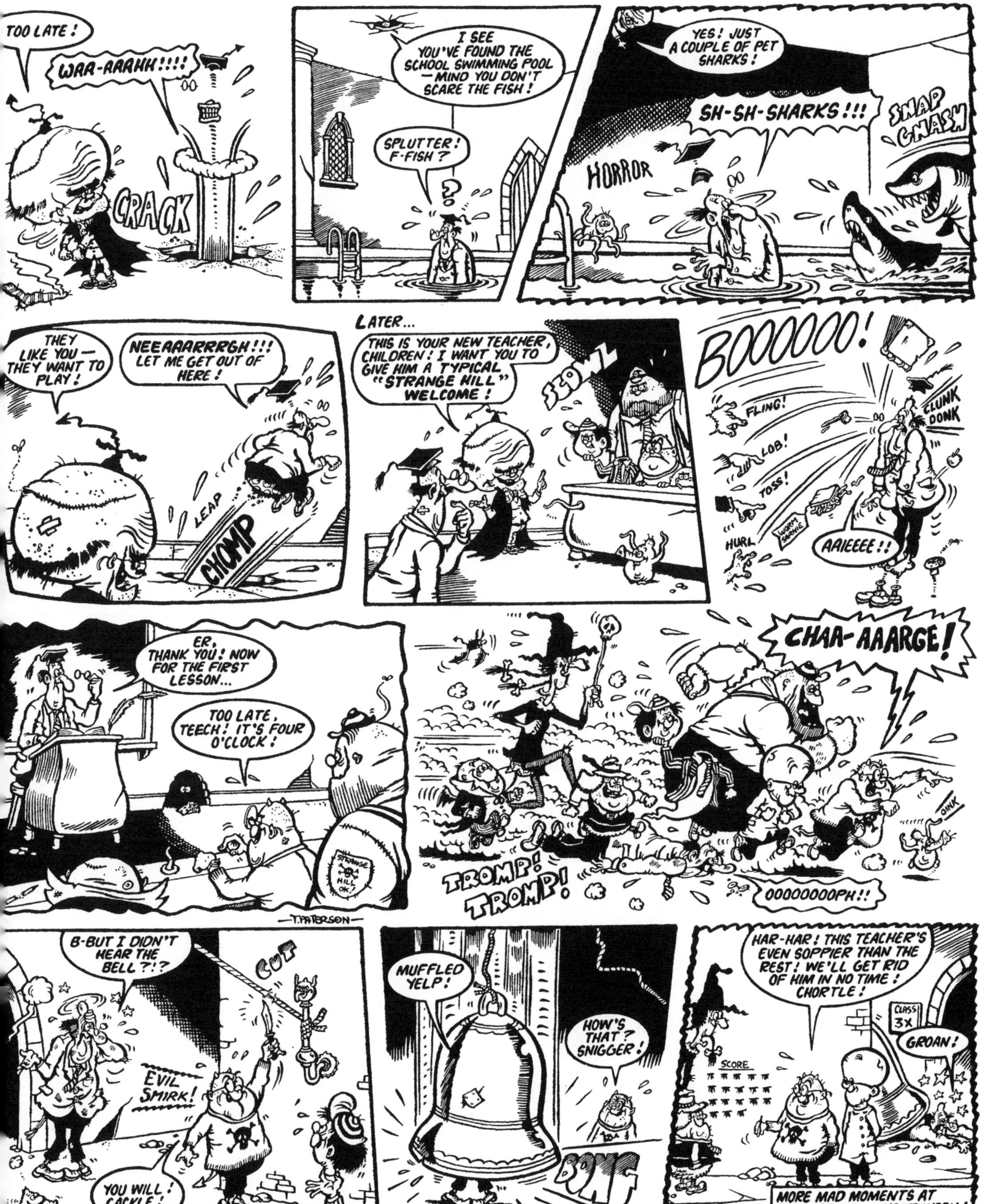
TOO LATE!
WAR-AAAHH!!!!
CRACK
I SEE YOU'VE FOUND THE SCHOOL SWIMMING POOL — MIND YOU DON'T SCARE THE FISH!
SPLUTTER! F-FISH?
?
YES! JUST A COUPLE OF PET SHARKS!
SH-SH-SHARKS!!!
SNAP GNASH
HORROR
THEY LIKE YOU — THEY WANT TO PLAY!
NEEAAARRRGH!!! LET ME GET OUT OF HERE!
LEAP
CHOMP
LATER...
THIS IS YOUR NEW TEACHER, CHILDREN! I WANT YOU TO GIVE HIM A TYPICAL "STRANGE HILL" WELCOME!
SCOWL
BOOOOOO!
FLING!
LOB!
TOSS!
HURL
WORM SARNIE
CLUNK DONK
AAIEEEE!!
ER, THANK YOU! NOW FOR THE FIRST LESSON...
TOO LATE, TEECH! IT'S FOUR O'CLOCK!
STRANGE HILL OK!
CHAA-AAARGE!
TROMP! TROMP!
OINK
OOOOOOOOPH!!
T. PATERSON
B-BUT I DIDN'T HEAR THE BELL?!?
CUT
EVIL SMIRK!
YOU WILL CACKLE!
MUFFLED YELP!
HOW'S THAT? SNIGGER!
BONG
HAR-HAR! THIS TEACHER'S EVEN SOPPIER THAN THE REST! WE'LL GET RID OF HIM IN NO TIME! CHORTLE!
CLASS 3X
GROAN!
SCORE
MORE MAD MOMENTS AT STRANGE HILL — NEXT WEEK!

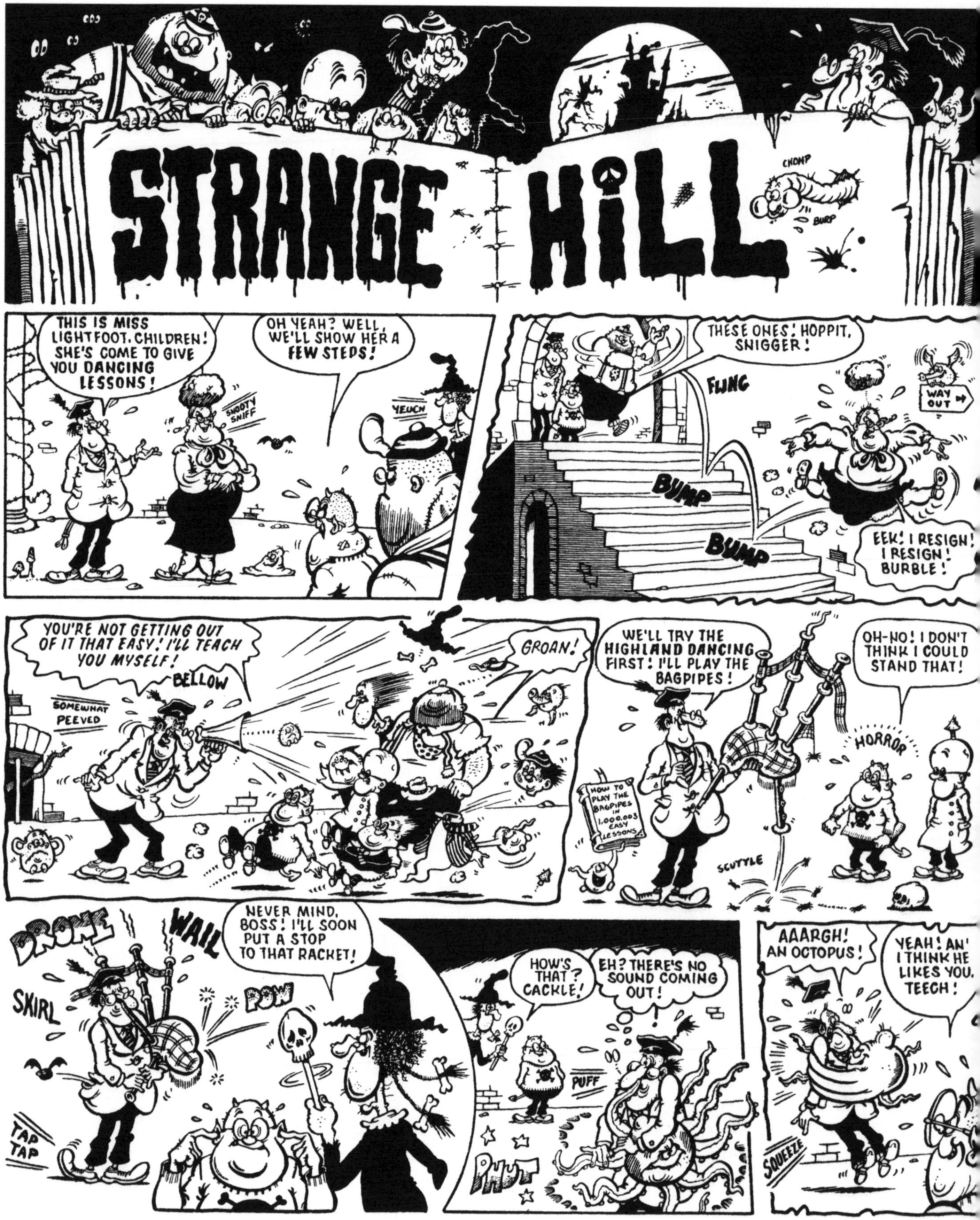
STRANGE HILL
CHOMP
BURP
THIS IS MISS LIGHTFOOT, CHILDREN! SHE'S COME TO GIVE YOU DANCING LESSONS!
SNOOTY SNIFF
OH YEAH? WELL, WE'LL SHOW HER A FEW STEPS!
YEUCH
THESE ONES! HOPPIT, SNIGGER!
FLING
WAY OUT
BUMP
BUMP
EEK! I RESIGN! I RESIGN! BURBLE!
YOU'RE NOT GETTING OUT OF IT THAT EASY! I'LL TEACH YOU MYSELF!
BELLOW
SOMEWHAT PEEVED
GROAN!
WE'LL TRY THE HIGHLAND DANCING FIRST! I'LL PLAY THE BAGPIPES!
HOW TO PLAY THE BAGPIPES IN 1,000,003 EASY LESSONS
SCUTTLE
OH-NO! I DON'T THINK I COULD STAND THAT!
HORROR
DRONE
WAIL
SKIRL
TAP TAP
NEVER MIND, BOSS! I'LL SOON PUT A STOP TO THAT RACKET!
POW
HOW'S THAT? CACKLE!
EH? THERE'S NO SOUND COMING OUT!
PUFF
PHUT
AAARGH! AN OCTOPUS!
YEAH! AN' I THINK HE LIKES YOU, TEECH!
SQUEEZE

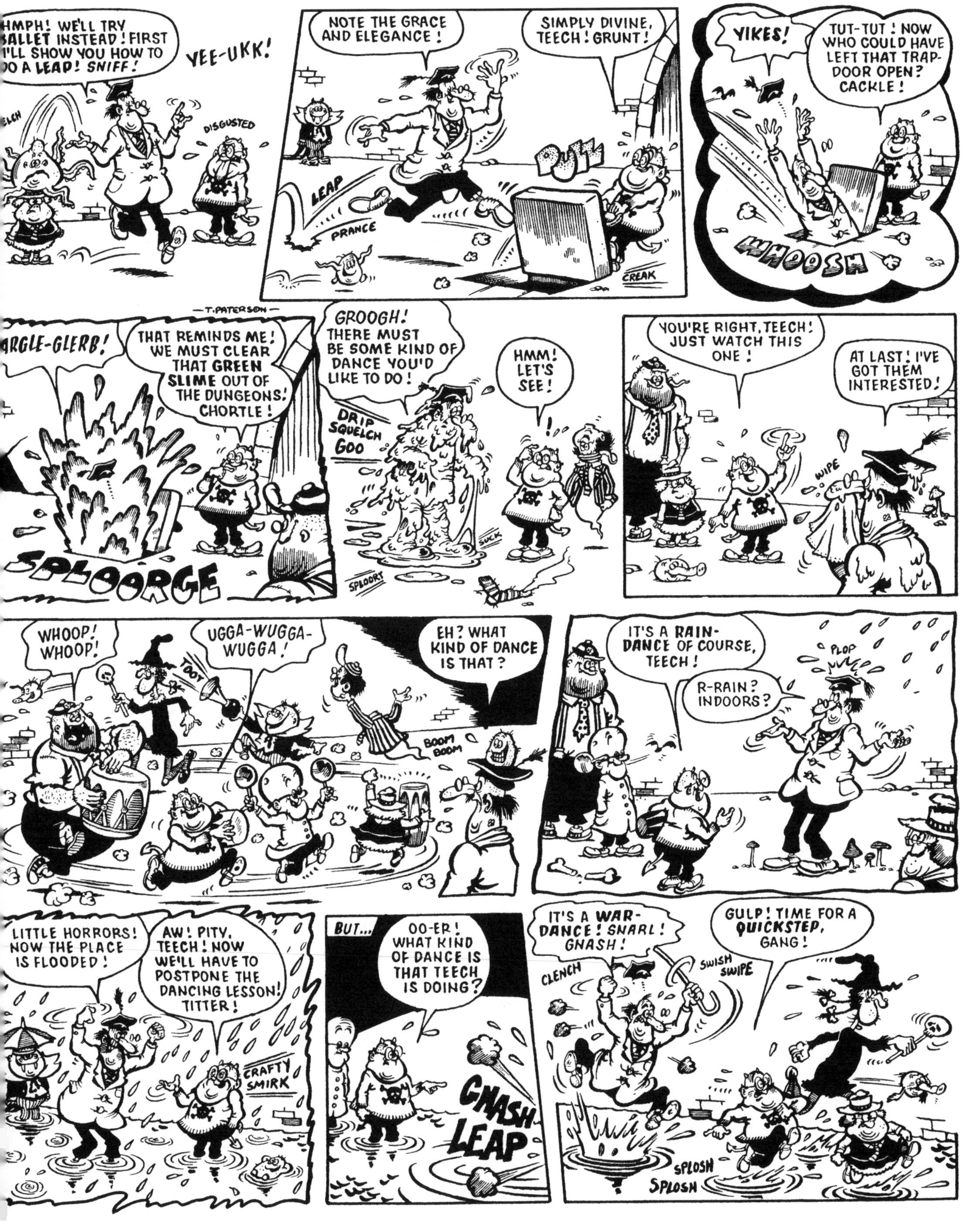
HMPH! WE'LL TRY BALLET INSTEAD! FIRST I'LL SHOW YOU HOW TO DO A LEAP! SNIFF!
YEE-UKK!
DISGUSTED
NOTE THE GRACE AND ELEGANCE!
SIMPLY DIVINE, TEECH! GRUNT!
LEAP
PRANCE
CREAK
YIKES!
TUT-TUT! NOW WHO COULD HAVE LEFT THAT TRAP-DOOR OPEN? CACKLE!
WHOOSH
T. PATERSON
ARGLE-GLERB!
THAT REMINDS ME! WE MUST CLEAR THAT GREEN SLIME OUT OF THE DUNGEONS! CHORTLE!
SPLOORGE
GROOGH! THERE MUST BE SOME KIND OF DANCE YOU'D LIKE TO DO!
HMM! LET'S SEE!
DRIP SQUELCH GOO
SUCK
SPLOORT
YOU'RE RIGHT, TEECH! JUST WATCH THIS ONE!
AT LAST! I'VE GOT THEM INTERESTED!
WIPE
WHOOP! WHOOP!
UGGA-WUGGA-WUGGA!
TOOT
EH? WHAT KIND OF DANCE IS THAT?
BOOM BOOM
IT'S A RAIN-DANCE OF COURSE, TEECH!
R-RAIN? INDOORS?
PLOP
LITTLE HORRORS! NOW THE PLACE IS FLOODED!
AW! PITY, TEECH! NOW WE'LL HAVE TO POSTPONE THE DANCING LESSON! TITTER!
CRAFTY SMIRK
BUT...
OO-ER! WHAT KIND OF DANCE IS THAT TEECH IS DOING?
GNASH LEAP
IT'S A WAR-DANCE! SNARL! GNASH!
CLENCH
SWISH SWIPE
GULP! TIME FOR A QUICKSTEP, GANG!
SPLOSH
SPLOSH

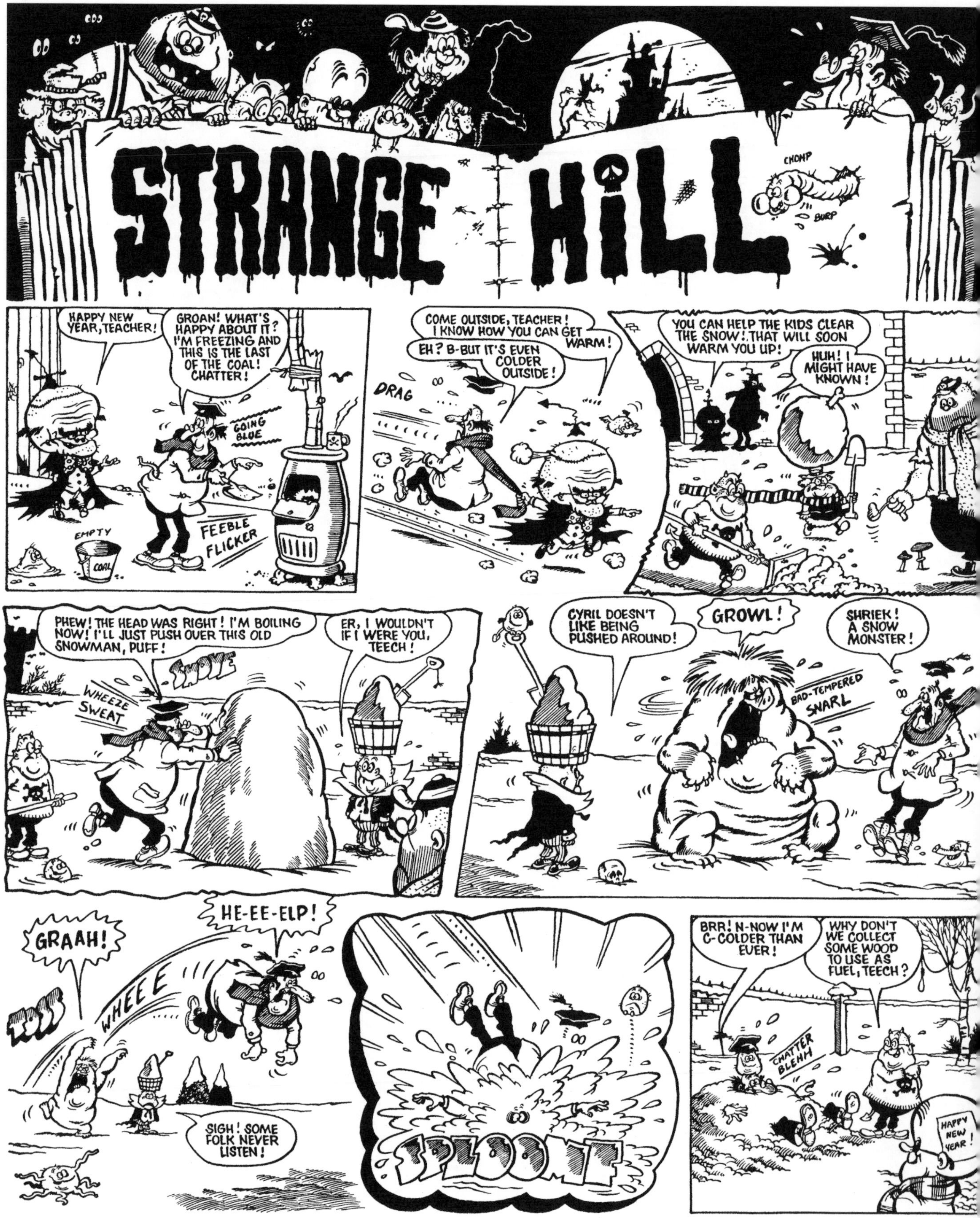
STRANGE HILL
CHOMP
BURP
HAPPY NEW YEAR, TEACHER!
GROAN! WHAT'S HAPPY ABOUT IT? I'M FREEZING AND THIS IS THE LAST OF THE COAL! CHATTER!
GOING BLUE
EMPTY
COAL
FEEBLE FLICKER
COME OUTSIDE, TEACHER! I KNOW HOW YOU CAN GET WARM!
EH? B-BUT IT'S EVEN COLDER OUTSIDE!
DRAG
YOU CAN HELP THE KIDS CLEAR THE SNOW! THAT WILL SOON WARM YOU UP!
HUH! I MIGHT HAVE KNOWN!
PHEW! THE HEAD WAS RIGHT! I'M BOILING NOW! I'LL JUST PUSH OVER THIS OLD SNOWMAN, PUFF!
ER, I WOULDN'T IF I WERE YOU, TEECH!
WHEEZE SWEAT
SHOVE
CYRIL DOESN'T LIKE BEING PUSHED AROUND!
GROWL!
SHRIEK! A SNOW MONSTER!
BAD-TEMPERED SNARL
GRAAH!
HE-EE-ELP!
TOSS
WHEEE
SIGH! SOME FOLK NEVER LISTEN!
SPLOOMF
BRR! N-NOW I'M C-COLDER THAN EVER!
WHY DON'T WE COLLECT SOME WOOD TO USE AS FUEL, TEECH?
CHATTER BLEHH
HAPPY NEW YEAR!

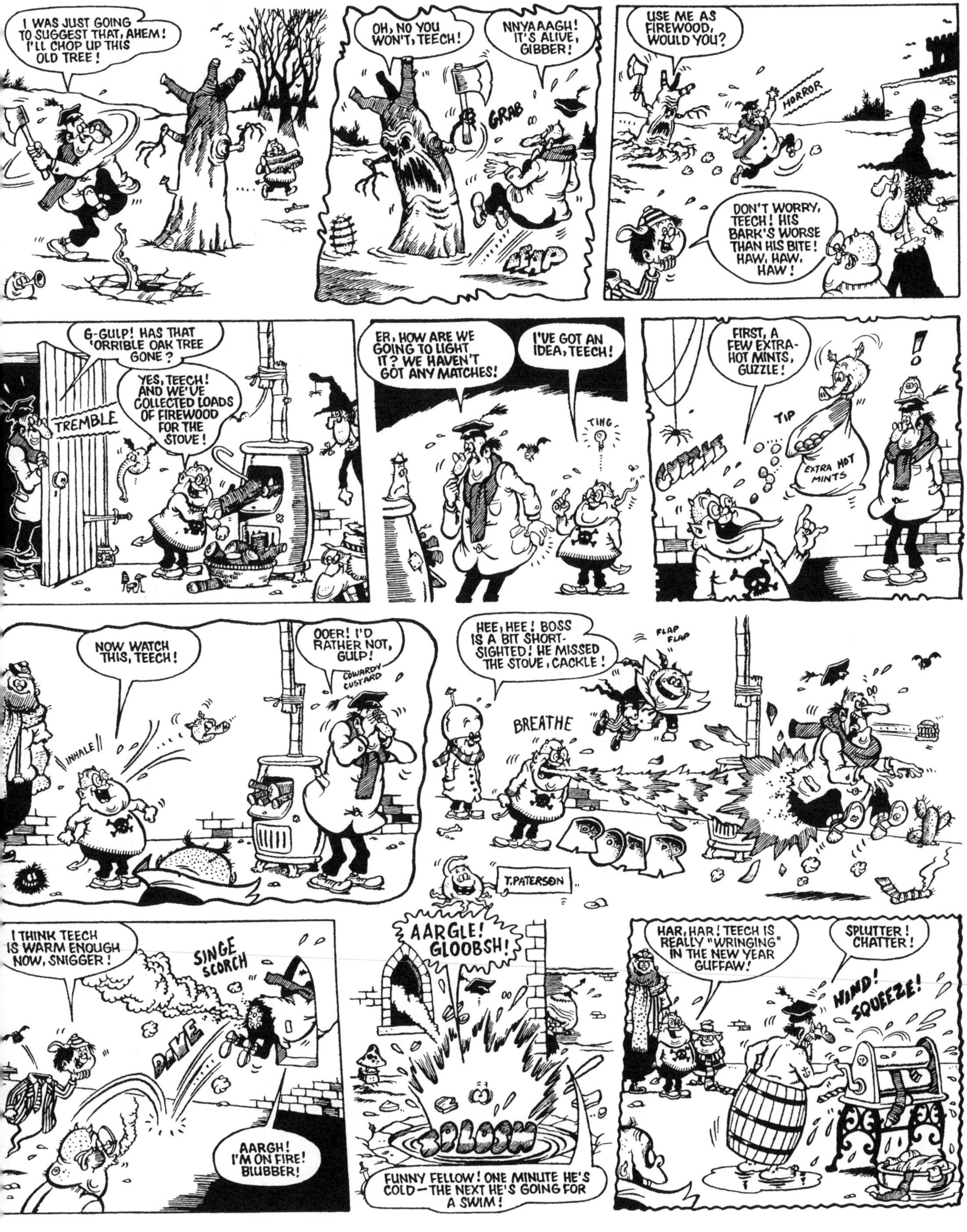

I WAS JUST GOING TO SUGGEST THAT, AHEM! I'LL CHOP UP THIS OLD TREE!
OH, NO YOU WON'T, TEECH!
NNYAAAGH! IT'S ALIVE, GIBBER!
GRAB
USE ME AS FIREWOOD, WOULD YOU?
HORROR
DON'T WORRY, TEECH! HIS BARK'S WORSE THAN HIS BITE! HAW, HAW, HAW!
G-GULP! HAS THAT 'ORRIBLE OAK TREE GONE?
TREMBLE
YES, TEECH! AND WE'VE COLLECTED LOADS OF FIREWOOD FOR THE STOVE!
ER, HOW ARE WE GOING TO LIGHT IT? WE HAVEN'T GOT ANY MATCHES!
I'VE GOT AN IDEA, TEECH!
TING
FIRST, A FEW EXTRA-HOT MINTS, GUZZLE!
TIP
EXTRA HOT MINTS
NOW WATCH THIS, TEECH!
INHALE
OOER! I'D RATHER NOT, GULP!
COWARDY CUSTARD
HEE, HEE! BOSS IS A BIT SHORT-SIGHTED! HE MISSED THE STOVE, CACKLE!
FLAP FLAP
BREATHE
T. PATERSON
I THINK TEECH IS WARM ENOUGH NOW, SNIGGER!
SINGE SCORCH
DIVE
AARGH! I'M ON FIRE! BLUBBER!
AARGLE! GLOOBSH!
SPLOOSH
FUNNY FELLOW! ONE MINUTE HE'S COLD—THE NEXT HE'S GOING FOR A SWIM!
HAR, HAR! TEECH IS REALLY "WRINGING" IN THE NEW YEAR GUFFAW!
SPLUTTER! CHATTER!
WIND! SQUEEZE!

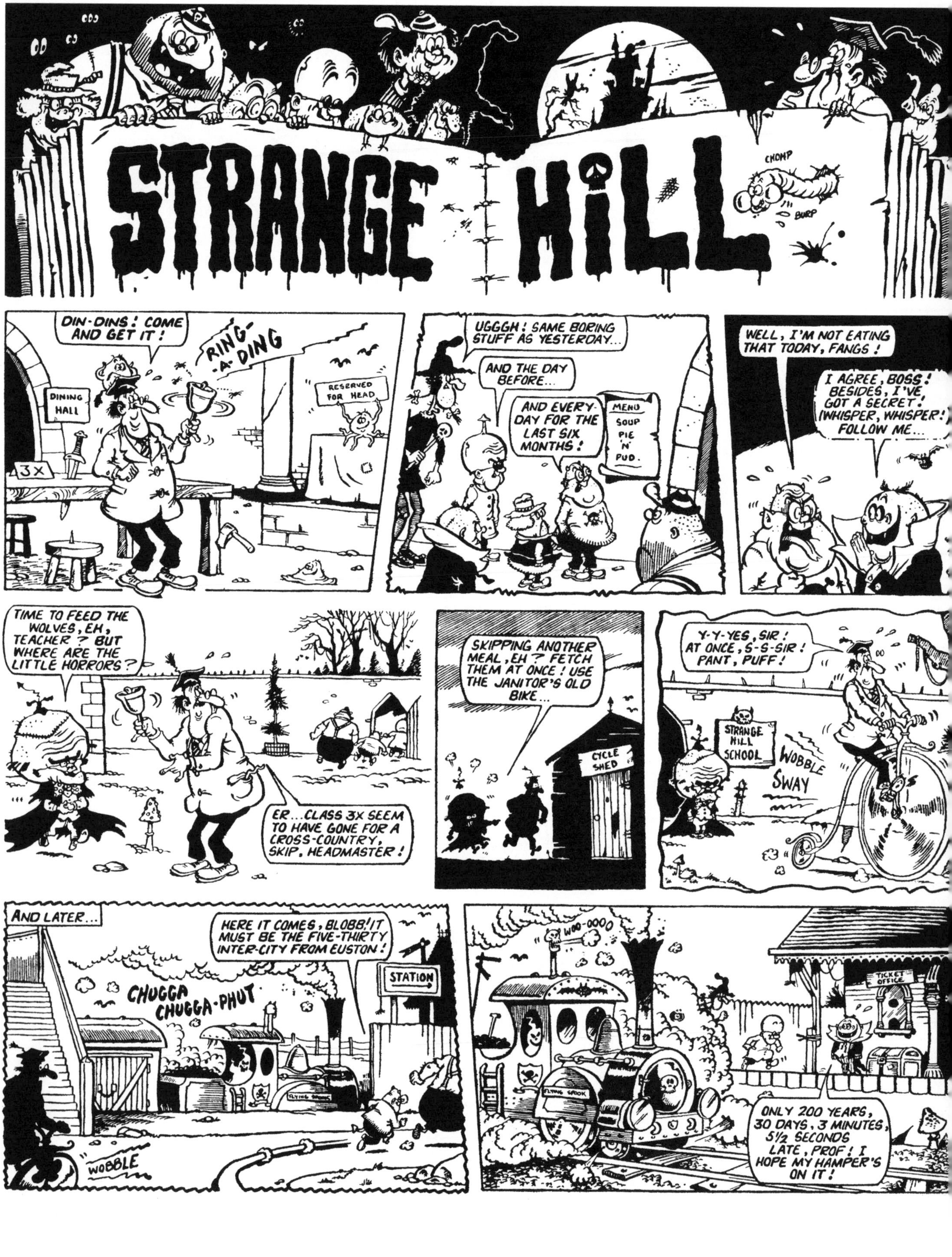
STRANGE HILL
CHOMP
BURP
DIN-DINS! COME AND GET IT!
RING-A-DING
DINING HALL
3X
RESERVED FOR HEAD
UGGGH! SAME BORING STUFF AS YESTERDAY...
AND THE DAY BEFORE...
AND EVERY DAY FOR THE LAST SIX MONTHS!
MENU
SOUP
PIE 'N' PUD.
WELL, I'M NOT EATING THAT TODAY, FANGS!
I AGREE, BOSS! BESIDES, I'VE GOT A SECRET! WHISPER, WHISPER! FOLLOW ME...
TIME TO FEED THE WOLVES, EH, TEACHER? BUT WHERE ARE THE LITTLE HORRORS?
ER...CLASS 3X SEEM TO HAVE GONE FOR A CROSS-COUNTRY, SKIP, HEADMASTER!
SKIPPING ANOTHER MEAL, EH? FETCH THEM AT ONCE! USE THE JANITOR'S OLD BIKE...
CYCLE SHED
Y-Y-YES, SIR! AT ONCE, S-S-SIR! PANT, PUFF!
STRANGE HILL SCHOOL
WOBBLE
SWAY
CHOMP
AND LATER...
HERE IT COMES, BLOBB! IT MUST BE THE FIVE-THIRTY INTER-CITY FROM EUSTON!
STATION
CHUGGA CHUGGA-PHUT
WOBBLE
WOO-OOOO
TICKET OFFICE
ONLY 200 YEARS, 30 DAYS, 3 MINUTES, 5½ SECONDS LATE, PROF! I HOPE MY HAMPER'S ON IT!

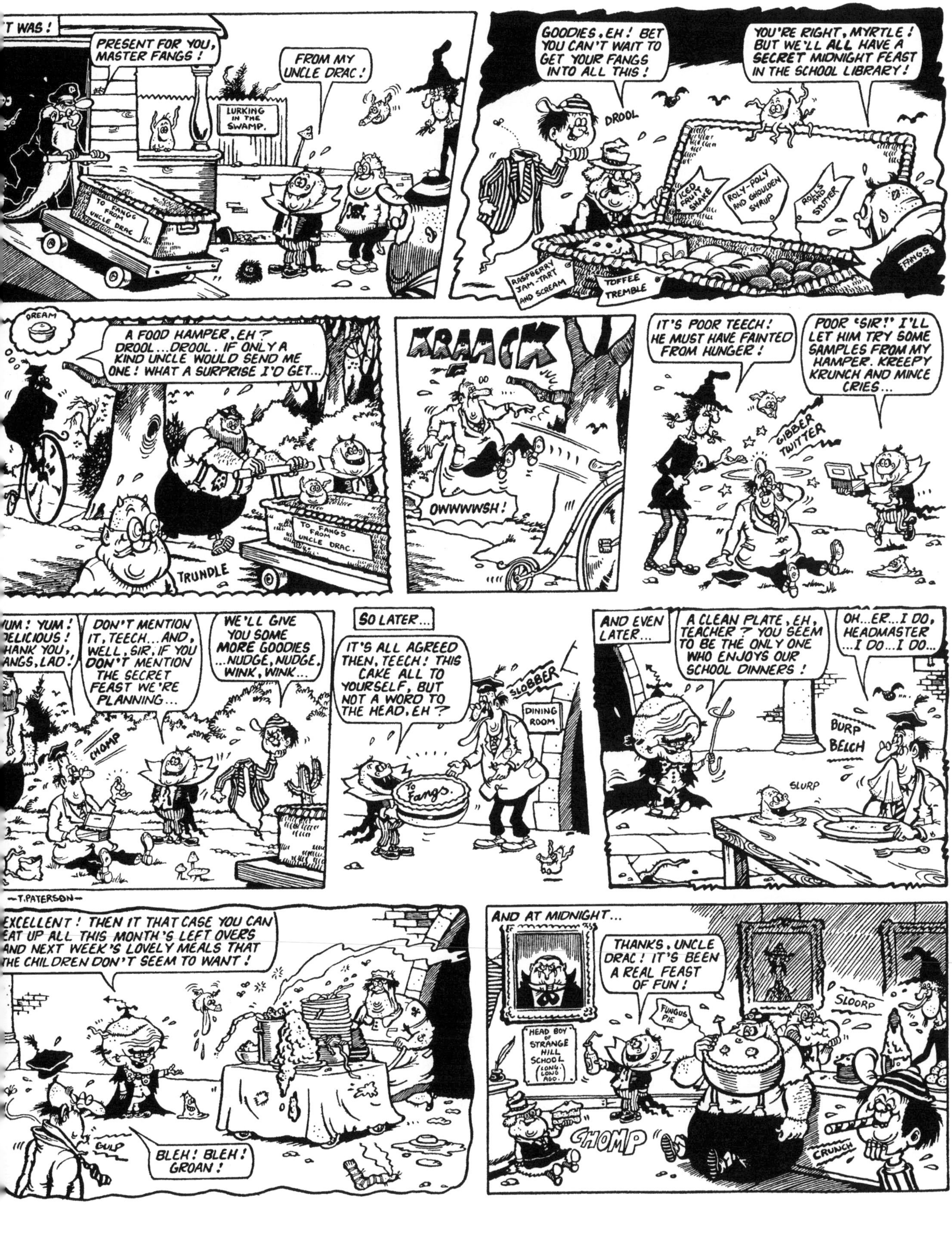
T WAS !
PRESENT FOR YOU, MASTER FANGS !
FROM MY UNCLE DRAC !
LURKING IN THE SWAMP.
TO FANGS FROM UNCLE DRAC
GOODIES, EH! BET YOU CAN'T WAIT TO GET YOUR FANGS INTO ALL THIS !
YOU'RE RIGHT, MYRTLE ! BUT WE'LL ALL HAVE A SECRET MIDNIGHT FEAST IN THE SCHOOL LIBRARY !
DROOL
ICED FRUIT SHAKE
ROLY-POLY AND GHOULDEN SYRUP
ROLLS AND STUTTER
RASPBERRY JAM-TART AND SCREAM
TOFFEE TREMBLE
FANGS
DREAM
A FOOD HAMPER, EH? DROOL... DROOL. IF ONLY A KIND UNCLE WOULD SEND ME ONE! WHAT A SURPRISE I'D GET...
TRUNDLE
TO FANGS FROM UNCLE DRAC.
KRAACK
OWWWWSH !
IT'S POOR TEECH ! HE MUST HAVE FAINTED FROM HUNGER !
POOR 'SIR!' I'LL LET HIM TRY SOME SAMPLES FROM MY HAMPER. KREEPY KRUNCH AND MINCE CRIES...
GIBBER TWITTER
UM ! YUM ! ELICIOUS ! HANK YOU, ANGS, LAD !
DON'T MENTION IT, TEECH... AND, WELL, SIR, IF YOU DON'T MENTION THE SECRET FEAST WE'RE PLANNING...
WE'LL GIVE YOU SOME MORE GOODIES ...NUDGE, NUDGE. WINK, WINK...
CHOMP
SO LATER...
IT'S ALL AGREED THEN, TEECH ! THIS CAKE ALL TO YOURSELF, BUT NOT A WORD TO THE HEAD, EH?
SLOBBER
DINING ROOM
To Fangs
AND EVEN LATER...
A CLEAN PLATE, EH, TEACHER? YOU SEEM TO BE THE ONLY ONE WHO ENJOYS OUR SCHOOL DINNERS !
OH...ER...I DO, HEADMASTER ...I DO...I DO...
BURP
BELCH
SLURP
T. PATERSON
EXCELLENT ! THEN IT THAT CASE YOU CAN EAT UP ALL THIS MONTH'S LEFT OVERS AND NEXT WEEK'S LOVELY MEALS THAT THE CHILDREN DON'T SEEM TO WANT !
GULP
BLEH ! BLEH ! GROAN !
AND AT MIDNIGHT...
THANKS, UNCLE DRAC ! IT'S BEEN A REAL FEAST OF FUN !
FUNGUS PIE
HEAD BOY OF STRANGE HILL SCHOOL. (LONG LONG AGO.)
SLOORP
CHOMP
CRUNCH

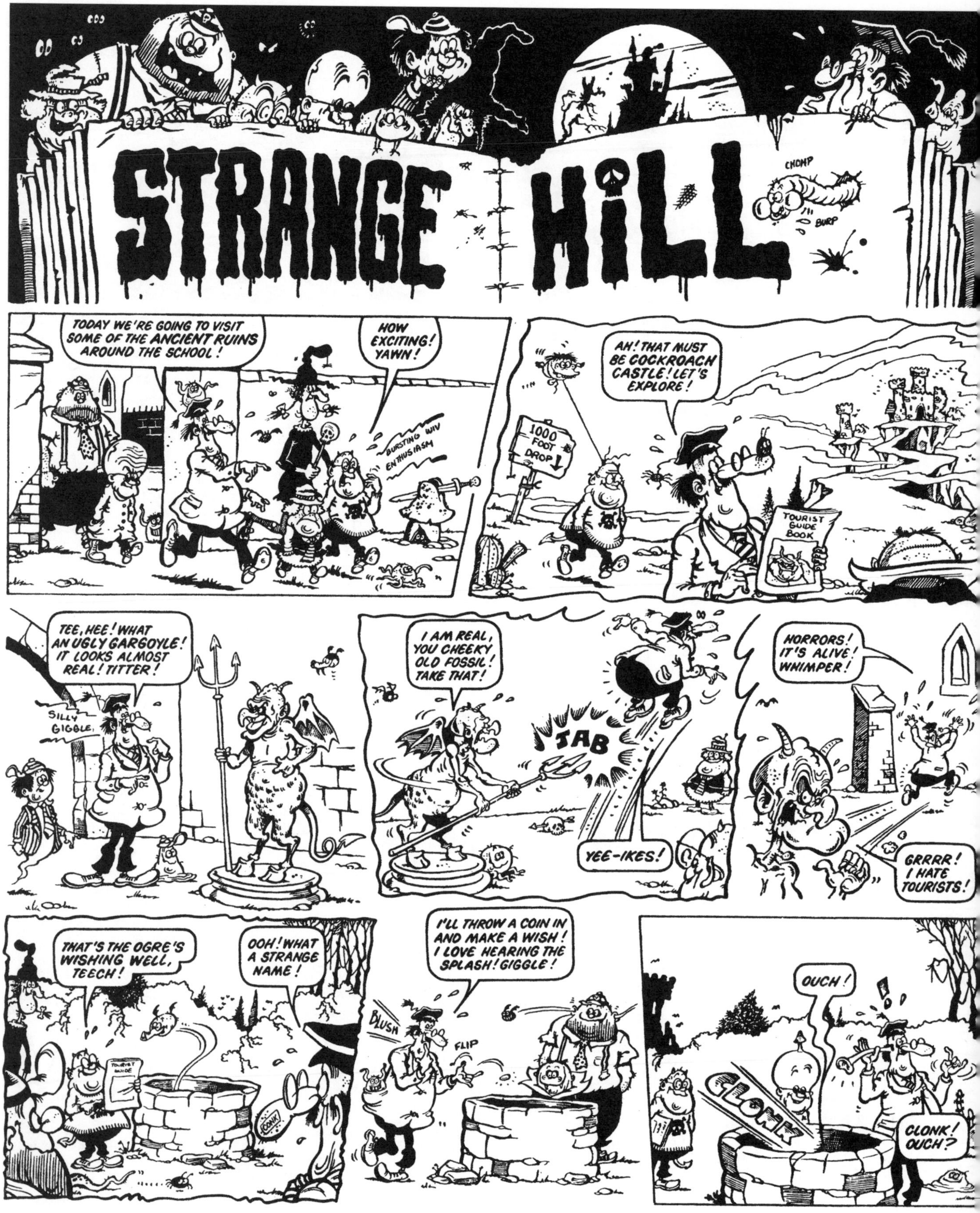
STRANGE HILL
CHOMP
BURP
TODAY WE'RE GOING TO VISIT SOME OF THE ANCIENT RUINS AROUND THE SCHOOL!
HOW EXCITING! YAWN!
BURSTING WIV ENTHUSIASM
AH! THAT MUST BE COCKROACH CASTLE! LET'S EXPLORE!
1000 FOOT DROP
TOURIST GUIDE BOOK
TEE, HEE! WHAT AN UGLY GARGOYLE! IT LOOKS ALMOST REAL! TITTER!
SILLY GIGGLE
I AM REAL, YOU CHEEKY OLD FOSSIL! TAKE THAT!
JAB
YEE-IKES!
HORRORS! IT'S ALIVE! WHIMPER!
GRRRR! I HATE TOURISTS!
THAT'S THE OGRE'S WISHING WELL, TEECH!
OOH! WHAT A STRANGE NAME!
CONK
I'LL THROW A COIN IN AND MAKE A WISH! I LOVE HEARING THE SPLASH! GIGGLE!
BLUSH
FLIP
OUCH!
CLONK
CLONK! OUCH?

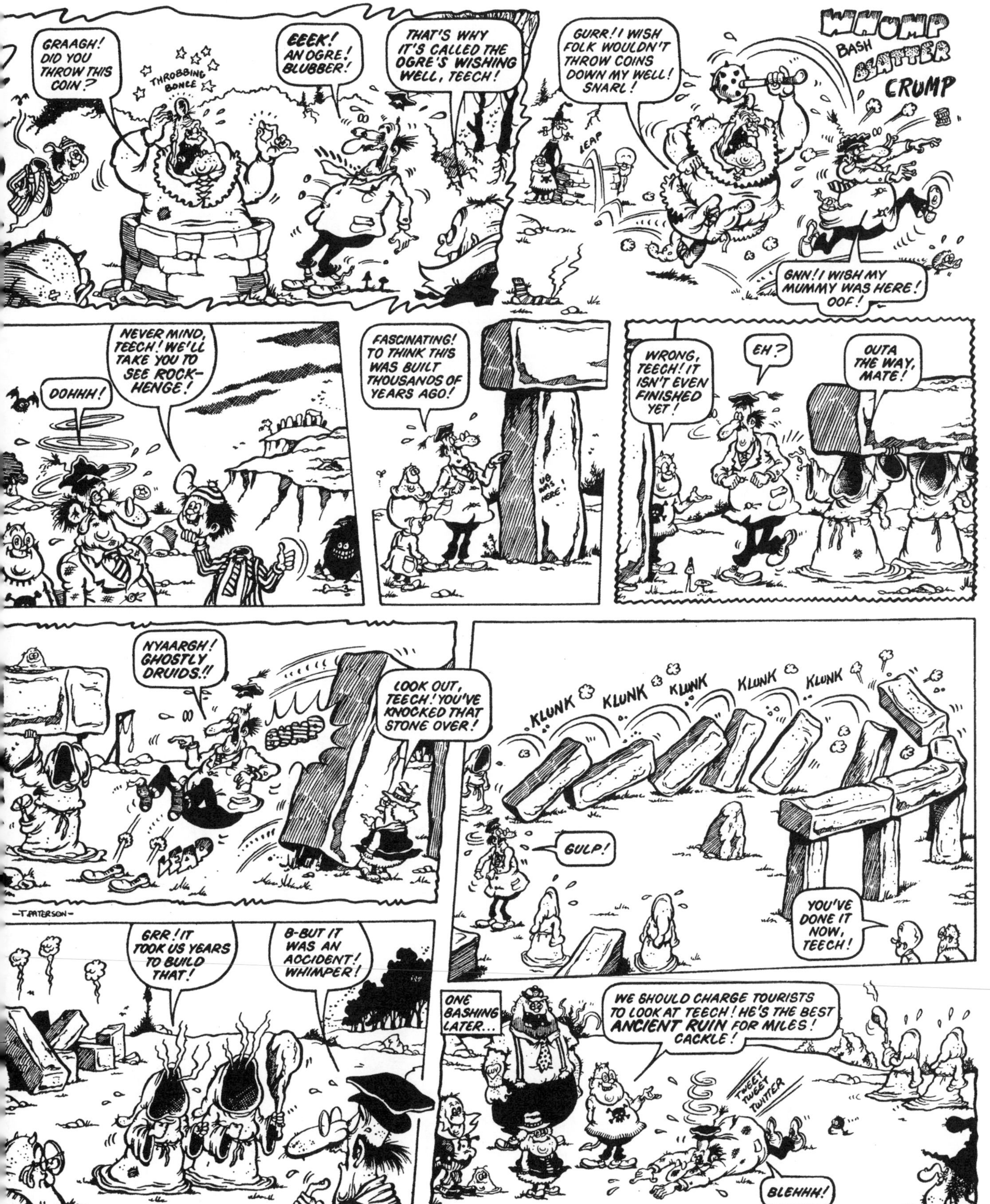
GRAAGH! DID YOU THROW THIS COIN?
THROBBING BONCE
EEEK! AN OGRE! BLUBBER!
THAT'S WHY IT'S CALLED THE OGRE'S WISHING WELL, TEECH!
GURR! I WISH FOLK WOULDN'T THROW COINS DOWN MY WELL! SNARL!
LEAP
WHUMP
BASH
SLATTER
CRUMP
GNN! I WISH MY MUMMY WAS HERE! OOF!
NEVER MIND, TEECH! WE'LL TAKE YOU TO SEE ROCK-HENGE!
DOHHH!
FASCINATING! TO THINK THIS WAS BUILT THOUSANDS OF YEARS AGO!
UG WAS HERE!
WRONG, TEECH! IT ISN'T EVEN FINISHED YET!
EH?
OUTA THE WAY, MATE!
NYAARGH! GHOSTLY DRUIDS!!
LOOK OUT, TEECH! YOU'VE KNOCKED THAT STONE OVER!
LEAP
KLUNK
KLUNK
KLUNK
KLUNK
KLUNK
GULP!
YOU'VE DONE IT NOW, TEECH!
-T.PATERSON-
GRR! IT TOOK US YEARS TO BUILD THAT!
B-BUT IT WAS AN ACCIDENT! WHIMPER!
ONE BASHING LATER...
WE SHOULD CHARGE TOURISTS TO LOOK AT TEECH! HE'S THE BEST ANCIENT RUIN FOR MILES! CACKLE!
TWEET TWEET TWITTER
BLEHHH!

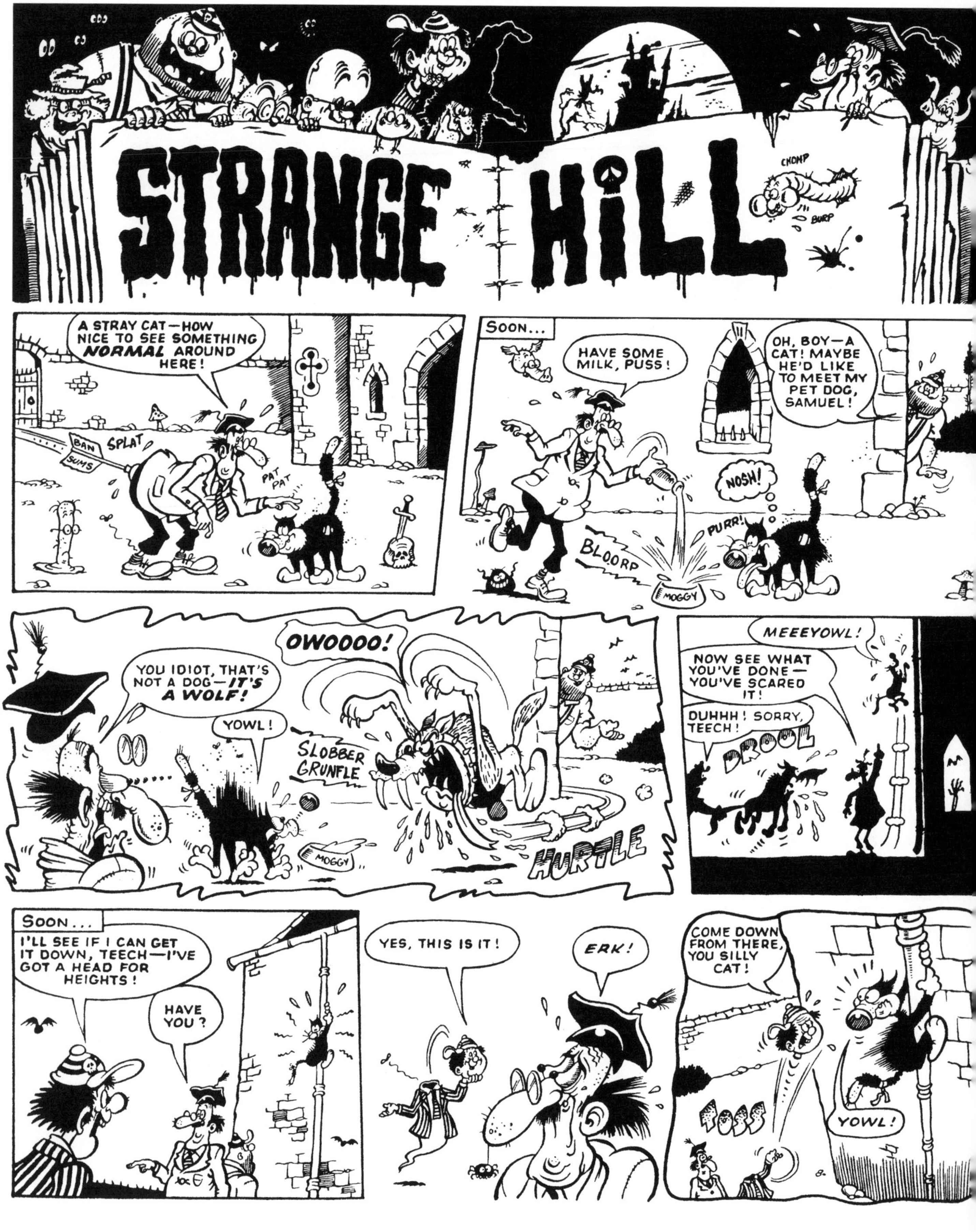
STRANGE HILL
CHOMP
BURP
A STRAY CAT—HOW NICE TO SEE SOMETHING NORMAL AROUND HERE!
BAN SUMS
SPLAT
PAT PAT
SOON...
HAVE SOME MILK, PUSS!
OH, BOY—A CAT! MAYBE HE'D LIKE TO MEET MY PET DOG, SAMUEL!
NOSH!
PURR!
BLOORP
MOGGY
OWOOOO!
YOU IDIOT, THAT'S NOT A DOG—IT'S A WOLF!
YOWL!
SLOBBER GRUNFLE
MOGGY
HURTLE
MEEEYOWL!
NOW SEE WHAT YOU'VE DONE—YOU'VE SCARED IT!
DUHHH! SORRY, TEECH!
DROOL
SOON...
I'LL SEE IF I CAN GET IT DOWN, TEECH—I'VE GOT A HEAD FOR HEIGHTS!
HAVE YOU?
YES, THIS IS IT!
ERK!
COME DOWN FROM THERE, YOU SILLY CAT!
YOWL!

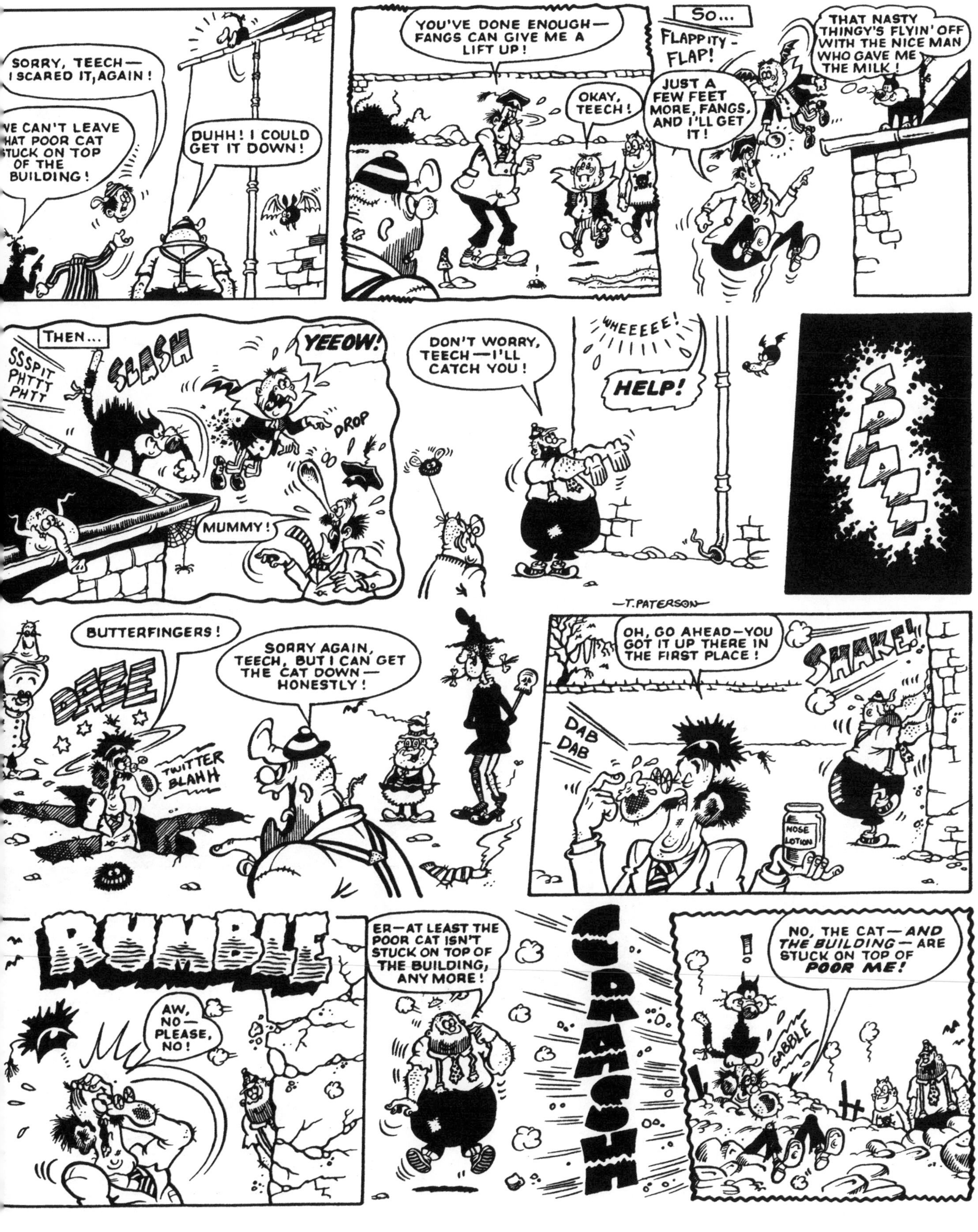
SORRY, TEECH— I SCARED IT, AGAIN!
VE CAN'T LEAVE HAT POOR CAT TUCK ON TOP OF THE BUILDING!
DUHH! I COULD GET IT DOWN!
YOU'VE DONE ENOUGH— FANGS CAN GIVE ME A LIFT UP!
OKAY, TEECH!
SO...
FLAPPITY-FLAP!
JUST A FEW FEET MORE, FANGS, AND I'LL GET IT!
THAT NASTY THINGY'S FLYIN' OFF WITH THE NICE MAN WHO GAVE ME THE MILK!
THEN...
SSSPIT PHTTT PHTT
SLASH
YEEOW!
DROP
MUMMY!
DON'T WORRY, TEECH—I'LL CATCH YOU!
WHEEEEE!
HELP!
T. PATERSON
BUTTERFINGERS!
DAZE
TWITTER BLAHH
SORRY AGAIN, TEECH, BUT I CAN GET THE CAT DOWN— HONESTLY!
OH, GO AHEAD—YOU GOT IT UP THERE IN THE FIRST PLACE!
SHAKE!
DAB DAB
NOSE LOTION
RUMBLE
AW, NO— PLEASE, NO!
ER—AT LEAST THE POOR CAT ISN'T STUCK ON TOP OF THE BUILDING, ANY MORE!
CRASH
NO, THE CAT—AND THE BUILDING—ARE STUCK ON TOP OF POOR ME!
GABBLE

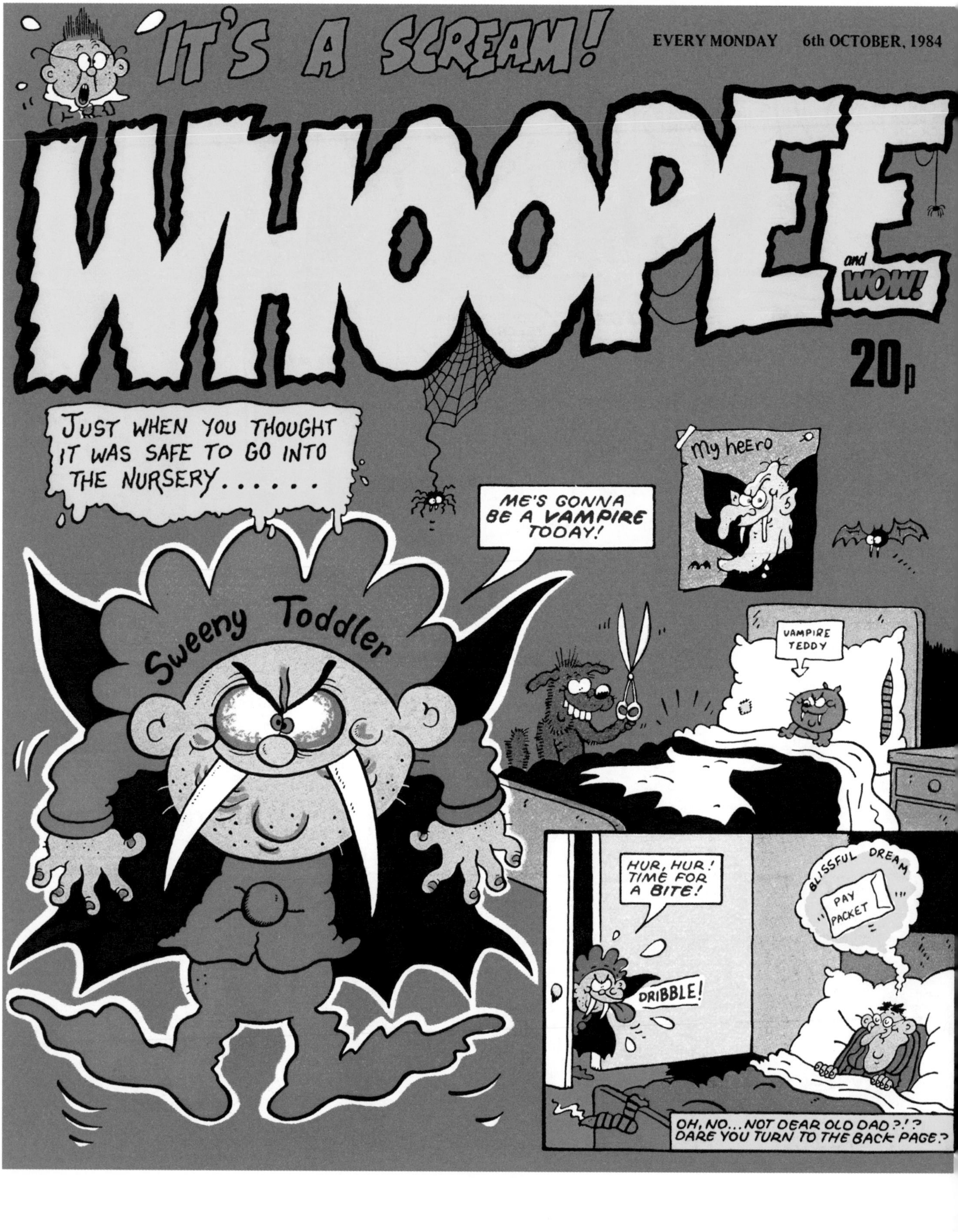
IT'S A SCREAM!
EVERY MONDAY 6th OCTOBER, 1984
WHOOPEE
and WOW!
20p
JUST WHEN YOU THOUGHT IT WAS SAFE TO GO INTO THE NURSERY......
ME'S GONNA BE A VAMPIRE TODAY!
My heero
Sweeny Toddler
VAMPIRE TEDDY
HUR, HUR! TIME FOR A BITE!
BLISSFUL DREAM
PAY PACKET
DRIBBLE!
OH, NO... NOT DEAR OLD DAD ?!? DARE YOU TURN TO THE BACK PAGE?

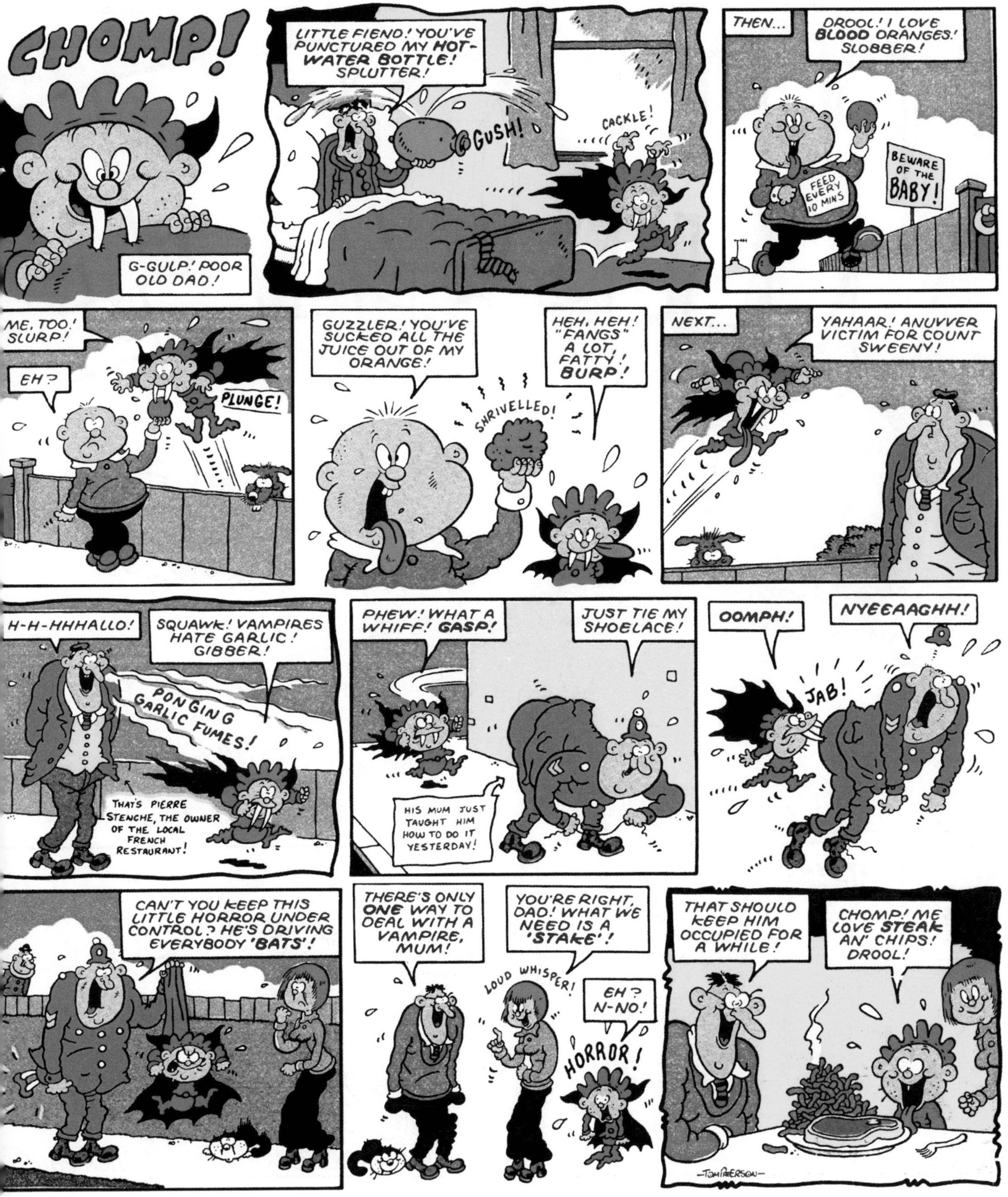
CHOMP!
G-GULP! POOR OLD DAD!
LITTLE FIEND! YOU'VE PUNCTURED MY HOT-WATER BOTTLE! SPLUTTER!
GUSH!
CACKLE!
THEN...
DROOL! I LOVE BLOOD ORANGES! SLOBBER!
FEED EVERY 10 MINS
BEWARE OF THE BABY!
ME, TOO! SLURP!
EH?
PLUNGE!
GUZZLER! YOU'VE SUCKED ALL THE JUICE OUT OF MY ORANGE!
SHRIVELLED!
HEH, HEH! "FANGS" A LOT, FATTY! BURP!
NEXT...
YAHAAR! ANUVVER VICTIM FOR COUNT SWEENY!
H-H-HHHALLO!
SQUAWK! VAMPIRES HATE GARLIC! GIBBER!
PONGING GARLIC FUMES!
THAT'S PIERRE STENCHE, THE OWNER OF THE LOCAL FRENCH RESTAURANT!
PHEW! WHAT A WHIFF! GASP!
JUST TIE MY SHOELACE!
HIS MUM JUST TAUGHT HIM HOW TO DO IT YESTERDAY!
OOMPH!
NYEEAAGHH!
JAB!
CAN'T YOU KEEP THIS LITTLE HORROR UNDER CONTROL? HE'S DRIVING EVERYBODY 'BATS'!
THERE'S ONLY ONE WAY TO DEAL WITH A VAMPIRE, MUM!
YOU'RE RIGHT, DAD! WHAT WE NEED IS A 'STAKE'!
LOUD WHISPER!
EH? N-NO!
HORROR!
THAT SHOULD KEEP HIM OCCUPIED FOR A WHILE!
CHOMP! ME LOVE STEAK AN' CHIPS! DROOL!
TOM PATERSON

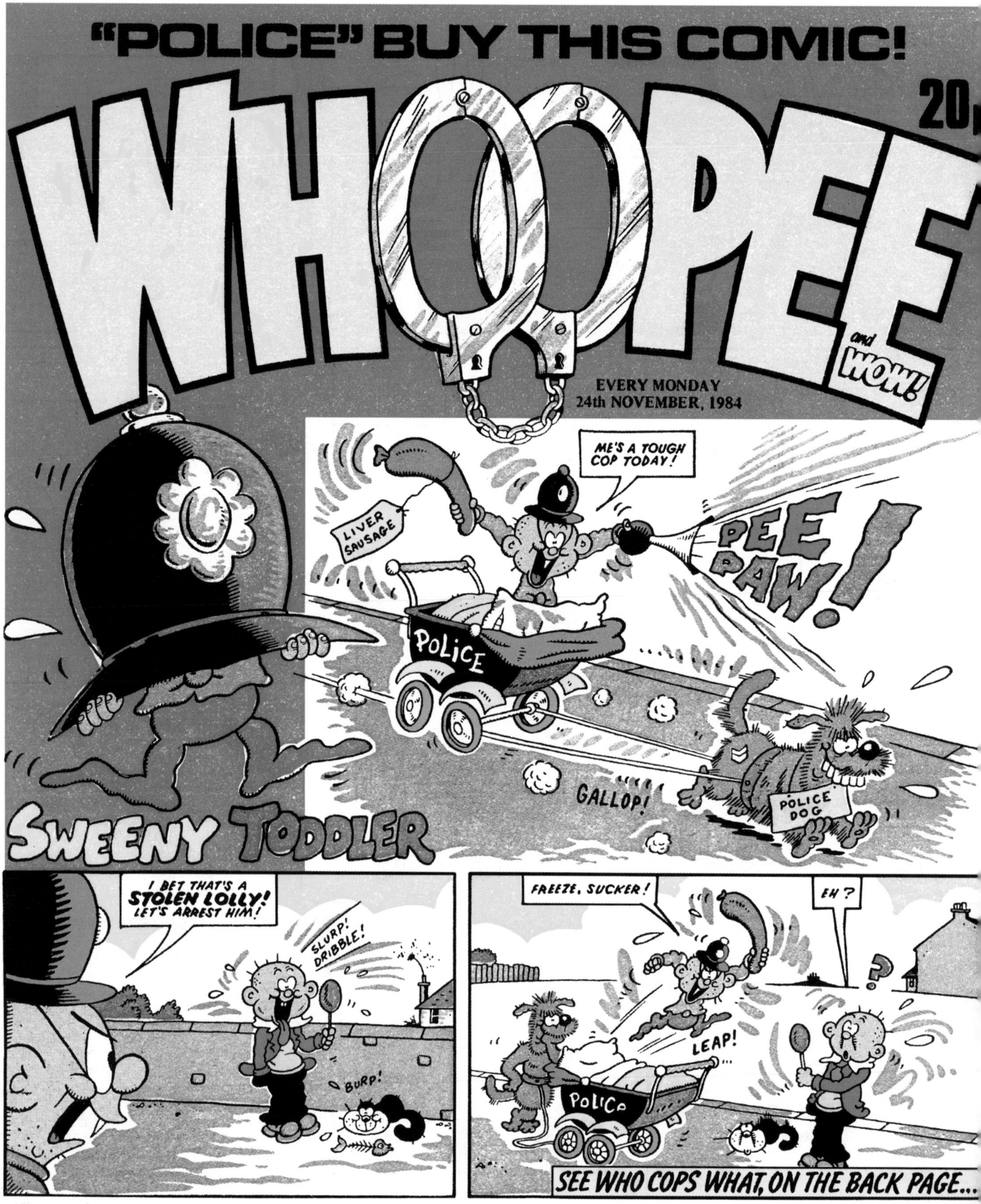
"POLICE" BUY THIS COMIC!
WHOOPEE
20p
and WOW!
EVERY MONDAY
24th NOVEMBER, 1984
ME'S A TOUGH COP TODAY!
LIVER SAUSAGE
PEE PAW!
POLICE
GALLOP!
POLICE DOG
SWEENY TODDLER
I BET THAT'S A STOLEN LOLLY! LET'S ARREST HIM!
SLURP! DRIBBLE!
BURP!
FREEZE, SUCKER!
EH?
LEAP!
POLICE
SEE WHO COPS WHAT, ON THE BACK PAGE...

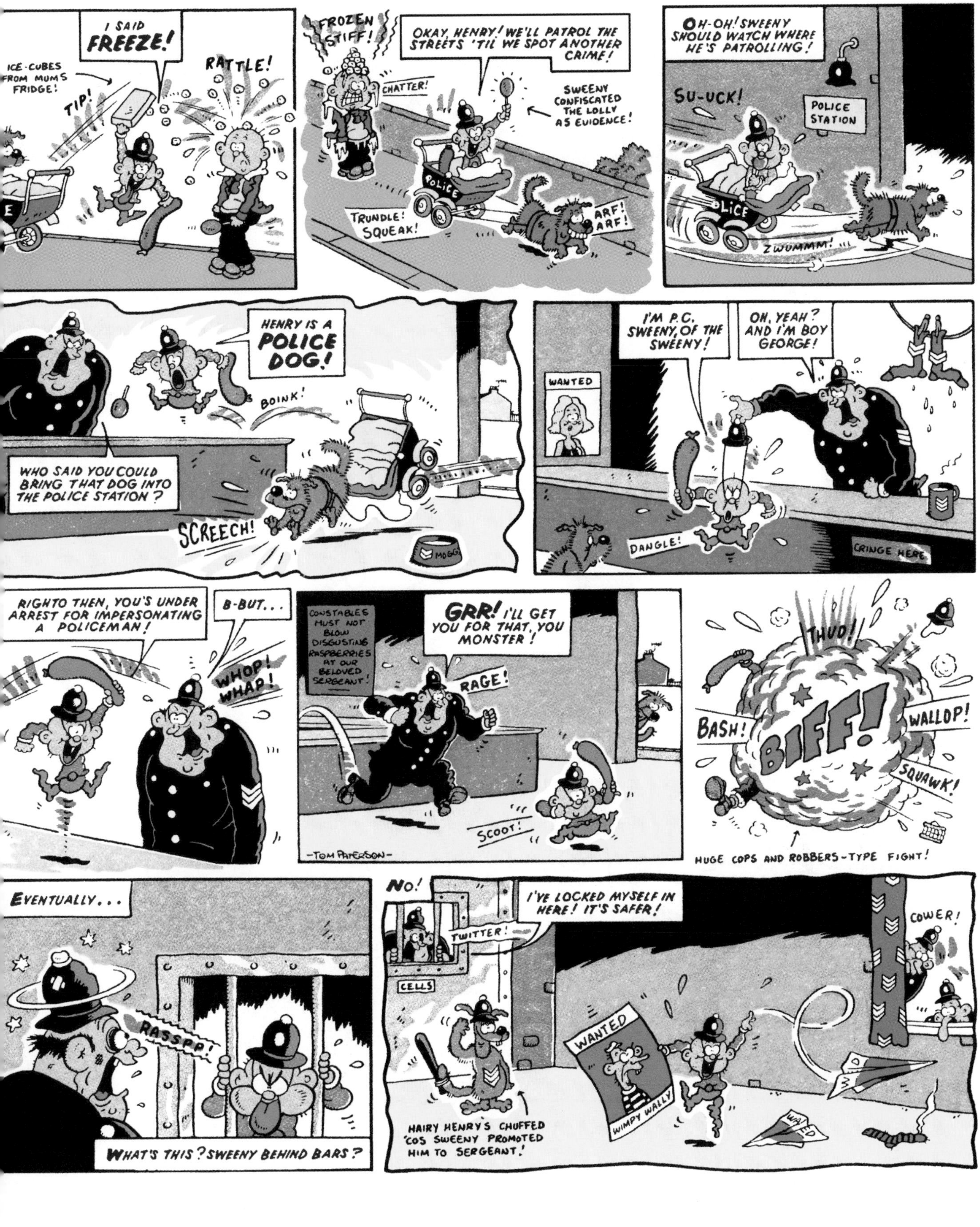

I SAID FREEZE!
ICE-CUBES FROM MUM'S FRIDGE!
TIP!
RATTLE!
FROZEN STIFF!
OKAY, HENRY! WE'LL PATROL THE STREETS 'TIL WE SPOT ANOTHER CRIME!
CHATTER!
SWEENY CONFISCATED THE LOLLY AS EVIDENCE!
POLICE
TRUNDLE! SQUEAK!
ARF! ARF!
OH-OH! SWEENY SHOULD WATCH WHERE HE'S PATROLLING!
SU-UCK!
POLICE STATION
LICE
ZWUMMM!
HENRY IS A POLICE DOG!
BOINK!
WHO SAID YOU COULD BRING THAT DOG INTO THE POLICE STATION?
SCREECH!
MOGGY
I'M P.C. SWEENY, OF THE SWEENY!
OH, YEAH? AND I'M BOY GEORGE!
WANTED
DANGLE!
CRINGE HERE
RIGHTO THEN, YOU'S UNDER ARREST FOR IMPERSONATING A POLICEMAN!
B-BUT...
WHOP! WHAP!
CONSTABLES MUST NOT BLOW DISGUSTING RASPBERRIES AT OUR BELOVED SERGEANT!
GRR! I'LL GET YOU FOR THAT, YOU MONSTER!
RAGE!
SCOOT!
-TOM PATERSON-
THUD!
BASH!
BIFF!
WALLOP!
SQUAWK!
HUGE COPS AND ROBBERS-TYPE FIGHT!
EVENTUALLY...
RASSPP!
WHAT'S THIS? SWEENY BEHIND BARS?
NO!
I'VE LOCKED MYSELF IN HERE! IT'S SAFER!
TWITTER!
CELLS
COWER!
WANTED
WIMPY WALLY
HAIRY HENRY'S CHUFFED 'COS SWEENY PROMOTED HIM TO SERGEANT!

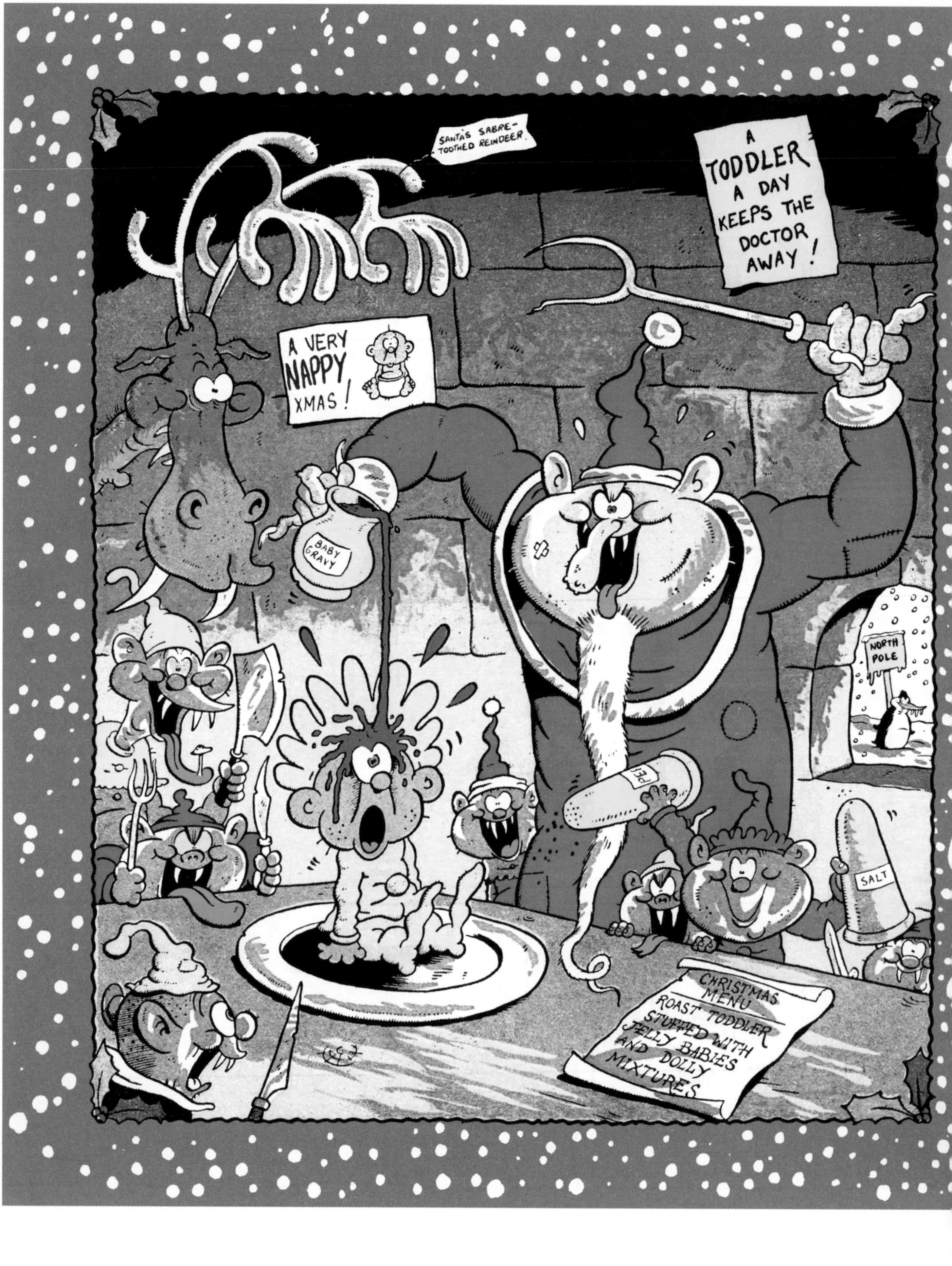
SANTA'S SABRE-TOOTHED REINDEER
A TODDLER A DAY KEEPS THE DOCTOR AWAY!
A VERY NAPPY XMAS!
BABY GRAVY
NORTH POLE
PEA
SALT
CHRISTMAS MENU
ROAST TODDLER STUFFED WITH JELLY BABIES AND DOLLY MIXTURES

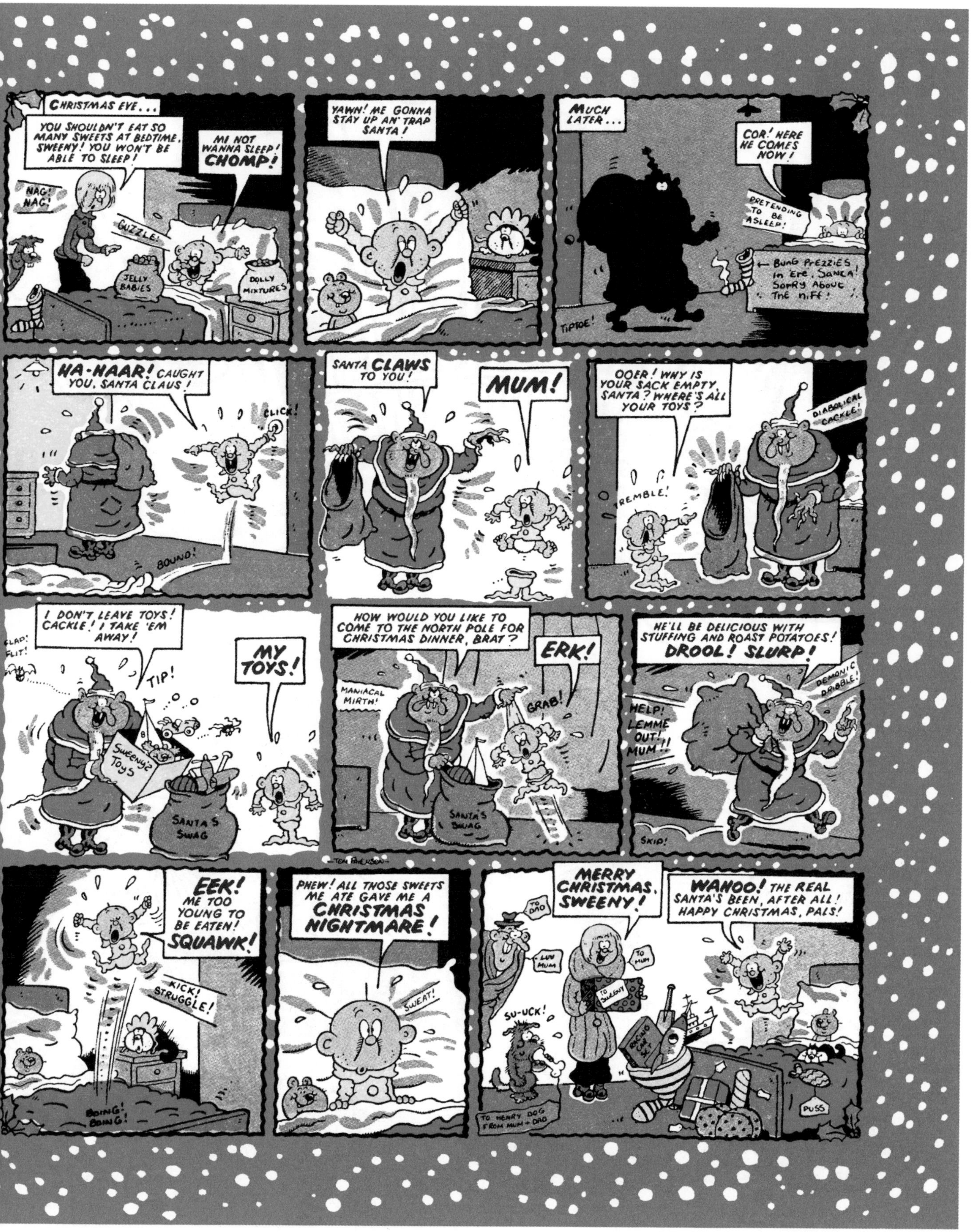
CHRISTMAS EVE...
YOU SHOULDN'T EAT SO MANY SWEETS AT BEDTIME, SWEENY! YOU WON'T BE ABLE TO SLEEP!
MI NOT WANNA SLEEP! CHOMP!
NAG! NAG!
GUZZLE!
JELLY BABIES
DOLLY MIXTURES
YAWN! ME GONNA STAY UP AN' TRAP SANTA!
MUCH LATER...
COR! HERE HE COMES NOW!
PRETENDING TO BE ASLEEP!
← BUNG PREZZIES IN 'ERE, SANTA! SORRY ABOUT THE NIFF!
TIPTOE!
HA-HAAR! CAUGHT YOU, SANTA CLAUS!
CLICK!
BOUND!
SANTA CLAWS TO YOU!
MUM!
OOER! WHY IS YOUR SACK EMPTY, SANTA? WHERE'S ALL YOUR TOYS?
DIABOLICAL CACKLE!
TREMBLE!
I DON'T LEAVE TOYS! CACKLE! I TAKE 'EM AWAY!
SLAP! FLIT!
TIP!
MY TOYS!
SWEENY'S TOYS
SANTA'S SWAG
HOW WOULD YOU LIKE TO COME TO THE NORTH POLE FOR CHRISTMAS DINNER, BRAT?
ERK!
MANIACAL MIRTH!
GRAB!
SANTA'S SWAG
HE'LL BE DELICIOUS WITH STUFFING AND ROAST POTATOES! DROOL! SLURP!
DEMONIC DRIBBLE!
HELP! LEMME OUT! MUM!!
SKIP!
EEK! ME TOO YOUNG TO BE EATEN! SQUAWK!
KICK! STRUGGLE!
BOING! BOING!
PHEW! ALL THOSE SWEETS ME ATE GAVE ME A CHRISTMAS NIGHTMARE!
SWEAT!
MERRY CHRISTMAS, SWEENY!
WANOO! THE REAL SANTA'S BEEN, AFTER ALL! HAPPY CHRISTMAS, PALS!
TO DAD
LUV MUM
TO MUM
TO SWEENY
SU-UCK!
RACING CAR SET
PUSS
TO HENRY DOG FROM MUM + DAD

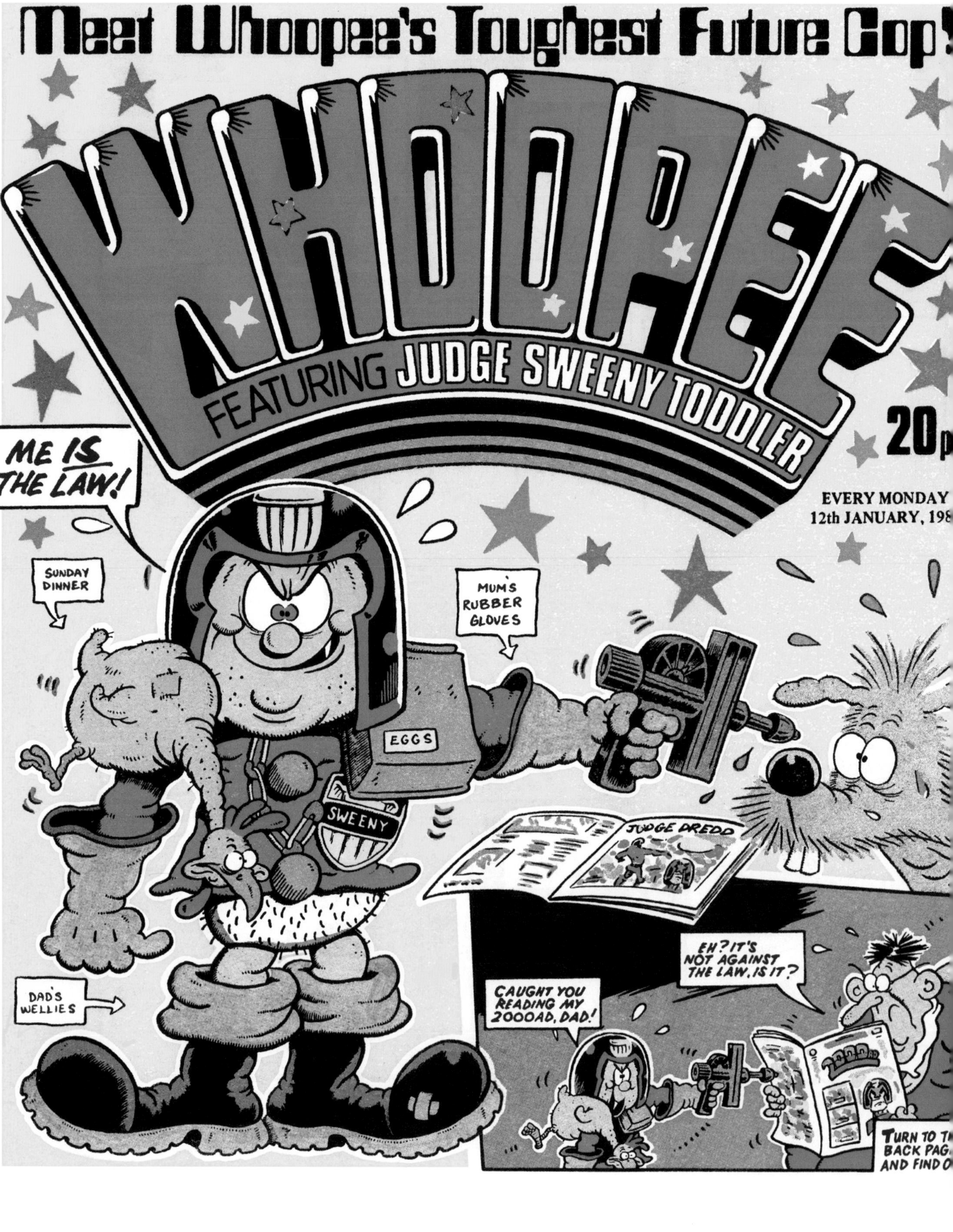
Meet Whoopee's Toughest Future Cop!
WHOOPEE
FEATURING JUDGE SWEENY TODDLER
20p
EVERY MONDAY
12th JANUARY, 198
ME IS THE LAW!
SUNDAY DINNER
MUM'S RUBBER GLOVES
EGGS
SWEENY
JUDGE DREDD
DAD'S WELLIES
EH? IT'S NOT AGAINST THE LAW, IS IT?
CAUGHT YOU READING MY 2000AD, DAD!
TURN TO TH
BACK PAG
AND FIND O

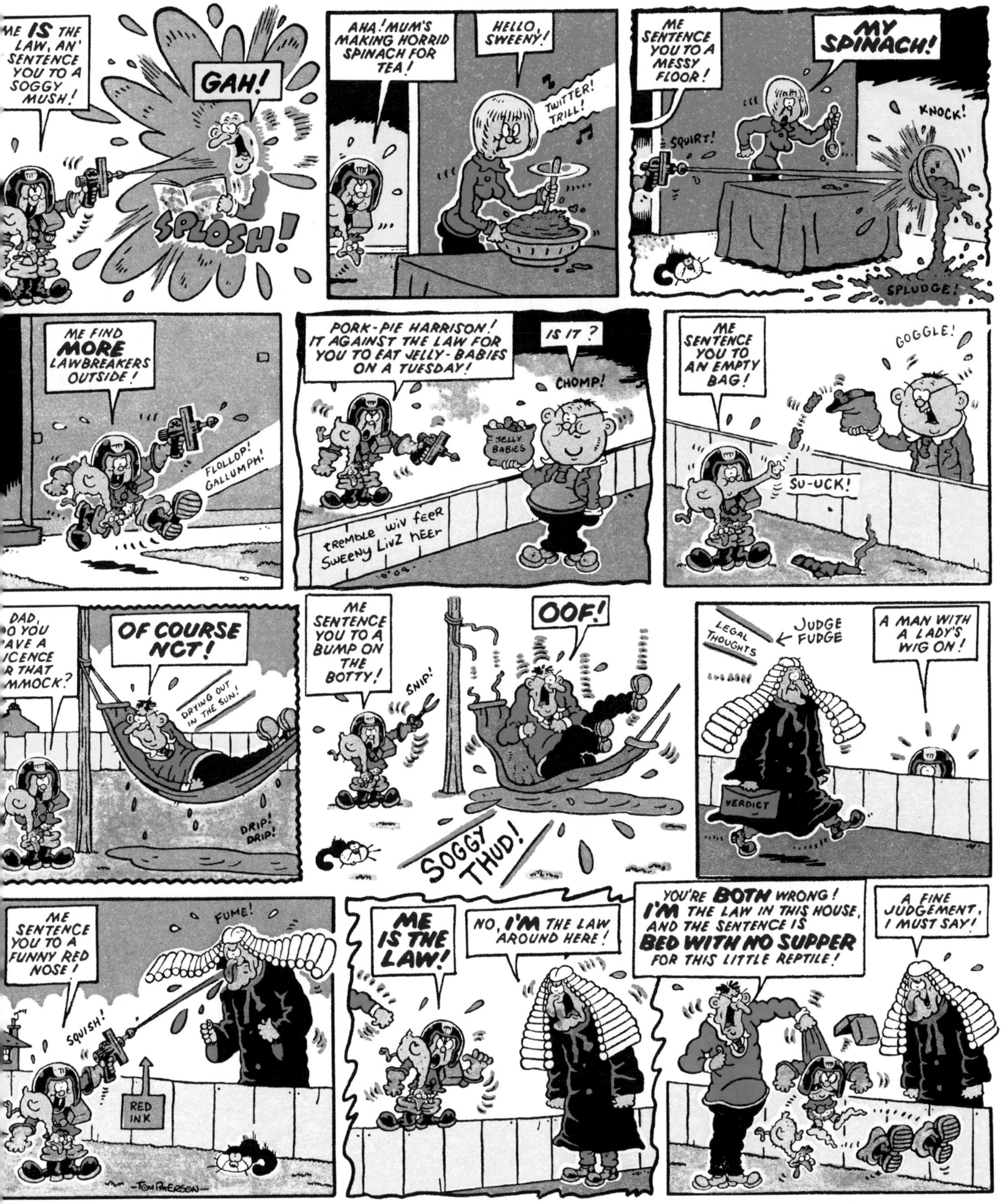

ME IS THE LAW, AN' SENTENCE YOU TO A SOGGY MUSH!
GAH!
SPLOSH!
AHA! MUM'S MAKING HORRID SPINACH FOR TEA!
HELLO, SWEENY!
TWITTER! TRILL!
ME SENTENCE YOU TO A MESSY FLOOR!
MY SPINACH!
SQUIRT!
KNOCK!
SPLUDGE!
ME FIND MORE LAWBREAKERS OUTSIDE!
FLOLLOP! GALLUMPH!
PORK-PIE HARRISON! IT AGAINST THE LAW FOR YOU TO EAT JELLY-BABIES ON A TUESDAY!
IS IT?
CHOMP!
JELLY BABIES
tremble wiv feer Sweeny LivZ heer
ME SENTENCE YOU TO AN EMPTY BAG!
GOGGLE!
SU-UCK!
DAD, O YOU AVE A ICENCE R THAT MMOCK?
OF COURSE NCT!
DRYING OUT IN THE SUN!
DRIP! DRIP!
ME SENTENCE YOU TO A BUMP ON THE BOTTY!
SNIP!
OOF!
SOGGY THUD!
LEGAL THOUGHTS
JUDGE FUDGE
A MAN WITH A LADY'S WIG ON!
VERDICT
ME SENTENCE YOU TO A FUNNY RED NOSE!
FUME!
SQUISH!
RED INK
-TOM PATERSON-
ME IS THE LAW!
NO, I'M THE LAW AROUND HERE!
YOU'RE BOTH WRONG! I'M THE LAW IN THIS HOUSE, AND THE SENTENCE IS BED WITH NO SUPPER FOR THIS LITTLE REPTILE!
A FINE JUDGEMENT, I MUST SAY!

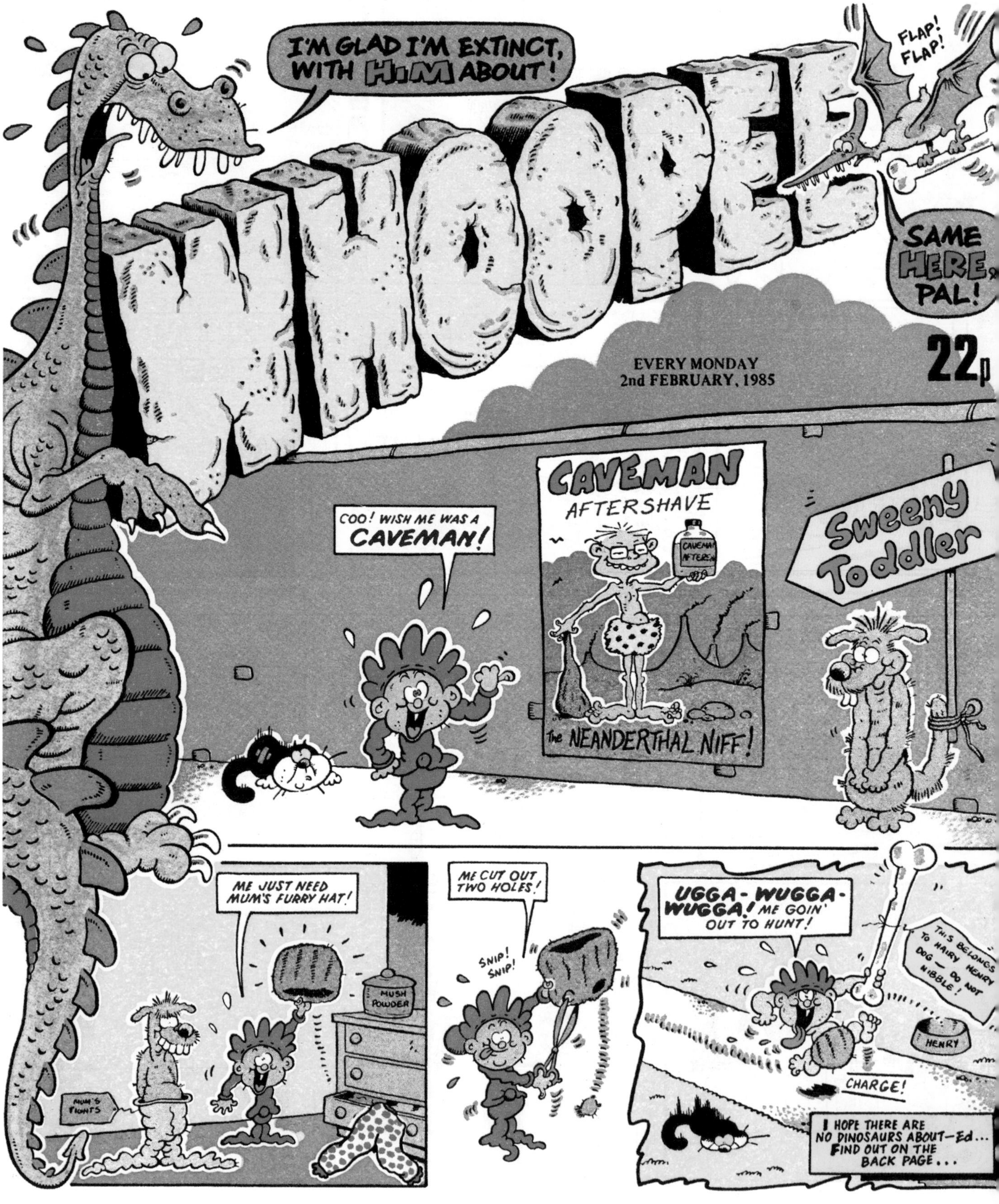
I'M GLAD I'M EXTINCT, WITH HIM ABOUT!
WHOOPEE
FLAP! FLAP!
SAME HERE, PAL!
EVERY MONDAY
2nd FEBRUARY, 1985
22p
COO! WISH ME WAS A CAVEMAN!
CAVEMAN AFTERSHAVE
The NEANDERTHAL NIFF!
Sweeny Toddler
ME JUST NEED MUM'S FURRY HAT!
MUSH POWDER
ME CUT OUT TWO HOLES!
SNIP! SNIP!
UGGA-WUGGA-WUGGA! ME GOIN' OUT TO HUNT!
THIS BELONGS TO HAIRY HENRY DOG — DO NOT NIBBLE!
HENRY
CHARGE!
I HOPE THERE ARE NO DINOSAURS ABOUT—Ed... FIND OUT ON THE BACK PAGE...

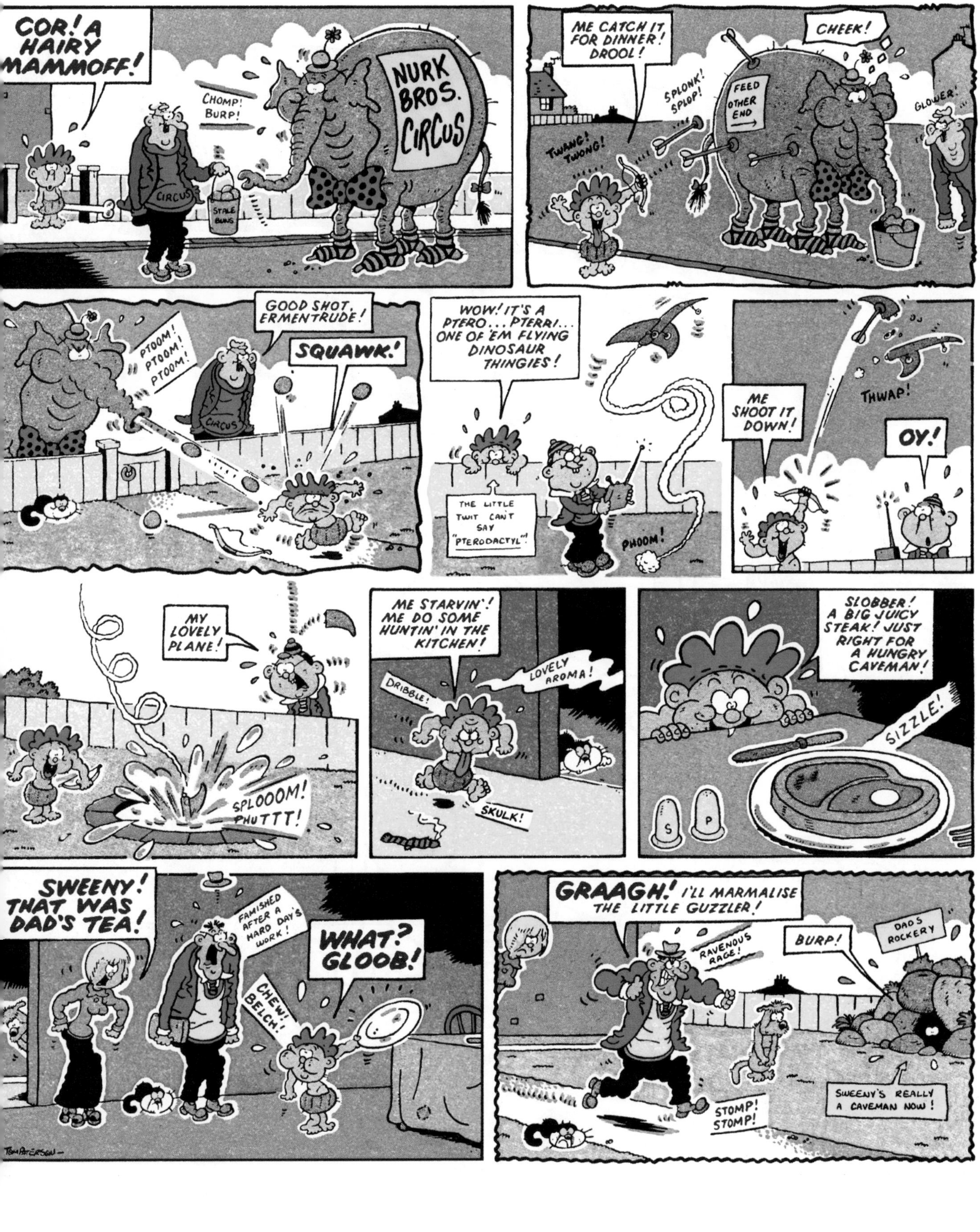
COR! A HAIRY MAMMOFF!
CHOMP! BURP!
NURK BROS. CIRCUS
CIRCUS
STALE BUNS
ME CATCH IT FOR DINNER! DROOL!
CHEEK!
SPLONK! SPLOP!
FEED OTHER END
TWANG! TWONG!
GLOWER!
GOOD SHOT, ERMENTRUDE!
PTOOM! PTOOM! PTOOM!
SQUAWK!
CIRCUS
WOW! IT'S A PTERO... PTERR!... ONE OF 'EM FLYING DINOSAUR THINGIES!
THE LITTLE TWIT CAN'T SAY "PTERODACTYL"!
PHOOM!
ME SHOOT IT DOWN!
THWAP!
OY!
MY LOVELY PLANE!
SPLOOOM! PHUTTT!
ME STARVIN'! ME DO SOME HUNTIN' IN THE KITCHEN!
LOVELY AROMA!
DRIBBLE!
SKULK!
SLOBBER! A BIG JUICY STEAK! JUST RIGHT FOR A HUNGRY CAVEMAN!
SIZZLE!
S
P
SWEENY! THAT WAS DAD'S TEA!
FAMISHED AFTER A HARD DAY'S WORK!
WHAT? GLOOB!
CHEW! BELCH!
TOM PATERSON
GRAAGH! I'LL MARMALISE THE LITTLE GUZZLER!
RAVENOUS RAGE!
BURP!
DAD'S ROCKERY
SWEENY'S REALLY A CAVEMAN NOW!
STOMP! STOMP!

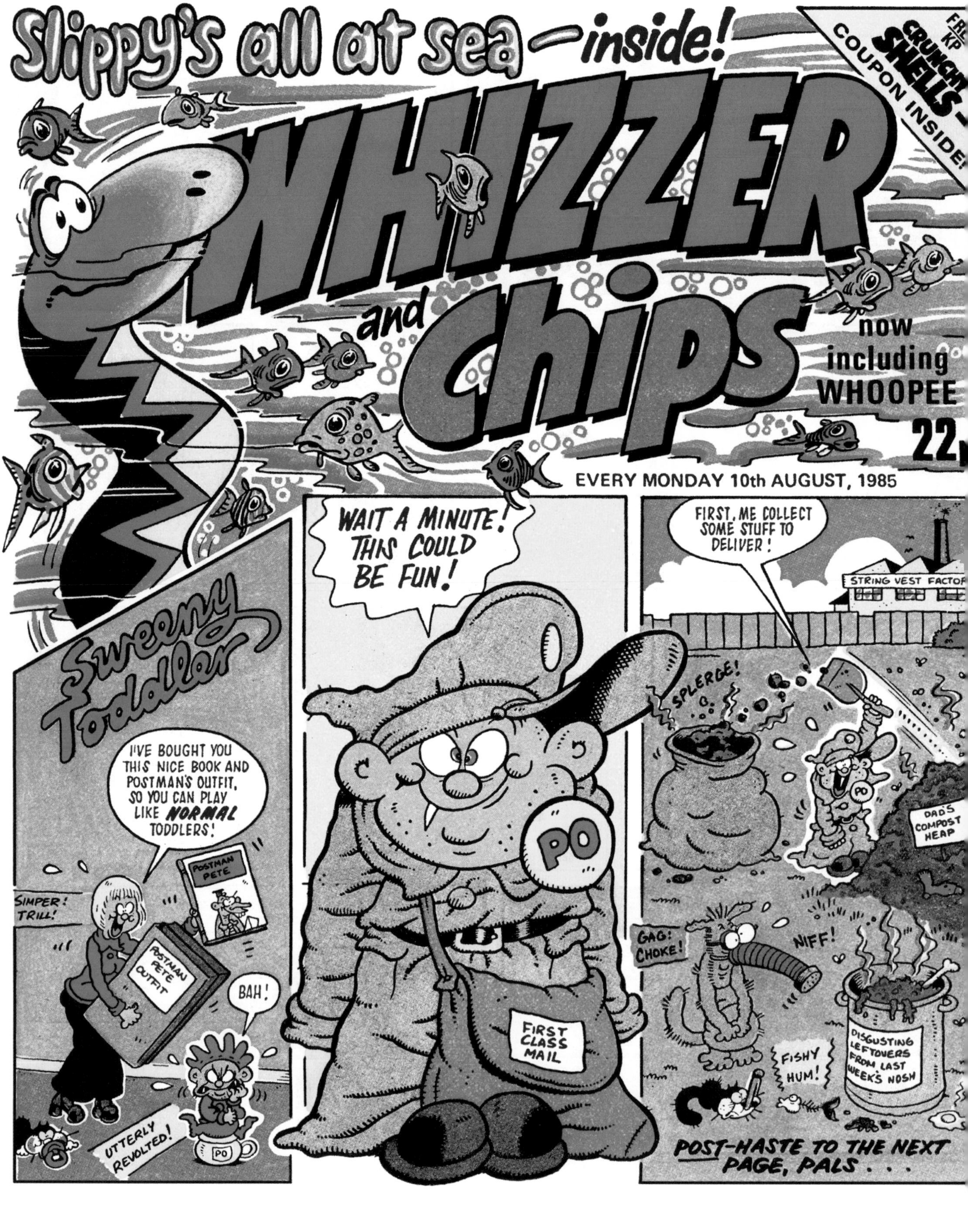
Slippy's all at sea—inside!
FREE KP CRUNCHY SHELLS — COUPON INSIDE!
WHIZZER and Chips
now including WHOOPEE
22p
EVERY MONDAY 10th AUGUST, 1985
Sweeny Toddler
I'VE BOUGHT YOU THIS NICE BOOK AND POSTMAN'S OUTFIT, SO YOU CAN PLAY LIKE NORMAL TODDLERS!
POSTMAN PETE
SIMPER! TRILL!
POSTMAN PETE OUTFIT
BAH!
UTTERLY REVOLTED!
PO
WAIT A MINUTE! THIS COULD BE FUN!
PO
FIRST CLASS MAIL
FIRST, ME COLLECT SOME STUFF TO DELIVER!
STRING VEST FACTOR
SPLERGE!
PO
DAD'S COMPOST HEAP
GAG: CHOKE!
NIFF!
FISHY HUM!
DISGUSTING LEFTOVERS FROM LAST WEEK'S NOSH
POST-HASTE TO THE NEXT PAGE, PALS . . .

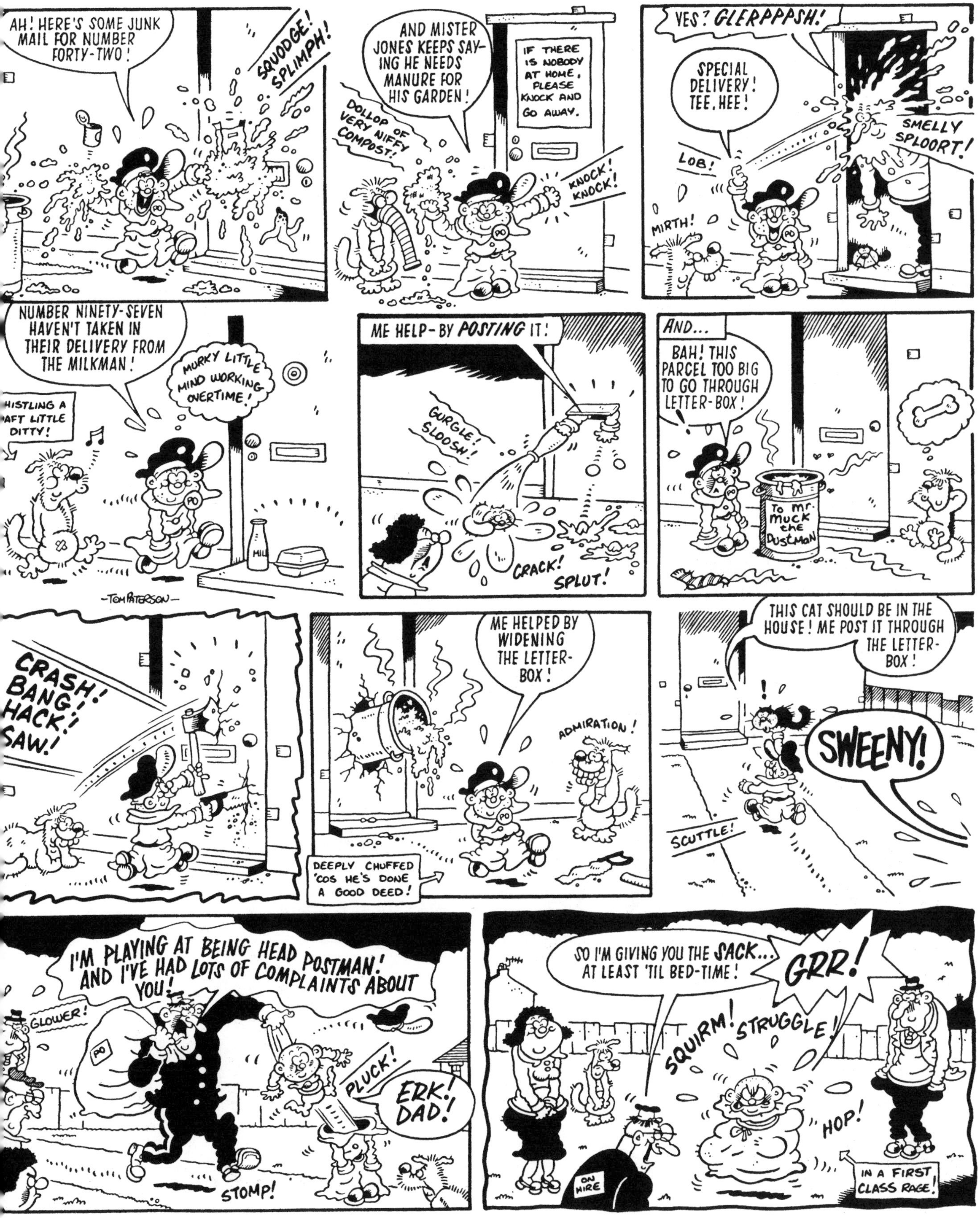

AH! HERE'S SOME JUNK MAIL FOR NUMBER FORTY-TWO!
SQUODGE! SPLIMPH!
AND MISTER JONES KEEPS SAYING HE NEEDS MANURE FOR HIS GARDEN!
DOLLOP OF VERY NIFFY COMPOST!
IF THERE IS NOBODY AT HOME, PLEASE KNOCK AND GO AWAY.
KNOCK! KNOCK!
YES? GLERPPPSH!
SPECIAL DELIVERY! TEE, HEE!
LOB!
SMELLY SPLOORT!
MIRTH!
NUMBER NINETY-SEVEN HAVEN'T TAKEN IN THEIR DELIVERY FROM THE MILKMAN!
MURKY LITTLE MIND WORKING OVERTIME!
HISTLING A AFT LITTLE DITTY!
TOM PATERSON
ME HELP-BY POSTING IT!
GURGLE! SLOOSH!
CRACK! SPLUT!
AND...
BAH! THIS PARCEL TOO BIG TO GO THROUGH LETTER-BOX!
To mr. muck the Dustman
CRASH! BANG! HACK! SAW!
ME HELPED BY WIDENING THE LETTER-BOX!
ADMIRATION!
DEEPLY CHUFFED 'COS HE'S DONE A GOOD DEED!
THIS CAT SHOULD BE IN THE HOUSE! ME POST IT THROUGH THE LETTER-BOX!
SWEENY!
SCUTTLE!
I'M PLAYING AT BEING HEAD POSTMAN! AND I'VE HAD LOTS OF COMPLAINTS ABOUT YOU!
GLOWER!
PO
PLUCK!
ERK! DAD!
STOMP!
SO I'M GIVING YOU THE SACK... AT LEAST 'TIL BED-TIME!
GRR!
SQUIRM! STRUGGLE!
HOP!
ON HIRE
IN A FIRST CLASS RAGE!

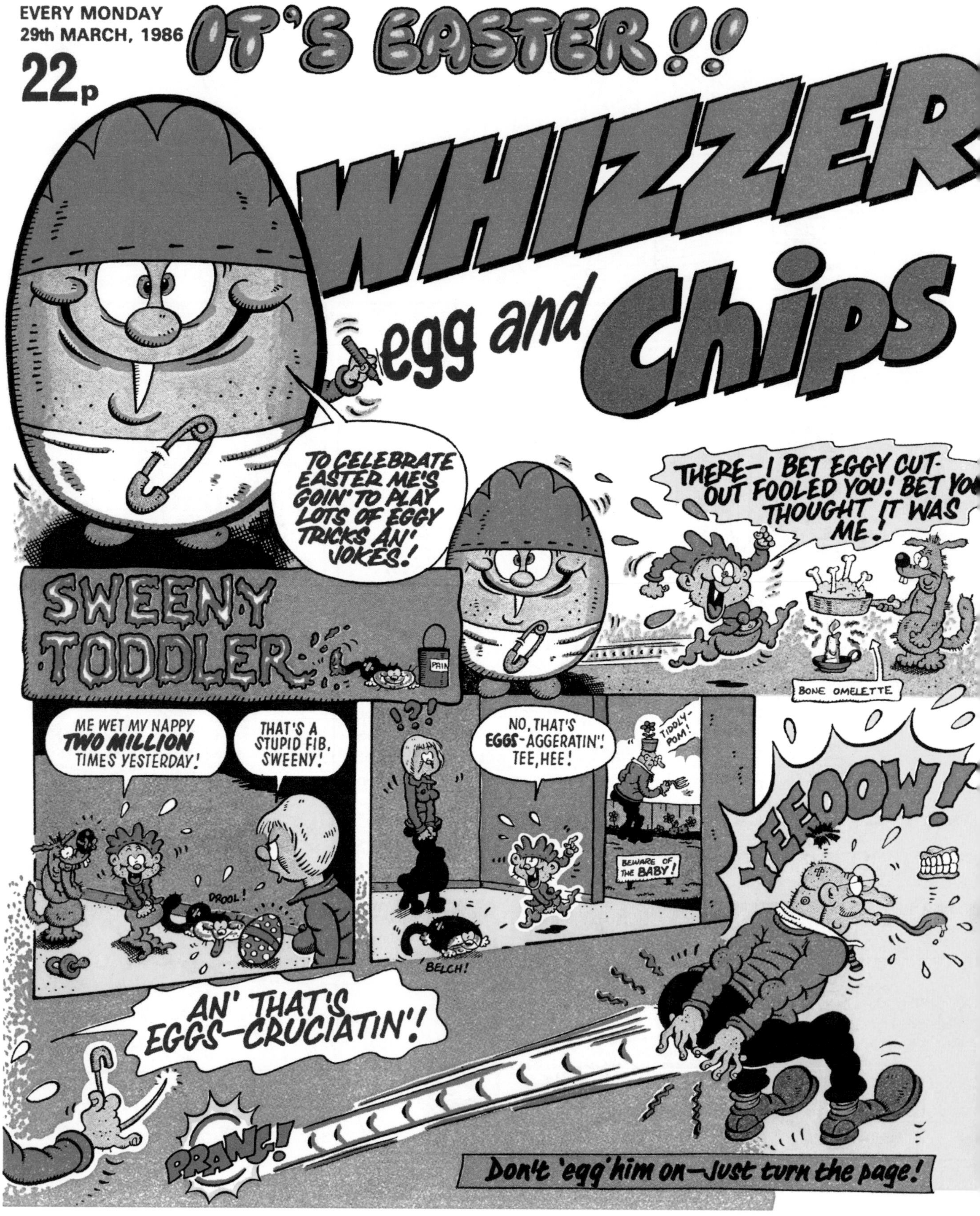
EVERY MONDAY
29th MARCH, 1986
22p
IT'S EASTER!!
WHIZZER egg and Chips
TO CELEBRATE EASTER ME'S GOIN' TO PLAY LOTS OF EGGY TRICKS AN' JOKES!
THERE—I BET EGGY CUT-OUT FOOLED YOU! BET YOU THOUGHT IT WAS ME!
BONE OMELETTE
SWEENY TODDLER
PAIN
ME WET MY NAPPY TWO MILLION TIMES YESTERDAY!
THAT'S A STUPID FIB, SWEENY!
DROOL!
!?!
NO, THAT'S EGGS-AGGERATIN'! TEE, HEE!
TIDDLY-POM!
BEWARE OF THE BABY!
BELCH!
YEEOOW!
AN' THAT'S EGGS-CRUCIATIN'!
PRANG!
Don't 'egg' him on—Just turn the page!

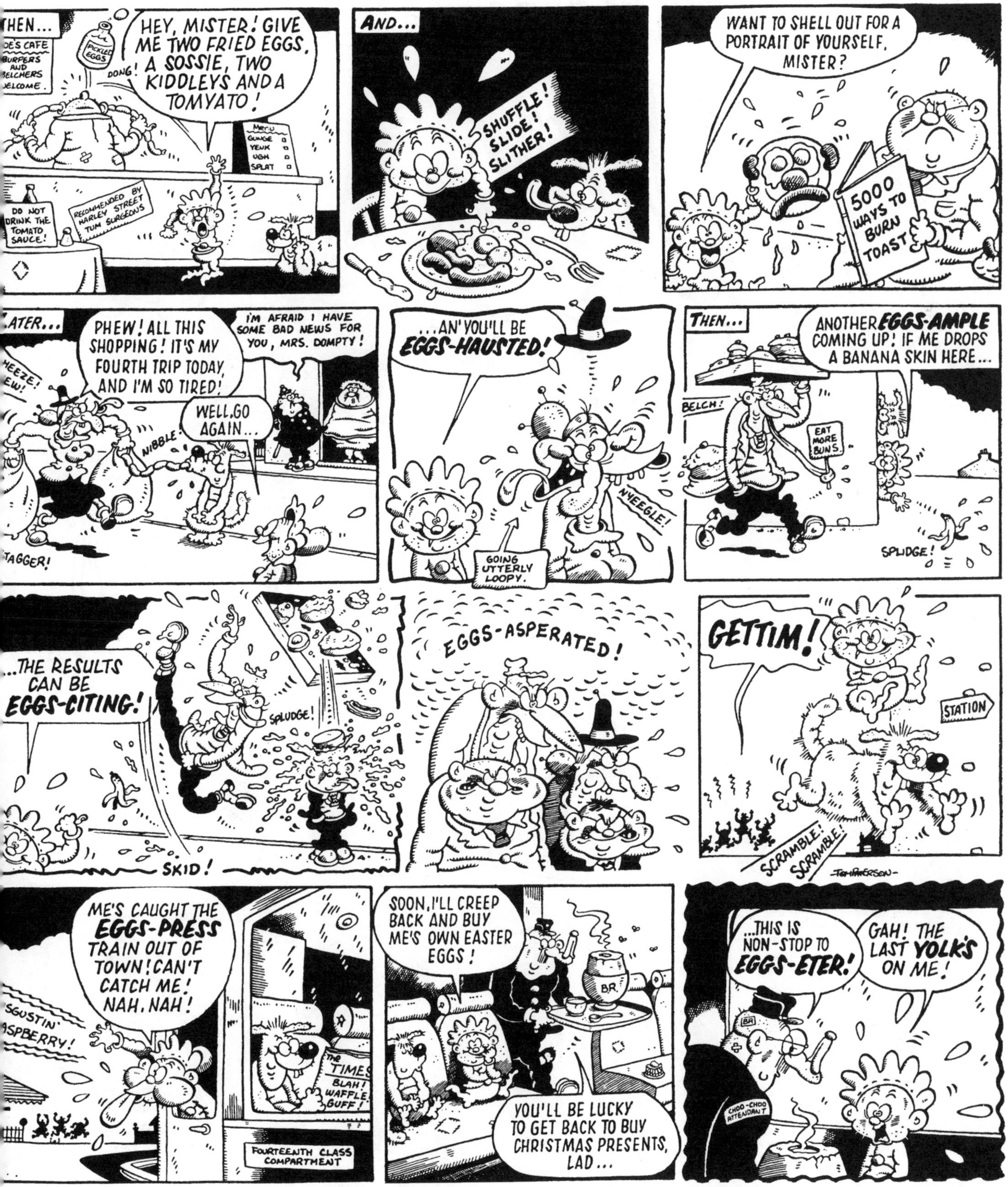
THEN...
JOE'S CAFE BURPERS AND BELCHERS WELCOME.
PICKLED EGGS
DONG!
HEY, MISTER! GIVE ME TWO FRIED EGGS, A SOSSIE, TWO KIDDLEYS AND A TOMYATO!
MENU GUNGE YEUK UGH SPLAT
DO NOT DRINK THE TOMATO SAUCE!
RECOMMENDED BY HARLEY STREET TUM SURGEONS
AND...
SHUFFLE! SLIDE! SLITHER!
WANT TO SHELL OUT FOR A PORTRAIT OF YOURSELF, MISTER?
5000 WAYS TO BURN TOAST
LATER...
PHEW! ALL THIS SHOPPING! IT'S MY FOURTH TRIP TODAY, AND I'M SO TIRED!
I'M AFRAID I HAVE SOME BAD NEWS FOR YOU, MRS. DOMPTY!
WELL, GO AGAIN...
NIBBLE
STAGGER!
...AN' YOU'LL BE EGGS-HAUSTED!
GOING UTTERLY LOOPY.
NYEEGLE!
THEN...
ANOTHER EGGS-AMPLE COMING UP! IF ME DROPS A BANANA SKIN HERE...
BELCH!
EAT MORE BUNS.
SPLUDGE!
...THE RESULTS CAN BE EGGS-CITING!
SPLUDGE!
SKID!
EGGS-ASPERATED!
GETTIM!
STATION
SCRAMBLE! SCRAMBLE!
TOM PATERSON
ME'S CAUGHT THE EGGS-PRESS TRAIN OUT OF TOWN! CAN'T CATCH ME! NAH, NAH!
DISGUSTIN' RASPBERRY!
THE TIMES BLAH! WAFFLE GUFF!
FOURTEENTH CLASS COMPARTMENT
SOON, I'LL CREEP BACK AND BUY ME'S OWN EASTER EGGS!
BR
YOU'LL BE LUCKY TO GET BACK TO BUY CHRISTMAS PRESENTS, LAD...
...THIS IS NON-STOP TO EGGS-ETER!
GAH! THE LAST YOLK'S ON ME!
BR
CHOO-CHOO ATTENDANT

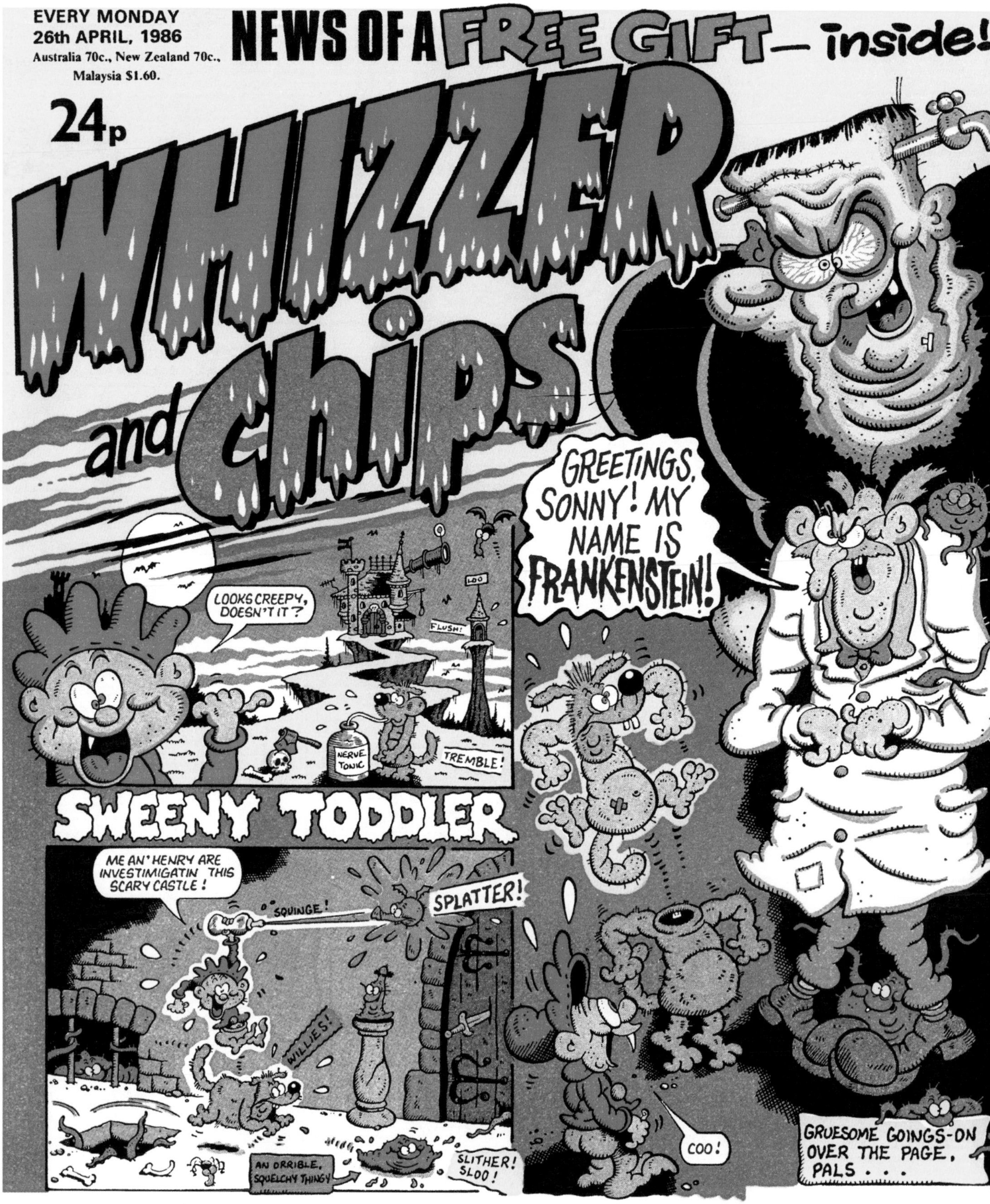
EVERY MONDAY
26th APRIL, 1986
Australia 70c., New Zealand 70c., Malaysia $1.60.
NEWS OF A FREE GIFT — inside!
24p
WHIZZER and CHIPS
GREETINGS, SONNY! MY NAME IS FRANKENSTEIN!
LOOKS CREEPY, DOESN'T IT?
LOO
FLUSH!
NERVE TONIC
TREMBLE!
SWEENY TODDLER
ME AN' HENRY ARE INVESTIMIGATIN THIS SCARY CASTLE!
SQUINGE!
SPLATTER!
WILLIES!
AN ORRIBLE, SQUELCHY THINGY
SLITHER! SLOO!
COO!
GRUESOME GOINGS-ON OVER THE PAGE, PALS . . .

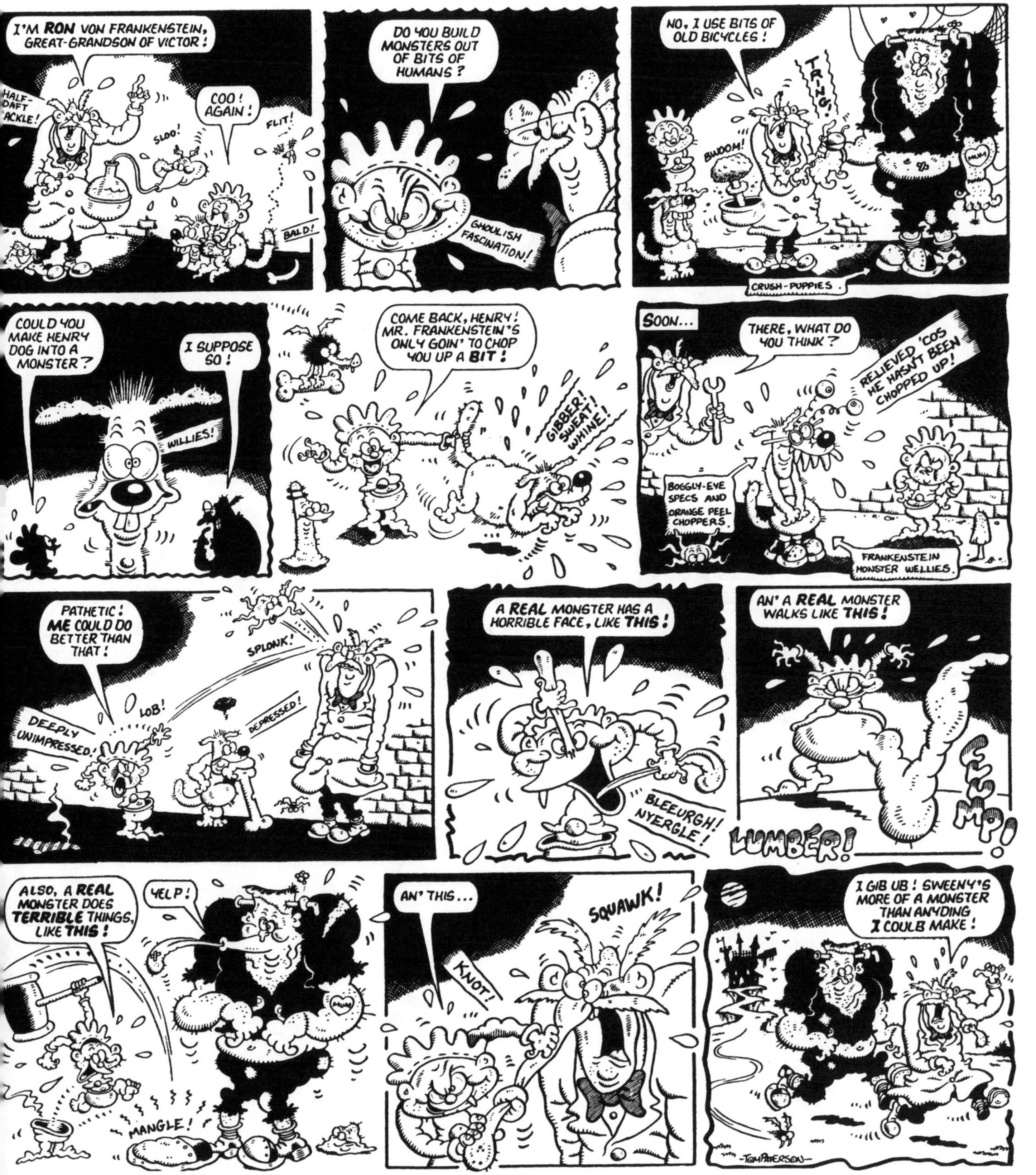

I'M RON VON FRANKENSTEIN, GREAT-GRANDSON OF VICTOR!
HALF-DAFT ACKLE!
COO! AGAIN!
SLOO!
FLIT!
BALD!
DO YOU BUILD MONSTERS OUT OF BITS OF HUMANS?
GHOULISH FASCINATION!
NO, I USE BITS OF OLD BICYCLES!
TRING!
BWOOM!
CRUSH-PUPPIES
COULD YOU MAKE HENRY DOG INTO A MONSTER?
I SUPPOSE SO!
WILLIES!
COME BACK, HENRY! MR. FRANKENSTEIN'S ONLY GOIN' TO CHOP YOU UP A BIT!
GIBBER! SWEAT! WHINE!
SOON...
THERE, WHAT DO YOU THINK?
RELIEVED 'COS HE HASN'T BEEN CHOPPED UP!
BOGGLY-EYE SPECS AND ORANGE PEEL CHOPPERS
FRANKENSTEIN MONSTER WELLIES
PATHETIC! ME COULD DO BETTER THAN THAT!
SPLONK!
LOB!
DEEPLY UNIMPRESSED!
DEPRESSED!
A REAL MONSTER HAS A HORRIBLE FACE, LIKE THIS!
BLEEURGH! NYERGLE!
AN' A REAL MONSTER WALKS LIKE THIS!
LUMBER!
CLUMP!
ALSO, A REAL MONSTER DOES TERRIBLE THINGS, LIKE THIS!
YELP!
MANGLE!
AN' THIS...
SQUAWK!
KNOT!
I GIB UB! SWEENY'S MORE OF A MONSTER THAN ANYDING I COULB MAKE!
TOM PATERSON

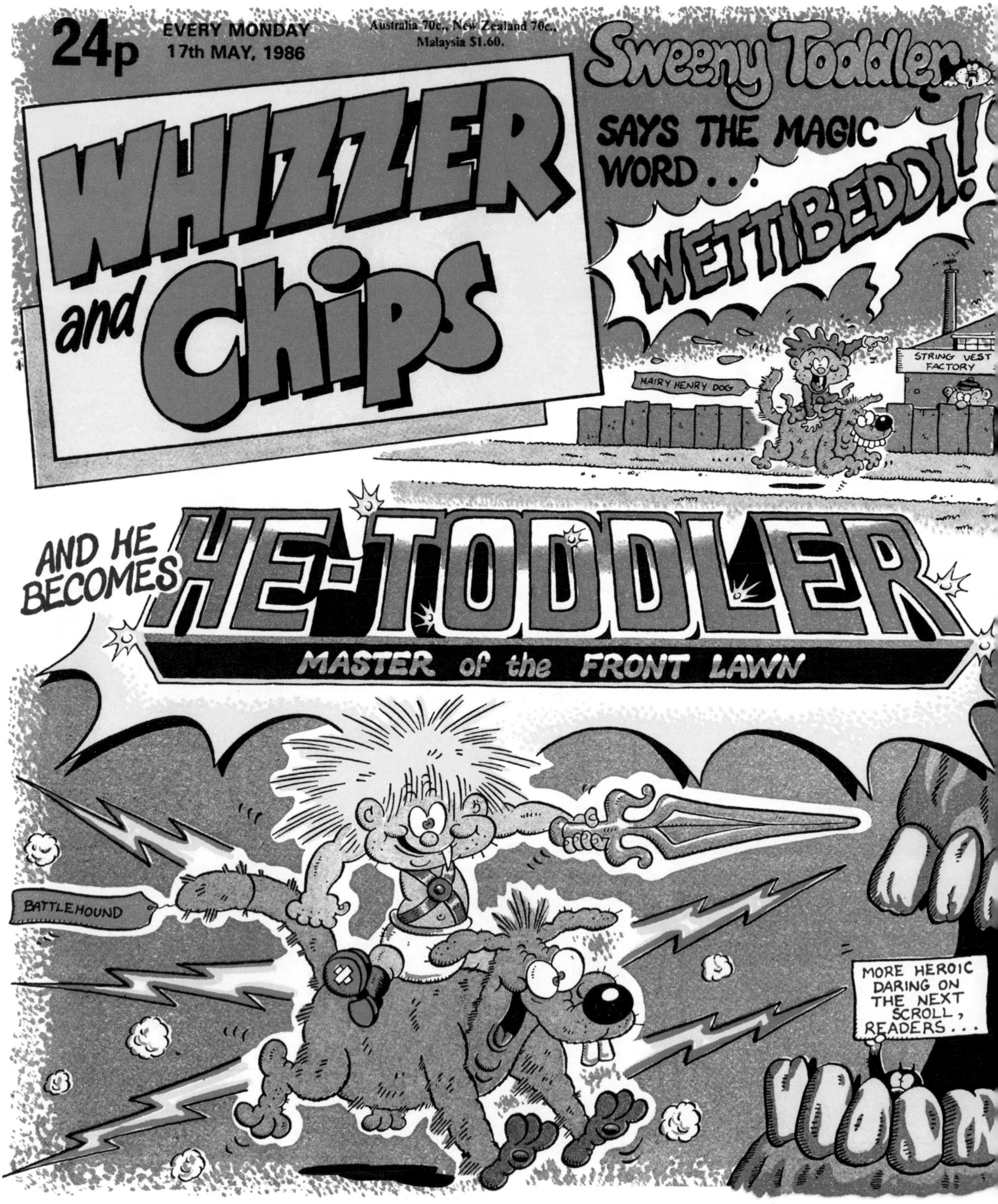
24p
EVERY MONDAY
17th MAY, 1986
Australia 70c., New Zealand 70c., Malaysia $1.60.
WHIZZER and Chips
Sweeny Toddler
SAYS THE MAGIC WORD . . .
WETTIBEDDI!
STRING VEST FACTORY
HAIRY HENRY DOG
AND HE BECOMES
HE-TODDLER
MASTER of the FRONT LAWN
BATTLEHOUND
MORE HEROIC DARING ON THE NEXT SCROLL, READERS . . .

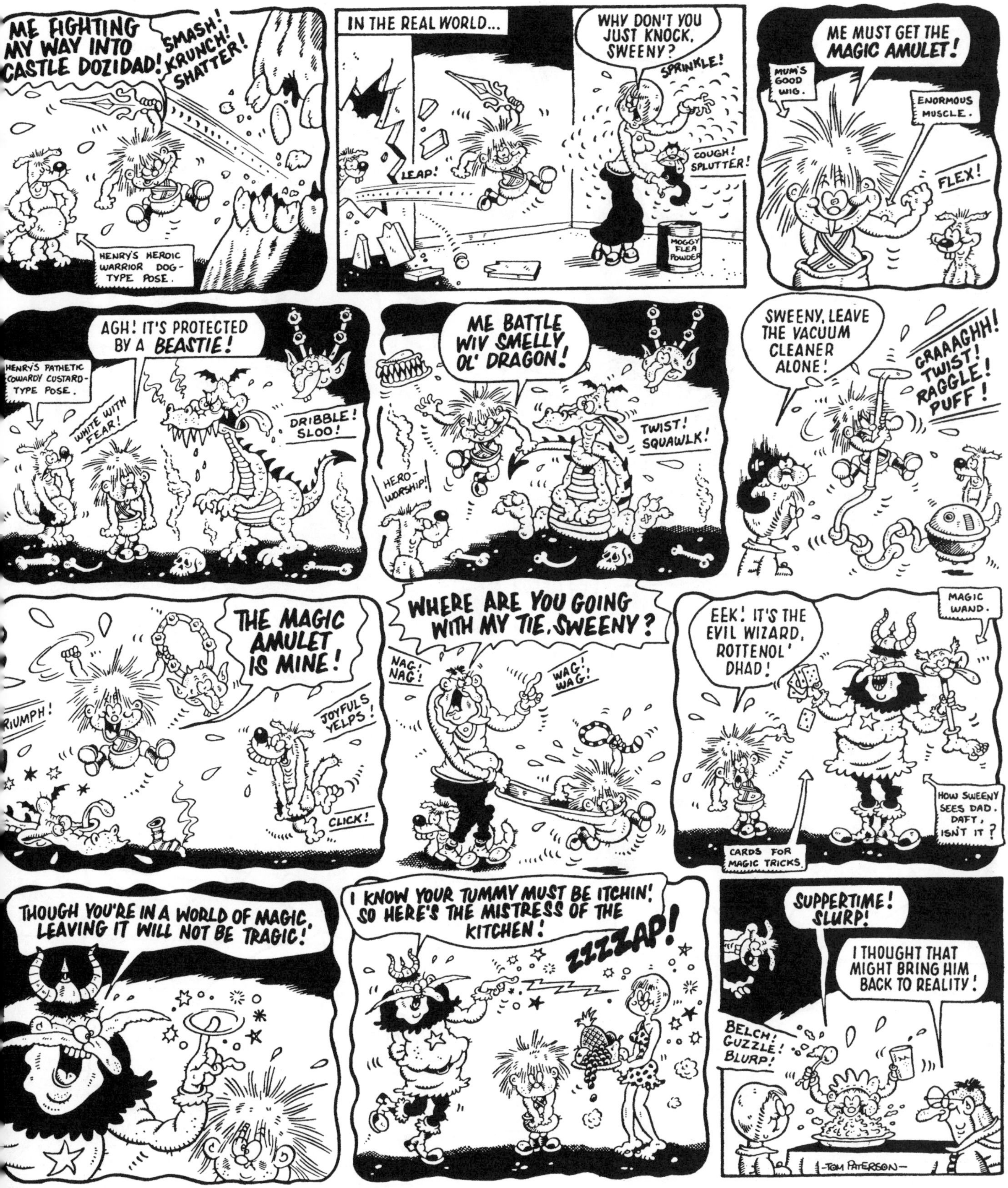
ME FIGHTING MY WAY INTO CASTLE DOZIDAD!
SMASH! KRUNCH! SHATTER!
HENRY'S HEROIC WARRIOR DOG-TYPE POSE.
IN THE REAL WORLD...
LEAP!
WHY DON'T YOU JUST KNOCK, SWEENY?
SPRINKLE!
COUGH! SPLUTTER!
MOGGY FLEA POWDER
ME MUST GET THE MAGIC AMULET!
MUM'S GOOD WIG.
ENORMOUS MUSCLE.
FLEX!
AGH! IT'S PROTECTED BY A BEASTIE!
HENRY'S PATHETIC COWARDY CUSTARD-TYPE POSE.
WHITE WITH FEAR!
DRIBBLE! SLOO!
ME BATTLE WIV SMELLY OL' DRAGON!
TWIST! SQUAWLK!
HERO-WORSHIP!
SWEENY, LEAVE THE VACUUM CLEANER ALONE!
GRAAAGHH! TWIST! RAGGLE! PUFF!
THE MAGIC AMULET IS MINE!
RIUMPH!
JOYFULS YELPS!
CLICK!
WHERE ARE YOU GOING WITH MY TIE, SWEENY?
NAG! NAG!
WAG! WAG!
EEK! IT'S THE EVIL WIZARD, ROTTENOL' DHAD!
MAGIC WAND.
CARDS FOR MAGIC TRICKS.
HOW SWEENY SEES DAD. DAFT, ISN'T IT?
THOUGH YOU'RE IN A WORLD OF MAGIC, LEAVING IT WILL NOT BE TRAGIC!
I KNOW YOUR TUMMY MUST BE ITCHIN', SO HERE'S THE MISTRESS OF THE KITCHEN!
ZZZZAP!
SUPPERTIME! SLURP!
I THOUGHT THAT MIGHT BRING HIM BACK TO REALITY!
BELCH! GUZZLE! BLURP!
-TOM PATERSON-

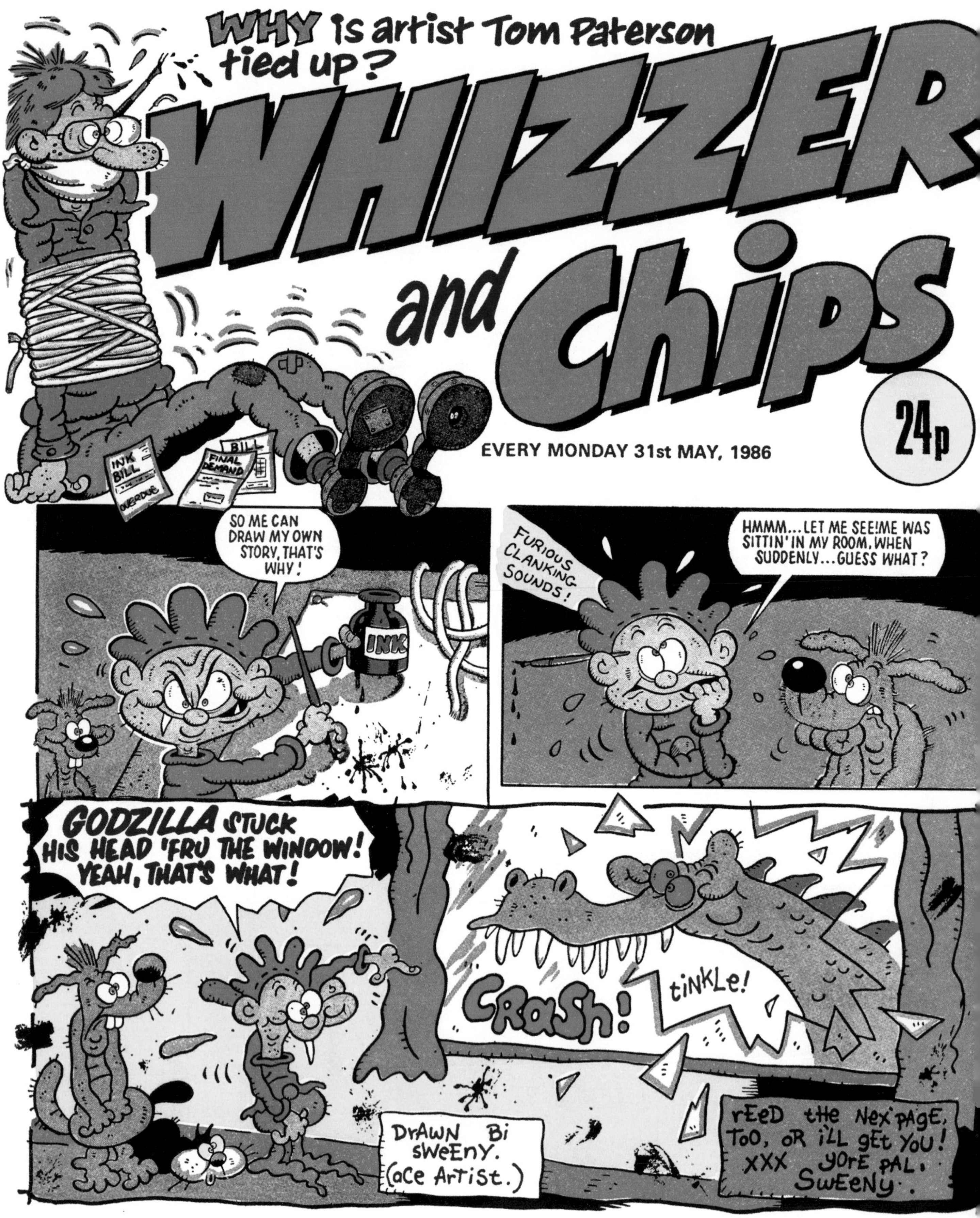
WHY is artist Tom Paterson tied up?
WHIZZER and Chips
24p
EVERY MONDAY 31st MAY, 1986
INK BILL OVERDUE
BILL FINAL DEMAND
SO ME CAN DRAW MY OWN STORY, THAT'S WHY!
INK
FURIOUS CLANKING SOUNDS!
HMMM... LET ME SEE! ME WAS SITTIN' IN MY ROOM, WHEN SUDDENLY... GUESS WHAT?
GODZILLA STUCK HIS HEAD 'FRU THE WINDOW! YEAH, THAT'S WHAT!
CRASH!
tinkle!
DrAWN Bi sWeEny. (aCe ArTiSt.)
rEeD tHe Nex'pAGE, TOO, oR i'LL gEt YOU! XXX yOrE PAL. SwEENy.

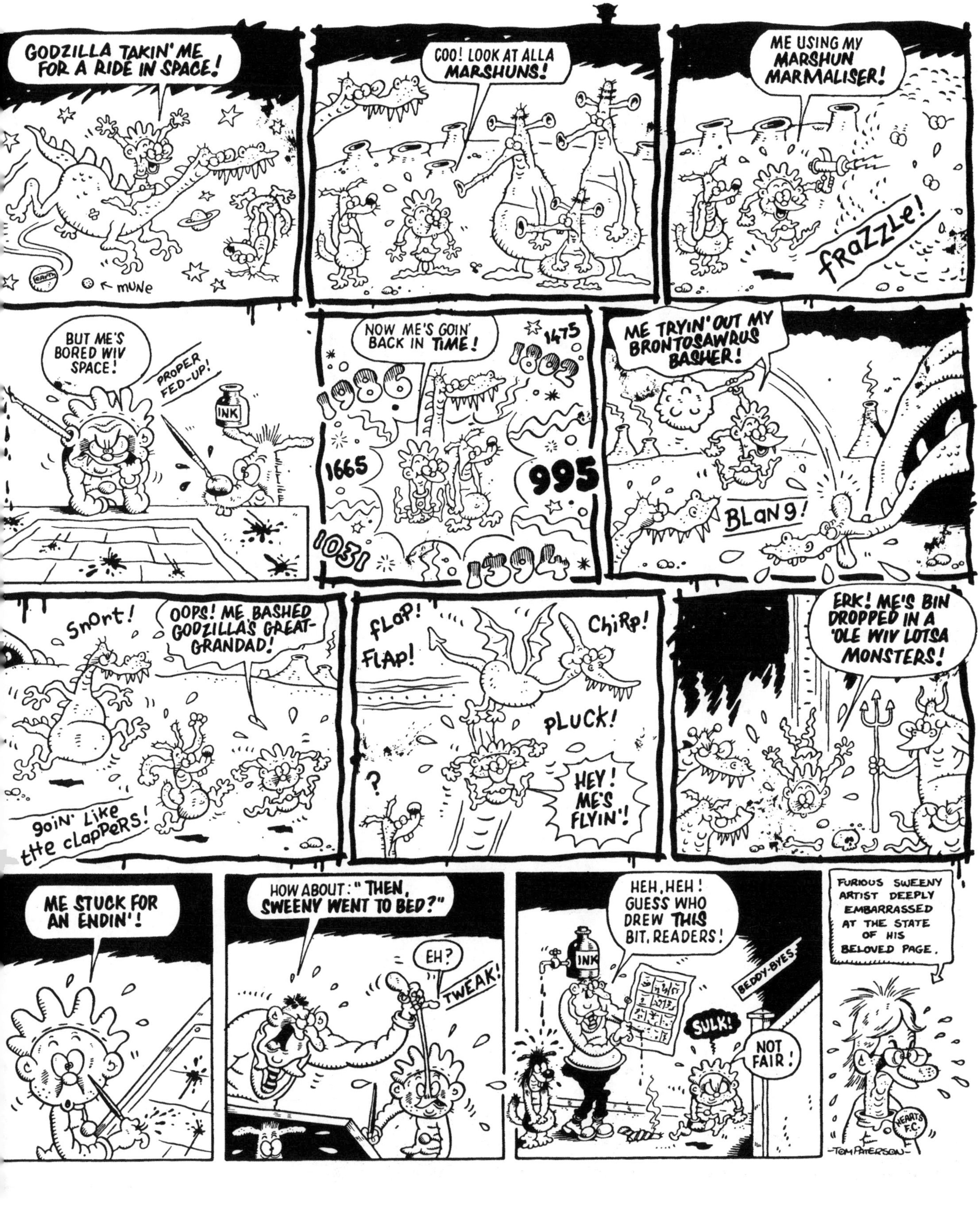
GODZILLA TAKIN' ME FOR A RIDE IN SPACE!
EARTH
← MUNE
COO! LOOK AT ALLA MARSHUNS!
ME USING MY MARSHUN MARMALISER!
FRAZZLE!
BUT ME'S BORED WIV SPACE!
PROPER FED-UP!
INK
NOW ME'S GOIN' BACK IN TIME!
1475
1802
1986
1665
995
1031
1394
ME TRYIN' OUT MY BRONTOSAWRUS BASHER!
BLANG!
SNORT!
OOPS! ME BASHED GODZILLA'S GREAT-GRANDAD!
GOIN' LIKE THE CLAPPERS!
FLAP!
FLAP!
CHIRP!
PLUCK!
?
HEY! ME'S FLYIN'!
ERK! ME'S BIN DROPPED IN A 'OLE WIV LOTSA MONSTERS!
ME STUCK FOR AN ENDIN'!
HOW ABOUT: "THEN, SWEENY WENT TO BED?"
EH?
TWEAK!
HEH, HEH! GUESS WHO DREW THIS BIT, READERS!
INK
BEDDY-BYES
SULK!
NOT FAIR!
FURIOUS SWEENY ARTIST DEEPLY EMBARRASSED AT THE STATE OF HIS BELOVED PAGE.
HEARTS F.C.
-TOM PATERSON-

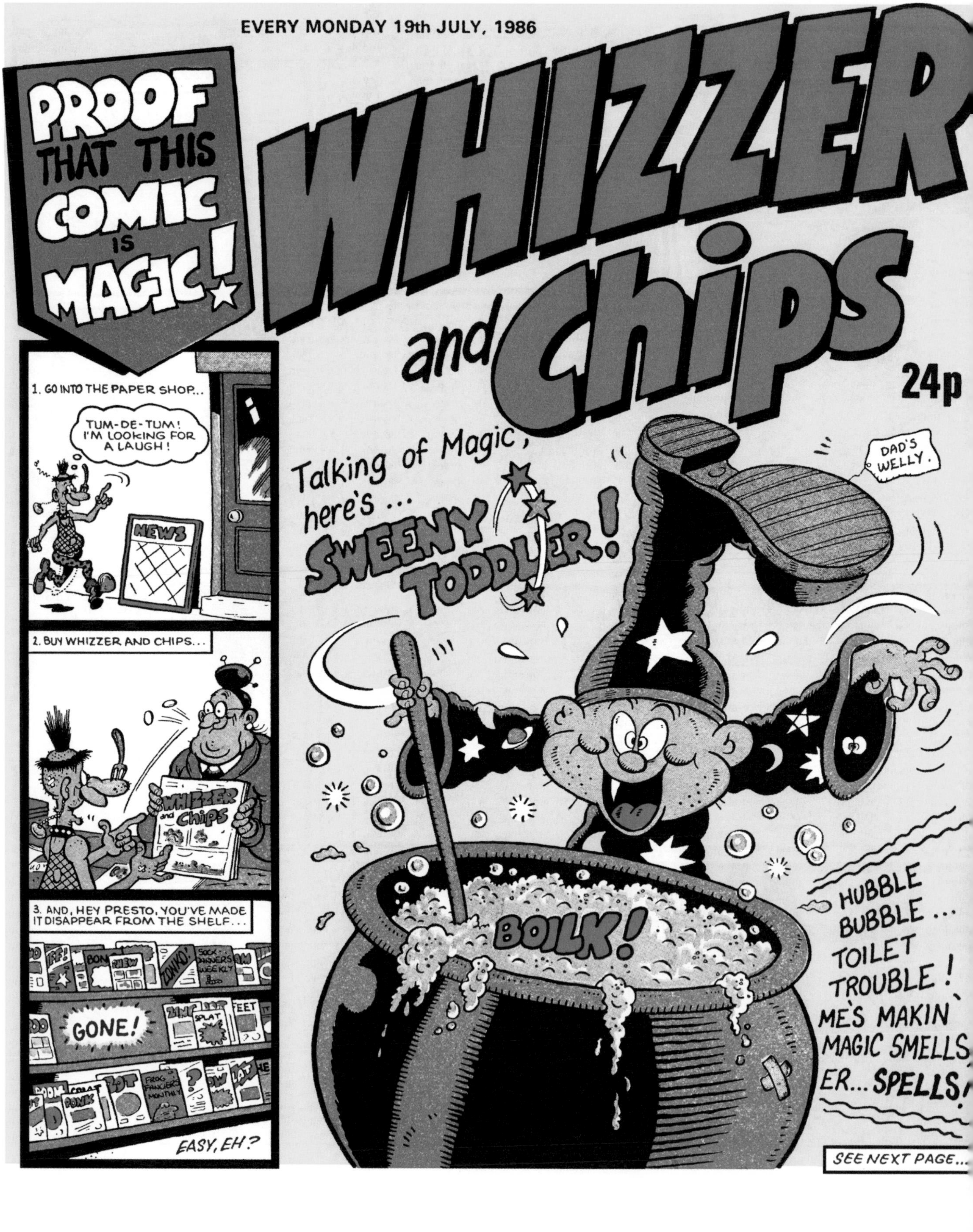
EVERY MONDAY 19th JULY, 1986
PROOF THAT THIS COMIC IS MAGIC!
WHIZZER and Chips
24p
1. GO INTO THE PAPER SHOP...
TUM-DE-TUM! I'M LOOKING FOR A LAUGH!
NEWS
2. BUY WHIZZER AND CHIPS...
WHIZZER and Chips
3. AND, HEY PRESTO, YOU'VE MADE IT DISAPPEAR FROM THE SHELF...
ZONKO!
SOCK-DARNERS WEEKLY
GONE!
SPLAT
FROG FANCIERS MONTHLY
EASY, EH?
Talking of Magic, here's ... SWEENY TODDLER!
DAD'S WELLY.
BOILK!
HUBBLE BUBBLE ... TOILET TROUBLE! ME'S MAKIN' MAGIC SMELLS, ER... SPELLS!
SEE NEXT PAGE...

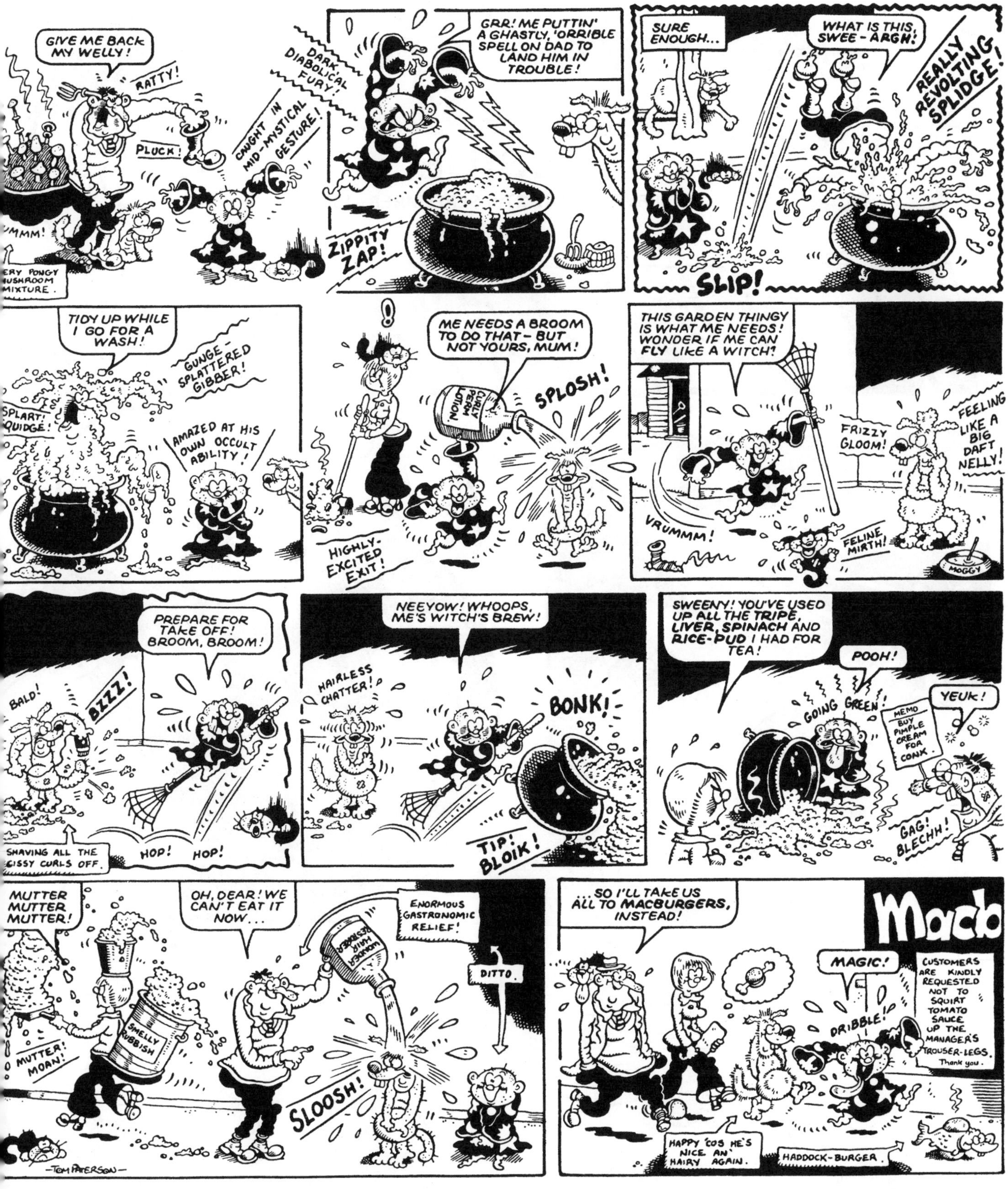
GIVE ME BACK MY WELLY!
RATTY!
PLUCK!
UMMM!
ERY PONGY USHROOM MIXTURE.
CAUGHT IN MID-MYSTICAL GESTURE!
DARK DIABOLICAL FURY!
GRR! ME PUTTIN' A GHASTLY, 'ORRIBLE SPELL ON DAD TO LAND HIM IN TROUBLE!
ZIPPITY ZAP!
SURE ENOUGH...
WHAT IS THIS, SWEE - ARGH!
REALLY REVOLTING SPLIDGE!
SLIP!
TIDY UP WHILE I GO FOR A WASH!
GUNGE-SPLATTERED GIBBER!
SPLART! QUIDGE!
AMAZED AT HIS OWN OCCULT ABILITY!
ME NEEDS A BROOM TO DO THAT - BUT NOT YOURS, MUM!
CURLY PERM LOTION
SPLOSH!
HIGHLY-EXCITED EXIT!
THIS GARDEN THINGY IS WHAT ME NEEDS! WONDER IF ME CAN FLY LIKE A WITCH!
FRIZZY GLOOM!
FEELING LIKE A BIG DAFT NELLY!
VRUMMM!
FELINE MIRTH!
MOGGY
PREPARE FOR TAKE OFF! BROOM, BROOM!
BALD!
BZZZ!
SHAVING ALL THE CISSY CURLS OFF.
HOP!
HOP!
NEEYOW! WHOOPS, ME'S WITCH'S BREW!
HAIRLESS CHATTER!
BONK!
TIP! BLOIK!
SWEENY! YOU'VE USED UP ALL THE TRIPE, LIVER, SPINACH AND RICE-PUD I HAD FOR TEA!
POOH!
GOING GREEN!
YEUK!
MEMO BUY PIMPLE CREAM FOR CONK.
GAG! BLECHH!
MUTTER MUTTER MUTTER!
OH, DEAR! WE CAN'T EAT IT NOW...
ENORMOUS GASTRONOMIC RELIEF!
WONDER HAIR RESTORER
DITTO.
SMELLY RUBBISH
MUTTER! MOAN!
SLOOSH!
-TOM PATERSON-
...SO I'LL TAKE US ALL TO MACBURGERS, INSTEAD!
Macb
MAGIC!
CUSTOMERS ARE KINDLY REQUESTED NOT TO SQUIRT TOMATO SAUCE UP THE MANAGER'S TROUSER-LEGS. Thank you.
DRIBBLE!
HAPPY 'COS HE'S NICE AN' HAIRY AGAIN.
HADDOCK-BURGER.

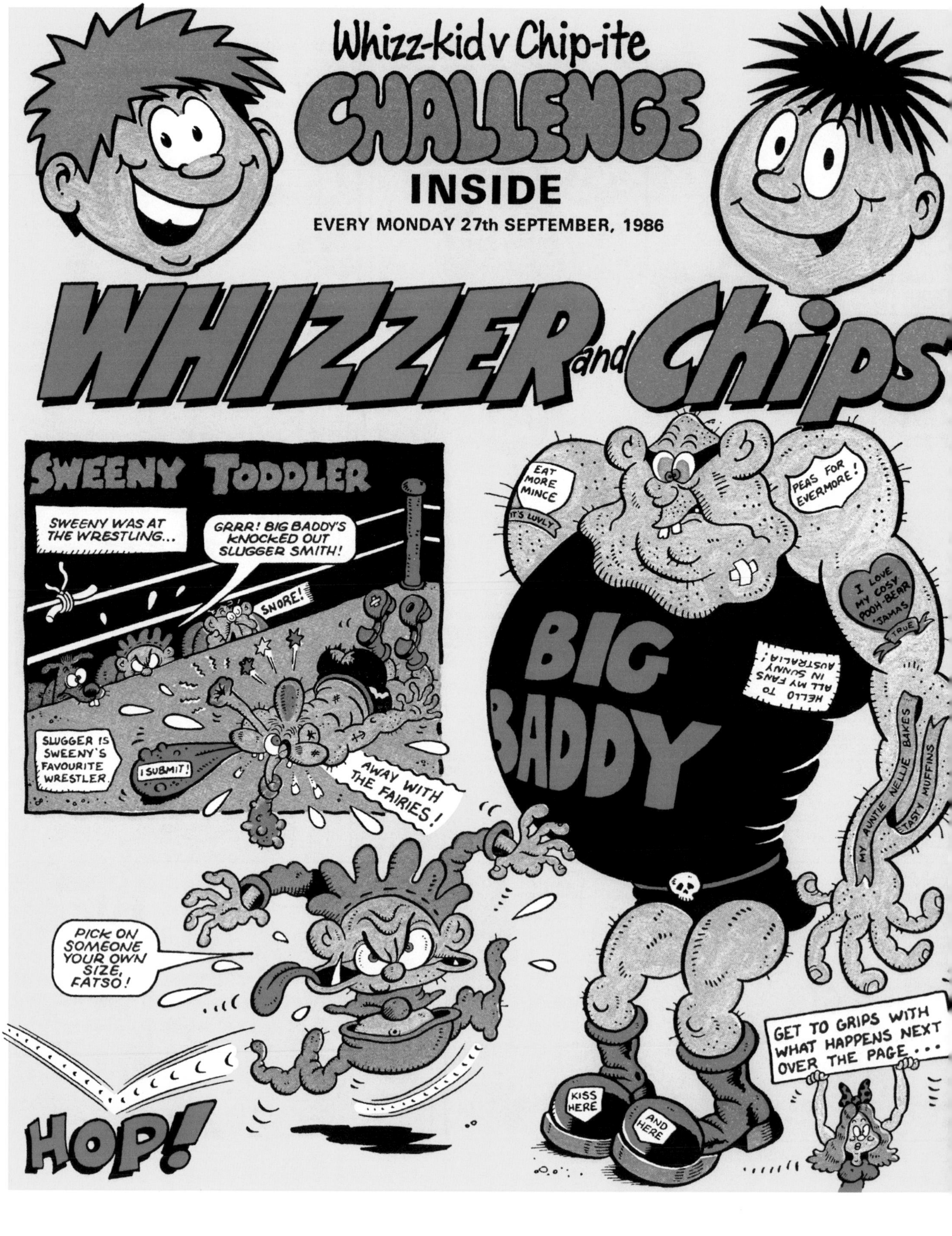
Whizz-kid v Chip-ite
CHALLENGE
INSIDE
EVERY MONDAY 27th SEPTEMBER, 1986
WHIZZER and Chips
SWEENY TODDLER
SWEENY WAS AT THE WRESTLING...
GRRR! BIG BADDY'S KNOCKED OUT SLUGGER SMITH!
SNORE!
SLUGGER IS SWEENY'S FAVOURITE WRESTLER
I SUBMIT!
AWAY WITH THE FAIRIES!
EAT MORE MINCE
IT'S LUVLY
PEAS FOR EVERMORE!
I LOVE MY COSY POOH-BEAR JAMAS
TRUE
HELLO TO ALL MY FANS IN SUNNY AUSTRALIA!
BIG BADDY
MY AUNTIE NELLIE BAKES TASTY MUFFINS
PICK ON SOMEONE YOUR OWN SIZE, FATSO!
GET TO GRIPS WITH WHAT HAPPENS NEXT OVER THE PAGE...
KISS HERE
AND HERE
HOP!

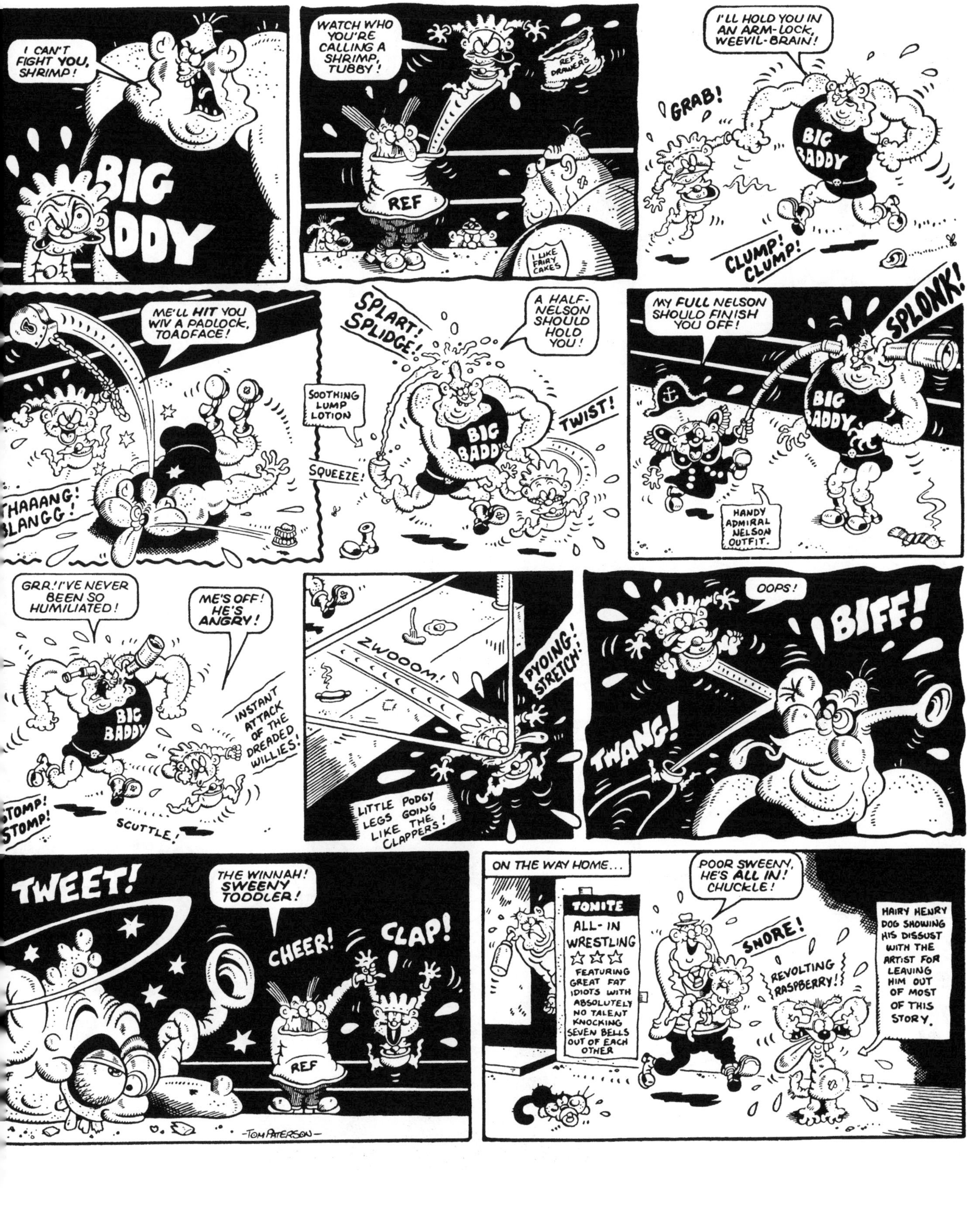

I CAN'T FIGHT YOU, SHRIMP!
BIG BADDY
WATCH WHO YOU'RE CALLING A SHRIMP, TUBBY!
REF'S DRAWERS
REF
I LIKE FAIRY CAKES
I'LL HOLD YOU IN AN ARM-LOCK, WEEVIL-BRAIN!
GRAB!
BIG BADDY
CLUMP! CLUMP!
ME'LL HIT YOU WIV A PADLOCK, TOADFACE!
THAAANG! BLANGG!
SPLART! SPLIDGE!
A HALF-NELSON SHOULD HOLD YOU!
SOOTHING LUMP LOTION
SQUEEZE!
BIG BADDY
TWIST!
MY FULL NELSON SHOULD FINISH YOU OFF!
SPLONK!
BIG BADDY
HANDY ADMIRAL NELSON OUTFIT.
GRR! I'VE NEVER BEEN SO HUMILIATED!
ME'S OFF! HE'S ANGRY!
BIG BADDY
INSTANT ATTACK OF THE DREADED WILLIES!
STOMP! STOMP!
SCUTTLE!
ZWOOOM!
PYOING! STRETCH!
LITTLE PODGY LEGS GOING LIKE THE CLAPPERS!
OOPS!
BIFF!
TWANG!
TWEET!
THE WINNAH! SWEENY TODDLER!
CHEER!
CLAP!
REF
-TOM PATERSON-
ON THE WAY HOME...
TONITE
ALL-IN WRESTLING
FEATURING GREAT FAT IDIOTS WITH ABSOLUTELY NO TALENT KNOCKING SEVEN BELLS OUT OF EACH OTHER
POOR SWEENY, HE'S ALL IN! CHUCKLE!
SNORE!
REVOLTING RASPBERRY!
HAIRY HENRY DOG SHOWING HIS DISGUST WITH THE ARTIST FOR LEAVING HIM OUT OF MOST OF THIS STORY.

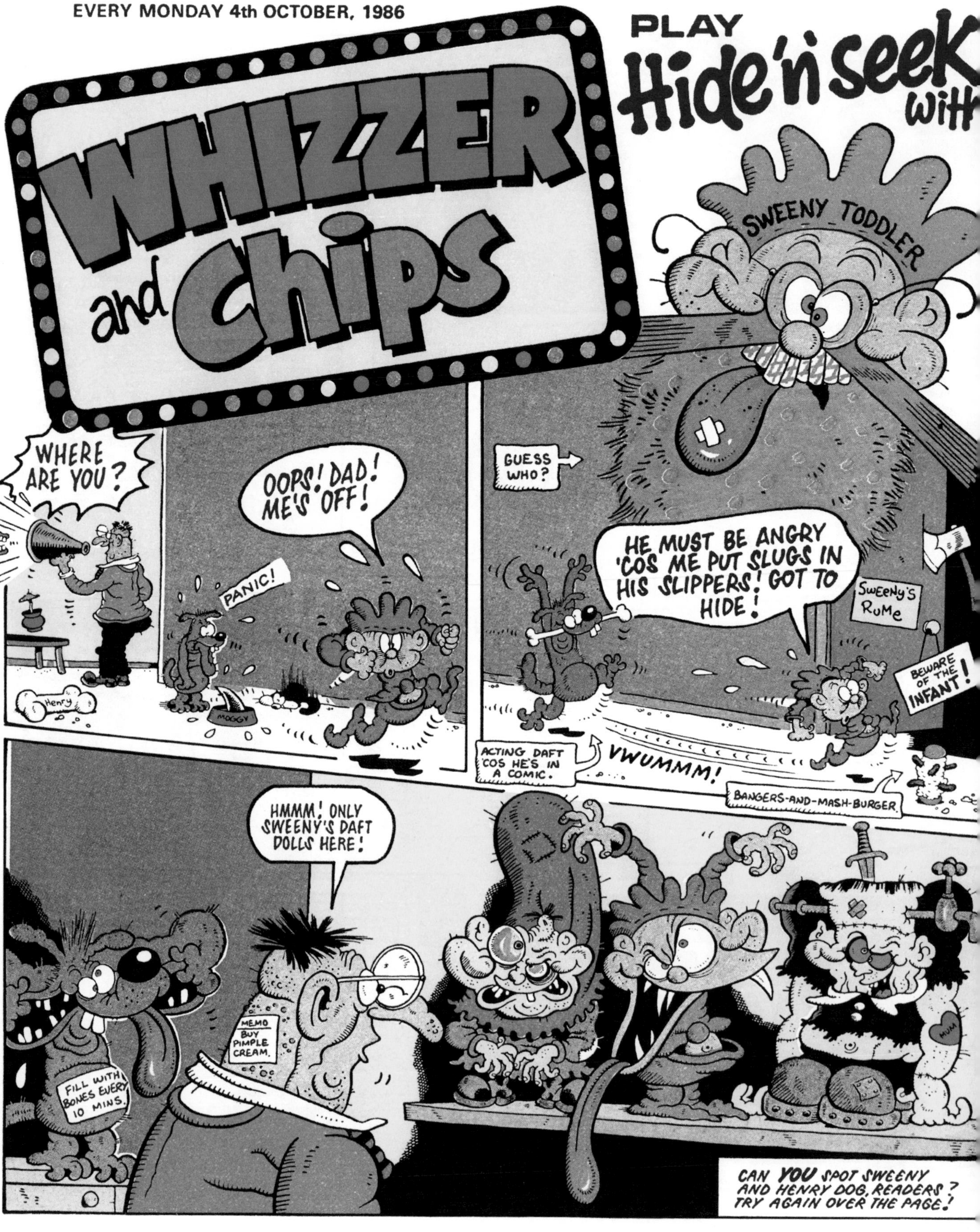
EVERY MONDAY 4th OCTOBER, 1986
WHIZZER and Chips
PLAY Hide 'n seek with
SWEENY TODDLER
WHERE ARE YOU?
OOPS! DAD! ME'S OFF!
PANIC!
Henry
MOGGY
GUESS WHO?
HE MUST BE ANGRY 'COS ME PUT SLUGS IN HIS SLIPPERS! GOT TO HIDE!
SWEENY'S RUME
BEWARE OF THE INFANT!
ACTING DAFT 'COS HE'S IN A COMIC.
VWUMMM!
BANGERS-AND-MASH-BURGER
HMMM! ONLY SWEENY'S DAFT DOLLS HERE!
MEMO BUY PIMPLE CREAM.
FILL WITH BONES EVERY 10 MINS.
MUM
CAN YOU SPOT SWEENY AND HENRY DOG, READERS? TRY AGAIN OVER THE PAGE!

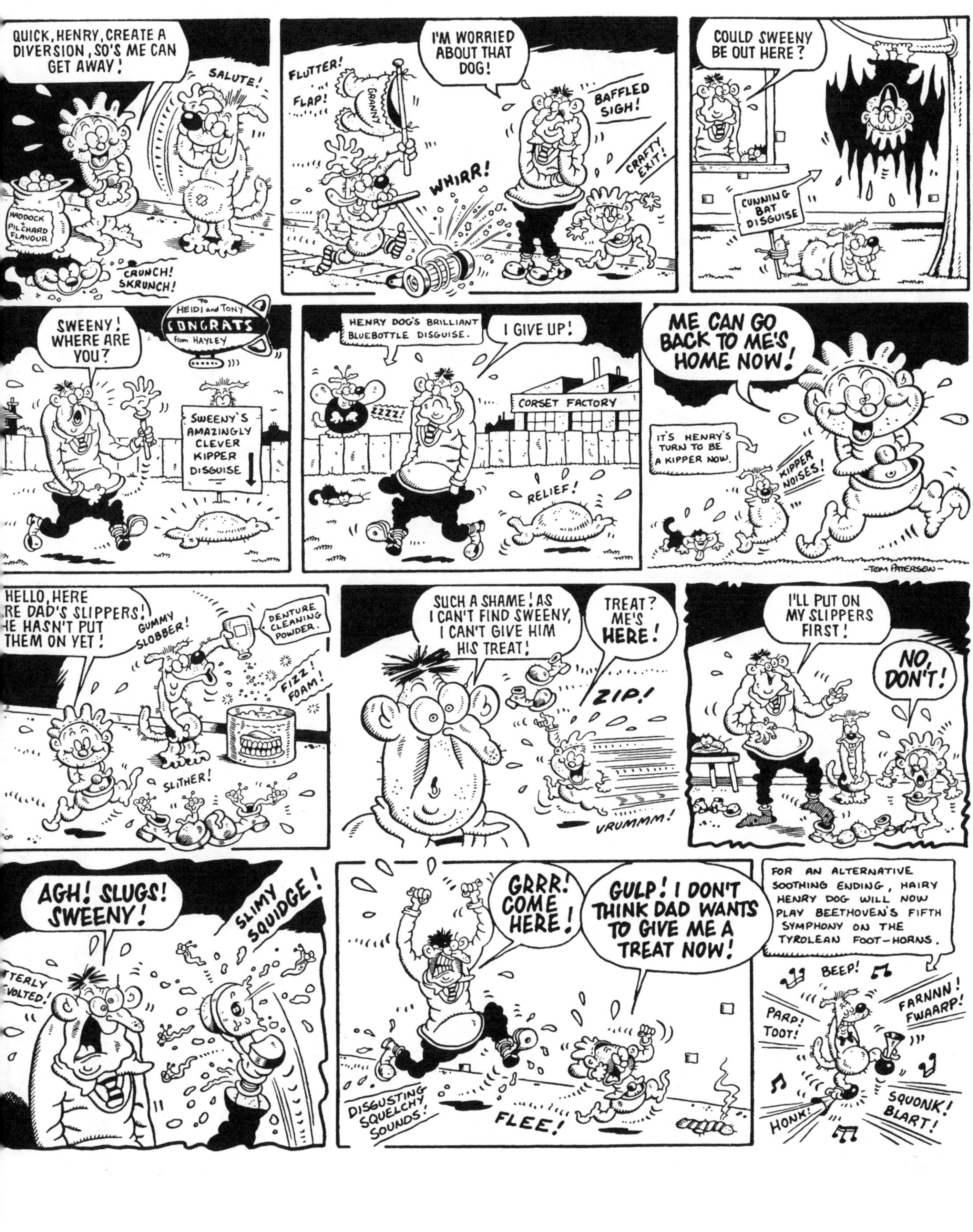
QUICK, HENRY, CREATE A DIVERSION, SO'S ME CAN GET AWAY!
SALUTE!
HADDOCK & PILCHARD FLAVOUR
CRUNCH! SKRUNCH!
I'M WORRIED ABOUT THAT DOG!
FLUTTER!
FLAP!
GRANNY
WHIRR!
BAFFLED SIGH!
CRAFTY EXIT!
COULD SWEENY BE OUT HERE?
CUNNING BAT DISGUISE
SWEENY! WHERE ARE YOU?
TO HEIDI and TONY CONGRATS from HAYLEY
SWEENY'S AMAZINGLY CLEVER KIPPER DISGUISE
HENRY DOG'S BRILLIANT BLUEBOTTLE DISGUISE.
I GIVE UP!
ZZZZ!
CORSET FACTORY
RELIEF!
ME CAN GO BACK TO ME'S HOME NOW!
IT'S HENRY'S TURN TO BE A KIPPER NOW.
KIPPER NOISES!
-TOM PATERSON-
HELLO, HERE ARE DAD'S SLIPPERS! HE HASN'T PUT THEM ON YET!
GUMMY SLOBBER!
DENTURE CLEANING POWDER.
FIZZ! FOAM!
SLITHER!
SUCH A SHAME! AS I CAN'T FIND SWEENY, I CAN'T GIVE HIM HIS TREAT!
TREAT? ME'S HERE!
ZIP!
VRUMMM!
I'LL PUT ON MY SLIPPERS FIRST!
NO, DON'T!
AGH! SLUGS! SWEENY!
SLIMY SQUIDGE!
UTTERLY REVOLTED!
GRRR! COME HERE!
GULP! I DON'T THINK DAD WANTS TO GIVE ME A TREAT NOW!
DISGUSTING SQUELCHY SOUNDS!
FLEE!
FOR AN ALTERNATIVE SOOTHING ENDING, HAIRY HENRY DOG WILL NOW PLAY BEETHOVEN'S FIFTH SYMPHONY ON THE TYROLEAN FOOT-HORNS.
BEEP!
PARP! TOOT!
FARNNN! FWAARP!
HONK!
SQUONK! BLART!

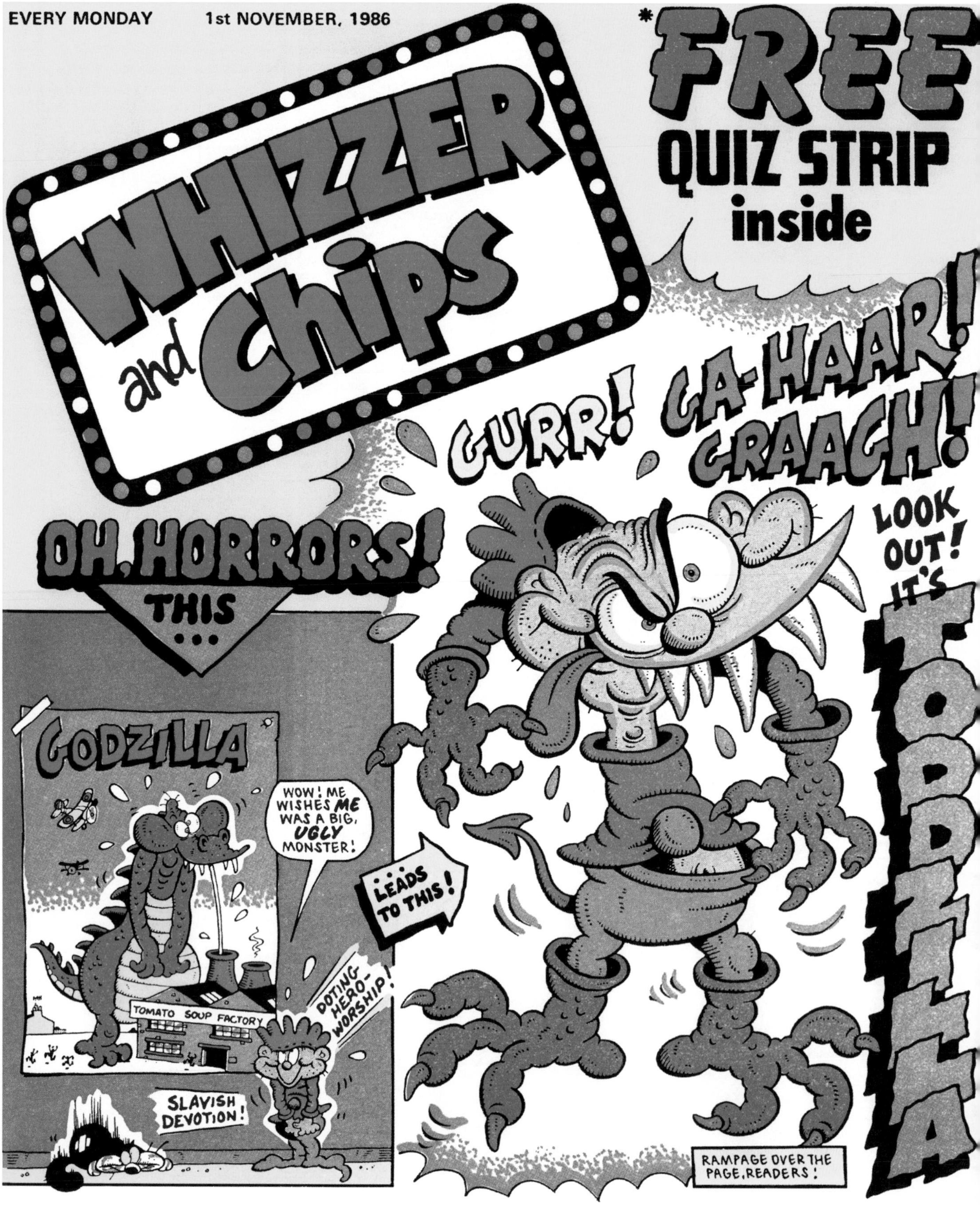
EVERY MONDAY
1st NOVEMBER, 1986
WHIZZER and Chips
*FREE QUIZ STRIP inside
GURR! CA-HAAR! CRAACH!
OH, HORRORS! THIS...
GODZILLA
WOW! ME WISHES ME WAS A BIG, UGLY MONSTER!
...LEADS TO THIS!
TOMATO SOUP FACTORY
DOTING HERO-WORSHIP!
SLAVISH DEVOTION!
LOOK OUT! IT'S TODZILLA
RAMPAGE OVER THE PAGE, READERS!

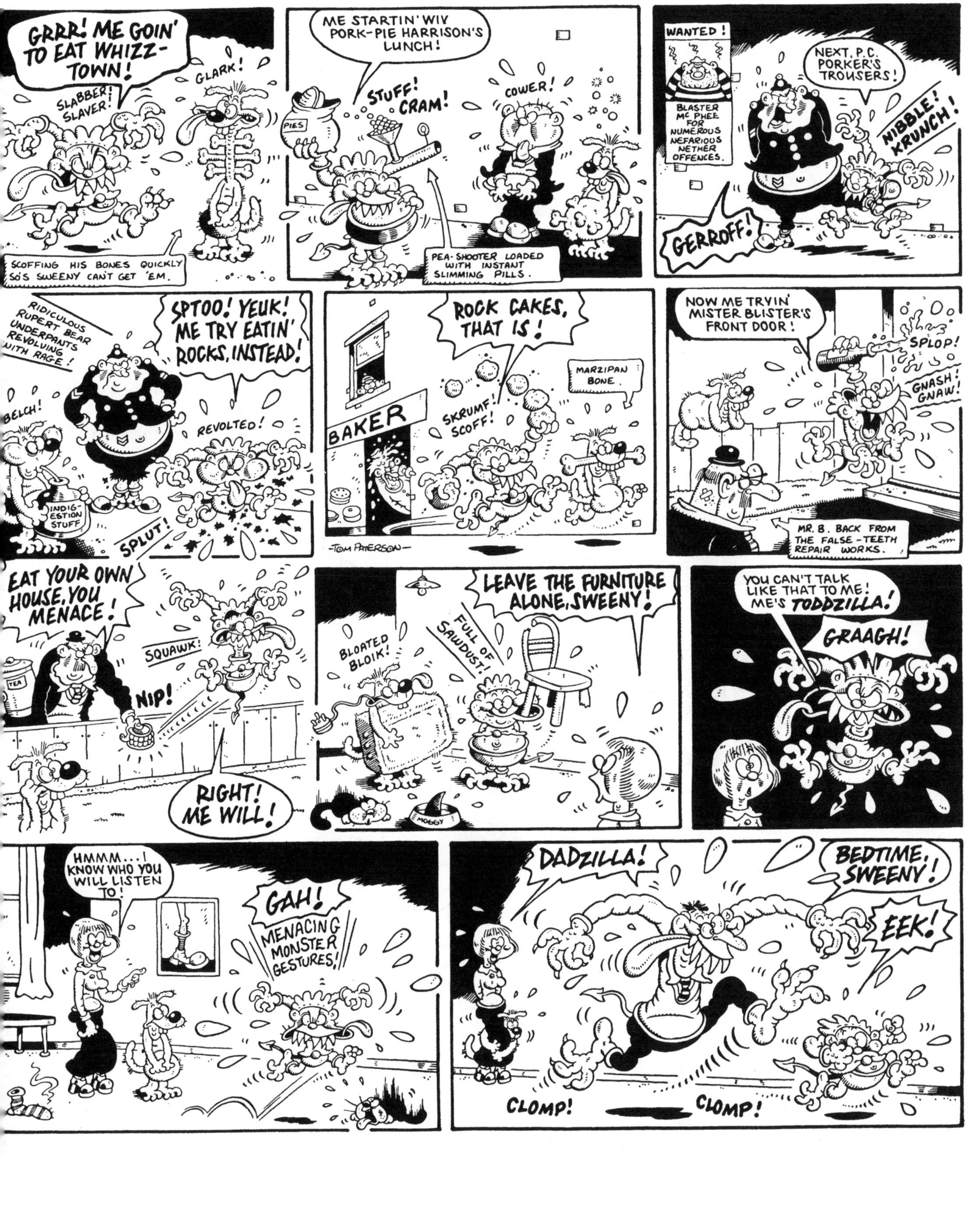
GRRR! ME GOIN' TO EAT WHIZZ-TOWN!
SLABBER! SLAVER!
GLARK!
SCOFFING HIS BONES QUICKLY SO'S SWEENY CAN'T GET 'EM.
ME STARTIN' WIV PORK-PIE HARRISON'S LUNCH!
PIES
STUFF! CRAM!
COWER!
PEA-SHOOTER LOADED WITH INSTANT SLIMMING PILLS.
WANTED!
BLASTER Mc PHEE FOR NUMEROUS NEFARIOUS NETHER OFFENCES.
NEXT, P.C. PORKER'S TROUSERS!
NIBBLE! KRUNCH!
GERROFF!
RIDICULOUS RUPERT BEAR UNDERPANTS REVOLVING WITH RAGE!
SPTOO! YEUK! ME TRY EATIN' ROCKS, INSTEAD!
BELCH!
REVOLTED!
INDIG-ESTION STUFF
SPLUT!
ROCK CAKES, THAT IS!
MARZIPAN BONE
BAKER
SKRUMF! SCOFF!
-TOM PATERSON-
NOW ME TRYIN' MISTER BLISTER'S FRONT DOOR!
SPLOP!
GNASH! GNAW!
MR. B. BACK FROM THE FALSE-TEETH REPAIR WORKS.
EAT YOUR OWN HOUSE, YOU MENACE!
SQUAWK!
TEA
NIP!
RIGHT! ME WILL!
LEAVE THE FURNITURE ALONE, SWEENY!
BLOATED BLOIK!
FULL OF SAWDUST!
MOGGY
YOU CAN'T TALK LIKE THAT TO ME! ME'S TODDZILLA!
GRAAGH!
HMMM...I KNOW WHO YOU WILL LISTEN TO!
GAH!
MENACING MONSTER GESTURES!
DADZILLA!
BEDTIME, SWEENY!
EEK!
CLOMP!
CLOMP!

EVERY MONDAY 3rd JANUARY, 1987

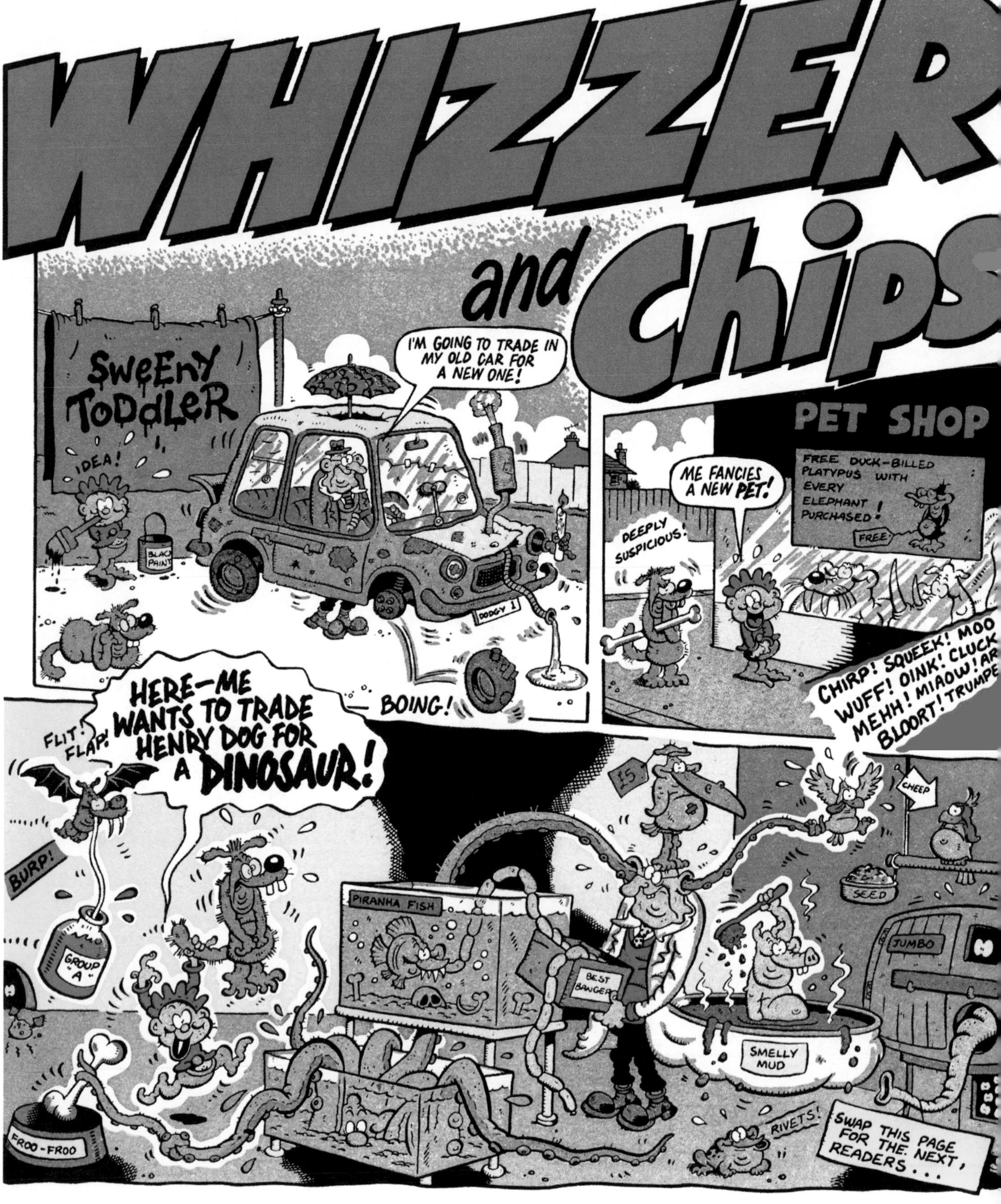
WHIZZER
and Chips
SWEENY TODDLER
IDEA!
BLACK PAINT
I'M GOING TO TRADE IN MY OLD CAR FOR A NEW ONE!
DODGY 1
BOING!
PET SHOP
FREE DUCK-BILLED PLATYPUS WITH EVERY ELEPHANT PURCHASED!
FREE
ME FANCIES A NEW PET!
DEEPLY SUSPICIOUS.
CHIRP! SQUEEK! MOO
WUFF! OINK! CLUCK
MEHH! MIAOW! AR
BLOORT! TRUMPE
FLIT! FLAP!
HERE—ME WANTS TO TRADE HENRY DOG FOR A DINOSAUR!
BURP!
GROUP "A"
£5
CHEEP
SEED
PIRANHA FISH
BEST BANGERS
JUMBO
SMELLY MUD
FROO-FROO
RIVETS!
SWAP THIS PAGE FOR THE NEXT, READERS...

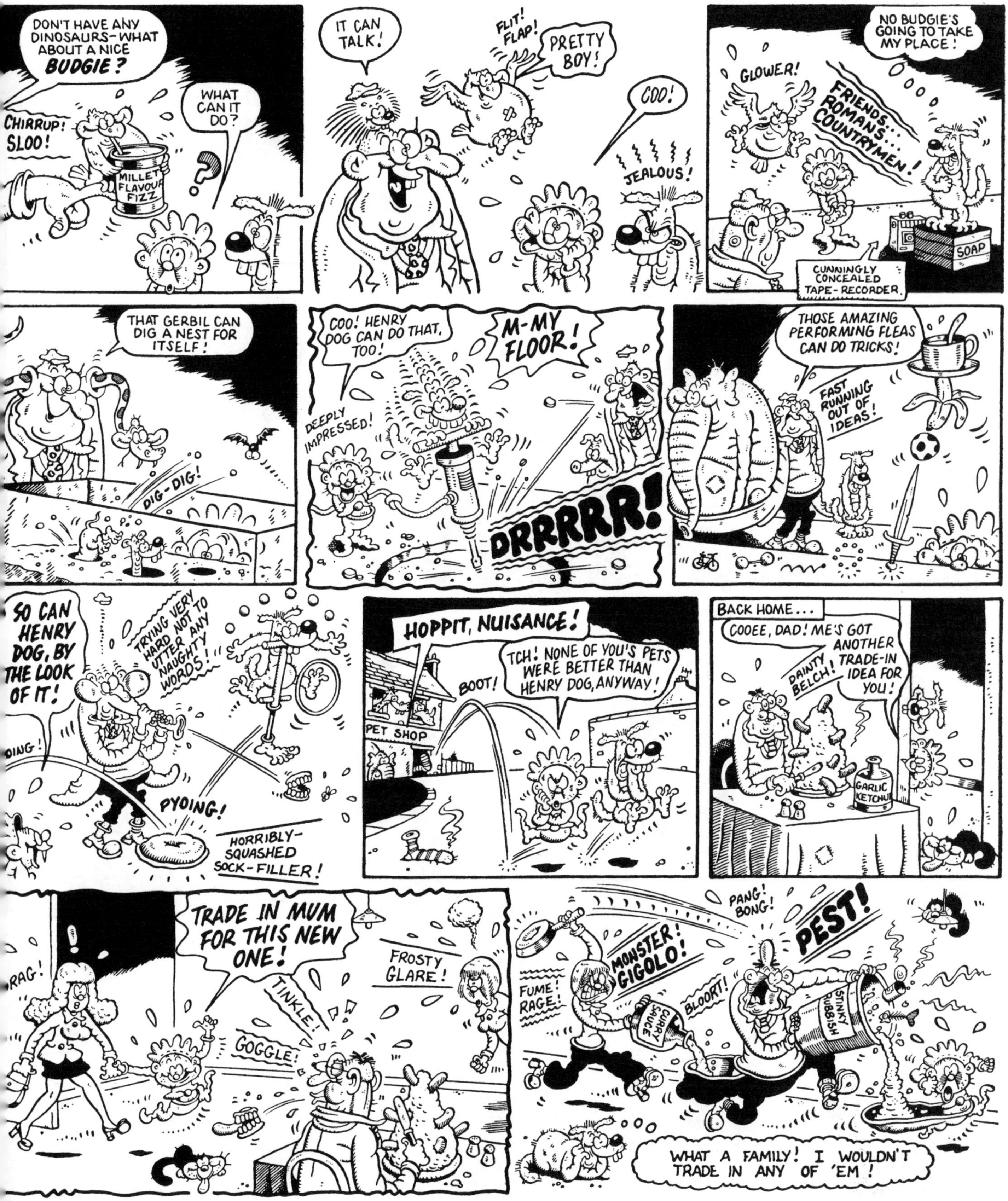
DON'T HAVE ANY DINOSAURS– WHAT ABOUT A NICE BUDGIE?
CHIRRUP! SLOO!
MILLET FLAVOUR FIZZ
WHAT CAN IT DO?
IT CAN TALK!
FLIT! FLAP!
PRETTY BOY!
COO!
JEALOUS!
NO BUDGIE'S GOING TO TAKE MY PLACE!
GLOWER!
FRIENDS... ROMANS... COUNTRYMEN!
SOAP
CUNNINGLY CONCEALED TAPE-RECORDER
THAT GERBIL CAN DIG A NEST FOR ITSELF!
DIG-DIG!
COO! HENRY DOG CAN DO THAT, TOO!
M-MY FLOOR!
DEEPLY IMPRESSED!
DRRRRR!
THOSE AMAZING PERFORMING FLEAS CAN DO TRICKS!
FAST RUNNING OUT OF IDEAS!
SO CAN HENRY DOG, BY THE LOOK OF IT!
TRYING VERY HARD NOT TO UTTER ANY NAUGHTY WORDS!
PYOING!
HORRIBLY-SQUASHED SOCK-FILLER!
HOPPIT, NUISANCE!
BOOT!
TCH! NONE OF YOU'S PETS WERE BETTER THAN HENRY DOG, ANYWAY!
PET SHOP
BACK HOME...
COOEE, DAD! ME'S GOT ANOTHER TRADE-IN IDEA FOR YOU!
DAINTY BELCH!
GARLIC KETCHUP
TRADE IN MUM FOR THIS NEW ONE!
FROSTY GLARE!
TINKLE!
GOGGLE!
PANG! BONG!
PEST!
MONSTER GIGOLO!
FUME! RAGE!
BLOORT!
CURRY SAUCE
STINKY RUBBISH
WHAT A FAMILY! I WOULDN'T TRADE IN ANY OF 'EM!

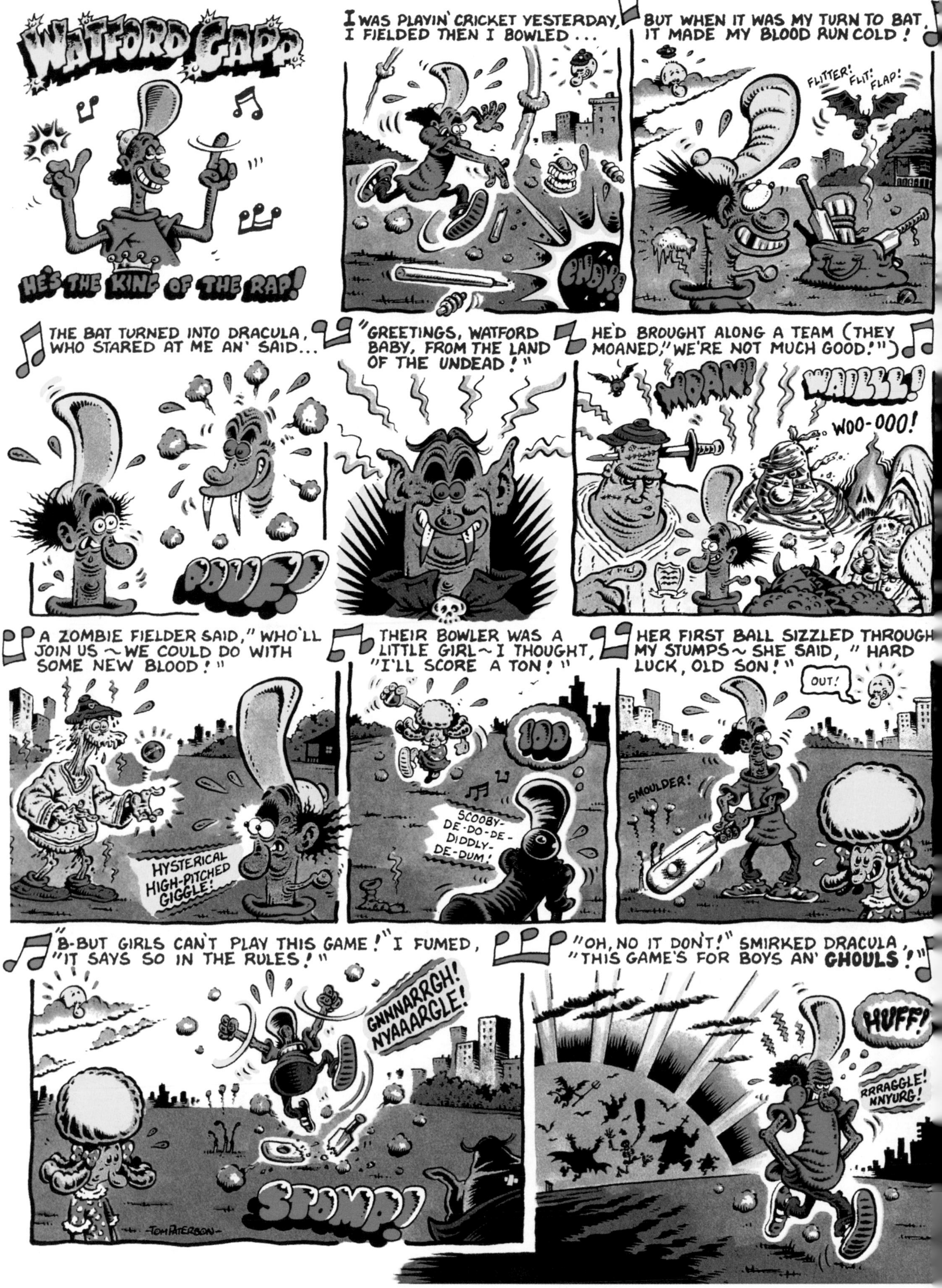
WATFORD GAPP
HE'S THE KING OF THE RAP!
I WAS PLAYIN' CRICKET YESTERDAY, I FIELDED THEN I BOWLED ...
CHOK!
BUT WHEN IT WAS MY TURN TO BAT, IT MADE MY BLOOD RUN COLD!
FLITTER! FLIT! FLAP!
THE BAT TURNED INTO DRACULA, WHO STARED AT ME AN' SAID...
POUF!
"GREETINGS, WATFORD BABY, FROM THE LAND OF THE UNDEAD!"
HE'D BROUGHT ALONG A TEAM (THEY MOANED, "WE'RE NOT MUCH GOOD!")
MOAN!
WAILLL!
WOO-OOO!
A ZOMBIE FIELDER SAID, "WHO'LL JOIN US ~ WE COULD DO WITH SOME NEW BLOOD!"
HYSTERICAL HIGH-PITCHED GIGGLE!
THEIR BOWLER WAS A LITTLE GIRL ~ I THOUGHT, "I'LL SCORE A TON!"
100
SCOOBY-DE-DO-DE-DIDDLY-DE-DUM!
HER FIRST BALL SIZZLED THROUGH MY STUMPS ~ SHE SAID, "HARD LUCK, OLD SON!"
OUT!
SMOULDER!
"B-BUT GIRLS CAN'T PLAY THIS GAME!" I FUMED, "IT SAYS SO IN THE RULES!"
GNNNARRGH! NYAAARGLE!
STOMP!
-TOM PATERSON-
"OH, NO IT DON'T!" SMIRKED DRACULA, "THIS GAME'S FOR BOYS AN' GHOULS!"
HUFF!
RRRAGGLE! NNYURG!

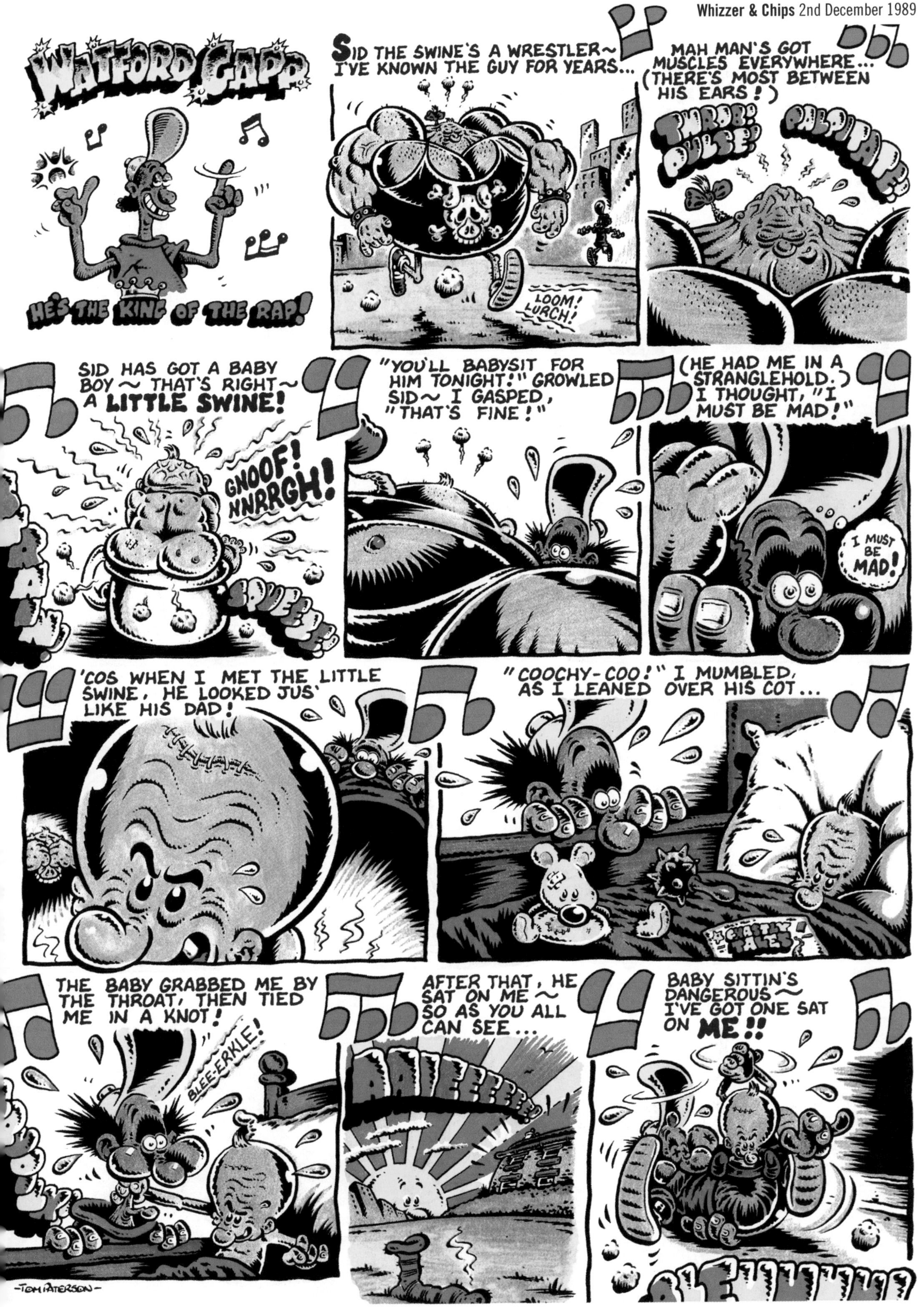
WATFORD GAPP
HE'S THE KING OF THE RAP!
SID THE SWINE'S A WRESTLER~ I'VE KNOWN THE GUY FOR YEARS...
LOOM! LURCH!
MAH MAN'S GOT MUSCLES EVERYWHERE... (THERE'S MOST BETWEEN HIS EARS!)
THROB! PULSE! PALPITATE!
SID HAS GOT A BABY BOY ~ THAT'S RIGHT~ A LITTLE SWINE!
GNOOF! NNRRGH!
"YOU'LL BABYSIT FOR HIM TONIGHT!" GROWLED SID~ I GASPED, "THAT'S FINE!"
(HE HAD ME IN A STRANGLEHOLD.) I THOUGHT, "I MUST BE MAD!"
I MUST BE MAD!
'COS WHEN I MET THE LITTLE SWINE, HE LOOKED JUS' LIKE HIS DAD!
"COOCHY-COO!" I MUMBLED, AS I LEANED OVER HIS COT...
GHASTLY TALES
THE BABY GRABBED ME BY THE THROAT, THEN TIED ME IN A KNOT!
BLEE-ERKLE!
AFTER THAT, HE SAT ON ME~ SO AS YOU ALL CAN SEE...
BABY SITTIN'S DANGEROUS~ I'VE GOT ONE SAT ON ME!!
-TOM PATERSON-

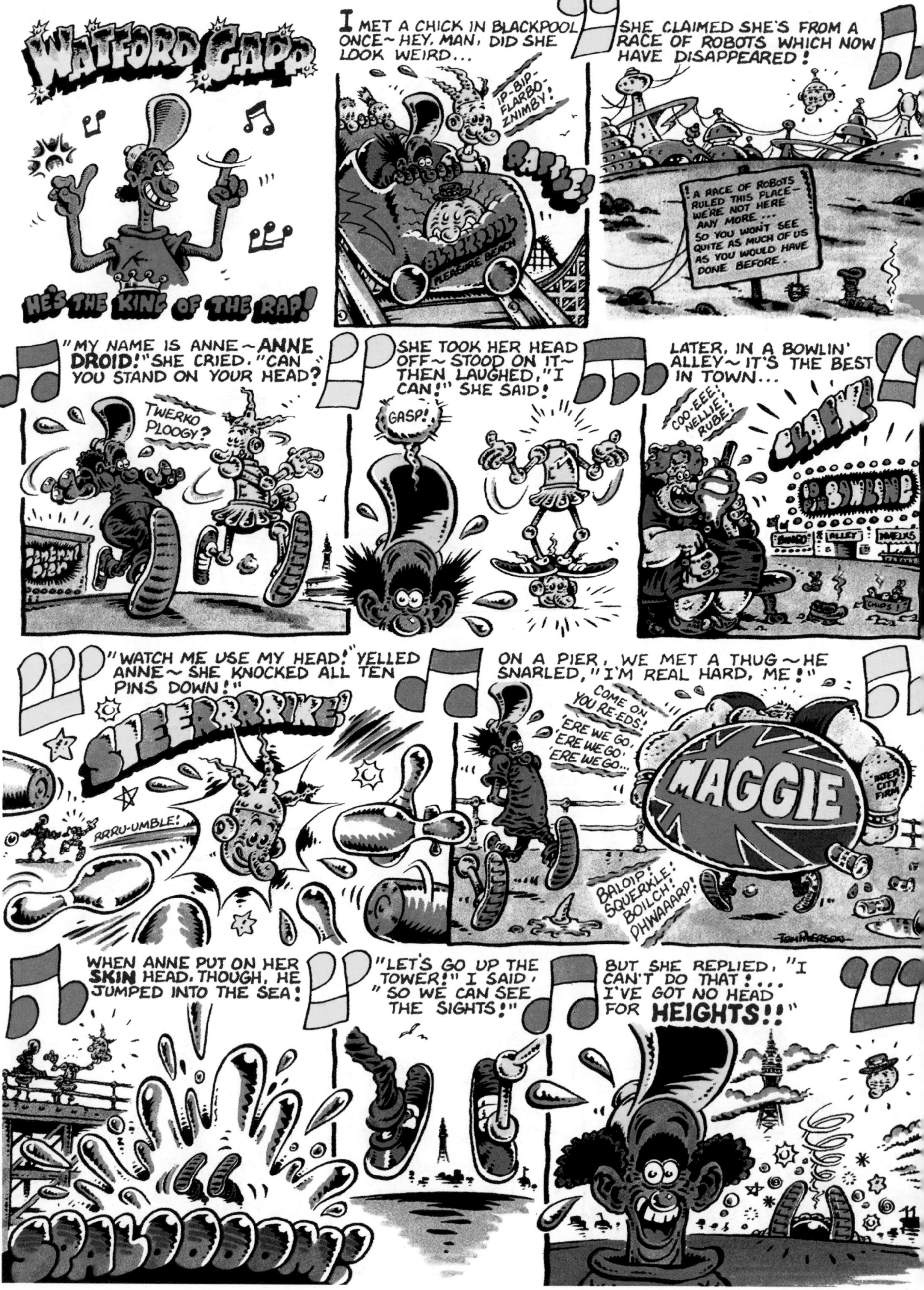
WATFORD GAPP
HE'S THE KING OF THE RAP!
I MET A CHICK IN BLACKPOOL ONCE~ HEY, MAN, DID SHE LOOK WEIRD...
IP-BIP-FLARBO-ZNIMBY!
RATTLE!
BLACKPOOL PLEASURE BEACH
SHE CLAIMED SHE'S FROM A RACE OF ROBOTS WHICH NOW HAVE DISAPPEARED!
A RACE OF ROBOTS RULED THIS PLACE— WE'RE NOT HERE ANY MORE... SO YOU WON'T SEE QUITE AS MUCH OF US AS YOU WOULD HAVE DONE BEFORE.
"MY NAME IS ANNE~ANNE DROID!" SHE CRIED. "CAN YOU STAND ON YOUR HEAD?
TWERKO PLOOGY?
Central Pier
SHE TOOK HER HEAD OFF~ STOOD ON IT~ THEN LAUGHED, "I CAN!" SHE SAID!
GASP!
LATER, IN A BOWLIN' ALLEY~ IT'S THE BEST IN TOWN...
COO-EEE NELLIE RUBE!
CLANK!
BOWLING
BINGO
ALLEY
CHIPS
"WATCH ME USE MY HEAD!" YELLED ANNE~ SHE KNOCKED ALL TEN PINS DOWN!"
STEERRRRIKE!
RRRU-UMBLE!
ON A PIER, WE MET A THUG~HE SNARLED, "I'M REAL HARD, ME!"
COME ON YOU RE-EDS!
'ERE WE GO, 'ERE WE GO, 'ERE WE GO...
MAGGIE
INTER CITY FIRM
BALOIP! SQUERKLE! BOILCH! PHWAAARP!
WHEN ANNE PUT ON HER SKIN HEAD, THOUGH, HE JUMPED INTO THE SEA!
SPLOOSH!
"LET'S GO UP THE TOWER!" I SAID, "SO WE CAN SEE THE SIGHTS!"
BUT SHE REPLIED, "I CAN'T DO THAT!... I'VE GOT NO HEAD FOR HEIGHTS!!"

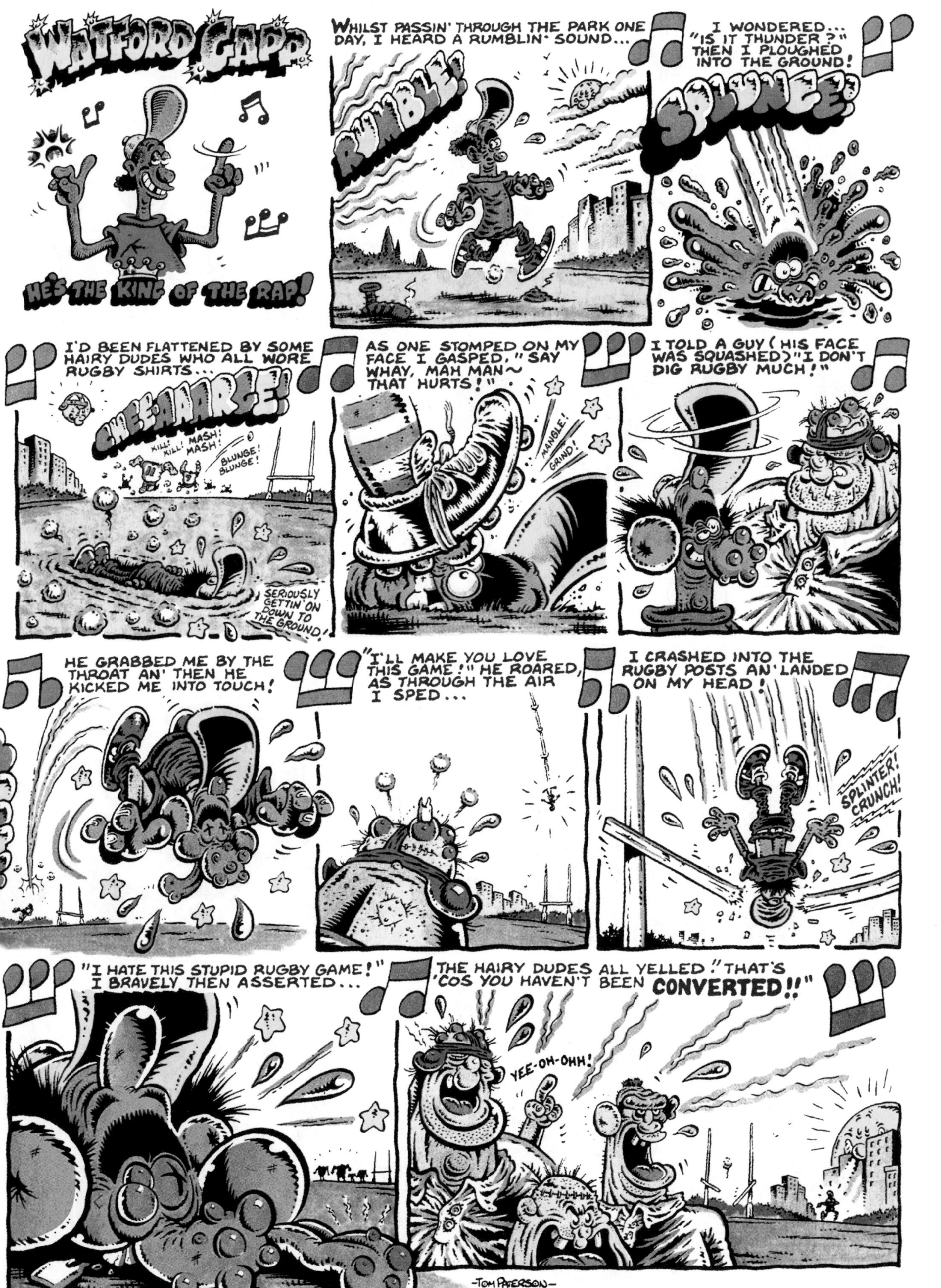
WATFORD GAPP
HE'S THE KING OF THE RAP!
WHILST PASSIN' THROUGH THE PARK ONE DAY, I HEARD A RUMBLIN' SOUND...
RUMBLE!
I WONDERED... "IS IT THUNDER?" THEN I PLOUGHED INTO THE GROUND!
SPLUNGE!
I'D BEEN FLATTENED BY SOME HAIRY DUDES WHO ALL WORE RUGBY SHIRTS...
CHEE-AAARGE!
KILL! KILL! MASH! MASH!
BLUNGE! BLUNGE!
SERIOUSLY GETTIN' ON DOWN TO THE GROUND!
AS ONE STOMPED ON MY FACE I GASPED, "SAY WHAY, MAH MAN~ THAT HURTS!"
MANGLE! GRIND!
I TOLD A GUY (HIS FACE WAS SQUASHED) "I DON'T DIG RUGBY MUCH!"
HE GRABBED ME BY THE THROAT AN' THEN HE KICKED ME INTO TOUCH!
"I'LL MAKE YOU LOVE THIS GAME!" HE ROARED, AS THROUGH THE AIR I SPED...
I CRASHED INTO THE RUGBY POSTS AN' LANDED ON MY HEAD!
SPLINTER! CRUNCH!
"I HATE THIS STUPID RUGBY GAME!" I BRAVELY THEN ASSERTED...
THE HAIRY DUDES ALL YELLED "THAT'S 'COS YOU HAVEN'T BEEN CONVERTED!!"
YEE-OH-OHH!
-TOM PATERSON-

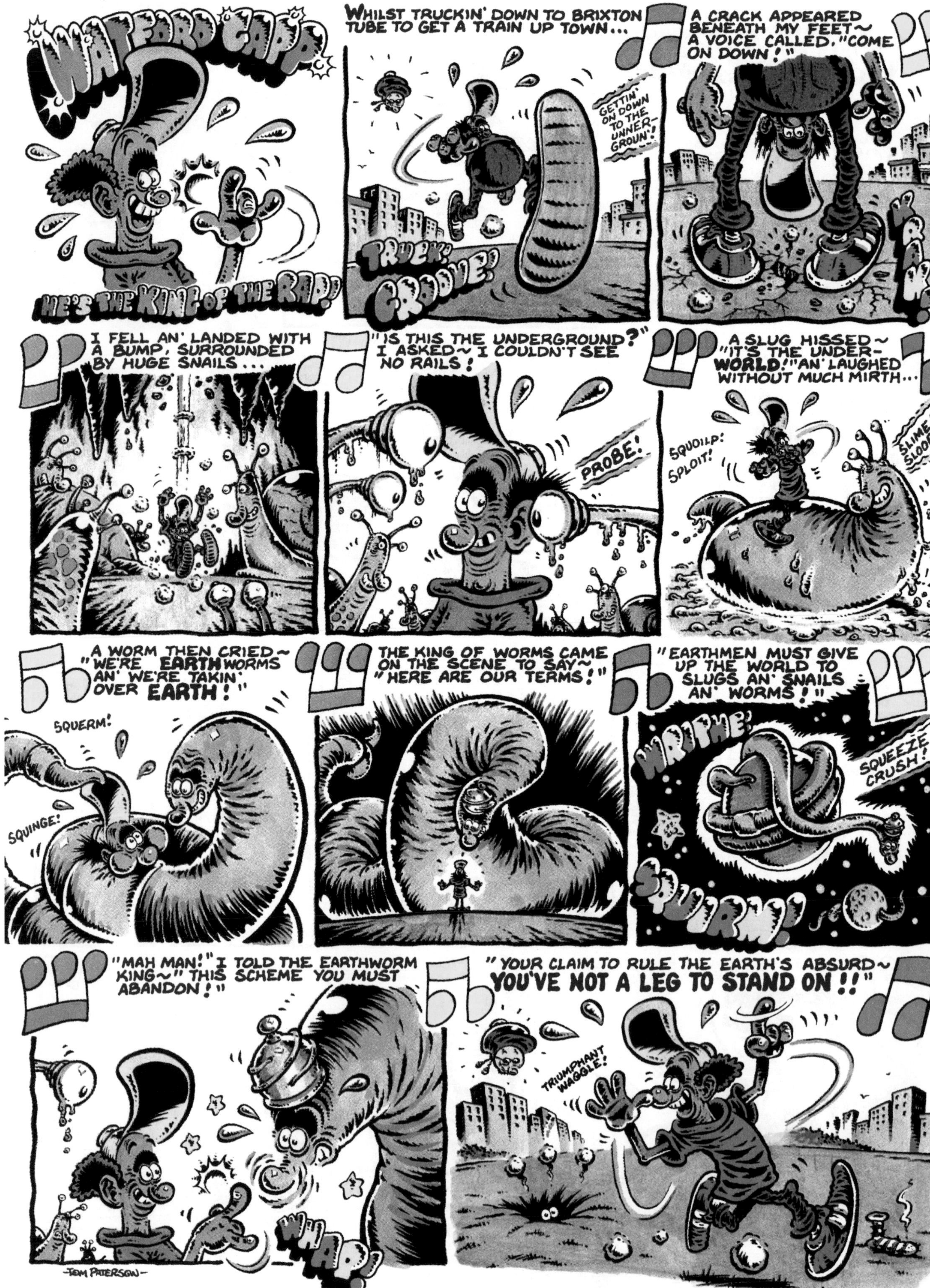
WATFORD CAPP
HE'S THE KING OF THE RAP!
WHILST TRUCKIN' DOWN TO BRIXTON TUBE TO GET A TRAIN UP TOWN...
GETTIN' ON DOWN TO THE UNNER-GROUN'!
TRUCK! GROOVE!
A CRACK APPEARED BENEATH MY FEET~ A VOICE CALLED, "COME ON DOWN!"
I FELL AN' LANDED WITH A BUMP, SURROUNDED BY HUGE SNAILS...
"IS THIS THE UNDERGROUND?" I ASKED~ I COULDN'T SEE NO RAILS!
PROBE!
A SLUG HISSED~ "IT'S THE UNDER-WORLD!" AN' LAUGHED WITHOUT MUCH MIRTH...
SQUOILP! SPLOIT!
SLIME! SLOOB!
A WORM THEN CRIED~ "WE'RE EARTHWORMS AN' WE'RE TAKIN' OVER EARTH!"
SQUERM!
SQUINGE!
THE KING OF WORMS CAME ON THE SCENE TO SAY~ "HERE ARE OUR TERMS!"
"EARTHMEN MUST GIVE UP THE WORLD TO SLUGS AN' SNAILS AN' WORMS!"
WRITHE!
SQUEEZE! CRUSH!
SQUIRM!
"MAH MAN!" I TOLD THE EARTHWORM KING~ "THIS SCHEME YOU MUST ABANDON!"
WHAP!
-TOM PATERSON-
"YOUR CLAIM TO RULE THE EARTH'S ABSURD~ YOU'VE NOT A LEG TO STAND ON!!"
TRIUMPHANT WAGGLE!

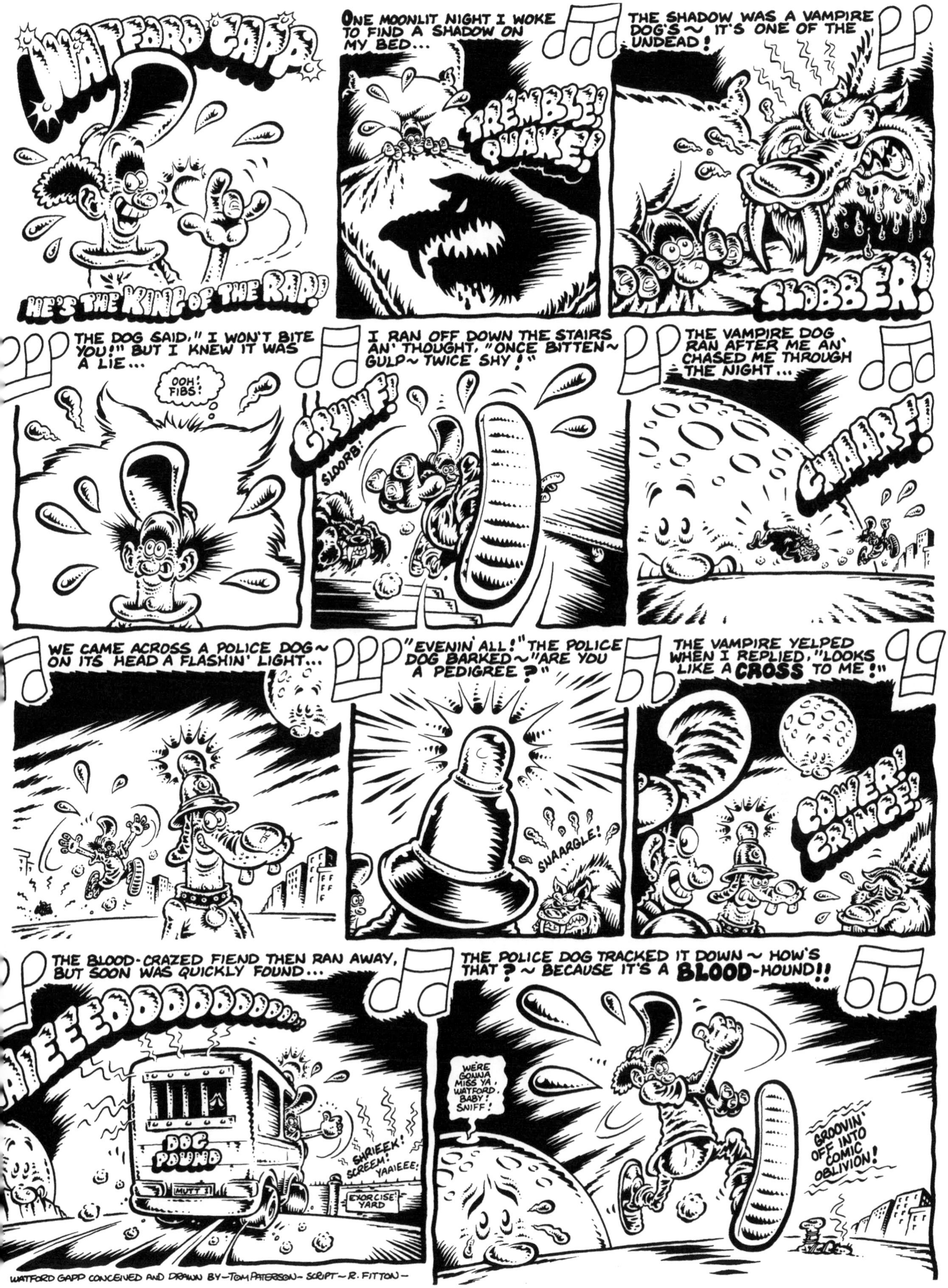
WATFORD GAPP
HE'S THE KING OF THE RAP!
ONE MOONLIT NIGHT I WOKE TO FIND A SHADOW ON MY BED...
TREMBLE! QUAKE!
THE SHADOW WAS A VAMPIRE DOG'S ~ IT'S ONE OF THE UNDEAD!
SLOBBER!
THE DOG SAID, "I WON'T BITE YOU!" BUT I KNEW IT WAS A LIE...
OOH! FIBS!
I RAN OFF DOWN THE STAIRS AN' THOUGHT, "ONCE BITTEN ~ GULP ~ TWICE SHY!"
GRUNF!
SLOORB!
THE VAMPIRE DOG RAN AFTER ME AN' CHASED ME THROUGH THE NIGHT...
SNAARF!
WE CAME ACROSS A POLICE DOG ~ ON ITS HEAD A FLASHIN' LIGHT...
"EVENIN' ALL!" THE POLICE DOG BARKED ~ "ARE YOU A PEDIGREE?"
SNAARGLE!
THE VAMPIRE YELPED WHEN I REPLIED, "LOOKS LIKE A CROSS TO ME!"
COWER! CRINGE!
THE BLOOD-CRAZED FIEND THEN RAN AWAY, BUT SOON WAS QUICKLY FOUND...
DOG POUND
MUTT 1
SHRIEEK! SCREEM! YAAIEEE!
EXORCISE YARD
THE POLICE DOG TRACKED IT DOWN ~ HOW'S THAT? ~ BECAUSE IT'S A BLOOD-HOUND!!
WE'RE GONNA MISS YA, WATFORD, BABY! SNIFF!
GROOVIN' OFF INTO COMIC OBLIVION!

WATFORD GAPP CONCEIVED AND DRAWN BY—TOM PATERSON— SCRIPT— R. FITTON—

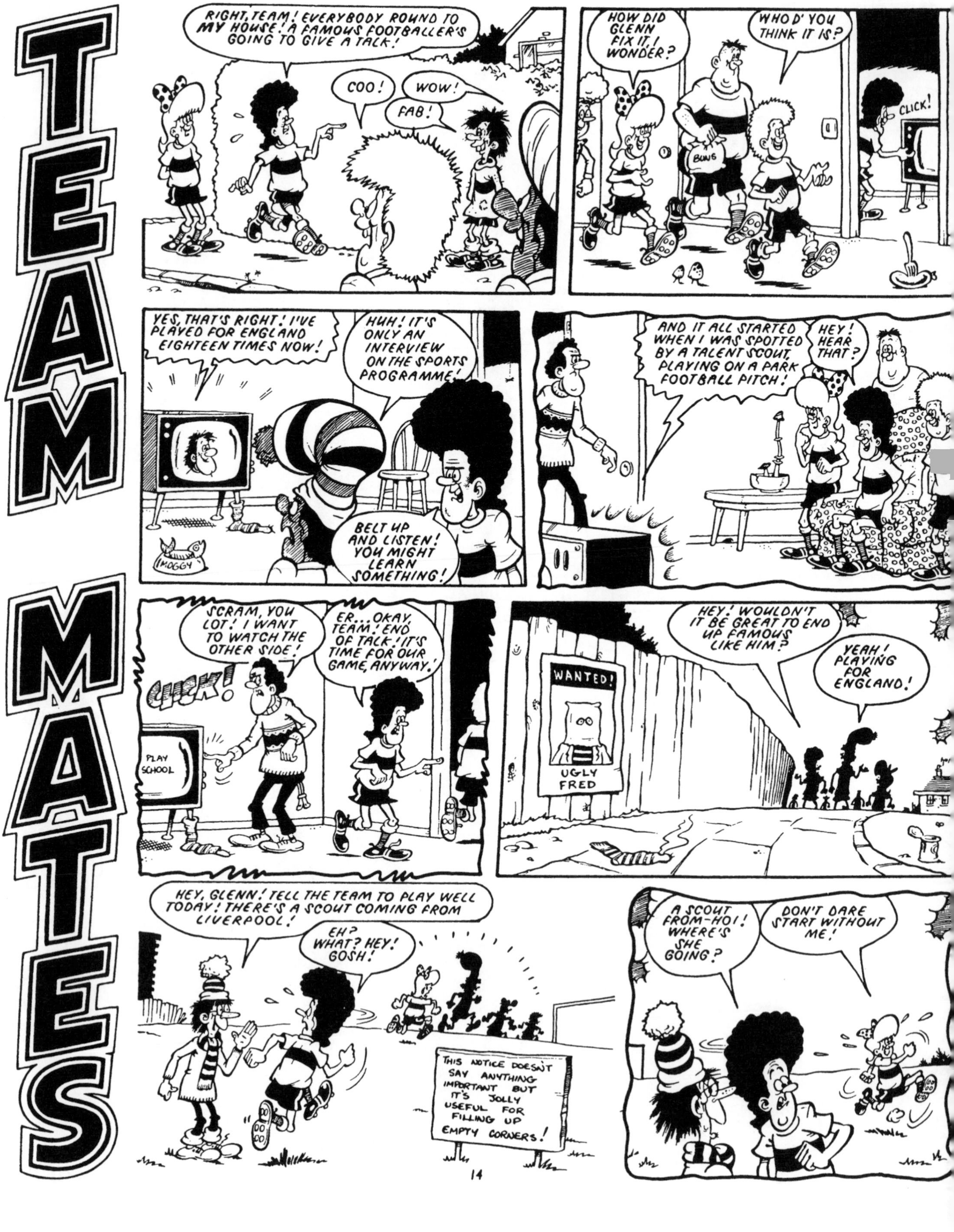
TEAM MATES
RIGHT, TEAM! EVERYBODY ROUND TO MY HOUSE! A FAMOUS FOOTBALLER'S GOING TO GIVE A TALK!
COO!
WOW!
FAB!
HOW DID GLENN FIX IT, I WONDER?
WHO D' YOU THINK IT IS?
BUNS
CLICK!
YES, THAT'S RIGHT! I'VE PLAYED FOR ENGLAND EIGHTEEN TIMES NOW!
HUH! IT'S ONLY AN INTERVIEW ON THE SPORTS PROGRAMME!
BELT UP AND LISTEN! YOU MIGHT LEARN SOMETHING!
MOGGY
AND IT ALL STARTED WHEN I WAS SPOTTED BY A TALENT SCOUT, PLAYING ON A PARK FOOTBALL PITCH!
HEY! HEAR THAT?
SCRAM, YOU LOT! I WANT TO WATCH THE OTHER SIDE!
ER... OKAY, TEAM! END OF TALK! IT'S TIME FOR OUR GAME, ANYWAY.
CLICK!
PLAY SCHOOL
HEY! WOULDN'T IT BE GREAT TO END UP FAMOUS LIKE HIM?
YEAH! PLAYING FOR ENGLAND!
WANTED!
UGLY FRED
HEY, GLENN! TELL THE TEAM TO PLAY WELL TODAY! THERE'S A SCOUT COMING FROM LIVERPOOL!
EH? WHAT? HEY! GOSH!
THIS NOTICE DOESN'T SAY ANYTHING IMPORTANT BUT IT'S JOLLY USEFUL FOR FILLING UP EMPTY CORNERS!
A SCOUT FROM—HOI! WHERE'S SHE GOING?
DON'T DARE START WITHOUT ME!
14

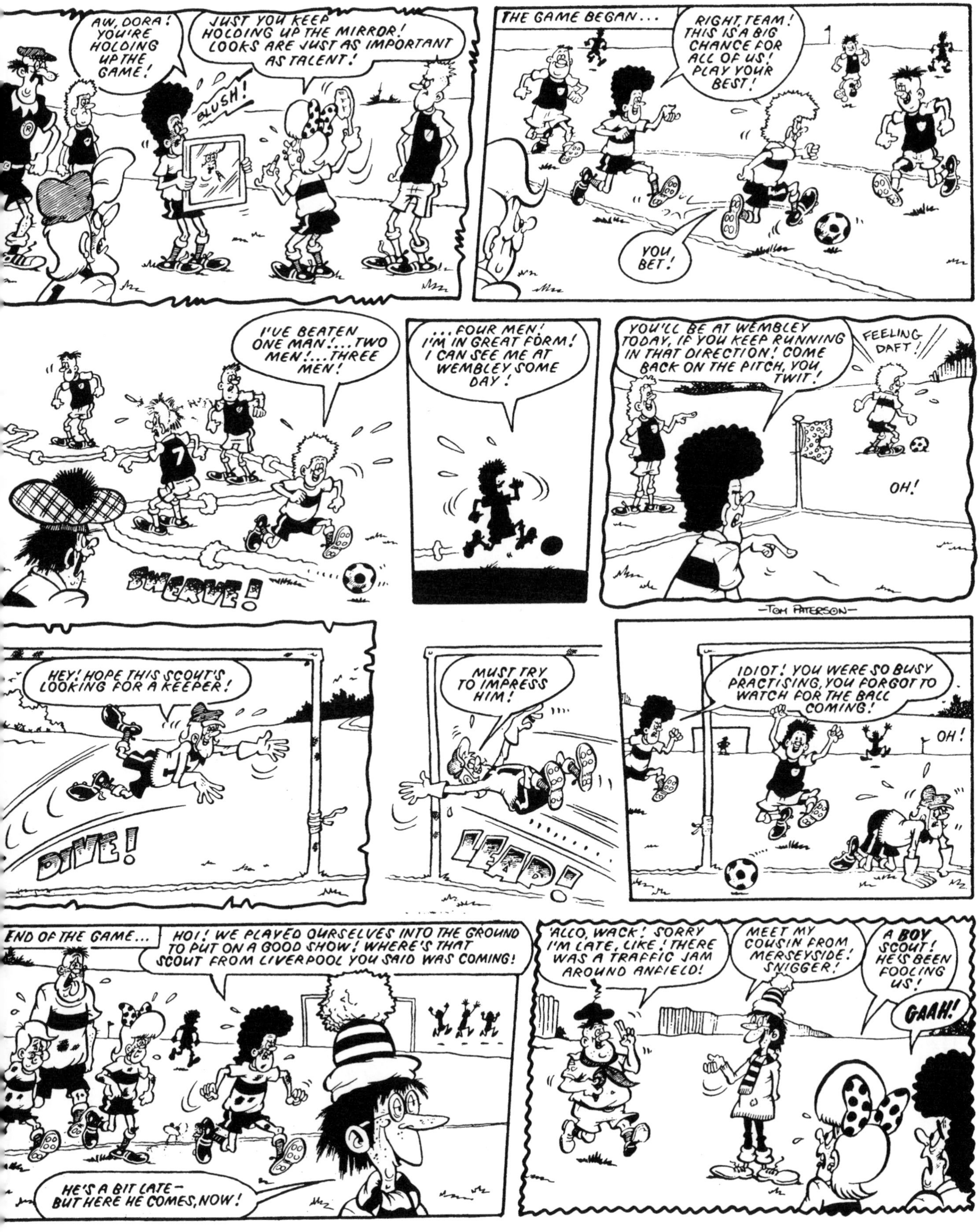
AW, DORA! YOU'RE HOLDING UP THE GAME!
JUST YOU KEEP HOLDING UP THE MIRROR! LOOKS ARE JUST AS IMPORTANT AS TALENT!
BLUSH!
THE GAME BEGAN...
RIGHT, TEAM! THIS IS A BIG CHANCE FOR ALL OF US! PLAY YOUR BEST!
YOU BET!
I'VE BEATEN ONE MAN!...TWO MEN!...THREE MEN!
SWERVE!
...FOUR MEN! I'M IN GREAT FORM! I CAN SEE ME AT WEMBLEY SOME DAY!
YOU'LL BE AT WEMBLEY TODAY, IF YOU KEEP RUNNING IN THAT DIRECTION! COME BACK ON THE PITCH, YOU TWIT!
FEELING DAFT!
OH!
—TOM PATERSON—
HEY! HOPE THIS SCOUT'S LOOKING FOR A KEEPER!
DIVE!
MUST TRY TO IMPRESS HIM!
LEAP!
IDIOT! YOU WERE SO BUSY PRACTISING, YOU FORGOT TO WATCH FOR THE BALL COMING!
OH!
END OF THE GAME...
HOI! WE PLAYED OURSELVES INTO THE GROUND TO PUT ON A GOOD SHOW! WHERE'S THAT SCOUT FROM LIVERPOOL YOU SAID WAS COMING!
HE'S A BIT LATE— BUT HERE HE COMES, NOW!
'ALLO, WACK! SORRY I'M LATE, LIKE! THERE WAS A TRAFFIC JAM AROUND ANFIELD!
MEET MY COUSIN FROM MERSEYSIDE! SNIGGER!
A BOY SCOUT! HE'S BEEN FOOLING US!
GAAH!

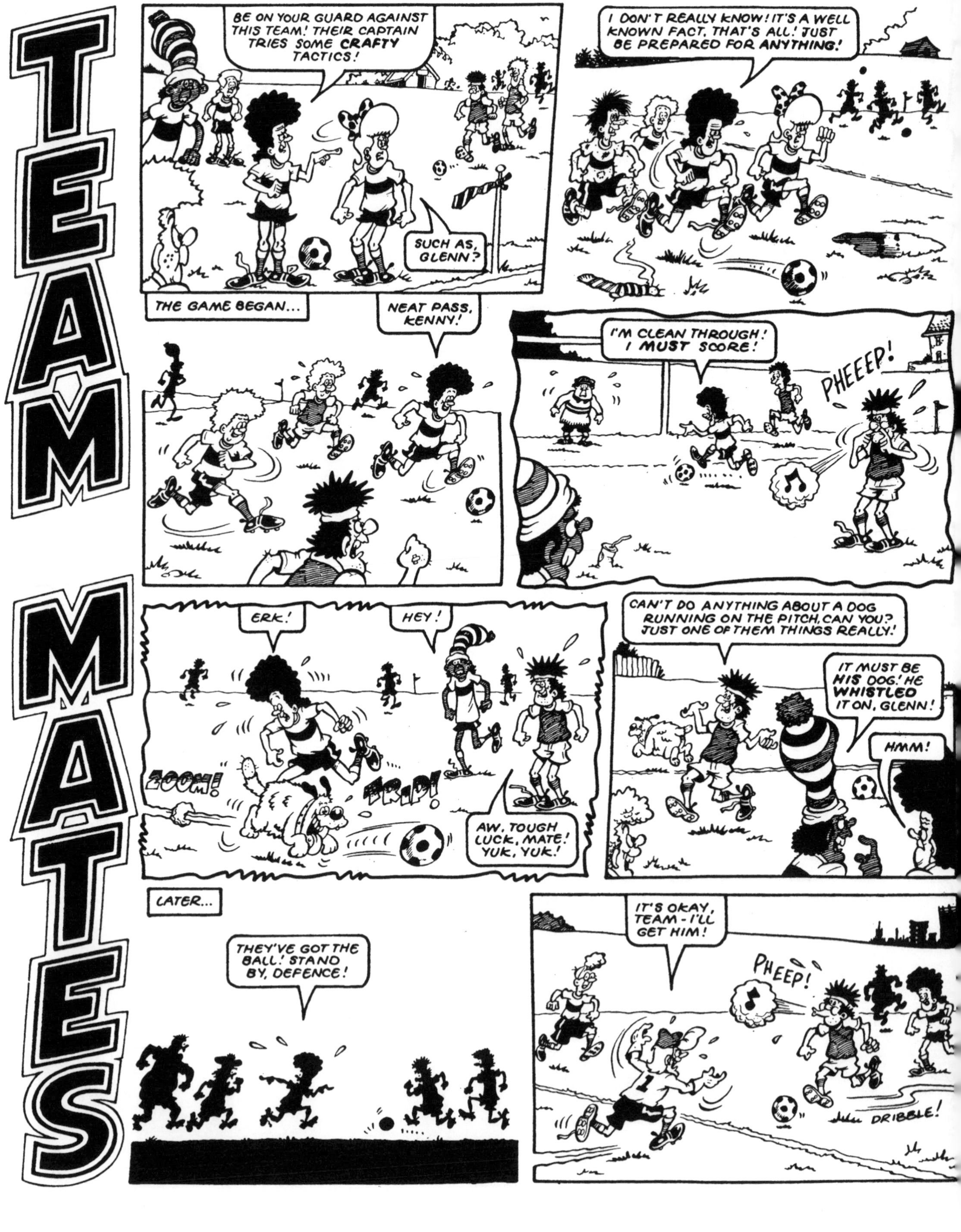
TEAM MATES
BE ON YOUR GUARD AGAINST THIS TEAM! THEIR CAPTAIN TRIES SOME CRAFTY TACTICS!
SUCH AS, GLENN?
I DON'T REALLY KNOW! IT'S A WELL KNOWN FACT, THAT'S ALL! JUST BE PREPARED FOR ANYTHING!
THE GAME BEGAN...
NEAT PASS, KENNY!
I'M CLEAN THROUGH! I MUST SCORE!
PHEEEP!
ERK!
HEY!
ZOOM!
AW, TOUGH LUCK, MATE! YUK, YUK!
CAN'T DO ANYTHING ABOUT A DOG RUNNING ON THE PITCH, CAN YOU? JUST ONE OF THEM THINGS REALLY!
IT MUST BE HIS DOG! HE WHISTLED IT ON, GLENN!
HMM!
LATER...
THEY'VE GOT THE BALL! STAND BY, DEFENCE!
IT'S OKAY, TEAM - I'LL GET HIM!
PHEEP!
DRIBBLE!

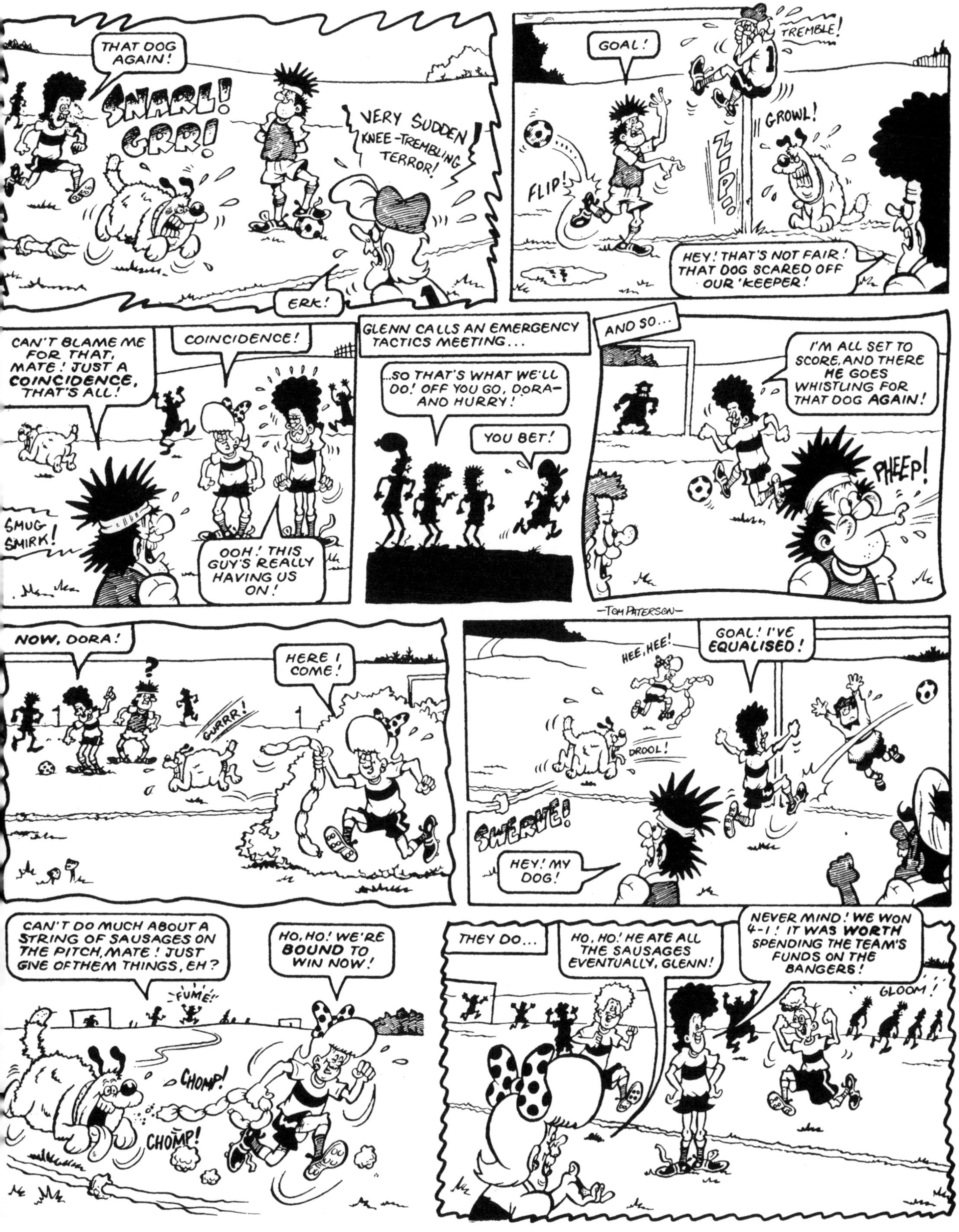
THAT DOG AGAIN!
SNARL! GRR!
VERY SUDDEN KNEE-TREMBLING TERROR!
ERK!
GOAL!
TREMBLE!
FLIP!
ZIP!
GROWL!
HEY! THAT'S NOT FAIR! THAT DOG SCARED OFF OUR 'KEEPER!
CAN'T BLAME ME FOR THAT, MATE! JUST A COINCIDENCE, THAT'S ALL!
COINCIDENCE!
SMUG SMIRK!
OOH! THIS GUY'S REALLY HAVING US ON!
GLENN CALLS AN EMERGENCY TACTICS MEETING...
...SO THAT'S WHAT WE'LL DO! OFF YOU GO, DORA-AND HURRY!
YOU BET!
AND SO...
I'M ALL SET TO SCORE, AND THERE HE GOES WHISTLING FOR THAT DOG AGAIN!
PHEEP!
-TOM PATERSON-
NOW, DORA!
GURRR!
HERE I COME!
HEE, HEE!
GOAL! I'VE EQUALISED!
DROOL!
SWERVE!
HEY! MY DOG!
CAN'T DO MUCH ABOUT A STRING OF SAUSAGES ON THE PITCH, MATE! JUST GIVE OF THEM THINGS, EH?
FUME!
HO, HO! WE'RE BOUND TO WIN NOW!
CHOMP!
CHOMP!
THEY DO...
HO, HO! HE ATE ALL THE SAUSAGES EVENTUALLY, GLENN!
NEVER MIND! WE WON 4-1! IT WAS WORTH SPENDING THE TEAM'S FUNDS ON THE BANGERS!
GLOOM!

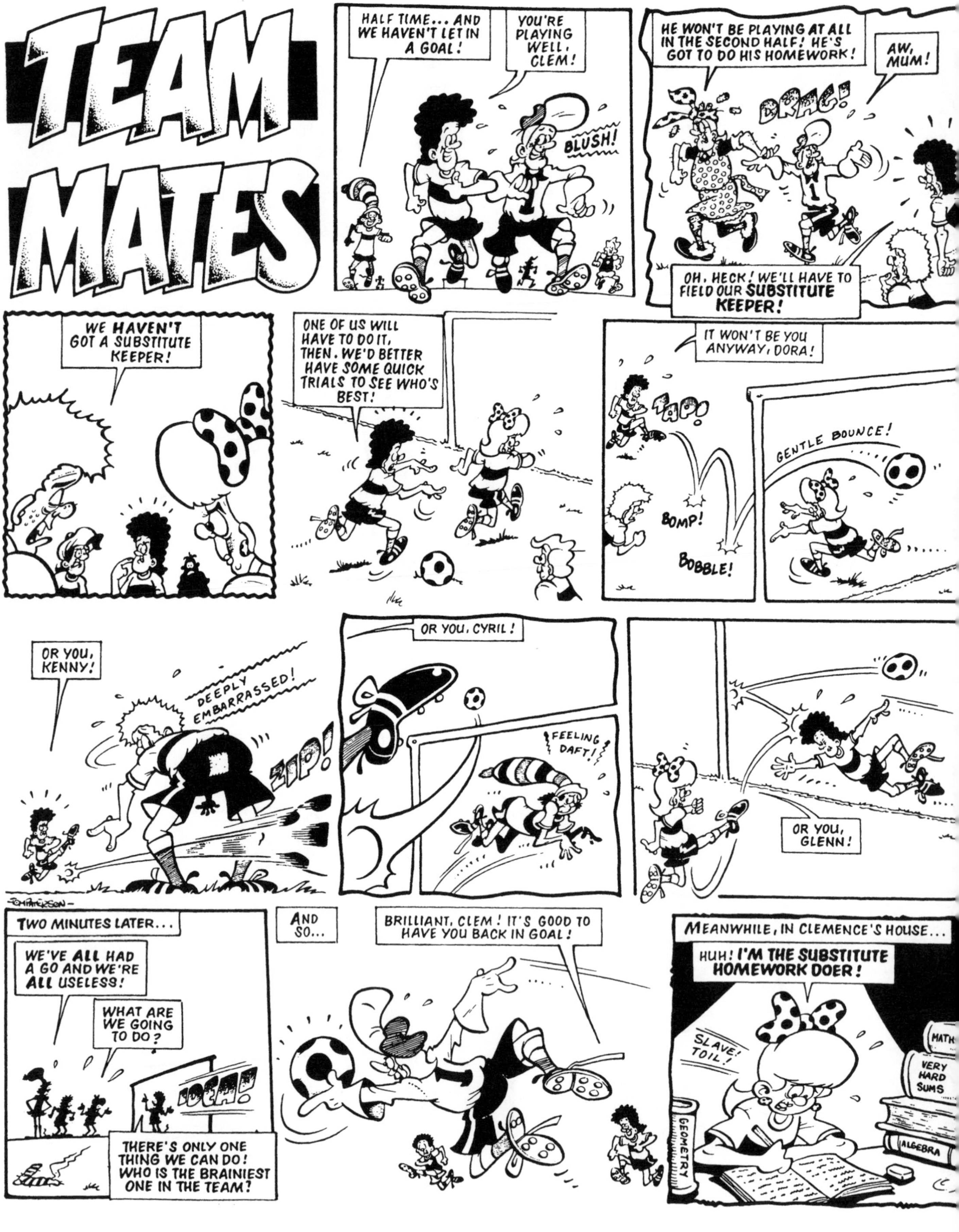
TEAM MATES
HALF TIME... AND WE HAVEN'T LET IN A GOAL!
YOU'RE PLAYING WELL, CLEM!
BLUSH!
HE WON'T BE PLAYING AT ALL IN THE SECOND HALF! HE'S GOT TO DO HIS HOMEWORK!
AW, MUM!
DRAG!
OH, HECK! WE'LL HAVE TO FIELD OUR SUBSTITUTE KEEPER!
WE HAVEN'T GOT A SUBSTITUTE KEEPER!
ONE OF US WILL HAVE TO DO IT, THEN. WE'D BETTER HAVE SOME QUICK TRIALS TO SEE WHO'S BEST!
IT WON'T BE YOU ANYWAY, DORA!
TAP!
BOMP!
BOBBLE!
GENTLE BOUNCE!
OR YOU, KENNY!
DEEPLY EMBARRASSED!
ZIP!
OR YOU, CYRIL!
FEELING DAFT!
OR YOU, GLENN!
TWO MINUTES LATER...
WE'VE ALL HAD A GO AND WE'RE ALL USELESS!
WHAT ARE WE GOING TO DO?
THERE'S ONLY ONE THING WE CAN DO! WHO IS THE BRAINIEST ONE IN THE TEAM?
AND SO...
BRILLIANT, CLEM! IT'S GOOD TO HAVE YOU BACK IN GOAL!
MEANWHILE, IN CLEMENCE'S HOUSE...
HUH! I'M THE SUBSTITUTE HOMEWORK DOER!
SLAVE! TOIL!
MATHS
VERY HARD SUMS
ALGEBRA
GEOMETRY

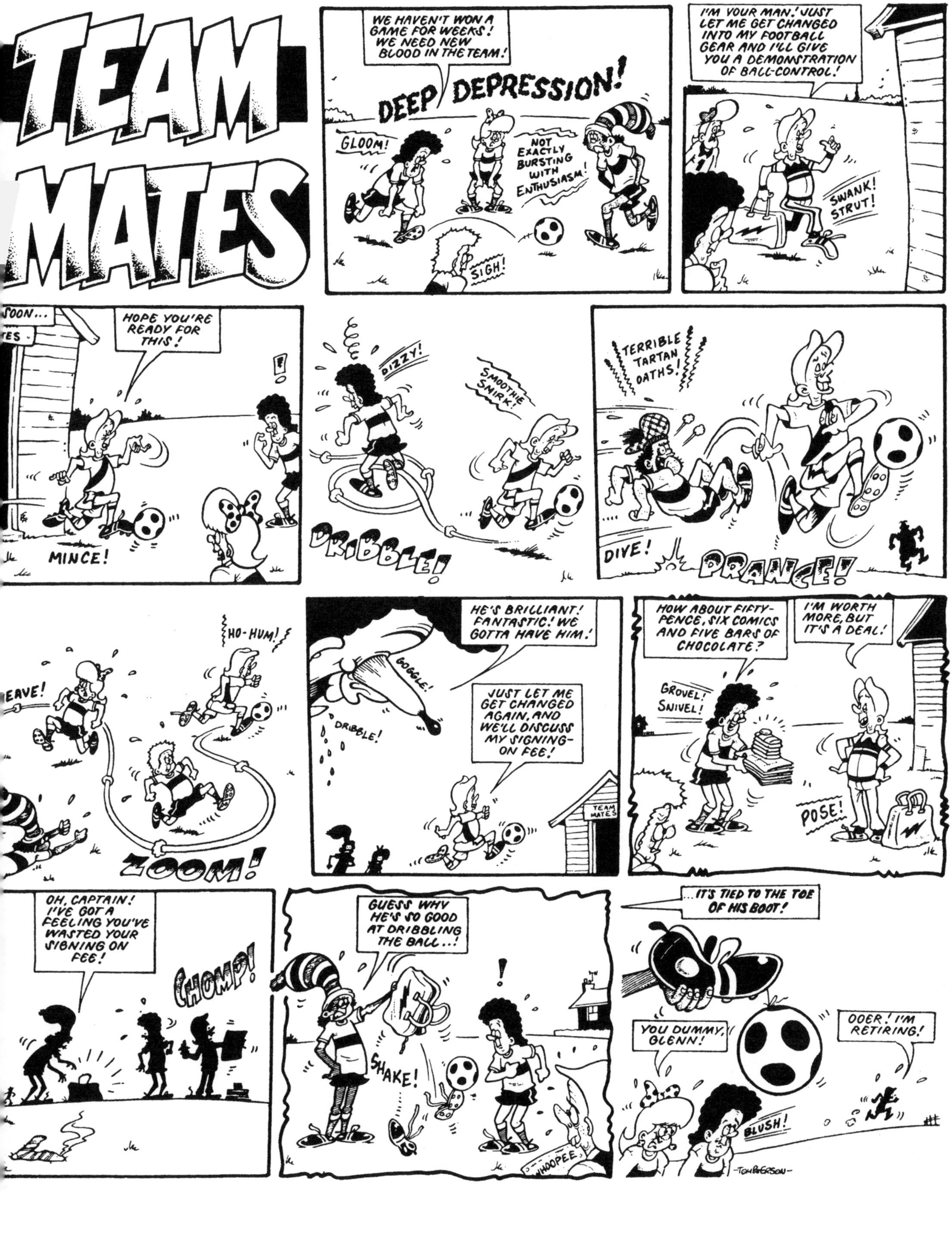
TEAM MATES
WE HAVEN'T WON A GAME FOR WEEKS! WE NEED NEW BLOOD IN THE TEAM!
DEEP DEPRESSION!
GLOOM!
NOT EXACTLY BURSTING WITH ENTHUSIASM!
SIGH!
I'M YOUR MAN! JUST LET ME GET CHANGED INTO MY FOOTBALL GEAR AND I'LL GIVE YOU A DEMONSTRATION OF BALL-CONTROL!
SWANK! STRUT!
SOON...
HOPE YOU'RE READY FOR THIS!
!
MINCE!
DIZZY!
SMOOTHIE SNIRK!
DRIBBLE!
TERRIBLE TARTAN OATHS!
DIVE!
PRANCE!
HO-HUM!
ZOOM!
HE'S BRILLIANT! FANTASTIC! WE GOTTA HAVE HIM!
GOGGLE!
DRIBBLE!
JUST LET ME GET CHANGED AGAIN, AND WE'LL DISCUSS MY SIGNING-ON FEE!
TEAM MATES
HOW ABOUT FIFTY-PENCE, SIX COMICS AND FIVE BARS OF CHOCOLATE?
I'M WORTH MORE, BUT IT'S A DEAL!
GROVEL! SNIVEL!
POSE!
OH, CAPTAIN! I'VE GOT A FEELING YOU'VE WASTED YOUR SIGNING ON FEE!
CHOMP!
GUESS WHY HE'S SO GOOD AT DRIBBLING THE BALL...!
!
SHAKE!
WHOOPEE
...IT'S TIED TO THE TOE OF HIS BOOT!
YOU DUMMY, GLENN!
OOER! I'M RETIRING!
BLUSH!
-TOM PATERSON-

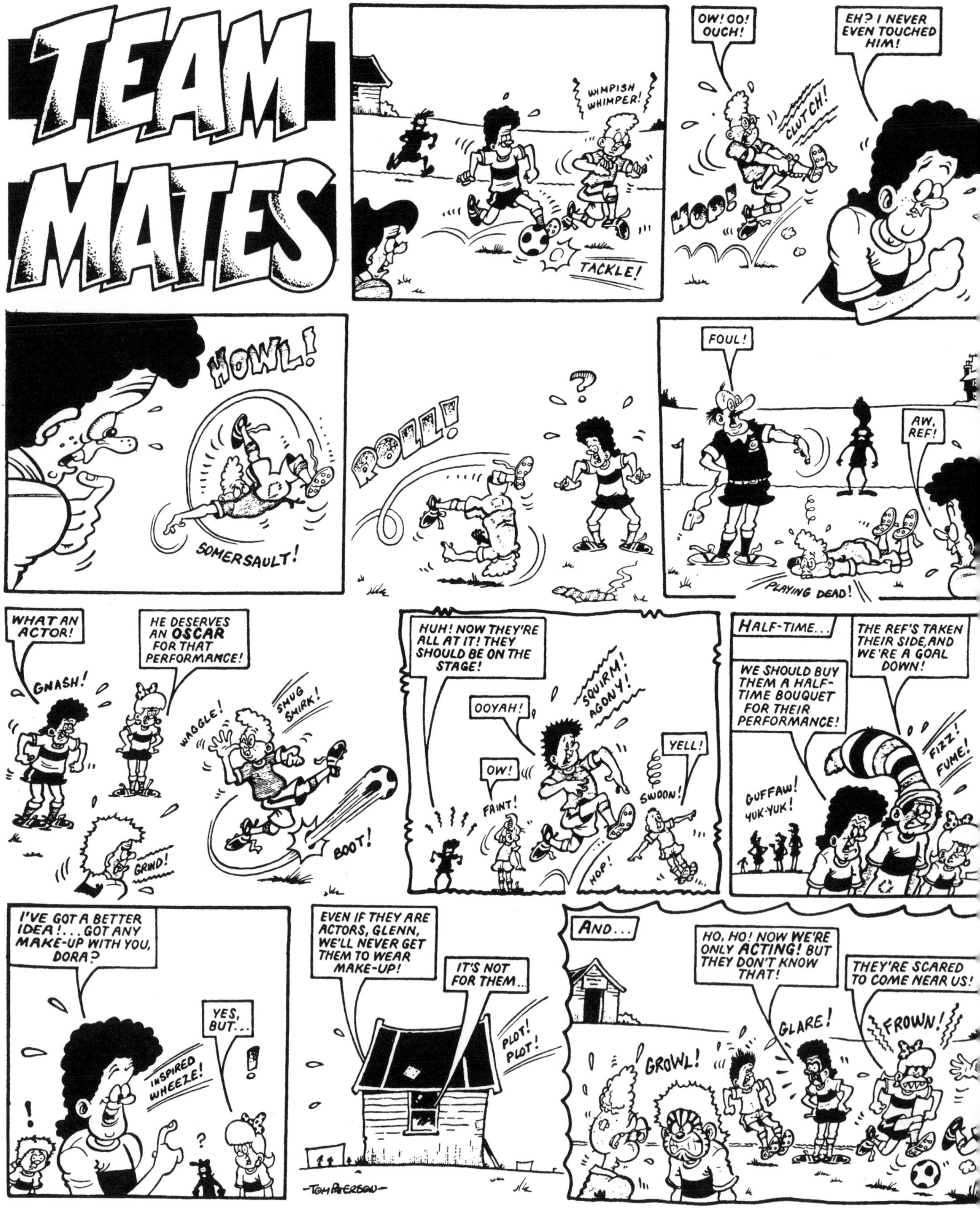
TEAM MATES
WIMPISH WHIMPER!
TACKLE!
OW! OO! OUCH!
CLUTCH!
HOP!
EH? I NEVER EVEN TOUCHED HIM!
HOWL!
SOMERSAULT!
ROLL!
?
FOUL!
AW, REF!
PLAYING DEAD!
WHAT AN ACTOR!
GNASH!
HE DESERVES AN OSCAR FOR THAT PERFORMANCE!
WAGGLE!
SMUG SMIRK!
BOOT!
GRIND!
HUH! NOW THEY'RE ALL AT IT! THEY SHOULD BE ON THE STAGE!
OOYAH!
SQUIRM! AGONY!
OW!
FAINT!
YELL!
SWOON!
HOP!
HALF-TIME...
THE REF'S TAKEN THEIR SIDE, AND WE'RE A GOAL DOWN!
WE SHOULD BUY THEM A HALF-TIME BOUQUET FOR THEIR PERFORMANCE!
GUFFAW! YUK-YUK!
FIZZ! FUME!
I'VE GOT A BETTER IDEA!... GOT ANY MAKE-UP WITH YOU, DORA?
YES, BUT...
INSPIRED WHEEZE!
!
?
EVEN IF THEY ARE ACTORS, GLENN, WE'LL NEVER GET THEM TO WEAR MAKE-UP!
IT'S NOT FOR THEM...
PLOT! PLOT!
TOM PATERSON
AND...
HO, HO! NOW WE'RE ONLY ACTING! BUT THEY DON'T KNOW THAT!
THEY'RE SCARED TO COME NEAR US!
GROWL!
GLARE!
FROWN!

DANGER!
EMERGENCY DESTRUCT MECHANISM

# EXTRAS

**SCRIPTS**

Scripts by Tom Paterson

COR!!

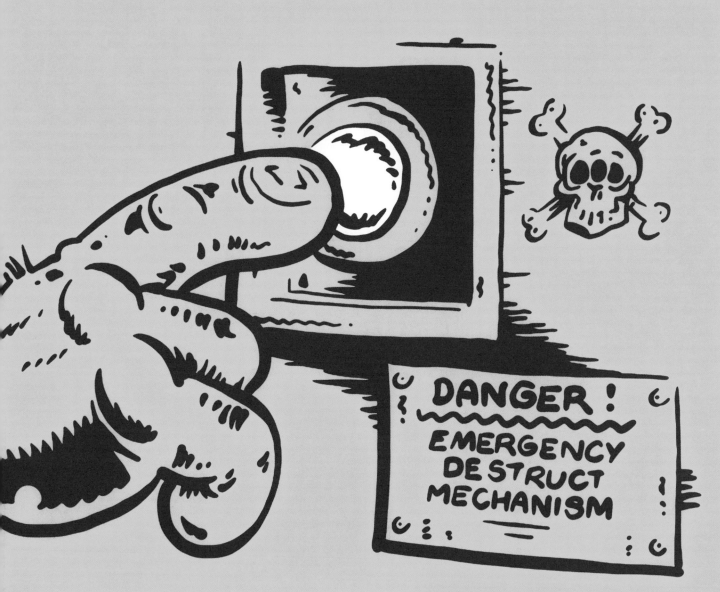

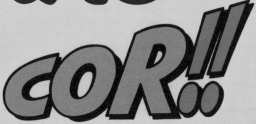

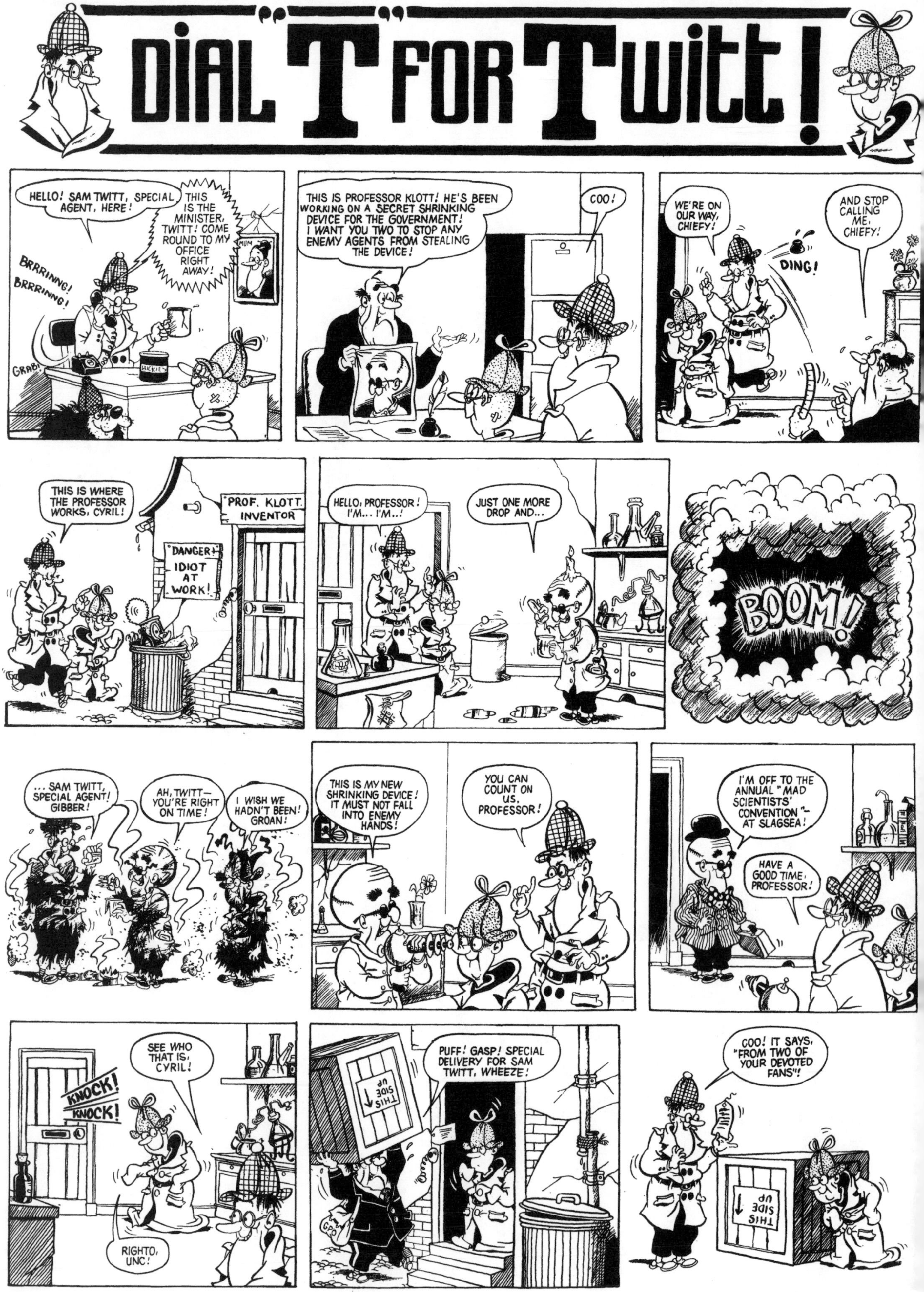
DIAL "T" FOR TWITT!
HELLO! SAM TWITT, SPECIAL AGENT, HERE!
THIS IS THE MINISTER, TWITT! COME ROUND TO MY OFFICE RIGHT AWAY!
BRRRINNNG! BRRRINNNG!
MUM
BICKIES
GRAB!
THIS IS PROFESSOR KLOTT! HE'S BEEN WORKING ON A SECRET SHRINKING DEVICE FOR THE GOVERNMENT! I WANT YOU TWO TO STOP ANY ENEMY AGENTS FROM STEALING THE DEVICE!
COO!
WE'RE ON OUR WAY, CHIEFY!
AND STOP CALLING ME, CHIEFY!
DING!
THIS IS WHERE THE PROFESSOR WORKS, CYRIL!
PROF. KLOTT. INVENTOR
"DANGER!" IDIOT AT WORK!
HELLO, PROFESSOR! I'M... I'M...!
JUST ONE MORE DROP AND...
BOOM!
... SAM TWITT, SPECIAL AGENT! GIBBER!
AH, TWITT— YOU'RE RIGHT ON TIME!
I WISH WE HADN'T BEEN! GROAN!
THIS IS MY NEW SHRINKING DEVICE! IT MUST NOT FALL INTO ENEMY HANDS!
YOU CAN COUNT ON US, PROFESSOR!
I'M OFF TO THE ANNUAL "MAD SCIENTISTS' CONVENTION"— AT SLAGSEA!
HAVE A GOOD TIME, PROFESSOR!
KNOCK! KNOCK!
SEE WHO THAT IS, CYRIL!
RIGHTO, UNC!
PUFF! GASP! SPECIAL DELIVERY FOR SAM TWITT, WHEEZE!
THIS SIDE UP
GPO
COO! IT SAYS, "FROM TWO OF YOUR DEVOTED FANS"!
THIS SIDE UP

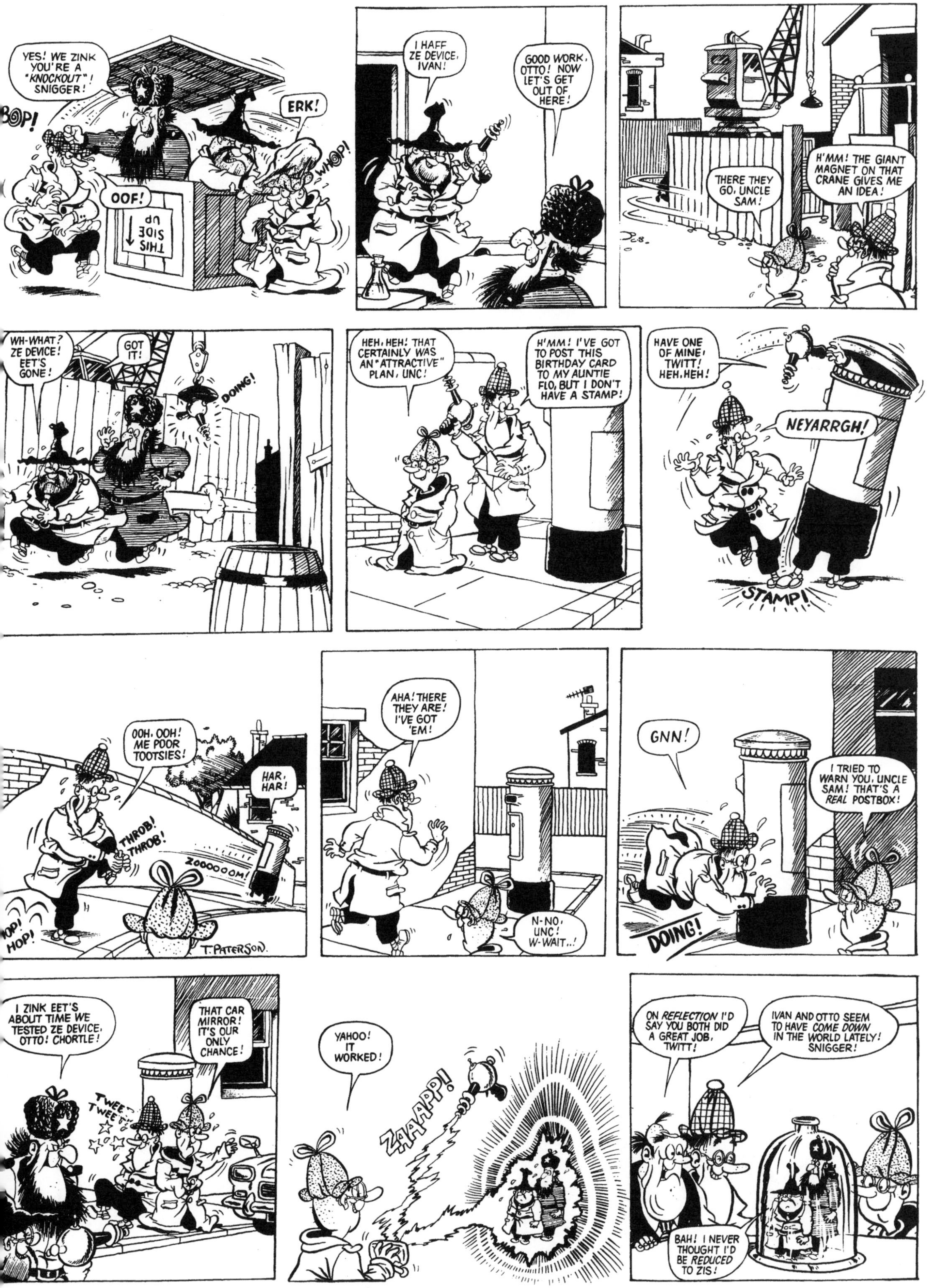

YES! WE ZINK YOU'RE A "KNOCKOUT"! SNIGGER!
BOP!
ERK!
WHOP!
OOF!
THIS SIDE UP
I HAFF ZE DEVICE, IVAN!
GOOD WORK, OTTO! NOW LET'S GET OUT OF HERE!
THERE THEY GO, UNCLE SAM!
H'MM! THE GIANT MAGNET ON THAT CRANE GIVES ME AN IDEA!
WH-WHAT? ZE DEVICE! EET'S GONE!
GOT IT!
DOING!
HEH, HEH! THAT CERTAINLY WAS AN "ATTRACTIVE" PLAN, UNC!
H'MM! I'VE GOT TO POST THIS BIRTHDAY CARD TO MY AUNTIE FLO, BUT I DON'T HAVE A STAMP!
HAVE ONE OF MINE, TWITT! HEH, HEH!
NEYARRGH!
STAMP!
OOH, OOH! ME POOR TOOTSIES!
HAR, HAR!
THROB! THROB!
ZOOOOOOM!
OP! HOP!
T. PATERSON.
AHA! THERE THEY ARE! I'VE GOT 'EM!
N-NO, UNC! W-WAIT...!
GNN!
I TRIED TO WARN YOU, UNCLE SAM! THAT'S A *REAL* POSTBOX!
DOING!
I ZINK EET'S ABOUT TIME WE TESTED ZE DEVICE, OTTO! CHORTLE!
THAT CAR MIRROR! IT'S OUR ONLY CHANCE!
TWEE TWEE
YAHOO! IT WORKED!
ZAAAPP!
ON *REFLECTION* I'D SAY YOU BOTH DID A GREAT JOB, TWITT!
IVAN AND OTTO SEEM TO HAVE *COME DOWN* IN THE WORLD LATELY! SNIGGER!
BAH! I NEVER THOUGHT I'D BE *REDUCED* TO ZIS!

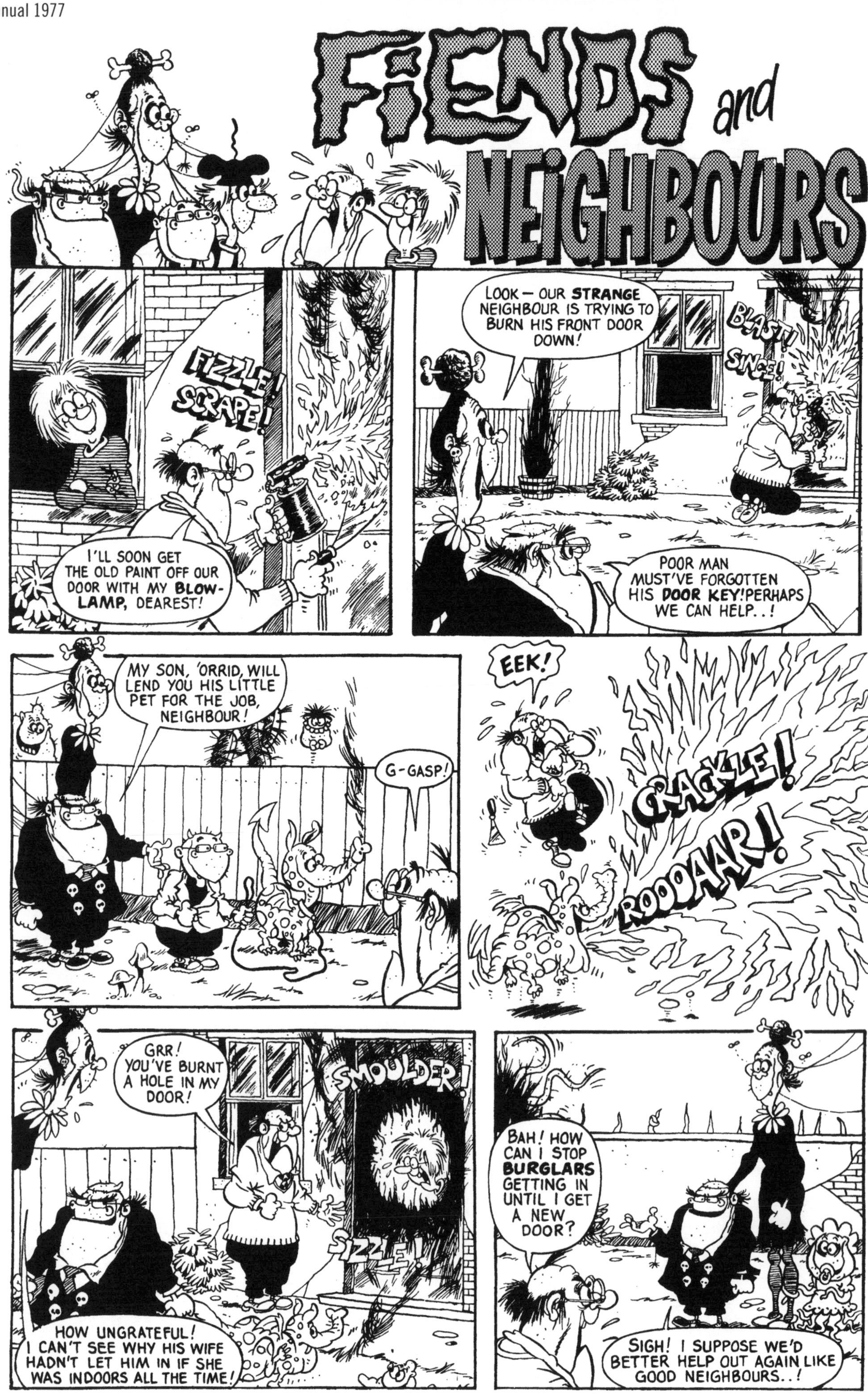
FIENDS and NEIGHBOURS
FIZZLE! SCRAPE!
I'LL SOON GET THE OLD PAINT OFF OUR DOOR WITH MY BLOW-LAMP, DEAREST!
LOOK – OUR STRANGE NEIGHBOUR IS TRYING TO BURN HIS FRONT DOOR DOWN!
BLAST! SINGE!
POOR MAN MUST'VE FORGOTTEN HIS DOOR KEY! PERHAPS WE CAN HELP..!
MY SON, 'ORRID, WILL LEND YOU HIS LITTLE PET FOR THE JOB, NEIGHBOUR!
G-GASP!
EEK!
CRACKLE!
ROOOAAR!
GRR! YOU'VE BURNT A HOLE IN MY DOOR!
SMOULDER!
SIZZLE!
HOW UNGRATEFUL! I CAN'T SEE WHY HIS WIFE HADN'T LET HIM IN IF SHE WAS INDOORS ALL THE TIME!
BAH! HOW CAN I STOP BURGLARS GETTING IN UNTIL I GET A NEW DOOR?
SIGH! I SUPPOSE WE'D BETTER HELP OUT AGAIN LIKE GOOD NEIGHBOURS..!

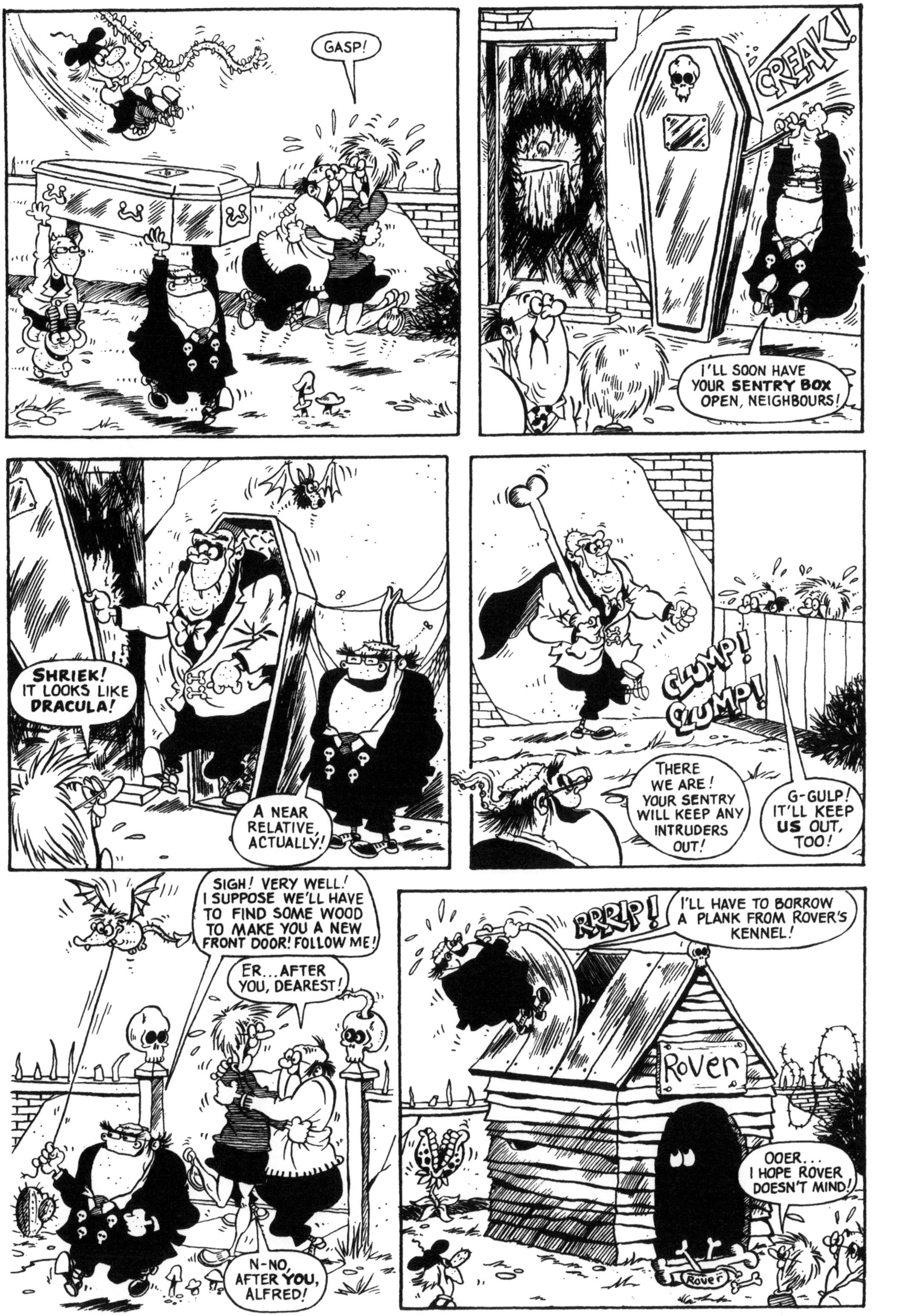
GASP!
CREAK!
I'LL SOON HAVE YOUR SENTRY BOX OPEN, NEIGHBOURS!
SHRIEK! IT LOOKS LIKE DRACULA!
A NEAR RELATIVE, ACTUALLY!
CLUMP! CLUMP!
THERE WE ARE! YOUR SENTRY WILL KEEP ANY INTRUDERS OUT!
G-GULP! IT'LL KEEP US OUT, TOO!
SIGH! VERY WELL! I SUPPOSE WE'LL HAVE TO FIND SOME WOOD TO MAKE YOU A NEW FRONT DOOR! FOLLOW ME!
ER... AFTER YOU, DEAREST!
N-NO, AFTER YOU, ALFRED!
RRRIP!
I'LL HAVE TO BORROW A PLANK FROM ROVER'S KENNEL!
Rover
OOER... I HOPE ROVER DOESN'T MIND!
Rover

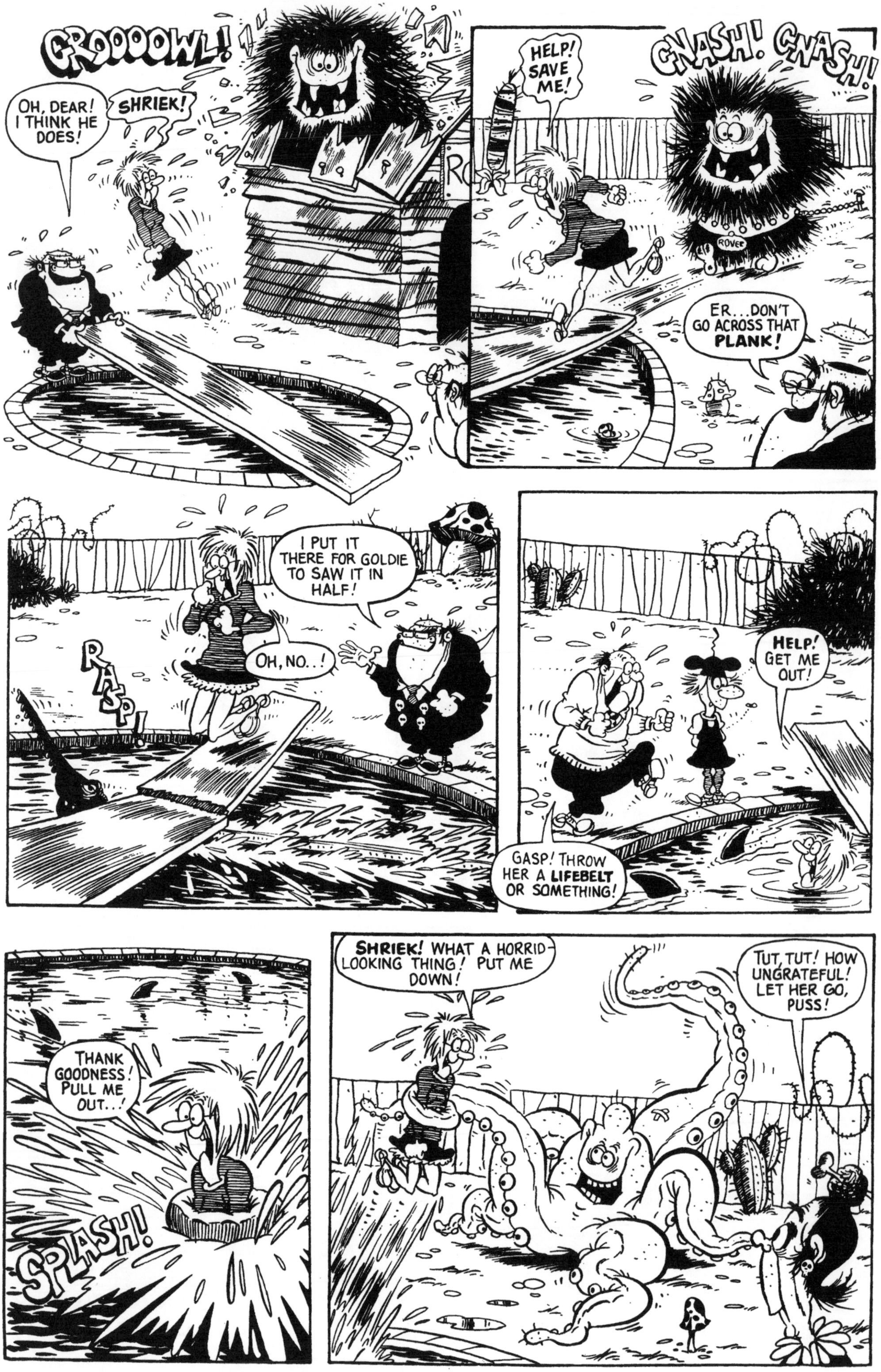
GROOOOWL!
OH, DEAR! I THINK HE DOES!
SHRIEK!
HELP! SAVE ME!
GNASH! GNASH!
ROVER
ER...DON'T GO ACROSS THAT PLANK!
I PUT IT THERE FOR GOLDIE TO SAW IT IN HALF!
OH, NO..!
RASP!
HELP! GET ME OUT!
GASP! THROW HER A LIFEBELT OR SOMETHING!
THANK GOODNESS! PULL ME OUT...!
SPLASH!
SHRIEK! WHAT A HORRID-LOOKING THING! PUT ME DOWN!
TUT, TUT! HOW UNGRATEFUL! LET HER GO, PUSS!

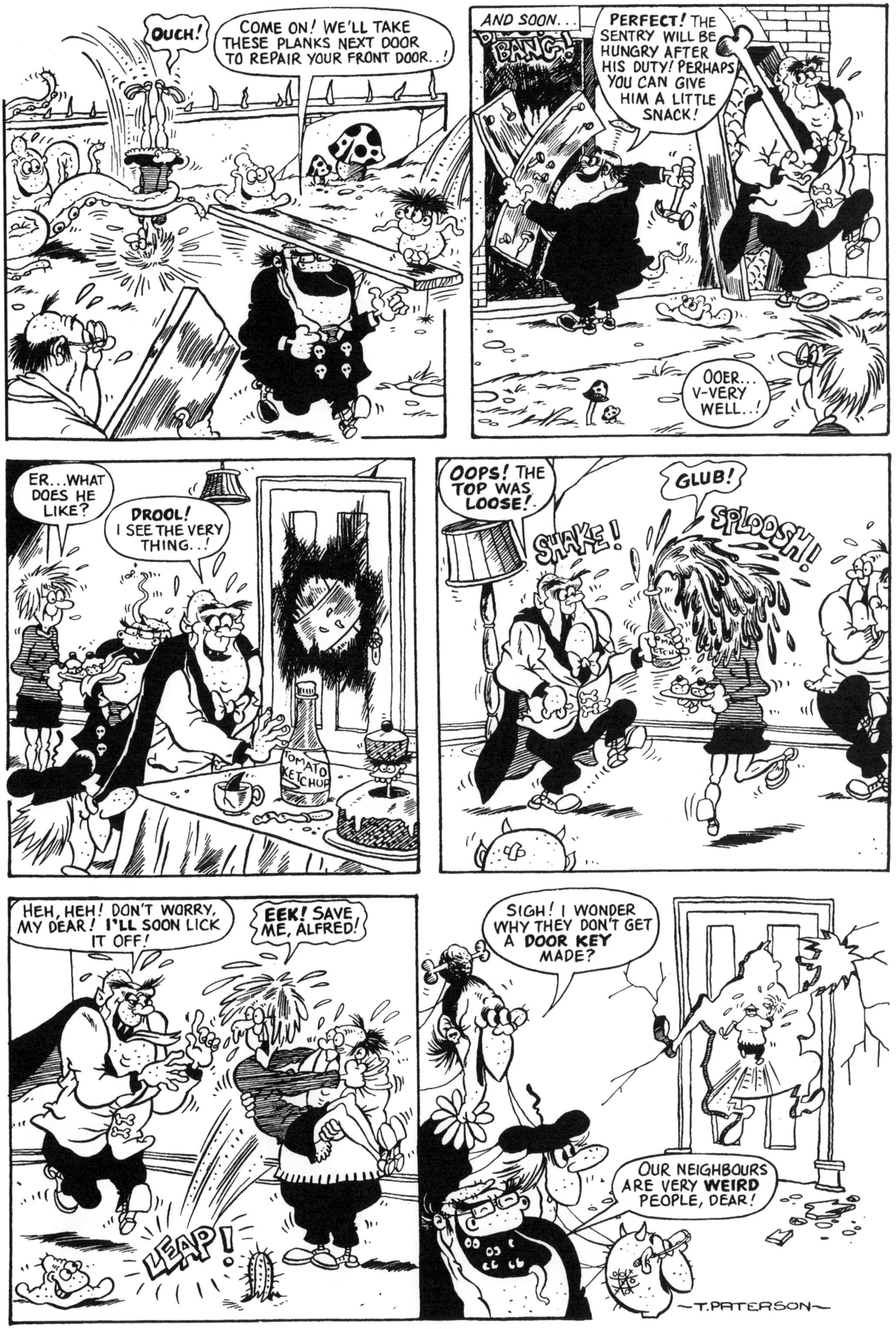
OUCH!
COME ON! WE'LL TAKE THESE PLANKS NEXT DOOR TO REPAIR YOUR FRONT DOOR..!
AND SOON...
BANG!
PERFECT! THE SENTRY WILL BE HUNGRY AFTER HIS DUTY! PERHAPS YOU CAN GIVE HIM A LITTLE SNACK!
OOER... V-VERY WELL..!
ER...WHAT DOES HE LIKE?
DROOL! I SEE THE VERY THING..!
TOMATO KETCHUP
OOPS! THE TOP WAS LOOSE!
SHAKE!
GLUB!
SPLOOSH!
HEH, HEH! DON'T WORRY, MY DEAR! I'LL SOON LICK IT OFF!
EEK! SAVE ME, ALFRED!
LEAP!
SIGH! I WONDER WHY THEY DON'T GET A DOOR KEY MADE?
OUR NEIGHBOURS ARE VERY WEIRD PEOPLE, DEAR!
T.PATERSON

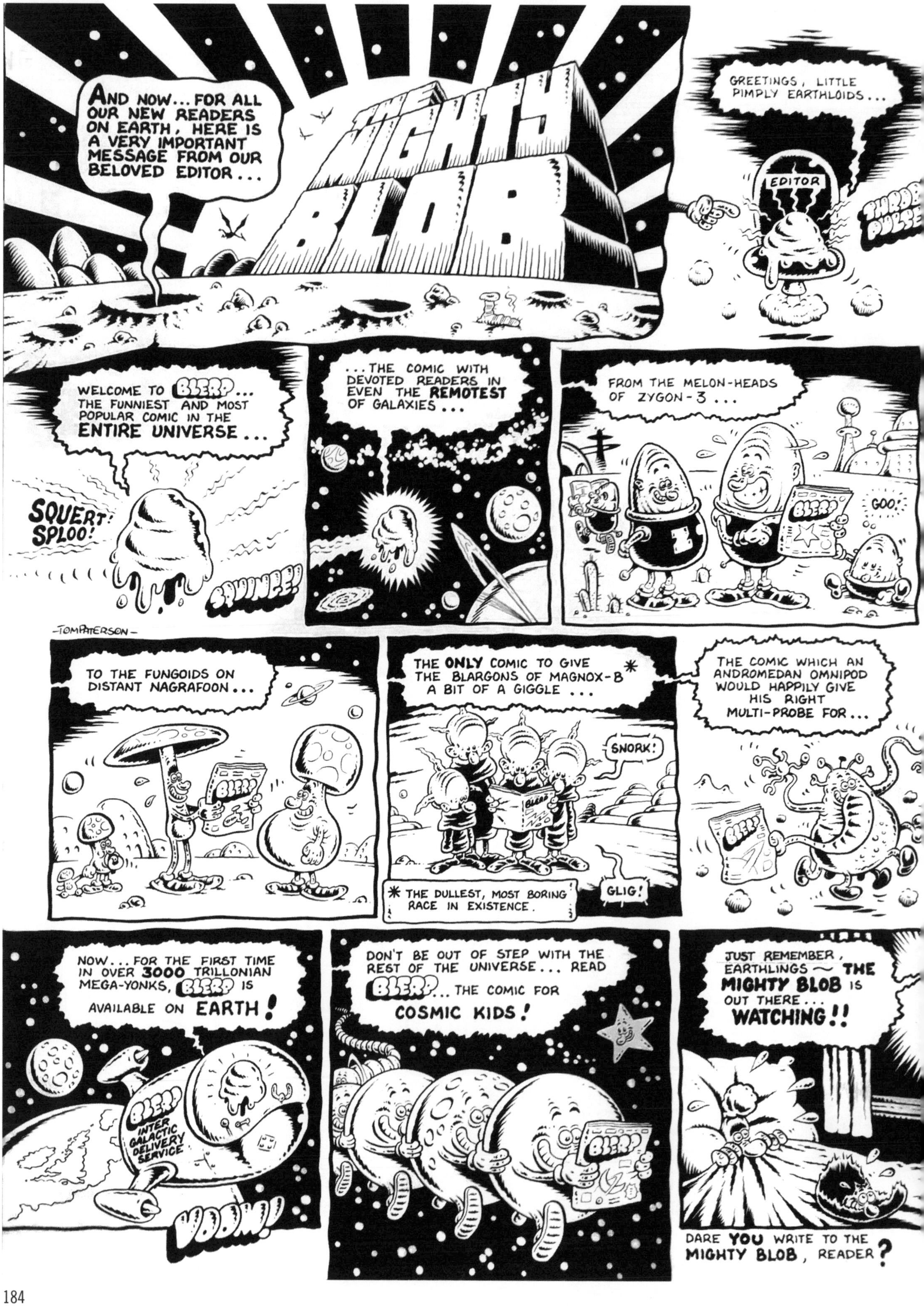
AND NOW... FOR ALL OUR NEW READERS ON EARTH, HERE IS A VERY IMPORTANT MESSAGE FROM OUR BELOVED EDITOR...
THE MIGHTY BLOB
GREETINGS, LITTLE PIMPLY EARTHLOIDS...
EDITOR
THROB PULSE
WELCOME TO BLERP... THE FUNNIEST AND MOST POPULAR COMIC IN THE ENTIRE UNIVERSE...
SQUERT! SPLOO!
SQUINCE!
-TOMPATERSON-
...THE COMIC WITH DEVOTED READERS IN EVEN THE REMOTEST OF GALAXIES...
FROM THE MELON-HEADS OF ZYGON-3...
BLERP
GOO!
TO THE FUNGOIDS ON DISTANT NAGRAFOON...
BLERP
THE ONLY COMIC TO GIVE THE BLARGONS OF MAGNOX-B * A BIT OF A GIGGLE...
SNORK!
* THE DULLEST, MOST BORING RACE IN EXISTENCE.
GLIG!
THE COMIC WHICH AN ANDROMEDAN OMNIPOD WOULD HAPPILY GIVE HIS RIGHT MULTI-PROBE FOR...
BLERP
NOW... FOR THE FIRST TIME IN OVER 3000 TRILLONIAN MEGA-YONKS, BLERP IS AVAILABLE ON EARTH!
BLERP INTER GALACTIC DELIVERY SERVICE
VOOM!
DON'T BE OUT OF STEP WITH THE REST OF THE UNIVERSE... READ BLERP... THE COMIC FOR COSMIC KIDS!
BLERP
JUST REMEMBER, EARTHLINGS ~ THE MIGHTY BLOB IS OUT THERE... WATCHING!!
DARE YOU WRITE TO THE MIGHTY BLOB, READER?

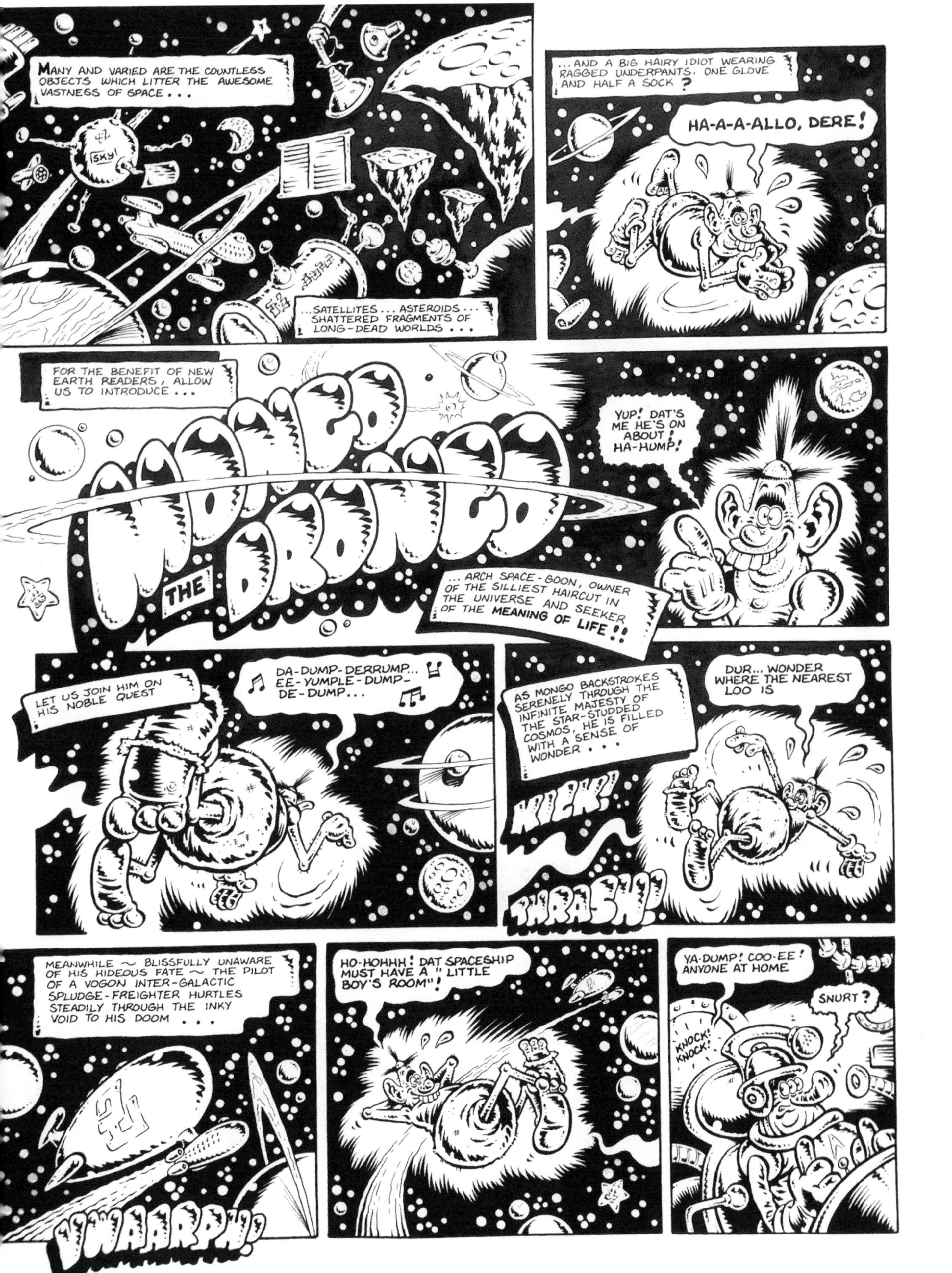
MANY AND VARIED ARE THE COUNTLESS OBJECTS WHICH LITTER THE AWESOME VASTNESS OF SPACE . . .
SKY!
. . . SATELLITES . . . ASTEROIDS . . . SHATTERED FRAGMENTS OF LONG-DEAD WORLDS . . .
. . . AND A BIG HAIRY IDIOT WEARING RAGGED UNDERPANTS, ONE GLOVE AND HALF A SOCK ?
HA-A-A-ALLO, DERE!
FOR THE BENEFIT OF NEW EARTH READERS, ALLOW US TO INTRODUCE . . .
MONGO THE DRONGO
YUP! DAT'S ME HE'S ON ABOUT! HA-HUMP!
. . . ARCH SPACE-GOON, OWNER OF THE SILLIEST HAIRCUT IN THE UNIVERSE AND SEEKER OF THE MEANING OF LIFE!!
LET US JOIN HIM ON HIS NOBLE QUEST
DA-DUMP-DERRUMP... EE-YUMPLE-DUMP-DE-DUMP . . .
AS MONGO BACKSTROKES SERENELY THROUGH THE INFINITE MAJESTY OF THE STAR-STUDDED COSMOS, HE IS FILLED WITH A SENSE OF WONDER . . .
DUR... WONDER WHERE THE NEAREST LOO IS
KICK!
THRASH!!
MEANWHILE ~ BLISSFULLY UNAWARE OF HIS HIDEOUS FATE ~ THE PILOT OF A VOGON INTER-GALACTIC SPLUDGE-FREIGHTER HURTLES STEADILY THROUGH THE INKY VOID TO HIS DOOM . . .
VWAARPH!!
HO-HOHHH! DAT SPACESHIP MUST HAVE A "LITTLE BOY'S ROOM"!
YA-DUMP! COO-EE! ANYONE AT HOME
KNOCK! KNOCK!
SNURT ?

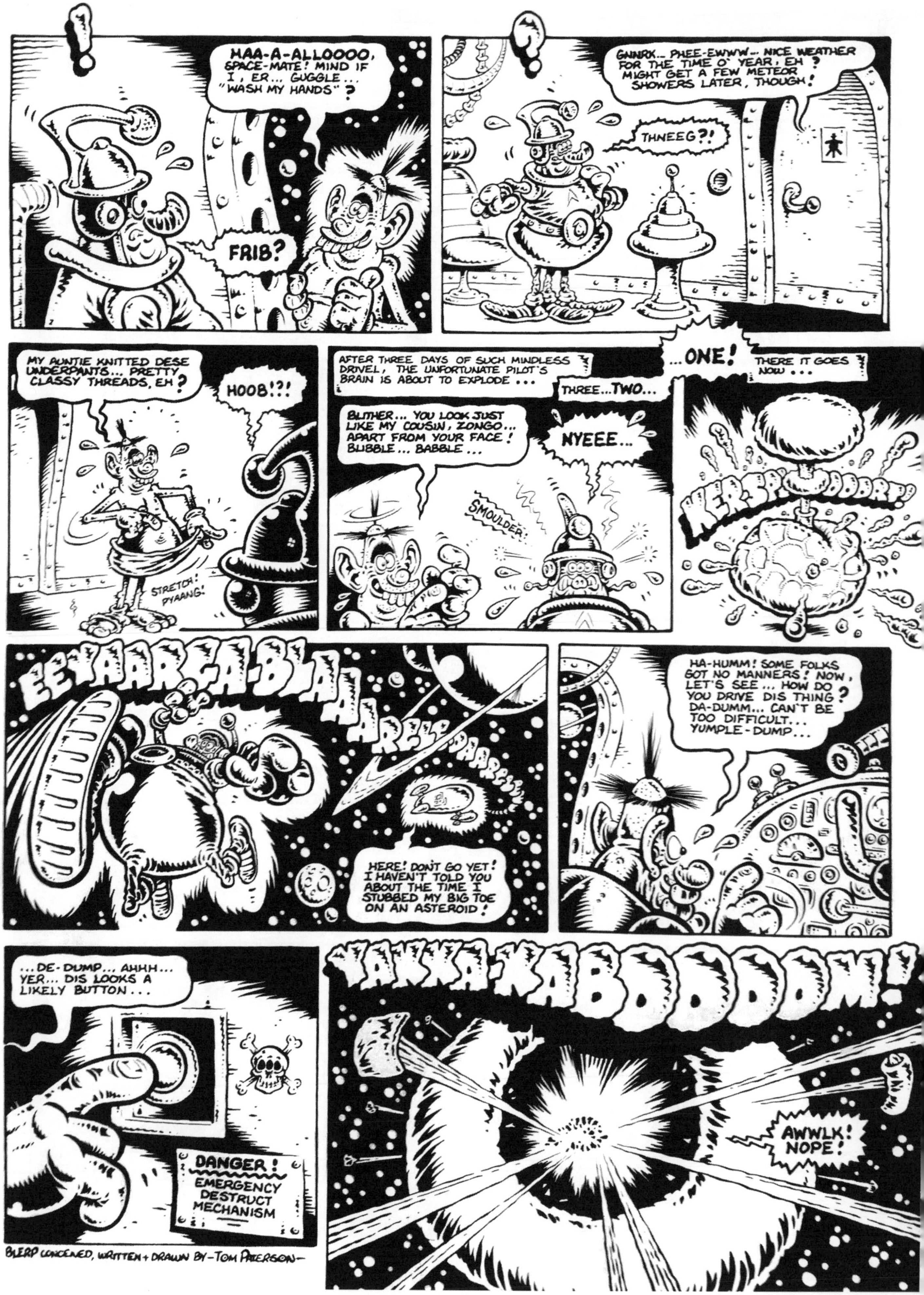
HAA-A-ALLOOOO, SPACE-MATE! MIND IF I, ER... GUGGLE... "WASH MY HANDS"?
FRIB?
GNNRK... PHEE-EWWW... NICE WEATHER FOR THE TIME O' YEAR, EH? MIGHT GET A FEW METEOR SHOWERS LATER, THOUGH!
THNEEG?!
MY AUNTIE KNITTED DESE UNDERPANTS... PRETTY CLASSY THREADS, EH?
HOOB!?!
STRETCH! PYAANG!
AFTER THREE DAYS OF SUCH MINDLESS DRIVEL, THE UNFORTUNATE PILOT'S BRAIN IS ABOUT TO EXPLODE...
BLITHER... YOU LOOK JUST LIKE MY COUSIN, ZONGO... APART FROM YOUR FACE! BUBBLE... BABBLE...
THREE...TWO...
NYEEE...
SMOULDER
...ONE!
THERE IT GOES NOW...
HERE! DON'T GO YET! I HAVEN'T TOLD YOU ABOUT THE TIME I STUBBED MY BIG TOE ON AN ASTEROID!
HA-HUMM! SOME FOLKS GOT NO MANNERS! NOW, LET'S SEE... HOW DO YOU DRIVE DIS THING? DA-DUMM... CAN'T BE TOO DIFFICULT... YUMPLE-DUMP...
...DE-DUMP... AHHH... YER... DIS LOOKS A LIKELY BUTTON...
DANGER! EMERGENCY DESTRUCT MECHANISM
YAKKA-KABOOOOOM!
AWWLK! NOPE!
BLERP CONCEIVED, WRITTEN + DRAWN BY -TOM PATERSON-

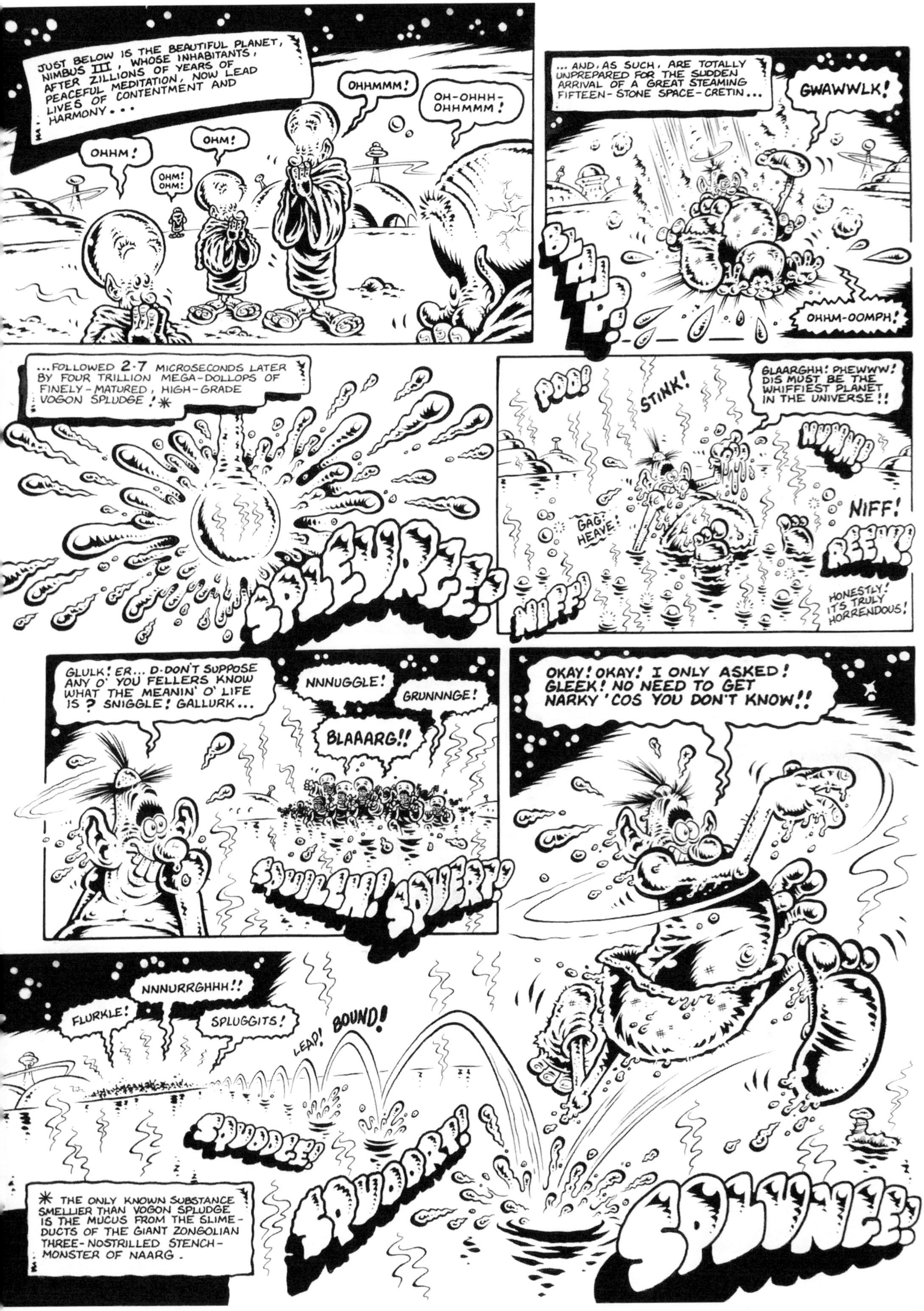
JUST BELOW IS THE BEAUTIFUL PLANET, NIMBUS III, WHOSE INHABITANTS, AFTER ZILLIONS OF YEARS OF PEACEFUL MEDITATION, NOW LEAD LIVES OF CONTENTMENT AND HARMONY...
OHHMMM!
OH-OHHH-OHHMMM!
OHHM!
OHM!
OHM! OHM!
... AND, AS SUCH, ARE TOTALLY UNPREPARED FOR THE SUDDEN ARRIVAL OF A GREAT STEAMING FIFTEEN-STONE SPACE-CRETIN...
GWAWWLK!
OHHM-OOMPH!
...FOLLOWED 2·7 MICROSECONDS LATER BY FOUR TRILLION MEGA-DOLLOPS OF FINELY-MATURED, HIGH-GRADE VOGON SPLUDGE! *
SPLEURGE!
POO!
STINK!
GLAARGHH! PHEWWW! DIS MUST BE THE WHIFFIEST PLANET IN THE UNIVERSE!!
GAG! HEAVE!
NIFF!
REEK!
NIFF!
HONESTLY! IT'S TRULY HORRENDOUS!
GLULK! ER... D-DON'T SUPPOSE ANY O' YOU FELLERS KNOW WHAT THE MEANIN' O' LIFE IS? SNIGGLE! GALLURK...
NNNUGGLE!
GRUNNNGE!
BLAAARG!!
SPLUERT!
OKAY! OKAY! I ONLY ASKED! GLEEK! NO NEED TO GET NARKY 'COS YOU DON'T KNOW!!
NNNURRGHHH!!
FLURKLE!
SPLUGGITS!
LEAP!
BOUND!
SPLUNGE!
* THE ONLY KNOWN SUBSTANCE SMELLIER THAN VOGON SPLUDGE IS THE MUCUS FROM THE SLIME-DUCTS OF THE GIANT ZONGOLIAN THREE-NOSTRILLED STENCH-MONSTER OF NAARG.

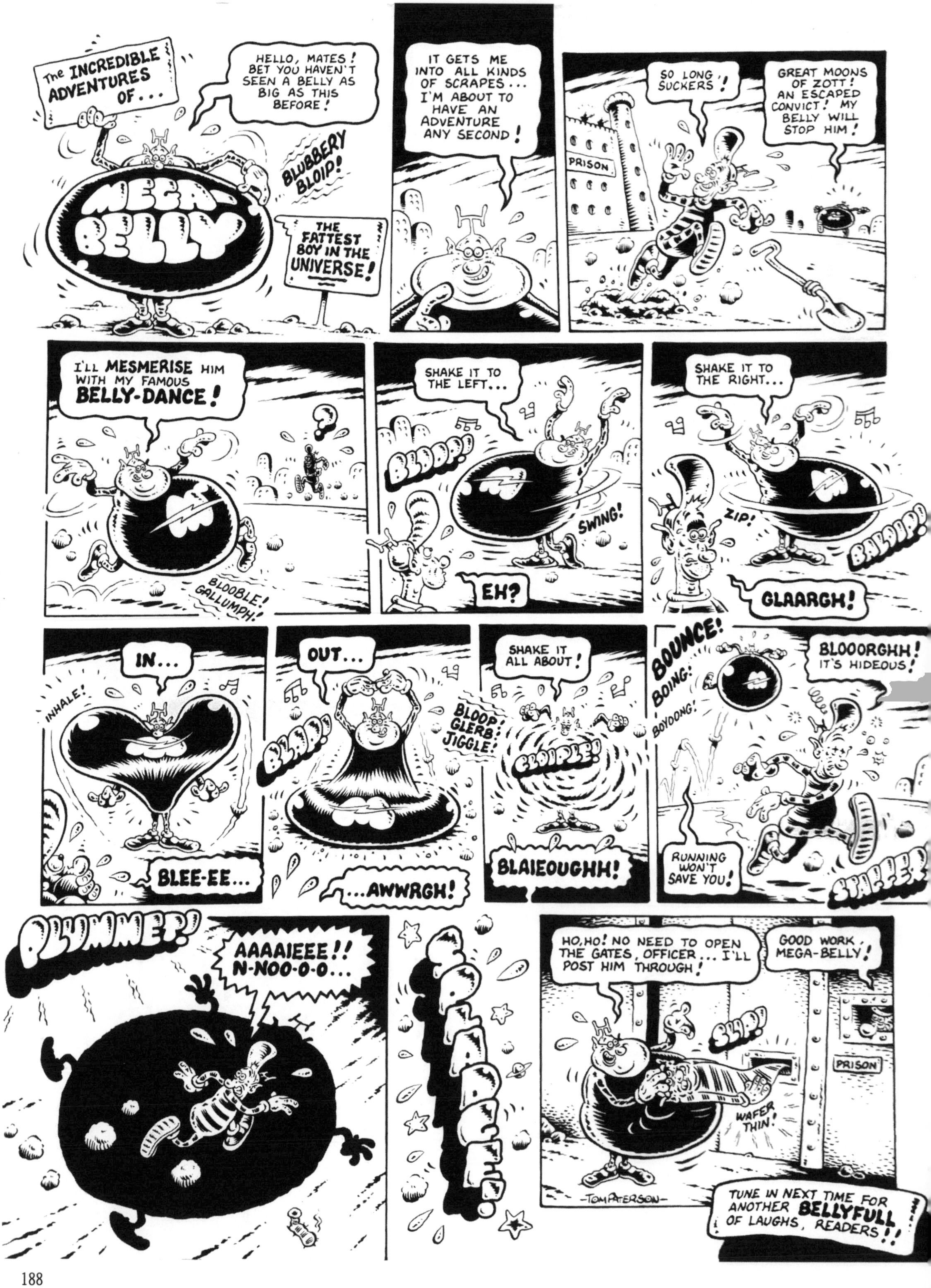
The INCREDIBLE ADVENTURES OF...
HELLO, MATES! BET YOU HAVEN'T SEEN A BELLY AS BIG AS THIS BEFORE!
MEGA-BELLY
BLUBBERY BLOIP!
THE FATTEST BOY IN THE UNIVERSE!
IT GETS ME INTO ALL KINDS OF SCRAPES... I'M ABOUT TO HAVE AN ADVENTURE ANY SECOND!
SO LONG SUCKERS!
GREAT MOONS OF ZOTT! AN ESCAPED CONVICT! MY BELLY WILL STOP HIM!
PRISON
I'LL MESMERISE HIM WITH MY FAMOUS BELLY-DANCE!
BLOOBLE! GALLUMPH!
SHAKE IT TO THE LEFT...
SWING!
EH?
SHAKE IT TO THE RIGHT...
ZIP!
GLAARGH!
IN...
INHALE!
BLEE-EE...
OUT...
...AWWRGH!
SHAKE IT ALL ABOUT!
BLOOP! GLERB! JIGGLE!
BLAIEOUGHH!
BOUNCE!
BOING!
BOYOONG!
BLOOORGHH! IT'S HIDEOUS!
RUNNING WON'T SAVE YOU!
PLUMMET!
AAAAIEEE!! N-NOO-O-O...
HO, HO! NO NEED TO OPEN THE GATES, OFFICER... I'LL POST HIM THROUGH!
GOOD WORK, MEGA-BELLY!
PRISON
WAFER THIN!
-TOM PATERSON-
TUNE IN NEXT TIME FOR ANOTHER BELLYFULL OF LAUGHS, READERS!!

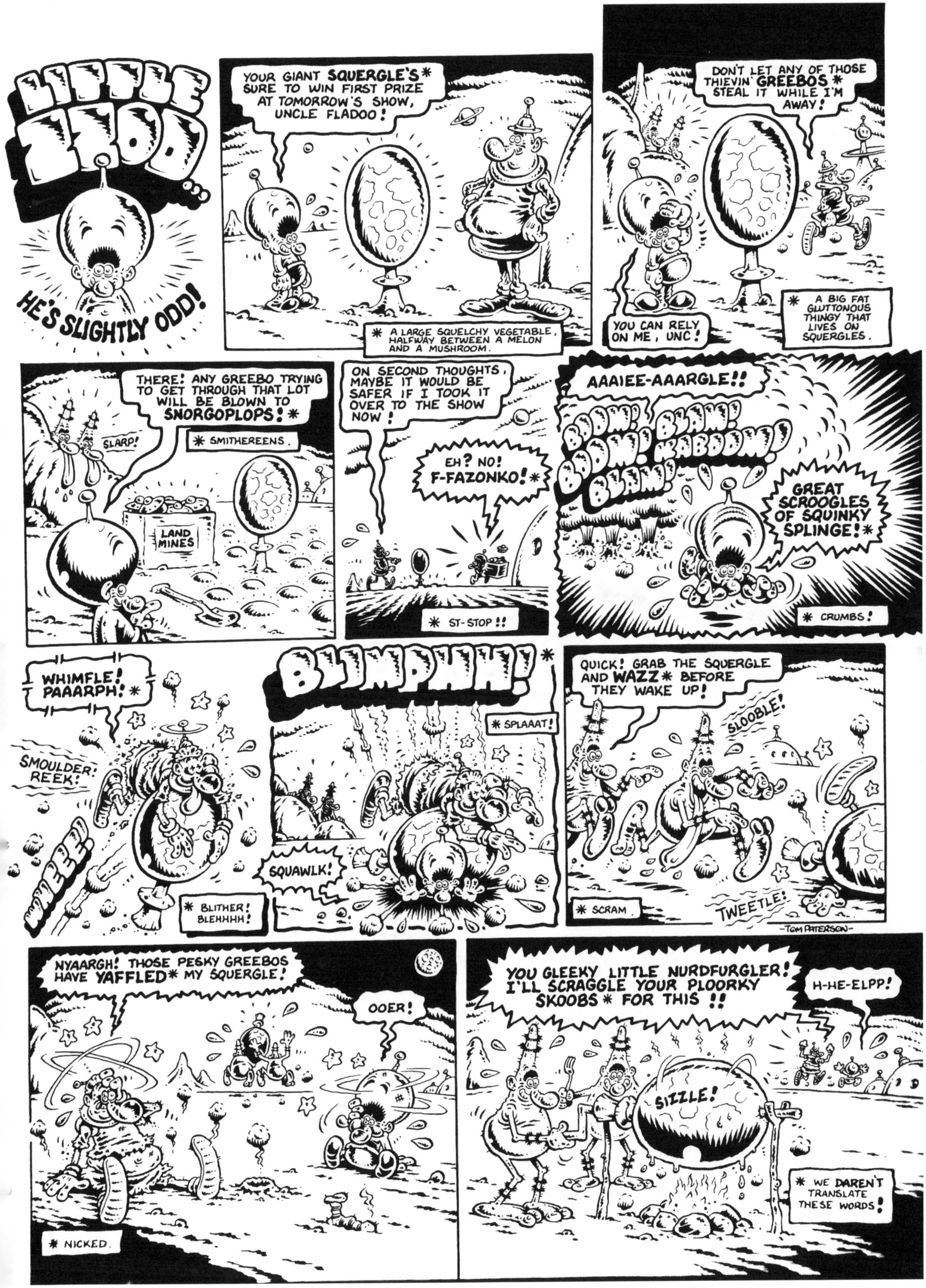
LITTLE ZZOD...
HE'S SLIGHTLY ODD!
YOUR GIANT SQUERGLE'S* SURE TO WIN FIRST PRIZE AT TOMORROW'S SHOW, UNCLE FLADOO!
* A LARGE SQUELCHY VEGETABLE, HALFWAY BETWEEN A MELON AND A MUSHROOM.
DON'T LET ANY OF THOSE THIEVIN' GREEBOS* STEAL IT WHILE I'M AWAY!
YOU CAN RELY ON ME, UNC!
* A BIG FAT GLUTTONOUS THINGY THAT LIVES ON SQUERGLES.
THERE! ANY GREEBO TRYING TO GET THROUGH THAT LOT WILL BE BLOWN TO SNORGOPLOPS!*
SLARP!
* SMITHEREENS.
LAND MINES
ON SECOND THOUGHTS, MAYBE IT WOULD BE SAFER IF I TOOK IT OVER TO THE SHOW NOW!
EH? NO! F-FAZONKO!*
* ST-STOP!!
AAAIEE-AAAARGLE!!
BOOM! BOOM! BLAM! BLAM! KABOOM!
GREAT SCROOGLES OF SQUINKY SPLINGE!*
* CRUMBS!
WHIMFLE! PAAARPH!*
SMOULDER! REEK!
WHEEE!
* BLITHER! BLEHHHH!
BLUMPHH!*
* SPLAAAT!
SQUAWLK!
QUICK! GRAB THE SQUERGLE AND WAZZ* BEFORE THEY WAKE UP!
SLOOBLE!
* SCRAM.
TWEETLE!
-TOM PATERSON-
NYAARGH! THOSE PESKY GREEBOS HAVE YAFFLED* MY SQUERGLE!
OOER!
* NICKED.
YOU GLEEKY LITTLE NURDFURGLER! I'LL SCRAGGLE YOUR PLOORKY SKOOBS* FOR THIS!!
H-HE-ELPP!
SIZZLE!
* WE DAREN'T TRANSLATE THESE WORDS!

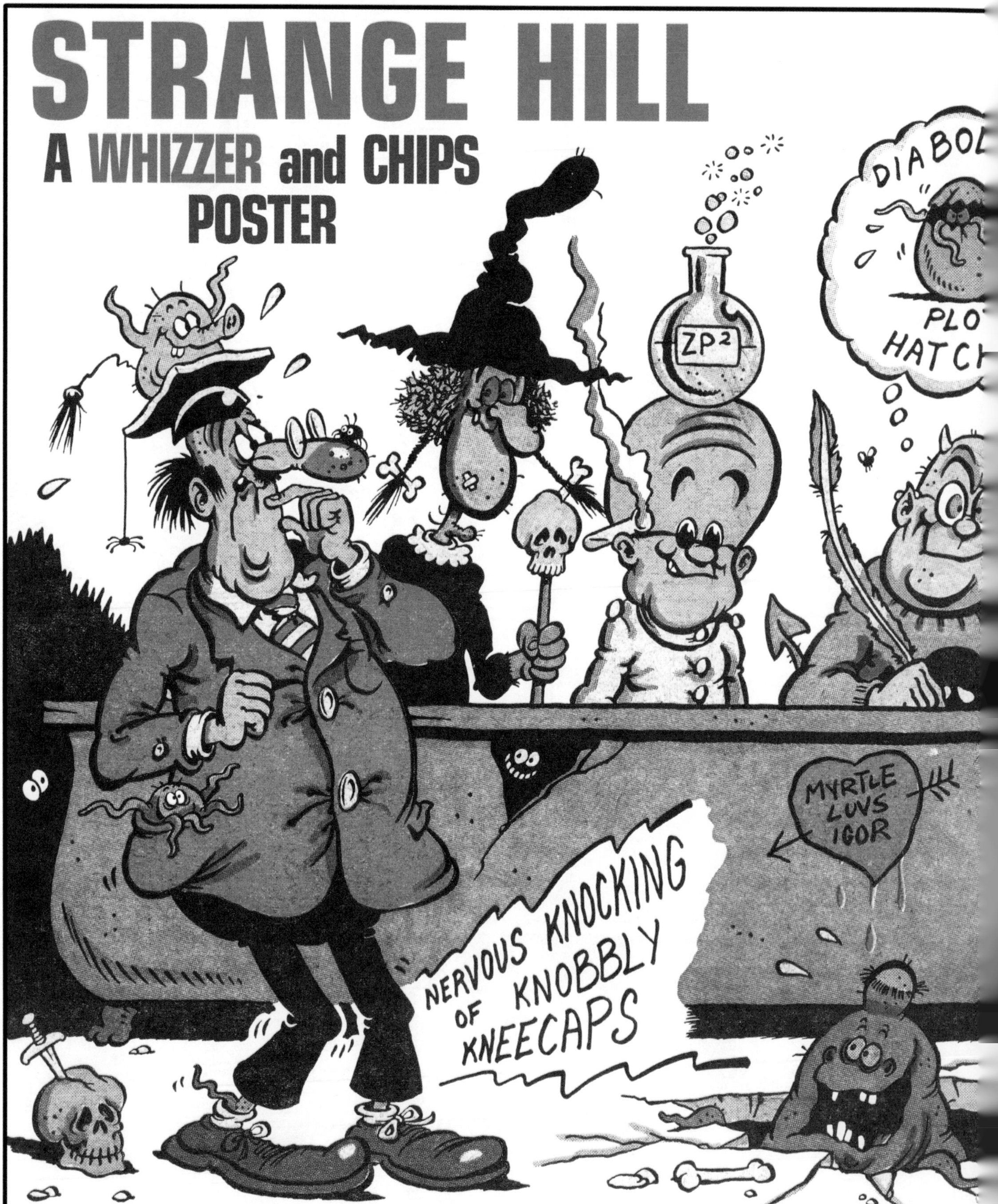
STRANGE HILL
A WHIZZER and CHIPS POSTER
ZP²
MYRTLE LUVS IGOR
NERVOUS KNOCKING OF KNOBBLY KNEECAPS

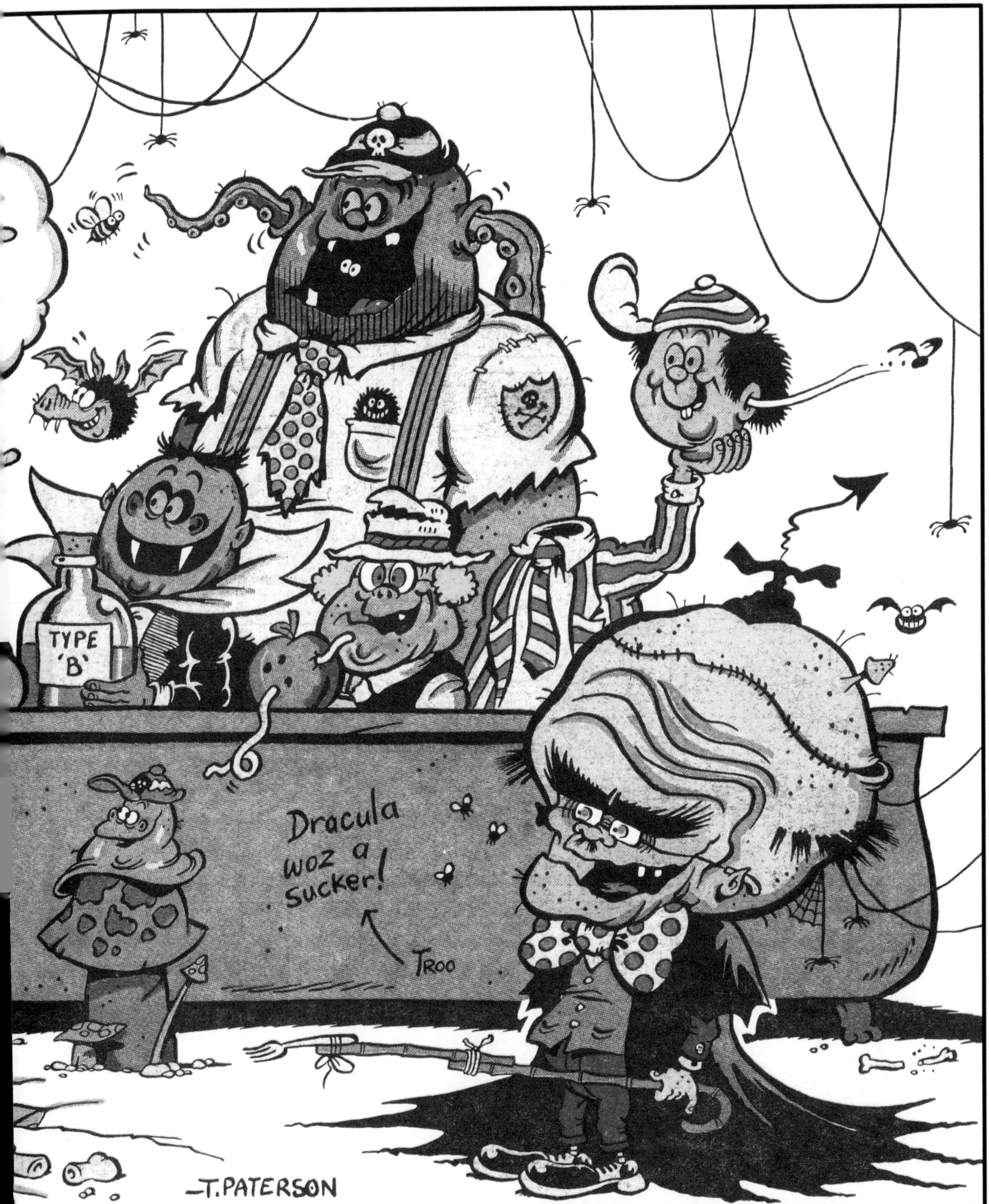
TYPE 'B'
Dracula woz a sucker!
TROO
T.PATERSON

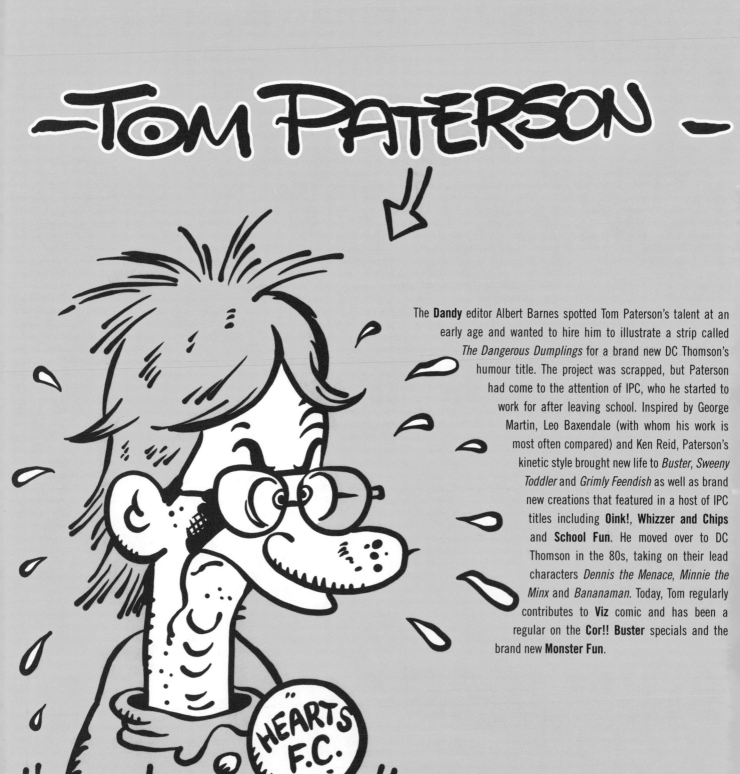

# TOM PATERSON

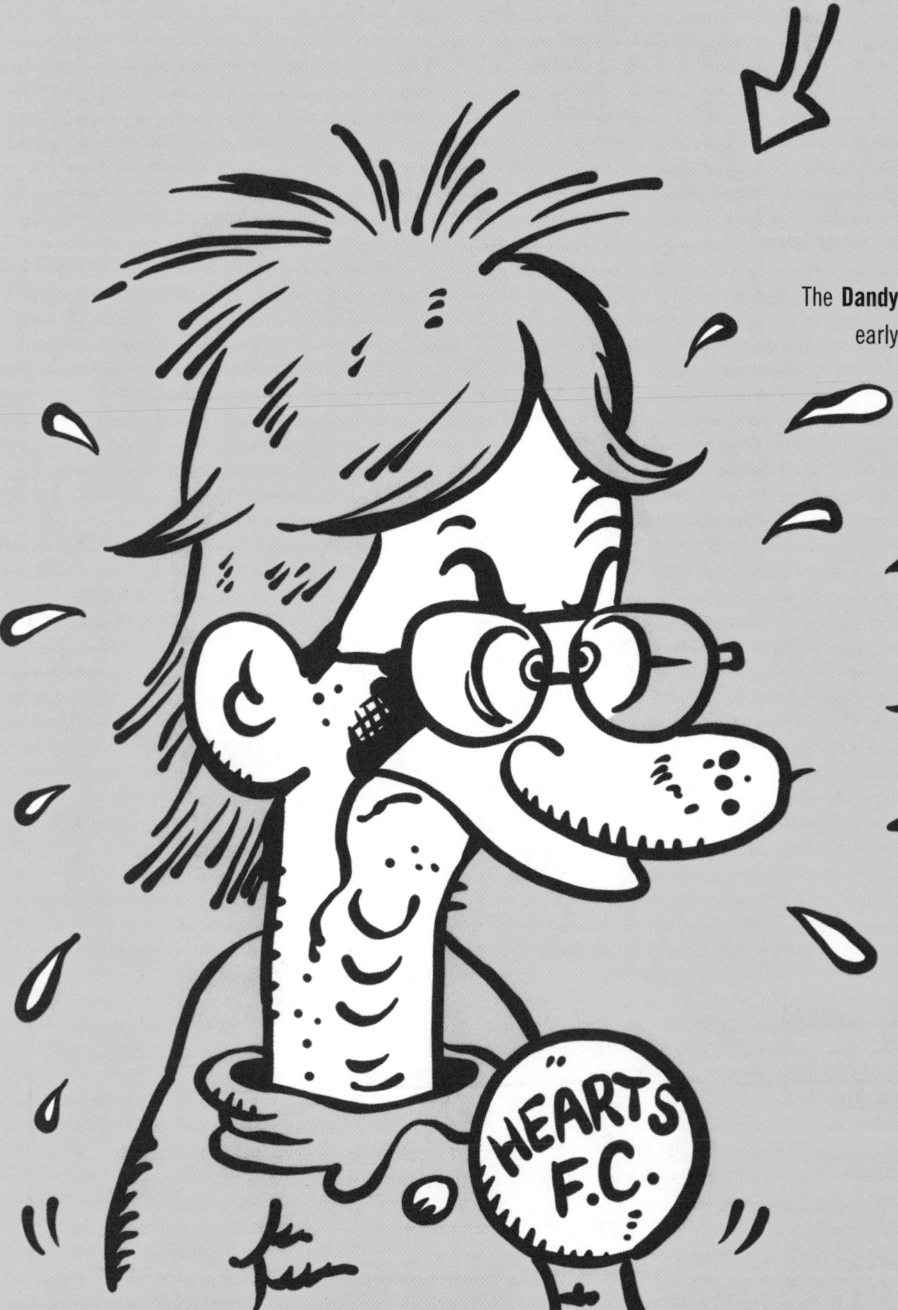
HEARTS F.C.

The **Dandy** editor Albert Barnes spotted Tom Paterson's talent at an early age and wanted to hire him to illustrate a strip called *The Dangerous Dumplings* for a brand new DC Thomson's humour title. The project was scrapped, but Paterson had come to the attention of IPC, who he started to work for after leaving school. Inspired by George Martin, Leo Baxendale (with whom his work is most often compared) and Ken Reid, Paterson's kinetic style brought new life to *Buster*, *Sweeny Toddler* and *Grimly Feendish* as well as brand new creations that featured in a host of IPC titles including **Oink!**, **Whizzer and Chips** and **School Fun**. He moved over to DC Thomson in the 80s, taking on their lead characters *Dennis the Menace*, *Minnie the Minx* and *Bananaman*. Today, Tom regularly contributes to **Viz** comic and has been a regular on the **Cor!! Buster** specials and the brand new **Monster Fun**.

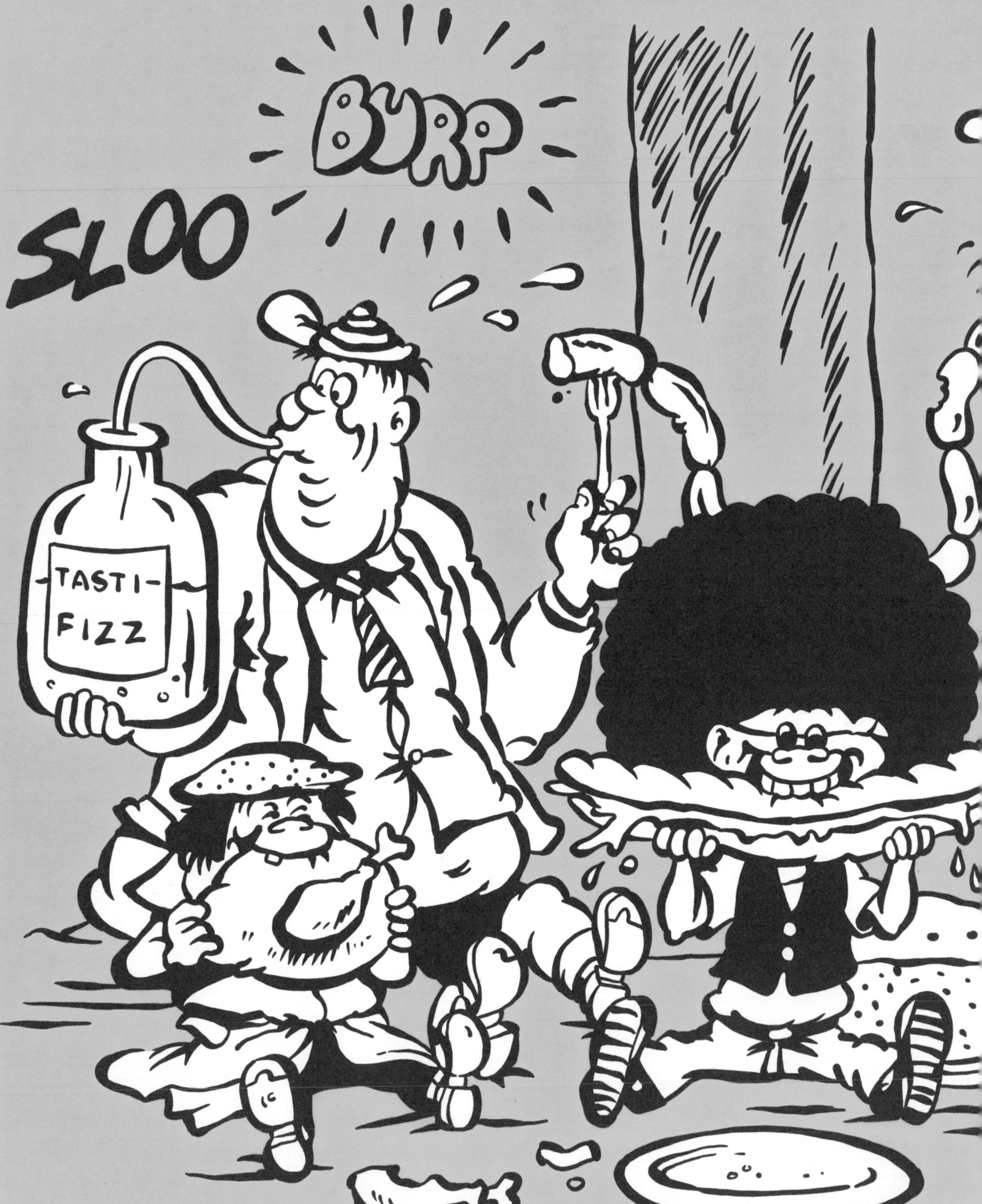
SLOO
BURP
TASTI-
FIZZ